"A SUSPENSE WRITER WHO KNOWS HOW TO MIX CHUCK-
LES WITH THRILLS." —*The Wall Street Journal*

McNally's Secret

"Clever . . . witty . . . a good read!" —Copley News Service

"A page-turner." —The Associated Press

"YOU CAN'T HELP FALLING FOR ARCHY McNALLY."
—*The Washington Times*

McNally's Luck

"Entertaining . . . Sophisticated wit. This is a fun book!"
—*South Bend Tribune*

"McNally is a charmer." —*Orlando Sentinel*

"It's nice to have Sanders back, twisting plots and turning phrases."
—Press

"SAND Times

McNally's Risk

"Keeps the reader guessing . . . relax and enjoy."
—*The Virginian-Pilot*

"A rollicking tale." —*The Indianapolis Star*

"Fast paced . . . thoroughly engaging . . . as crisp as a gin and tonic."
—*St. Petersburg Times*

The McNally Novels

McNALLY'S SECRET

McNALLY'S LUCK

McNALLY'S RISK

McNALLY'S CAPER

McNALLY'S TRIAL

McNALLY'S PUZZLE

McNALLY'S GAMBLE

McNALLY'S DILEMMA, AN ARCHY McNALLY NOVEL BY VINCENT LARDO

McNALLY'S FOLLY, AN ARCHY McNALLY NOVEL BY VINCENT LARDO

McNALLY'S CHANCE, AN ARCHY McNALLY NOVEL BY VINCENT LARDO

McNALLY'S ALIBI, AN ARCHY McNALLY NOVEL BY VINCENT LARDO

McNALLY'S DARE, AN ARCHY McNALLY NOVEL BY VINCENT LARDO

McNALLY'S BLUFF, AN ARCHY McNALLY NOVEL BY VINCENT LARDO

Also by Lawrence Sanders

GUILTY PLEASURES

THE SEVENTH COMMANDMENT

SULLIVAN'S STING

CAPITAL CRIMES

TIMOTHY'S GAME

THE TIMOTHY FILES

CAPER

THE EIGHTH COMMANDMENT

THE FOURTH DEADLY SIN

THE PASSION OF MOLLY T.

THE SEDUCTION OF PETER S.

THE CASE OF LUCY BENDING

THE THIRD DEADLY SIN

THE TENTH COMMANDMENT

THE SIXTH COMMANDMENT

THE TANGENT FACTOR

THE SECOND DEADLY SIN

THE MARLOW CHRONICLES

THE TANGENT OBJECTIVE

THE TOMORROW FILE

THE FIRST DEADLY SIN

LOVE SONGS

THE PLEASURES OF HELEN

THE ANDERSON TAPES

PRIVATE PLEASURES

STOLEN BLESSINGS

THE LOVES OF HARRY DANCER

THE DREAM LOVER

THE
McNALLY
FILES

Lawrence
SANDERS

BERKLEY BOOKS, NEW YORK

THE BERKLEY PUBLISHING GROUP
Published by the Penguin Group
Penguin Group (USA) Inc.
375 Hudson Street, New York, New York 10014, USA
Penguin Group (Canada), 90 Eglinton Avenue East, Suite 700, Toronto, Ontario M4P 2Y3, Canada
(a division of Pearson Penguin Canada Inc.)
Penguin Books Ltd., 80 Strand, London WC2R 0RL, England
Penguin Group Ireland, 25 St. Stephen's Green, Dublin 2, Ireland (a division of Penguin Books Ltd.)
Penguin Group (Australia), 250 Camberwell Road, Camberwell, Victoria 3124, Australia
(a division of Pearson Australia Group Pty. Ltd.)
Penguin Books India Pvt. Ltd., 11 Community Centre, Panchsheel Park, New Delhi—110 017, India
Penguin Group (NZ), Cnr. Airborne and Rosedale Roads, Albany, Auckland 1310, New Zealand
(a division of Pearson New Zealand Ltd.)
Penguin Books (South Africa) (Pty.) Ltd., 24 Sturdee Avenue, Rosebank, Johannesburg 2196,
South Africa

Penguin Books Ltd., Registered Offices: 80 Strand, London WC2R 0RL, England

THE MCNALLY FILES

This is a work of fiction. Names, characters, places, and incidents either are the product of the author's imagination or are used fictitiously, and any resemblance to actual persons, living or dead, business establishments, events, or locales is entirely coincidental.

PRINTING HISTORY
Berkley trade paperback edition / December 2006

Library of Congress Cataloging-in-Publication Data

Sanders, Lawrence, 1920–
  The McNally files / Lawrence Sanders.—Berkley trade paperback ed.
  Contents: McNally's secret—McNally's luck—McNally's risk.
  ISBN 0-425-21503-2 (trade pbk.)
  1. McNally, Archy (Fictitious character)—Fiction. 2. Private investigators—Florida—Palm Beach—
Fiction. 3. Palm Beach (Fla.)—Fiction. I. Title.

  PS3569.A5125A6 2006
  813'.54—dc22   2006049885

PRINTED IN THE UNITED STATES OF AMERICA

10 9 8 7 6 5 4 3 2 1

CONTENTS

McNALLY'S SECRET

Chapter 1

I poured a few drops of an '87 Mondavi Chardonnay into her navel and leaned down to slurp it out.

Jennifer's eyes closed and she purred. "Do you like that?" she breathed.

"Of course," I said. "Eighty-seven was an excellent year."

Her eyes popped open. "Stinker," she said. "Can't you ever be serious?"

"No," I said, "I cannot."

That, at least, was the truth. In my going-on thirty-seven years I had lived through dire warnings of nuclear catastrophe, global warming, ozone depletion, universal extinction via cholesterol, and the invasion of killer bees.

After a while my juices stopped their panicky surge and I realized I was bored with all these screeched predictions of Armageddon due next Tuesday. It hadn't happened yet, had it? The old world tottered along, and I was content to totter along with it. I am an amiable, sunnily tempered chap (and something of an ass, my father would undoubtedly add), and I see no need to concern myself with disasters that may never happen. The world is filled with kvetchers, and I have no desire to join the club.

I could have explained all this to Jennifer, but didn't. She might think I was serious about it, and I wasn't. I mean I wasn't even serious about not being serious, if you follow me.

So I took up where I had left off, and the next hour was a larky interlude of laughs and high-intensity moans. This was the first time we had bedded and, though I cannot speak for the lady, I know I was delighted; it was one of those rare sexual romps when realization exceeds expectation.

Part of my joy was due to pleased surprise. Jennifer Towley was almost as tall as I, and had impressed me as being a rather reserved, elegant, somewhat austere lady who dressed smartly but usually in black—and this is South Florida, where *everyone* favors pastels.

That was the clothed Jennifer. Stripped to the tawny buff and devoid of her gray contact lenses, she metamorphosed into an entirely different woman. What a jolly lady she turned out to be! Enthusiastic. Cooperative. Acrobatic. I felt a momentary pang over how I was deceiving her. But it was momentary.

Later, a bit after midnight, I regretfully dragged myself from her warm embrace and dressed. She rose and donned an enormous white terry robe that bore the crest of a Monte Carlo hotel.

"Thank you for a super evening," I said politely.

"The dinner was splendid," she said. "And the dessert even better. But wait; I have a gift for you."

I felt a perfect cad. Here I was deluding the poor girl, and she was about to give me a present. Perhaps a gold lighter or cashmere pullover—something expensive she could ill afford. I was shattered by shame.

But she brought me a packet of letters tied with a bit of ribbon. She had replaced her contacts, and gave me the full force of a direct, chilling stare. I glanced at the letters and knew immediately what they were: the reason for my duplicity.

"I believe these may be what you want," she said sternly.

I looked at her. "How long have you known?" I asked.

"I suspected you from the start," she said. "I don't ordinarily attract the attention of handsome, charming men my own age. Most of them are looking for teen-aged centerfolds. And then you claimed to be a tennis pro. Your game is good, but not *that* good. So tonight, while you were in the john, I went through your wallet."

"You didn't!"

"I did," she said firmly. "And discovered you are Archibald McNally, attorney-at-law."

"Not so," I said, shaking my head. "If you examine my business card closely, you'll see it says McNally and Son, Attorney-at-Law, not Attorneys-at-Law. Singular, not plural. My father, Prescott McNally, is the lawyer. I am not."

"Then what *are* you?"

"I am the Son, in charge of a department called Discreet Inquiries. It consists of me."

"But why *aren't* you an attorney?" she persisted.

"Because I was expelled from Yale Law for not being serious enough. During a concert by the New York Philharmonic I streaked across the stage, naked except for a Richard M. Nixon mask."

Then she laughed, and I knew everything was going to be all right.

"If you had asked for the letters at the beginning," she said, "I would have been happy to hand them over. The man is obviously demented. But I had no idea what your game was, and I was curious."

I sighed. "Our client, Clarence T. Frobisher, is a nice old gentleman, but not buttoned-up too tightly, as you've noticed. How did you meet him?"

"At a charity benefit. He seemed harmless enough. A bit vague perhaps, but nothing to scare a girl out of her wits. When I found out he was loaded, I thought of him as a potential customer for my antiques. We had a few dinners together—nothing more—and then I began to get these incredible letters from him. He loved me passionately, wanted to marry me, would give me as much money as I wanted if only I would let him nibble my beautiful pink toes. My toes may or may not be beautiful—that's in the eye of the beholder—but they are certainly not pink, as you well know."

I nodded. "Mr. Frobisher has a thing for toes. I must tell you, Jennifer, this is not the first time he has written to women much younger than he, offering to buy, or rent, their toes. In three other cases we have bought back his letters to prevent his being sued or exposed to publicity that would make him the giggle of Palm Beach. It is a pleasant shock to have one of his toe targets return his letters voluntarily. I thank you."

She looked at me thoughtfully. "If I hadn't given you the letters, or sold them back to you, would you have stolen them?"

"Probably," I said. "Now there is one final matter to discuss."

"Oh? And what might that be?"

"When may I see you again?" I asked.

Once more that cool, level gaze was aimed at me.

"I'll think about it," she said.

I drove home in my red Mazda Miata, one of the first in South Florida. As I headed eastward, I whistled the opening bars of Beethoven's Fifth. Or perhaps it was "Tiptoe Thru the Tulips." I wasn't sure and didn't much care. I was puffed with satisfaction: a job accomplished, a fine dinner and, most important, I had been intimate with a splendid woman.

I will not say I was smitten; that would be a bit much. My devotion to triviality as a way of life had taught me to automatically suspect and shun strong feelings. But still, I was intrigued by Ms. Jennifer Towley, no doubt about it. I wanted to see her again. Dine with her again. And then, I confess, the thought occurred to me that Clarence T. Frobisher may have had a perfectly reasonable and understandable fantasy. Forgive me.

We lived on A1A, right across the road from the Atlantic Ocean. Our manse was quite different from neighboring homes. They were mostly two-floor faux Spanish haciendas with red tile roofs; ours was a three-story faux Tudor with mullioned windows and a leaky copper mansard roof.

It was no Mar-a-Lago, but we had five bedrooms, which were sufficient to accommodate the annual visit of my married sister from Tucson with her family. In addition, our five acres included a two-story, three-car garage. Our houseman and cook-housekeeper, a married couple of Scandinavian origin, occupied an apartment on the upper floor.

There was a small greenhouse where my mother cultivated six million varieties of begonias—or so it seemed. There was also a formal garden, a potting shed, a Victorian-styled gazebo, and a doghouse that had once sheltered our golden retriever. He had gone to the Great Kennel in the Sky, but his home remained.

There was no swimming pool.

Actually, I thought the McNally estate was rather pukka. The main building was boxy with awkward lines, but ivy covers a multitude of sins. The entire place projected moneyed ease—costly comfort without flash. The weathered buildings and ample grounds bespoke old family and old wealth. It was all a stage set, of course, but only I knew that.

I parked the Miata between my father's black Lexus LS-400 and my mother's old wood-bodied Ford station wagon. There were no lights burning in the servants' quarters and none on the upper floors of the main house. But the portico lamp was on, and I caught slivers of light coming from between the drawn drapes of my father's first-floor study.

I went directly there. The heavy oaken door was ajar, and when I peeked in, I saw him comfortably ensconced in his favorite leather club chair, a port decanter and glass at his elbow. He was reading from a leather-bound volume, and I'd have bet it was Dickens. For years he had been digging through the entire oeuvre, and at the rate he was going, he'd be a Dear Departed before he got to *Bleak House*.

He looked up when I entered. "Good evening, Archy."

"Evening, father," I said, and tossed the tied packet onto his desk. "The Frobisher letters," I explained.

"Excellent," he said. "How much did they cost?"

"A dinner at Cafe L'Europe. The lady handed them over voluntarily. No charge."

"She *is* a lady," he said. "Will she accept a small gift in gratitude?"

"I suspect she will," I said. "She's a tennis nut, but her racquet looks like an old banjo. I think a new Spalding graphite would be appreciated."

He nodded. "Take care of it. You look bushed. A port?"

"Thank you, sir," I said gratefully, and poured myself a generous tot in a glass that matched his.

"Better sit down," he advised. "I have a new assignment for you, and it'll take some telling."

"It can't wait until tomorrow?"

"No," he said shortly, "it can't. It's not something I care to discuss in the office."

So I lounged limply in an armchair and crossed my legs. He cast a baleful look at my lavender socks but made no comment. He'd never persuade me to emulate him by wearing knee-high hose of black wool, wingtip brogues, and a vested suit of gray tropical worsted.

He sat a few moments in silence, and I knew he was considering what to say and how to say it. My father *always* thought long and carefully before speaking. It was a habit I was used to, but I can tell you it sometimes caused awkward moments with clients and acquaintances who feared the old man was woolgathering or had gone daft.

"Lady Cynthia Horowitz came to the office this evening," he said. "After you left."

"Good Lord!" I said. "Don't tell me the old bird is changing her will again?"

"Not today," he said with a faint smile. "She had something more urgent to discuss. She wouldn't come upstairs—because of the air conditioning, you know—so I had to go downstairs and sit in that antique Rolls of hers. Roomy enough, but stifling. She made her chauffeur take a stroll while we conferred in private. She was quite upset."

"And what's bothering her now?"

My father sighed and took a small sip of his port. "She alleges that an important part of her estate has vanished."

"Oh? Lost, strayed, or stolen?"

"She believes it was stolen. It was kept in a wall safe in her bedroom. It is no longer there."

"What exactly is it?"

"A block of four U.S. postage stamps."

I was amused. "And this was an important part of her estate?"

My father looked at me thoughtfully. "A similar block of four was recently auctioned at Christie's in New York for one million dollars."

I hastily took a gulp of wine. "Then I gather they're not the type of stamps one sticks on a letter to the IRS."

"Hardly. They are part of a sheet of one hundred 24-cent airmail stamps issued in 1918. The stamps are red with a blue biplane framed in the center. Due to a printing error, the plane was reproduced upside down on this particular sheet. Since the biplane pictured was popularly known as the Jenny, the misprinted stamp is famous in philatelic circles as the Inverted Jenny. Why are you laughing?"

"The lady I dined with tonight," I said, "the one who surrendered the Frobisher letters—apparently you don't recall, father, but her name is Jennifer Towley. I suppose some people might address her as Jenny."

He raised one eyebrow—a trick I've never been able to master. "And was she inverted?" he asked. Then, apparently fearing he had posed an imprudent question, he hurriedly continued: "In any event, Lady Horowitz doesn't wish to take the problem to the police."

I stared at him. "She thinks someone in her household might have snaffled the stamps?"

"I didn't ask her. That's your job."

"Why on earth didn't she keep them in her bank's vault? That's where she stores her furs in the summer."

"She kept them at home," my father explained patiently, "for the same reason she keeps her jewelry there. She enjoys wearing her diamonds, and she enjoyed showing the misprinted stamps to guests."

I groaned. "So everyone in Palm Beach knew she owned a block of Inverted Jennies?"

"Perhaps not *everyone,* but a great number of people certainly."

"Were they insured?"

"For a half-million. She has not yet filed a claim, hoping the stamps may be recovered. Since she desires no publicity whatsoever, this is obviously a task for the Discreet Inquiries Department. Archy, please get started on it tomorrow morning. Or rather, this morning."

I nodded.

"I suggest," he went on, "you begin by interviewing Lady Horowitz. She'll be able to provide more details of the purported theft."

"I'm not looking forward to that meeting," I said, and finished my port. "You know what people call her, don't you? Lady Horrorwitz."

My father gave me a wintry smile. "Few of us are what we seem," he said. "If we were, what a dull world this would be."

He went back to his Dickens, and I climbed the stairs to my third-floor suite: bedroom, sitting room, dressing room, bathroom. Smallish but snug. I showered, pulled on a pongee robe, and lighted a cigarette, only my third of the past twenty-four hours, for which I felt suitably virtuous.

I'm a rather scatterbrained bloke, and shortly after I joined my father's law firm and was given the responsibility for Discreet Inquiries, I thought it wise to start a private journal in which I might keep notes. That way, you see, I wouldn't forget items that, seemingly unimportant, might later prove significant. I tried to make daily entries, but on that particular night I merely sat staring at my diary and thinking of my father's comment: "Few of us are what we seem." That was certainly true of Prescott McNally.

My father's father, Frederick McNally, was not, as many believed, a wealthy member of the British landed gentry. Instead, *mirabile dictu,* my grandfather had been a gapping-trousered, bulb-nosed burlesque comic, billed on the Minsky circuit as Ready Freddy McNally. He never achieved stardom, but his skill with dialects and his raunchy trademark laugh, "Ah-oo-gah!," had earned him the reputation of being the funniest second banana in burley-cue.

In addition to his dexterity with pratfalls and seltzer bottles, plus his ability to leap like a startled gazelle when goosed onstage, Ready Freddy turned out to be a remarkably astute investor in real estate. During the Florida land boom of the 1920s, my grandfather purchased beachfront property (wonderfully inexpensive in those days) and lots bordering the canal that later became the Intracoastal Waterway.

By the time he retired from the world of greasepaint, he was moderately well-to-do, rich enough certainly to purchase a home in Miami and send his son, my father, off to Yale University to become a gentleman and eventually an attorney-at-law.

Shortly after Ready Freddy made his final exit, my paternal grandmother, a former showgirl, also passed from the stage. Whereupon my father sold the Miami home (at a handsome profit) and moved his family to Palm Beach. He had been admitted to the Florida bar and knew exactly how he wanted to live. Had known, as a matter of fact, since his first days as a Yale undergraduate.

The world my father envisioned—and this was years before Ralph Lauren created a fashion empire from the same dream—was one of manor homes, croquet, polo, neatly trimmed gardens, a wine cellar, lots of chintz, worn leather and brass everywhere, silver-framed photographs of family members, and cucumber sandwiches at tea.

That was the life he deliberately and painstakingly created for himself and his family in Palm Beach. He was Lord of the Manor, and if this necessitated buying an antique marble fireplace and mantel from a London dealer and having it crated and shipped to Florida at horrendous expense, so be it. He believed in his dream, and he realized it beautifully and completely. Gentility? It was coming out our ears.

That made me not merely a son but a scion. (Lords of the Manor had heirs or scions.) And if I recognized my father's spurious life-style at an early age, that didn't prevent me from taking full advantage of the perks it offered.

I recalled a conversation with comrades at Yale Law before I was booted out. We were discussing how sons often followed in the footsteps of their fathers, not only adopting pop's vocation, but frequently his habits, hobbies, and vices.

"The apple never falls far from the tree," someone remarked sententiously.

To which someone else added, "And the turd never falls far from the bird."

I didn't wish to brood too deeply on how that latter aphorism might apply to me. But I want you to know that I was aware of what I considered my father's masquerade. And although I might regard it with lofty scorn, I was willing to profit from it. Perhaps I was as much an actor as my father.

I put all these heavy ruminations in a mental deep six and resolutely turned to making suitable entries in my daily journal. To accomplish this, I was forced to don reading glasses. Yes, at the tender age of thirty-six-plus, the peepers had shown evidence of bagging at the knees, and I needed the horn-rimmed cheaters for close-up work. Naturally I never wore them in public. One doesn't wish to wobble about resembling a nuclear physicist, does one?

I made notes regarding the recovery of the Clarence T. Frobisher letters. Then I jotted down what little I had learned from my father regarding the claimed theft of the Inverted Jenny stamps from the wall safe in the bedroom of Lady Cynthia Horowitz. I scrawled a reminder to phone Horowitz and set up an early appointment.

Then, staring at my diary, I made a final note that amazed me. It read as follows:

"Jennifer Towley!!!"

Chapter 2

I overslept and by the time I trooped downstairs my father had already left for the office (we usually drove in together), and my mother was pottering about in the potting shed, which seemed logical. I learned all this from Olson, our houseman, who was seated in the kitchen smoking a pipe and working on a mug of black coffee to which he may or may not have added a dram of aquavit. He also told me his wife, Ursi, had taken the station wagon to seek fresh grouper for our dinner that night.

You would think, wouldn't you, that a man with the red corpuscles of the Vikings dancing through his veins would have a given name of Lars or Sven. But Olson's first name was Jamie, and it was not a diminutive of James; it was just Jamie. He was a wrinkled codger, about my father's age, and he and his wife had been with us as long as I could remember. They were childless and both seemed content to go on working at the Chez McNally for as long as they could get out of bed in the morning.

"Eggs?" he asked.

I shook my head. "Rye toast and coffee. I'm dieting."

He set to work in that slow, deliberate way of his. Both the Olsons were good chefs—good, not great—but neither would ever qualify for a fast-food joint. They didn't dawdle, they were just unbrisk.

"Jamie," I said, "do you know Kenneth? He drives for Lady Horowitz."

"I know him."

"What's his last name?"

"Bodin."

"What kind of a guy is he?"

"Big."

I sighed. Getting information from Olson isn't difficult, but it takes time. "How long has he been with Horowitz—do you know?"

He paused a moment to think. "Mebbe five, six years."

"That sounds about right," I said. "A few years ago there was talk going around that he was more than just her chauffeur. You hear anything about that?"

"Uh-huh," Jamie said. He brought my breakfast and poured himself more coffee.

"You think there was anything to it?" I persisted.

"Mebbe *was*," he said. "Then. Not now."

His taciturnity didn't fool me; he enjoyed gossip as much as I did.

You must understand that Palm Beach is a gossiper's paradise. It is, in fact, the Gossip Capital of the World. In Palm Beach everyone gossips eagerly and constantly. I mean we *relish* it.

"Is this Kenneth Bodin married?" I pressed on, slathering my toast with the mango jelly Jamie had thoughtfully set out.

"Nope."

"Girlfriend?"

"Mebbe."

"Anyone I might know?"

He slowly removed his cold pipe from his dentures and regarded me gravely. "She gives massages," he said.

"No kidding?" I said, interested. "Well, at the moment I'm not acquainted with any masseuses. She work in West Palm Beach?"

"Did," Olson said. "Till the cops closed her down."

"And what is she doing now?"

He was still staring at me. "This and that," he said.

"All right," I said hurriedly, "I get the picture. Ask around, will you, and see if you can find out her name and address."

He nodded.

I finished my breakfast and went into my father's study to use his directory and phone. The old man puts covers on his telephone directories. Other people do that, of course, but most use clear plastic. My father bound his directories in genuine leather. I mention this merely to illustrate how meticulous he was in his pursuit of gentility.

I looked up the number of Lady Cynthia Horowitz and dialed. Got the housekeeper, identified myself, and asked to speak to the mistress. Instead, as I knew would happen, I was shunted to Consuela Garcia. She was Lady Cynthia's social secretary and general factotum.

I knew Consuela, who had come over from Havana during the Mariel boatlift. A few years previously she and I had a mad, passionate romance that lasted all of three weeks. Then she discovered that when it comes to wedding bells I am tone-deaf, and she gave me the broom. Fair enough. But we were still friends, I thought, although now when we met at parties and dances, we shook hands instead of sharing a smooch.

"Archy," she said, "how nice to hear from you."

"How are you, Connie?"

"Very well, thank you."

"I saw you out at Wellington last Saturday," I told her. "That was a very handsome lad you were with. Is he new?"

"Not really," she said, laughing. "He's been used. What can I do for you, Archy?"

"An audience with Lady C. Half-hour, an hour at the most."

"What's it about?"

"Charity subscription," I said, not knowing if Horowitz had told her of the disappearance of the Inverted Jennies. "We've simply *got* to do something to save the hard-nosed gerbils."

"The *what?*"

"Hard-nosed gerbils. Delightful little beasties, but they're dwindling, Connie, definitely dwindling."

"I don't know," she said doubtfully. "Everyone's been hitting on her lately to help save something or other."

"Give it a try," I urged.

She came back on the phone a few moments later. "If you can come over immediately," she said, sounding surprised, "Lady Cynthia will see you."

"Thank you, Connie," I said humbly. I can do humble.

The Miata is not a car whose door you open to enter. As with the old MG, you vault into the driver's seat as if you were mounting a charger. So I vaulted and headed northward on A1A. Lady Horowitz's estate was just up the road a piece, as they say in Florida, and traffic was mercifully light, so I could let my charger gallop.

As I drove I mentally reviewed what I knew about the woman I was about to interview.

Her full name was Lady Cynthia Kirschner Gomez Stanescu Smythe DuPey Horowitz. If she was not a clear winner in the Palm Beach marital sweepstakes, she was certainly one of the contenders. Around her swimming pool, in addition to Old Glory, she flew the six flags of her ex-husbands' native lands. Everyone said it was a sweet touch; the divorce settlements had left her a very wealthy woman indeed.

She had won her title from her last husband, Leopold Horowitz, who had been knighted for a lifetime of research on the mating habits of flying beetles.

Unfortunately, a year after being honored, he had fallen to his death from a very tall tree in the Amazon while trying to net a pair of the elusive critters *in flagrante delicto*. His bereaved widow immediately flew to Paris to purchase a black dress (with pouffe) from Christian Lacroix.

Long before I met Lady Cynthia I had heard many people speak of her as a "great beauty." But when I was finally introduced, it was difficult to conceal my shock. It would be ungentlemanly to call a woman ugly. I shall say only that I found her excessively plain.

While not a crone, exactly, she had a long nose with a droopy tip and a narrow chin that jutted upward. Drooping nose and jutting chin did not touch, of course, but I had this dream that you might clamp a silver dollar vertically between nose and chin tips and, by flicking it with your forefinger, set it a-twirling. I could not understand how old age could so ravage the features of a "great beauty."

"Why, she must be over eighty," I remarked to my father.

"Nonsense," he said, rather stiffly. "She's a year younger than I."

I still could not comprehend the "great beauty" legend or how she had been able to snare so many husbands. The mystery was solved when a national tabloid (published in nearby Lantana, incidentally) printed a sensationalized article on Lady Cynthia and her myriad marriages and extracurricular affairs. The article was, as they say, profusely illustrated, and it provided the reason for her allure.

She had been born Cynthia DiLuca in Chicago, daughter of a butcher, and even at an early age it was observed that she had a face that would stop a Timex. But to make up for this, she was blessed with a body so voluptuous that her first published nude photos made every geezer in the world snap his braces.

During the 1940s and 1950s she posed for many photographers and artists. Her face was usually turned away, masked in shadow, or concealed beneath a gauze scarf. One photographer even went so far as to graft a more attractive feminine head onto Cynthia's body, but viewers weren't deceived; her figure was as unique, universally recognized, and dearly beloved as a Coca-Cola bottle. Even the immortal Picasso painted her portrait, converting her divine form into a stack of shingles that was much admired.

Now, at the age of seventy-plus, she apparently retained the body that had electrified the world fifty years ago. She also retained more spleen than anyone, woman or man, had a right to possess. Her temper tantrums were legendary. She was notorious for a long list of peeves that included cigars, dogs, and men who wore pinky rings. But tops on her roster of grievances were air conditioning and direct sunlight—which made it difficult to understand why she had decided to spend her remaining years in South Florida.

All in all, she had the reputation of being a nasty old lady, short-tempered and, when provoked, foul-mouthed. But she was tolerated, even treasured, by Palm Beach society as a genuine "character." Part of her popularity was due to her generosity. She held wondrous parties and galas, and few rejected her invitations, mostly because they knew that one of the things she found unacceptable was dining at other people's homes or in public restaurants, and her guests would not be expected to return her hospitality.

She had an excellent reason for reclusive dining: She employed the best French chef in South Florida.

Having said all this, I must also add that Lady Cynthia Horowitz had never treated the McNally Family with anything less than charming civility. My mother, father, and I had dined with her privately several times, and she couldn't have been a more gracious hostess and fascinating raconteuse over postprandial brandies. You figure it out.

Her home looked like an antebellum southern plantation: Tara transplanted to Florida's Gold Coast. The only anachronisms in this idyllic scene were the high wall of coral blocks topped with razor wire surrounding the estate and a large patio and swimming pool area at the rear of the main house.

It was to poolside that the black housekeeper conducted me, and I was happy to see the ex-husbands' flags snapping merrily in the breeze. Lady C. was reclining on a chaise lounge in the shade of an umbrella table. Not only was she lying in the shade, but she was swaddled in a voluminous white flannel robe, wore white socks to protect feet and ankles, and long white gloves to shield wrists and hands from that old devil sun. And, of course, she wore a wide-brimmed panama straw hat that provided even deeper shadow for her face and neck.

There were two phones, cordless and cellular, in view as I approached. Horowitz was using the cellular and waved me to a nearby canvas director's chair while she continued her conversation. I could not help but overhear.

"No, no, and no," she was saying wrathfully. "Just forget it. I don't want to hear another word about it. Listen, sweetie, if I thought it was humanly possible, I'd tell you to go fuck yourself. Am I coming through loud and clear?"

She hung up and glared angrily at me through green-tinted sunglasses. "Have you met Mercedes Blair?" she demanded.

"I don't believe I've had the pleasure," I said.

"Believe me, lad," she said bitterly, "it's no pleasure. That woman is one of the great bubbleheads of Palm Beach. The last time I was in Cairo, I bought this absolutely divine ivory dildo. After I got back I made the mistake of showing it to Mercedes, not knowing she's one of these save-the-elephant people. Well, she turned positively livid, and ever since she's been busting my chops. She wants me to throw it away! Can you imagine? I just can't get it through her tiny, tiny brain that the elephant croaked centuries ago. That ivory dildo is ancient Egyptian, a beautiful antique, and besides, it's quite useful. But she keeps insisting I get rid of it. I'll never speak to that stupe again as long as I live."

Years ago I had come to the conclusion that life is strange. I decided then that the only way to hang on to one's sanity with a sweaty grasp is to acknowledge the incomprehensibility of life. Accept all—and just nod knowingly.

So I listened to this tale of the ivory dildo, nodded knowingly, and made sympathetic noises. Lady Cynthia finished her tirade, leaned down to pick up a tumbler alongside her chaise. It contained what I guessed to be her first gin-and-bitters of the day. She took a sip and visibly relaxed.

"Want a drink, lad?" she asked pleasantly.

"Not at the moment, thank you."

"That jazz you gave Connie about the hard-nosed gerbils—that was all bullshit. Right?"

"Right," I said.

"And you want to ask about my missing stamps. Prescott said you'd be looking into it. Ask away."

"Who knows about the disappearance of the Inverted Jennies?"

"Me, your father, you."

"You haven't told Consuela or anyone else on your staff?"

She shook her head. "Maybe one of them pinched the stamps," she said darkly.

"Maybe," I said. "Let's see . . . in addition to Connie, you've got a butler, housekeeper, two maids, chef, and chauffeur. Right?"

"Wrong," she said. "The butler and one of the maids quit about two weeks ago. Claimed they couldn't stand the summer in Florida. Idiots!"

"So that leaves a staff of five," I said. "Anyone else staying in the house?"

"My son Harry Smythe and his wife, Doris. Also my son Alan DuPey and his bride, Felice. They've only been married a month. And my daughter, Gina Stanescu. Also Angus Wolfson, an old friend. He's down from Boston for a couple of weeks. He's gay—but so what?"

"A full house," I commented. "They were all here when the stamps disappeared?"

She nodded.

"Who knew the combination to the wall safe besides you?"

"No one. But that doesn't matter. I never locked it."

I looked at her and sighed. "I'll have that drink now, please," I said, figuring the sun had to be over the yardarm somewhere in the world.

"Of course. What?"

"Vodka and tonic will do me fine."

She used the cordless phone to call her kitchen and order up my drink.

"Lady Cynthia," I said, "why didn't you lock your wall safe?"

"I couldn't be bothered," she said. "That stupid combination—I kept forgetting it and had to rummage through my desk to find it. Besides, I trusted people."

I didn't make the obvious reply to that. We waited in silence until the housekeeper, Mrs. Marsden, a motherly type, brought my drink. It had a thick slice of fresh lime—just the way I like it.

After the housekeeper departed, I said, "I don't mean to get picky about this, but if you couldn't remember the combination to your safe, isn't it possible you forgot where you put the stamps?"

She shook her head. "They weren't just in an envelope or anything like that. They were between clear plastic pages in a little book about the size of a diary. A thin book bound in red leather specially made to hold the Inverted Jennies. It's not something you'd easily misplace. Also, I've torn the house apart looking for it. It's just gone."

"Would you object if I asked how you came into possession of those stamps in the first place?"

"No," she said, "I wouldn't object. Go ahead and ask."

I laughed. "Lady Cynthia, you're pulling my leg."

"I'd love to, lad," she said, leering like Groucho Marx, "but people might talk. I received those silly upside-down stamps as part of my divorce settlement from my first husband, Max Kirschner. Dear old Max. He loved to wear my lingerie, but he really knew how to manage a bank. He bought the stamps in Trieste. I think he paid ten thousand American for the block of four. But of course that was years and years ago."

"Was he a stamp collector?"

"No, he just liked to own rare things. Like me."

I wasn't making great progress—perhaps because she seemed to be treating her loss so lightly. But that was her way—the dictum of haut monde: Never complain and never explain.

"All right," I said, "if the stamps weren't misplaced, let's assume they were nicked. Anyone in particular you suspect might have sticky fingers?"

The question troubled her. "I'd hate to think it was one of my staff. They've all been with me for years."

"But you said the butler and one of the maids quit. Was this before the stamps disappeared or after you became aware they were missing?"

She thought about that a moment. "No, the stamps were still here after the butler and maid left. I remember now: They quit, and the next day Alan DuPey showed up with his bride. Felice had never seen the stamps, so that night at dinner I brought them down to show her. Then, after dinner, I took them back upstairs and put them in the wall safe. That was the last time I saw them."

"Any signs around the house of a break-in? Jimmied doors or broken windows—anything like that?"

"No. And after the gate is locked at night, Mrs. Marsden always turns on the electronic alarm system."

"Are you certain she turns it on every night?"

"Absolutely. If it's not turned on by midnight, I get a phone call from the security agency to remind me."

"What do you do when you have a party that lasts until the wee small hours?"

"I always hire one or two guards for the occasion. Then, after everyone has gone home, the guards leave, the gate is locked, and the alarm activated."

"Very efficient," I observed, and looked into my half-empty glass. No clues there. "Okay, let's put aside the idea of a break-in or someone on your staff pinching the stamps. Now what about your houseguests?"

"Don't be silly," she snapped at me. "My God, lad, they're *family*. Except for Angus Wolfson, and I've known him for ages."

"Uh-huh," I said. "And are they all well-off?"

"Not one of them is hurting." She paused to finish her drink, then crunched the ice between her teeth. "But of course when it comes to money, enough is never enough—if you know what I mean."

I nodded. "Lady Cynthia, if you expect McNally and Son to make a complete investigation of this matter, you'll have to tell your staff and houseguests about the theft."

She stared at me, outraged. Then: "Shit! If I do that, it'll be all over Palm Beach within two hours."

"True," I agreed, "but that can't be helped."

"But that's why I didn't go to the police. I wanted to keep the whole thing private."

"Can't be done," I said, shaking my head. "How on earth can I make discreet inquiries if people don't know what I'm talking about?"

She considered that. "I guess you're right," she said finally, sighing. "But it means cops, reporters, and maybe the TV people. What am I going to tell them?"

"Lie," I said cheerfully. "Tell them the stamps weren't stolen at all but have been sent to a New York auction house for appraisal."

She laughed. "You're a devious lad, you know that? All right, I'll tell the staff and guests."

"Good. Then I can get the show on the road." I put my empty glass on the umbrella table and stood up. "One more request: I'd like to take a look at the so-called scene of the crime, if I may. Do you mind if I go poking about in your bedroom for a few minutes?"

"Go ahead and poke," she said. "You know your way around the place, don't you?"

"Only the ground floor."

"My bedroom is on the second. South wing. It stretches the width of the house. The east windows overlook the ocean and the west windows look down on the pool and patio. There . . ."

She gestured, and I looked to the second floor where opened windows, screened, were framed by French blue shutters.

"You can pry into anything you like," she said. "Nothing's locked."

"It won't take long," I promised. "Thank you for the drink."

I started away but she called, "Archy," and I turned back, surprised that she had used my name. Usually I was "lad" or, when speaking of me to others, "Prescott's son."

She stared at me a moment, and I waited. "Last night you dined at L'Europe," she said, almost accusingly. "With Jennifer Towley."

"Oh-ho," I said, "the grapevine has been working overtime."

"Are you seeing her?" she demanded.

"Not yet."

"Watch your back, lad," she said. "There's more to her than meets the eye. If I were you, I'd bring that association to a screeching halt. The lady could turn out to be a problem."

I grinned at her. "One never knows, do one?" I said.

I continued on to the house, wondering just what the hell she was implying—and deciding it was merely Palm Beach gossip.

The interior of the Horowitz home was gorgeous, right out of *Southern Accents,* and all the more impressive because I knew the mistress had done the decorating herself. It was an eclectic mix of Victorian, Louis Quinze, Early American, and even a few Bauhaus touches. I know that sounds like a mishmash, but everything fit, nothing clashed, and the predominant colors were rich wine shades, a welcome relief from the sorbet pastels of most South Florida mansions', many of which resemble the lobby of a Miami Beach hotel.

Lady Cynthia's bedroom was large enough to accommodate an enormous four-poster bed lacquered in claret red, a tall wardrobe of carved pine, an escritoire painted with gamboling putti, and much, much more.

There were three huge crystal vases of fresh flowers, one in her dressing room. The walk-in closet contained enough costumes to outfit the female cast of *My Fair Lady,* and the racks of shoes would have made Imelda Marcos gnash her teeth. The bathroom was golden yellow: tile, tub, sink, john, bidet—everything. The faucets were tarnished gold: a nice touch, I thought. One strives for careless elegance, doesn't one?

I didn't search through the desk or turn over chair cushions—nothing like that. I was interested only in the wall safe, and that was easy to spot since it was not concealed behind a painting or camouflaged in any way. It projected slightly from the wall just to the left of the canopied bed. It was nothing special: single dial, single handle. The door opened easily and noiselessly. Inside were several manila envelopes tied with what appeared to be old shoelaces. I didn't inspect the contents, but closed the safe door again, latching it with a twist of the stainless steel handle.

What I was interested in was the distance from the bedroom door to the wall safe. I paced it off. Fourteen long steps. I estimated an intruder could slip into the bedroom, open the safe door, extract the small red leather book containing the Inverted Jennies, close the safe door, and whisk from the bedroom within a minute. Two at the most. It was a cakewalk. But who took the walk?

Then I found another problem. On a bedside table, almost directly below the wall safe, was a large suede jewel case. I lifted the lid: It was like looking into a Tiffany display case. Question: What self-respecting crook would swipe the stamps and then not pause a sec to grab up a handful of those glittering gems? A puzzlement.

Hands in my pocket, I strolled about the bedroom, thinking it was spacious enough to swallow my entire suite at the McNally manse. I believe I was whistling "I've Never Been in Love Before" when I wandered to the west windows and looked down.

Lady Cynthia was paddling around in the swimming pool, obviously naked but still wearing her panama hat and sunglasses. Mrs. Marsden stood waiting on the tiled border of the pool, holding a big bath towel. As I watched, Lady C. came slowly wading out, white body gleaming wetly, and I saw how extraordinary she was.

Usually in the presence of great beauty, one has the urge to leap into the air accompanied by the clicking of heels. But now, seeing that incredible nude emerging from the pool—Venus rising from the chlorine—I felt only an ineffable sadness, realizing I had been born forty years too late.

Chapter 3

Of all the counties in Florida, Palm Beach is the Ace of Clubs. There is a superabundance: golf clubs, tennis clubs, yacht clubs, polo clubs. Probably the most elegant and exclusive social clubs on Palm Beach Island are the Bath & Tennis and the Everglades. But about five years previously, I got together with a bunch of my wassailing pals, and we agreed what the town needed was another club, so we decided to start one. We called it the Pelican Club in honor of Florida's quintessential bird. Also, most of the roistering charter members resembled the pelican: graceful and charming in flight, lumpish and dour in repose.

We found an old two-story clapboard house out near the airport that we could afford. It was definitely not an Addison Mizner but it had the advantage of being somewhat isolated: no close neighbors to complain about the sounds of revelry. We all chipped in, bought the house, fixed it up (sort of), and the Pelican Club opened for business.

And almost closed six months later. We were lawyers, bankers, stockbrokers, realtors, doctors, etc., but we knew nothing about running a club bar and restaurant. We were facing Chapter 7 when we had the great good fortune to hire the Pettibones, an African-American family who had been living in one of the gamier neighborhoods of West Palm Beach and wanted out. All of them had worked in restaurants and bars, and they knew how an eating-drinking establishment should be run.

They moved into our second floor, and the father, Simon Pettibone, became club manager and bartender. Son Leroy was our chef, daughter Priscilla our waitress, and wife Jas (for Jasmine) was appointed our housekeeper and den mother. Within a month the Pettibones had the club operating admirably, and so many would-be Pelicans applied for membership that eventually we had to close the roster and start a waiting list.

The Pelican Club was not solely dedicated to merrymaking, of course. We were also involved in Good Works. Once a year we held a costume ball at The Breakers: our Annual Mammoth Extravaganza. All the proceeds from this lavish blowout were contributed to a local home for unwed mothers, since so many of our members felt a personal responsibility. In addition we formed a six-piece jazz combo (I played tenor kazoo), and we were delighted to perform, without fee, at public functions and nursing homes. A Palm Beach music critic wrote of one of our recitals, "Words fail me." You couldn't ask for a better review than that.

It was to the Pelican Club that I tooled the Miata after my stimulating morning with Lady Horowitz. It was then almost eleven-thirty, but traffic crossing Lake Worth on the Royal Park Bridge was heavy, and it was a bit after noon when I arrived at the club.

No members were present when I entered the Pelican, but Simon Pettibone was behind the bar, polishing glasses and watching the screen of a television set displaying current stock quotations.

I swung onto a barstool. "Are you winning or losing, Mr. Pettibone?" I inquired.

"Losing, Mr. McNally," he replied. "But I prefer to think of it as a learning experience."

"Very wise," I said. "A vodka-tonic for me, please, with a hunk of lime."

He began preparing the drink, and I headed for the phone booth in the rear of the barroom. Did you guess I intended to call Jennifer Towley? You will learn that when duty beckons, there is stern stuff in the McNally male offspring; I phoned the Palm Beach Police Department. I asked to speak to Sergeant Al Rogoff.

"Rogoff," he answered in his phlegmy rasp.

"Archy McNally here." I said.

"Yes, sir, how may I be of service?"

When Al talks like that, I know someone is standing at his elbow—probably his lieutenant or captain.

"Feel like a nosh?" I asked. "I'll stand you a world-class hamburger and a bucket of suds."

"Your Alfa-Romeo is missing, sir?" he said. "I'm sorry to hear that. It will be necessary for you to file a missing vehicle report. Where are you located, sir?"

"I'm in the barroom at the Pelican."

"Yes, sir," he said, "I am familiar with that office building. Suppose I meet you there in a half-hour, and you can give me the details of the alleged theft."

"Hurry up," I said. "I'm hungry."

I returned to the bar where my drink was waiting on a clean little mat. I took a sip. Just right.

"Mr. Pettibone," I said, "life is strange."

"Bizarre is the word, Mr. McNally," he said. "*Bee*-zar."

"Exactly," I said.

Sgt. Al Rogoff owned that adjective. I had worked a few cases with him in the past—to our mutual benefit—and had come to know him better than most of his professional associates. He deliberately projected the persona of a good ol' boy: a crude, profane "man's man" who called women "broads" and claimed he would like nothing better than a weekend on an airboat in the Everglades, popping cans of Bud and lassoing alligators. He even drove a pickup truck.

I think he adopted this Joe Six-pack disguise because he thought it would further his career as an officer of the law in South Florida. Actually, he knew who Heidegger was; could quote the lines following "Shall I part my hair behind? Do I dare to eat a peach?"; and much preferred an '82 Médoc to sour mash and branch water. He looked and acted like a redneck sheriff, but enjoyed Vivaldi more than he did Willie Nelson.

He hadn't revealed the face behind the mask voluntarily. I had slowly, patiently, discovered who he really was. He knew it, and rather than be offended, I think he was secretly relieved. It must be a tremendous strain to play a role continually, always fearful of making a gaffe that will betray your impersonation. Al didn't have to act with me, and I believe that was why he was willing to provide official assistance when my discreet inquiries required it.

By the time he came marching through the front door, uniform smartly pressed, the Pelican barroom was thronged with the lunchtime crowd and people had started to drift to the back area where a posted warning said nothing about jackets and ties but proclaimed: "Members and their guests are required to wear shoes in the dining room."

I noticed a few patrons glancing warily at the uniformed cop who had invaded the premises. Did they fear a bust—or were they just startled by this armed intruder who was built like a dumpster? Al Rogoff's physical appearance was perhaps the principal reason for the success of his masquerade. The man was all meat, a walking butcher shop: rare-beef face, pork chop jowls, slabs of veal for ears. And unplucked chicken wing sideburns.

I conducted him to the dining room where Priscilla was holding a corner table for me. We both ordered medium-rare hamburgers, which came with country fries and homemade coleslaw. We also ordered steins of draft Heineken. While waiting for lunch to be served, we nibbled on spears of kosher dill pickles placed on every table in mason jars. The Pelican Club did not offer haute cuisine, but Leroy Pettibone's food adhered to the ribs.

"How much time do you have?" I asked Rogoff.

"An hour tops," he said. "What's up?"

"I want to report a crime."

"Oh?" he said. "Have you sexually abused a manatee?"

"Not recently," I said. "But this may not be a crime at all. It is an *alleged* crime. And the alleged victim will not report it to the police. And if you hear or read about it and question the alleged victim, she will claim no crime has been committed."

"Love it," the sergeant said. "Just love it. Alleged crime. Alleged victim. And I've got to listen to this bullshit for a free hamburger? Okay, I'm not proud. Who's the alleged victim?"

"Lady Cynthia Horowitz."

He pursed his lips in a soundless whistle. "Mrs. Gotrocks herself? That makes the cheese more binding. She's got clout. And what's the alleged crime?"

"Possible theft of a valuable possession."

"The Koh-i-noor diamond?"

"No," I said. "Four postage stamps."

He looked at me sorrowfully. "You never come up with something simple," he said. "Like a multiple homicide or a supermarket bombing. With you, everything's got to be cute. All right, buster, tell me about the four postage stamps."

But then our food was served, and we were silent until Priscilla left. Between bites and swallows, I told him the whole story of the Inverted Jenny and how a block of four of the misprinted stamps was missing from the wall safe in Lady Horowitz's bedroom. The sergeant listened without interrupting. Then, when I finished, he spoke.

"You know," he said, "this hamburger is really super. What does Leroy put in the meat?"

"Probably minced Vidalia onion this time of year. Sometimes he uses chopped red and yellow peppers. The man is the Thomas Alva Edison of hamburgers. What about the Inverted Jennies?"

"What about them? What do you want us to do?"

"Nothing," I said. "If you go to Lady Cynthia, she'll tell you the stamps weren't stolen but have been sent to a New York auction house for appraisal."

"Uh-huh," Rogoff said. "And who gave her that idea—as if I didn't know."

"I did," I admitted. "But she doesn't want any publicity."

The sergeant pushed back his empty plate and stared at me. "You're a devious lad, you know that?"

"You're the second person who's told me that today."

"Who was the first—Lady Horowitz?"

I nodded. "But it's not true," I protested. "I'm not devious. I just want to maintain civility in the world."

"Of course," Rogoff said. "And I'm the Tooth Fairy. So if you're not demanding the PBPD get involved, what *do* you want?"

"A little information."

"It figures," he said mournfully. "There's no free lunch."

"Have another beer," I urged.

"Nope. Coffee and a wedge of Leroy's key lime pie will be fine. I deserve it for listening to your blather."

Priscilla cleared our table, and I gave her Al's order. I settled for just coffee. Black.

"Getting a little tubby?" she teased.

"Nonsense," I said. "I'm still the slender, lithe, bronzed Apollo you've always known."

"Oh sure," she said. "And I'm the Tooth Fairy."

"Two 'devious lads' in one day," I complained to Rogoff, "and now two Tooth Fairies in one day. Does everything come in twos?"

"Everything comes in threes," he said. "You should know that. Now cut the drivel. What kind of information do you want?"

"Those Inverted Jenny stamps," I said. "They're extremely rare. Only a hundred of them were originally sold. I imagine all stamp dealers and most collectors know about them. A block of four recently went at auction for a million bucks. I mean they're valuable and they're famous. So, assuming Lady Cynthia's stamps were pinched, what's the thief going to do with them? It's been bothering me since I was handed the job. He can't sell them to a legitimate dealer; he'd want to know where they came from—the provenance. Ditto for auction houses. So how does the criminal profit from his crime?"

Silence while Priscilla served our coffee and Rogoff's dessert. Then:

"Lots of possibilities," Al said, digging into his pie. "One is ransom. The perp contacts Lady Horowitz and offers to sell her stamps back to her for X number of dollars. Were they insured?"

"Half a million."

"All right, if Horowitz won't play ball, the crook calls the insurance company and tries to make a deal. The insurance people would rather pay out a hundred grand than a half-mil.

"Another possibility is that it was a contract heist. Some collector just *had* to have those cockamamie stamps. He can't afford a million at auction, but he can afford, say, fifty thousand to hire some experienced burglar to lift them. Believe me, there are collectors like that. They'd never put the Jennies on public display; it would be enough to drool over them in private.

"A third possibility is that the thief will use the stamps as collateral for a bank loan. Take my word for it, there are banks here and abroad that accept collateral like stolen bearer bonds without inquiring too closely how the loan applicant got possession. So the crook gets his loan, defaults, and the bank is stuck with hot merchandise while the bad guy is tanning his hide on the French Riviera."

"Fascinating," I said. "I didn't realize it would be so easy to convert the stamps into cash."

"Not easy," Rogoff said, "but it can be done. The simplest way, of course, would be to sell the stamps to a crooked dealer."

"Talking about dealers," I said, "do you know of any local experts who could provide more information about the Inverted Jennies?"

He thought a moment. "There's a guy on the island named Bela Rubik. As in Cube. He's got a stamp and coin shop off Worth Avenue. He knows his stuff. I've used him to help identify stolen property."

"Is he straight?" I asked.

"As far as I know."

"Thanks, Al. You've been a big help. I'll take it from here."

He stared at me. "Why do I have this antsy feeling that I haven't heard the last of the Inverted Jennies?"

"Beats me," I said, shrugging. "I can't see why the Department should get involved."

"The last time you told me that, I ended up in a shoot-out with two crackheads. Remember that?"

"I remember," I said. "You performed admirably."

"Oh sure. And almost got blown away. Thanks for the banquet. Don't call us; we'll call you."

We shook hands and he tramped away. I signed tabs for the lunch and my drinks at the bar, then headed back to Palm Beach. I was satisfied with what I had learned from Rogoff. I don't claim to be yours truly, S. Holmes. I mean I can't glance at a man and immediately know he is left-handed, constipated, has a red-haired wife, and slices lox for a living. I do investigations a fact at a time. Eventually they add up—I hope. I'm very big on hope.

I found Rubik's Stamp & Coin Shop without too much trouble. It was a hole-in-the-wall but appeared clean and prosperous. There was an attractive display of Morgan silver dollars in the front window.

But the door was locked, and I rattled the knob a few times before the man inside came forward and inspected me carefully through the glass. Then he unlocked, let me enter, locked the door behind me. He went back behind the showcase and shoved his glasses, a curious pair of linked jeweler's loupes, atop his bald head.

"Mr. Rubik?" I asked.

He nodded. I fished out a business card and handed it over. He read it slowly, then handed it back.

"I don't need a lawyer," he said. "I already got a will."

I smiled as pleasantly as I could. "I'm not drumming up business, Mr. Rubik. I just need a little information."

He stared at me, silent and expressionless. I figured he was on the down-side of sixty, and if his grayish pallor was any indication, he'd never hit seventy. He had a puffy face and his gaze was unfocused and nearsighted. He reminded me of someone I had seen before. Suddenly it came to me: He was Mr. Magoo.

"Information?" he said finally, in a creaky voice. "You lawyers bill by the hour, don't you?"

"That's correct."

"For information," he said, "I do the same. My fee is fifty dollars an hour. Payable in advance for the first consultation."

I took out my wallet, picked out a fifty, and handed it over. "I'll need a receipt for that," I said, trying not to show how miffed I was.

"Of course," he said. "What information do you want?"

"I want to learn something about the Inverted Jenny airmail stamps."

His stare was making me nervous. "Why do you want to know about that issue?" he asked.

I could have demanded, "What the hell do you care? You got paid, didn't you?" Instead I said, "My firm is handling the will of a Boca Raton real estate developer who passed away recently. His estate includes a block of four Inverted Jennies. We'd like to establish an approximate evaluation."

"You want me to make an appraisal without seeing the stamps? Impossible. What condition are they in? Are they glued in an album or what? Are they faded, torn, folded? All these things affect the value."

I sighed. "I don't want you to appraise this particular block of stamps, Mr. Rubik. I just want some general information about Inverted Jennies."

"Nine sheets of the twenty-four-cent airmail stamps were issued in 1918. The printing plate of the blue biplane in the center had been put on the press backwards. Eight sheets were destroyed after the error was discovered. The ninth was sold over the counter in a Washington, D.C., post office to a broker's clerk for twenty-four dollars. A week later he sold the sheet of a hundred stamps to a dealer for fifteen thousand. The sheet was then broken up into blocks and singles. Over the years the value has greatly increased. The block of four that was recently auctioned in New York for a million showed the plate number. A block of four with a printing-plate guideline through the middle went for less than half of that."

"Are there any Inverted Jennies for sale now?"

Rubik shrugged. "Everything is for sale—if the price is right. But many of the Jennies have deteriorated. Like I told you, the value depends on the condition of the stamps."

I tried again. "Are there any on the market now?"

"That I can't say."

"Could you find out? You have contacts with other dealers, I presume. Do you have an association?"

"Yes."

"Will you inquire and see if any Inverted Jennies are being offered for sale?"

"That's a big job," he said. "It'll take time."

"Fifty dollars an hour," I reminded him.

"All right," he said grudgingly, "I'll ask around."

I waited patiently while he pulled down his crazy glasses and wrote out a receipt for fifty dollars in a spidery scrawl. Actually, prorated, he had given me about twenty dollars' worth of time. But I said nothing. If he wanted to believe he had diddled me, so much the better. I have profited mightily by letting people think I am a tap-dancer when, in reality, I am capable of *Swan Lake*.

I took the bill and handed back my business card. "If you hear of any Jennies for sale," I said, "give me a call. If I don't hear from you, I'll stop by again in a week or so."

"I'll have my bill ready," he said without smiling.

He may have been straight, as Sgt. Rogoff had said, but I thought Bela Rubik was a surly character with a galloping case of cupidity. I vowed he would never get my vote for Mr. Congeniality.

My next step was at a nearby sporting goods emporium. In the tennis section I picked out a Spalding graphite racquet I thought would please Jennifer Towley. The clerk promised she could exchange it if the weight and balance didn't suit her. I had it gift-wrapped with a wide ribbon and bow, tossed it into the Miata, and headed for home.

I arrived in time to change and go down to the ocean for my daily plunge. When the surf wasn't too high, I tried to swim a mile up the shore and a mile back. I am not a graceful swimmer, I admit, but I plow along and I get there. Swimming two miles in the late afternoon is an extremely healthful exercise and makes one eager for the cocktail hour.

The gentry must have their ceremonies, of course, and the cocktail hour was one of ours. Actually, it rarely lasted more than thirty minutes, but it wouldn't be posh to call it the cocktail half-hour, would it?

My mother, father, and I met in the second-floor sitting room, and there the senior McNally would go through the ritual of mixing a pitcher (not too large) of gin martinis. I know it is fashionable to demand *dry* martinis; the drier the better. Some insist on a mixture of eight or ten parts gin to one of vermouth. In fact, I know fanatics who believe having an unopened bottle of vermouth somewhere in the neighborhood is sufficient.

But my father is an ardent traditionalist, and his martinis were mixed in the classic formula: three parts gin, one part vermouth. The result was so odd and unusual that I found it enjoyable. The sire did relax his stern standards to the extent of using olives stuffed with a bit of jalapeño pepper.

On that particular day he had come home early to enjoy the family cocktail hour and then change into black tie since he was scheduled to be the main speaker that evening at a testimonial dinner of our local bar association.

After the martini rite was completed, my father departed, and mother and I dined alone downstairs. That night, as I recall, we had lamb chops with fresh mint sauce. Different from Leroy Pettibone's hamburgers, but not necessarily better. Just different.

Now I must tell you something about my mother since she was fated to play an important role in what I later came to call "The Direful Case of the Inverted Jenny."

Her name was Madelaine, and she was the dearest, sweetest woman who ever lived but, like all mothers, slightly dotty. She was a native Floridian, which is very rare; most Floridians were born in Ohio. She met my father-to-be when she worked as a secretary in the Miami law firm he joined after becoming a full-fledged attorney. It turned out to be a splendid match.

Not that there weren't disagreements, but they were mostly of a minor nature. My parents could never, ever, agree on the proper temperature setting for their bedroom air conditioner. And my father decried mother's insistence on drinking sauterne with meat and fish courses, while she could never understand why on earth he demanded starch in the collars and cuffs of his dress shirts.

A more serious personal problem was Madelaine McNally's health. My mother was overweight, not obese but definitely much, much too plump. In addition, she suffered from high blood pressure, which probably accounted for her somewhat florid complexion and occasional shortness of breath. Our family physician had put her on a strict diet, and we were bewildered that it resulted in no weight loss. Then we discovered she had been sneaking chocolate truffles while working amidst her begonias in the greenhouse.

But she really was a wonderful woman, and I loved her. I shall always treasure the profound advice she gave me in the first letter I received at New

Haven. "Archy," she wrote, "live as if every day may be your last, and always have on clean underwear."

That night, during the minty lamb chops, mother and I chatted of this and that, laughed, and then clappped our hands when Ursi Olso brought us fresh, chilled raspberries topped with a sinful dollop of whipped cream.

"No-cal," Ursi assured my mother.

"I don't care," she said. "I just don't *care*. Life is too short."

Over coffee, I remarked that I had seen Lady Cynthia Horowitz that morning.

"Oh? I hope you gave her our best wishes."

"Of course I did," I said, though I hadn't.

"What an unhappy woman," my mother said, suddenly saddened. "I feel sorry for her."

"Mother! That woman's got everything!"

"No," she said, "she doesn't. She wants it all, and no one can have it all."

I thought she was talking goofy nonsense and made no response. We left the table, and mother returned to the sitting room for an evening of television. I went upstairs to my suite to enter the day's events in my journal.

But first I phoned Jennifer Towley on my private line. I got her answering machine, and after the *beep,* I said, "Jennifer, this is Archibald McNally. It is vitally, urgently, desperately important that I speak to you. Please call me at any hour of the day or night." Then I recited my unlisted number, said, "Thank you," and hung up.

I lighted my *first* English Oval of the day (I was so proud) and wondered again what Lady Horowitz had been hinting about Jennifer. I could not believe that cool, complete woman could be guilty of anything more serious than an ingrown toenail, but it was mildly unsettling to discover she was the subject of Palm Beach gossip.

I had worked on my journal for more than an hour, jotting down what I had learned that day, when my phone rang about nine-thirty, and I grabbed it up and said, "H'lo?"

"Jennifer Towley," she said crisply. "What on earth is so vitally, urgently, desperately important?"

"Have you decided to see me again?" I asked eagerly.

"I'm still considering it."

"Well, you *must*," I said. "The Board of Directors of McNally and Son, in solemn conclave assembled, voted to reward you with a gift for your splendid cooperation in the affair of the Frobisher letters. I have made the gift selection and now must make delivery. And that is why it's necessary to see you as soon as possible."

She laughed. "What a devious lad you are," she said.

"Three," I said. "Rogoff was right. Now don't tell me you're the Tooth Fairy."

There was a brief silence. Then: "What *are* you gibbering about?"

"Nothing," I said. "Just idle chatter. Well, when is it to be?"

"I don't know," she said doubtfully. "I'm going to be awfully busy. I've landed a new client who wants her bedroom done over in Art Nouveau. It'll take me forever to find the right pieces."

"Then you'll need a few hours of relaxation," I said. "Dinner tomorrow night would be nice. Ever been to the Pelican Club?"

"No, but I've heard a lot of weird things about it."

"They're all true," I assured her. "Dress informally. I'll stop by for you around seven. Okay?"

"All right," she said faintly.

"And I'll bring your gift," I said. "If I can get three men to help me load it onto the truck."

She was giggling when I hung up. That was a delight, to hear that restrained woman giggle. I went back to my journal with a song in my heart.

I finished making notes and drew up a tentative plan of how I intended to proceed in the Inverted Jenny investigation. Then I poured myself a very small marc from a private stock of spirits and liqueurs I kept in an old sea chest in my sitting room. Pony in hand, I settled down to watch a rerun of *Columbo* on my portable TV set. I had seen that particular segment twice before, but it was still fun.

One more marc and one more English Oval, and I was ready to kiss the day goodbye. I undressed, brushed my teeth, and showered. If I thought of Jennifer Towley—and I did, continually—they were innocent thoughts. Mostly.

I pulled on my pajama shorts, set the air conditioner at 75°, turned out the lights, and went to bed. I slept the untroubled sleep of the pure at heart.

Chapter 4

I phoned Lady Horowitz after breakfast and asked if she had told her employees and house-guests that the Inverted Jenny stamps had disappeared. She said she had.

"And now *everyone* knows," she said bitterly. "I've already had a dozen phony sympathy calls—including one from a cousin in Sarasota. Bad news certainly travels fast."

"Always has," I said cheerfully. "There's nothing more enjoyable than other people's troubles."

Then I asked if it would be all right if I spent most of the day at her place, making discreet inquiries. She said to come ahead, she would tell everyone I'd be nosing around. But she would not be present.

"I'll be gone all day, lad," she said. "I have scads of things to do."

I asked if that meant Kenneth, the chauffeur, would also be absent.

"No," she said, "I'll take the Jag."

I love it. That casual "I'll take the Jag" meant she would not be chauffeured in her antique Rolls-Royce (a rare 1933 Tourer) but would pilot her spanking-new bronzy Jaguar XJ-S convertible.

I was musing on the unique traits of the affluent when I pulled into the white graveled driveway of the Horowitz mansion. I drove to the left, past the guesthouse, to the broad turnaround in front of the five-car garage. Now *there* was a prime example of conspicuous consumption.

When the long, low building had been erected in the early 1920s, it had been designed as a stable, to house the original owner's riding and carriage horses. Would you believe that this habitat for nags was floored with gorgeous tiles from the palazzo of a bankrupt Venetian nobleman and walled with oak panels from an abandoned Spanish monastery? Money, I decided, has no conscience and no memory.

I climbed out of the Miata and strolled into the shadowy garage where a large, muscular young man (about my age) was sponging down the Rolls. He was wearing the trousers of a chauffeur's uniform but had taken off the jacket. His upper torso was tightly sheathed in one of those tailored T-shirts body-builders affect: nipped-in at the waist and with abbreviated cap sleeves, to display their biceps, triceps and, for all I know, forceps.

"Kenneth Bodin?" I asked.

He looked at me, and for a moment I wasn't sure if he would answer or snap my spine just for the fun of it.

"That's right," he said finally in a high-pitched voice that was shocking to hear issuing from the mastodon.

"I'm Archibald McNally," I said. "Did Lady Horowitz tell you I'd be around asking questions about her missing stamps?"

"She said," he acknowledged and tried a smile. I wished he hadn't; his teeth weren't all that great. "I hope she don't think I swiped them."

"Of course not," I assured him. "She doesn't believe anyone in the house had a thing to do with it. Probably someone from outside."

"Sure," he said. "A cat burglar." When I nodded, he went back to washing the Rolls.

"Just a few questions, Mr. Bodin," I said. "When was the last time you saw the stamps?"

He stopped his work and appeared to think a moment. If he was capable of it. Which I doubted.

"Oh lordy," he said, "I haven't seen those things in years. Maybe two or three."

"You live on the premises?"

"Nope." He gestured toward the end of the garage where a lavender '69 Volkswagen Beetle was slumbering peacefully on the Venetian tiles. "That's mine."

"Beautiful car," I said politely.

"I keep it up," he said proudly. "Anyway, I drive in every day. I live in Delray."

"Long way to commute," I observed.

"Not really," he said. "I start out early. Not much traffic, so I can make time. That's a Miata you got—right?"

"Uh-huh."

"Nice," he said. "I wish I could afford one."

"Mr. Bodin," I said, "you suggested the stamps might have been lifted by a cat burglar. Have you seen anyone casing the place recently? You know—lurking about or driving past frequently?"

He shook his head. "No one like that. You could ask the Beach Patrol."

"Good idea," I said. "Can you think of anyone—staff or houseguests—who might have been tempted?"

He stopped wiping off the Rolls with a shammy and turned to face me. God, he was a bruiser! Even his muscles had muscles. If the gossip was true—that he had once been Lady C.'s lover—I could understand her brief fling. The guy was a hulk.

But my admiration for his physique stopped at his thick neck. I thought he had the face of a dyspeptic terrier, and his blond hair was too metallic to be credited to the Florida sun. It was carefully coiffed and artfully streaked. Clairol, I was certain, had provided assistance.

"Why no," he said. "To my way of thinking there's no one around here who'd rob the Lady. She's a good boss, and the guests are all family."

"What about the friend, Angus Wolfson?"

"Shit!" he said with unnecessary vehemence. "That old guy's a butterfly. But he seems to be loaded. So why should he cop the stamps?"

"Why indeed?" I said, and couldn't think of any more questions to ask that he might be willing to answer. "Thank you for talking with me, Mr. Bodin. I appreciate it."

"Sure," he said. "Why not? I got nothing to hide."

He turned away, and I saw he had an unlighted cigarette tucked behind his ear. Why he wasn't sucking on a toothpick I'll never know.

I wandered out into the sunlight, heard soft laughter coming from the pool area, and ambled over there. A man and a woman were seated at an umbrella table, working on what appeared to be iced black coffees and a plate of mini-croissants. They looked up as I approached, and the ancient male rose slowly to his feet.

"Good morning," I said, taking off my white linen cap and giving them a 75-watt smile (my max is 150). "I hate to disturb you, but I wonder if I might join you for a few moments. My name is Archibald McNally. I hope Lady Horowitz warned you I might come puttering around asking questions about the missing Inverted Jennies."

"Of course, my dear chap," the man said, offering a halibut handshake. "I am Angus Wolfson, an old friend of Cynthia's. And I do mean *old*—but please don't ask me to be more precise about my age. Growing old is a dreadful thing—until you consider the alternative!" He paused and waited for my laugh.

I gave him a 25-watter. "Maurice Chevalier," I said.

Something changed in his face. "Oh-ho," he said, "an erudite detective."

"Not very," I said, and then tried to make amends for squelching his big boffola. "That's a marvelous jacket you're wearing, Mr. Wolfson."

It was, too: burgundy velvet in the belted Norfolk style. He wore it over creamy flannel trousers. There was a flowered ascot looped casually around his chicken neck. Quite the aged peacock.

"Thank you," he said, regaining his good humor. "And this lovely lady is Gina Stanescu, daughter of Cynthia and her—which was it, darling? Third or fourth husband?"

"Third," Ms. Stanescu said with a faint smile and offered me a cool hand to shake. "So nice to meet you, Mr. McNally. Do join us."

I pulled up a webbed patio chair and placed it so I was facing both of them.

"We're having iced coffee," Wolfson said. "Would you care for a glass?"

"Thank you, no," I said. "I never drink on duty." I meant it as a joke, of course—a feeble joke, I admit—but it didn't earn so much as a snigger.

"Shocking thing about those stamps," Wolfson said. "Absolutely shocking."

"It is so unpleasant," Stanescu said in a small voice. "It makes one look at other people with new eyes—wondering."

"Could you tell me the last time you saw the stamps."

They looked at each other. Then Wolfson replied:

"Let me see . . . It was at dinner the night Alan DuPey and his bride arrived. Felice had never seen the Inverted Jennies, so Cynthia brought them downstairs to show. Is that correct, Gina?"

She nodded.

"Did everyone see the stamps at dinner?"

"I believe so," Wolfson said. "The book was passed around the table."

"Yes," Stanescu said. "I looked at them and passed the book along."

"And then? After everyone had seen the stamps?"

"I couldn't swear to it," Wolfson said, "but I believe that after we all left the table, Cynthia took them back upstairs to her bedroom."

"She did," the Lady's daughter said definitely. "I walked up the stairs with her. I was going to my room to get a light sweater because we had all decided to sit outside awhile and have a brandy. I saw mother take the little red book into her bedroom."

"And neither of you saw the stamps after that?"

"No," they said in unison.

"Have either of you noticed any strangers prowling about? Anyone who apparently doesn't belong on the estate?"

Wolfson laughed. "You mean some chappie dressed in black and wearing a mask? No, I've seen no one who even remotely resembles a villain. Gina?"

"No," she said, "no one. Everything has been quite normal."

"Do either of you have any doubts about any member of the staff? I assure you, any accusation you may make will be held in strictest confidence."

"I accuse the chef of putting too much saffron in the rice last night," Wolfson said, "but that's hardly criminal. No, to the best of my knowledge everyone on the staff is honest—and remarkably efficient, I might add."

"I agree with Angus," Stanescu said. "All of mother's people seem to be trustworthy and very loyal to her."

Wolfson gave me a derisive smile. "We're not much help, are we?" he said.

"No," I agreed, "not much."

He took a sip of his iced coffee, started on another croissant, and I had a moment to eyeball him directly. He must have been a dandy fifty years ago, but now the Barrymore profile had softened. His entire face, in fact, had melted downward, pulling at a broad, high brow that was now pale and shiny with stretched skin.

"Mr. Wolfson," I said, "this has nothing to do with the stamps, and if you feel I am prying unnecessarily, please tell me, but are you retired?"

"Semi," he said. "I was somewhat of a bookman. Had a sweet little shop on the Square. I am also somewhat of a bibliophile, and somewhat of an antiquarian. I have been a somewhat all my life, Mr. McNally, and have done very well at it, I might add. These days my professional activities are limited. Occasionally I am called upon to serve as a consultant to librarians, private and public, and to make appraisals of rare books prior to sale or auction."

"Interesting," I said. "I have a first edition of Mad Comics. Should I sell it, sir?"

"No," he said. "Hold."

We all laughed.

"What about me," Gina Stanescu said. "I feel left out. Don't you want to know about me?"

"I do indeed," I said.

"I am forty-one and unmarried," she stated flatly, "and well on my way to becoming what in your country is called an old maid. A strange fate for the daughter of a mother who has been married six times—is it not? I live in France, in Rouen, where I am the director of an orphanage. And that is the whole story of my life, total and complete."

"An orphanage?" I said. "That must be very rewarding work."

"Rewarding and frustrating. There is never enough money."

"You shouldn't have said that, Gina," Wolfson chided. "Now Mr. McNally will suspect you pinched your mother's stamps to support your home for bastards."

I was offended but she wasn't. She reached out to place a soft hand on one of his veined claws. "Dear Angus," she said fondly. "You talk like a devil, but I know you have a heart of gold."

He snorted. "Of tarnished brass you mean," he said, and lifted her hand to kiss her knuckles.

This Gina Stanescu seemed to me a curious woman. She was swathed in a summery gown of miles and miles of white chiffon and wore a woven straw hat with a wide, floppy brim that sometimes obscured her dark eyes. The floating dress and garden hat gave her a wispy look as if she might go galloping through the heather bellowing, "Heathcliff! Heathcliff!"

But despite that vaporish appearance, her features were as sharp as her mother's. She had a no-nonsense manner, and I suspected those orphans in

Rouen did their lessons and cleaned their plates. I wondered, idly, what the body of Lady Cynthia's daughter might be like, hidden beneath those yards of billowing silk. The image that sprang to mind was that of a very elegant Japanese sword.

Wolfson suddenly turned to me. "You are the son of Cynthia's attorney, Prescott McNally, are you not?"

"Yes, sir."

"I have met your father," he said. "A gentleman of the old school." His smile held more than irony but less than scorn.

"He is that," I agreed and rose to make my farewells. I thanked them for their cooperation and warned I might return with more questions. They couldn't have been more gracious, but when I returned to the Miata, I heard their muted laughter drifting across the manicured lawn.

Since no one had invited me to stick around for a spot of lunch, I raced home with a terrible craving for a cold ale and a corned beef sandwich on the sour rye Ursi Olson baked once a week. There was no corned beef in the fridge, but Ursi provided smoked salmon topped with slices of onion, which added up to a very satisfactory substitute.

Sandwich in hand, I sauntered around to the garage where Jamie was planting a few dwarf palms to make the place look less like a barrack.

"What's new?" I asked him.

"Nuthin," he said, so I gave him a nudge.

"I talked to Kenneth Bodin this morning," I said. "You were right; he's a big one."

"Uh-huh." '

"And not too much between his ears," I added.

"Air," Jamie said.

I waited patiently.

"Girlfriend's name is Sylvia," he said finally. "Sylvia Montcliff or Montgrift or Montgrief. Something like that. Lives in Delray Beach."

"Sure she does," I said. "So does he. Thanks, Jamie."

I took what remained of my sandwich up to my lair and scribbled in my journal awhile. I figured I might not have the energy after what I hoped would be an enjoyable engagement with Jennifer Towley that evening.

By two-thirty I was back at the Horowitz estate, and this time I entered the main house by the back door and went directly to the kitchen. Jean Cuvier, the chef, was seated at a stainless steel table, the usual Gitane dangling from his lower lip. He was poring over a handicap sheet for the races at Calder. Instead of the white toque of his calling, he wore a New York Yankee baseball cap, the beak turned to the rear.

If girth was any indication of culinary talent he should have been a Cordon Pourpre instead of a Cordon Bleu. I mean he was a *humongous* man with three chins, two bellies and, I presumed, jowls on his kneecaps. He was also living refutation of the popular belief that all fat men are jolly, being peevish and cranky. But his genius with a saucepan excused all.

"Bonjour, maître," I said.

He squinted up at me through a swirl of blue smoke. "Bonjour, Ar-chay," he said.

The following conversation was entirely in French. My years at Yale weren't a total loss.

I asked him when was the last time he had seen the Inverted Jenny stamps. He shrugged and said years and years ago. I asked if he had seen a small red book being passed around the dinner table on the night Alan DuPey and his wife arrived. He shrugged and said no.

I asked if he thought anyone on the staff might have taken the stamps. He shrugged. I asked if he had seen any nogoodnik-types skulking about. He shrugged and said no. Then I asked if he thought any of the houseguests might be capable of such a nefarious deed. This time he didn't shrug, but slowly stubbed out the minuscule butt of the Gitane in a white china saucer.

"Perhaps," he said.

"Who?"

"The English son," he said. "Harry Smythe and his wife."

"Why them?"

Then he shrugged. "They are very cold people. And the last time they were here, they left me no tip. A month of meals, and no tip. I thought they were tight people. Cold and tight. But perhaps they are in need of money. They see the stamps and think the madam is rich and will not miss them. So they collar the stamps. Simple, no?"

I was about to shrug when a young woman in a maid's uniform entered the kitchen. I recognized her from those dinners my family had enjoyed at the Chez Horowitz. I knew she was addressed as Clara but didn't know her last name. I introduced myself and learned she was Clara Bodkin—and you didn't have to be a Shakespearean scholar for the phrase "bare bodkin" to leap to mind, for she was a toothsome creature, a bit plumpish but excellently proportioned. Her flawless, sun-blushed complexion was especially attractive.

I ran through my list of questions, in English, with meager results. Yes, she had seen the stamps being passed around the table at the DuPey dinner. That was the last time she had seen them. No, she did not believe anyone on the staff or any of the houseguests was capable of the theft. And while she had seen no strangers hanging about, it was her theory that some fiend had sneaked into the house while everyone slept, and took the Inverted Jennies from madam's wall safe. It gave her, Clara, chills to think about it.

I listened to all this somewhat absently. My attention was elsewhere. For as Clara spoke so volubly, she stood alongside Jean Cuvier's chair, and he was steadily stroking her rump in a thoughtful fashion. She did not move away.

He must have seen astonishment in my face, for after Clara finished talking, he lighted another Gitane and said to me, in French, "It is all right, Ar-chay. Clara and I are to be married."

"Congratulations," I said heartily.

"For one night," he added, and gave a great shout of laughter.

"What did he say?" Clara demanded of me. "Is the blimp talking dirty again?"

"Not at all," I said hastily. "He told me that I can accept every word you say as gospel since you know everything that's going on in this house."

"That I do," she said, nodding. "But I see no evil, hear no evil, speak no evil."

"Very wise," I assured her.

When I left, she was tickling the back of his fat neck. I do believe she might have seated herself on his lap—if he had one.

I decided I had earned my salary for the day, and besides, asking the same questions continually had the same effect as the Chinese water torture. I drove home, changed, and went down to the beach for a swim. I resolutely did my two miles and returned home in time to dress for the family cocktail hour 'and my date with Jennifer Towley.

Mother remarked how handsome I looked, father stared disgustedly at my acid green polo shirt, and I ingested my share of the martini pitcher's contents. Then I bid them good night and departed for what I hoped would be an evening of a thousand delights. I didn't forget Jennifer's tennis racquet. Talk about Greeks bearing gifts!

She lived across Lake Worth, south of the Royal Park Bridge. It was an old neighborhood of short streets west of Flagler Drive. The homes were small but pleasant, the grounds limited but neatly groomed. Jennifer rented the ground floor of a two-story stucco building painted a sky blue. Her apartment was her antique shop; everything in the place was for sale—except the lady herself, of course.

She greeted me at the door, and I entered into a foyer (Edwardian) and then was ushered into the living room (Victorian). I had suggested she dress informally, but she was impeccably upholstered in a black dress so simple and *nothing* that it must have cost a fortune. The only jewelry she wore was a pale amethyst choker. Elegant? On a scale of 1 to 10, I'd rate her a 12.

The tennis racquet was an instant success; after hefting it and trying a few swings, she declared the weight and balance were perfect. I received a kiss in gratitude. It was a very small kiss but much appreciated.

I held the Miata door for her, and she slid in with a flash of bare tanned legs that made me want to turn cartwheels on her lawn. But I controlled my rapture and we sped off to the Pelican Club. I called her attention to the full moon I had ordered for the occasion.

"I may turn into a werewolf," I cautioned.

"I'll get some garlic at the restaurant," she said.

"Garlic is for vampires," I told her. "And frogs' legs. There is no known defense against a werewolf."

"I have a black belt in karate," she claimed.

"I have a white belt in Indian wrestling," I said. "Perhaps later this evening you will permit me to demonstrate."

She laughed. "What am I going to do with you?" she asked.

"Love me," I replied, but I did not say it aloud.

We were early enough to beat the usual dinner crowd, and Priscilla showed us to my favorite corner table. Jennifer looked about with interest.

"It resembles a fraternity house," she said.

"It was intended to," I said. "Strictly stag. But shortly after the club was organized, the ladyfriends and wives of several founding members threatened a lawsuit if they were not allowed to join. They said they would claim sex discrimination because we were carrying on business networking at the club. Actually, the only networking going on was an active exchange of hangover remedies, but we surrendered graciously to their demands. Now the Pelican Club is a coed establishment. The roster is full, but I chair the Membership Committee and might be able to finagle a quid pro quo and get you a card if you're interested in joining."

"Thank you," she said, giving me the cool, level gaze, "but I think not. If I want to visit I'll ask you to invite me."

"Splendid idea," I said, and looked around for Priscilla. She was standing at the kitchen door, and when she caught my eye she pointed at Jennifer and made a loop with thumb and forefinger in the A-OK sign. It was gratifying to have her approval.

She came over to the table and posed, hip-sprung. "Something to wet the whistle, folks?" she said.

"Let's have a champagne cocktail," I suggested to Jennifer.

"Oh my," she said, "you'll spoil me."

"That's my intent," I said. "We'll have champagne cocktails, Priscilla. And what is Leroy pushing tonight?"

"Roast pork or broiled yellowtail."

"How's the yellowtail?"

"I wouldn't know," she said. "I eat at McDonald's."

Jennifer smiled.

"Priscilla," I said, "behave yourself."

She grinned and sashayed away to fetch our cocktails.

It turned out to be a very pleasant dinner indeed. We both had the yellowtail, shared a big Caesar salad, and had lemon ice for dessert.

Jennifer ate like a trencherwoman—which always pleases the guy who's picking up the tab. She spoke very little but that was okay; I like to talk, as you may have guessed, and I kept her laughing throughout the meal.

I do not consider myself a womanizer. Most of my relationships with women have been lasting, some as long as three or four months, and one for an entire year, almost. I have always favored jolly ladies who are not too intent on trotting up the aisle while an adenoidal soprano belts out "Oh Promise Me."

We moved out to the bar where we had a brandy stinger because it seemed the glam thing to do. I had a vague romantic notion of suggesting a long drive down the coast during which the full moon shining off a calm sea would work its libidinous magic. But Jennifer, now suddenly serious, if not solemn, said she'd like to return home since she had an important appointment early the next morning. The moon promptly went behind a cloud.

So I drove her back to her pad, disappointed but not devastated. In addition to playing the clown, one must have an endless reserve of patience. We pulled in front of her trig little house, and I killed the engine, hoping against odds that she might invite me in for a nightcap.

She turned on the seat to face me and took up my hand. Good start.

"Archy," she said, "there is something I must tell you."

"Oh?"

"I'm divorced."

It was my turn to laugh. "Jennifer, you say that as if it was an awful perversion, like collecting thimbles. A lot of people are divorced. Some of my best friends are divorced. It's really not a mortal sin."

"I just wanted you to know."

"Thank you. Now I know."

She hesitated, and I thought she was about to reveal more. But apparently she changed her mind. Instead, she said, "Then it won't change things between us?"

I stared at her, and my mouth might have fallen open just a wee bit. "Of course not," I said, thinking that this *couldn't* be what Lady Horowitz warned me about. Divorce is as widespread in Palm Beach as jock itch in the Major Leagues. "I don't see why it should change anything."

"Would you like to come in for a nightcap?" she asked.

Strange, enigmatic woman!

Chapter 5

On the following morning I went to the office with my father. He drove his Lexus the way he did everything else: slowly, carefully, and with a deep respect for thou-shalt-nots. I mean we'd come to a red light, no traffic to be seen in either direction, and he'd stop and wait for the green. What an upright man he was! But never a prig; he was simply worshipful of the law. His tombstone might justifiably bear the inscription: "Prescott McNally: He never stole a hotel towel."

"About Lady Horowitz's missing stamps," he said, eyes determinedly on the road. "Are you making any progress?"

"Not really, sir," I said. "So far I've spoken to three of the staff and two houseguests and learned very little."

He was silent a moment, and I knew the gears were turning. Not meshing yet, but turning.

"What is your feeling about this, Archy? Have the stamps merely been misplaced or were they stolen?"

"All I can do right now is guess," I told him. "I'd guess they were pinched."

Then the gears meshed, and he nodded. "I think it would be prudent to act on that assumption. I'll call Lady Cynthia and suggest she report the disappearance of the Inverted Jennies to the police immediately. Or, if she prefers, I'll do it for her."

"Father!" I said, offended. "I've just started my investigation."

He gave me a brief glance, then hastily turned his attention back to the road. "Archy, I don't mean to bruise your ego, but if the stamps are not recovered—a possibility, you'll admit—and Lady Horowitz puts in a claim for the insurance, it is vitally important that there is a police record attesting to the fact that she reported the theft. You can understand that, can't you?"

"Yes, sir," I said resignedly. "Does this mean I'm off the case?"

"Not at all. I want you to continue your discreet inquiries."

"That means the cops and I will be walking up each other's heels," I said. "Interviewing the same people twice."

"You've worked with the police before," he pointed out. "And very successfully, I might add. Besides, as you well know, it is frequently wise to ask a witness to repeat his or her story twice or more. It's an effective method of uncovering discrepancies."

"All right then," I said, "I'll keep at it. You might suggest to Lady Cynthia that she report the theft to Sergeant Al Rogoff. If he catches the squeal, he may be assigned the investigation. Al and I get along well together."

I didn't think it necessary to tell him that Rogoff already knew of the theft. We drove along in silence a few minutes while I debated whether the injection of officialdom into what I considered *my* case would prove a help or a hindrance.

"Pleasant evening last night?" my father asked idly.

"What?" I said, startled. "Oh yes, sir, very pleasant."

"Anyone your mother and I know?"

"I don't think so. Jennifer Towley, the lady who returned the Frobisher letters. I gave her the tennis racquet."

"And was she appreciative?"

"Extremely."

"You are attracted to her?"

"Exceedingly."

He sighed. "It seems to me I have heard that several times in the past."

I laughed. "Father, I know very well that you and mother would like to see me happily married, settled down, and producing grandchildren at regular intervals. That time may come—but not yet."

"We'll try to be patient," he said dryly.

McNally & Son was not a rinky-dink operation. We occupied (and owned) a five-story edifice of glass and stainless steel on Royal Palm Way. The architecture was not to my father's taste, but he admitted the gleaming modernism seemed to impress clients, potential clients, and IRS auditors.

Most of the firm's work was in estate planning, taxes, revocable and charitable trusts, and dull stuff like that. But we also had associates skilled in litigation; real estate; copyrights, trademarks and patents; divorce; malpractice;

personal and product liability; and even one old codger who knew more maritime law than anyone south of Chesapeake Bay. McNally & Son was, in fact, a legal supermarket.

My office was possibly the smallest in the building, and I often thought I was condemned to that cell so that Prescott McNally could easily refute any charges of nepotism. But I really didn't mind since I rarely occupied the office. Naturally I wasn't assigned a secretary, but on those rare occasions (about once a year) when I had to compose a letter, my father's personal secretary, Mrs. Trelawney, helped me out and corrected my spelling. I never could remember if there were one or two c's and m's in "accomodate."

The reason I visited headquarters that morning was to prepare my monthly expense account, which might be a contender for the Pulitzer Prize for Fiction. I dug out all my bar and restaurant tabs, the bill for Jennifer's tennis racquet, the signed receipt from Bela Rubik (the stamp and coin man), bills for dues paid to various clubs, and bits of this and that. I added them all up, and the total seemed to me woefully inadequate.

So I tacked on a few imaginary cash expenditures: cab rides I had never taken, bribes to informants I had never made, gas purchases for the Miata. I did not go hog-wild, of course; I am not a swindler. But as I added more fanciful items, my swindle sheet grew satisfyingly.

I was still hard at it when my phone rang. I was shocked. I mean, my phone almost *never* rings. And then it's usually a wrong number.

"Archibald McNally," I answered.

"The Machiavelli of Palm Beach?" Sgt. Al Rogoff said. "I just wanted to check that you're in. What a pleasant surprise! I'll be right over."

"What for?" I asked.

"Hah!" was all he said before hanging up.

A half-hour later he was squirming uncomfortably on the one folding steel chair allotted to me for visitors, regarding me more in anger than in sorrow.

"Rat fink," he said accusingly. "Oh, excuse me. I should have addressed someone who's a pal of Lady Horowitz as *Mister* Rat Fink."

I held up my palms in surrender. "Al, I swear I didn't know until this morning that she was going to file a complaint. I really thought it was going to be my headache. I had no idea it would end up on your plate."

"Yeah?" he said, staring at me. "Maybe. And maybe not. You been looking into it?"

"Only for two days."

"What have you got?" he demanded, taking out his notebook.

I gave him the names of the staff and guests residing at the Horowitz home. I recited the gist of the conversations I had with Kenneth Bodin, Angus Wolfson, Gina Stanescu, Jean Cuvier, and Clara Bodkin. I described Lady Cynthia's bedroom, and told him about the unrifled jewelry box close to the wall safe.

He scribbled rapid notes in his little book, and when I finished, he looked up at me suspiciously. "And that's all you've got?"

"That's all."

"Come on, Archy, don't try to kid a kidder. You're holding out on me."

I had already polished the bone I intended to toss him.

"Well, there is something," I said hesitantly, "but I don't think it's important."

"Let me play the judge. What is it?"

I told him that a few weeks before the stamps disappeared, a butler and a maid had left Lady Horowitz's employ, claiming they couldn't stand the heat of a Florida summer.

"But the Inverted Jennies were seen after they left," I pointed out, "so they couldn't be involved in the snatch. Unless they sneaked back in."

"Uh-huh," Al said. "Or told some light-fingered buddy about the stamps. Okay, I'll look into it." He closed his fat notebook and put a rubber band around it. "You figure to keep sherlocking on this thing?"

I nodded. "I planned to go out there this afternoon and check out some of the people I haven't talked to yet."

He considered that awhile, and I awaited his decision. If he ordered me off the case, I'd have to take a walk. He had the badge, not me.

"All right," he said finally, "you keep nosing around and we'll compare notes. Nothing held back. Is that understood?"

"Of course," I said. "I wouldn't have it any other way."

He sighed and hauled himself to his feet. "I hate Beach cases," he said. "Those richniks treat me like the hired help."

"Don't give it a second thought," I advised him. "They're just as innocent and just as guilty as anyone else. And don't forget the gifts at Christmastime."

"Yeah," he said sourly. "A box of stale Girl Scout cookies." He started for the door, then paused and looked about my infinitesimal office. "You really rate," he said.

"The boss's son," I reminded him.

He was laughing when he left.

What I hadn't told him, of course—and didn't intend to—was the rumor that a few years ago Lady Horowitz had been enjoying fun and games with her chauffeur. It seemed to me the doyenne was the type of woman who'd terminate that relationship; it wouldn't be Kenneth Bodin who split; he'd never want the gravy train to stop.

And, assuming he was unceremoniously dumped, it was possible he had entertained dim-witted thoughts of revenge against the wealthy woman who had suddenly taken him up and then just as suddenly dropped him, either from boredom or because she found another lover with Bodin's physical excitement plus the brains he lacked. So the muscleman, enraged by this slight to his machismo, decided to swipe the Inverted Jennies to teach the rich bitch a lesson.

Thin stuff, you say? Of course it was. I knew it was. But it was all I had so far, and I wanted to check it out before handing over the results to Sgt. Al Rogoff.

I finished composing my expense account, dropped it off at our treasurer's office, and then stopped by the employees' cafeteria. The luncheon specialty of the day was something called a "mushburger," apparently made of minced mushrooms, carrots, black olives, and rhubarb. What, no turnips? Anyway I passed. But I did drink a glass of unsalted tomato juice and ate two rice cakes. Feeling healthy as all get-out, I leaped into the Miata and headed for the Horowitz domain.

I rang the front-door chimes and, as I had hoped, the oak portal was opened by the housekeeper, Mrs. Marsden. We exchanged pleasantries, and I asked if we could talk privately for a moment.

"I was wondering when you'd get around to me," she said—a steely smile there—and led the way into the first-floor sitting room, which could have held the Boston Pops. We sat in chintz-covered armchairs in a secluded corner and leaned toward each other, speaking in hushed voices as if we were trading state secrets.

She was a majestic woman with the posture and manner of a sergeant major. She was a widow, and I happened to know she had put two kids through college by enduring all the craziness of the Horowitz ménage. She had been with Lady C. a long time, and I doubted if any outrage her mistress might commit would surprise her. She knew she was working for a loony and accepted it.

I took her through the usual questions, and she gave a firm negative to all. Then I sat back and regarded her gravely.

"Mrs. Marsden, you know I'm not a lawyer, but I do represent my father, Lady Cynthia's attorney. So in a sense I am bound by the same rules of lawyer-client confidentiality. What I'm trying to say is that it's the job of McNally and Son to protect the interests of Lady Horowitz. With that in mind, is there anything at all you can tell me about the disappearance of the stamps? I assure you it'll be held in strictest confidence."

She was silent for a long while, which was a tipoff in itself. If there was nothing, she would have said so immediately.

Finally she stirred restlessly. "It's nothing I can spell out," she said. "Nothing definite—you understand?"

I nodded.

"A feeling," she said. "That's all it is, a feeling. I see people talking, and they shut up when I come close. And people meeting people they shouldn't be meeting."

"Which people?" I asked.

But she ignored my question. "Just the mood," she said, almost ruminating. "Like something's happening, something's going down, but I don't know what it is. That's not much help, is it?"

"More than you think," I told her. "I trust your instincts. If things become a little clearer, will you contact me?"

"Yes, I could do that."

"I know you have our phone numbers, at home and the office. I'd really appreciate it if you'd give me a call. This business is nasty."

"That it is," she said, nodding vigorously. "I-do-not-like-it-one-bit."

"I won't take up any more of your time, Mrs. Marsden. Anyone else around I can talk to?"

"Harry Smythe and his wife are out on the north terrace. Playing chess."

"Nice people?" I asked her.

"I wouldn't know, sir," she said, the perfect servant.

I found my way to the north terrace—the one in the shade—and walked into a family squabble. Nothing vulgar, but as I arrived he swept the chessboard clear with a sweep of his arm and she gave him a high-intensity glare. If looks could kill, he would have been dead on the scene. And these were the people chef Jean Cuvier had described as "cold"?

I stooped to pick up a rook and a pawn, and set them upright on the board. "Checkmate," I said with what I hoped was a soothing smile. It wasn't.

"And just who the hell are you?" he demanded in a BBC accent.

I was tempted to give him a brash response like "Mickey Mouse" or "King Tut" but obviously neither of them was in the mood for levity.

"Archibald McNally," I said. "And you must be Doris and Harry Smythe. Surely Lady Horowitz told you I'd be around asking questions about her missing stamps."

"It's got nothing to do with us," the woman said in the surliest way imaginable. "So bug off."

Unbidden, I pulled up a chair, sat down, crossed my legs, and gave them a taste of the McNally insolence. "Of course it concerns you," I said stonily. "You were on the premises when the Inverted Jennies disappeared. So naturally you are suspect. The theft has now been reported to the local authorities. If you refuse to answer my questions, I shall be forced to report your uncooperative attitude to Sergeant Al Rogoff, who is heading the official investigation. He has been known to make recalcitrant witnesses talk by beating them about the kidneys with a rubber truncheon."

I really thought I had gone too far, and they'd immediately dismiss me as a demented freak. But perhaps it was the influence of American movies and TV shows that caused them to stare at me in horrified astonishment, wondering if I might be telling the truth about the interrogative techniques of Florida cops.

"We know absolutely nothing about it," Harry Smythe said, tugging at his ridiculously wispy Vandyke.

"Not a thing," his wife chimed in.

I looked at them. What a pair they were! Both long and stretched, all pale skin and tendons. Both wore their hair parted in the middle, but his was sparse and straw yellow while hers was thick chestnut and quite long. And both had the dazed eyes and clenched jaws of the luckless. I hoped Mrs. Marsden would count the silver before they left.

I spent an unpleasant twenty minutes putting the Smythes through my inquisition. But as I seemingly accepted all their answers without objection, their aplomb returned, and Harry took to staring at my pastel silk sports jacket with chilly disdain. He was wearing a Harris tweed with suede patches on the elbows—in South Florida yet!

I didn't find it bothersome if he thought me foppish. That was his opinion—and my father's. *His* idea of sartorial splendor is wearing a Countess Mara tie.

"There is nothing you can add to what you've already told me?" I asked finally.

"I think someone on the staff took the stamps," he offered.

"Thank you both very much," I said, rising. "I'll probably be back with more questions, and I imagine Sergeant Rogoff will want to hear your story as well. Now go back to your chess game. It's such a lovely day for it."

I marched back into the house and met Lady Cynthia Horowitz entering from the front door. She looked like a million dollars. But I speak metaphorically. Actually she looked like a hundred million dollars which, according to Palm Beach gossip, was her approximate net worth. Anyway, she was smashing in a Donna Karan sheath of beige linen. She also had a tennis bracelet of diamonds around one bare ankle.

"Hi, lad," she said breezily. "How's the snooping coming along?"

"Slowly," I said. "I've just been talking to Doris and Harry Smythe."

"Monsters, aren't they?" she said. "I just can't believe that stiff is my son. And that shrew he married! The two of them are so dull."

"You invited them," I pointed out.

"Come with me," she ordered, crooking a forefinger.

I followed her down the long hallway to a shadowed game room complete with billiard table, card tables, and a small roulette wheel. There was also a zinc wet bar built into one wall, and that's where Lady Cynthia headed.

"What'll you have?" she asked.

"Nothing, thank you," I said. "But you go ahead."

"I intend to," she said, and I watched with fascination as she swiftly and expertly constructed a gin-and-bitters.

"Let me tell you about my son Harry," she said, "and my sweet daughter-in-law. They're professional guests. That's how they live: London to Paris to Antibes to Monte Carlo to Palm Beach to Newport—wherever they have acquaintances, friends, or relatives who'll put up with them for a weekend, a week, a month—whatever. Neither Harry nor Doris has ever worked and probably never will. The only capital they have can be packed in four suitcases. I give Harry a yearly allowance, just enough so they can fly tourist-class to their next invitation. Sponges, both of them."

"A sad way to live," I observed. "What kind of a future can they have?"

She gave me a crooked grin. "They're waiting for me to die," she said, then hoisted her glass. "Cheers!" she said.

I wished then I had asked for a drink because what she said touched me. Sad bravery always does.

"Ma'am," I said, "I'd like to ask you something I hope won't offend you. If the Smythes are constantly on their uppers, as you say, do you think it possible they might have stolen the Inverted Jennies?"

She considered that a moment, head cocked to one side.

"Nope," she said at last. "Out of character. Petty stuff maybe, but not a *big* crime. They just don't have the balls for it. They're really small people, lad. Which is why I have Mrs. Marsden count the silver before they leave."

I laughed. "The idea had occurred to me. You and I think the same way."

She looked at me strangely. I could not interpret that look.

"Do we?" she said.

I departed soon afterward, having had my fill of the Inverted Jenny Case for one day. I drove home, took my swim, attended the family cocktail hour, and dined with my parents.

I announced my intention of spending the evening in my den getting caught up on personal correspondence. My father suggested I might like to take a break later and come downstairs for a nightcap in his study. Prescott McNally never commanded, he suggested.

I brought my journal up to date, paid a bill for a tapestry waistcoat (couldn't put *that* on my expense account), and dashed off a few short notes.

I also phoned Jennifer Towley and got her answering machine. While waiting for the *beep* I wondered idly if it was a Victorian or Edwardian model. I left a message thanking her for an invigorating evening and asking that she call so that we might arrange an encore. I hung up, curious about where she might be at that hour. I am not afraid of competition, you understand, but I would much prefer the cool Towley gaze be leveled only at me. And my ego is such that I refused to believe she could have found a more ardent swain. Grumbling with frustration, I clumped downstairs to my father's study for that nightcap.

He was still fighting his way through *Little Dorrit*, but put the volume aside when I entered and invited me to help myself from his port decanter. He waited until I was fueled and seated before he spoke:

"I suppose you know that the police have been notified about the disappearance of Lady Horowitz's stamps."

I nodded.

"As you had hoped, Sergeant Rogoff has been assigned to the investigation."

"Yes, sir," I said. "I had a talk with him this morning and gave him what I have, which isn't much."

He looked at me narrowly. "You gave him *everything?*"

"Not *quite* everything," I said, and told my father the wild theory I had that Kenneth Bodin, the chauffeur, might have pinched the stamps to get back at the rich lady who had an affair with him and then gave him the boot.

My father rose from his club chair and strode over to the pipe rack on his marble-topped sideboard. He selected a handsome silver-banded Comoy and began to pack it from a walnut humidor. His back was turned to me.

"You really believe that, Archy?" he asked. "About the chauffeur?"

"I'll have to check it out," I said, "but at the moment it's all I have."

He lighted his pipe with a wooden kitchen match and returned, puffing, to his chair.

"Sounds farfetched to me," he said.

"Yes, sir, it does," I agreed. "And if I had anything better I'd zero in on that. But I still have three more people to talk to, and something might turn up. By the way, I spoke to Lady Horowitz this afternoon. She seemed remarkably chipper."

"She doesn't appear devastated by her loss," he admitted. "But as I'm sure you're aware, it represents a small fraction of her net worth. Couldn't that rumor about Lady Cynthia and her chauffeur be merely idle gossip, with no truth to it?"

"It could be," I acknowledged. "But I'm always amazed at how often local gossip turns out to have at least a kernel of truth. And she does have the reputation of being rather free with her favors, in addition to her six husbands."

"Yes," he said, "I suppose so."

And then he said nothing more about the Inverted Jenny Case. I made some idle conversation about the dwarf palms Jamie had planted about the garage, and he responded mechanically. I finished my port, thanked him, and rose to leave. He didn't urge me to stay.

He said merely, "Keep at it, Archy."

I went back upstairs and prepared for bed. My father is a deep, deep man, and I couldn't help wondering why he had quizzed me in such detail about the missing stamps. Usually he hands me an assignment and never asks questions until I bring him the results. I could only assume he wanted McNally & Son to provide exemplary service to a valued client. There are a lot of hungry attorneys in South Florida, where many wealthy people switch lawyers as often as they do proctologists.

Chapter 6

The following morning I overslept (a not infrequent occurrence) and dashed down to the kitchen where I found Ursi Olson doing something violent to a pot of yams. Our cook-housekeeper is a stalwart woman who looks as if she could plow a field, pause to drop a foal, and then continue plowing.

"Breakfast?" she asked.

"Sure," I said. "But I'm on a diet."

"No eggs Benedict?"

"I lied to you," I said. "I'm not on a diet. Eggs Benedict, by all means."

"You got a phone call from your father's office," she said. "Mrs. Trelawney. She wants you to call her."

While Ursi rustled up my eggs, I used the kitchen phone to call my father's secretary.

"I have your expense account check," she told me.

"Bless you!" I said fervently.

"Can you pick it up?"

"You betcha," I said. "Later today. Okay?"

"Whenever," she said.

Sounds like a silly, innocuous phone call, doesn't it? But later I was to reflect on how important it turned out to be. Because if Mrs. Trelawney hadn't called me, and I hadn't agreed to stop by the office and pick up my check, then I—but I'm getting ahead of myself. At the time it happened I felt nothing but joy at the news that funds awaited me. My checking account had become a bit emaciated. I don't mean that poverty loomed, but one sleeps better with a few shekels under the mattress, doesn't one?

After breakfast I hustled to the Horowitz mansion. I wanted to talk to the remaining residents before they were braced by Sgt. Rogoff and his henchmen. Al is a very capable investigator, but subtlety is not his long suit. First of all, he *looks* menacing, which makes a lot of people lockjawed—especially the guilty. I look like a twit, which fools many into telling me more than they intended.

I headed directly for the ground-floor office of Consuela Garcia, Lady Cynthia's social secretary and my lost love. She was on the phone when I entered and motioned me to a chair.

"But I mailed the invitation myself, Mrs. Blair," she was lying smoothly. "I really can't understand why you didn't receive it. Our dreadful postal service! Well, Lady Horowitz is planning a big Fourth of July bash, and I'll make every effort to make certain you receive your invitation. And again, I'm so sorry you were disappointed last time."

She hung up and grinned at me.

I rubbed one stiff forefinger against the other in the "shame on you" gesture. "Liar, liar, pants on fire," I said.

"Listen, you," she said, "I hear you were at the Pelican with a looker. Who is she?"

"My sister," I said.

"Since when does a guy buy his sister champagne cocktails?"

"Oh-ho," I said. "Priscilla's been talking."

Connie, who's a member of the Pelican Club, said, "Priscilla never blabs and you know it. But my spies are everywhere. How are you, Archy?"

"If I felt any better I'd be unconscious. And you?"

"Surviving, barely. Half the calls I get are from yentas who want to know who snatched the madam's stamps. I suppose that's why you're here."

"You suppose correctly. Have the cops been around?"

"Not yet."

"They will be."

"That's all I need," she said mournfully. "The reporters are bad enough. Okay, let's get it over with."

I ran her through my shortened version of Twenty Questions and learned nothing important. Consuela had last seen the Inverted Jennies about six months ago when Lady Cynthia passed them around at a charity benefit. Everyone knew they were kept in an unlocked wall safe, and anyone could have snaffled them: staff, houseguests, or even brief visitors.

I stared at her as she spoke and saw what had attracted me originally: She was a shortish, perky young lady with cascading black hair. Once, in our brief escapade, I had the joy of seeing her in a string bikini. The memory lingered. But there was more to her than just a bod; she had a brain as well. She ditched me, didn't she?

"Connie," I said, "give me something, no matter how wild. Who do *you* think could have stolen those stupid stamps?"

She pondered a long while. "Not an outsider," she said finally. "Not an over-the-wall crook. I don't buy that. It was an inside job."

I groaned. "Thanks a lot," I said. "Five people on the staff, six houseguests. That's eleven suspects."

"Including me," she said, grinning again.

"That's right," I agreed. "And the cops know it."

"Oh, that's beautiful."

"What about Harry Smythe and his wife?"

"What about them?"

"I don't like them," I said.

"Who does?" she asked, reasonably enough.

"But if I had to make guesses, they wouldn't head the list. They're too mean."

"Who would head the list?"

She hesitated just a moment. Then: "Alan DuPey and his wife."

"Why them?"

"They're too nice."

I came close to slapping my thigh in merriment. "The FBI could use you, Connie. What a sleuth you are!"

"Well, you asked me for wild ideas."

"So I did," I said. "I haven't talked to the DuPeys yet. Are they around?"

"No one's around. The madam is at the hairdresser's and the rest of the crowd has gone out for the day on Phil Meecham's yacht."

"That old roué?" I said. "He'll make a play for all the women and most of the men. All right, I'll catch the DuPeys another time. Thanks for your help, Connie."

I was starting out when she called, "Archy," and I turned back.

"Who is she?" she asked again.

"You never give up, do you?" I said. "Well, it's no secret; her name is Jennifer Towley."

Connie's smile faded. "Oh-oh," she said. "You've got trouble, son."

I stared at her. "What *is* this?" I demanded. "You're the second person who's warned me. Why have I got trouble? What's wrong with my dating Jennifer?"

"Nothing," she said, busying herself with papers on her desk. "Now get the hell out of here. I have work to do."

I knew there was no use pushing it so I got the hell out of there as ordered. I drove to headquarters debating which mystery was more maddening: the missing stamps or Jennifer Towley. About equal, I reckoned.

In the cool lobby of the McNally & Son Building, the receptionist, a white male heterosexual (we were an equal opportunity employer), handed me a pink message note. It stated that Bela Rubik had phoned me about an hour previously and wanted me to call him as soon as possible.

But first things first: I went upstairs and collected my check from Mrs. Trelawney. She was a delightful old bird who obviously wore a wig and looked like everyone's maiden aunt. But she loved raunchy jokes, so I spent ten minutes with her, relating the most recent I had heard. She had a couple of good ones herself. Then I went to my office and phoned Rubik.

"Archibald McNally," I said, "returning your call. Do you have anything for me, Mr. Rubik?"

"Yes," he said. "Something important."

"What is it?"

"Not on the phone," he said. "Come over as soon as you can."

"All right," I said. "I'll be there shortly."

I stopped at my bank, a block away, and deposited the expense account check. I could have ambled down to Rubik's shop—it was a nice stroll—but the day was becoming brutally hot, and I decided to drive. I found a place to park near Worth Avenue and walked over to the stamp and coin store, wishing I had worn my panama.

There was a cardboard sign taped to the glass door: BACK IN AN HOUR. I am not ordinarily a profane man, but I admit I may have uttered a mild oath, pianissimo, when I read that. Not only had I told the idiot I was on my way, but the sign gave no indication of when Rubik had left. Back in an hour could mean I'd have to wait three minutes or fifty.

Not at all gruntled, I started to walk away, then stopped. Suddenly I realized that stupid sign had been taped to the *outside* of the glass door. How often have you seen a merchant do that? Never. They fasten their signs on the *inside* of the glass so they can be removed and used again. Tape it outside and some nut will come along, rip it off, and toss it in the gutter just for the fun of it.

I retraced my steps and inspected the sign more closely. It seemed to have been hastily scrawled and was attached to the glass with a ragged piece of masking tape. I shielded my eyes and tried to peer within. I saw no movement, but on the tile floor alongside the showcase I spotted the stamp dealer's crazy spectacles with the twin loupes. They were twisted and one of the lenses had popped out.

"Oh Jesus," I said aloud.

I tried the doorknob. It turned easily. I opened the door a few inches. "Mr. Rubik," I called, "are you here?"

No answer.

I entered cautiously, moving very, very slowly. He was lying on the floor behind the showcase. His bald skull had been dented so many times it looked like a crushed paper bag. It was clear that his spirit had flown. And next to his smashed skull lay what seemed to be the weapon: a crystal paperweight. There was very little blood coming from the shattered skull.

I am not a stranger to violent death, but I don't think I'll ever get used to it. I hope not. I looked around, then stepped carefully over the corpse to a back office that was large enough to hold a big double-doored safe. No one was in sight and no one was crouched behind the desk ready to leap out and shout, "Boo!" The tiny lavatory was also empty.

I used the phone on Rubik's desk, handling it lightly with my silk foulard pocket square. I called the PBPD, praying Al would be in. He was.

"Sergeant Rogoff," he said.

"Archy McNally," I said. "I'm in Rubik's Stamp and Coin Shop. He's on the floor waiting for the meat wagon. Someone smashed in his skull."

Al didn't miss a beat. "All right," he said. "I'm on my way."

"Make it fast, Al," I urged. "I'm lonely."

"Don't touch a thing," he ordered. "Go outside and wait for me on the sidewalk."

"I know the drill," I said crossly, but he had already hung up.

I went back outside and stood guard at the door. I stuck my hands in my pockets to hide the tremble. There were pedestrians moving lazily along, and some of them gave me a friendly nod the way people do in Florida. One old codger said, with a perfectly straight face, "I don't think it's too cold, do you, partner?" I wanted to top him by casually mentioning, "Hey, partner, there's a murdered man in this store." But I didn't.

It seemed like an eternity but it probably wasn't much more than ten minutes before I heard the sound of an approaching siren. What a sweet song that was! Then the police car pulled up with a squeal of brakes. Al and another uniformed officer climbed out, taking their time. The other cop was a stranger to me, but he seemed awfully young, which means I'm getting awfully old—right? Anyway, he was trying to look stern and purposeful, and he kept his hand resting on his gun butt.

We all moved inside and looked down at the crumpled remains of Bela Rubik.

"Thanks a lot, Archy," Al said to me. "And it's not even my birthday."

The young officer squatted by the corpse and fumbled at the neck. I don't know what he thought he was doing—probably feeling for the carotid. He looked up at Rogoff. "He's stiff, sarge."

"No kidding?" Al said. "Are you sure he's not faking it?" He turned to me. "Go back to your office, Archy," he ordered, "and don't leave it even to take a pee. After I get the wheels turning here, I'll give you a call and you come over to the palace and dictate your statement."

I nodded. "That paperweight—" I offered. "It's called a millefiori. It's made by cutting cross sections of glass rods of different colors and shapes."

"Thank you, professor," the sergeant said. "That certainly is a valuable clue. Now beat it."

I didn't go directly back to my office. I stopped at the nearest bar and had a double Pinch. My shaking finally stopped. When I arrived at headquarters, I went to my father's office, but Mrs. Trelawney said he had left for lunch with a client. So I retired to my cubbyhole and lighted my first English Oval of the day. I thought I deserved it.

I sat there for more than an hour, counting the walls and trying not to think about *anything*. But it didn't work. I couldn't stop reflecting on chance. If Mrs. Trelawney hadn't phoned me about that expense account check, I wouldn't have come into the office that morning. And if I hadn't come into the office, I wouldn't have received the message that Rubik had called. And if I hadn't wasted time trading jokes with Mrs. Trelawney, I'd have left sooner. And if I hadn't paused to deposit the check but hustled over to Rubik's shop immediately, I might have walked in on a horrendous murder.

But what was the use of imagining. Life is all ifs, is it not?

Then Sgt. Rogoff called. "All right," he said, "come over now. We're ready for you."

I drove over to the building on County Road Al liked to call the "palace." His office was larger than mine (whose wasn't?), and the decor was Police Station Moderne. I sat in an uncomfortable wooden armchair and dictated my statement into a tape recorder, with Al and two witnesses in attendance.

This time I omitted absolutely nothing. I told of my first meeting with Bela Rubik and how he had agreed to ask other dealers if a block of four Inverted Jenny stamps had suddenly come on the market. Then I stated how he phoned me that morning, saying he had something of importance to tell me that he didn't want to discuss on the phone.

I described how the sign attached to the outside of the glass had aroused my curiosity. I said I had entered after seeing Rubik's broken glasses on the floor. I noted that when I first visited the shop, the door had been locked and apparently the proprietor would not admit anyone he didn't know who appeared threatening.

I said I had touched nothing but the doorknob and the phone on Rubik's desk. I had seen no one leaving the shop as I approached. I had smelled no perfume, cologne, or any other scent inside the store. The stamp dealer had mentioned nothing to me of prior robberies or assaults. And that was all I knew.

The tape was taken away to be transcribed, and Sgt. Rogoff and I were left alone. He pulled out a cigar, sliced off the tip with a penknife, and began to juice it up.

"You come up with some doozies, you do," he said. "You figure it had something to do with the Inverted Jennies?"

"I think that's a reasonable assumption," I said. "Unless it was plain and simple robbery. Was anything missing?"

"Didn't look like it. The showcase was locked and intact. So was the safe in the back office. Rubik still had his wallet, untouched."

"Al, was he married?"

"Yeah," the sergeant said softly. "His wife's in a nursing home. Alzheimer's. He's got one daughter with the Peace Corps in Africa. We're trying to notify her. He had two sons but both were killed in a light-plane crash last year. 'When troubles come, they come not singly but in battalions.' "

"Why, Sergeant Rogoff," I said, "that's beautiful. But you've got it wrong. It's 'When sorrows come, they come not single spies, but in battalions.' "

"Troubles or sorrows," he said, "what's the diff? So you figure it was someone he knew?"

"Someone he recognized," I said. "Someone he had dealt with before."

"What do you think was important that he wanted to talk to you about?"

I shrugged. "I asked him to find out if any Inverted Jennies were being offered for sale. Maybe he found out."

"And was killed for it?"

"It's possible."

Al grinned at me. "Anything is possible," he said. "It's even possible that you're holding out on me."

"I wouldn't do that," I protested. "Not about murder."

Rogoff thought a moment. "How are you coming along with the Horowitz clan?" he asked suddenly.

"Still at it. Nothing to report."

"Stick with it," he said. "You handle the stamp theft—those people will tell you more than they'll tell us—and I'll concentrate on the Rubik homicide. How does that sound?"

"Makes sense," I said. "And I think eventually we'll discover we're working the same case."

"You think someone in the Horowitz group offed Rubik?"

"Yes," I said. "Don't you?"

But "Could be" was all he'd say. The stenographer came in with my typed statement: original and four photocopies. I signed them all, and Rogoff gave me one of the copies for my file.

"If you think of anything else," he said, "let me know."

"I just did," I said. "That sign on the door—did the killer bring it with him? I mean, was the whole thing planned?"

The sergeant shook his head. "I doubt it. There was a stack of cardboard like that in the bottom drawer of Rubik's desk. He probably used it to stiffen envelopes when he mailed stamps. He also had a roll of masking tape."

"So it was a spur-of-the-moment thing?"

"I'd say so. He and the perp got in an argument about something, and it ended up with him getting his skull cracked."

"And the killer hung out the sign to give himself more time to get far away?"

"That's the way I see it."

"Did they dust the sign? The tape? The paperweight?"

"They're still at it," Al said. "Don't hold your breath."

"May I go now?" I asked.

"Sure," he said. "You better go home, have a belt, and lie down. You don't look so great."

"I don't feel so great," I said. "Thanks for your prompt assistance, sergeant. Sorry I had to dump this on you."

"If not this," he said, sighing, "it would be something else. It never ends." He paused a moment. Then: "I didn't much like Rubik, did you?"

"No," I said. "Still . . ."

I drove slowly and carefully back to the McNally spread. I wondered why I was driving in that Medicare fashion and realized it was a whiff of mortality that had inspired my caution. One never knows, do one?

I garaged the Miata and entered the house through the side door. My mother was standing at the sink in the kitchen, arranging cut flowers from our garden in a crystal vase. She looked up as I came in.

"Hello, Archy," she said brightly. "Isn't it a splendiferous day!" She paused a beat, doubting. "Did I use the right word?"

"Exactly the right word," I assured her.

"Good! And what have you been doing today?"

"Oh," I said, "this and that. Right now I'm going to change and take my swim."

"Do be careful," she said. "It's rough out there. Now these are the last of the roses, Archy. The heat just eats them up."

I watched a moment as she worked, bending over the sink and smiling as she clipped stems and placed the blooms in the vase just so.

"Mother," I said, "how have you been feeling lately?"

"Tiptop," she said. "Couldn't be better."

"Are you taking your medication?"

"Of course. Every day."

I swooped suddenly to kiss her velvety cheek, and she looked at me with pleased surprise.

"Oh my!" she said. "What was that for?"

"I got carried away," I said, and left her laughing with her flowers. She had a little girl's laugh.

I changed, took up my beach bag and towel, and trotted across A1A to the ocean. I saw at once that mother had been right; it was rough out there, with a pounding surf and big patches of seaweed lifting and falling on the waves farther out. I decided not to dare it.

So I smeared on sunblock and sat on the sand in the latticed shade of a palm tree. I stared out at that turbulent sea and tried to review the events of the day. I did all right with my mental rerun until I got to the strip of film where I stood staring down at the crushed skull of Bela Rubik. And that became a freeze-frame; I couldn't get past it.

I never thought I could shiver on a blazing late-May afternoon in South Florida, but I did. It required almost a physical wrench to dissolve that morbid scene from my memory. I did it by resolutely focusing my mind's camera on more positive images. Jennifer Towley's classic elegance. Consuela Garcia in a string bikini. And similar recollections of love, joy, and calm seas. All to keep the specter of sudden death at bay.

Listen, I'm no hero.

Chapter 7

My parents had a local couple in for a rubber of bridge that evening, and I didn't have a chance to speak to my father. But after breakfast the next morning I asked if we could talk for a few minutes before he left for the office. He led the way into his study.

"What is it, Archy?" he asked rather testily. The governor hates to have his routine disturbed.

I told him about the murder of Bela Rubik. His face grew bleak. He pondered a long time.

"Distressing," he finally pronounced. "Do you think the homicide is connected with the theft of Lady Horowitz's stamps?"

"Yes, sir," I said. "I'd bet on it."

"Sergeant Rogoff also thinks so?"

I nodded.

He moved slowly about his den, picking things up and putting them down. "I hope he won't reveal the possible connection to the media."

"I doubt if he will, sir. Al is an intelligent man, and prudent when it comes to dealing with Beach millionaires. He'll tell the reporters Rubik's death was probably due to an attempted robbery. The stamp dealer put up a fight and was killed. That will protect Lady Horowitz and also give the perpetrator a false sense of security. Rogoff likes to come on as a heavy, but he can be foxy when it's called for."

"I'm glad to hear that. In view of the murder, do you wish to continue your discreet inquiries?"

I was offended. "Of course," I said heatedly.

My father turned to face me. "I am not questioning your courage, Archy," he said quietly. "I am merely suggesting that this case has taken on a gravity we didn't anticipate. Our firm will do its best to protect our clients' interests, but I am not certain that includes a homicide investigation."

"Sergeant Rogoff will handle that," I told him, "and I will try to solve the Inverted Jenny theft. Al and I agreed on that."

Another long pause for heavy ratiocination.

"Very well," the lord of the manor said at last. "Let's do it that way. Please keep me informed."

I nodded, and he started out, then paused to look back at me.

"Be careful," was all he said, but I appreciated even that small expression of his concern.

I waited a few moments, watching out the window. When I saw the Lexus pull away, I dug out his telephone directories again. This time I consulted the

Yellow Pages for North Broward County. There were a half-dozen stamp dealers listed. I tore the whole page out of the directory and stuffed it in my pocket.

This was my reasoning:

If Rubik had discovered that a block of Inverted Jennies was suddenly being offered for sale, there seemed to be no reason why another stamp dealer couldn't do the same thing. But I didn't want to endanger the skull of another local philatelist. I figured employing a dealer miles away from the scene of the crime would offer sufficient protection—unless I was followed, and I intended to make certain I wasn't.

Usually the trip from Palm Beach to Fort Lauderdale along A1A is one of the most scenic drives in the Sunshine State. As you proceed south, the Atlantic Ocean is on your left, and on your right are the lavish dormitories of the *rich* rich. On one side: nature; on the other: civilization. But the depredation of the beachfront didn't bother me. I figured that sooner or later nature would even the score with a juicy hurricane.

But that morning I had little time for environmental musings. As I drove along at a lively clip, I revised the agenda I had drawn up for my investigation. The brutal killing of Bela Rubik had shuffled my priorities and, despite my agreement with Sgt. Rogoff, I decided the homicide took precedence over the theft.

Incidentally, during my trip southward I passed through Delray Beach and made a mental note to get cracking on Kenneth Bodin, to prove or disprove that Mr. Deltoids was involved in this meshugass. I also remembered to check my rearview mirror frequently to see if I could spot a tracker. Nothing.

I had selected the Lantern Stamp & Coin Shop in Fort Lauderdale only because I found the name attractive. And when I found the place on East Commercial Boulevard, I was pleased to see an antique lantern hanging over the entrance. I approved of that since I am a great fan of Diogenes. But lettered on the plate-glass window in gilt script was the legend prop.: H. LANTERN. So apparently the store had been named for the owner, not the lamp.

The door was locked, and when I rattled the knob a formidable fiftyish lady came forward and peered at me through the glass. I held up my business card so she could read it. She unlocked the door and allowed me to enter.

"Yes?" she said.

"May I speak to the owner, please?"

She stiffened. "*I* am the owner," she said haughtily.

"I beg your pardon," I said. "I assumed that—"

"I know what you assumed," she interrupted. "That it's impossible for a woman to own and run an independent business, and therefore I must be a salesclerk or the wife or daughter of the owner."

"Nothing of the sort," I said. "It's just that—"

"Let me tell you something," she carried on. "There are no secrets of business management known only to the male gender. There are many women who own and manage successful enterprises."

"Very admirable, I'm sure," I said, "but you are inferring a prejudice that simply doesn't exist. I have known several stamp dealers in my lifetime, and without exception they have all been old, crotchety gentlemen. So naturally I was surprised to find a young, attractive female in the trade."

And I gave her a 100-watt smile that had no effect whatsoever. She stared at me with narrowed eyes, obviously debating whether or not I was conning her, which, of course, I was. Finally she relented.

"All right," she said, "I'll accept your apology."

I wasn't aware that I had offered one, but didn't dare tempt this gorgon's wrath by mentioning it.

"Now then," she continued, all business, "what can I do for you?"

I gave her the same song and dance I had given Bela Rubik: My law firm was handling the estate of a recently deceased Boca Raton real estate developer. Included in the inventory of his personal effects was a block of four Inverted Jenny postage stamps. For tax purposes we would like to establish the value of the stamps by determining the market price of a similar block currently being offered for sale.

H. Lantern shook her head. "Can't be done," she said decisively. "All stamps have different values, even those of the same issue. The value depends on the condition of the stamps."

"You know that," I said, "and I know that, but the IRS doesn't know that. Quite frankly, we fear they are aware that a block of four Inverted Jennies was recently auctioned for a million dollars, and they are liable to insist that value be placed on the stamps included in the estate of our deceased client."

"I could do an appraisal for you," she offered.

I uttered a short, bitter laugh. "You think the IRS would accept that? Never! Right now their estimate of market value is the million-dollar sale in New York that received so much publicity. The only way we can counter that is by quoting the price of Inverted Jennies currently being offered for sale. We will pay fifty dollars per hour for your time if you would be willing to take on the job of discovering if any blocks of Inverted Jennies have recently come on the market and, if so, what the asking price is. I'm sure it's less than a million dollars."

I could see she wasn't totally convinced by my scam, but the fifty dollars an hour was alluring, and I'm certain she asked herself what possible harm could she suffer by agreeing to my proposal. I could have enlightened her, but didn't.

"A down payment?" she asked, and I knew I had her.

I gave her fifty in cash, took a signed receipt, and left her my business card. She promised to call as soon as she had made inquiries, talked to other dealers, and consulted philatelic periodicals. We shook hands, and she smiled before I departed. What a pleasant surprise!

Because I was so close, I cut over to Oakland Park Blvd. and took it eastward to the ocean. I decided to have a small lunch at Ireland's Inn, a place I recalled from previous excursions to Lauderdale.

The day had started out clear and bright, but Florida's weather is mercurial, and now the air was clotting up, a dark cloud bank was moving in from the south. So instead of lunching outside, practically on the beach, I opted to sit indoors at a window facing the sea. I ordered a turkey club sandwich, which I dearly love, and a bottle of nonalcoholic beer, for which I was developing a taste, and I hope you will not think the less of me for it.

There is no delicate method of eating a thick club sandwich; one must gobble. So while I gobbled and swigged my Buckler, I reviewed the interview with H. Lantern, whose given name turned out to be Hilda. She was a prickly woman (she would be incensed by that adjective), but I thought her competent enough and was convinced she'd do a conscientious job.

The rainsquall came over as I lunched. It really poured, then suddenly stopped, the sky blued, the sun shone. I paid my bill, went outside, and found to my delight that the parking valet had had the great good sense to move my open Miata under the portico before the deluge. I gave him a heavy tip and assured him that one day he would be president.

I was back in Palm Beach by three o'clock, drove past my home, admiring that dignified, stately edifice, and turned into the driveway of the Horowitz fiefdom. I asked Mrs. Marsden if the DuPeys were present, and she directed me to a Georgian-styled gazebo framed in a small grove of bottle palms beyond the pool area.

There I found the newlyweds lounging at a set of cast-iron garden furniture. On the table was a pitcher of what appeared to be iced sangria, along with a stack of plastic tumblers. I introduced myself, they introduced themselves and invited me to help myself to a drink. I did and sipped cautiously. It was intended to be sangria, all right, but made with some awful plonk. Dreadful stuff.

I congratulated the DuPeys on their recent nuptials, and they laughed heartily as if the marriage had been a lark and no one appreciated the joke more than they. They were holding hands when I arrived, and they continued to clasp paws during the entire interview. It was easy to see they were both sappy with love.

I started to address them in French, but Felice asked me prettily to speak English as she wasn't certain of the syntax and also wanted to learn as many American idioms as possible. I obliged. I would have granted her every wish, for she was charming, a kitten with a mischievous grin and a full inventory of pouts and moues.

Alan, the benedict, was onion soup personified. I mean, give him a beret and a pencil-thin mustache and you'd have Lucky Pierre in the flesh. But he was bubbling with gaiety that not infrequently slopped over into hilarity. Did I hear the pitch of desperation there, as if he thought it better never to stop laughing or he might start screaming?

They were perfectly willing to answer questions about their personal lives. He wrote book reviews for a monthly Parisian literary journal, and she was an apprentice at Chanel, and wasn't life grand? I began to understand what Consuela Garcia meant when she had condemned them for being "too nice." The DuPeys' happiness seemed excessive, almost cloying. You wouldn't make an entire meal of caviar, would you? You would?

I resolutely turned to business, asked the usual questions, and heard nothing new. Chuckling Alan had seen his mother's misprinted stamps several times in the past. Giggling Felice had seen them for the first time at dinner the evening they arrived. Neither had the slightest notion of who, staff or guests, might have nobbled the Inverted Jennies. And it was obvious from their manner that the theft ranked far down on their anxiety list.

It seemed nothing was to be learned from these lovebirds, and I was about to withdraw when I casually asked if they had enjoyed the cruise on Phil Meecham's yacht the previous day. My innocent query elicited another eruption of uncontrolled glee.

"We never went," Alan explained after his spasm of mirth had subsided. "The captain of the yacht—a splendid vessel!—said the sea was much too rough and we would all suffer mal de mer. So Monsieur Meecham proposed we remain tied to the dock and have a party right there."

"Ooo, la!" his wife cried.

"And what a party," Alan went on, rolling his eyes. "Four cases of a very good champagne—Moët Brut Impérial, you know—and the food! An *orgie!*"

"Four cases for the six of you?" I said. "I'd say that was ample."

"More than six," Felice said. "There were also fourteen other guests."

"Ten," her husband corrected her gently. "Because the Smythes, Gina, and Angus left after the cruise was canceled. But I can tell you that those of us who remained put a big dent in Monsieur Meecham's wine supply."

"He was so fonny," his wife added. "He wanted to make love to *all* of us!"

"I can imagine," I said, bid them farewell, and departed while they were still convulsed with laughter and still holding hands.

I tried to tumble-dry my thoughts and realized that last bit of information was a lone sock. Here's the scenario:

The time of the murder was reasonably well established. The clobbering of Bela Rubik's occiput had occurred between the moment I spoke to him on the phone from my office and the moment I found the corpus delicti.

I had previously learned that all the six Horowitz houseguests were afloat on a cruise aboard Phil Meecham's yacht the previous day.

That meant that if anyone in the Horowitz household was the killer, it had to be one of the staff.

But now I had learned that Doris and Harry Smythe, Gina Stanescu, and Angus Wolfson had left the moored yacht when the cruise was canceled. That meant I had to restore them to the list of suspects.

I consoled myself by reflecting that the original roster of eleven possibles had now dwindled to nine.

It's called progress.

I drove away in a melancholy mood, wondering if I might achieve a more fulfilling life by becoming a real estate agent like everyone else in South Florida. Then I had another mournful thought: If Lady Cynthia's butler hadn't quit two weeks before the crimes were committed, he would have been the prime suspect. All the tomes I had read on criminal behavior were quite firm on that point: The butler *always* did it.

But my spirits rose when I arrived home, for Mrs. Olson informed me that Jennifer Towley had phoned while she was cleaning my suite.

"She sounds nice," she said.

"She *is* nice," I shouted back as I dashed upstairs to phone.

I lay back on my bed as I spoke to Jennifer and kicked my heels in the air, thinking the DuPeys' happiness might be contagious. We talked of weighty things like the weather, the cost of fresh snapper, and the outrageous attempts by the State of Florida to ban thong bikinis on public beaches.

"Enough of this idle chitchat, Jennifer," I said finally. "When may I see you again?"

"That's why I called," she said. "I'm having dinner with a client tonight, but I should be home by ten o'clock at the latest. Could you come over for a drink? There is something very important I want to say to you."

"You're going to propose?" I asked.

"No," she said, not laughing. "This is very serious, Archy. I should have told you sooner, but I didn't have the courage. Now I've decided to tell you before you hear it from someone else."

"All right," I said, my joy balloon deflating, "I'll be there at ten."

"I won't keep you long," she promised.

"Keep me as long as you like," I told her.

Then she did laugh, but it was a feeble one.

I hung up somewhat disquieted. It was her statement "This is serious, Archy" that put the quietus to my brief felicity. I've already told you what a carefree cove I am, or strive to be. I blame most of society's ills on seriousness. Believe me, if everyone would sit on a whoopee cushion at least once a day, it would be a better world.

I know I was uncharacteristically withdrawn and silent that evening because my mother remarked on it. She asked if I was coming down with something. I was tempted to reply, "Love," but instead I assured her I was in perfect health but merely distracted by the press of business. I don't believe mother knew exactly what it was I did, but she accepted my explanation, although advising that a nice glass of warm milk before bedtime would enable me to sleep better.

I was at Jennifer Towley's home a few minutes after ten o'clock, and she had something better to offer than warm milk: a liter of Absolut plunged into a crystal bucket of ice cubes. She had set out two tall shot glasses that looked like bud vases.

She was wearing one of her elegant Little Black Dresses. This one appeared to be conservatively cut, with a high neck and long sleeves. But when she turned around, I saw that it had no back whatsoever. As Felice DuPey might say, "Ooo, la!"

"I shall pour your first drink, Archy," she said, "and then you must help yourself to more. I think you may need it."

"Oh-oh," I said, "that sounds ominous."

"Not ominous," she said. "Perhaps upsetting."

She seated herself in a low armchair and tugged her skirt down to cover her bare knees. Now *that* was upsetting.

"I told you I was divorced," she stated. "Towley is my maiden name. My married name was Bingham. My husband was Thomas Bingham. Does the name mean anything to you?"

I shook my head.

She sighed. "Several years ago he was arrested and convicted of felony theft. He stole about fifty thousand dollars from his employer, a wholesaler of plumbing supplies."

I took a heavy gulp of my vodka. "Where did this happen?"

"Boca Raton. He did three years and four months at Raiford."

It was my turn to sigh. "Jennifer, were you divorced before or after he was convicted?"

"About a year before," she said. "Thank God. If I hadn't, I wouldn't have divorced him after he went to prison, would I?"

"I suppose not," I said, thinking there were many women who would have, and admiring her.

"He was a gambler," she said. "Absolutely addicted. He was handsome, well-educated, well-spoken. And a dynamite salesman. At a party one night the president of the company told me that Tom had a bright future: sales manager and then into the executive suite. He might even become CEO. He could have had all that, but he couldn't stop gambling."

"On what?"

"On everything! Horse races; dog races; baseball, football, and basketball games; lotteries; elections; the weather—you name it. And on his selling trips he always managed to get to Las Vegas or Atlantic City."

"You were aware of his addiction?"

"Of course I was aware," she said angrily. "How could I *not* be aware? I saw what was happening to our bank accounts, a second mortgage on our home, the dunning letters from creditors. And the interest on his credit card charges! It was a horrendous situation. I pleaded with him to get professional help: a psychologist, Gamblers Anonymous, talk to our minister—anything. But he refused to admit that he had a problem, that he was hopelessly addicted. You don't have any addictions, do you, Archy?"

"One," I said. "You."

I do believe she blushed, but it may have been the rosy glow coming from the Tiffany lamp on the table. I helped myself to more Absolut. I couldn't serve Jennifer; her full glass was untouched.

"I did everything I could," she continued. "I loved Tom, I really did. He could be a splendid husband: kind, gentle, understanding. Except he had this terrible sickness."

"I had a friend who was like that," I said, lying but trying to be sympathetic. "And it is a sickness."

"Things began to disappear from our home," she went on. "Crystal, silverware, a few of my antiques. He was selling them. He was involved with loan sharks, and rough men began coming to our house or parking outside all night. I really couldn't take any more of it so I filed for divorce. He wept and begged and swore he would stop betting. But he had done that a dozen times before, and I knew it was no good. I think the final straw was when I realized he was stealing money from my purse. So I divorced him. And a year later he went to prison."

"A sad story," I said.

"A soap opera," she said with a strained smile. "It happens all the time, all over the country. I talked to a counselor who specialized in treating addictions, and he said no improvement could be expected until the addict acknowledged he was out of control and sought help voluntarily. Tom wouldn't do that."

There was silence awhile. She sat with her head lowered, and I hoped she wasn't going to cry. I'm an absolute klutz when it comes to dealing with weeping women.

"Something I haven't asked you," I said. "Any children?"

"No," she said, lifting her chin to look at me, and I saw she was clear-eyed; her calm, direct gaze had returned. "Do you think it would have changed Tom if we had?"

"I don't know," I said. "Who can predict human behavior? Did you say he's out of prison?"

"Yes. He was released about a month ago."

"Did you visit him while he was inside?"

"No."

"Write to him?"

"Not really," she said. "Just birthday and Christmas cards. But he wrote me frequently. He said being behind bars had made him realize how he had screwed up his life, and mine. He swore he was a changed man, and when he was released he'd never gamble again as long as he lived."

"Do you believe him, Jennifer?"

"No."

"Has he called you since he's been out?"

"Four times."

"And he wants you to take him back?"

Her eyes grew round. "How did you know?" she asked.

"Because that's exactly what I'd do if I were in his place. Will you take him back?"

"Never!" she cried. "Archy, have you ever had nightmares?"

"Not often. Perhaps a half-dozen in my lifetime."

"Well, I had a nightmare that lasted almost four years. I don't want to go through that again."

I asked, almost idly, "Where did he call you from—Boca?"

"No," she said, "he's living in Delray Beach."

I think I stared at her with a look akin to the wild surmise of the men of stout Cortez, silent upon a peak in Darien. Although how they managed to spot the Pacific Ocean from Connecticut I've never been able to understand.

"Delray Beach?" I repeated, and my voice sounded like a croak. "What's he doing there?"

"He says he has a good job selling hurricane shutters, mostly to people who live in high-rise condos. He claims his boss knows about his prison record but is willing to give him a chance. Tom says he makes a small salary but does well on commissions. I believe that. I told you he's a super salesman."

I nodded, thinking that Jennifer was probably his toughest prospect. She leaned forward and took my hands in hers.

"Archy," she said, "I'm sorry to dump this on you. I realize it's depressing. But I know how people talk, and I wanted to tell you myself rather than have you hear it secondhand."

"I appreciate that," I said.

She sat back and slumped. "I feel wrung-out. Just talking about it brings back so many memories. All of them painful."

"I can understand that," I said. I stood up. "I suppose you want me to go."

Finally, finally, she took a sip of her vodka, then looked up at me with that cool, level gaze. "Whatever gave you that silly idea?" she said.

There was something demonic in her love-making that night, as if she sought to exorcise thoughts, feelings, perhaps those painful memories. I profited shamelessly from her anguish.

Popular wisdom has it that the way to a man's heart is through his stomach. Don't you ever believe it.

Chapter 8

I banished all my problems for the weekend and lived the life of a blade-about-town. On Saturday I played tennis at a friend's private court. After he scuttled me in straight sets, he phoned a couple of jolly ladies. They came over, and we all frolicked in his pool, had a few drinks, and laughed a lot.

On Saturday night after dinner (tournedos with foie gras), I headed for the Pelican Club. I found a few of my cronies already in attendance, and I won five dollars throwing darts. That made me the big winner, and I had to stand a round of drinks that cost me twenty.

On Sunday I took my ocean swim early, then drove out to Wellington where I watched a polo match from my father's box. I had brought my Tasco zoom binocs along, but I saw no one in the stands who excited my interest. Jennifer Towley, I decided, had elevated my taste. How ya gonna keep 'em down on the farm after they've seen Paree?

On Sunday night my parents and I made a short trip down A1A to a Palladian-style mansion owned by a wealthy client of McNally & Son. Along with thirty other guests we enjoyed a boisterous cocktail party and cookout that featured Maine lobsters and Louisiana prawns. The grill was presided over by a uniformed butler wearing white gloves and a topper.

But Monday rolled around all too quickly, and then it was back to the Sturm und Drang.

You may think a detective's best friend is his revolver, magnifying glass, or bloodhound. Wrong. It is a telephone directory—the handiest aid to any inquiry, discreet or otherwise. I looked up the home address and phone number of Kenneth Bodin in Delray Beach, and scrawled them on the inside of a book of matches. Then, just for the fun of it, I tore out the Yellow Pages listing places that sold hurricane shutters. There were a lot of them, but most seemed to be located north of Boynton Beach. I found only a few in the Delray–Boca Raton area.

By ten o'clock I was on the road again, and it was not a day that would bring a prideful smile to the mug of Florida boosters. The sky had the color and weight of a wet army blanket, not a wisp of air was moving, and even the palm fronds looked dejected. It was an oppressive atmosphere, as if a storm was lurking nearby and might pounce at any moment.

I stopped for gas in Delray Beach and made my phone call to Kenneth Bodin's residence from the station. As I had hoped, a woman answered.

"Hello?" she said in a squeaky little voice.

"Sylvia?" I asked.

"Yes. Who's this?"

"My name is Dooley, and I'm in South Florida for a convention. I threw my back out, and I need a massage. A friend suggested you might be able to help."

"Yeah?" she said suspiciously. "What friend?"

I named the most active roué I knew. "Phil Meecham," I said. It worked. She squealed with delight. "What a crazy guy!" she said. "How is Phil?"

"Sitting up and taking nourishment," I said. "How about that massage?"

"Aw, I'm sorry, Dooley, but I'm not in that line of work anymore. My boyfriend won't let me."

"Well, I can understand that," I said. "But is he home right now?"

"No. He works up at Palm Beach."

"Well, then . . . ?" I suggested.

"No can do," she said firmly. "I gave him my sacred promise. And besides, he might come home unexpectedly."

"That's too bad," I said, sounding disappointed. "Then I guess I made the trip for nothing."

"Listen, Dooley," she said. "I'm working as a cocktail waitress at a lovely place on the beach. The joint opens at noon. Why don't you stop by, have a few drinks, and maybe we can work something out."

"Sounds good to me," I said, and she gave me the name of the lovely place on the beach and told me how to find it.

I killed an hour by driving around to stores that sold and installed hurricane shutters. I hit pay dirt on the fourth. Yes, Thomas Bingham worked there, but at the moment he was out estimating a job. I was relieved to hear it, having absolutely no idea of what I would have said to him if he had been present. I think I just wanted to size him up, see what a man looked like who would sacrifice Jennifer Towley for the sake of a dog race.

I left no message for Bingham but said I'd stop by again. Then I headed for Sylvia's place of employ, wishing I knew what the hell I was doing. But sometimes chance and accident prove more valuable than the most detailed plan. That's what I told myself.

At least I had sense enough to park my car a few blocks away and walk back. I had no desire for Sylvia to remark casually to Bodin, "A young buck stopped by today, driving a flag-red Miata." His porcine ears would have perked up immediately.

When I entered Hammerhead's Bar & Grill, I was tempted to do a Bette Davis impersonation: flap my elbows, suck an imaginary cigarette, and utter those immortal words: "What-a-*dump!*" I suppose I was being elitist, but it was a bit of a culture shock, after that deluxe weekend at Palm Beach, to be faced by so much Formica with naked fluorescent tubes flickering overhead.

The bar was crowded with what appeared to be a fraternity of construction workers and commercial fishermen. I took a bandanna-sized table in the corner, and in a moment a zoftig blond lady came jiggling over to me. She was wearing a hot-pink miniskirt and a hot-green tank top that may have been sprayed on with an atomizer.

"Hiya," she said.

"Sylvia?" I said. "I'm Dooley."

"Well!" she said, giving me a really nice smile. "Pleased to make your acquaintance, I'm sure. In town for long?"

"Oh, maybe a week or so," I said. "I'm staying in Boca with a friend."

"Man or woman?" she asked, leering at me.

"Man," I said. "Unfortunately."

"Maybe we can do something about that," and she actually winked at me. "What can I bring you?"

I know that in a place like that, the only safe choice would be something with a cap on the bottle. But I feared if I asked for nonalcoholic beer, the proprietor and patrons might toss me to the sharks skulking offshore.

"A bottle of beer, please," I said. "Do you have Heineken?"

"Of course," she said. "This is a high-class joint."

She brought my beer and a bowl of salted peanuts. Then, unbidden, she took the chair opposite me, and I was aware that a few customers at the bar glanced at me enviously.

"You're awfully young to be a pal of Phil Meecham," she said.

"You know Phil," I said. "He never discriminates because of age, sex, color, creed, or country of national origin."

"You can say that again," she said, laughing. "Once I saw him try to make a chimpanzee. Can you believe it?"

"Easily," I said. "May I buy you a drink?"

"Maybe a diet Coke," she said. "Okay? I'm trying to lose weight."

"Don't you dare," I said.

"Oh *you!*" she said.

She came back with her drink and then dug into my bowl of peanuts.

"What time do you get off work, Sylvia?" I asked.

"Well, that's the problem," she said. "I leave around eight when the night girl comes on. Then I have to go right home or my boyfriend will have the pip. Or sometimes he comes in here when he gets off work, and then we go home together. He keeps me on a short leash."

"What's doing there?" I asked her. "Wedding bells?"

"Maybe," she said, scoffing more peanuts. "It depends on my mood."

"So really the only time you have free is in the mornings?"

"That's about it," she agreed. "Ken leaves for work early to beat the traffic. And I have to get up early to make him breakfast."

"I'll be around awhile," I said. "May I call you some morning?"

"Of course you can, Dooley," she said. "We could take a ride down to your friend's place in Boca."

"Good idea," I said, and finished my beer. "I'll give you a ring." I stood up. "How much do I owe you, Sylvia?"

"It's on the house," she said. "Maybe you'll come back. You've got class; I can tell."

"Thank you," I said, and slipped her a ten for her keen discernment. I waved and started away. Then I had one of my wild ideas that always shock me because I can't understand where they come from.

"By the way," I said, turning back, "my friend in Boca lives in a high-rise condo, and he's thinking of installing hurricane shutters. You know anyone around here who sells them?"

"Sure," she said. "Tom Bingham. He drops by almost every evening when he gets off work."

"Fine," I said. "The next time you see him, will you get me a business card?"

"A pleasure," she said. "Tom's a good guy. Him and Ken and me spend a lot of time together."

See what I mean about chance and accident? But sometimes you have to nudge them a bit.

I drove home through a darkling day. It hadn't yet started to rain, but the sky pressed lower, and gulls were straining to beat their way against a freshening wind. Where *do* gulls go during a storm?

But I had more on my mind than the homing habits of sea gulls. I was computing that if Kenneth Bodin, girlfriend Sylvia, and Thomas Bingham were buddies, maybe all three—or at least the two men—had planned and carried out the theft of the Inverted Jennies. My main reason for considering this a distinct possibility was that Bingham had served time for stealing fifty thousand dollars.

That may sound prejudicial to you, but law enforcement officers the world over know that if a former felon is anywhere near the scene of a crime, the odds are good that he or she was actively involved. It's not bigotry; it's a knowledge of recidivist rates. Leopards don't change their spots, and ex-cons rarely change their stripes.

You may smugly believe that I had a more personal reason for suspecting Bingham, that I hoped to end what I thought was a determined effort on his part to win back the affection of his ex-wife. And if you ask if that was indeed my motive, or an important part of my motive, I plead the Fifth Amendment—the one dealing with self-incrimination.

I was a short distance from home when I felt the first spatters of rain. I gave the Miata the automotive equivalent of giddyap and made it into our garage just before the deluge. Sgt. Al Rogoff's pickup truck was parked outside on the gravel, and he lowered the window of the cab long enough to beckon me over.

I dashed through the rain and climbed in. It was air conditioned but rank with old cigar smoke.

"You don't have to light up a fresh stogie," I told him. "You can just drive around inhaling yesterday's smoke."

"Talking about cigars," he said, "I spent all day at the Horowitz place, and that crazy dame wouldn't let me flame a cigar anywhere. Not just in the house, she said, but nowhere on the grounds. She's only got a hundred acres—right?"

"Maybe a little less."

"Well, I couldn't even go out in the woods and grab a puff. She's a bird, that one."

"A rich bird," I said. "Is that why you're wearing civvies and driving your own heap?"

"Yeah. She didn't want any uniforms or police cars hanging around. I guess she thought it would lower the tone of the neighborhood. Where have you been?"

"Down in Delray Beach checking out Kenneth Bodin, the chauffeur."

"Learn anything?" Al asked.

"Less than a soupçon," I said. "He's living with a cupcake, but if that's a crime, half the guys in South Florida would be behind bars. No signs or talk of sudden wealth."

"Heavy debts?"

"I can check that out through bank and credit agencies up here. How did you make out on the homicide?"

"Not too bad," the sergeant said. "We're lucky because the time of death can definitely be established within an hour or so. At that time the five members of the staff were all on the estate. I admit they alibi each other, which could be a conspiracy, but I doubt it. Lady Horowitz says she was at the hairdresser's. I'll have to check that out. As for the houseguests, the DuPeys claim they were partying on a docked yacht and were seen by dozens of people. Something else to check out. That leaves Mr. and Mrs. Smythe, Gina Stanescu, and Angus Wolfson. All four claim they left the yacht after the cruise was canceled and were wandering around the shops on Worth Avenue at the time Bela Rubik got pasted in the Great Stamp Album in the Sky. The actual whereabouts of those four at the time of death will be a migraine to pin down, but I guess it can be done with a lot of legwork."

"You're convinced that the homicide and the theft of the Inverted Jennies are connected?"

"The only reason I'm convinced," Al said, "is that I've got nothing else. There's no evidence at all pointing to an attempted robbery. Maybe it was a weirdo, a serial killer on the loose, but I don't buy that. Those missing stamps and what Rubik said to you on the phone are the only leads I've got. Archy, what's your guess—was it a man or a woman?"

I considered a moment. "I'd guess it was a man. Look, the human skull isn't an eggshell, you know. You can give it a pretty sharp bop without breaking it. So there was physical power behind that paperweight."

"It could have been a strong woman."

"Could have been," I agreed, "but bashing in a skull just doesn't seem to me something a woman would do, even if she was insane with rage."

"Yeah," Rogoff said, "it doesn't seem likely, does it? By the way, he didn't die of a bashed skull."

I stared at him. "Would you run that by me again."

"Bela Rubik didn't die from repeated blows to the cranium. According to the ME, they would have knocked him out for sure, and they damaged the brain, but he actually died of cardiac arrest, a massive heart failure brought on by the assault. That still makes it a homicide, of course."

"Of course," I said, "but it opens up a whole new can of worms. Maybe the attacker didn't intend to kill him. Just knock him out or hurt him."

"I'm not interested in the killer's intent," Al said. "That's for the courts to decide. I just want to nab the perp and then let the lawyers argue about intent."

"I'm not sure that's the way to go," I said slowly. "Perhaps knowing the intent is the only way to find the killer."

The sergeant groaned. "You know, you have a taste for complexity. I'll bet you like black olives, too."

"Love 'em," I admitted.

"It figures." Al said mournfully. "All right, the rain's letting up, you can run for the house without getting soaked. I have to get back to work. Keep in touch."

"For sure," I said. "I expect to be in all night. Give me a call if anything breaks."

That evening my parents left to attend a dinner being given for a septuagenarian couple celebrating their 50th wedding anniversary. I was invited but begged off. Long hours of fruit punch and charades are not my idea of a hot time in the old town tonight.

So I had dinner in the kitchen with the Olsons. Ursi dished up a concoction she called McNally Stew: a spicy mix of chunks of beef, chicken, hot Italian sausage, and shrimp, all in a red wine sauce and served over a bed of wide noodles. Kiss your diet farewell.

After that gluttonous debauch I went upstairs, thankful I was wearing an expandable belt, and set to work on my journal, with the original cast album of *Guys and Dolls* playing on my stereo. I may even have sung along with "Sue Me." This was after I phoned Jennifer Towley, got her answering machine, and hung up without leaving a message.

I was still scribbling when *my* phone rang. It was Sgt. Rogoff.

"Wake you up?" he asked.

"Come on, Al," I said, "it's not even ten o'clock. What's up?"

"After I left you I hit the streets. First I went to the hairdresser where Lady Horowitz claims she had an appointment at the time Rubik was aced."

"And?"

"She had an appointment all right, but she never showed up."

I was silent.

"Hello?" Rogoff said. "You there?"

"I'm here," I said. "Just trying to catch that curve ball."

"Yeah," he said. "It's screwy, isn't it? Listen, Archy, do me a favor, will you? I don't want to brace that old dame with what I know and demand she spill the truth. She scares me; I admit it. She's got a lot of clout in this town and could make things sticky for me if she wanted to. You follow?"

"I follow," I said. "All right, Al, I'll try to find out where she was at the time Rubik was killed. Did you tell her that the theft of her stamps was connected to a homicide?"

"Hell, no! I didn't tell her or any of the others there was probably a link. I just said we had a good lead on the identity of the stamp thief, and I had to check out their whereabouts at a specific time to eliminate the innocent."

"You think they bought that?"

"Everyone but the killer," Al said. "Talk to the old biddy for me, will you, Archy? She likes you."

"She does?" I said, somewhat surprised.

"Sure. She told me so herself. Something else you can do for me . . ."

I sighed. "And I get a piece of your salary—right?"

"Wrong. Your father drew up Lady Horowitz's will, didn't he?"

"That's correct," I said, knowing what was coming.

"Can you find out who inherits if she croaks?"

"Probably," I said, "but I'm not going to tell you. That's privileged information."

"What do I have to do to get it?"

"Get her permission first. I'll ask my father."

"Do that, will you?"

"Sure. But why do you want to know who inherits?"

"Because maybe someone, family or friends, perhaps one of the houseguests, *doesn't* inherit, knows it, and decided to pinch the stamps to get what they could. And that led to the homicide."

"Sergeant Rogoff," I said, "you're brilliant."

"It's taken you this long to find out? What a lousy detective. Let me know what your father says."

It was about ten-thirty when I heard the crunch of gravel, went to the window, and saw the Lexus pulling into the garage. I waited another half-hour, smoked my first cigarette of the day, and brooded about what Rogoff had told me. I wasn't looking forward to telling Lady Cynthia she had been caught in a lie. She was quite capable of canning McNally & Son instanter.

The door of my father's study was closed, but when I knocked I heard his murmured, "Come in." He was plumped down in his club chair, still wearing his dinner jacket, but he had loosened tie and collar. I thought he looked old and tired.

"Good party?" I asked.

"Wearing," he said with a wan smile. "You were wise not to attend. Not your cup of vodka at all."

"Speaking of that, sir," I said, "may I bring you a glass of port? You look a mite bushed."

He stared a brief moment. "I think a tot of brandy would do more good. Thank you, Archy, and help yourself."

I poured us small snifters of cognac from his crystal decanter and seated myself in an armchair facing him. We raised glasses to each other, took small sips.

"Sorry to bother you at this hour, father," I said, "but Sergeant Rogoff just called and asked me to speak to you."

I explained what Rogoff wanted and why he wanted it. The guv listened closely.

"I couldn't possibly release that information," he said, "without Lady Horowitz's permission."

"I told Al that. He wants you to try to get it."

Long pause for heavy thought. Then: "I can understand Rogoff's reasoning. It's a nice point: A disinherited relative or friend might wish to profit immediately. You were right, Archy; the sergeant is a foxy man."

"Yes, sir. Will you ask Lady Horowitz if details of her will may be given to the police? On a confidential basis, of course."

He sighed wearily. "All right, I'll ask."

"Do you think she'll agree?"

He looked at me with rueful amusement. "Who can possibly predict what that extraordinary woman might or might not do? I'll ask her; that's all I can tell you."

"Good enough," I said, finished my brandy, and rose. "Sorry to have disturbed you, sir."

"Not at all," he said.

I tramped upstairs, thinking he was not so much wearied as troubled. And seeing my father troubled was like viewing a statue of a worried Buddha.

Chapter 9

I had a lot of important things to do the next morning—such as dumping the contents of my wicker laundry hamper into a big canvas bag, adding four pairs of slacks to be dry cleaned, and lugging everything downstairs to be picked up by our laundry service. I also balanced my checkbook, which came out three dollars more than my bank statement. Close enough. And I called a florist to deliver an arrangement of whatever was fresh to Jennifer Towley.

So it was a bit past ten-thirty before I headed for the Horowitz empire. I knew quite well that all those putzy things I had busied myself with that morning were sheer cravenness on my part: an attempt to postpone the moment when I'd have to face Lady C. and ask, "Why did you lie to Sergeant Rogoff?" When Al told me she scared him, I could empathize; she scared me, too. She was a woman of strong opinions and fierce determination. And her millions gave muscle to her whims.

I found Lady Horowitz lying on a chaise at poolside. In the shade, of course. She was wearing a mint-green silk burnoose, the hood pulled up, and I soon learned she was in a scratchy mood.

"That policeman," she said wrathfully, "that insufferable *cop,* positively *reeks* of cigar smoke."

"I know," I said, "but he—"

"And his idiotic questions!" she ranted on. "Why, he treated me like a common criminal."

"He's just trying to do his job," I said as soothingly as I could. "He's really on your side, you know. He'd like to recover the stamps as much as you would."

"Cowpats!" she said. "He's just trying to make my life miserable because I gave him work to do when he'd rather be somewhere else swilling beer and belching."

"He's really a very efficient police officer."

She stared at me. "He's a friend of yours, lad?" she demanded.

"We've worked together several times," I acknowledged. "And successfully, I might add."

But she'd have none of it. "That's all I need," she fumed, "two amateur sherlocks stumbling around on their flat feet. I suppose that's why you're here—to ask more questions."

She hadn't invited me to sit down, so I didn't. But I moved into the shade of a beach umbrella and leaned on the back of a chair, looking down at her.

"Well, yes," I admitted. "I'd just like to get a clarification of something you told Sergeant Rogoff."

"A clarification?" she said suspiciously. "Of what?"

"The sergeant has a good lead on the identity of the thief, but needs to pin down the whereabouts of everyone involved at the time the crime was apparently committed. You told him you were at your hairdresser's. But when Rogoff checked, he discovered you had an appointment but didn't show up. Would you care to comment?"

"My first comment is that I'm going to get a new hairdresser," she said. "The stupid snitch!"

"Please, Lady Horowitz," I said, "where were you?"

"I've had a touch of arthritis in my knees, and didn't want anyone to know I was going to an acupuncturist. That's where I was." She looked at me. "You're not buying that, are you?"

"No," I said.

"All right," she said almost cheerfully, "let's try this one: I was sitting in a dyke bar slugging Black Russians. No? How about this: It was such a lovely day I decided to drive the Jag up the coast to the country club. How does that grab you?"

I sighed. "I gather you're not going to tell me where you were."

"You gather correctly, lad. The whole thing is so moronic it's sickening. Does Rogoff think I swiped my own stamps?"

"Of course not."

"Then why in hell should I tell him where I was at such and such a time? My private life is my private life, and I don't have to account for it to anyone. Period. That includes you, lad."

I nodded. "Thank you for your time."

She tried to smile but couldn't. "You're pissed at me, aren't you?"

"Somewhat," I admitted. "It seems to me you're making Mount Everest out of a very small molehill indeed."

"That's what you think," she said, and I looked at her with perplexity because she appeared to be stiff upperlipping it, and I couldn't understand why. But then she waved me away with a gesture of dismissal, and I went.

Ordinarily I am an even-tempered johnny. I don't curse when a shoelace snaps. Stepping on a discarded wad of chewing gum might elicit a mild "Tsk." And I've been known to laugh merrily after spattering the front of my white shirt with marinara sauce. But that go-around with Lady Cynthia definitely cast a shadow on the McNally sunniness. It was not, I felt, going to be my day. How right I was.

I went into the main house to search for Mrs. Marsden, hoping she might be willing to describe in more detail those forebodings she had mentioned. But as I passed the game room, I heard the unmistakable sounds of a female sobbing, and since the door was ajar I had no scruples about entering and looking about for the sobber.

I found Gina Stanescu leaning against the billiard table and trying to stanch a freshet of tears with a hanky no larger than a cocktail napkin. I've told you that I'm usually a klutz when dealing with lacrimating ladies, but in this case I believe I responded sympathetically if not nobly.

"Hi, Miss Stanescu," I said. "What's up?"

Her answer was more sobs, and I reacted to the crisis in my usual fashion by heading directly for the nearest source of spirits—in this case, the wet bar. The first bottle I put my hand on was ouzo, which I thought would be excellent shock therapy. I poured the tiniest bit into a snifter, brought it to her, and pressed it into her hand.

It worked to the extent that she found she couldn't cough and weep at the same time. The weeping stopped and, eventually, so did the coughing.

"What is wrong?" I asked. "Is there anything I may do to help?"

She shook her head, then took another sip of the ouzo, which emptied the glass.

"More?"

She cleared her throat. "Thank you, no. You have been most kind, Mr. McNally. I should have closed the door. But it came upon me very suddenly. Do you have a handkerchief, please? I'm afraid mine is a mess."

I supplied the linen, happy it was fresh and unwrinkled. She used it to dab her eyes dry, but they remained swollen.

"I received some bad news," she said. "The Rouen authorities wish to close my orphanage. The roof leaks dreadfully, you see, and the plumbing is in very bad repair. Also, the electrical wiring must be replaced. It would all cost a great deal of money."

"That's a shame," I said, suddenly wary, I admit, because I feared this might be a prelude to an attempted financial bite. "Surely your patrons or contributors would be willing to provide the funds."

"I think not," she said, now speaking evenly and decisively. "We have just been scraping by as it is. People give what they can afford. I will not beg."

"Very admirable," I said, "but sometimes it's necessary. What about your mother?"

She looked at me as if questioning my IQ. "Who do you think has been making up the losses all these years? I will not ask her for more. I cannot. She has been so generous. Just incredible."

Why did I feel this was the first false note in what she was telling me? I knew that her mother made small annual contributions to several charities, but she was Lady Horowitz, not Lady Bountiful. Unless, of course, she splurged on her daughter's orphanage. That was possible, but after the morning's snappish interview I found it difficult to credit her mother with any generosity, of spirit or purse.

"I don't know about France," I said, "but in this country there are fundraising organizations. For a fee, they recommend methods of increasing the income of worthwhile charities. Direct mail campaigns, for instance. Auctions of donated art objects. Even lotteries."

She shook her head again. "We are too small," she said, "and too local. We can only exist with the kindness of our benefactors. But the cost of the repairs far exceeds what we can expect."

"Surely you don't intend to close down?"

"No," she said determinedly, "not yet." And her sharp features hardened. Then she did resemble her mother. "Not until the very last moment. There is still a slim chance we may pull through."

"And what is the slim chance?"

"A miracle," she said solemnly. "Mr. McNally, thank you for your interest, and the loan of your handkerchief. I shall have it laundered and returned to you."

"No need," I said, but she was already sweeping from the room. She was wearing one of her voluminous white gowns, and it billowed out behind her. But now it made her look less like a romantic heroine than a fleeing ghost.

Nothing was making much sense to me. First, Lady Cynthia refused to reveal her whereabouts at the time Bela Rubik was killed. Now Gina Stanescu refused to ask her mother for funds to repair her orphanage although, according to her, mommy dearest had been a generous contributor in the past. I suspected Ms. Stanescu had been telling me the truth, but not the *whole* truth.

What I needed at the moment, I decided, was one of Leroy Pettibone's creative hamburgers and a pail of suds. A lunch like that would goose the disposition and bring roses back to my cheeks.

But when I arrived at the Pelican Club, I found it mobbed with the midday crowd, all apparently ravenous, because when I glanced into the dining room, I saw no vacant tables. I concluded I would be forced to lunch at the bar, but then a bare feminine arm was raised, waved, and beckoned me. I peered and saw it was Consuela Garcia, sitting alone at a table for two. I dodged over immediately.

"Hiya, babe," I said huskily, twirling an imaginary mustache. "You come here often?"

"Oh, shut up and sit down," she said. "You look hungry."

"*And* thirsty," I said, sitting. "How are you, Connie?"

"Miserable," she said.

"Well, you look great," I assured her. "Just great."

That was the truth. She was wearing a white linen sundress that enhanced her deep tan beautifully. Big gold hoop earrings dangled, and her glossy black hair was unbound. I happened to know it was long enough to touch her buns.

Priscilla came over to take our order and glanced at me. "Connie," she said, "you're not allowed to pick up strange men in the club."

"You're going to get it," I said to her threateningly.

"I hope so," she said. "But when?"

Connie and I laughed, ordered hamburgers and beers, and started nibbling on the pickle spears.

"Why are you miserable?" I asked her.

"It's that nuthouse I work in," she said. "I had to get away for an hour or I'd be climbing walls."

"What's the problem? Lady Cynthia?"

"You've got it, Archy. She's been in a snit lately."

"Oh?" I said, suddenly curious. "Since when? Since her stamps were stolen?"

"No," Connie said, "that didn't seem to bother her. It's only been in the last few days that she's become a holy terror. You know what I heard her called the other day?"

"Lady Horrorwitz?"

"That's old stuff. I was at a cocktail party and heard some old bitch refer to her as Lady Whorewitz. People can be awfully cruel."

"Awful *and* cruel," I said. "Ah, here's our lunch."

Connie asked for hot salsa to put on her burger, but I passed. I recalled that during our brief and intimate joust she amazed me by nibbling on chipotles, those peppers that can scorch your tonsils. Connie popped them like macadamia nuts.

"Tell me something," I said casually, working on my food, "when the madam takes off alone in her Jag, does she tell you where she's going?"

"Sometimes," Connie said, "and sometimes not. And she hates it if anyone asks. She's really a very secretive person."

"Maybe too secretive. Sergeant Al Rogoff asked her where she was at a particular time, and she lied to him. Then I asked her, and she as much as told me to stuff it."

"That sounds like her."

"She lied to you, too," I said quietly.

Connie stopped eating long enough to stare at me. "When was this?"

"The day everyone was supposed to go out on Phil Meecham's yacht. You told me Lady C. went to her hairdresser's."

"That's where she said she was going."

"I'm sure she did. But she never showed up at the salon."

"That's odd," Connie said, frowning. "As I told you, she either tells me where she's going or she doesn't. But I can't recall her ever lying to me. How do you figure it?"

"I can't," I said. "Perhaps she enjoys being a mystery woman."

"Archy, that's nonsense. She's about as mysterious as a fried egg. She has only one rule: Just do everything exactly her way, and you'll get along fine with her."

"I don't suppose you'd care to ask her where she went instead of the hairdresser's."

"No, I would not," Consuela said firmly. "In spite of my kvetching I happen to like my job and want to keep it."

We cleaned our plates and sat a moment in silence, finishing our beers.

"You still seeing Jennifer Towley?" Connie asked idly.

I nodded.

"Did she tell you her history?"

"She did."

"That her ex-husband is also an ex-con?"

"She told me," I said patiently.

"You ever see him, Archy?"

"No, I never have."

"I have," Connie said. "He was pointed out to me last Saturday."

"Oh?" I said, interested. "What kind of a dude is he?"

"Well, he certainly doesn't look like he's done time. I mean he's well-dressed, got a nice tan, looks to be in good shape. I'd guess he's an inch or two shorter than you. No flab. Pleasant-looking. Not a matinee idol, but presentable enough. He laughs a lot."

"Where did you see him, Connie?"

"Down at Dania Jai Alai."

"What on earth were you doing there?"

"My Significant Other and I decided to do something different on Saturday, so we drove down to catch the games."

"And that's where you saw Thomas Bingham?"

"Oh-ho," she said, "so you know his name. Yes, he was there. My guy knew who he was."

"Connie," I said, "was he betting?"

"Bingham? Like there was no tomorrow."

I signed the tab, we left the club, and Connie gave me a warm kiss on the cheek and thanked me for lunch. I waved when she drove away in her Subaru. A sterling lady, I reflected, and our abbreviated affair was something I'd remember when I was playing checkers in a nursing home.

I got into the Miata and squirmed a bit on the sun-heated cushions. I lighted an English Oval and pondered my next move. Al Rogoff was wrong; I did not enjoy complexity. I liked things clear and uncomplicated. But now I seemed to be involved in a maze of maybes. The uncertainties were so overwhelming that I was tempted to take off for Hong Kong immediately and not return until all problems had been solved.

But instead of flying to Hong Kong, I drove to a car rental agency in West Palm Beach. I flashed my plastic and hired a black Ford Escort GT for a week. I asked the clerk if I could leave it right there on the lot.

He looked at me as if I were a new variety of nut. "For a week?" he asked incredulously.

I nodded. "I'll pick it up every now and then." I told him. "Whenever I feel the urge." And I gave him a twenty-buck tip.

"Of course, sir!" he cried heartily. "Absolutely no problem."

I didn't wish to explain my motive to him. To wit: The Miata is a spiffy little car that catches the eye, especially when it's a screaming red. If I was going to do any tailing, I wanted wheels that wouldn't attract a second glance.

I drove back to the McNally & Son Building and parked the Miata in our underground garage. I went upstairs and asked Mrs. Trelawney if my father was available. She said he was in, but conferring with a client; she'd give me a buzz when he was free. So I went to my office which, for some reason, seemed smaller than ever. I thought of it as an Iron Maiden without the spikes.

I sat there for more than a half-hour reviewing the morning's tête-à-têtes with Lady Cynthia, Gina Stanescu, and Consuela Garcia. Very frustrating. Instead of clarifying matters, all three women had succeeded in adding to my professional and personal woes. They had tossed me more oddly shaped pieces on the table, the jigsaw puzzle kept getting larger, and I hadn't yet found two parts that fit.

Mrs. Trelawney phoned and said the boss could give me fifteen minutes before his next appointment, so make it snappy. Before I left for my audience, I tugged out my breast pocket handkerchief a bit to display it more conspicuously. It happened to be a square of brightly colored Pucci silk in a wildly abstract pattern, and I knew it would make my father's teeth ache. I really don't know why it pleased me to rile the old man occasionally. Perhaps it was just a sophomoric way of asserting my independence.

He was standing alongside his big rolltop desk when I entered his office, and I saw his gaze go immediately to the Pucci square. He made no comment, but one hairy eyebrow rose a good half-inch.

"Sorry to bother you, sir," I said, "but I wondered if you've had a chance to speak to Lady Horowitz about her will."

"I have," he said, "and she absolutely refuses to reveal any of its contents to the police."

"I expected that," I said, "but as you observed, she's unpredictable, and there was always a chance she might agree. Sergeant Rogoff will be disappointed."

There was silence, and I could tell by his thousand-yard stare that he was conducting one of those long inner debates that always preceded his dicta.

"I trust your discretion, Archy," he said finally. "If I didn't, you would not occupy the position you do in this organization. For your information—and I emphasize, *only* for *your* information—approximately half of Lady Horowitz's estate will go to several charities. Then there is a long list of specific bequests to individuals, including servants, friends, and even, I might add, all her ex-husbands who are still alive. The remainder of the estate is to be divided equally amongst her five children, three of whom are presently her houseguests."

I nodded. "I appreciate your confidence in my discretion, father. Without revealing any of the details to Sergeant Rogoff, may I tell him that you informed me there is nothing in Lady Cynthia's will that would aid his investigation?"

Again that long pause while he considered all the possible consequences of granting my request. Prescott McNally was one great muller.

"Yes," he said at last, "you may tell him that, but no more. How is the investigation proceeding?"

" 'A riddle wrapped in a mystery inside an enigma,' " I quoted. "Winston Churchill."

"*Sir* Winston Churchill," he corrected me gravely, always the stickler for titles. "No suspects at all?"

"Too many suspects," I said. "Including Lady Horowitz herself."

He stiffened and almost glared at me. "Surely you are not suggesting our client stole her own stamps and murdered the dealer."

"Oh no, sir," I said hastily, "nothing like that. But she refuses to reveal her whereabouts at the time Rubik was killed." Then I told him of the inability of Al Rogoff to determine where she was, capped by my own failure that morning. "Not necessarily guilty conduct," I admitted, "but worth a little more digging, wouldn't you say, father?"

"I suppose so," he said slowly, and I sensed the return of that troubled state of mind I had noted the previous evening.

"One final question, sir," I said. "You told me that approximately half of Lady Horowitz's estate will go to several charities. Do you happen to recall if one of them is an orphanage in Rouen operated by her daughter Gina Stanescu?"

He thought about that, but only for a moment this time. "No," he said definitely, "it is not."

"Thank you, father," I said.

I drove home in a pensive mood; "pensive" meaning that I devoted no thought at all to the Inverted Jenny Case, but spun my mental wheels trying to decide whether or not to tell Jennifer Towley that her ex was gambling again. If I did tell, was it to save her from potential heartbreak or further my own romantic prospects? There was a nice moral choice involved there, and I solved the problem in my usual fashion: I postponed my decision.

I found my mother standing at the wooden workbench in the potting shed. She was sorrowfully regarding what was possibly the most decrepit plant I had ever seen: stalk drooping, leaves withered, the soil in the white pot dried and cracked.

"Mother," I said, "what on earth is that thing?"

"Isn't it sad, Archy?" she said, and I feared she might weep. "It's a 'Dancing Girl' begonia. Sarah Bogart brought it over to see if I could save it."

"What did she *do* to it—feed it Drano?"

"Neglect," mother said angrily. "Just sheer, brutal neglect. The sick little thing is on its last legs."

"Can you save it?"

"I'm certainly going to try," she said determinedly. "I shall repot it in proper soil, water and fertilize, coddle it—and talk to it, of course."

She set to work with a marvelous set of stainless steel gardening tools my father had sent her during a business trip to Edinburgh. Her ministrations were slow, gentle, and purposeful. I had no doubt at all that the "Dancing Girl" would be kicking up its heels within a fortnight.

"Mother," I said, "have you noticed that father seems unusually troubled lately?"

"The poor thing," she said, and it took me a beat to realize she was referring to the bedraggled begonia.

"I realize he works very hard," I went on, "and is probably under a great deal of stress. But that's nothing new, and I've always felt he was coping."

"Tender, loving care is what's needed," mother said.

"But recently," I continued, "he seems almost distraught. Do you know of anything in particular that might be disturbing him?"

"You're going to be well again real soon," my mother promised the plant.

"You'll have gorgeous, healthy leaves and all the scarlet flowers you could want."

I gave up and started away, but she called me back. "You must think positively, Archy," she said, "and always look on the bright side of things."

"Yes, mother," I said.

Chapter 10

I really hated to scam Consuela Garcia. I thought her a lovely woman, perhaps not as sophisticated as she believed, but there was no malice in her. And I knew that despite her complaints, she was intensely loyal to her employer. So I had a swindle devised and rehearsed before I tooled up to the State of Horowitz on Wednesday morning.

I found Connie in her office, talking on the phone as usual. She waved me to a chair and continued her conversation. Apparently it involved a reception Lady Cynthia planned for a famous tenor who was about to visit Palm Beach.

Connie hung up and rolled her eyes heavenward. "The first crisis of the morning," she said, "and now you. What's on your mind, Archy?"

"A request," I said. "But please hear me out before you decide. Yesterday at lunch you told me that sometimes when Lady Horowitz takes off alone in her Jag, she doesn't tell you where she's going. Right?"

Connie nodded.

"What I'd like you to do," I said, "is the next time that happens, give me a quick telephone call."

"So you can follow her?" she said, outraged.

"Please listen a moment. You know I've been working closely with the police on the theft of the Inverted Jennies. We have good reasons to believe Lady Horowitz is being blackmailed, and she turned over the stamps as part payment."

"Blackmail!" Connie gasped, but she sounded more dismayed than disbelieving. She had been around long enough to know that Palm Beach is to a blackmailer as a chicken coop to a fox.

"All the evidence points to it," I lied on. "Regular cash withdrawals from her bank account, for instance. Now you know that if the cops or I ask her the direct question, 'Are you being blackmailed?' she'll tell us to get lost. Our best bet to stop this nastiness is to follow her to the blackmailers, identify them, and either put them behind bars or kick them out of the county. With no publicity; I can promise you that."

She looked at me, then took a deep breath. "I don't know," she said slowly. "I suppose she's done some things in her life she could be blackmailed for."

"Haven't we all?" I said. "Will you do it, Connie? Will you call me the moment you learn she's taking off in the Jag?"

"I'll think about it."

"Please do that," I said, rising. "I know you want to end this dirty business as much as I do."

I left her shaken and fumbling for a cigarette with trembling hands. Did I feel guilty about giving her that song and dance? No. The end doesn't *always* justify the means, but sometimes it does.

I exited the main house and heard sounds of laughter and splashings coming from the pool area. I strolled over there and found Felice and Alan DuPey frolicking in the water like baby dolphins. The newlyweds were wearing matching mauve swimsuits and aqua bathing caps.

I waved to them, and they waved to me. Their terry robes were piled on an umbrella table, and I pulled up a chair there and sat in the shade. I watched them cavort, yelping and dunking each other. Why did I feel so old? And why did I feel faint stirrings of envy? Tinged with a smidgen of regret, of course.

They came scrambling out of the pool laughing and peeling off their caps. They pulled on their robes, joined me, and we all exchanged greetings.

"Having a good time?" I asked. A silly question; they both looked like they had found Eden in South Florida.

"Oh, it is so lovely here," Felice said, looking about with shining eyes. "I never want to leave."

"But we must," her husband said, clasping her hand. He turned to me. "We depart Saturday morning."

"Sorry to hear it," I said. "Can't you stay a bit longer?"

He shook his head. "Sadly, no. We must return to our jobs. Back to the salt mines."

"You go, Alan," his wife said saucily, "and I shall stay. Mr. McNally will take care of me."

"I'd be delighted," I said, and we all laughed.

But it disturbed me. The DuPeys ranked close to the bottom of my list of suspects, but I didn't want to see them gone from the scene. If they were somehow involved in the theft and subsequent homicide, it would be extremely difficult if not impossible to prove their guilt if they were half a globe away.

Even more important, if they were totally innocent, as I believed, they still might have information they hadn't yet divulged, information they thought insignificant but which could be useful. Alan gave me the opening I needed.

"Tell me, Mr. McNally," he said, "have you discovered who stole mother's stamps?"

"Not yet," I said. "The investigation goes on. Perhaps you and Felice can help. When you all went aboard Phil Meecham's yacht, you were told the cruise was canceled because of high seas. Is that correct?"

"Yes," he said, "but we stayed to party."

"You and Felice did," I said. "But the Smythes, Gina Stanescu, and Angus Wolfson took off. I believe that's what you said. Have I got it right?"

They both nodded.

"Did they tell you where they were going?"

"Shopping," Felice said promptly, paused, then jabbered at her husband in such rapid French I couldn't follow it.

"Window-shopping," Alan explained. "I don't think they were planning to buy anything, but they said they wanted to see the shops on Worth Avenue."

"Such expensive shops!" his wife said. "Ooo, la!"

"Aren't they," I agreed. "So as far as you know, they were just going to wander about and do the tourist bit?"

The two looked at each other, then nodded again, vigorously this time.

"They all left the yacht in a group—the four of them?"

He frowned, trying to recall, but his wife supplied the answer.

"No," she said, "not all together. Gina and Angus departed first and then, perhaps a half-hour later, the Smythes. I remember because . . ."

Suddenly both burst out laughing, sharing a mutual joke.

"What's so amusing?" I asked.

Alan calmed down long enough to reply. "I shouldn't peach on them," he said, "but when Harry and Doris left, they took a bottle of Monsieur Meecham's champagne with them."

"We saw it," Felice said. "It was so fonny. Harry tried to hide it under his jacket."

"In case they got thirsty while window-shopping," I suggested. "Well, I'm sure Phil Meecham never missed it. But Gina and Angus went off together?"

"Oh yes," Alan said. "They are very close, those two."

"Do you suppose—" his wife started, then stopped and bit her knuckle.

"Suppose what?" I urged her.

"It's nonsense," Alan said, looking at his new wife fondly. "Felice believes there may be more than friendship there."

"Oh?" I said. "A romance?"

"It is not nonsense," Felice said, pouting prettily. "A woman knows these things, and I say there is definitely a feeling, an emotion between them."

"Impossible," the husband said firmly. "First of all, he is at least twenty years older than she, and also he is gay."

"Those things are of no importance," the wife said just as firmly. "Perhaps they are both lonely."

"That's possible," I admitted. "I hoped to have a talk with Mr. Wolfson this morning. Do you know if he's around?"

"No, he is not," Alan said. "He went down to the beach about an hour ago."

"I hope he's not going to swim," I said. "It's choppy out there today, and the radio warned of an undertow."

"Oh no," Felice said. "He can't swim; he told us so. He said he's just going to take a walk and perhaps pick up a few shells."

I nodded and stood up. "I'll see if I can find him. Thank you for the talk. I'm sure I'll see you again before you leave."

"You are not married, Mr. McNally?" she asked suddenly.

"No," I said, "I am not."

Felice looked at me speculatively. "I have a beautiful cousin," she said. "About your age I would say. Also unmarried."

"Felice!" her husband cried, and clapped a palm lightly over her mouth. "Please to excuse," he said to me. "She is *such* a matchmaker."

His wife took his hand away. "I just want everyone to be as happy as we are," she said.

I left them holding hands and gazing at each other with bedroom eyes. Enough already!

The Horowitz estate fronted on Ocean Boulevard. Across the road was a paling of sea grape and then a waist-high concrete wall. Beyond that was the beach, the Atlantic Ocean and, eventually, Morocco.

But I wasn't going that far. I walked northward to a break in the wall where a weatherworn wooden staircase led down to the sand. During the season you might see dozens of bathers in both directions. In late May I saw a family group of four swimmers to the north and two supine sun-worshipers to the south. Palm Beach Island is definitely not Coney.

I also saw, to the north, the distant, approaching figure of a solitary stroller I decided could very well be Angus Wolfson. I kicked off my loafers (no socks) and plodded through the sand. As we came closer it indeed proved to be the Boston bibliophile, carrying his sandals and sloshing through the shallows like a kid kicking his way through puddles of rain.

He was wearing white flannel bags and a silk shirt with flamboyant collar and billowing sleeves that Lord Byron might envy. Atop his head was a yellowed boater with a tatty band that he wore with an insouciance I admired, and he stabbed at the sand with the tip of a Malacca cane.

As I came up, he recognized me and swept off his ridiculous hat with a gesture of mock politesse and bowed slightly. "Mr. McNally," he said, "what a delightful surprise."

"Planned," I told him. "I heard you were walking the beach and hoped to have a talk. May I accompany you, sir?"

"Only if you cease calling me 'sir.' It's one notch from 'pop.' "

"Old habits die hard," I said. "I was taught to address male elders as 'sir' as a mark of respect."

"Sometimes we don't deserve it," he said lightly. "By all means, walk along. An absolutely *brilliant* day."

It was. An ocean breeze took the edge off the sun's heat, and the blue sky was mottled with popcorn clouds. But the sea was undeniably choppy with a steady surf that came pounding in to swirl milky foam about our bare ankles.

We meandered slowly southward, Wolfson occasionally leaning heavily on his cane. I didn't think he looked at all well. The sagging flesh of his face had a grayish tinge, and once or twice he pressed his free hand to his abdomen as if to restrain a persistent pain.

"Are you feeling all right?" I asked.

"A temporary malady," he said blithely. "It will soon pass."

"What is it, Mr. Wolfson?"

"Living," he said and looked to me for an appreciative chuckle. I obliged as best I could. He asked: "And are you still snooping about after those silly stamps?"

I was offended by that derisive description of my discreet inquiries, but let it pass. "I'm still investigating, yes."

He stopped a moment to lean on his cane and stare out at the dim horizon. "I really don't understand why you're making such a fuss about the disappearance of those misprinted bits of paper. I assure you that Lady Cynthia is not losing any sleep over their loss."

"If the stamps are not recovered, an insurance claim will be filed. My father wants to make certain that both his office and the police have made a good-faith effort to find the stamps or the thief or both."

He made no reply but resumed his slow walk. His head was lowered, the wide brim of his hat hid his eyes.

"And why did you wish to talk to me?" he inquired. "I've already told you what little I know of the matter."

"Just a few more questions," I said. "You left Phil Meecham's yacht with Gina Stanescu after the cruise was canceled. Do you mind telling me where you went?"

"Yes, I do mind," he said. "I resent this interrogation since it seems to imply there may have been something suspicious in my activities that day. However, I have nothing to hide so I shall answer. Gina and I found our way to Worth Avenue and visited several shops. We separated in a department store because I was weary of walking about. We made plans to meet in an hour. I stopped briefly in a bookstore but found nothing that interested me. I then went to the Cafe L'Europe, sat at the bar and had an excellent vodka gimlet, ice cold and razor-sharp. Gina eventually joined me and had a glass of white wine. We finished our drinks—I had a second—and phoned Kenneth. He came for us in that marvelous Rolls, and we rode home in style. Satisfied?"

"I am," I said, "but you know what the police are like; they'll want to check your story with Gina, the clerk at the bookstore, the bartender at L'Europe, and Kenneth."

"Let them do all the bloody checking they want," he cried with unexpected fury. "I don't give a good goddamn!"

I looked at him with astonishment. The sudden spasm of anger seemed to have weakened him. He swayed, I feared he might fall, and put a hand on his elbow to steady him.

"Are you all right?" I asked anxiously.

"I'm beginning to feel the heat," he said with what I can only describe as a vulpine grin. "I think we better go back."

"Of course," I said. "Would you care to lean on my arm?"

He glared at me. "I am stronger than you may think," he said coldly. "I am not yet decrepit, I do assure you."

But we retraced our steps slowly, Wolfson with his head bowed and using his cane. He stopped abruptly, lowered his head a little more to peer at the sand.

"Look at that!" he said. "A lovely shell! Will you retrieve it for me, please."

I bent to pick it up, shake out the sand and hand it to him. It was a common whelk, chipped and encrusted, but he turned it tenderly in his fingers as if he had found a treasure.

"Is it rare?" he asked.

I could not lie but I could dissemble. "All shells are rare along this stretch of coast," I told him. "We've had very slim pickings for the past few years."

"I shall give it to Gina," he said. "She'll love it."

We finally got back to the Horowitz mansion, and Wolfson left me to go to his room. "A short nap," the antiquarian said, "to recharge my batteries."

I went out to the Miata and saw Kenneth Bodin puttering about in the garage. He was wearing one of his skimpy T-shirts, muscles popping in all directions. I joined him and proffered my box of cigarettes. He selected one and examined it closely.

"English Ovals, huh?" he said. "I never smoked one. Imported?"

"Yes," I said. "From Virginia."

"I'll have it after lunch," he said, and tucked the cigarette behind his ear. "You find those stamps yet?"

"Not yet," I said. "Perhaps you can help. On the day all the houseguests were supposed to go for a yacht cruise, did you get a call around one o'clock to pick up Gina Stanescu and Angus Wolfson?"

"That's right," he said. "The cruise was canceled, so they went shopping. Then they wanted a ride back. They could have called a cab, I guess, but that's what I'm here for—right?"

"Right," I said. "Where did you pick them up?"

"Outside the Cafe L'Europe," he said promptly. "They were waiting for me on the sidewalk."

"And you drove them directly back here?"

"Sure. Hey, has this got something to do with the stamps?"

"One never knows, do one?" I said, and left him flummoxed.

I returned home for lunch. But before digging into the chef's salad Ursi had prepared, I made two phone calls. The first was to Sgt. Al Rogoff.

"Hiya, sherlock," he said. "What's up?"

"You're having lunch," I said. "I can hear you masticating."

"Nah," he said, "I haven't done that since I was in the navy."

"Not a bad pun," I admitted. "What are you eating?"

"Anchovy pizza."

"Rather you than me," I said. "Can you chew pizza and make notes at the same time?"

"Sure."

I repeated what Angus Wolfson had told me of his activities during the time Bela Rubik was getting his skull smashed.

"Okay," Al said. "Thanks. I'll check it out."

"I've already questioned the chauffeur," I told him. "He says yes, he picked up Stanescu and Wolfson about one o'clock. Do you believe him?"

"I don't believe anyone," Rogoff said.

"Does that include me?" I asked.

"Especially you," he said.

My second call was to Jennifer Towley, and I was pleasantly surprised when she replied instead of her answering machine.

"Sorry," I said, "but I can't talk until you *beep.*"

"*Beep,*" she said.

"How about dinner tonight?"

"Love to," she said at once.

"Are you sure you wouldn't like to consider it for—oh, say two seconds?"

"I did," she said, "and I'd love to have dinner with you tonight. What shall I wear?"

"Clothes would be nice—but if you'd rather not . . ."

"I'll wear clothes," she said firmly.

"Listen," I said, "I just had an earthshaking idea. I haven't done the black-tie bit in ages. Why don't we glam it up just for the fun of it?"

"Groovy," she said. Then: "Do people still say groovy?"

"No."

"Well, I think glamming it up for an evening is a marvy idea."

"No one says marvy anymore either."

"Keep it up," she warned, "and you and your black tie will end up alone at the Pelican Club."

"See you around seven," I said.

"That's keen," she said. "Also neat."

I hung up, thinking she was in a delightfully antic mood.

At the family cocktail hour that evening, father eyed my white dinner jacket with his usual distaste for my duds. He once observed that wearing a white dinner jacket made a man look like a trombonist in Guy Lombardo's band.

Mother had news. She had received a handwritten note from Lady Cynthia Horowitz. The three of us were invited to attend an informal dinner for Felice and Alan DuPey on Friday night. It was to be a farewell party prior to their departure for France on Saturday morning.

"Shall we accept, Prescott?" she asked. (She had once addressed him as "father," and he had instructed her in no uncertain terms that since he was not her father, he did not appreciate the designation. All very well and good, and I agreed with him, but I noted that on more than one occasion he had addressed her as "mother." How do you figure that?)

"I think we should," he said, and turned to me. "You've met the DuPeys, Archy?"

"Yes, sir. I spoke to them today."

"A pleasant couple?"

"Newlyweds," I said, "and disgustingly in love. It can't last."

"Don't be so sure of that, Archy," my mother said, sipping her martini.

I know it's fashionable to be late, but early in our relationship I had sensed that Jennifer was a woman who preferred punctuality in her business and personal dealings. So I rang her bell a minute or two after seven o'clock, duded up in dinner jacket, black tie and cummerbund, as promised.

She came to the door, and I almost shouted with delight. If that wasn't a Hanae Mori she was wearing, it was an awfully good ripoff. The beaded gown fell to her ankles and looked as if it had been painted by van Gogh, perhaps as a study for "Starry Night." It was all swirls of vibrant colors that caught the light and gave it back deepened and intensified.

Jennifer must have seen my admiration, for she struck a model's pose and twirled. "Glamorous enough for you?" she asked.

"Magnificent," I said. "I think I better cancel our reservation at Burger King. We'll go to a fancier place."

"We better," she said. "I shot my bank account on this little number."

Actually, I had made a reservation at The Ocean Grand, a new hotel down the road a piece. It's an elegant resort, and if anything could top the painted silk murals on the walls of the dining room, it could only be that scintillant gown Jennifer was wearing.

I'm not going to describe our dinner in detail because you'd gain weight just reading about it. I'll merely mention our entrees: Jennifer had sautéed breast of pheasant with kumquats, and I had wood-grilled tenderloin flavored with tamarind and guava. Isn't that enough to set your salivary glands atwitter?

After dessert and espresso, we moved to the lounge, where a harpist was strumming something that sounded suspiciously like "The Darktown Strutters' Ball." We sat at the bar and ordered S.O.B.s. You may not be familiar with that drink. The full name is Sex on the Beach, and I believe it's indigenous to South Florida. I don't wish to reveal the ingredients lest it achieve wide popularity and undermine the democratic institutions of this great nation.

"Oh Archy," Jennifer said, sighing, "what a scrumptious dinner! I must have put on five pounds."

"Nonsense," I said. "It was all no-cal—didn't you know?"

"Liar," she said. "But I don't care; I'll go on a diet tomorrow."

"Famous last words. Just play a few sets of tennis in the hot sun; that'll melt the avoirdupois. Jennifer, have you used your new racquet yet?"

"Not yet. I can't tell you how busy I've been. I was hoping to take an hour off yesterday for a lesson with the club pro, but something came up."

I didn't ask.

"As a matter of fact," she said, looking down at her drink, "my ex phoned. He was going to be in West Palm Beach and wanted to have lunch."

"Uh-huh," I said. "And did you?"

She nodded. "I thought about it and decided there was no point in being uncivil. After all, we were married. And having a quick lunch with Tom didn't send a signal that I wanted him back, did it?"

I didn't answer that. "It's your decision," I said, but suddenly the evening didn't seem quite as perfect as it had ten minutes ago.

"Well, I saw him," she went on. "I think it was more curiosity than anything else. I wondered if those years in prison had changed him."

"And?"

She gave a short laugh. "I think they helped. Physically, at least. He's thinner and has a good tan. He looks very fit. And he's as optimistic as ever. I suppose salesmen have to be that way."

"What about the gambling?"

"He says that's all finished. He claims he hasn't made a bet since his release, and he swears he'll never gamble again as long as he lives."

"Do you believe him?"

"Oh Archy, how can I? He told me the same thing so many times when we were married, and he always broke his promise. No, I don't believe him."

"I think that's wise."

"I hope he means it this time," she said thoughtfully. "For his sake. But I wouldn't bet on it."

"Good," I said. "Don't you start betting."

She gave me a sad smile.

We finished our drinks and left. I drove slowly on the trip homeward while Jennifer chattered on about her crazy clients and their wild decorating ideas. I had never known her to be so voluble, and it suddenly occurred to me that she—like Gina Stanescu and Angus Wolfson—might be lonely. Lonely in the sense of lacking someone in her life with whom to share intimacies, even if they were only the mundane details of living: What did you have for lunch? Did you get caught in the rain? Is your headache better? Did you remember to pick up the dry cleaning?

In other words, she lacked a partner. And I wasn't yet certain I wanted to apply for the job. The reason is obvious, isn't it? Cowardice.

She invited me in for a nightcap, and I accepted gratefully because I did admire this woman. She really demanded nothing from me, and I knew she wouldn't. She gave generously and in return, I think, she wanted me to respect her independence. And so we circled each other in comfortable orbit, but never collided. That would have meant destruction or merger, and I don't believe either of us had the moxie to chance it.

That evening, in her Victorian four-poster, her horizontal aerobics were as fervid as ever. At least her body responded enthusiastically to stimuli. But I had the feeling that her thoughts were away and drifting.

Chapter 11

I had Thursday carefully planned: things to do, people to see, questions to ask. And then my carefully crafted schedule just fell apart, and chance and accident took over again, with no help from me this time.

I was heading out to the garage after breakfast when the phone rang. I scampered back into the kitchen with a premonition that the day was not going to proceed as planned.

"The McNally residence," I said.

"May I talk to Mr. Archibald McNally, please."

A woman's voice, deep and throaty. I had heard it before but couldn't place it.

"Speaking," I said. "Who is calling?"

"This is Mrs. Agnes Marsden."

"Mrs. Marsden! How nice to hear from you. Sorry I didn't recognize your voice. How are you?"

"Very well, thank you. Mr. McNally, are you coming over today?"

"I intend to," I said, "but later this afternoon."

"Could you come right away?" she said, almost pleading. "There's something I should tell you, and I want to get it off my chest now. If I wait till this afternoon, I might change my mind again."

"Don't do that," I said. "I'll be there in ten minutes. Thank you, Mrs. Marsden."

She opened the door of the Horowitz mansion while I had my hand raised to use that enormous brass knocker: the head of Bacchus surrounded by vine leaves. The housekeeper led me into the mammoth first-floor sitting room, and we occupied a corner as we had before. She sat stiffly upright, but her fingers were interlaced and gripped tightly.

"Young man," she started, "can I trust you?"

"Of course you can," I said, oozing sincerity. "Whatever you tell me is strictly confidential. It will go no farther, I promise you."

"See that you keep your promise," she said tartly. "I mentioned to you that I have seen strange goings-on that disturb me."

I nodded.

"I have decided to tell you about them. They may mean nothing, and I hope they do. But a crime has been committed in this house, Mr. McNally, and something of great value has been stolen. Being black, I am naturally the one the police will suspect."

"No, no," I protested, infinitely saddened.

"Yes, yes," she said ironically. "Don't attempt to teach me the ways of the world, young man. So I have a personal reason for helping your investigation any way I can."

"I appreciate that," I said, "and I welcome it. But believe me, Mrs. Marsden, you are not a suspect and never have been."

She ignored that, obviously not believing it. "First of all," she said, "Gina Stanescu and Angus Wolfson have become very close. Closer than you might expect for two people who have known each other such a short time. I see them together frequently: taking walks, sitting on the terrace or in the game room. Once or twice she was crying, and he was comforting her."

I nodded again, not wanting to interrupt her recital.

"That could be completely innocent," she said. "A man and a woman getting close—nothing wrong about that. What is wrong is the way Wolfson has been carrying on with Ken Bodin, the chauffeur."

I was surprised at Wolfson's temerity, but not shocked. "Carrying on?" I said.

Her back became ramrod straight and she looked sternly at me. "People's personal lives are their own. I don't interfere, and I don't expect them to interfere with me. But private things should be kept private. They can do anything they wish, but I don't want to know about it. Do you understand what I'm saying?"

"Yes, Mrs. Marsden, I think I do."

"That Mr. Wolfson just doesn't care who sees what he's doing or who hears what he's saying to Kenneth. I don't like it one bit."

"And how does Kenneth take all this?"

She made a grimace. "That boy is a noodle," she said. "Nothing between his ears. He just eats it up when Mr. Wolfson comes on to him. He grins and laughs and shows off his muscles."

"I get the picture," I said, and thought a moment. Then: "Do you think Wolfson is giving Kenneth money?"

"I wouldn't be a bit surprised," the housekeeper said, stood suddenly, and smoothed the wrinkles from her bombazine dress.

I rose also. "Thank you for the information, Mrs. Marsden. It may be of help. One final question: Do you think Lady Horowitz has been acting oddly lately?"

She stared at me, face expressionless. "Oddly?" she asked. "What do you mean?"

"Oh, driving off in the Jaguar by herself without telling anyone where she's going."

"No," she said firmly, "I've noticed nothing like that."

And she swept swiftly from the room, leaving me standing there with more unlinked pieces to add to my jigsaw puzzle.

I drove the Miata to the McNally Building on Royal Palm Way, foolishly believing I was going to get back to my planned schedule. I parked in the underground garage and strolled over to the glass-enclosed booth inhabited by Herb, our security guard. He's a spindly, hipless bloke whose gunbelt always seems in danger of slipping down around his knees.

"Herb," I said, "may I use your phone?"

"Sure thing, Mr. McNally," he said. "It's a scorcher out there today."

"True," I said. "It gets hot in the summer and cold in the winter. I don't understand it."

I called for a cab to come pick me up. While I waited, I chatted with Herb about tropical fish. According to what I had heard, his mobile home was wall-to-wall aquaria, and he liked nothing better than to debate the virtues of Black Tetras versus Mickey Mouse Platies. I am not an expert on tropicals, but I once owned a Zebra Danio named Irving. It died.

The cab finally showed up, and I asked the driver to take me to that car rental agency in West Palm Beach where I intended to pick up the black Ford Escort GTI had hired for tailing purposes. This was what I was thinking:

If I received a call from Consuela Garcia telling me that Lady Horowitz was going to take off alone in her Jaguar, destination unknown, I wanted my anonymous car closer than West Palm Beach. And I couldn't park it in the McNally driveway or my father would be sure to ask me its purpose. And if I told him I had rented it so that I could follow McNally & Son's wealthiest client without fear of detection, he would have had me committed.

I switched from cab to Escort and drove back to Royal Palm Way. I parked next to the Miata and told Herb I was going upstairs to get a windshield sticker issued to employees. All cars parked in our underground garage must have them or they get towed away. We had a small outside parking area for visitors and clients.

I asked Mrs. Trelawney for a numbered decal, and she wanted to know why I needed it since I already had one for the Miata. I told her it was for my new skateboard. She hooted one laugh and handed it over. I stopped at my office and found two telephone messages on my desk. One was from Sgt. Al Rogoff, the other from Hilda Lantern, the stamp dealer in Fort Lauderdale. Both asked me to call as soon as possible.

I phoned Hilda Lantern first. She sounded excited for such a dour woman and told me she had a report regarding the current market value of a block of four Inverted Jenny stamps, and thought it important that I be informed at once.

"That's fine," I said. "What is it?"

"Not on the phone," she said sharply. "You better come here."

I wasn't about to argue with that dominative lady and assured her I'd be delighted to spend three hours driving to and from Fort Lauderdale to hear what she had to relate. I hung up and may have screamed, "Drat!" Or possibly some other four-letter word.

I stuffed Al Rogoff's message in my jacket pocket, returned to the garage, and slapped the identification sticker onto the corner of the Escort's windshield. Then I headed the rented car southward to Lauderdale, glumly reflecting that when R. Burns penned his aphorism regarding the best laid schemes o' mice and men, he must have been referring to the Thursday schedule of A. McNally.

The drive south didn't lift my mood. It was a hot day all right, but humid and cloudy. So instead of beaching, everyone in South Florida decided to go malling. Traffic was horrendous, and by the time I hit East Commercial Boulevard I was as cantankerous as Hilda Lantern and figured I could match her peeve for peeve.

But I found the lady in a dulcet mood. Of course that may have been due to the whopping bill she handed me for her labors to date on behalf of McNally & Son. The charges, she claimed, were for time spent and phone calls made to stamp dealers, trying to establish the current market price of a block of four Inverted Jenny stamps.

"None of them ever handled such a rarity," she reported. "I couldn't get any quotes."

That was understandable. Asking the average stamp dealer what he would pay for an Inverted Jenny was akin to asking the average jeweler for a quote on the Star of India.

"But then," she went on, "I got a return call from a dealer out on Powerline Road near Palm Aire. He said that early this morning, right after he opened, a woman showed up with a block of four Jennies and asked if he wanted to buy."

I tried to conceal my rush. "Did she mention how much she wanted?"

"Half a million. He examined the stamps and told her they were too rich for his blood; he just couldn't swing the deal."

"How were the stamps presented? Mounted? In an envelope? Or what?"

"Between plastic sheets in a small red book," Ms. Lantern said. "About the size of a daily diary."

"Uh-huh," I said. "And did the dealer describe the would-be seller?"

Hilda delivered a short, scornful laugh. "Not your run-of-the-mill stamp collector," she said. "A young blond woman wearing short-shorts and a halter top. I suppose she was what you men would call well-endowed."

"I suppose," I agreed. "Did the dealer happen to note the car she was using?"

"He didn't mention it," Lantern said, looking at me curiously. "Why do you ask?"

"Just wondering," I said, naturally hoping it had been a lavender Volkswagen Beetle. "So she left with her stamps, and that was that?"

"Not quite," she said almost triumphantly. "The block of four Inverted Jennies she tried to sell him were counterfeit."

I clenched my teeth to keep the old jaw from drooping. "Counterfeit?"

She nodded.

"A forgery?"

"Absolutely. No doubt about it."

"How could the dealer be so sure after such a brief inspection?"

"You know anything about the history of the Inverted Jennies?" she demanded.

"Some," I said. "The original sheet of a hundred stamps was bought in 1918 at a Washington, D.C., post office by a broker's clerk. He paid twenty-four dollars. About a week later he sold the sheet to a stamp dealer for fifteen thousand."

"That's right," Lantern said. "And a week after that, the dealer sold the stamps to a collector for twenty thousand. But the collector kept only twenty of the stamps and gave the dealer permission to break up the remainder of the sheet into singles and blocks and sell them. When the dealer did that, he made light pencil marks on the back of each stamp, showing the name of the buyer. Practically all the Inverted Jennies in existence have those penciled notations on the back. If they don't, the chances are good that they're counterfeits. In this case, the Palm Aire dealer who called me said there were no marks on the backs of the stamps. And when he examined the face with a magnifying glass, the printing appeared slightly fuzzy and the inverted biplane in the center was slightly off register. Also, the number of perforations along the edges of each stamp was one less than the government printing office uses. Those stamps were definitely fakes."

I drew a deep breath. "Did the dealer tell that to the woman who was trying to sell them?"

"No. He didn't want to get involved. He just told her that he couldn't afford them and got her out of his shop as quickly as possible."

"That was probably the smart thing to do," I said. "Well, I don't think we can use the asked-for price of forged stamps as a benchmark for our deceased client's block of four, but I certainly appreciate the information. Will you continue your inquiries, please."

"If you want me to," she said. "When can I expect payment?"

"You'll have a check within a week," I promised. "Or I can pay now by credit card if you'd prefer."

"I'll wait for the check," she said, and we parted with a firm handshake.

I drove back to Delray Beach as speedily as traffic and the law allowed. Of course you know what I was thinking: In all of South Florida there couldn't be more than one blond young woman, wearing short-shorts and halter top (and "well-endowed"), trying to peddle a block of four Inverted Jenny stamps. And those placed between plastic sheets in a small red book. Tallyho!

I entered Hammerhead's Bar & Grill and looked about for Sylvia. Not present, which pleased me. I stood at the Formica bar and ordered a beer from a T-shirted bartender who appeared to be in the full flower of middle-aged louthood.

"Sylvia around?" I asked casually.

"Nah," he said. "It's her day off."

"Oh," I said, "I didn't know. Maybe I'll try her at home."

"Won't do you no good," he said with a louche laugh. "It's her boyfriend's day off, too. They was going to drive down to the Keys."

"Thank you very much," I said, and meant it.

I finished my beer, left a tip large enough to shock the publican, and headed for the hurricane-shutter emporium where Thomas Bingham was employed. Now if it was also *his* day off, my happiness would be complete.

My motive was contemptible; I admit it. I wanted desperately to involve Bingham in the snatch of Lady Cynthia's stamps and the subsequent murder of Bela Rubik. My excuse was simply that I was smitten by Jennifer Towley. I had felt similar emotions about other women—similar but far less intense. Then it had been mostly a matter of testosterone. Now it was a matter of heart. I wanted that cool, elegant woman for my very own, and the ex-husband represented a threat to my felicity.

Not a very noble reason for hounding a man, is it? But I make no claims to nobility. After all, my grandfather was an expert at pratfalls.

My luck foundered with Tom Bingham. He was in the store, and when I asked for him, he came forward smiling.

"Yes, sir," he said, "what can I do for you?"

Vanish, I wanted to say, but didn't.

"Mr. Bingham," I said, "I'm from out of town, but I'm staying with a friend in Boca. He's got a condo in a high-rise and wants to get hurricane shutters. He asked me to find someone who could do the job."

"And how did you get on to me?" he asked, still smiling.

"I was having a drink at Hammerhead's," I said, "and Sylvia suggested I contact you."

"Good for Sylvia," he said. "She's great people, isn't she?"

"She certainly is."

"I party with her and her boyfriend," he went on in the most open and honest way imaginable. "We have a lot of laughs together. Would you like me to come to your friend's condo and give you an estimate? No charge."

"The problem is that he works during the day," I explained, "and I'm about ready to head up north. Could you possibly come out in the evening?"

"Of course," he said promptly. "Anytime. And that includes Saturday or Sunday. Whatever's convenient for him."

Connie Garcia had been right; he was a pleasant man, not terribly handsome but with more than his share of easy charm. I could understand why he was a dynamite salesman; he gave the impression that satisfying your every wish was his foremost priority. There was something almost puppyish in his desire to please.

"Suppose I have my friend give you a call," I said. "Then the two of you can set up a time."

"Sounds good to me," he said, and I wondered if he slept with that genial smile.

"Thank you, Mr. Bingham," I said, started to leave, then turned back. "Oh, by the way," I said, "is there any place nearby where I can buy lottery tickets?"

The smile expanded. "You play the lottery, do you?"

I nodded. "Since I've been in Florida I've been hooked."

"Me, too," he said cheerfully. "Totally addicted. I play Lotto, Fantasy Five, the scratch-offs—everything. It keeps me poor. Sure, there's a liquor store on the corner that has a computer. They'll sell you as many tickets as you want. As they say in the commercials, 'You never know.' "

"That's right," I agreed. "Hit once and you're set for life."

"Now you're singing my song," he said, and I left him with his smile intact.

I still wasn't ready to forget his complicity in the Horowitz heist. If playing the lottery kept him poor, he could be in as deep as Kenneth Bodin and Sylvia, and the two men had elected the woman to try to sell the swag. But one thing I definitely knew to be true: Thomas Bingham hadn't been cured of his compulsion to gamble by those years he had spent in the slammer.

I pondered these things on my homeward drive. I decided the biggest puzzle was this: What on earth did Jennifer Towley, a lady of taste and discernment, *see* in this guy? There was nothing exceptional about him that I could spot. He was a loser, a salesman of plumbing supplies and hurricane shutters, an ex-convict with a monkey on his back. But Jennifer had married him, sent him birthday cards in prison, taken his phone calls after his release, met him for lunch. She was demeaning herself and I couldn't compute it.

Does that make me an elitist snob? I guess so.

I drove directly to the Pelican Club. It was then about three-thirty, and the place was deserted except for Simon Pettibone behind the bar. He was reading *The Wall Street Journal* through his B. Franklin specs. I waved to him, went to the public phone, and called Sgt. Al Rogoff.

"So nice to hear from you," he said. "Have you had a pleasant day? A tennis match perhaps? A chukker of polo?"

"Oh, shut up," I said. "I think you and I better get together and have a talk."

"No kidding?" he said. "What a brilliant idea. Where are you now?"

"In the bar of the Pelican Club."

"I should have known. Can you stay sober for a half-hour until I get there?"

"I never drink to excess," I said stiffly.

"Now you *are* kidding. If I ever need a liver transplant, with my luck I'll get yours. Wait for me."

I returned to the bar and swung onto a stool. "Mr. Pettibone," I said, "you have a few years on me and infinitely more wisdom. Tell me, what do *you* do when life threatens to overwhelm and problems become too heavy to be borne?"

He thought a moment, peering at me over his square glasses. "I usually kick my cat, Mr. McNally," he said.

"Good suggestion," I said. "I must purchase a cat. Meanwhile I'll have a wee bit of the old nasty in the form of an Absolut on the rocks, splash of water, chunk of lime. And if I attempt to order a refill, I want you to eighty-six me. An officer of the law has just cast aspersions on my liver."

I carried my drink over to a booth and nursed it until Sgt. Rogoff came stalking in. He looked around, saw me, and came lumbering. He slid in opposite me and stared stonily.

"What are you drinking?" I asked.

"Hemlock," he said. "I know you're not totally to blame, but every time you drop something on my plate I start thinking about early retirement. You know how I spent yesterday?"

"Haven't the slightest."

"Checking out the whereabouts of Doris and Harry Smythe at the time Rubik was iced. They claimed they left Meecham's yacht and went to Testa's for what Harry called 'a spot of lunch.' Bushwa! No one at Testa's remembered them. So I went back to the Smythes, and they finally admitted they had lunch at a Pizza Hut. So I checked on that, and the people at the Pizza Hut remembered them all right. You know why?"

"They left a nickel tip?"

"That, too. But mostly they were remembered because they asked for two plastic glasses and uncorked a bottle of champagne they had brought along. Archy, can you believe this insanity?"

"Easily," I said, laughing. "They swiped the bubbly from Meecham's yacht. So you figure they're cleared?"

"Looks like it."

"Al, have you started checking out Gina Stanescu and Angus Wolfson?"

"Not yet. You believe Wolfson's story?"

"Not completely," I said. "He flared up when I started to ask questions. There really was no need for it if he was totally innocent. But maybe he was just being crotchety. I think the man is sick."

"Sick?"

"Ill. He seems to be in pain. Get out your notebook, Al; I have more for you."

While I had waited for him, sipping my vodka daintily, I had decided how much to tell him. Everything about Hilda Lantern, Kenneth Bodin and Sylvia, but nothing about Thomas Bingham. That's all Rogoff would have to hear: an ex-con possibly implicated in crimes under investigation. He'd have zeroed in on Bingham like a gundog on point. And I didn't want Jennifer Towley involved in any manner whatsoever.

When I completed my recital, Al looked at me thoughtfully. "What made you go to the stamp dealer in Lauderdale?"

I pondered my answer carefully. I really needed the sergeant's cooperation and didn't want to stiff him or send him sniffing along false trails. But there were things I didn't wish to reveal at this stage of the investigation. My reasons will, I trust, become apparent later.

"Take your time," Al said, peeling the cellophane from a cigar. "Meditate. Cogitate. Consider all the permutations and combinations. And what about your karma? I can wait."

"Look," I said, hunching forward, "when I hired Rubik I fed him a farrago. I told him my firm was handling an estate that included Inverted Jenny stamps, and we wanted to establish an evaluation. I asked Rubik to make inquiries and see if he could determine the current price. That's what I *told* him. What I hoped was that he'd discover a block of Inverted Jennies had recently come on the market. You follow?"

"Way ahead of you," Rogoff said, lighting his cigar. "You figured the thief would try to unload as soon as possible. Right?"

"Right. And Rubik obviously discovered something of importance but was killed before he could pass it along to me. So I decided that if Rubik could get the information, another stamp dealer might be able to do the same thing. I just happened to pick Hilda Lantern's name out of the Yellow Pages, and she came through. How do you like that bit about the stamps being counterfeit?"

"Love it," Al said. "You think that was the important information Bela Rubik uncovered and wanted to tell you before he was iced?"

"Possibly," I said.

Rogoff thought a moment, then puffed a plume of blue smoke over my head. "That Palm Aire dealer who examined the stamps—do you think he told Bodin's girlfriend they were fakes?"

"Hilda Lantern said he didn't."

"That means the villains still believe they're holding loot worth half a million. I think what I better do is contact every stamp dealer from Miami to Fort Pierce and tell them to stall anyone who comes in and tries to sell a block of Inverted Jennies. They can say they need a day or two to raise the cash. Then the dealer can give me a panic call, and I'll have someone in the store and the place staked out when the crook returns. How does that sound?"

"It's got to be done," I agreed. "It's a big job, but it's doable. I think you'll nab Bodin and Sylvia, but that's my opinion—not something you can take to the SA. The only way you're going to make a case is to pinch the thieves in the act of trying to sell. The fact that the stamps are fakes doesn't change things; they're still stolen property."

"Yeah," Al said, sighing, "all that work for itty-bitty pieces of worthless paper. Well, I better get back to the palace and start the wheels turning."

"Just two more short items," I said. "I struck out with Lady Horowitz. She just won't tell me where she was when Bela Rubik was killed. And she refuses to let you take a look at her last will and testament. But my father said I could tell you that there's nothing in that document that could have any possible effect on your investigation."

"How does he know?" the sergeant said bitterly. "He's no cop."

"True," I said, "but he's no simp either. And he's also a man of probity with a high regard for the law. Believe me, Al, if there was anything at all in the will that would help solve a theft and a homicide, he'd reveal it even if it meant breaching client-attorney confidentiality. My father's morals are stratospheric. Sometimes I think he's training to take over God's job in case He resigns."

Rogoff laughed, flipped a hand at me, and strutted out, chewing on his cigar. I went back to the bar and slid my empty glass toward Mr. Pettibone.

"Another, please," I said.

"You told me to cut you off," he reminded me.

"I lied," I said.

But the second was a sufficiency. Florida police are rough on even slightly tipsy drivers, and I had no desire to get racked up on a DUI charge. I drove the Escort back to the McNally Building at a sedate pace, switched to the Miata, and continued my homeward journey.

I had time for an abbreviated ocean swim and arrived bright-eyed and bushy-tailed at the family cocktail hour. I dined with my parents that night and made a mindless jape about feeling exactly like our entree—soft-shelled crabs. Mother and father smiled politely.

I retired to my suite and scribbled furiously in my journal until I had recorded everything that had happened, including my last conversation with Rogoff. Then I phoned Jennifer Towley and was happy to find her at home.

"I miss you," I told her.

"And I miss you, too," she replied. Divine female!

"Good," I said. "Then how about lunch tomorrow?"

"Oh Archy, I'd love to," she said, "but I just can't. I've *got* to get caught up on my bookkeeping: billing, clients' accounts, my own checkbook, and nonsense like that. I simply *must* spend the day at it."

Suspicion flared, and I wondered if she was actually meeting her ex-husband for lunch.

"You've got to take a break in your accounting chores," I said. "Why don't I pick up some edible takeout food and show up at your place around noon. We can have a nosh together, and then I'll take off and leave you to your ledgers."

"Marvelous idea," she said at once. "Absolute genius."

"I thought so," I said with a considerably leavened heart. "See you at noon tomorrow. Sleep well, dear."

"You, too," she said, then added faintly, "darling."

I hung up delighted with her response and mortified at my initial jealous reaction. I must, I thought, learn to trust this woman who had invaded my right and left ventricles. It was not yet a Grand Passion but, like my mother's begonias, my love needed only TLC to flower.

I idly flipped the pages of my journal, resolutely turning my thoughts back to the theft of the Inverted Jennies. I set to work brooding, an activity aided by a very small tot of marc and the haunting wails of a Billie Holiday tape.

Maybe, I acknowledged, Sgt. Al was right after all, and I did have a taste for complexity. Because I found I could not really believe that this whole foofaraw was simply a case of a lamebrained and resentful chauffeur stealing from his employer. I didn't *want* to believe that, perhaps because it reduced the entire investigation to banality and my own role to that of an office manager catching a junior clerk swiping paper clips.

But it wasn't complexity I favored so much, I finally decided, as intrigue and the convolutions of human hungers. I wished the Case of the Inverted Jennies to hold hidden surprises, unexpected revelations, and a startling denouement.

I should have remembered what Aesop once told me:

"We would often be sorry if our wishes were gratified."

Chapter 12

I breakfasted with my parents on Friday. Then my father departed for the office in his Lexus, mother scampered into the greenhouse to bid a bright "Good morning!" to her begonias, and I moved to the kitchen to have a heart-to-heart with our cook-housekeeper.

"Ursi, luv," I said, "I've contracted for a picnic today—a very special picnic for two. What would you suggest?"

She accepted my question as a serious challenge, as I knew she would, and inspected her refrigerator and the shelves of her cupboards.

"Lemon chicken," she decided. "Baked, then chilled. German potato salad. The greens should be arugula and radicchio. For dessert, maybe a handful of those chocolate macaroons your mother bought."

"Sounds super to me," I said. "I'm hungry already. Where's our picnic hamper?"

"In the utility room," she said. "And don't forget a bottle of wine."

"Fat chance," I said.

I brought her the wicker picnic hamper that had been in our family since Year One and contained enough cutlery, accessories, and china to supply an orgy of eight. I also selected a bottle of white zinfandel which I tucked onto the bottom shelf of the fridge. Our table wine was stacked in the utility room. The vintage stuff was kept in a massive temperature-controlled cabinet in my father's study, protected by a combination padlock. R5-L8-R4, as well I knew.

I hopped into the Miata and, as usual, turned its nose toward the Horowitz manse. There was one little question I had to ask Lady C. It had been bedeviling me since that talk with Rogoff.

I banged the brass Bacchus on the front door, and eventually it was opened by the saucy housemaid, Clara Bodkin. She still had sleep in her eyes and looked all the more attractive for it.

"Good morning, Clara," I said.

"Hi, Mr. McNally," she said, and yawned. "The party's not till tonight."

"I know," I said, smiling, "and we'll certainly be here. Is Lady Horowitz up and about?"

"She's in the sauna."

"Oh," I said, disappointed. "I guess I better come back another time."

"You can talk to her through the intercom," Clara offered. "In the north wing just inside the terrace."

"Thank you," I said. "I'll find it."

"I love the way you smell," she said suddenly.

I remembered Simon Pettibone's observation: Life is not merely strange, it is *bee*-zar.

"It's not me, Clara," I said, "it's Royal Copenhagen. But I appreciate the thought."

Lady Cynthia had two built-in saunas, dry and wet (if you're going to do it, do it *right*), and the red light was burning over the door of the latter. The door itself was thick redwood planks and inserted at eye-level was a judas window of heavy glass. Alongside the door, fixed to the wall, was the intercom transmitter-receiver: a round knob of metal mesh.

I tried to look through the glass, but it was so fogged with steam that I could see nothing. I addressed the intercom.

"Lady Horowitz," I called, "it's Archy McNally. May I speak to you for a moment?"

A brief wait, then she replied, her voice sounding thin and tinny. "You don't have to shout," she said. "I can hear you perfectly well. How are you, lad?"

"Very well, thank you," I said, and watched as her fingers wiped away the steam from the inside of the glass, and she peered out at me.

"Care to join me?" she asked.

"Not right now," I said, laughing. "Just one short question and I'll be on my way."

She disappeared from the window, but I continued staring inside with nary a qualm. I was certain she was aware of my scrutiny and just didn't give a damn.

She moved slowly through swirling clouds of vapor like an Isadora Duncan dancer, seeming to float. She appeared to be performing a private exercise, for her knees rose high and her extended arms waved languidly. She was a white wraith; all I could see was that wondrous body pearled with steam. It made me forget age and believe in immortality.

"What's the question?" she asked.

"Did you ever examine the back of those Inverted Jenny stamps?"

Her face came close to the glass again and she stared at me. "Examine the *back*? Whatever for? Have you gone completely bonkers, lad?"

"Just wondering," I said hastily. In a moment the glass was fogged again and she was lost to view.

I drove into town wondering if Lady Cynthia had been telling me the truth. People do lie, you know. I do. Frequently.

I had been delegated by my parents to purchase an inexpensive going-away gift for Felice and Alan DuPey, to be presented that evening at the party. So I wandered Worth Avenue, viewing and regretfully rejecting all the glittering baubles that Street of Impossible Dreams has to offer.

Finally, in a tiny shop on Hibiscus Avenue, I found something for the DuPeys I thought they'd cherish: two lovely polished seashells, as a remembrance of their stay in South Florida. One was a Banded Tulip, the other a Flame Auger. In size and shape, there was a definite physical symbolism in those shells, and I thought them a fitting gift for randy newly-weds. I admit my sense of humor sometimes verges on the depraved.

I returned home and helped Ursi pack the picnic hamper, complete with a linen tablecloth and napkins. I added the chilled bottle of zinfandel (not forgetting a corkscrew) and set out for the home of Jennifer Towley across the lake.

Her reaction to the picnic hamper was all I had hoped for.

"You scoundrel!" she cried. "You told me it would be takeout food."

"So it is," I said. "From the spotless kitchen of the Chez McNally."

"How wonderful everything looks," she said, inspecting all the viands neatly packed in covered dishes. "Shall I set the dining room table?"

"Don't you dare," I said. "This is an indoor picnic. We'll eat on the floor."

And so we did, spreading the tablecloth over the worn dhurrie in her small office. We sat cross-legged, surrounded by file cabinets, books of fabric and wallpaper samples, a desk cluttered with documents, her word processor, and all the other odds and ends of a littered sanctum devoted to business.

We lunched with enthusiasm, exclaiming over the flavor of the lemon chicken, the taste of oregano in the greens, the touch of garlic in the German potato salad. We were down to the macaroons and the remainder of the wine before we collapsed against furniture and talked lazily of this and that.

Jennifer looked especially attractive that afternoon, hair piled up and tied with a mauve ribbon. Her face was free of makeup and seemed shockingly young. She wore an oversized sweatshirt with nothing printed on the front—thank God!—and pleated Bermuda shorts. Her feet were bare, and I saw once again those toes that had driven Clarence T. Frobisher mad with lust.

"Have you heard from your ex lately?" I asked casually.

"A few times," she said just as casually. "He seems to be doing wonderfully. The man he works for is thinking of opening a branch store in West Palm Beach and asked Tom if he'd like to manage it."

"Sounds like a great opportunity. Has he mentioned anything about his gambling?"

"Continually. He keeps assuring me that he's cured."

"But you've heard those assurances before, haven't you?"

"Yes," she said. "May I have another macaroon, please."

I watched her white teeth bite into the cookie, and I went through the now-familiar mental wrestle: tell or not tell. If she meant nothing to me, I would have told her at once that Thomas Bingham was up to his old tricks again. But she did mean something to me, a great deal, and so there would be a selfish motive in my revelation, and that would be base.

One day I must try to draw up a blueprint of my moral code. Then, perhaps, I might know what the hell I'm doing and why I do it.

"He wants me to have dinner with him," Jennifer said in a low voice, not looking at me. "And he wants to visit me. Here."

"Oh?" I said. "And how do you feel about that?"

"I don't know how I feel," she said, almost angrily, and raised her eyes to look directly at me. "And I don't want to talk about it anymore."

"All right," I said equably. "Then we shan't."

"Let's talk about you," she said.

"My favorite subject."

"What do you want to do with your life, Archy?"

"I can't write, paint, sculpt, compose, or play the piccolo. So I want to make my life a creation. I want to elevate artificiality into a fine art."

She laughed. "You're putting me on."

I raised a palm. "Scout's honor. And now let's talk about you. What do you want to do with your life?"

"I wish I knew," she said. "I'm betwixt and between. A crazy, mixed-up kid. May I finish the wine?"

"Of course. But there's only a drop left. I should have brought two bottles."

"Oh no," she said. "That would have pushed me over the edge. And I've got to get back to my bookkeeping; I'll need a clear head."

I nodded. "I'll pack up and be on my way."

She stared at me, and I couldn't interpret that look. Something heavy was going on behind those luminous eyes, but I didn't even guess what it might be.

"No," she said finally in a steady voice, "don't do that. Not yet."

What a delicious afternoon that turned out to be, the most paradisiacal I had ever spent in my life. Most of the credit, of course, was due to Jennifer, who seemed to be a woman bereft of her senses. But if it was within my power to award a medal for actions above and beyond the call of duty, I would have pinned a gold star and ribbon to her sweatshirt—or affixed it to her bare bosom with a Band-Aid.

I returned home so fatigued that I knew an ocean swim would risk instant immolation. So I took a nap, slept fast, and awoke in time to shower, dress, and join my parents for the ceremonial cocktail. Then we all set off for Lady Horowitz's party, my father driving the Lexus and humming something that sounded vaguely like "On the Street Where You Live."

It was a sterling night, absolutely cloudless. And if there was no full moon, there were a jillion stars spangling the sky. A cool ocean breeze caressed, and the whole world seemed to have been spritzed by Giorgio. Perfect weather for an outdoor party. That was the luck of the wealthy—right? Remember the old Yiddish joke? A guy gets splattered by a passing bird, looks up and says, "For the rich you sing."

The pool-patio area was strung with Chinese lanterns. There was a hurricane lamp with scented candle on each table, plus a bowl of fresh narcissi. As they say in New York, "Gawjus!"

A small portable bar had been set up in one corner, and service was provided by temps. Chef Jean Cuvier, wearing a high white toque, presided over the grill. All the other staff members were present as well as houseguests and about a dozen invited couples in various degrees of "informal dress," from tailored jeans to sequined minidresses. For the record: I wore my silver-gray Ultrasuede jacket.

Two small added notes on that night's festivities: A three-piece combo played old show tunes amongst the palms, and a small red neon sign set atop the bar proclaimed: NO SMOKING.

Since the McNallys knew most of the other guests present, there were many air-kisses and handshakes. My mother handed our gift to Felice and Alan DuPey, and they were delighted with the shells. I could see they made a polite effort to conceal their hilarity for, being French, they immediately saw the symbolism of those shapes. I was happy they hid their mirth; mother would have been horrified if they had tried to explain why the shells were so "fonny."

I headed for the bar to get in a party mood and was waiting for the ham-handed keep to mix a vodka gimlet when my elbow was plucked. I turned to find the hostess, radiant in flowered evening pajamas and a silk turban that looked like a charlotte russe.

"Good evening, Lady Cynthia," I said. "Lovely party."

"Is it?" she said. "I hadn't noticed. Listen, lad, what was that business this morning about my looking at the back of my Inverted Jennies?"

"Oh, that was just nonsense," I said.

"Of course it was," she said. "You ninny." And she stroked my cheek with such a smarmy smile that I was certain she was lying. But for what purpose I could not fathom.

She moved away and I sampled my drink. Passable but not notable. Carrying my glass, I joined the chattering throng and greeted several friends and acquaintances. I garnered two dinner invitations. Single women (mostly widows and divorcees) outnumber single men in Palm Beach, and hostesses are continually searching for the odd man to complete their table—and I'm as odd as they come.

I spotted Angus Wolfson standing apart, observing the scene with what I imagined he thought was amused detachment. He was wearing an embroidered guayabera shirt that hung in folds on his shrunken frame, making him look like an emaciated barber. He was holding an opened Perrier, no glass, and I wondered if he was drinking directly from the bottle. I strolled over.

"Good evening, Mr. Wolfson," I said. "How are you feeling tonight?"

He didn't exactly glare at me but he came close. "You seem to have an obsessive interest in my health, young McNally," he said.

"Not obsessive," I said, "but certainly concerned."

I thought he was about to give me the knife, but he caught himself, chuffed a small laugh, and took a swig from his bottle. "If you can't become mean, nasty and grumpy," he said, "what's the point of growing old?"

"I'll remember that," I said, laughing.

"Oh, you have a few years to go," he said, looking at me with a peculiar expression. "Spend them wisely. Don't try to set the world to right. No one can do that. Just accept it."

Either he was playing the Ancient Guru or his Perrier bottle was filled with gin. In either case, I had no desire to hear more of his homilies, so I smiled, nodded, and sauntered away. Besides, I had a bit of business to do.

When we drove through the opened gate in the Lexus, we found that Kenneth Bodin was parking guests' cars. He was doing a fine job, too, maneuvering all those Cadillacs, Lincolns, and BMWs on the driveway until they were within inches of each other with no scraped fenders. I found him leaning against the trunk of a white Excalibur, sucking on a cigarette and simultaneously prying into one ear with a matchstick. That young man was obviously in need of a couth IV.

"Having fun, Mr. McNally?" he asked me.

"Not yet," I said, "but I plan to."

"How's the Miata doing?"

"Taking the jumps like a thoroughbred," I said, pleased at having found a reasonable segue to the question I needed to ask. "As a matter of fact, I'm thinking of taking a drive down to the Keys. Have you ever been there?"

"Never have," he said, "and don't want to go. Disney World is what I like. I was there last year and had a helluva time. Did you know you can—"

But I was saved from listening to how he shook hands with Mickey Mouse by the melodious sound of dinner chimes coming from the patio.

"Got to run," I said hastily, "while the food lasts."

"You're having ribs," he said. "My favorite. I'll get mine later."

He was correct: Jean Cuvier was grilling big racks of pork spareribs along with ears of corn in the husk. There were kabobs of onions, mushrooms, green peppers, and cherry tomatoes, a salad of romaine and escarole with an anchovy dressing, and loaves of crusty French bread heated on the grill. Also bottles of a very decent merlot.

There was just one thing wrong with that feast: my dining partners. It happened this way:

I returned to the patio and found most of the tables already occupied. I was looking about for a seat with jovial companions when Consuela Garcia grabbed my arm. She was wearing a long-sleeved, off-the-shoulder crimson cashmere sweater that ended at midthigh. Tanned thigh. She looked sensational, and I started to tell her so but she cut me short.

"Listen, Archy," she said, leaning close, "you've got to eat with Harry and Doris Smythe."

I looked at her with horror. "Why do I have to ruin a perfectly splendid evening by eating with the Smythes?"

"Because no one else will eat with them."

"No, no, and no," I said. "What am I—a second-class citizen?"

She stared at me. "You want me to tell you when the madam takes off alone in her Jag?"

I sighed. "I get the picture, Connie. You are one cruel, cruel lady. All right, where are Loeb and Leopold?"

"Who?"

"The nasties," I said. "Where are they stuffing their ravenous maws?"

And that's how I was forced to share a culinary masterpiece by Jean Cuvier. The barbecue sauce was tangy without being too spicy. I learned later that its smoothness was due to a dash or two of bourbon. I only wish my dining partners had been as mellow.

The Smythes went through that dinner like a plague of locusts, devouring everything in sight. (I craftily moved the bowl of fresh flowers beyond their reach.) And as they munched, gnawed, and gulped, they complained. Nothing pleased them. The ribs were too fatty, barbecue sauce too mild, kabobs undercooked, salad dressing too salty, bread not *quite* warm enough, the wine corky.

For most of the meal I had to listen to their litany of kvetches as an audience of one. The fourth chair at our table belonged to Connie Garcia, but she had to play the social secretary and was constantly disappearing to solve minor crises. So I was left alone to endure the Smythes' endless bitching.

After a while I began to get a glimmer of why they claimed to be so dissatisfied. Lady Horowitz had called them "professional guests," and they were that. But they had the wit to recognize it, and the only way they could hang on to shreds of their ego was to disparage the charity provided. Viewed in that light, their carping was understandable. Unpleasant, but so human it made one want to weep.

However, I had no intention of spending the remainder of the evening weeping. Dessert was served—warmed New Orleans pralines and chilled Krug—and I excused myself. I carried a handful of the buttery confections and a flute of bubbles to the table where my parents were seated alone, the couple they had dined with having risen to dance to the combo's rendition of "June Is Bustin' Out All Over"—which indeed it was.

"Did you enjoy dinner?" I asked mother.

"So good," she said, patting her tummy, "but I'm afraid I ate too much. And drank too much."

"Mother is feeling a bit faintish," my father said, looking at her anxiously. "I think perhaps we better go home."

"Are you really ill?" I asked her, taking up her hand. "Shall I call Doc Semple?"

"Don't be silly," she said. "I just stuffed myself, that's all. I'll have a nice cup of hot tea, and I'll be right as rain in the morning."

"You're sure?"

"Absolutely. Don't worry so, dear."

"No point in your leaving early, Archy," my father said. "Will you be able to get a lift?"

"Of course," I said. "Plenty of wheels around. I'll be along in an hour or so. Mother, have a bit of blackberry brandy with your tea. It's wonderful for the grumbles. Believe me, I know."

She reached up to stroke my cheek, and then my parents rose to seek the hostess and make their farewells. I finished my pralines, returned to the bar with my empty champagne glass, and asked for a refill. For a few moments I watched dazed couples dancing on the verge of the pool and wondered who would be the first drunk to fall in. Or jump.

I craved a cigarette but that red neon sign was staring at me. So I wandered back into the wooded section of the estate, hoping that if I got far enough away from the patio, Lady C. would be unable to sniff my transgression and call the cops.

That area of the Horowitz empire was flippantly called "the jungle" by its monarch. But it was far from that, being artfully landscaped with hundreds of tropical plants, including a few orchids if you knew where to look. Paths meandered, garden statuary was half-hidden in the thick foliage, and benches of weathered teak were placed here and there to rest the weary.

It was on one of those slatted seats that I paused to light an English Oval, sip my Krug, and wonder what more life could hold. I soon found out. I became aware of a murmur of voices coming from the direction of the lake. Once I heard a raucous laugh and once a sharp cry as if someone had suffered a sudden pain.

As you may have guessed, I am not totally innocent of nosiness. I stubbed out my cigarette butt and moved slowly toward the sound of the voices, careful to keep off the pebbled path and step only on the spongy earth.

I cautiously approached a place where old, gnarled ficus trees encircled a greensward with a concrete birdbath in the center. Concealed in shadow, I could see the people I had indistinctly overheard. Illumined by the light of the starry sky, the scene was clear enough and startling enough: Angus Wolfson and Kenneth Bodin locked in a fierce embrace, lips pressed.

I retraced my steps as noiselessly as I could, returned to the party, and exchanged my empty flute for a snifter of Rémy Martin. I downed that in two gulps.

"Again," I said hoarsely to the bartender.

He looked at me warily, but poured another ounce.

"You driving tonight, sir?" he asked.

"Of course not," I said. "I'm the designated drinker. The people I came with are sticking to Pepsi."

I left him to puzzle that out and went to a deserted corner where I could sit, stretch out my legs, and ponder. Instead, I sat, stretched out my legs, and sipped my cognac. At the moment I was incapable of pondering.

And that's how Connie Garcia found me a half-hour later, staring into my empty snifter and wondering if I should give up a career of discreet inquiries and learn how to flip hamburgers at McDonald's.

"So there you are," she said. "Dinner with the Smythes wasn't so bad, now was it?"

"I loved it," I said. "Just as I love root canal work. Connie, when are you leaving?"

"Very soon," she said. "Why do you ask?"

"Can you give me a lift home? My parents left early."

"Of course," she said. "Just give me a few minutes to make sure everything's under control."

I wanted to express my gratitude and bid a fond farewell to mine hostess, but Lady Cynthia had discarded her turban and was dancing an insane Charleston with a partner who appeared to be seven feet tall. I left them to their madness and walked slowly out to the deserted driveway. Connie appeared in about ten minutes and we climbed into her Subaru.

She looked at me. "You okay?" she asked.

"Tiptop," I said. "Wonderful party."

"Do you really think so?" she said eagerly. "I thought it went well."

"A joy," I assured her. "An absolute joy."

We drove home in silence. I leaned my head back and closed my eyes. Connie pulled into the McNally driveway, killed the engine, and turned to face me.

"You're uncommonly quiet tonight, Archy," she said. "Are you sure you're all right?"

"Just a bit weary," I said. "After ten thousand and forty winks I'll be ready for a fight or a frolic."

"Something I wanted to tell you . . . I think your idea about Lady Horowitz being blackmailed is all wet."

"Then where is she going on those solo jaunts?"

"I think she's got a new lover."

"Man, woman, or cocker spaniel?"

"No, I'm serious," Connie said. "You probably think a woman's instinct is all b.s., but I definitely have the feeling that she's found someone new. She's been buying lingerie you wouldn't believe. Kinky stuff."

"So?" I said. "She's entitled. We're all entitled; the Declaration of Independence guarantees it. Life, liberty, and the pursuit of happiness—remember? Of course it doesn't guarantee you'll find it, but you can pursue the hell out of it."

Connie laughed and reached to stroke my cheek. It was certainly my night for cheek-stroking. First Lady Cynthia, then mother, now Connie.

Then she stretched to kiss me, which was a lot nicer than a pat on the mandible.

"Take care of yourself, Archy," she said lightly. "You mean a lot to me."

"And you to me, sweet," I said. "Thanks for the lift."

My father's study was darkened, so I locked up and plodded bedward. In truth I *was* weary. It had been a long, eventful day, and I didn't even want to think about it, let alone scribble an account in my journal.

I undressed and crawled between the sheets. Sleep was a mercy. I didn't even have the strength to stroke my cheek.

Chapter 13

During my undergraduate days at Yale I studied Latin for two years and did quite well—with the aid of some wonderful trots. As I recall (don't quote me on this), *"Hie in spiritum sed non incorpore"* means "Here in spirit but not in body." Turn that around and you've got a clue to my mood and behavior that weekend. I was there in body all right, but where the spirit was, the deponent knoweth not.

Confusion reigned supreme, and I waltzed through those two days with a glassy smile that probably convinced my golf-, tennis-, and poker-playing companions that McNally was finally over the edge. Well, I wasn't—but I was teetering. There were just too many bits and pieces, and I couldn't see any grand design to the Case of the Inverted Jennies—if there was one.

I returned home late Sunday night after a subdued dinner with a couple of cronies at the Pelican Club. I was in such an anomic mood that, to give myself the illusion I was capable of working purposefully, I scrawled notes in my journal for almost an hour, jotting down everything that had happened since the last entry. Then I spent another hour reading over the entire record of the Inverted Jenny Case. No light bulb flashed on above my head. I groaned and went to bed.

It must have been a shallow sleep because when my phone rang I awoke almost instantly. I glanced at the bedside clock; the luminous dial showed 4:40 A.M. At that dark hour it had to be Death calling. I answered warily.

"Hello?"

"Archy? Al Rogoff. I just got a wake-up call from the Beach Patrol. They pulled a floater out of the surf near the Horowitz place. Elderly male Caucasian. He was naked, but there were clothes stacked on the sand. They tentatively ID him as Angus Wolfson."

I swallowed. "Dead?"

"Very," Rogoff said. "Want to meet me there and positively ID the body?"

I really didn't want to. "Sure," I said. "I'll get dressed."

"Take your time," the sergeant said. "It'll take me at least twenty minutes. Listen, any chance of your bringing some hot coffee along?"

"Yes, I can do that. We've got a thermos."

"Good," Al said. "No sugar or cream. Black will be fine."

I dressed as quietly as I could because my bedroom is directly above my parents'. I tiptoed down the stairs to the kitchen, switched on the light, put a kettle of water on to boil. I went into the pantry for the thermos and a stack of plastic cups. When I returned to the kitchen my father was standing there.

Was he the last man in America to wear a full pajama suit: long-sleeved jacket and drawstring pants? Under a robe of maroon silk, of course. With matching leather mules on his long feet.

"Trouble, Archy?" he asked.

I repeated what Sergeant Rogoff had told me.

Father nodded once. "Keep me informed," he said, turned, and went back to bed.

The unflappable Prescott McNally.

I was at the scene within a half-hour after Al's call. It wasn't hard to find; three police cars, a fire-rescue truck, and an ambulance were parked on Ocean Boulevard. I pulled up, and Rogoff came over before I could dismount from the Miata.

"You bring the coffee?" he asked eagerly.

I nodded.

"We better have a slug," he said. "There's a cold wind down on the beach."

He did the pouring, for which I was grateful; I didn't want him to see that I had the shakes.

"How did they happen to find him?" I asked.

"Some dentist from Lake Worth wanted to try out his new ATV, a three-wheeler. He figured he could get away with driving on the beach at four in the morning. He spotted the body bobbing around in the shallows and decided to be a good citizen. He had a cellular phone with him and called 911. Good coffee, Archy."

"Thanks. Was it suicide?"

"Could be. But does a suicide stack his clothes neatly on the sand under a palm tree before he takes the long walk?"

"I don't believe suicides are thinking rationally in their last few minutes."

"You may be right. But there are some other things."

"What things?"

"You'll see. Finished your coffee? Let's go."

We walked down that same flight of wooden stairs I had taken to stroll the beach with Angus Wolfson. He had looked like a rakish boulevardier then. I tried not to imagine what he looked like now.

The body lay on the sand, covered with a blue blanket. There was a group of officers nearby, smoking cigarettes, conversing, occasionally laughing. Rogoff had been right; it was chilly down near the water. The wind was kicking up whitecaps, and clouds were moving swiftly across the night sky.

"Can I get some light here?" Rogoff called.

A woman from the fire-rescue truck came over with a big lantern. She turned the beam onto the blanketed corpse. The sergeant leaned down and uncovered the naked body to the waist.

The face was remarkably peaceful. Almost serene. A few wet strands of thin, grayish hair were plastered to his cheeks. He was so pale, so pale. But I had the irreverent notion that he looked younger in death than he had in life.

"Yes," I said steadily, "this is the body of a man I knew as Angus Wolfson. He was a house-guest at the home of Lady Cynthia Horowitz."

The sergeant turned to the woman holding the lantern. "You hear that?" he demanded.

She nodded.

"Al," I said, "what are those blotches on his neck and chest?"

"The things I mentioned to you—bruises. Could have been caused by the body banging around in the surf. But look at this."

He beckoned, and we both squatted alongside the remains. "What do you make of that?" Rogoff asked, pointing.

Four faint parallel scratches ran down the torso from clavicle to navel.

I peered closely. "Looks like fingernails did that," I said.

The sergeant grunted. "Could be," he said. "Made by himself in the final moment when he was gasping for air. Or made by someone else. Or made by shells on the bottom of the sea. We'll let the ME figure it out. Let's go finish that coffee."

I started back to the stairway.

"Take him away," Al called to the waiting officers and followed me up to the corniche.

We sat in the Miata and sipped coffee. It was lukewarm now, but we drank it.

"What I've got to do now," Rogoff said, "is go to the Horowitz place, wake up the dear Lady, and tell her what happened. Care to come with me?"

"No, thanks," I said.

He laughed. "Didn't think you would. What I want to do is see if he left a suicide note. Not that it means a helluva lot. Sometimes they do, sometimes they don't."

"So you think it *was* a suicide."

"I didn't say that. But you told me he was ill."

"That was my idea. He didn't tell me, and I don't have a medical degree."

"How old did you say he was?" the sergeant asked.

"I didn't say because I don't know," I said, a trifle peevishly I admit. "I'd guess about seventy-five. Around there."

Al turned to stare at me. "That's amazing."

"Being seventy-five? What's so amazing about that?"

"Because when we were going through that neat stack of his clothes on the beach, in the hip pocket of his slacks we found a condom."

"Oh lord," I said.

"Unused," Rogoff added. "Still in a sealed packet."

I drew a deep breath. "I better tell you something, Al," I said. "On Friday night my parents and I went to a party at Lady Cynthia's. After dinner . . ."

I described the scene I had witnessed between Angus Wolfson and Kenneth Bodin deep within "the jungle" of the Horowitz property. The sergeant listened intently without interrupting. When I finished, he drained his last few drops of coffee and tossed the plastic cup onto the roadside.

"You're littering," I pointed out.

"I know," he said. "Listen, what I want you to do right now, even before you go home, is drive to the palace and dictate a statement. I'll radio ahead and set it up. I want you to include what you just told me about Wolfson, and also everything you told me at the Pelican Club about Bodin, his girlfriend Sylvia, and that Fort Lauderdale stamp dealer—what's her name?"

"Hilda Lantern."

"Well, make sure you describe your dealings with her: what you said and what she said. Go into detail. Even the stuff you don't think is important. I want everything."

"Al, that'll take hours!"

"Sure it will," he said. "But you're pulling down a nice buck, aren't you? Now earn it."

But despite his instructions, I did go home first—to shower, shave, change my clothes, and have an early morning breakfast with the Olsons at the kitchen table.

I was leaving for the palace to dictate my statement when I encountered my father coming downstairs for *his* breakfast. He saluted me by elevating one bushy eyebrow, and I gave him a precis of what had happened at the scene of Wolfson's death.

"Dreadful business," he said in magisterial tones. Then, dryly: "I expect I shall hear from Lady Horowitz this morning."

"I think you probably will, sir," I said. "If I learn anything more from Sergeant Rogoff, I'll get word to you."

"Yes, do that," he said. "Thank you, Archy."

As I drove into town through the June after-dawn, I rehearsed in my mind what I would reveal in my statement. It seemed to me that up to this point I had been reasonably straight with Al Rogoff. I had given him all the facts as I knew them, with the exception of any mention of Thomas Bingham. And his implication in the crimes was iffy.

What I hadn't told the sergeant, of course, were my personal feelings about the people involved, my no doubt prejudicial reactions to their personalities, and certain wild ideas I entertained that had absolutely no hard evidence to sustain them. I was sure Al had as many private fancies. And there was little point in either of us going public with them until we had some solid facts to quote. You can't convict on opinions, except those of judge or jury.

I was correct about spending hours providing that statement. After I finished dictating, I waited for the transcription. Then I read the eight-page manuscript carefully, making some minor changes, deletions, and additions. I was signing all eight pages when Rogoff came in and plopped down wearily in the wooden armchair behind his desk.

"Not even noon," he said, "and already my ass is dragging."

"You spoke to Lady Horowitz?"

He nodded. "You know what spooked her the most? Not the death of an old friend. But she was upset at how this 'unpleasantness'—her word—might affect a reception she's giving tomorrow afternoon for a visiting Italian tenor. Can you believe it?"

"Lady Cynthia," I said carefully, "is a rather self-centered woman."

"No kidding?" Rogoff said. "And all this time I thought she was a selfish bitch. Anyway, I didn't find a suicide note. But like I told you, that means zilch."

"Who is next of kin?"

"A sister in Boston. Horowitz phoned your father while I was there, and he agreed to notify the sister. Thank him for me. Informing the next of kin of victims is not my favorite pastime. You finished here?"

"All done," I said, and slid the signed statement across the desk to him. "That's everything."

He stared at me. "You sure?"

"Absolutely. Except for my hat size, which is seven and three-eighths. Al, have you contacted all the local stamp dealers?"

"We're working on it. But some are out to lunch, some are on vacation, some are retired. It's a miserable job. But we should have it finished in a day or two."

"Good," I said. "I still think you'll pick up Kenneth Bodin or Sylvia or both."

Rogoff looked at me thoughtfully. "You think Wolfson might have been in on it?"

"The possibility had occurred to me," I admitted. "Wolfson steals the stamps and gives them to Bodin to sell. Then they split the take. There's only one thing wrong with that scenario."

"What?"

"Wolfson wasn't a thief. I didn't particularly cotton to him, but he was trying hard to be a gentleman. He just wouldn't steal."

Al stared at me. "Would he kill?"

"Anyone can murder if the time and circumstances are right. You've told me that yourself, many times."

"So I have," the sergeant said, sighing. "Thank you for your keen perceptions, Hercule Poirot. I wish with all my heart that we may soon meet again."

"I pray we shall, Inspector Maigret," I said, and departed.

I drove to the McNally Building, intending to ask my father to fill me in on his conversation with Lady C. But the lobby receptionist handed me a message: Consuela Garcia had phoned and wanted me to call her immediately.

"She said it was important," the receptionist told me. "She repeated three times: Urgent! Urgent! Urgent!"

"Probably heard a new Polish joke," I said.

I called Connie from my office. She sounded harried.

"Archy," she said breathlessly, "did you hear about Angus Wolfson?"

"Yes," I said, "I heard."

"And on top of that," she went on, "the caterer called and said he can't get any fresh pineapples for the reception tomorrow. What a morning!"

"And that's why you called?" I asked. "To tell me about the pineapples?"

"Oh, don't be such a schnook," she said. "I called to tell you the madam is taking off about one o'clock. She said she'd be gone a few hours. She didn't tell me where she was going, and I didn't ask."

"Thank you, Connie," I said gratefully.

"If you follow her, will you tell me later where she went?"

"No."

"I didn't think you would," she said. "You still seeing that Jennifer Towley?"

"Occasionally."

"Well, my guy gave me the brush."

"Why would the idiot do that?"

"He found some tootsie with mucho dinero. Her father owns a used-car lot."

I laughed. "I'm looking for a nymphomaniac whose father owns a liquor store."

Connie giggled. "Well, if you break up with the Towley woman, put me back in your little black book."

"You've never been out," I assured her.

I glanced at my watch, saw it was a bit past twelve-thirty, and decided to put my talk with father on hold. I went down to the garage, waved to Herb, and crawled into my rented Ford Escort. I headed for Ocean Boulevard, hoping Lady Cynthia hadn't decided to leave early. If she had, I was snookered.

As I drove I wondered how I was going to handle this. I don't claim to be an expert at shadowing, but I had read enough espionage novels to know how it's done—or how the novelists *think* it's done. You hang back, occasionally let a car or two get between you and your quarry, and you might even speed up and tail from in front of your target. It all seemed so simple I was certain I'd bollix it up.

I drove past the Horowitz mansion. The gate was open but I saw no activity within. I went northward a few hundred yards, made an illegal U-turn, and passed the house again, going southward. I repeated this maneuver twice more with no results.

Finally, on my fourth drive south, I observed the bronze Jaguar convertible pull out of the Horowitz driveway, turn, and also proceed southward. I distinctly saw Lady Cynthia driving, her hair bound with a periwinkle scarf.

"Thank you, God," I said aloud.

She headed down the coast and surprised me by staying within the speed limit. I was several car lengths behind her, and there seemed no need for tricky tactics; she never once turned her head to look back and gave no indication whatsoever that she sensed a nose was on her trail.

The Jag went on and on and on, and I was beginning to wonder if our destination was Miami. But then we came to a stretch of the corniche south of Manalapan Beach. This area of the island, between the Atlantic Ocean and Lake Worth, is so narrow that a long-ball hitter (say Mickey Mantle) might stand on the beach and swat one into the lake.

Lady Horowitz slowed, and I slowed right along with her. Then she signaled a right and turned into a driveway, through opened gates. I drove past at a crawl and took a good peep.

It was a frumpy place, a mansion gone to seed. The wrought-iron gates were rusted, grass sprouted from the brick driveway, and several red tiles were missing from the roof. The house, designed in a vaguely Spanish style, had a sad, sheepish look about it, as if its dilapidation was its own fault and not that of the neglectful owner.

The Jaguar was nowhere in sight when I drove past. From this, Monsieur Poirot deduced that the driveway led down to the rear of the house, facing Lake Worth. Perhaps a garage was there. Certainly a turnaround. And probably a lawn, patio, or terrace giving a loverly view of the lake. I imagined a dock, rotting now, that was large enough to accommodate a thirty-five-foot cabin cruiser.

I made a U-turn again and headed northward. This time, on a slow pass, I noted the un-trimmed shrubbery, a broken window, paint peeling from the portico columns. Even more perplexing was no sign of habitation; the entire place was silent, deserted, and so melancholy it could have been a set for *The Exorcist XII.*

I also made certain to memorize the house number, painted on a weathered shingle dangling by a single nail from one of the stained stucco entrance pillars.

I drove home sedately, ruminating on my next move. I wasn't about to hang around Manalapan until Lady Cynthia emerged from the Castle of Otranto, and then follow her back to Palm Beach. What was the point of that? I even considered the possibility of renting a boat with the intention of approaching from the lake side, on her next visit, and observing any activities taking place in the rear of the house. But even with an advance alert from Connie, I could never arrive in time.

What on earth was the wealthy Lady Horowitz doing in such a ruin? Could my original wild scam turn out to be correct? Was she really meeting blackmailers to make a payment? The whole idea was absurd, but I could conjure no other explanation, except that possibly she had flipped her wig, joined a coven of witches, and drove to that shabby house to engage in satanic rites.

The truth turned out to be even more unbelievable.

Chapter 14

I returned to the McNally Building, parked the Escort in the underground garage, and waved to the security guard. Then I rode the elevator to the second floor, occupied by our real estate department. We didn't hawk homes and condos, of course, but represented our clients at closings, advised on leases and, when requested, suggested investments in raw land and commercial properties.

The woman I sought, Mrs. Evelyn Sharif, was chief of the department. She was married to a Lebanese who sold Oriental rugs from a very elegant shop on Worth Avenue. At the moment, Evelyn was obviously, almost embarrassingly, pregnant.

"Archy," she said, "if you ask me if I've swallowed a watermelon, I'll never speak to you again as long as I live."

"I'd never be guilty of such gross humor," I said. "A cantaloupe?"

She laughed and punched my arm. It hurt. Evelyn was a jovial lady but very physical. When she slapped you lightly on the back, your knees sagged.

"When is the Little One due?" I asked her.

"In about six weeks," she said. "Did you drop by to hear details of my morning sickness?"

"Thank you, no," I said. "A small favor is all I ask."

I explained that I had the number of a property on Ocean Boulevard down near Manalapan and wanted to find out who owned the place. With Evelyn's contacts in Palm Beach County real estate circles, that should be duck soup.

"Why do you want to know?" she asked.

"Discreet inquiries," I said. "Cloak-and-dagger stuff. Absolutely, positively top secret."

She smirked. I knew what she was thinking: that I had seen a centerfold entering the house and wanted her name. Ridiculous! I had done that only once before.

She was silent a moment, and I could see she was debating whether or not to grant my request. But after all, I was Prescott McNally's son, and she didn't want to endanger her paid maternity leave.

"All right, Archy," she said, sighing, "give me the number and I'll see what I can do. Maybe I'll have something for you tomorrow."

"Thank you, dear," I said. "And may your Blessed Event be twice blessed."

"It is," she said, grinning. "The doc says twins."

"Mazel tov!" I cried.

I went up to my very own cul-de-sac and phoned my father's office. But Mrs. Trelawney said he was at a protracted lunch with a client. So I headed down to the garage and waved at Herb for the third time that day. I drove the Miata toward the beach, brooding about Lady Cynthia's motives for traveling miles to spend a sunny afternoon in the House of Usher.

I learned a long time ago that in any investigation it was goofy to devise a theory early on and then try to fit the facts to your hypothesis. You find yourself disregarding important evidence simply because you can't cram it into your harebrained idea. The best method, by far, is to collect as many facts as possible, even the most trivial, and let them form their own pattern. Logic beats conjecture every time.

I was still in the fact-collecting phase when I turned into the Horowitz driveway. The place appeared to be abandoned; not a soul in sight and no sounds of human presence. Great security. Jesse James could have waltzed in there and carted off the patio furniture.

No one answered my knocks at the front door, so I wandered around to the swimming pool. Gina Stanescu was seated at one of the umbrella tables. She was wearing another of her voluminous gowns, and a floppy-brimmed panama hid her eyes. But she looked up when I approached, and I was glad to see she wasn't weeping.

"Ma'am," I said, "I'm sorry about Mr. Wolfson. I'm sure you and everyone else are devastated by what happened."

She nodded without speaking and motioned for me to sit down. I pulled up a canvas director's chair and moved it so that I was facing her.

"Life is sad, Mr. McNally," she said. "Is it not?"

"Frequently," I said. "I don't wish to add to your sorrow, but it seemed to me that in the short time you had known Mr. Wolfson, you and he had established a special rapport."

"Yes, yes," she said eagerly. "He was a dear man, very gentle. He liked to act the bugbear, but he was really kind and understanding. He was ill—did you know?"

"I thought he was," I said, thinking that sadness had softened her sharp features.

"He refused to speak of it, but I saw several times that he was in pain. But he was a gallant." Her smile was faint. "An aged gallant."

"That was my impression," I said. "That in spite of his problems, he was determined to face the world with a fresh flower in his lapel."

She knew immediately what I meant and looked at me with approval. But I wanted to get away from Wolfson eulogies and asked if she would care for something to drink; I would bring it from the kitchen. She declined, which disappointed me. At the moment I could have endured a stiff wallop of 80-proof.

"The last time we spoke," I said, "in the game room, you mentioned the possibility of a miracle rescuing your orphanage. I hope it has occurred."

Whatever animation she had shown a moment ago disappeared, and her face became stony and set.

"No," she said, "that miracle dissolved when Angus died. *Pouf!*"

"I don't understand."

She tried to smile. A miserable failure. "I spoke to Angus of my problems at the orphanage. He said he could help. A relative had recently died, and Angus would inherit a great deal of money. He said he had no need for it and would be happy to donate it to the orphans of Rouen. Wasn't that magnificent of him?"

"Very," I said. "Did he happen to mention how much his inheritance might amount to?"

"Much," Stanescu said. "Perhaps a half-million American dollars. That would have been my salvation."

"Yes," I said. "Now I understand."

"Mr. McNally, you are an attorney, are you not?"

"Not, I'm afraid. But my father is, and I work for him. And I have studied law. Why do you ask?"

"The promise Angus made to contribute his inheritance to the orphanage, is that a legal agreement? May I claim his inheritance?"

"Did Mr. Wolfson state his intentions in writing?"

"No."

I pulled a face. "Then his inheritance becomes part of his estate, to be distributed according to the terms of his last will and testament."

"Yes," she said, "I thought that might be so." She attempted a brave smile again, and again it didn't work. "Then I must find another miracle for my children."

I wasn't thinking of the orphans of Rouen at that moment; something was stirring in that moist mass of Roquefort I call my brain.

"Ma'am," I said, "remember the day you and the others were to go on a yacht cruise but it was canceled because of high seas?"

"Yes," she said, looking at me curiously, "of course I remember."

"Mr. Wolfson told me that you and he left the party early, went window-shopping on Worth Avenue, and then later met at the Cafe L'Europe."

"Yes," she said, still puzzled, "that is correct."

"Could you tell me what shape Mr. Wolfson was in when you met for a drink?"

"Oh, he was in a dreadful condition. It was an extremely hot day. He was exhausted, obviously in pain, and I had to hold his arm while we waited for Kenneth to come get us. Why do you ask?"

"He was upset?" I persisted. "Disturbed? Unusually so?"

She considered a moment. "Yes, I would say so. Pale and trembling. I remember suggesting he might wish to see a doctor immediately, but he'd have none of that. Again, why do you ask?"

I shook my head. "I really don't know. We're still trying to solve the theft of your mother's stamps, and this may possibly have something to do with it. Miss Stanescu, I thank you for speaking to me so openly. I hope I may see you again under happier circumstances."

She smiled—and this time it was the McCoy. "I hope so, too, Mr. McNally," she said. "I enjoy your company. You are so pleasant."

"Thank you," I said, and left her.

Do you recall my telling you that on the previous night, Sunday, I had reviewed my notes on the Inverted Jenny Case and no light bulb had suddenly flashed above my head? Well, now the bulb was there. It wasn't burning brightly, but it was glowing dimly and flickering.

I remounted the Miata and was heading out when the bronze Jaguar pulled in. I stopped, and Lady Horowitz braked the Jag next to me. I was mortified: a schlump in a rubber dinghy moored alongside the USS *Iowa*.

"Hello, lad," she called. "What are you doing here—still snooping around?"

I was offended. "I came to express my condolences," I said. "On the death of Angus Wolfson."

"Well, people do die, you know," she said blithely. "One way or another."

She seemed in a radiant mood. The periwinkle scarf was gone, and her white hair, wind-whipped, formed a springy halo as if she had stuck her big toe in an electric outlet.

"Something I'd like to ask . . ." I said. "Did you know Wolfson was ill?"

"Was he?" she said. "Well, I can believe it. The idiot just didn't take care of himself. I once saw him swallow a live goldfish. He was drunk, of course—Angus, not the goldfish—but that's no excuse. I'm going to live forever; I'm too mean to die."

I thought her levity in poor taste, but I knew it was foolish to expect delicate sensibility from that woman. Might as well expect a curtsy from King Kong.

"Lady Cynthia," I said, "what was Wolfson doing down here? A vacation?"

"Of course," she said quickly. "A holiday. The poor man couldn't afford Antibes so he grabbed at the chance to spend a few weeks on the Gold Coast."

"Couldn't afford?" I asked. "I thought you told me he was well-off."

"Did I?" she said. "I don't think so. I probably said he wasn't hurting. Meaning he wasn't rooting through garbage cans or anything like that. But he did have to count his nickels and dimes. Why this sudden interest in his finances?"

"I was just wondering if he was on his uppers. And if he was, if he pinched your stamps."

She shrugged. "I wouldn't put it past him. He liked the lush life but just couldn't buy it. Fortunately I can. But I've paid my dues. My life would make a book."

"I can imagine," I said.

"No, you can't," she said. "Ta-ta, lad. I've got to grab a bath."

I drove home. The light bulb was still glowing. But the flickering had ceased.

I had plenty of time for a swim before the family cocktail hour. And the ocean was calm and brilliant under the westering sun. So why did I feel such a disinclination for plunging into those warm waters? Because, I realized, I was unnerved by the persistent image of the pale corpse pulled from that same sea.

But if I didn't conquer that fear, I might never dare the ocean again, and that would be shameful. So I resolutely changed, went down to the beach, and doggedly completed my two miles. I can't say I enjoyed it, and when I emerged, the image of the dead Angus Wolfson had not been banished. Never would be, I acknowledged.

It was a strange dinner that night. My father and I were in a rather subdued mood, but mother was almost hyper, laughing and yakking on and on about a flower show she had attended that afternoon. She had served as one of three judges, and apparently a contestant (an also-ran) had thrown a snit and loudly accused the judges of racial prejudice against African violets.

The guv and I listened to this account with small smiles. I think we were both happy to have mother monopolize the conversation. If it hadn't been for her, it would have been a dinner of grunts and mumbles, and Mrs. Olson might have wondered if we were dissatisfied with her poached salmon and dill sauce. Far from it.

After coffee and a dessert of fresh strawberries marinated in white crème de menthe, my father drew me aside.

"Are you planning to go out tonight, Archy?" he asked.

"No, sir. I'm staying in."

"Good. I brought some work home, but I should be finished by ten o'clock. Could you stop down? There are a few matters to discuss."

"I'll be there," I promised.

I went upstairs and worked on my journal awhile in a desultory fashion. Then I took off my reading specs and stared at the far wall. Not much inspiration there, but I didn't expect any. One thing bothering me was that Lady Cynthia had been so quick to agree that Angus Wolfson might have stolen her stamps. She had identified him as an "old friend." Surely she knew as well as I that the man was incapable of the crime. He may have been many things, not all of them noble, but I was convinced he was not a thief.

And I kept recalling that unlocked jewel box close to the rifled wall safe. Surely any crook, man or woman, would have paused long enough to lift the lid and grab up a handful of gems.

There was a third puzzle I had not yet brought to the attention of Sgt. Al Rogoff. It concerned the murderous assault on Bela Rubik. Kenneth Bodin was a likely suspect, since apparently the purloined Inverted Jennies were now in his possession, or girlfriend Sylvia's.

But as I well knew, the stamp dealer kept his door locked and carefully inspected visitors before allowing them entrance. Would he have unlocked for Bodin, who even in his chauffeur's uniform looked like an 800-pound gorilla in a purple Nehru jacket?

But even those three questions, important though they might be, paled before an enigma that had troubled me since I had uttered, "Yes, this is the body of a man I knew as Angus Wolfson." To wit: Did he really commit suicide, or did his nakedness, neatly stacked clothing, and the unused condom all indicate a sex scene that had gone awry, ending in murder instead of rapture?

But I was not such a beginner at criminal investigation as to believe that *all* riddles can be solved, *all* snarls untangled, *all* questions answered. Ask any law enforcement officer and he or she will tell you that some mysteries remain so forever—mysteries. I went downstairs a few minutes after ten. I found the lord of the manor seated behind the desk in his study. He looked weary but, as usual, he was dressed as if he expected a visit from a Supreme Court justice at any moment. As I entered, he was replacing files in his Mark Cross calfskin briefcase.

"Perfect timing, Archy," he said with a pinched smile. "I've done all I can do tonight. Interesting case. It concerns the estate of the late Peter Richardson. Did you know him?"

"No, sir. But I know Eddie Richardson. I think he's the youngest of three sons."

Father nodded. "Three sons and two daughters. All are contesting Peter Richardson's bequest of approximately two million dollars to a California organization that allegedly freezes the recently deceased in liquid nitrogen with the claim that they may be thawed and restored to sentient life at some future date. The children are denouncing the claim as fraudulent and petitioning that the bequest be ruled invalid."

"What is your opinion, sir?"

"Oh, we've just started," he said. "This will require extensive research." He smiled coolly. "And many hours of billing. I think I deserve a glass of port. Will you do the honors, Archy? And help yourself, of course."

A few moments later I was seated in a leather armchair alongside his desk. We raised glasses to each other, then sipped. I thought the port was a bit musty but made no comment.

"As we anticipated," my father began, "I received a phone call from Lady Horowitz early this morning. She informed me of the death of her house-guest, Angus Wolfson. I already knew it, of course, from your report, but didn't feel it necessary to tell her that. She gave me the name, address, and telephone number of the next of kin and requested that McNally and Son handle all the 'gruesome details.' Those are her words."

"She just can't be bothered," I said.

"I suspect you're correct. In any event, the next of kin is an unmarried sister, Roberta Wolfson, who shared an apartment with her brother in Boston. She is flying down to identify the body, claim the personal effects, and make funeral arrangements."

"And you want me to squire the lady about?"

"Very perspicacious of you, Archy. Yes, that is exactly what I wish. Lady Horowitz volunteered to pay all expenses, including burial costs."

"That was decent of her."

"Yes," he said. "In some ways she is a very generous woman. Mrs. Trelawney has arranged a round-trip airline ticket for Miss Wolfson. I understand she is an elderly lady, a year older than her brother. I know you will offer what sympathetic assistance you can."

"Yes, sir. When is she arriving?"

"Around noon tomorrow. Mrs. Trelawney will give you the details."

"Will she be staying with Lady Cynthia?"

He was silent a moment. "No," he said finally. "Apparently Miss Wolfson met Lady Horowitz once and was not favorably impressed. She prefers to stay elsewhere. Mrs. Trelawney has taken a comfortable suite at The Breakers for her use."

"Seems to me Mrs. Trelawney has been doing most of the donkeywork," I said. "What about the undertaker? Won't Angus have to be iced and boxed for shipment?"

Father sighed. "Not the terminology I would have used. Miss Wolfson insists on cremation. She says that was her late brother's wish and is so stated in his will. She will carry his ashes back to Boston."

"How did she sound, father? Tearful? Hysterical?"

"No, she seemed remarkably self-possessed. As if she had been expecting a phone call like mine for some time. Very cool, very formal. A proper Bostonian. She treated me with what I can only describe as condescension."

"It figures," I said, nodding. "Proper Bostonians believe anyone who lives beyond Beacon Hill is a peasant. All right, I shall meet and escort Miss Wolfson. How long does she plan to stay?"

"As briefly as possible. She hopes to return to Boston on Wednesday."

I was dubious. "I'm not certain the police will release the body that quickly. I'll check with Rogoff in the morning."

"That would be wise. Now then, the other matter I wanted to discuss with you is the theft of Lady Horowitz's stamps and the murder of Bela Rubik. How is that investigation coming along?"

I told him about Kenneth Bodin and Sylvia, Hilda Lantern, and the attempt to sell Inverted Jennies to a Palm Aire dealer who stated they were forgeries.

Mein papa seemed stunned. When he spoke, his voice was not quite steady. "I think we could use another glass, Archy," he said.

While I poured, he rose and went over to the sideboard. He began to pack a pipe, his favorite James Upshall. His back was to me.

"Have you told Lady Horowitz that her stamps are counterfeit?"

"No, sir."

"Why not?" he said sharply.

"Because I don't know for certain that they *are* counterfeit. All I have is hearsay. When the Inverted Jennies are recovered, an independent examination can be made by experts."

He came back to his chair and flamed his pipe. I took that as a signal that I could light up an English Oval, and did.

"But what if the stamps are not recovered?" he asked.

"I think they will be, sir," I said, and explained how Sgt. Al Rogoff was alerting all the dealers along the Gold Coast.

"I hope he'll be successful," father said, calming down as he puffed. "The reason I am so concerned is that Lady Horowitz has become insistent on filing an insurance claim. She mentioned it again this morning. But if the stamps are counterfeit, obviously no legitimate claim for a half million dollars can be made."

"Can you stall her awhile? If the stamps are recovered and prove to be forgeries, she'll have no claim. And if they are recovered and prove to be genuine, she'll still have no claim since they'll be returned to her."

"Yes, that's true," he said slowly. "I'll try to convince her to hold off filing, but she is a very strong-minded woman."

"As well I know," I said. "Something else about this case is troubling me, father, and I'd like your opinion."

He nodded.

I described the passionate embrace between Angus Wolfson and Kenneth Bodin I had witnessed the night of Lady Cynthia's party. Then I related how Wolfson had been found: naked, clothes neatly stacked, unused condom in pocket. These were details I had not previously told my father, and he listened intently.

"Are you suggesting," he said when I concluded, "that the chauffeur murdered Angus Wolfson?"

"I'm suggesting it's a possibility."

"Have you informed Sergeant Rogoff?"

"Yes, sir."

"And what was his reaction?"

"Nothing immediate. Knowing Al, I'm sure he'll dig into it. But unless he can find a witness or Bodin confesses—both highly unlikely—I doubt if the sergeant will be able to make a homicide case. Then he'll label it suicide and close the file."

The master went into one of his reflective trances, and I waited patiently. I thought he would be offended by the story of Wolfson's predilection, but when he spoke it was more in sadness than distaste.

"I hope Rogoff does close the file," he said. "What possible good could it do to make public that poor man's past? He is dead now; I would not care to see details of his life exploited in the tabloids."

He surprised me. "And let a murderer escape?" I asked.

"If he *was* murdered. You are not certain and, from what you say, the police will not be able to prove a homicide."

"They might," I argued. "If the Medical Examiner's report indicates an assault or a struggle, or Rogoff finds additional evidence to prove the presence of a killer."

He looked at me somberly. "Archy, don't let your desire for justice overcome your good sense. It seems to me this is a matter to be quietly swept under the rug. We are all guilty of actions in our lives which, while not illegal, may be morally reprehensible and which we would certainly not wish to be made public."

I was shocked. My father is usually the most logical and coldly judicial of men when forming and expressing his opinions. Now it seemed to me his reasoning was confused and his pronouncements perilously close to blather. I could not understand this crumbling of his Olympian standards.

"Homicide is illegal," I reminded him.

"I am quite aware of that," he said. "I am merely pointing out that sometimes the law must yield to decency and the protection of human dignity. It is a fine line, I admit, but there is a gray area where the rights of society conflict with the rights of the individual. Try not to be too rigorous in the defense of society. The day may come, Archy, when you will plead for mercy for yourself rather than justice."

I grinned. "One never knows, do one?"

"And that's another thing," he said testily. "I do wish you would stop saying that. Not only is it ungrammatical, but it is a superficial observation on the uncertainties of existence."

"I'll try not to use it again in your presence, father," I said gravely, wondering if there had ever been such a stodgy man.

I returned to my quarters, smiling at the final go-around with the pater. I don't know why I derived such pleasure from stirring him up occasionally. Perhaps I fancied I was saving him from priggery. Or it may have been a very small declaration of independence. I was well aware that only my father's largess enabled me to drive a snazzy sports car, dine young ladies, and wear silk briefs emblazoned with images of *Tyrannosaurus rex*. But even the lowliest of serfs must assert himself now and then. (But not too often and not too loudly.)

I phoned Jennifer Towley, and to my horror I woke her up.

"I'm sorry," I said. "I really am. Please go back to sleep and I'll call you tomorrow."

"No, no," she said. "I'm awake now, and I haven't spoken to you in ages."

"I know," I said. "Last Friday."

"Well, it *seems* like ages. That was a fabulous indoor picnic."

"The best," I agreed. "How about dinner tomorrow night?"

Pause. Then: "Oh, I can't, Archy. I'm so sorry, but I promised a client she could come over and we'd select a fabric for her Louis Something-or-other love seat."

"What a shame," I said. "May I call you late tomorrow? Maybe you'll feel like dashing out to the Pelican Club for some light refreshment."

"Well . . ." she said doubtfully, "all right. I should be finished around nine o'clock."

"I'll call," I promised. "Sleep well, dear."

"You, too," she said. This time she didn't add "darling."

She hung up, and I sat there with the dead phone in my hand, the green-eyed monster gnawing away like a mastiff. But after a while I convinced myself she really was going to spend the evening with a client discussing the upholstering of a love seat.

Did you say you had a bridge in Brooklyn for sale?

Chapter 15

After my father departed for work on Tuesday morning, I moved into his study and sat in his swivel chair behind the big, leather-topped desk, feeling like a pretender to the throne.

My first phone call was to Mrs. Trelawney. She gave me the number and time of arrival of Miss Roberta Wolfson's flight from Boston. Also the number of the suite at The Breakers that had been reserved for her use.

"Those charges will be billed directly to the company," Mrs. T. explained. "If there are any other expenses, pay with your plastic and add them to your next swindle sheet, Mr. Dillinger."

"Bless you," I said. "I'll call you from Saint-Tropez."

I then phoned The Breakers and arranged for fresh flowers to be placed in the suite reserved for Miss Roberta Wolfson. I figured if Lady Horowitz was picking up the tab, there was no point in scrimping.

My third call was to Sgt. Al Rogoff, who sounded a mite churlish. From this I deduced he had not yet had his fourth cup of black coffee that morning.

"Anything new on Wolfson?" I asked.

"Some," he admitted. "The doc says he drowned all right, but he was also full of painkillers. Heavy stuff. You told me you thought he was sick. So maybe he went for a midnight swim and couldn't fight the undertow. The doc says that stuff he was taking could have weakened him."

"It didn't happen that way, Al," I said. "Wolfson couldn't swim; the DuPeys told me that. He'd never take a dip, especially in the ocean at night."

"Then it was definitely suicide," he said.

"Don't be so sure," I said. "What about those bruises?"

"The ME says they could have been made in the surf, the body banging around on the bottom."

"And those scratches that looked as if they had been made by finger-nails?"

"There was stuff under Wolfson's nails indicating he might have scratched himself, clawing at his chest in that last minute."

"Did you search the beach?"

"Of course we searched the beach," he said crossly. "A mile north and a mile south. Nothing. By the way, Wolfson had a surgical scar on his ab-domen. The doc estimates the operation was done about a year ago. He couldn't say positively what it was for."

"But Wolfson did drown?"

"Sure he did."

"Al, he could have been dragged underwater."

"What's with you, Archy?" he demanded. "You're really trying to pin a killing on the chauffeur, aren't you? What have you got against the guy?"

"He carries a cigarette behind his ear."

Al roared. "And if he used a salad fork on steak, you'd want me to charge him with rape—right?"

"Bodin's a nogoodnik; I just know it."

"Beautiful. I go to my boss and tell him I'm arresting Bodin for first-degree murder because Archibald McNally says he's a nogoodnik. Will you please, for God's sake, talk sense."

"I guess you're right," I said, sighing. "Maybe I'm just trying to inject a little drama into this."

"You're trying to complex things up is what you're doing. As usual."

I told him the next of kin, a sister, Miss Roberta Wolfson, would be ar-riving at the Palm Beach International Airport a few minutes after noon. I would meet her and drive her to The Breakers. After she was settled, I would deliver her to police headquarters.

"She wants to claim the body and personal effects," I said. "All right?"

"I guess so," Rogoff said slowly. "What time do you figure to be here?"

"Around two o'clock or so."

"Well, if I'm not here I'll have a policewoman standing by to help her with the paperwork."

"And you'll release the body?"

"I'll have to get the okay of the brass on that, but I don't think they'll have any objections. I still think it was a suicide, and that's the way I'm going to sell it."

"Al, it's just the ambiguities that bother me."

"Ambiguities?" he said. "The story of my life. If you can't live with them, you really should be in another line of business."

My final phone call was to the airline Roberta Wolfson was flying. They reported her flight was on time. I had heard that fairy tale before but thought it better to hie myself out to the airport in case they were correct this time.

I had dressed as conservatively as my wardrobe allowed: navy tropical worsted suit, white shirt, maroon tie, black penny loafers. I even tucked a chaste white handkerchief into the breast pocket of my jacket. My sartorially retarded father would have been proud.

I thought the screaming-red Miata might be a bit too animated for the occasion, so I drove to the office garage and switched to the black Ford Escort, a sober and more suitable vehicle. I needn't have bothered. Roberta Wolfson turned out to be such a self-possessed woman I think she would have been at ease if I had shown up in a two-horse chariot.

I arrived at the airport in time to see her plane taxi up to the gate. I waited for the passengers to disembark, and hoped it would not be necessary to have her paged. It wasn't. All the others were wearing T-shirts and Bermuda shorts, and then appeared this tall, stately lady, confident and aloof.

I recognized immediately the image she called to mind: the Gibson Girl. She had that forthright, don't-give-a-damn air about her, and I could see her in an ankle-length middy dress, wearing a boater, or, in the evening, a wine-dark velvet gown by Worth. Her posture was splendid, her features pleasantly horsey. She was carrying an enormous tapestry portmanteau with bone handles.

I approached her. "Miss Roberta Wolfson?" I inquired.

She looked down at me from what seemed a tremendous height. "I am," she said in a deep, resonant voice. "And who might you be, young man?"

"Archibald McNally," I said. "I believe you spoke to my father yesterday." I proffered a business card.

She was wearing a lightweight tweed suit (with sensible brogues), and beneath the jacket was a frilly jabot with a high neckband of lace. Pearls, of course. Dangling from her wishbone was a pince-nez framed in gold wire. It was attached to a fine chain released from a spring-loaded disk pinned to her bodice. I had never seen a gadget like that before.

She used the small spectacles to examine my card. "McNally and Son, Attorney-at-Law," she read aloud. She caught it at once. "Two individuals, one attorney. Which one?"

"My father," I said. She requested no further explanation, for which I was grateful. "Miss Wolfson, may I express the condolences of my father and myself on the passing of your brother."

"Thank you," she said. "I appreciate your solicitude. May we go now?"

I attempted to relieve her of that huge bag she was schlepping but she would not relinquish it. So we marched out to the Escort. She made no comment on the heat, which was a welcome surprise. Usually, arriving visitors say, "Oof!"

As we drove eastward she looked about with interest. "Is this Palm Beach?"

"West Palm Beach, ma'am."

"Oh? Tell me something about the geography of this region."

"We are in Palm Beach County. This is the City of West Palm Beach on the mainland. We are going to the island of Palm Beach, which is separated from the United States by Lake Worth, crossed by bridges. There is also North Palm Beach and South Palm Beach."

"But no East Palm Beach?"

"No, ma'am. Only the Atlantic Ocean."

"And what is the population of Palm Beach?"

"At this time of year, the off-season? About fifteen thousand."

"And during the season?"

"Zillions," I said, and she laughed for the first time, a nice, throaty sound.

We didn't speak again until we arrived at The Breakers, that glorious remembrance of things past. I left the car with the parking valet and accompanied Miss Wolfson to the desk, where she registered.

"Ma'am," I said, "would you care for lunch before I drive you to make arrangements?"

"Thank you," she said, "but I had breakfast on the plane."

"Surely not very satisfying," I commented.

She looked at me as if I were demented. "Naturally I brought my own food," she said. "Yogurt, a cucumber sandwich, and herbal tea which the attendant was kind enough to heat for me. What I would enjoy, after I freshen up, is a glass of sherry."

"Of course," I said. "Suppose you meet me at the Alcazar Lounge. Any of the hotel employees will be happy to direct you there."

"I shan't be long," she said and left, still lugging that huge satchel, which she refused to yield to the bellhop.

I headed for the Alcazar and took a seat at the bar. I ordered a vodka-tonic with lime from a comely barmaid who provided a bowl of salted nuts to keep my thirst at a fever pitch. I had scarcely finished half my drink when Miss Wolfson appeared. I hopped from the barstool and asked if she'd care to sit at a table.

"No, this is fine," she said and swung aboard the stool next to mine with a practiced movement that made me think barstools were not an unfamiliar perch.

She ordered a glass of Harvey's Bristol Cream, took a small sip when it was served, and nodded approvingly. She gazed out the picture windows at the sea but said nothing about the beauty of the scene. After all, she was from Boston and had seen the Atlantic Ocean before—but not framed in palm trees.

"Miss Wolfson," I said, "are your accommodations satisfactory?"

"Perfectly," she said, then turned to gaze at me. "The flowers are lovely. Were they your idea?"

I nodded.

"You are a very *nice* young man," she said, and took another sip of sherry.

"Thank you," I said, happy this proper Bostonian didn't think me a rube. "Ma'am, I'd like to ask you a question about your brother, but if speaking of him will distress you, I'll say nothing more."

"It won't distress me, I assure you. You knew Angus?"

"Briefly. I found much to admire in him."

She gave me a look of wry amusement. "And much *not* to admire, I'm sure. My brother was a difficult man to know, Mr. McNally. He would be the last to deny it. What did you wish to ask?"

"Was he ill?"

"Mortally. A year ago he was operated on for prostatic cancer. They were unable to remove the entire malignancy because of possible damage to other organs. But the doctors felt that with radiation and chemotherapy his life could be extended. But Angus refused treatment."

I was aghast. "Why on earth did he do that?"

"He said it would be undignified. He said he had enjoyed a good life, and it would be humiliating to attempt to prolong it for a few miserable years by intrusive medical means. He was told that without treatment he would probably be dead within a year. He accepted that."

I finished my drink in two gulps and ordered another, and a second sherry for Miss Wolfson. She made no demur.

"Yes," I said, "that sounds like him. He was a brave man."

"Was he?" his sister said. "Possibly. He was certainly a foolish man because he had discounted the pain, although the doctors had warned him. The pain became fierce. Drugs lost their effectiveness until I believe he was constantly in agony."

"It must have been difficult for you," I offered.

She made the tiniest of shrugs. "I nursed both parents through lingering illnesses. I have become inured to suffering."

I didn't believe her for a minute. Here was a woman, I thought, hanging on to sanity with a slippery grasp. And perhaps a bottle of sherry.

"So his suicide really didn't come as a shock?" I asked.

"Not at all," she said, and now she was sipping her wine at a faster pace. "I was surprised it hadn't come sooner. He spoke of it frequently. I didn't attempt to dissuade him. He would have considered it effrontery on my part. As he said, who can feel another's pain?"

"Who indeed," I said. "Miss Wolfson, I think we better finish up and be on our way. I took the liberty of telling the authorities we'd meet them at about two o'clock."

"Of course," she said, draining her glass. "Mustn't be late for a funeral. Correct, young man?"

She was absolutely steady on her feet, her speech was still crisp and well-articulated, she gave no evidence whatsoever of having downed two glasses of sherry in a short time. We drove to police headquarters slowly while I pointed out places of interest and she asked lucid and intelligent questions. I hoped that when I was her age I might hold my schnapps as well as she did her wine.

"By the way," I mentioned as casually as I could, "Lady Horowitz has volunteered to pay the expenses of your trip to Palm Beach as well as all funeral costs."

I saw her expression change ever so slightly, and I had the feeling this news had come as a great relief. But the only words she uttered were a murmured, "Dreadful woman."

Sgt. Rogoff was not there to greet us, but we were met by a policewoman I knew, Tweeny Alvarez. (That really was her name.) Like Consuela Garcia, she was a Marielito, but about ten years older and fifty pounds heavier than Connie. Al couldn't have picked a better woman to assist Roberta Wolfson, for Tweeny was soft-spoken and *muy simpática.*

"You're in good hands," I assured Miss Wolfson. "We call Officer Alvarez 'Mother Tweeny.' "

"Oh you!" the policewoman said.

"I'm going back to my office now," I said. "Please call when you're ready to return to the hotel or if you need transportation elsewhere. I'm at your service."

"You're very kind," Miss Wolfson said faintly.

To tell you the truth, I was relieved to be absent while she viewed the remains and made arrangements for her brother to be cremated. This line of duty was not my cup of tea at all. I shine at games of darts and an occasional chugalug contest. But funeral stuff is not exactly a bowl of cherries, is it?

When I arrived back at my office, I found a note taped to my telephone handset. Printed on the top was the legend: *From the desk of Evelyn Sharif.* Notepaper like that sends me right up the wall. I mean, desks can't communicate. People, not furniture, write notes. I once contemplated having a notepad printed up that read: *From the bed of Archy McNally.* I didn't do it, of course. The senior would have taken a very dim view.

But the message itself raised my spirits. It stated: "Got an answer to your inquiry. Stop by. Evelyn."

I clattered down the back stairwell to the real estate department where I found Mrs. Sharif performing some sort of esoteric exercise.

"It strengthens the abdominal muscles," she informed me.

"Keep it up," I said, "and you're liable to drop the twins on your fax machine. What did you find out about that property down at Manalapan?"

"Interesting story," she said. She moved behind her desk and began flipping through a sheaf of notes. "A retired couple came down from Michigan in the late fifties. They had plenty of loot. He had made a fortune manufacturing portable johns, those white closets you see at construction sites. They bought the raw land between the ocean and the lake and had a house built. They called it Hillcrest."

"Love it," I said. "There isn't a hill worth the name within five hundred miles."

"Well, that's what they called it," Evelyn went on. "The man died in the seventies, and the widow died about three years ago. They had two grown children who inherited a bundle. But the house and acreage were left to the woman's alma mater, a small college in Ohio. The children are contesting the bequest. They want that house as a place to vacation with *their* children. So the whole question of ownership has been tied up in litigation for almost three years, and since no one was living there, the place went to rack and ruin. But about a year ago, all the litigants agreed that until the court case is decided, the house could be rented on a month-to-month basis. And that's the way things stand now."

"What's the monthly rental?" I asked.

"Five thousand."

"Cheap enough for that location," I said, "even though the place looks like a slum. Who's renting it now—did you find out?"

She consulted her notes again. "A single woman," she reported. "Clara Bodkin. Does the name mean anything to you?"

"Negative," I lied smoothly. "Never heard it before. Thank you, Evelyn; you did your usual bang-up job."

"Be sure and tell daddy," she said, only half-joking.

"I will," I promised.

I didn't laugh until I returned to my office. Clara Bodkin indeed! Lady Cynthia's maid could no more afford five thousand a month than I could. It seemed obvious to me that Horowitz herself had rented the empty house under her maid's name. A silly deception—but then she hadn't expected a Nosy Parker like me to come sniffing around.

It was at least ninety minutes before Roberta Wolfson phoned. I spent the time recalling everything she had told me of her brother's illness and mental state. I came to the regretful conclusion that I had been wrong and Al Rogoff right. Angus Wolfson did take that determined hike into the sea voluntarily. And, under the circumstances, it was difficult to blame him. People usually say of suicides, "He (or she) had so much to live for." That could hardly be said of Angus Wolfson.

After his sister phoned, I drove back to police headquarters. But this time, knowing the lady's temperament, I took the Miata. Miss Wolfson was waiting for me on the sidewalk and looked at my racing sloop with some amazement.

"Do you own two cars, Mr. McNally?" she asked.

"No, ma'am," I said, "the black Escort is a company car. This one is mine."

"Very nice," she said, and slid into the bucket seat with no trouble. She was an agile spinster.

On the trip back to The Breakers, I said, "I hope things went as well as could be expected."

"Oh yes," she replied. "Everyone was most cooperative. And you were quite right about Officer Alvarez. That woman is a treasure. She insisted on driving me to a funeral home. In a police car—can you imagine!" Unexpectedly she laughed. "I must tell my friends in Boston that I arrived at a mortuary in a police car! They'll be much amused."

"Yes," I said.

"In any event," she continued, "everything has been settled. Angus will be cremated tonight, and his ashes will be delivered to me at the hotel tomorrow."

She said this as matter-of-factly as if she was expecting a package from Saks. It has been my experience that women are much more capable of coping with illness and death than men. But I must say Roberta Wolfson's attitude approached a sangfroid I found somewhat off-putting.

We pulled up in front of the hotel.

"Ma'am," I said, "would you care to have dinner with me this evening?"

"Oh no," she said. "Thank you but no. It's been a long, tiring day, and I believe I shall have dinner brought to my suite, write a few letters, and then go to bed."

"As you wish," I said. "Suppose I come by at one o'clock tomorrow to drive you to the airport."

"One o'clock?" she said. "But my plane leaves at two."

"An hour will be plenty of time to get to the airport."

"I prefer to leave nothing to chance," she said severely. "I suggest we leave at noon."

"All right," I agreed. "No problem. I'll be here at noon."

She put a soft hand on my arm. "I do appreciate all you're doing for me, young man."

"I'm happy to be of help. Sleep well."

"I intend to," she said firmly, and I had no doubt she would.

I drove home, had my swim, and after dinner that night I delivered a condensed report of my day's activities to father. He listened closely and then went into a study—not *his* study but a brown study.

Finally he asked, "Then you are satisfied that Angus Wolfson committed suicide?"

"Yes, sir."

"I'm glad to hear you say that, Archy. There has been quite enough gossip and rumormongering as it is. How is Miss Wolfson taking all this?"

"Remarkably well," I said. "A very staunch lady."

"Yes," he said. "I phoned a friend in Boston to inquire about her family. She comes of good stock. Blood will tell."

And he was absolutely serious. Can you believe it? This from a man whose own father was Ready Freddy McNally, the most roguish second banana on the Minsky burlesque circuit!

I went to my aerie to scribble in my journal for an hour until it came time to call Jennifer Towley. The events of the day had been wearing, no doubt about it, and I was sorely in need of a spot of R&R. I had a vision of a delightfully mellow evening with Jennifer.

But it was not to be. She came on the phone distraught and close to tears.

"What's wrong?" I asked.

"Nothing," she said. "Or everything. I don't think I better see you tonight, Archy."

"I think you should," I told her. "I listen very well."

She didn't speak for a beat or two, then said, "Yes, I need a sympathetic ear. Will you come soon?"

"On my way," I said.

I sped to her home wondering at the cause of her distress. Something to do with her ex-husband, I had no doubt. The realization was growing that she was as hooked as he—but on different habits, of course.

I knew at once she had been weeping: eyes swollen, tissues crumpled in one fist. We sat in her shadowed living room, leaning toward each other. She offered no refreshment, and I wanted none. I was unsettled by her mood and appearance. I had always thought of her as a marmoreal woman, and learning a statue could suffer and cry was a stun.

"I lied to you," she said at once. "I didn't spend the evening with a client. I had dinner with Tom and then we came back here for a talk. Just a talk. He left only a few minutes before you called."

"He wants you to take him back?"

"Yes," she said. "Archy, he cried, he actually cried. He sat where you're sitting right now and sobbed his heart out."

"And you did, too," I pointed out. "A weepy meeting."

"I didn't cry until he left," she said. "I was proud of keeping control while he was here. But then, after he was gone, I lost it. Dear God, I don't know what to do."

"Jennifer, I can't tell you. No one can. It's your decision to make; you know that. Did he say anything about his gambling?"

"He said he hadn't made a bet since he was released. He was so forceful about it, so anxious that I believe him."

"And do you?" I asked, realizing that Thomas Bingham was indeed a demon salesman.

"I don't know what to believe. My mind is going like a Cuisinart. Everything is all chopped up. Archy, help me."

I reached forward to take her hand. I knew then I was in a no-win situation. If I told her that her ex was gambling as heavily as ever, she'd probably ditch him—but I don't believe she'd ever forgive me. She'd think I had acted out of jealousy (a reasonable assumption) and that I had robbed her of possible happiness. For what had I to offer?

And if I didn't tell her that Bingham was still a compulsive gambler, she would probably take him back and her nightmare would begin again.

If I had drawn up that blueprint of my moral code, as I intended to do but hadn't, I doubt if it would have given me any clues on how to resolve this dilemma.

It had been a gloom-and-doom kind of day, and I was stressed-out, physically and emotionally.

"Jennifer," I said finally, "I can't help you. I wish I could, but I can't. It's a heavy, heavy decision. It's your life and you must decide how you want to live it."

She tried to smile. "Yes," she said, "of course. I'm acting like a simpleton. It's my responsibility, isn't it?"

"It surely is," I said. "And you must decide on the basis of what is best for you. Be completely selfish. Don't even consider the wants and needs of Thomas Bingham or Archibald McNally or anyone else. Decide what you really want—and then go for it."

She nodded dumbly and I stood up to leave.

There was just nothing more to say.

Hours later, lying awake in bed, waiting for sleep that was slow in coming, I suddenly remembered that weeks ago Lady Cynthia and Connie Garcia had warned me that Jennifer Towley would be a problem. How did they know? How do women *know*?

Chapter 16

I recall those last few days of the Inverted Jenny Case as taking on a momentum of their own, whirling toward a resolution no one could have predicted, least of all me. Events governed, and neither I nor the police nor anyone else could control them. We all had to sit back, as it were, and watch with fascination as everything unraveled.

It began with a telephone call from Sgt. Al Rogoff on Wednesday morning while I was having a late breakfast in the kitchen with Jamie Olson. It was then about ten o'clock.

"Hiya, sherlock," Al said, sounding jubilant. "I think we fell in the crapper and came up with a box lunch. I just got a call from a stamp dealer up in Stuart. Early this morning, right after he opened, a bimbo breezes in and tries to sell him a block of four Inverted Jenny stamps. He described her as young, blond, pretty, with all her doodads in place. Sounds like our pigeon—right?"

"Right," I said. "It's got to be Sylvia."

"She's asking a half-million for the stamps. The dealer told her he'd have to see if he could raise the cash and to come back around noon. She said she would. I've got a car on the way with three heavies. I just changed to civvies, and I'm taking off. I'll play a clerk in the store, and the others will be backup. How's it sound?"

"Sounds great. Good hunting, Al, and give me a call as soon as it goes down. Or I'll call you."

"Sure thing," he said. "I've got something else to tell you, but it can wait. Keep your fingers crossed, old buddy."

He hung up, and I finished my breakfast. Rogoff was a brainy cop, and I was confident he'd grab Sylvia in the act of trying to sell stolen property. But then what? Would she talk or wouldn't she? I reckoned she had enough street smarts to cut a deal with the SA. I hoped she'd rat on Kenneth Bodin in return for a slap on the wrist.

.I had time to kill before heading for The Breakers to pick up Roberta Wolfson, so I wandered out to the greenhouse, where my mother was wielding a watering can and humming contentedly.

"Good morning, Mrs. McNally," I said. "Sorry I overslept. Did you rest well?"

"Splendidly," she said, "just splendidly. Now give me a kiss."

She held up her tilted face, and I kissed a velvety cheek.

"There!" she said, beaming. "Now wasn't that nice? I always say one should start the day with a kiss. It brings good luck."

I laughed. "Who told you that?"

"No one," she said, giggling. "I made it up. Archy, are you still seeing that nice lady you told us about, the interior decorator?"

"She's really an antique dealer, and yes, I'm still seeing her."

"Oh my," mother said, going on with her sprinkling chores. "Is it serious?"

"It is with me," I said without thinking, and then suddenly realized it was the truth: I *was* serious about Jennifer. "But I'm not sure how she feels about me. She's also seeing someone else."

"Have you told her how you feel?"

"No, not really."

Mother stopped her work and turned to face me. "Oh Archy," she said sorrowfully, "if you are serious about her, you should tell her. Isn't there some saying about unspoken love?"

"Love unspoken is love denied," I said.

"Exactly," mother said, nodding. "Who said that?"

"I did," I said, "just now. You're not the only one who can make things up."

"Well, it's completely true. You simply *must* tell her how you feel."

"You really think so?"

"Absolutely," she said firmly. "If you don't, you'll lose her."

"You're probably right," I said. "I'll think about it. Thank you for the advice."

"That's what mothers are for," she called gaily after me.

I did think about it—thought of what a dunce I had been not to have realized it myself. A sincere, passionate avowal of love, followed by a marriage proposal, might very well solve Jennifer's problem and my dilemma.

There was only one thing wrong with that scenario: I wasn't sure I was up to it. I did love the woman, I really did, but I could not decide if I wanted to give up the life of a happy rake for a till-death-do-us-part intimacy with one woman. After all, I was the man whose pals had considered nominating for a Nobel Prize in philandering.

In other words, I dithered.

When I arrived at the hotel, Miss Wolfson was waiting outside, still clutching that gigantic catchall. I slung the bag into the back of the Miata, and she made a little yip of protest.

"Do be careful," she said. "Angus is in there."

"What?" I said.

"Well, I thought the urns at the funeral parlor were in dreadful taste. Angus would be horrified. I'll find something more suitable in Boston."

"I see," I said. "And what are the ashes in now?"

"A mason jar," she said. "May we go?"

She was unusually voluble on the ride to the airport. She said it was her first trip to semi-tropical climes, and the weather, flora, the dress of inhabitants, and the colors of homes were all new to her. I found her comments quite discerning. She even noted the pace at which pedestrians moved along the streets, so much slower than in the northeast.

We arrived at the airport in plenty of time, of course. We checked the gate number of her departing flight, then found a nearby cocktail lounge for a farewell drink. I had a vodka gimlet, and she ordered a glass of her usual.

"Thank you," she said, "and please thank your father for me. You both have been enormously supportive. I also intend to write a letter to the mayor of Palm Beach commending the diligence and sympathetic assistance of Officer Tweeny Alvarez."

"That's very kind of you," I said. "I'm sure the letter will go into her file and may help her career."

"I believe in giving credit where credit is due," she said sternly. "I also have no hesitation in voicing criticism when it is deserved."

I could believe that. I would not care to be a waiter who served lukewarm coffee to Miss Roberta Wolfson.

"I am only sorry," I said, "that we have met under such unhappy circumstances. What a shame that your brother's holiday ended as it did."

I swear that's all I said. I wasn't prying. I didn't intend to ask any questions. I was merely trying to express a conventional sentiment to an elderly lady who, despite her courage, had obviously been under a strain. But what my comment elicited was a shocker.

"Oh, Angus wasn't on a holiday," she said casually. "It was a business trip."

That was my first alert, and no way was I going to let it pass without learning more.

"A business trip?" I said, trying to be as casual as she.

"Yes," she said, sipping her wine primly. "Lady Horowitz had sent him some old stamps she owned. She wanted Angus to have an appraisal made in Boston. I believe she intended to find a private buyer or put them up for auction."

"Oh?" I said. "And did Angus have an appraisal made?"

"He didn't have to. My brother was an antiquarian and very talented in his field. He saw at once that the stamps Lady Horowitz had sent him were counterfeit."

"Goodness gracious," I said.

"Oh yes," she said, nodding. "They were forgeries and completely worthless except as a curiosity. Whatever profit that unpleasant woman expected simply went out the window."

She uttered those words with some satisfaction, and I saw that even to a proper Bostonian revenge is sweet.

"So Angus came down here to return the stamps to Lady Horowitz and give her the bad news?"

"May I have another glass of sherry?" she asked.

"Of course," I said, "and I shall keep you company."

We didn't speak until our fresh drinks were served, and then she took up her tale again. Please don't blame her for speaking so openly to a comparative stranger. She did so innocently; she had no knowledge of the theft of the Inverted Jennies and knew nothing of the roles her brother had played and I was playing.

"Yes, he came to Palm Beach to return the stamps and tell Lady Horowitz they were fakes. Poor Angus was in a funk. He knew that woman's terrible temper and feared she would blame the messenger for the news."

"Yes," I said, "I can imagine."

"However," she went on, "everything turned out well. Angus phoned me a few days after he arrived down here. He said he had already told Lady Horowitz her stamps were forgeries, and she had accepted it with little fuss. In fact, Angus said, she had invited him to stay a week or two and try to recover his strength."

"Thoughtful of her," I said. "Miss Wolfson, I believe I just heard the first call for your flight. Perhaps we should move to the boarding gate."

"Let's," she said, and polished off her second sherry like a longshoreman downing a boiler-maker.

"Ma'am," I said, "I travel occasionally and may get to Boston one day. If I do, may I call you? Perhaps we might have dinner together?"

"I'd enjoy that," she said, smiling. "You are a very dear young man." And she swooped to kiss my cheek.

I watched her stalk away from me, indomitable, head high and spine straight. And still lugging that enormous bag containing Angus Wolfson in a mason jar.

I drove back to the McNally Building in a broody mood, trying to assimilate what Roberta Wolfson had told me. Vital stuff. Some of those oddly shaped pieces of a jigsaw puzzle that had frustrated me for so long were beginning to snap together with an almost audible *click*. The picture they formed was not a sweet one—not something you'd care to hang over your mantel in place of that Day-Glo portrait of Elvis Presley on black velvet.

The problem with the scenario I envisioned was that, if proved valid, it was going to leave my father with an ethical dilemma as racking as the one I faced with Jennifer Towley. The future did not promise a million laughs for the McNallys, *père et fils*.

I arrived back in my office to find a message from Al Rogoff asking that I call him immediately. That I hastily did without even removing my panama.

"Got her!" he said exultantly. "Full name: Sylvia Montgrift. And guess what? She's got a sheet. Did you know that?"

"No," I lied, remorseful that I had neglected to tell him. "What's she done?"

"She was running an unlicensed massage parlor. The West Palm Beach cops closed her down. She got off with a suspended sentence. Hey, she's a real looker."

"Not my type," I said. "I suspect she may be a closet Hegelian. Al, may I come over?"

"Sure," he said, "but don't butt in. We're waiting for her lawyer to show up. Lou Everton. You know him?"

"Of course," I said. "Six-stroke handicap. He's skunked me many times. And he's also a very smart apple."

"He is that," Al agreed, "but I've worked with him before, and he'll cut a deal. He likes fast-food justice as much as I do. He'll tell her to talk and cop a plea. If he doesn't we've got a problem. I mean what if she insists she found the stamps in the gutter. Then where are we? No way can we prove burglary."

"Well, if she talks," I said, "there's something I'd like to ask her. I'm on my way."

The last thing in the world I wanted was a confrontation with Sylvia but, as we all know, fate delights in the unexpected rabbit punch.

I got over to headquarters and found Rogoff in the corridor chewing on a cold cigar.

"Where is she?" I asked.

"Right now? In the john. Tweeny is with her to make sure she doesn't climb out the window."

"How did the bust go?"

"Like silk," he said. "She showed up with the stamps at the Stuart dealer a few minutes after twelve. I flashed my tin and grabbed her. That was it. No muss, no fuss."

"Did she say anything?"

"Yeah, she said, 'Shit.' "

"Where are the stamps now?"

"We've got them. Crazy little things. I've contacted a retired professor in Lantana who's supposed to be a hotshot on questionable documents. He's going to take a look—at no cost to the county."

At that moment Sylvia came out of the loo, Tweeny clasping her by the elbow, and they walked toward us.

She took one look at me and gasped, "Dooley! What are you doing here? Have you been arrested, too?"

But Officer Alvarez escorted her firmly into the sergeant's office and closed the door.

Al looked at me. "Dooley?" he said. "What's that all about? You haven't been getting any massages lately, have you?"

"No, no," I said hurriedly. "It's just the name I used at Delray Beach."

"Dooley," Rogoff repeated, grinning. "Beautiful."

"Listen, Al," I said, "if Lou Everton lets you question her in his presence, ask her if Thomas Bingham was in on the deal."

"Who?"

"Thomas Bingham."

"Who the hell is he?"

"A friend of Bodin's. He might have been part of it."

The sergeant looked at me reproachfully. "Have you been holding out on me again?"

"Al," I said, "this Bingham is just a walk-on. He might or might not be involved. Ask Sylvia, will you?"

"All right," he said grudgingly, "I'll ask."

I saw Lou Everton coming through the front door and I went out the back, leaving the attorney and the police officer to their merry-go-round. I climbed into the Miata and headed for the Horowitz spread. I planned to do something exceedingly imprudent. If I had told Rogoff, he'd have had the pip.

Cut-rate justice, also known as plea bargaining, is as prevalent in Palm Beach as it is in Manhattan and everywhere else. Everton and the State Attorney would have disagreements, many arguments, and perhaps many drinks together. Eventually a quid pro quo would be forged: what Sylvia would deliver and the punishment she would receive.

My only problem with it, at the moment, was that it would take time. And there was always the possibility, of course, that Sylvia would refuse to peach on her muscleman. I could not believe loyalty was her strong suit, but I didn't want to chance it.

So I drove beachward, too impatient to wait for a done deal. When I banged the brass clapper on the Horowitz front door, Mrs. Marsden opened it and didn't even say hello.

"I hear the cops got the stamps back," she said immediately, "and arrested the one who took them."

"Mrs. Marsden," I said, "the grapevine in this town is astounding. NASA should latch on to it, and they'd be hearing from Jupiter in seconds."

"Then it's true?"

I nodded. "The Inverted Jennies have been recovered. Happy?"

"Very," she said, and led the way into the cavernous foyer.

I saw a set of matched luggage piled near the door. "Someone leaving?" I asked.

"Miss Stanescu," the housekeeper said. "That Ken Bodin is going to drive her to the airport."

"Then perhaps I'll see her for a moment and say goodbye, if I may."

"Sure, Mr. McNally," she said. "She's upstairs." Then she suddenly grabbed my arm tightly and looked directly into my eyes. "Is everything going to be all right?" she demanded.

"Everything is going to be fine," I assured her, wishing I was telling the truth. "Exactly the way it was before all this started."

She nodded, but I knew she didn't believe me. Things were never going to be exactly as they were before. But Mrs. Marsden had learned to endure change. I was still learning.

The door to Gina Stanescu's bedroom was ajar, and I glimpsed her packing toiletries into a small leather case. I rapped on the doorjamb. She looked up, smiled, beckoned me in.

"I understand you're departing, Miss Stanescu," I said, "and just wanted to stop by to say farewell."

"Not farewell," she said. "I prefer the German *auf Wiedersehen,* which means until we see each other again."

"Of course," I said, "and I hope we do. I wish you a safe and pleasant trip home, and Miss Stanescu—" I paused, not wanting to make a promise I might not be able to fulfill.

"Yes?" she said.

"Keep believing in a miracle," I said. "Even a very small one."

"A petite miracle?" she said, her smile strained.

"Sometimes they do happen, you know."

We shook hands and parted. It was my day for goodbyes. And I feared more lay ahead.

I went downstairs and out to the garage. Kenneth Bodin was wiping down the Rolls as gently as a groom might curry a derby winner. He turned around at my approach, glanced at me, went back to his task. His jacket was off, and in his form-fitting T-shirt with cutoff sleeves, he looked a proper anthropoid.

"I hear the cops got the stamps back," he said, still turned away from me.

"That's right," I said breezily, "and they nabbed the woman who was trying to sell them. Sylvia Something-or-other. They're questioning her now. They don't think she was the thief, so they want to know who gave her the stamps to sell. I understand she's singing like a bird."

I had him pegged as a rash lad with nothing but ozone in his bean. I wanted to provoke him into doing something exceptionally stupid, such as taking off as soon as possible: added evidence of his guilt. In his lavender Volkswagen Beetle, he wouldn't be hard to trace. And if I had any luck at all, he might even resist arrest. That would put the frosting on the éclair.

"How did the cops happen to catch her?" he asked in a low voice, buffing the brightwork on the Rolls.

"Oh, that was my doing," I boasted, hoping my braggadocio would infuriate him even more. "I told the police to alert every stamp dealer in South Florida. I figured the guy who had the Inverted Jennies was such a complete moron he'd try to convert them to cash locally as quickly as possible. And that's exactly what the imbecile did."

Then, reckoning I had pushed him as hard and as far as I could, I called cheerily, "See you around," and wandered away, well-pleased with myself.

I know it wasn't Confucius, but it may have been Charlie Chan who said, "Man who pats himself on back risks broken arm." Right on, Charlie.

I stopped at Consuela Garcia's office simply because I wanted to see her again. She always gave me a lift. If Jennifer Towley was a marmoreal woman, Connie was a warm, fuzzy type, as comforting as a teddy bear. Also, she laughed at my jokes: an admirable quality.

She was on the phone, as usual, and waved me to a chair.

"Yes, that is correct," she said in the cold, official tone she used when speaking to reporters. "We understand the police have recovered the stolen stamps. Naturally, Lady Horowitz is delighted. Yes, you may quote me on that. Thank you so much for calling."

She hung up and grinned at me. "All's well that ends well," she said.

"Uh-huh," I said. "Also, look before you leap versus nothing ventured, nothing gained—and where does that leave anyone? How did Lady C. *really* take the news that her stamps had been found?"

Connie frowned. "Not with wild jubilation," she said. "In fact, I thought she was shook. She snapped, 'Who the hell cares?' A typical Horowitz performance. Listen, Archy, if the stamps are back, it's obvious she didn't use them to pay off a blackmailer. So your whole plot is demolished—right?"

"Wrong," I said. "There's still plenty of evidence that someone is leaning on her."

"And you're going to keep following her?"

"Whenever I can. It's in her own interest, Connie," I added earnestly. "She may be in danger."

She looked at me suspiciously—but what could I tell her? That I was still curious as to why Lady Horowitz wouldn't reveal her whereabouts at the time Bela Rubik was killed? If I told Connie that, she'd tell me to get lost and probably never give me another *"Hola!"* as long as she lived.

"Well . . ." she said hesitantly, "just one more time. And that's it. She's taking off tomorrow at one o'clock; destination unknown—to me at least."

"Thanks, Connie," I said gratefully. "I do appreciate it. You seeing anyone regularly these days?"

"Yeah," she said in a doleful voice, "my periodontist—and that's not much fun. In case you ever break up with the Towley woman, I'm footloose and fancy-free."

"I'll remember that," I said. "One more question: The DuPeys have left and Gina Stanescu is on her way; when are Doris and Harry Smythe going to brighten Florida by their absence?"

"Those dolts?" Connie said, then giggled. "Listen to this, Archy: The madam knows a retired British couple who live in Kashmir. They're both horse people, and for years they've been trying to get Lady Horowitz to sell them a Remington bronze she owns. She's refused up to now, but yesterday she phoned and said she'd sell them the bronze, but they have to invite the Smythes for a two-week stay, beginning immediately. So on Monday, Doris and Harry take off for Kashmir."

I laughed. "Lady Cynthia is a professional conniver."

"Oh sure," Connie said. "And you don't do too badly in that game yourself. You're not in her class, of course, but I'd rank you as a talented amateur."

I was wounded. If she had known what I was planning, she'd have upped my rating. Semipro, at least.

Chapter 17

On Thursday morning, after breakfast, I futzed around in my nest for an hour or so. I was in a smug mood, believing I was going to set the world aright and eventually get my eternal reward in Heaven. Or, prior to that, a weekend in Paris. Surely there was *some* way I would be honored for the good deeds I intended.

I decided I would motor at a leisurely pace to the office and spend time bringing my swindle sheet up-to-date. I had tabs for all those sherries consumed by Roberta Wolfson, plus bills for money spent on gas and the rental of the Ford Escort. And, of course, a few expenses of a more creative nature.

I came out into a nothing morning, the sky as colorless as a slate pavement, the air unmoving and damp. It was bloody hot, and a nice, refreshing cloudburst would have been a blessing. But that leaden sky offered no shadows and no hope. All in all, a grayish scene—enough to depress the most chipper of do-gooders and make one ponder the value of crawling out of bed on such a blah day.

I drove into town, thinking of how I might improve my shadowing technique when, later in the day, I tailed Lady Horowitz to her rendezvous at that dump near Manalapan, if that was again her destination. I decided to transfer my zoom binoculars from the glove compartment of the Miata to that of the Escort. I do believe I had some foolish notion of doing Inspector Clouseau: skulking in the underbrush and spying like a demented bird-watcher.

I pulled into the underground garage and glanced at the glassed booth inhabited by Herb, the security guard. I waved but drew no response; he had his nose deep in a paperback book, probably *Fun with Piranha*. I stopped alongside the Escort and climbed out of the Miata. As I did, Kenneth Bodin straightened up from behind a parked car and advanced toward me with a ferocious grin.

He was wearing jeans and a black leather jacket decorated with steel studs. In this heat? I wondered. Does vanity have no bounds? But then his hands came from behind his back, and I saw he was grasping a baseball bat. It was either a Louisville Slugger or a reasonable facsimile thereof.

He stepped close to me, drew back his shillelagh, and swung. I suspect he had eyes for my kidneys.

He was large and muscular. But dreadfully slow. The bat came around no faster than one of Jennifer Towley's tennis serves. I leaned back, his cudgel whooshed past. I moved in, shifted my weight to my left leg, and kicked him briskly in the *cojones*. I am really not as effete as I may have given you reason to believe.

Bodin dropped the bat and fell to the concrete floor of the garage. He curled up into the fetal position, clutching the family jewels and making "Gaugh, gaugh, gaugh" sounds of pain and anguish I found delectable.

"Herb!" I shouted as loudly as I could, and the guard came lumbering.

He looked down at the writhing man on the floor, saw the baseball bat nearby and then, with some difficulty, drew his long-barreled Colt from a dogleg holster. He pointed his ancient weapon at Bodin.

"You okay, Mr. McNally?" he asked anxiously.

"I'm fine, thank you."

The chauffeur looked up at me accusingly. "You hurt me," he said between moans.

"That was my intention, old boy," I said. "Herb, I'm going to call the cops. You stay here and keep your howitzer trained on this vicious assassin."

"If he gives me trouble," the guard said, "where should I shoot him?"

"Oh, I don't know," I said. "I imagine the kneecaps would be satisfactory."

"Small target," Herb said doubtfully. "How about the brisket?"

Kenneth Bodin groaned.

Sgt. Al Rogoff was in, which was a relief. I explained briefly what had just happened.

"You all right?" he asked.

"A mite shook," I admitted. "But no injuries."

"Good," Al said. "You saved us a lot of trouble. We've been looking for that guy since last night. Sylvia talked. Hang on to him; I'll be right over."

Herb and I stood alongside the recumbent assailant, observing his physical agony with some satisfaction. We discussed how he had managed to sneak into the garage. The guard decided it had probably happened while he was on one of his periodic security tours throughout the building. I didn't argue. Herb was a nice enough chap but about as alert as a stuffed sailfish.

Two police cars came rolling down the ramp, sirens dying away to a whisper. Sgt. Rogoff got out of the lead car and two stalwarts exited from the second. All three officers joined us in a circle about the fallen chauffeur, watched his contortions, and listened to his laments.

"What happened to him?" Al asked me.

"Testicular trauma," I reported. "Resulting from a sudden, sharp blow from the toe of an Allen-Edmonds cordovan kiltie, size ten-and-a-half."

The sergeant grinned at me. "Thank you, Bruce Lee," he said. "Dollars to doughnuts he sues you for causing him emotional distress." He turned to the other two cops. "Get the bum out of here. Take him in and book him."

"What's the charge?" one of the officers asked.

"Impersonating a human being," Rogoff said. "Just sit on him till I get back."

We watched as the two hauled Bodin to his feet and dragged him to their car. He was crouched over, feet dragging, and he was still whimpering.

"Thank you, Herb," I said to the guard. "You behaved splendidly."

"Happy to be of service, Mr. McNally," he said. I believe that if he had a forelock he'd have tugged it.

Al and I sat in the Miata. He lighted a cigar and I an English Oval.

"The girlfriend talked?" I asked him.

"Yep," he said, "but didn't spill much we didn't already know. She claims Bodin gave her the stamps to sell."

"Did she know they were counterfeit?"

"She didn't say, and I didn't tell her. But I think both she and Bodin thought they were the real thing. By the way, those Inverted Jennies *are* fakes, according to the expert we called in."

"Did Sylvia tell you where Bodin got the stamps?"

"She says they were given to him by an elderly man who was staying at the Horowitz place. That would be Angus Wolfson—right? The deal was that Bodin was to get ten percent of whatever he sold the stamps for."

"You're telling me Wolfson lifted the Inverted Jennies?"

Rogoff laughed. "I know what a keen student of human nature you are, Dr. Freud. You already told me it would be completely out of character for Wolfson to steal anything. But in this case I'm afraid you have more crap than a Christmas goose. Wolfson pinched them, all right."

I thought he had it wrong, but I wasn't about to tell him that.

"Speaking of Wolfson," I said, "I hereby confess I was mistaken about his death. You were right; it was suicide."

He looked at me quizzically. "What convinced you?"

I related what Roberta Wolfson had told me about her brother's terminal illness, his refusal to undergo radiation and chemotherapy, the constant pain he suffered.

"Reason enough to shuffle off this mortal coil," I said.

"Uh-huh," the sergeant agreed. "But he had another reason."

"Oh? And what, pray, was that?"

"Guilt. While we had Wolfson's body, we took his fingerprints. They matched up pretty well with the prints we took off the glass paperweight that caved in Bela Rubik's skull."

I hadn't anticipated that, but I wasn't shocked. The stamp dealer would have unlocked his door for Angus Wolfson, but not for a bruiser like Bodin.

"You're sure, Al?" I asked. "About the prints, I mean."

"Seventy-five percent sure," he said, "and that's good enough for me. This case is officially closed as far as I'm concerned. Rubik's homicide is cleared. The killer, Wolfson, is dead. Lady Horowitz gets her fake stamps back. Maybe Bodin will do some time, but it won't be heavy. Now the PBPD can concentrate on important investigations, like who's been swiping kiwis and mangoes from the local Publix."

"Do me a favor," I urged. "Tell me how you figure the whole thing went down. From the top."

"Sure," he said genially, puffing away at his cigar. "Wolfson had a lot of medical expenses, and he wasn't a rich man to begin with. As you would say, he was getting a bit hairy about the heels. So he swiped the Inverted Jennies, figuring Lady Horowitz had zillions and could stand the loss. Then he does something stupid: he tries to peddle the stamps to a local dealer. I figure he left the Inverted Jennies with Bela Rubik, giving him a chance to make an appraisal. Rubik already had the stamps when you first met him.

"Wolfson goes back to Rubik's shop on the afternoon the yacht cruise was canceled. Rubik tells him his stamps are forgeries. Knowing Rubik, I'd guess he got hot about it and threatened to tell the police that Wolfson was trying to sell counterfeits. Wolfson panicked and bounced the paperweight off Rubik's skull. I don't think he meant to kill him. Just knock him out, get his stamps back, and lam out of there.

"Then Wolfson reads the local papers and realizes he's a murderer. Also, he hasn't got the wheels to get around to other dealers, and he knows he's getting weaker. So he makes a deal with Kenneth Bodin, a money-hungry sleaze if ever I saw one. The chauffeur agrees to sell the stamps for a piece of the take. It's the best Wolfson can do. The rest you know. How does it sound?"

"Did Wolfson tell Bodin the stamps were forgeries?"

"No. Bodin and Sylvia thought they were handling something of genuine value. Look, maybe even Wolfson himself thought Rubik was wrong, and that he had stolen the real thing. Well?"

He had some of it right, but not all of it. But I had no desire to point out his errors; most of the mistakes were due to information I had not revealed. If Al's scenario was going to be the official version, so be it. It hurt no one. And I had other fish to fry.

"Yes," I said, "everything sounds plausible."

"No objections?"

I knew he'd be suspicious of total agreement. "A few minor questions," I said. "Like Wolfson's relations with Kenneth Bodin. I think he really had a thing for that mug."

"Sure he did," Rogoff said, nodding. "That's why he picked him as an accomplice and offered a piece of the pie. Hoping for favors in return."

"Yes," I said, "that makes sense. Was Bela Rubik really going to turn Wolfson in?"

Al gave me a twisted smile. "Only after he examined the stamps and saw they were counterfeit. If they had been legit, Rubik would have made a deal even if he knew they were stolen property. He was that kind of guy."

I sighed. "Well, I guess that wraps it up. Sorry to have dumped this mess in your lap, sarge."

"It comes with the territory," he said shrugging. "I'm leaving it to your father to tell Lady Horowitz her stamps are forgeries. I'm taking a week of my vacation starting tomorrow. I want to be out of town when she hears that. There goes her insurance claim!"

I laughed along with him. He got out of the Miata, lifted a hand in farewell, and strutted toward his squad car, still chewing on his cigar. I had a brief pang at not revealing the whole truth, but consoled myself with the thought that it would cause no loss to him and might benefit others.

Suddenly I yelled, "Al!" I got out of the car and trotted after him. "Did you remember to ask Sylvia about Thomas Bingham?"

"I remembered," he said. "She claims Bingham is a drinking buddy but knows nothing about the Inverted Jennies. Disappointed?"

"Yes," I admitted. "Will you ask Kenneth Bodin?"

"You never give up, do you? All right, I'll ask the master criminal."

He got in his car and backed up the ramp. I glanced at my watch, muttered a curse (mild), and hurriedly transferred my binoculars to the Ford Escort. Then I set out in pursuit of Lady Cynthia Horowitz.

I just did make it. I was heading north on Ocean Boulevard and as I passed the Horowitz gate I saw the Jaguar heading out, Lady C. at the wheel. She turned south, and I averted my head as I went by, hoping she wouldn't spot me.

I continued north for about fifty yards, made a screaming U-turn, and set off after the Jag. It wasn't difficult to keep it in view; the madam's hair was bound with a fuchsia scarf, and on that dreary day it glowed like a beacon in the fog. Traffic was light, and I thought it wise to hang back. I knew where she was going; there was no need to tailgate.

Sure enough, she eventually turned into the driveway of Hillcrest. I drove slowly past and was delighted with what I saw: The Jaguar had not been driven around to the rear of the house, facing Lake Worth, but was parked in front on the brick driveway. Lady Cynthia was out of the car and just entering the front door as I went by.

I drove back and forth a few times, considering my options. Not many. My notion of lurking in the underbrush with my binocs was nutsy. The homes north and south of Hillcrest were occupied, and if I was seen slinking furtively about, the gendarmes would have been summoned for sure.

I finally decided my original fear of looking like a demented bird-watcher wasn't such a bad idea after all. So I drove north to a small area that provided parking space for beachgoers. I locked the car and hiked back to Hillcrest, the binoculars hanging from a strap around my neck. Occasionally I paused to use the glasses, scanning all the foliage in sight and sometimes peering eastward, pretending I was looking for seabirds. What a performance! Stanislavsky would have been proud of me.

I came to Hillcrest and casually examined the surrounding trees. In the process, of course, I took a good look at the house itself. The Jaguar was still parked in front, but I could discern no action, no one moving behind any of the windows.

I continued my impersonation of a birder, parading north and south, using my binoculars until my eyes began to ache. I wondered how long I would have to maintain this charade—an hour? Two? Three? It turned out to be exactly one hour and forty-three minutes. I knew; I looked at my watch often enough.

I was then south of the house, standing on the eastern verge of the corniche, partially concealed by a row of big-leafed sea grapes. I was watching the house when the front door opened and Lady Cynthia came out. Her hair was unbound; she was carrying the fuchsia scarf. She paused on the portico, turned around, and spoke animatedly through the opened door to someone within.

I used the zoom lever and adjusted the focus to bring her into closer and sharper view. She was laughing, shaking her head prettily, and once she pouted and stamped her foot. I saw her reach out to the person within.

"Come out, come out, whoever you are," I sang aloud. And then, unsure of my grammar, I sang again, "Come out, come out, whomever you are."

Out he came.

My father.

I watched, glasses trembling slightly, as the two clutched in a fervid embrace and kissed. That was no fond and friendly farewell between attorney and client; it was an impassioned grapple and the osculation seemed to go on forever.

What may amuse you (or possibly not) was that my most convulsive shock came from seeing my father tieless, vestless, and coatless. Prescott McNally in shirtsleeves at midday! I can't tell you how *lubricious* it made the scene appear to me.

Finally they drew regretfully apart. Lady Horowitz went down to the Jaguar and gave father a final wave. He waved in return, went back into the house, closed the door.

She turned northward, heading for home. I sprinted for my Escort. I figured my father had parked the Lexus behind the house and soon he too would be heading north. I wanted to be long gone before that.

I drove back to the McNally Building at an illegal speed. I couldn't seem to cease brooding on the fact that I had recently witnessed two illicit embraces: Angus Wolfson–Kenneth Bodin and Cynthia Horowitz–Prescott McNally. Sgt. Al Rogoff had claimed that things happened in threes. I had a gloomy premonition of who might be involved in the third doomed embrace.

I pulled into the garage, and Herb hustled over before I got out of the Escort.

"You feeling all right, Mr. McNally?" he inquired anxiously.

"Tiptop, thank you, Herb," I said. "Couldn't be better."

"Glad to hear it," he said. "I should have shot that no-good. He deserved it."

He went back to his booth, still muttering. I climbed into the Miata and lighted a cigarette. I was pleased to see my hands were steady. I slumped, put my head back, stared at the sprinkler pipes overhead. I found that my reactions to what I had just seen took the form of an interrogation, a personal Q-and-A.

"What amazes you most about the affair?"

"The logistics involved. The planning! They had to find a place relatively safe from public view and gossip. So she rented an old house away from Palm Beach. And he arranged his absences from the office so no one might suspect."

"Why didn't you? After all, on at least two occasions he was not available at the same time she was mysteriously gone. And he was quick to correct you when you thought her older than she really is."

"That's right, but it just never occurred to me that they might be having a thing."

"Why not? Because of their age?"

"Don't be ridiculous. You think there's a certain cutoff point in everyone's life when the dreams end? They never end. (I hope.)"

"How long do you think their liaison has been going on?"

"Oh, I don't know. Probably for months. I could find out by asking Evelyn Sharif how long Hillcrest has been rented. But what's the point of that?"

"Be honest: You really have a grudging admiration for your father, don't you?"

"I guess I do."

"Because you have inherited his propensities?"

"The turd never falls far from the bird."

"Are you going to tell him you know?"

"Good God, no! I happen to love the man, despite his faults. Maybe because of them. He and I have a very special relationship."

"What you just learned—won't that end the relationship?"

"Of course not. It may change it, but it'll remain special."

"Will you tell your mother?"

"She already knows. I realize that now, from things she's said recently. How do women *know?* But for all her nuttiness, she has a wisdom that eclipses mine. And she has love and patience. She knows he'll come back to her."

"So you're not going to tell anyone?"

"I didn't say that."

The questioning ended, and I knew what I was going to do. I derived a sour amusement from recalling the scam I had used with Connie Garcia—that someone was blackmailing Lady Horowitz. It had turned out to be true. The blackmailer was me.

I drove out into a mizzle that swaddled the world in a foggy mist the color of old pewter. It wasn't drizzling hard enough to put on the Miata's hat, but I could see moisture collecting in pearls on windshield and hood. It became thicker as I neared the coast, and when I turned into the Horowitz driveway I headed directly for the garage to get my baby under cover.

I entered the house through the back door, and in the kitchen I found chef Jean Cuvier and maid Clara Bodkin sparking up a storm. I think they were just trying to have a few laughs on a dismal day, but then again their flirting had an edge to it as if their banter might become serious at any moment.

"Ar-chay," he said, "tell this innocent she must not be frightened of life, of love, of passion, of romance."

"And you tell this whale I know all about those things," she said, "and I am very particular as to whom I bestow my favors."

I admired her syntax but held up my hands in protest. "Peace," I said. "I refuse to enlist in this war. I just stopped by to have a word with the lady of the manor. Is she receiving?"

"I don't know," Clara said doubtfully. "I think she's having a bath. Why don't you go up and knock on her door."

"So I shall," I said. "And try to be kind to each other, children. What the world needs is love, sweet love."

"Just what I've been telling her," the fat chef said.

I went out into the hallway and then up that magnificent staircase to the second floor. I rapped gently on the door of Lady Cynthia's suite.

"Who?" she called.

"Archy McNally. May I speak to you for a moment?"

"Come on in."

If it was pewter outside, her chambers were silver, steamy and scented from her bath. The windows were open, but the voile curtains were unmoving. I could hear the susurrus of a rain that was now falling steadily. There was an ambience of quiet intimacy: a secret place fragrant and isolated. What a setting for an orgy à deux! But it was not to be.

She was reclining on the chaise lounge, clad in a peignoir of some diaphanous stuff. It revealed almost as much as it concealed. One leg was extended, bare foot on the floor. Very naked, that leg.

"Pull up a seat," she said languidly. And so I did, moving a velvet-covered ottoman into a position where I could face her directly.

"What's on your mind, lad?" she asked.

"At the moment?" I said. "You. I'm sure you've heard by now that the police have recovered your counterfeit stamps."

"My *what?*" she cried, shock and horror oozing from every pore.

"Oh, cut the crap," I said as roughly as I could. "You're a great actress but not *that* great. You've known for weeks that your Inverted Jennies were fakes. Even while you were bugging my father to file an insurance claim for their loss. It's called fraud, dearie."

She didn't order me from the premises immediately. Just turned her head to stare out the window where the rain was still whispering.

"What a filthy thing to say," she said. "But it's only your mad fancy. You have no proof, of course."

"Of course I do. You sent the stamps to Boston, asking Angus Wolfson to have an appraisal made. You had read of that block of four Inverted Jennies being auctioned for a million bucks and you thought: Why not mine? But then Wolfson came to Palm Beach to return your stamps and tell you they were forgeries."

"You're just guessing," she said. "That's not proof. Go away."

"Do you take me for an idiot?" I said. "I am not an idiot. Wolfson told his sister your Inverted Jennies were fakes. Roberta Wolfson does not harbor a favorable opinion of you, m'lady. If push comes to shove, she'll be happy to testify that her brother had determined the stamps were forgeries. And further, he phoned her a few days after he arrived here and told her that he had informed you the stamps were worthless and that you had accepted the bad news calmly."

(I didn't bother mentioning that Roberta Wolfson's testimony, being hearsay, would probably be inadmissible in any litigation.)

Lady C. turned her head to face me. "He told his sister that? What a fool the man was!"

That angered me but I tried to suppress it. "I wondered why you would try to pull an insurance swindle; your net worth is hardly a secret. Then I remembered something you told me during our first conversation. You said, 'When it comes to money, enough is never enough.' Greedy, greedy, greedy."

"You know what happens to greedy people?" she asked. "They get rich. Tell me something, lad. Suppose you discovered that a twenty-dollar bill you were trying to spend was counterfeit. Would you turn it in and take the loss as the law requires, or would you try to pass it along to someone else? Be honest."

I didn't answer that. I was afraid to. "That's twenty dollars," I blustered. "We're talking half a million."

"No difference," she said. "You'd try to pass it along; you know you would. That's all I was trying to do. Why should I take the bite? The insurance company has oodles of cash. They should; my premiums are high enough."

"But it would be outright fraud," I argued.

"Fraud-schmaud," she said, shrugging. "What's the big deal?"

Her imperturbability disconcerted me. I had expected heated denials. But she was admitting everything with a cool calmness I found maddening.

"Here's what I think happened," I said, trying to regain the initiative. "Wolfson told you the stamps were fakes. It took you perhaps three seconds to cook up the idea of a fake theft and then file an insurance claim. Wolfson didn't steal the stamps; you *gave* them to him and told him to get rid of them. Instead, he decided to try to sell them."

"I told you the man was a fool. He turned out to be greedier than I."

"Not so," I said. "He didn't want the money for himself. He wanted to assist your daughter, Gina Stanescu. She told him her orphanage was in trouble, and he hoped to help by selling the stamps to some unsuspecting dealer and turn over the proceeds to Gina. He was as larcenous as you, but from somewhat purer motives."

Finally, she was rattled. "Gina's orphanage needs money? Why didn't she tell me?"

"She's frightened of you."

Her eyes went wide. "Why would anyone be frightened of me?"

"Maybe because they think you're a barracuda with bucks—a scary combination. Anyway, she told Angus, and he was determined to try to help her. What did he have to lose—he knew he was dying. But the stamps were recognized as counterfeits by dealers, so Angus was never able to deliver. Now, of course, the police think he was the thief."

That naked leg slipped a little farther from its filmy covering.

"Do they?" she said. "And I suppose you're going to tell them the truth."

"Not necessarily," I said.

She was amused. "Oh-ho," she said, "it's deal-making time, is it? All right, lad, what's your proposition?"

"Two things," I said. "First of all, give Gina Stanescu enough money to save her orphanage."

"Done," she said promptly. "No problem. I can deduct it. What's the second thing?"

"Give my father the brush."

I had been wrong about her thespian talents; she *was* a great actress. The most her features revealed was a small ironic smile.

"My, my," she said, "you *do* get around, don't you?"

I nodded. "Dump him, Lady Cynthia," I urged. "You know how little it means to you; just a pleasant interlude a few afternoons a week. You'll find someone else."

"And your father?"

"He'll probably suffer awhile—he deserves to—but eventually he'll recover. Losing you will not prove a mortal wound."

"It never does," she said, the paradigmatic woman of the world. "Although there was a young man in Venice who died after I kicked him out. But he was tubercular."

Then she was quiet a moment, and I could almost hear the IBM AS/400 in her gourd go into action, circuits clicking.

"And if I don't?" she asked finally.

"If you don't," I said, "I'd feel myself duty-bound to inform my father that you were attempting grand larceny by fraud and deception."

She was absolutely expressionless. "And I suppose the word would get around."

"I'd make sure it did," I said.

"You know, lad," she said, " 'devious' isn't the word for you. You're a solid-gold sonofabitch."

"I try," I said modestly.

Then there was a long silence while she pondered the risk-benefit ratio. I wondered if she had learned mulling from Prescott McNally.

"Your father is something of a bore," she said at last.

"I know," I agreed.

"Do you?" she challenged. "Do you also know that he happens to be a very passionate lover?"

"How on earth would I know that?" I asked, reasonably enough.

She made up her mind. "Very well," she said. "I'll give your father a pink slip. And in return, you'll keep your mouth shut and go along with the police opinion that Angus was the thief?"

"Agreed."

"And that I was unaware the Inverted Jennies were fakes?"

"Again, agreed."

"Then consider the contract signed," she said. She lifted her arms above her head in a long, lazy stretch. The peignoir gaped open, a little. It could have been an accident. She looked at me thoughtfully. "Now I must find a replacement," she said.

"Not me," I said hastily.

"You have no desire to pinch-hit for your father?"

"I think not. I am not in your class, Lady Cynthia. A lightweight wouldn't go up against a heavyweight, would he?"

She grinned at me. "I don't weigh so much," she said. "I wouldn't hurt you."

"Tell it to the Marines," I jeered.

"I have," she said. "Frequently. Are we still friends, lad?"

"I devoutly hope so," I said, and meant it. "I assure you that I have the greatest respect and admiration for you."

That naked leg inched toward total revelation.

"Well, it's a start," she said, and I got out of there as fast as I could.

I drove home in the rain, not caring that both I and the Miata were getting drenched. Along the way I sang, "Yes! We Have No Bananas," never wondering why it gave me so much pleasure to finagle other people's lives.

Chapter 18

But by Friday morning, my joy had evaporated, and I suffered a seizure of introspection and doubt.

For the sake of McNally family unity I had brought an end to my father's fling with Lady Horowitz. I termed it a "fling," but what if it had been the world's greatest romance since Bonnie and Clyde? In other words, I had played God—and who gave me the divine right to manipulate people? I was, I acknowledged briefly, guilty of hubris, if not chutzpah.

It was a miserable day, and I had a mood to match. Flurries of rain came boiling in from the sea, and if there was a sun up there behind that fat mattress of clouds, there was no sign of it.

After breakfast I went back to my haven and mooched around awhile. I decided there was no point in driving to the office and sitting in my cramped sepulcher creating fictions for my expense account. I came to the conclusion that to prevent a fatal onslaught of the megrims I absolutely had to see Jennifer Towley, for lunch or dinner. That wonderful woman would elevate my spirits and give me a reason to go on breathing.

I called instanter and was rewarded with a mechanical message from her answering machine, followed by that damnable *beep*. I recited a piteous statement, pleading with her to call me as soon as possible. After I hung up, I wondered where on earth she might be so early in the morning on such a venomous day.

I told myself that jealous suspicion was an unworthy emotion, perilously close to paranoia, and I would have none of it. So I resolutely set to work on my journal, completing the record of the Inverted Jenny Case. I didn't call Jennifer again for almost an hour. Then, hoping she might have returned home and neglected to replay her messages, I phoned. All I got for my effort was the machine. Derisive, that gadget. I hung up, gnashing my molars in frustration.

Finally, close to noon, my phone rang and I leaped for it.

"Hello!" I caroled as melodiously as I could.

"What the hell?" Sgt. Rogoff said. "Are you yodeling or something?"

"Hello, Al," I said sheepishly. "Just clearing my throat. What did you learn from Kenneth Bodin?"

"His story's the same as Sylvia's. He says Wolfson gave him the stamps to sell and promised him a ten percent commission."

"Did Wolfson tell him how he got the stamps?"

"He claims Wolfson said Lady Horowitz gave them to him to sell."

"Do you believe that?"

"You think I was born yesterday? Of course not. The chauffeur knew damned well that Wolfson had stolen the stamps. But he didn't care; he just wanted a piece of the action."

"Uh-huh. What are you going to do with Sylvia and Bodin?"

"Not a whole hell of a lot. You want to bring assault charges against him?"

"Good lord, no!"

"Then I think we'll just tell him to take his playmate and vamoose. If we get both of them out of the county I'll be satisfied. By the way, he says Thomas Bingham wasn't connected with the caper in any way, shape, or form. I think he's telling the truth."

"Probably," I said. "It was just a wacko idea. Thanks for checking it out. So you're closing the file?"

"You betcha. I gave the stamps to your father. He's going to return them to Lady Horowitz this afternoon and tell her they're fakes. Lucky man!"

"Yes," I said, "isn't he. When are you leaving on your vacation?"

"As soon as the rain lets up. And the way it's coming down, that might be next year."

"Where are you going?"

"Lourdes," he said. "My hemorrhoids are killing me."

It was the first laugh I had all day. "Have a jolly time, Al," I said. "Give me a call when you get back and we'll get hammered at the Pelican Club."

"Will do," he said and hung up.

It wasn't the telephone call I wanted, but it soothed the fantods a bit. I wasn't even depressed to learn that Tom Bingham had nothing to do with the theft of the Inverted Jennies. Thinking he might be involved had been a selfish wish on my part, very unprofessional, and I was happy to have been proved wrong before I made an even bigger ass of myself.

I went down for lunch about twelve-thirty. Mother and I sat in the kitchen with the Olsons, and we all shared a big salad bowl of shrimp, crabmeat, and chunks of sautéed scallops, along with a basket of garlic toast. Mother was in a frolicsome mood and drank a glass of sauterne. No use telling her it was the wrong wine; it was right for her.

I went back upstairs, looked out the window, and saw that the rain was slackening. But the sky was still clotted with clouds, and there was grumbling eastward and an occasional flash of lightning. It was not a scene to photograph for South Florida's tourist brochures.

I resolved to call Jennifer one more time, just once, and if she wasn't in, the solution was simple: I'd just slit my wrists. Her phone rang twice, was grabbed up, and she said breathlessly, "Hello?"

"Archy," I said. "What have you been doing wandering about in this monsoon?"

"Oh dear," she said, "please let me call you back. I just got in, I'm soaked and have to change. Are you home or at the office?"

"Home."

"Call you back in five minutes," she said and hung up.

It was more like fifteen minutes, but I waited patiently; I had no choice.

"Listen, Archy," she said, very businesslike, "I know it's a rotten day, but I must talk to you. Could you come over?"

"Now?" I said. "This minute? How about dinner tonight?"

"No," she said firmly, "no dinner. I'd like to speak to you as soon as possible."

"Is something wrong?"

"Archy," she said, voice tight, "let's not discuss it on the phone. Can you or can you not come over now?"

"All right," I said, wondering what the crisis was. "I'll be there within the hour."

I pulled on a nylon golf jacket and my rain-hat. I went downstairs and found my mother and the Olsons still in the kitchen, laughing up a storm and sharing a plate of Ursi's sinful chocolate-chip cookies.

"Mother," I said, "I've got to go out and don't want to waste time raising the Miata's roof. May I take the station wagon?"

"In this weather, Archy?" she said. "Whatever for?"

"An errand of mercy," I said.

She looked at me, suddenly worried. "I hope so," she said. "Of course, take the Ford." She paused. "I'm not sure about the gas," she said doubtfully. "I think there's some in the tank. You better check, dear."

"I shall," I promised, leaned to kiss her cheek, and snaffled two of the cookies.

She was right about the gas; the dial showed less than a quarter-tank. But the instruments on that antique vehicle had eroded over the years, and I could just as easily be starting out with Full or Empty. I took the chance, comforting myself with the old maxim that God protects fools and drunks.

Despite a few asthmatic coughs and wheezes, the old wood-bodied station wagon behaved admirably and, boasting high clearance, had no trouble navigating the flooded streets en route to Jennifer's home. It had stopped raining, but I was forced to leap a few deep puddles to reach her door. I didn't quite succeed; my Bally loafers were squishing.

Inside, with her permission, I kicked off the shoes and left them in the umbrella drip-pan of her Victorian hall-tree. Then we looked at each other with very small and very tentative smiles. Jennifer was wearing an enormous white terry robe with the crest of a Monte Carlo hotel—the same cover-up she had donned the first night we were intimate.

I wanted desperately to believe that a good omen, but her troubled appearance and agitated manner convinced me that there was to be no instant replay of our initial frolic. She led the way into her living room which, on the mournful day, seemed overdecorated with lumpish furniture and ancient tchochkes.

Before I quite knew what was happening, she had me seated and had thrust into my hand a double old-fashioned glass that appeared to contain ice cubes and a half-pint of vodka.

"What?" I said, looking at that enormous drink. "No blindfold and a final cigarette?"

"Archy," she said without preliminaries, still standing, "I can't see you anymore."

"Oh?" I said. "Ah?" Not a brilliant reply, I admit, but I felt as if I had just been examined by a doctor who then asked, "Mr. McNally, do you have a will?" I mean I was devastated. Talk about utterly; I was about as utter as one could get. "Why not?" I finally managed to croak.

"I've been seeing Tom Bingham. I was with him last night and all this morning. I promised to remarry him."

I stared at her. Suddenly I realized her distress was not caused by vacillation about her decision; she was concerned that I might be hurt. Very kind of her, of course, but at the moment the last thing in the world I wanted was her solicitude.

"Jennifer," I said as steadily as I could, "why are you going to remarry Bingham?"

She lifted her chin a trifle, once more the cool, complete woman she had been. "Because I love him," she said.

If there was an answer to that, I didn't know it. I have a smattering of several foreign languages, but love isn't one of them. When it comes to the tender passion, I am a total illiterate.

"You've given it a lot of thought?" I asked.

"Too much," she said. "It's had me in a whirl. And then I realized thought and logic can take you only so far. But if they don't make you happy, what's the point? Then it's time to trust feelings and faith. I must do what my heart tells me to do." Then, recognizing the soap-opera triteness of that final remark, she tried a timid smile.

"Jennifer, you told me that life with him was a nightmare."

"It was. But I'm willing to gamble that he's changed. He promised he has, that those years in prison have made him a different man."

"You're willing to gamble?" I said, trying not to sound bitter and not succeeding. "You're doing exactly what you divorced him for—compulsive betting."

I think she was startled, as if the idea had never occurred to her.

"I suppose you're right," she said. "But even if you are, it doesn't affect the way I *feel*. And if he begins gambling again, so be it. But this time I'll stick by him. I *must*. Don't you see that, Archy? Because life without him is simply unendurable to me. Empty and without meaning. I know that now."

Jennifer turned upside down! I listened to that brainy, self-possessed woman calmly tell me what she intended to do, and I couldn't believe it. Where was her dignity, her self-esteem, her independence, her keen, cutting intelligence? All demolished by the virus of love for which, I had heard, there was no known cure.

There were things I could have told her. I could have said that while we all may be created equal in the sight of God and the law, people have varying degrees of quality. There are such things as ambition, emotional depth, and intellectual curiosity. Some are born with these attributes, some acquire them over a lifetime, some remain deficient until they are deep-sixed. But we are *not* all equal.

Thomas Bingham, it seemed to me, was a lowlife, simply not in Jennifer's class. And if that is *snobisme,* I plead guilty. Yet here was this high-quality woman willing—nay, eager!—to sacrifice her life for a low-quality man. I swear I shall never fully comprehend the vagaries of human nature.

I didn't say all that to Jennifer, of course. Nor did I tell her that Bingham had already resumed his old habits. I realized that to her, at the moment, the truth was inconsequential. I merely put my drink aside without having tasted a sip, for which I was justly proud. I stood and in ringing tones I wished Jennifer Towley all the happiness in the world and thanked her for all the joy she had given me.

Tears came to her eyes, she rushed to hug me, kiss my lips, touch my cheek.

The third embrace.

I reclaimed my sodden shoes, golf jacket, rainhat, and exchanged a final wave with Jennifer. What brave smilers we were! Then I drove home, determinedly *not* brooding on what my dithering had cost me. But I could almost hear my mother's sorrowful, "Oh, Archy!"

I stopped on the way to fill up the Ford's tank (it had been half-full—or half-empty, depending on your philosophy) and then continued on to the McNally stage set. I garaged the station wagon and entered the house through the kitchen. Ursi was at the range stirring up a bouillabaisse in a big cast-iron pot.

"Smells sensational," I told her, "but unfortunately I'm going out for dinner tonight. If there's any left, will you put it aside for my breakfast tomorrow?"

"Sure," she said, seeing nothing unusual in someone wishing to breakfast on her fish stew.

"And also, Ursi," I added, "please tell my parents I'm feeling a bit mangy and won't be able to join them for the cocktail hour."

She stopped stirring the stew to look at me. "If you say so," she said.

I trudged up to my hideout, feeling like something the cat dragged in.

After I locked the door, which I rarely do, I stripped off damp jacket and hat, kicked off soaked loafers, peeled away sodden socks. Then I lay on my bed and wished for a quick and merciful quietus. People would cluck and say, "He died of unrequited love," little knowing that I had croaked from chronic indecision.

I am, as you may have gathered, a social creature. I can endure solitude, but it is not my favorite indoor sport. I much prefer the company of others and the reassurance that they are as screwed-up as I.

But now, staring at a water stain on the ceiling that resembled a map of Iceland, I told myself there was a lot to be said for solitude. I told myself that man is not necessarily a herd animal. I told myself that self-knowledge is of utmost importance and can only be achieved through solitary rumination, a sort of mental cud-chewing.

I therefore resolved to spend a quiet, reflective evening alone, pondering my shortcomings and planning how I might become a kinder, gentler human being.

After about twenty minutes of this mawkish self-flagellation, I decided the hell with it and spake aloud Popeye's admirable dictum: "I yam what I yam." Invigorated, I rose and poured myself a very small marc. Then, in honor of Jennifer Towley, I put on a tape of Frank Sinatra singing "It Was a Very Good Year." I needed to hear it. His reading of that line ". . . and it came undone" is the perfect elegy for a lost love.

I played more Sinatra, and Billie Holiday, Bessie Smith, early Bing Crosby ("Just a Gigolo"), and Ella Fitzgerald singing Cole Porter. Then I listened to my favorite balladeer: Fred Astaire. Most people remember Astaire as a dancer, but no one has ever done a better vocal of "A Fine Romance."

While I listened to all this swell stuff, I took a shower, washed my hair, trimmed my toenails, and generally reconstructed my life. The cocktail hour passed, the dinner hour passed, and I dressed and was thinking vaguely of making a run to the Pelican Club when I heard a tentative knock on my door. I unlocked to find my father standing on the landing.

I was surprised to see him because he infrequently invaded my sanctum. I stared at him, wondering if his hairy eyebrows and mustache were drooping dispiritedly. They definitely were, I decided—which meant that Lady Horowitz had given him his marching papers. Not as her attorney, as her paramour.

"Ursi said you were feeling peakish," he said. "Mother asked me to stop by. May I come in?"

"Of course," I said. "I was feeling somewhat bilious, but I'm better now."

"Glad to hear it," he said, entering.

He was carrying two crystal wineglasses and an opened bottle of Cockburn's port. Considering what had happened to both of us that afternoon, it seemed a fitting brand.

He poured us full glasses, then took the chair behind my desk. I sat on the edge of the bed. He offered no toast, nor did I.

"I saw Lady Horowitz today," he said. "I returned the Inverted Jennies and informed her they were counterfeit."

"And how did she take the news?"

"Amazingly well. Disappointed, naturally, but willing to accept the loss. We discussed whether the grantor—her first husband, Max Kirschner—had gulled her or if he himself was swindled when he purchased the stamps in Trieste."

"Perhaps both," I suggested.

Father smiled, stroking his mustache with a knuckle. "That's quite possible, but it's a moot point. I explained to Lady Horowitz that the insurance company will have to be notified, and the forgeries deleted from the list of her insured properties. She asked if that would result in lowered premiums. I advised her not to count on it."

I laughed. "She's wonderful," I said. "Always working the angles."

"Yes," father said. "Archy, I had a very brief conversation with Sergeant Rogoff this morning. Apparently he's leaving on a vacation and was in a hurry to get away. He told me the official police investigation has been terminated and the case closed. Could you fill me in on the details of the affair?"

I recited the police version of what had happened: Angus Wolfson had stolen the Inverted Jennies and had attempted to sell them to Bela Rubik. The dealer had recognized them as forgeries and threatened to call the police. Panicking, Wolfson had struck him down with the paperweight, reclaimed the stamps, and fled.

Realizing he was physically incapable of fencing the stamps himself, Wolfson had recruited Kenneth Bodin, promising the chauffeur ten percent of the sale price. In turn, Bodin had enlisted his girlfriend, Sylvia, to sell the stamps. She had failed in her first attempt in Fort Lauderdale and on her second, in Stuart, she had been arrested.

Meanwhile, in agony from his cancer and suffering from guilt because he had caused the death of Rubik, Wolfson had committed suicide.

"That's how the police have reconstructed it, sir," I finished.

My father looked at me narrowly. "But you don't entirely agree?"

I knew he would never accept my total agreement. "A few things bother me," I admitted. "What was Wolfson's motive for the theft? After all, Lady Cynthia was an old friend. The police say that because of medical expenses he was badly in need of money and didn't want to saddle his sister with debts. I suppose that's possible."

"Of course it is," father said decisively. "It makes perfect sense to me. What else bothers you?"

"The circumstances of Wolfson's suicide. The police ascribe it to his worsening physical condition and remorse for his assault on the stamp dealer. I'm sure those factors were important, but I think there was another reason. I believe he had made a date with Kenneth Bodin for that late hour on the deserted beach, anticipating a sex scene. I think Bodin showed up all right but laughed at the old man and told him that he, Bodin, intended to keep the entire amount of whatever the Inverted Jennies were sold for. And there was nothing Angus could do about it. If he went to the cops, Bodin would name him as the original thief. So Wolfson was left with nothing, his dreams of love shattered, knowing he would soon die, knowing he had killed a man, however inadvertently. So he walked naked into the sea."

Father sipped his wine. "Very imaginative," he pronounced. "But far-fetched, don't you think? You have no evidence that what you believe happened between Wolfson and Bodin actually occurred."

"No evidence," I agreed. "It's pure conjecture." My father smiled wanly as he always did when I attempted to use legalese. "But it's not totally improbable," I went on. "It's based on what I know of the personalities and weaknesses of the men involved."

He shook his head doubtfully. "It seems rather odd behavior to me."

I might have pointed out that his shenanigans with Lady Cynthia seemed rather odd behavior to *me*. I didn't, of course, or he'd have had my gizzard.

"But even if you're correct," he continued, "it doesn't affect the final result, does it? The stamps have been recovered, the thief identified, the case officially closed. Perhaps the police solution is not as tidy as you might wish, but these things always have loose ends."

"Yes, sir."

He finished his wine and sat a moment somberly regarding his empty glass. "A messy affair," he said finally. "I find the whole thing distasteful. I've been wondering if it might not be wise to end the relationship of McNally and Son with Lady Horowitz and advise her to seek legal counsel elsewhere. What is your opinion, Archy?"

What a shock that was! I could count on one finger the times he had asked for my opinion on matters affecting the family business.

"Oh, I wouldn't do that, sir," I said. "Admittedly she can be troublesome at times, but so can most of our clients. That's part of our job, is it not, to endure vexations and the sometimes wacky conduct of the people we represent. If they were all rational, intelligent, upright human beings, you and I would probably be chasing ambulances from a one-room office above a delicatessen."

He gave me a wry smile and stood up. "I suspect you're right. Very well, we'll keep Lady Horowitz on our roster of valued and honored clients." He appeared to notice for the first time how I was dressed. "You seem to be dandyish this evening, Archy," he observed. "Planning to visit your young lady?"

"No, sir," I said. "That's ended."

"Oh," he said, somewhat disconcerted, "sorry to hear it. Well, those things happen. But you're going out?"

"I thought I'd stop by the Pelican Club and see if there's any action."

He looked at me closely and said something that touched me: "Yes, I think that would do you good."

Did I catch an echo of envy in his voice? No matter; I felt closer to him at that moment than I had in a long time. Twin losers—right? He took his bottle of port with him when he departed, probably reckoning (correctly) that he needed it more than I.

I spent a few moments inspecting myself in the dresser mirror, wondering if I really did look dandyish. Actually, I decided, I was dressed conservatively. I was doing my silver-white-black bit, quiet but elegant: Ultrasuede jacket, white polo shirt, black silk trousers. I felt perhaps a spot of color would not be amiss so I carefully adjusted my new straw boater. It had a band of cerise silk shantung I thought rather swank.

I went downstairs. On the way, I passed the second-floor sitting room, heard the sound of the television set, and peeked in. My mother and father were seated on the couch watching a rerun of *Mrs. Miniver.* They were holding hands. Domestic bliss? Let's hear a chorus of "Silver Threads Among the Gold."

See what a devious lad with atrophied scruples can accomplish?

The night sky was not entirely clear but the cloud cover was breaking up, and as I tooled the Miata across the Royal Palm Bridge I was happy to see a few pale stars timidly peeping out. Best of all, the air had freshened; a cool sea breeze was blowing at about five knots and boded well for a golf-and-tennis weekend.

It was still relatively early but the Pelican Club was already jumping. It was the TGIF crowd of working stiffs, eager to relax after a week of strenuous labor in banks, boardrooms, and insurance offices. When I entered, heads swiveled in my direction, and my straw sailor with the cerise silk band inspired general hilarity, verging on hysteria. I accepted my friends' derisive gibes with my usual aplomb and headed directly for the bar.

"Good evening, Mr. McNally," Simon Pettibone said. "Nice hat."

"Thank you," I said. "You are a man of refined taste. What do these peasants know of casual elegance? Mr. Pettibone, tonight I yearn for something a bit more exotic than vodka, something that will clutch my palate with both fists and never let go. What do you suggest?"

"A margarita?" he asked.

"Excellent! Heavy on the salt, please."

I removed my hat and placed it on the bar-stool next to mine. A moment later it was whisked away and I turned to see Consuela Garcia with the boater atop her head, cocked rakishly. She looked charming.

"Archy," she said, "I simply *must* have this hat. What do you want for it?"

"Your innocence."

"Sorry," she said, "I'm broke. As you well know."

"Then have a drink with me," I said, "and the hat's yours."

"That's easy," she said and swung aboard the stool next to me. Just then Mr. Pettibone served my margarita. Connie picked it up immediately and sipped. "Divine," she said. "What are *you* drinking?"

Sighing, I ordered another margarita and turned my attention to Connie. She looked positively ripping. Her long black hair was down, splaying over a crocheted turtleneck of white wool. Her stone-washed jeans were so tight that they may not have been jeans at all but rather a hip-to-ankle tattoo. My new hat was the perfect complement to that costume. What a delicious crumpet she was!

"Are you baching it tonight?" I asked her.

"Yes, dammit," she said. "And on top of that, I had to take a cab here. My car's in the garage."

"What's wrong?"

"Faulty alternator."

I looked at her haughtily. "I'm not sure I want to associate with a woman who has a faulty alternator."

"Oh, shut up. Why aren't you squiring Jennifer Towley tonight?"

Just then my margarita arrived. Plenty of salt. I sampled it. Exactly right.

"Jennifer?" I said. "That's over."

"It is?" Connie said. "Want to talk about it?"

"No."

"Okay," she said equably, "we won't. But *please* tell me about Lady Horowitz. You followed her twice. Where did she go?"

"Oh, that was a false alarm. She wasn't being blackmailed."

"I *knew* she wasn't. But what was she up to?"

"You may find this hard to believe, Connie, but she's been doing volunteer work at a shelter for the homeless."

"You're kidding!"

"Scout's honor. That's where she's been going a few times a week. She passes out cheese sandwiches to the hungry and helps make soup."

"What about those regular withdrawals you told me she was making from her bank account?"

"Contributions to the shelter."

"I can't believe it," Connie marveled. "Why didn't she say something about it? It's nothing to be ashamed of."

I shrugged. "I guess she prefers to keep her charity private. Maybe she enjoys her reputation and doesn't want people to know just how sympathetic and generous she is."

"Amazing," Connie said. "And all this time she's been ministering to the needs of the deprived."

"Precisely," I said.

"She really has a heart of gold. I'll bet she's done a lot of good deeds no one knows about."

"I wouldn't be a bit surprised."

We sipped our margaritas thoughtfully. The club was filling up, with more noise, more laughter, a few voices raised in ribald song.

"Archy," Connie said, "I'm hungry. Can we have a hamburger here at the bar?"

"I have a better idea," I said. "It's clearing and there's a nice, fresh breeze. Let's take a drive down the coast. We'll stop at the first interesting place we come to and have dinner, a few drinks, a few giggles. How does that sound?"

"Sensational," she said. "Let's go."

We finished our margaritas. I signed the tab and we went outside, Connie wearing my new hat. It galled me, a little, that it looked better on her than it did on me.

I opened the door of the Miata for her, but she paused and gripped my arm. She looked into my eyes.

She said, "Do you think we might get back together again?"

I said, "One never knows, do one?"

McNALLY'S LUCK

Chapter 1

The cat's name was Peaches, and it was a fat Persian with a vile disposition. I knew that because the miserable animal once upchucked on my shoes. I was certain Peaches wasn't suffering from indigestion; it was an act of hostility. For some ridiculous reason the ill-tempered feline objected to my footwear, which happened to be a natty pair of lavender suede loafers. Ruined, of course.

So when my father told me that Peaches had been catnapped and was being held for ransom, I was delighted and began to believe in divine retribution. But unfortunately the cat's owner was a client of McNally & Son, Attorney-at-Law (father was the Attorney, I was the Son), and I was expected to recover the nasty brute unharmed. My premature joy evaporated.

"Why don't they report it to the police?" I asked.

"Because," the sire explained patiently, "the ransom note states plainly that if the police are brought in, the animal will be destroyed. See what you can do, Archy."

I am not an attorney, having been expelled from Yale Law, but I am the sole member of a department at McNally & Son assigned to discreet inquiries. You must understand that we represented some very wealthy residents of the Town of Palm Beach, and frequently the problems of our clients required private investigations rather than assistance from the police. Most denizens of Palm Beach shun publicity, especially when it might reveal them to be as silly and sinful as lesser folk who don't even have a single trust fund.

Peaches' owners were Mr. and Mrs. Harry Willigan, who had an estate on Ocean Boulevard about a half-mile south of the McNally manse. Willigan had made a fortune buying and developing land in Palm Beach and Martin counties, and specialized in building homes in the $50,000–$100,000 range. It was said he never took down the scaffolding until the wallpaper was up—but that may have been a canard spread by envious competitors.

With wealth had come the lush life: mansion, four cars, 52-ft. Hatteras, and a staff of three servants. It had also brought him a second wife, forty years younger than he.

The McNallys had dined at his home occasionally—after all, he *was* a client—but I thought him a coarse man, enamored of conspicuous consumption. He seemed to believe that serving beluga caviar on toast points proved his superiority to old-money neighbors, many of whom served Del Monte tomato herring on saltines. Laverne, his young wife, was not quite as crass. But she did flaunt chartreuse polish on her fingernails.

Willigan had children by his first wife, but he and Laverne were childless and likely to remain so if her frequent public pronouncements on the subject were to be believed. Instead of a tot, they had Peaches, and Harry lavished on that cranky quadruped all the devotion and indulgence usually bestowed on an only child. Laverne, to her credit, tolerated the cat but never to my knowledge called it Sweetums, as Harry frequently did.

And that's how the entire affair began, with the snatching of a misanthropic cat. It almost ended with the untimely demise of yrs. truly, Archibald McNally: bon vivant, dilettantish detective, and the only man in Palm Beach to wear white tie and tails to dinner at a Pizza Hut.

I left father's office in the McNally Building and drove my fire-engine-red Miata eastward toward the ocean. I had a brief attack of the rankles because my unique talents were being used to rescue a treacherous beast whose loathing of me was exceeded only by mine of her. But I am a sunny bloke, inclined to accentuate the positive, and my distemper did not last. It happened to be June 21st, and when Aristotle remarked that one swallow does not make a summer, he obviously wasn't thinking of frozen daiquiris. That was my plasma of choice from the June solstice to the September equinox, and I was looking forward to the first of the season.

Also, my regenerated romance with Consuela Garcia was going splendidly. Connie had made no alarming references to wedlock—the cause of our previous estrangement—and we had vowed to allow each other complete freedom to consort with whomever we chose. But we were so content with each other's company that this declaration of an open relationship had never been tested. As of that morning.

Finally, my spirits were ballooned by an absolutely smashing day: hot sun, scrubbed sky, low humidity and a fresh sea breeze as welcome as a kiss. I thought God had done a terrific job and I thanked Him. As my mother is fond of saying, it never hurts to be polite.

The Willigans' mansion was a *faux* Spanish hacienda with red tile roof, exposed oak beams, and a numbing profusion of terra-cotta pots. The place was called *Casa Blanco* and when you tugged the brass knob on the front door, you expected a butler to appear wearing sombrero and serape.

Actually, the butler who opened the door was wearing a black alpaca jacket over white duck trousers. He was an Australian named Leon Medallion, and when he came to work for the Willigans he had to be restrained from addressing all guests as "Mate."

"Good morning, Leon," I said. "How are you this loverly day?"

"Great, Mr. McNally," he said enthusiastically. "Couldn't be better."

That was a shock. Leon usually took a dour view of existence in general and life on the Gold Coast in particular. More than once I had heard him mutter, "Florida sucks."

"And how are the allergies?" I asked.

He looked about cautiously, then stepped close to me. "Would you believe it," he said in a hoarse whisper, "but since that rotten cat's been gone, I haven't sneezed once."

"Glad to hear it," I said, "but I'm sorry to tell you that's why I'm here. I've been ordered to try to find Peaches."

He groaned. "Please, Mr. McNally," he said, "don't try too hard. I suppose you want to see the lady of the house."

"If she's in."

"She is, but I gotta go through all that etiquette shit and see if she's receiving."

He left me standing in the tiled foyer and shambled away. He returned in a few moments.

"She's at the pool and wants you to come out there," he reported. "She also says to ask if you'd like a drink."

I glanced at my watch: almost eleven-thirty. Close enough.

"Yes, thank you, Leon," I said. "Can you mix me a frozen daiquiri?"

"Sure," he said. "My favorite. Mother's milk."

I walked down the long entrance hall, the walls unaccountably decorated with swords, maces, and a few old muskets. The hallway led to a screened patio, and the rear door of that opened to a lawned area and the swimming pool.

Laverne Willigan was lounging at an umbrella table on the grass, her face shaded by a wide-brimmed planter's hat. It may not have been the world's smallest bikini she was wearing, but it wouldn't have provided a decent meal for a famished moth. Her tanned legs were crossed, and one bare foot was bobbing up and down in time to music coming from a portable radio on the table. A rock station, of course.

She had the decency to turn down the volume as I approached, for which I was grateful. I am not an aficionado of rock. I much prefer classical music, such as "I Wish I Could Shimmy Like My Sister Kate."

"Hiya, Archy," Laverne said breezily. "Pull up a chair. You order a drink?"

"I did indeed, thank you," I said, doffing my pink linen golf cap. I moved a canvas sling to face her. "You're looking positively splendid. Glorious tan."

"Thanks," she said. "I work at it. What else have I got to do?"

I hoped she wasn't expecting an answer, but I was saved from replying by the arrival of Leon bearing my daiquiri on a silver salver. It was in a brandy snifter large enough to accommodate a hyacinth bulb.

"Good heavens," I said, "that must be a triple."

"Nah," Leon said, "it's mostly ice."

"Well, if I start singing, send me home. Aren't you drinking, Laverne?"

"Sure I am," she said and picked up a glass as large as mine from the grass alongside her chair. "Bloody Mary made with fresh horseradish. I like hot stuff."

She frequently said things like that. Not suggestive things, exactly, and not double entendres, exactly, but comments that made you wonder what she intended. I had the impression that she was continually challenging men, and if an eager stud wanted to think she was coming on to him and responded, she wouldn't be offended. But I doubted if it ever went beyond high-intensity flirting. She had it made as mistress of *Casa Blanco,* and I hoped she was shrewd enough to know it.

We raised glasses to each other and sipped.

She said, "Through the lips and past the gums; look out, stomach, here it comes."

She actually said that; I am not making it up. I am merely the scribe.

Suddenly I became aware of activity in the Olympic-size swimming pool behind me and turned to look. A young woman in a sleek black maillot was doing laps, brown arms flashing overhead, long legs moving from the hips in a perfect flutter kick.

I watched, fascinated, as she swam the length of the pool, made a racing turn, and started back. There was very little splash and her speed was impressive.

"Who on earth is that?" I asked.

"My sister," Laverne said. "Margaret Trumble. You can call her Meg if you like, but don't call her Maggie or she's liable to break your arm. She's very strong."

"I can see that," I said. "What a porpoise!"

"And she jogs, lifts weights, skis, climbs mountains, and does t'ai chi. She's staying with us until she decides what to do."

I looked at her and blinked. "About what?"

"Right now she teaches aerobics in King of Prussia. That's in Pennsylvania."

"I know," I said. "I once met the queen of Prussia."

Laverne looked at me suspiciously, but continued. "Anyway, Meg is thinking of moving to Florida. She thinks there are enough richniks here so she could do well as a personal trainer. You know: go to people's homes, teach them how to exercise, put them on diets, plan individual workout programs for them. Meg says all the big movie and TV stars have private trainers, and so do business bigshots. She thinks she could get plenty of clients just in Palm Beach."

"She probably could," I said, watching Ms. Trumble zip back and forth through the greenish water. "She seems like a very disciplined, determined young lady."

"Not so young," Laverne said. "She's three years older than I am."

"It's still young to me," I said. "But I was born old. Anyway, it must be fun having your sister here for company."

"Yeah," she said and took a gulp of her drink.

Suddenly she whisked away her straw hat and tossed it onto the grass. She shook her head a few times so her long blond hair swung free. It was not chemically brazen but softly tinted with reddish accents. I thought it quite attractive.

Her body, barely restrained by that minuscule bikini, was something else. It would be ungentlemanly to call it vulgar, but there was something fulsome about her flesh. There was just so *much* of it. It was undeniably sunned to an apricot tan, and certainly well-proportioned, but the very lavishness was daunting: whipped cream on chocolate mousse.

"Listen, Archy," she said, closing her eyes against the sun's glare. "Do you think you'll get Peaches back?"

"I'm certainly going to try. Could you show me the ransom note you received?"

"Harry's got it. He keeps it in the office safe. In the stockroom."

That was probably accurate since I happened to know she had worked for a year as receptionist in Harry Willigan's office. Then, discovering the boss's son was happily married, had children, and lived in Denver, she had done the next best thing: she had married the boss.

"All right," I said, "I'll see him later. How much are the catnappers asking?"

She opened her eyes and stared at me. "Fifty thousand," she said softly.

"Gol-*lee!* That's a lot of money for a cat."

"Harry will pay it if he has to," she said. "Sometimes I think he loves that stupid animal more than he does me."

"I doubt that," I said, but I wasn't certain. "When did Peaches disappear?"

"Last Wednesday. Harry was at work, I was at the beauty parlor, and Ruby Jackson—she's our housekeeper and cook—had the day off. So only Leon and Julie Blessington were here. She's the maid."

"Where was your sister?"

"Gone to town to look for a place to live. She wants her own apartment. Anyway, it was around one o'clock in the afternoon when Leon and Julie realized Peaches was gone. They searched all over but couldn't find her."

"Maybe she just wandered off or went hunting mice and lizards."

Laverne shook her head. "Peaches is a house cat. We never let her out, because she's been declawed and can't defend herself. Sometimes she went into the screened patio to get some fresh air or sleep on the tiles, but she never went outside. The back patio door is always kept closed."

"Locked?"

"No. But at night the door from the hallway to the patio is locked, bolted, and chained. So if anyone got into the patio at night, what could they steal—aluminum furniture?"

"But during the day, if Peaches was on the patio and no one was around, any wiseguy could nip in, stuff her in a burlap sack, and lug her away?"

"That's about it. Harry is fit to be tied. He screamed like a maniac at Leon and Julie, but it really wasn't their fault. They couldn't watch the damned cat every minute. Whoever thought she'd be kidnapped?"

"Catnapped," I said. "Leon and Julie are sure the outside door to the patio was closed?"

"They swear it was."

"No holes in the screening where Peaches might have slipped through?"

"Nope. Go look for yourself."

"I'll take your word for it. When did the ransom note arrive?"

"Thursday morning. Leon found it under the front door."

"I'll see it at Harry's office, but can you tell me what it said?"

She picked up her straw hat from the grass, clapped it on her head, tilted it far down in front to shade her eyes. She squirmed to find a more comfortable position in her canvas sling. I wished she hadn't done that. She took a deep breath and stretched, arching her back. I wished she hadn't done that.

"The note said they had taken Peaches and would return her in good health for fifty thousand dollars. If we went to the cops, they'd know about it and we'd never see Peaches alive again."

"Did they say how the payment was to be made?"

"No, they said we'd be hearing from them again."

"You keep using the plural. Did the note say *we* have the cat and you'd be hearing from *them?*"

"That's what it said."

"Uh-huh. Was the note in an envelope?"

"Yes. A plain white envelope."

"Was it typed or handwritten?"

"I thought it was typed, but Harry said it had been done on a word processor."

"That's interesting. Is Peaches on a special diet?"

"She eats people-type food, like sautéed chicken livers and poached salmon. Things like that."

"Lucky Peaches," I said. "Well, I can't think of any more questions to ask."

"What will you do now, Archy?"

"Probably go to Harry's office and get a look at the ransom note. It may have—"

I stopped speaking and rose to my feet as I became aware that Margaret Trumble was approaching from the pool, drying her hair with a towel. There wasn't much to dry. Her hair was fairer than her sister's, almost silver, and cut quite short. In fact, she had a "Florida flattop," clipped almost to the scalp at the sides and back, with the top looking like a truncated whisk-broom.

I must admit she wore this bizarre hairdo with panache, as if other people's opinions were not worth a fig. But I found her coiffure charming, perhaps because her face was strong enough to carry it. Good cheekbones there, and a chin that was assertive without being aggressive.

Laverne introduced us, lauding me as "one of my dearest friends"—which was news to me. Meg Trumble's handclasp was firm but brief. She coolly nodded her acknowledgment of my presence—obviously an exquisite joy to her—and began toweling her bare arms and legs.

"How do you like South Florida, Miss Trumble?" I inquired politely.

She paused to look about at the azure sky, green lawn, palms, and a sumptuous royal poinciana.

"Right now it's beautiful," she said. Her voice was deep and resonant, totally unlike Laverne's girlish piping.

"Oh yes," I said. " 'What is so rare as a day in June?' "

She looked directly at me for the first time. "Keats?" she asked.

"Lowell," I said, reflecting that though she might not know poetry, her pectorals were magnificent. "You're an excellent swimmer," I told her. "Do you compete?"

"No," she said shortly. "There's no money in it. Do you swim?"

"Wallow is more like it," I confessed.

She nodded again, as if wallowing was to be expected from a chap who wore a teal polo shirt and madras slacks.

"Laverne," she said, "I'd like to use the Porsche this afternoon. Can Leon drive me in?"

Her sister pouted. "I want Leon to get busy on the silver; it's getting so tarnished." She turned to me. "Archy, the Porsche is at the garage in West Palm for a tune-up. They phoned that it's ready. Could you drive Meg in to pick it up?"

"Of course," I said. "Delighted."

"That's a good boy," she said. "Meg, Archy will drive you to the garage and you can use the Porsche all afternoon. How does that sound?"

"Fine," the other woman said, expressing no gratitude to me. "I'll get dressed. I won't be long, Mr. McNally."

"Listen, you two," Laverne said. "Enough of that 'Miss Trumble' and 'Mr. McNally' crap. Be nice. Make it Meg and Archy. Okay?"

"Brilliant suggestion," I said.

The sister gave me a frosty smile and headed for the house.

"Don't mind her," Laverne advised me. "She's coming down off a heavy love affair that went sour."

"Oh? What happened?"

"It turned out the guy was married. Now she's in an 'All men should drop dead' mood. Treat her gently, Archy."

"That's the way I always treat women who lift weights," I said. "Thank you for the drink, Laverne. Please call me at my office or home if you hear from the catnappers. And I'll let you know if I learn anything about Peaches."

"I don't much care," she said, "but when Harry is miserable he makes sure everyone is miserable, if you know what I mean. So find that lousy cat, will you."

I bid her adieu and was standing next to the Miata puffing my first English Oval of the day when Meg Trumble came striding from the house. She was wearing a tank dress of saffron linen, and I saw again how slender and muscled she was. Her bare arms and legs were lightly tanned, and she had the carriage of a duchess—a nubile duchess.

I gave her the 100-watt smile I call my Supercharmer. My Jumbocharmer hits 150, but I didn't want to unnerve her. "You look absolutely lovely," I said.

"I would prefer you didn't smoke," she said.

I could have made a bitingly witty riposte and withered this haughty woman, but I did not lose the famed McNally cool. "Of course," I said, flicked my fag at a dwarf palm, and wondered why I had agreed to chauffeur Ms. Cactus.

We headed north on Ocean Boulevard, and when we passed the McNally home, I jerked my thumb. "My digs," I said.

She turned to stare. "Big," she said.

"I live with my parents," I explained, "with room enough for my sister and her brood when they come to visit. Laverne tells me you're thinking of moving down here."

"Possibly," she said.

And that was the extent of our conversation. Ordinarily I am a talkative chap, enjoying the give-and-take of lively repartee, especially with a companion of the female persuasion. But Meg Trumble seemed in an uncommunicative mood. Perhaps she believed still waters run deep. Pshaw! Still waters run stupid.

Then we were in West Palm Beach, nearing our destination when, staring straight ahead, she suddenly spoke. "I'm sorry," she said.

What a shock that was! Not only was she making a two-word speech, but she was actually apologizing. The Ice Maiden had begun to melt.

"Sorry about what?" I asked.

"I'm in such a grumpy mood," she said. "But that's no reason to make you suffer. Please pardon me."

If I had accepted that with a nod of forgiveness and said no more, I would have saved a number of people (including your humble servant) a great deal of tsores. But her sudden thaw intrigued me, and I reacted like Adam being offered the apple: "Oh boy, a Golden Delicious!"

"Listen, Meg," I said, "after I leave you I planned to have a spot of lunch and then go back to my office. But why don't you have lunch with me first, and then I'll drive you to the garage."

She hesitated, but not for long. "All right," she said.

We went to the Pelican Club. This is mainly an eating and drinking establishment, although it is organized as a private social club. I am one of the founding members, and it is my favorite watering hole in South Florida. The drinks are formidable and the food, while not haute cuisine, is tasty and chockablock with calories and cholesterol.

The place was crowded, and I waved to several friends and acquaintances. All of them eyeballed Meg; the men her legs, the women her hairdo. Such is the way of the world.

I introduced her to Simon Pettibone, a gentleman of color who doubles as club manager and bartender. His wife, Jas (for Jasmine), was housekeeper and den mother; his son, Leroy, was our chef, and daughter Priscilla worked as waitress. The Pelican could easily be called The Pettibone Club, for that talented family was the main reason for our success. We had a waiting list of singles and married couples eager to become full-fledged members, entitled to wear the club's blazer patch: a pelican rampant on a field of dead mullet.

Priscilla found us a corner table in the rear of the dining room. "Love your hair," she said.

"Thank you," I said.

"Not you, dummy," Priscilla said, laughing. "I'm talking to the lady. Maybe I'll get me a cut like that. You folks want hamburgers?"

"Meg?" I asked.

"Could I get something lighter? A salad perhaps?"

"Sure, honey," Priscilla said. "Shrimp or sardine?"

"Shrimp, please."

"Archy?"

"Hamburger with a slice of onion. French fries."

"Drinks?"

"Meg?"

"Do you have diet cola?"

"With your bod?" Priscilla said. "You should be drinking stout. Yeah, we got no-cal. Archy?"

"Frozen daiquiri, please."

"Uh-huh," she said. "Now I know it's summer."

She left with our order. Meg looked around the dining room. "Funky place," she observed.

"It does have a certain decrepit appeal," I admitted. "How come no hamburger? Are you a vegetarian?"

"No, but I don't eat red meat."

"I know you don't smoke. What about alcohol?"

"No."

"Then you must have a secret vice," I said lightly. "Do you collect cookie jars or plastic handbags?"

Suddenly she began weeping. It was one of the most astonishing things I've ever seen. One moment she was sitting there quite composed, and the next moment tears were streaming down her cheeks, a perfect freshet. Then she hid her face in her palms.

I can't cope with crying women. I just don't know what to do. I sat there helplessly while she quietly sobbed. Priscilla brought our drinks, stared at Meg, then glared at me. I knew she thought I had been the cause of the flood: Priscilla believed breaking hearts was my hobby. Ridiculous, of course. I may be a philanderer, but if there is one thing I have inherited from my grandfather (a burlesque comic) it is this inflexible commandment: Always leave 'em laughing when you say goodbye.

"Look, Meg," I said awkwardly, "did I say the wrong thing?"

She shook her head and blotted her face with a paper napkin. "Sorry about that," she said huskily. "A silly thing to do."

"What was it?" I asked. "A bad memory?"

She nodded and tried to smile. A nice try but it didn't work. "I thought I was all cried out," she said. "I guess I'm not."

"Want to talk about it?" I asked.

"It's so banal," she said. "You'll laugh."

"I won't laugh," I said. "I promise."

Priscilla brought our food, glanced at Meg, gave me a scowl, then left us again. While we ate our lunch, Meg told me the story of her demolished romance. She had been right: it *was* banal.

It had been a high-voltage affair with a handsome rogue. He had vowed undying love and proposed marriage, but continually postponed the date: he wanted to build up his bank account, his mother was ill, his business was being reorganized, etc. The excuses went on for almost two years.

Then a girlfriend brought Meg a newspaper from her swain's town. He had won a hefty prize in the state lottery. The front-page photograph showed him grinning at the camera, his arm about the waist of a woman identified as his wife. That was that.

"I was a fool," Meg said mournfully. "I don't blame him as much as I blame myself—for being such an idiot. I think that's what hurts the most, that I could have been tricked so easily."

"Did you enjoy the relationship?" I asked.

She toyed with her salad a moment, head lowered. "Oh yes," she said finally, "I did. I really liked him, and we had some wonderful times together."

"So it's really a bruised ego that makes you weep."

She sighed. "I guess I always had a high opinion of my intelligence. I know better now."

"Nonsense," I said. "Intelligence had nothing to do with it. It's your emotions that were involved, and you were too trusting, and so you were vulnerable and got hurt: a constant risk for the hopeful. But would you rather be a crusty cynic who denies all possibility of hopes coming true?"

"No," she said, "I don't want to be like that."

"Of course you don't," I said. "Meg, when one is thrown from a horse, the accepted wisdom is to mount and ride again as soon as possible."

"I don't think I'm ready for that."

"You will be," I assured her. "You're too young, too attractive to be grounded."

Then we finished our lunch in silence. I was happy to note that despite her sorrow she had a good appetite: she emptied the really enormous salad bowl.

"Basil," she said.

"I beg your pardon," I said. "The name is Archy."

She laughed. "In the salad, silly. It was delicious. Archy, are you really one of Laverne's dearest friends?"

I tried to raise one eyebrow (my father's shtick) and failed miserably. "Not quite," I said. "Your sister has a penchant for hyperbole."

"You mean she lies?"

"Of course not. She just exaggerates occasionally to add a little spice to life. Nothing wrong with that. No, my relationship with your sister and brother-in-law is more professional than personal."

I handed over my business card and explained that I had been assigned by McNally & Son to locate the missing feline—the reason for my visit to *Casa Blanco*. I asked Meg when she had last seen Peaches, and she corroborated what Laverne had told me: she had been apartment hunting on the day the cat disappeared.

"Meg, do you think anyone on the staff might have had a hand in the catnapping?"

"I really don't know," she said. "None of them liked Peaches. And I didn't either."

"Glad to hear it," I said, and told her the story of how the beast had regurgitated on my lavender suede loafers.

She laughed again and leaned forward to put a hand lightly on my arm. "Thank you for making me laugh, Archy," she said. "I was afraid I had forgotten how."

"Laughter is medicine," I pontificated. "Even better than chicken soup. You must promise to have at least one good giggle a day, preferably just before bedtime."

"I'll try, doctor," she vowed.

Coffee was another of her no-no's and neither of us wanted dessert, so I signed the tab and we went out to the Miata. I drove Meg to the garage and just before she got out of the car she thanked me for lunch.

"And for being such a sympathetic listener," she said. "I feel better. I hope I see you again."

"You shall indeed," I said, meaning that I would probably be nosing about *Casa Blanco* frequently in my search for Peaches.

But she looked intently into my eyes and repeated, "I do want to see you again," and then whisked away.

There was no misinterpreting that; it seemed evident Ms. Trumble was ready to ride a horse again, and I was the nag selected. I didn't know whether to be delighted or frightened. But I was certain I would not act wisely. Like most men, my life is often a contest between brains and glands. And you would do well to bet Gray Matter to place.

I returned to the McNally Building on Royal Palm Way, parked in our underground garage, and waved to Herb, the security guard. I took the elevator up to my tiny office and lo! on my desk was a telephone message: I was requested to call Consuela Garcia as soon as possible. I did.

"Hi, Connie," I said. "What's up?"

"Who was that baldy you had lunch with at the Pelican?" she demanded.

I believe it was Mr. Einstein who stated that nothing can move faster than the speed of light. It's obvious Albert had no knowledge of the Palm Beach grapevine.

Chapter 2

I spent at least fifteen minutes trying to placate Connie. I explained that the luncheon had been professional business, part of an investigation into a catnapping. I said that Margaret Trumble, sister of Mrs. Laverne Willigan, had valuable testimony to offer, and I needed to question her away from the scene of the crime.

"Is she living with the Willigans?" Connie asked.

"Visiting."

"For how long?"

"I have no idea."

"Are you going to see her again?"

"If my investigation requires it," I said. "Connie, I am shocked— *shocked!*—by your suspicious tone. I only met Meg this morning and—"

"Oh-ho," she said bitterly, "it's *Meg*, is it?"

"Holy cow!" I burst out. "Laverne insisted I address her sister as Meg, and I complied as a matter of courtesy. Connie, your attitude is unworthy of you. What happened to our decision to have an open relationship: both of us free to date whomever we choose?"

"So you *are* going to see her again!"

"Only in the line of business."

"Just make sure it's not monkey business, buster," she said darkly. "Watch your step; my spies are everywhere."

And she hung up.

I did not take lightly her warning of "spies." Consuela Garcia was secretary to Lady Cynthia Horowitz, one of our wealthiest and most socially active matriarchs. Connie knew everyone in Palm Beach worth knowing, and many who weren't. I had no doubt that she was capable of keeping tabs on my to-and-froing. After all, Palm Beach is a small town, especially in the off-season.

It was a sticky situation but, I reflected, there was more than one way to skin a cat. And recalling that old saw brought me back to the search for the missing Peaches. I only hoped the catnappers were also aware of the ancient adage.

I phoned Harry Willigan's office, and a male receptionist answered. His employment, I reckoned, was Laverne's doing; after marrying the boss, she wanted her hubby's office cleared of further temptations. Smart lady. Harry had the reputation of being a willing victim of satyriasis.

I identified myself and asked for a personal meeting with Mr. Willigan as soon as possible. The receptionist was gone a few moments and then came back on the line to say that if I could come over immediately, I would be granted an audience to last no longer than a half-hour. I told him I was on my way.

Willigan's office was only a block from the McNally Building. Ten minutes later I was seated alongside the tycoon's littered desk, trying hard to conceal my distaste for a man who apparently thought a silk cowboy shirt with bolo tie and diamond clasp, silver identification bracelet, gold Piaget Polo, and a five-carat pinky ring were evidence of merit and distinction.

He was built like a mahogany stump and, to carry the arboreal analogy farther, his voice was a rough bark. I imagined he might have been a good-looking youth, but a lifetime of sour mash and prime ribs had taken their toll, and now his face was a crumpled road map of burst capillaries. The nose had the hue and shape of a large plum tomato.

"What are you doing about Sweetums?" he screamed at me.

I quietly explained that I had barely started my investigation but had already visited his home to learn the details of the catnapping from his wife. I intended to return to question the servants and make a more detailed search of the premises.

"No cops!" he shouted. "Those bastards claim they'll kill Peaches if I go to the cops."

I assured him I would not inform the police, and asked to see the ransom note. He had taken it from the safe prior to my arrival and flung it at me across the desk. I questioned how many people had handled it. The answer: he, Laverne, his receptionist, Leon Medallion and perhaps the other servants at *Casa Blanco*. That just about eliminated the possibility of retrieving any usable fingerprints from the note.

It was neatly printed on a sheet of good paper, and appeared to have been written on a word processor, as Willigan had told his wife. What caught my eye was the even right-hand margin. The spacing between words had been adjusted so that all lines were the same width. Rather rare in a ransom note— wouldn't you say?

I asked if he had received any further communication from the catnappers, and Willigan said he hadn't. I then inquired if there was anyone he thought might have snatched the cat. Did he have any enemies?

He glowered at me. "I got more enemies than you got friends," he yelled. (A comparison I did not appreciate.) "Sure, I got enemies. You can't cut the mustard the way I done without making enemies. But they're all hard guys. They might shoot me in the back, but they wouldn't steal my Sweetums for a lousy fifty grand. That's penny-ante stuff to those bums."

I couldn't think of any additional questions to ask, so I thanked Willigan for his time and rose to leave. He walked me to the door, a meaty hand clamped on my shoulder.

"Listen, Archy," he said in his normal, raucous voice, "you get Peaches back okay and there's a nice buck in it for you."

"Thank you," I said stiffly, "but my father pays me a perfectly adequate salary."

"Oh sure," he said, trying to be jovial, "but a young stud like you can always use a little extra change. Am I right?"

Wretched man. How Laverne could endure his total lack of couth, I could not understand. But I suspected the Bloody Marys with fresh horseradish helped.

I walked back to the McNally Building, swung aboard the Miata, and headed for home. The old medulla oblongata had enough of the misadventure of Peaches for one day. I gave all those bored neurons a treat by turning my thoughts to Meg Trumble and Laverne Willigan.

I found it amazing that the two were sisters. I could see a slight resemblance in their features, but their carcasses were totally dissimilar. If they stood side by side, Meg on the left, they'd look like the number 18.

And their personalities were so unlike. Laverne was a bouncy extrovert, Meg more introspective, a *serious* woman. I thought she was not as coarsely woven as Laverne, not as many slubs. As of that moment I was not smitten, but she intrigued me. There was a mystery to her that challenged. Laverne was about as mysterious as a baked potato.

I pulled into the driveway of the McNally castle, a tall Tudorish pile with a mansard roof of copper that leaked. I parked on the graveled turn-around in front of our three-car garage, making sure I did not block the entrance to the left-hand bay where my father always sheltered his big Lexus. The middle space was occupied by an old, wood-bodied Ford station wagon, used mostly for shopping and to transport my mother's plants to flower shows.

I found her in the small greenhouse talking to her begonias, as usual. Her name was Madelaine, and she was a paid-up member of the Union of Ditsy Mommies. But she was an absolutely glorious woman, warm and loving. I had seen her wedding pictures, when she became Mrs. Prescott McNally, and she was radiant then. Now, pushing seventy, she was even more beautiful. I speak not as a dutiful son but as an eager student of pulchritude. (I carried in my wallet a small photo of Kay Kendall.)

Mother's specs had slipped down on her nose, and she didn't see me sneak up. I kissed her velvety cheek, and she closed her eyes.

"Ronald Colman?" she asked. "John Barrymore?"

"Tyrone Power," I told her.

"My favorite," she said, opening her eyes. "He was so wonderful in *The Postman Always Rings Twice*."

"Mother, that was John Garfield."

"I loved him, too," she said. "Where have they all gone, Archy?"

"To the great Loew's in the sky," I said. "But I'm still here."

"And I love you most," she said promptly, patting my cheek. "Ursi is baking scallops tonight. Isn't that nice?"

"Perfect," I said. "I'm in a scallopy mood. Ask father to open one of those bottles of muscadet he's been hoarding."

"Why don't you ask him, Archy?"

"Because he'll tell me that a jug chablis is good enough. But if you ask, he'll break out the good stuff. He's putty in your hands."

"He is?" she said. "Since when?"

I kissed her again and went up to my suite to change. "Suite" is a grandiloquent word to describe a small sitting room, cramped bedroom, and claustrophobic bathroom on the third floor. But you couldn't beat the rent. Zip. And it was my private aerie. I had no complaints whatsoever.

I pulled on modest swimming trunks (shocking pink), a terry coverup, and sandals. Then I grabbed a towel and went down to the beach. The Atlantic was practically lapping at our doorstep; just cross Ocean Boulevard and there it was, shimmering in the late afternoon sunlight. The chop was not strong enough to give me second thoughts.

I try to swim two miles a day. Not out and back; that's for idiots. I swam parallel to the shore, about fifty feet out. I go a mile north or south and then return. I don't exactly wallow, as I told Meg Trumble, but I sort of plow along. However, since it is the only physical exercise I get—other than an occasional game of darts at the Pelican Club—it makes me feel virtuous and does wonders for the appetite. And thirst.

My father is very big on tradition. One of the ceremonies he insists on honoring is the cocktail hour, a preprandial get-together that usually lasts thirty minutes during which we imbibe martinis he mixes to the original formula of three parts gin to one of vermouth. Not dry enough for you? Complain to Prescott McNally, but be prepared to face a raised eyebrow—and a hairy one at that.

"Are you going out tonight, Archy?" my father asked that evening at the family gathering.

"No, sir," I said, "I hadn't planned to."

"Good," he said. "Roderick Gillsworth phoned this afternoon and wants to come over at nine o'clock. It concerns some matter he didn't wish to discuss at the office."

"And you want me to be present?" I asked, somewhat surprised.

The governor chomped on his olive which, in a small departure from his love of the hallowed, had been stuffed with a sliver of jalapeño. "Yes," he said, "Gillsworth particularly asked that you sit in."

"And how is Lydia?" mother asked, referring to the client's wife.

Father knitted his brows which, considering their hirsuteness, might have resulted in a sweater. "I asked," he said, "but the man didn't give me a direct answer. Very odd. Shall we go down to dinner?"

The scallops were super, the flavor enhanced by a muscadet the lord of the manor had consented to uncork. He's inclined to be a bit mingy with his vintage wines. It makes little difference to mother, who drinks only sauterne with dinner—a dreadful habit my father and I have never persuaded her to break. But I like a rare wine occasionally: something that doesn't come in a bottle with a handle and screw-top.

For dessert, Ursi Olson, our cook-housekeeper, served big slices of a succulent honeydew with wedges of fresh lime. Surfeited, I climbed upstairs to my cave and did a spot of work before Roderick Gillsworth arrived.

During discreet inquiries in the past I had learned to keep a record of my investigations in a ledger. I have a tendency to forget things that may or may not turn out to be important.

So I scribbled short notes on the cases in which I was engaged. That evening I started a new chapter on the catnapping of the malevolent Peaches. I jotted down everything I had learned during the day, which wasn't a great deal. When finished, I put my completed notes aside and glanced at my Mickey Mouse wristwatch (an original, not a reproduction). I saw that I had a quarter-hour before my presence was required in my father's study, to listen to what was troubling our client. I spent the time recalling what I knew of Roderick Gillsworth.

He was a poet, self-proclaimed. His first book, *The Joy of Flatulence*, was so obscure and prolix that critics were convinced he was a genius, and on the strength of their ecstatic reviews *TJOF* sold 527 copies. But Gillsworth's subsequent volumes didn't do as well, and he accepted employment as poet-in-residence at an exclusive liberal arts college for women in New Hampshire.

There he married one of his students, Lydia Barkham. She was heiress to a fortune in old money accumulated by a Rhode Island family that began by making string, graduated to rope, moved on to steel cables, and eventually sold out to a Japanese conglomerate at such a humongous price that one financial commentator termed it "Partial revenge for Pearl Harbor."

Lydia and Roderick Gillsworth moved to Palm Beach in the late 1970s and, despite their wealth, bought a relatively modest home on Via Del Lago, about a block from the beach. They lived quietly, entertained infrequently, and apparently had little interest in tennis, golf, or polo. This did not make them pariahs, of course, but they were considered somewhat odd. According to Palm Beach gossips (the entire population) the Gillsworths had what the French label a *mariage blanc,* and what your grandmother probably called a "marriage in name only." Naturally I cannot vouch for that.

Roderick continued to write poetry, but now his slim volumes were privately printed, handsomely bound in calfskin, and given as Christmas gifts to personal friends. The McNally family had eight of his books, the pages still uncut. The most recent collection of his poems was titled *The Cross-Eyed Atheist.*

When I entered my father's study on the ground floor, Gillsworth was already lounging in a leather wing chair. I went over to shake his hand and he didn't bother rising. I was an employee and about ten years younger than he, but I still felt it was bad manners. My father sat behind his big leather-topped desk, and I drew up a straight chair and positioned it so that I could observe both men without turning my head back and forth.

"Archy," the don said, "Mr. Gillsworth apparently has a personal problem he wishes to discuss. He is aware of your responsibility for discreet inquiries and the success you have achieved in several investigations with a minimum of publicity."

"No publicity," the poet said sharply. "I must insist on that: absolutely no publicity. Lydia would never forgive me if this got out."

Father stroked his mustache with a knuckle. That mustache was as bristly as his eyebrows, but considerably wider. It was the Guardsman's type and stretched the width of his face, a thicket that was a sight to behold when he was eating barbecued ribs. "Every effort will be made to keep the matter confidential, Mr. Gillsworth," he said. "What exactly *is* it?"

Our client drew a deep breath. "About three weeks ago," he began, "a letter arrived at our home addressed to my wife. Plain white envelope, no return address. At the time Lydia was up north visiting cousins in Pawtucket. Fortunately she had left instructions to open her mail and forward to Rhode Island whatever I thought important and might require her immediate attention. I say 'fortunately' because this particular letter was a vicious threat against Lydia's life. It spelled out the manner of her murder in such gruesome and sickening detail that it was obviously the product of a deranged mind."

"Dreadful," my father said.

"Did the letter give any reason for the threat?" I asked.

"Only in vague terms," Gillsworth said. "It said she must die to pay for what she is doing. That was the phrase used: 'for what she is doing.' Complete insanity, of course. Lydia is the most innocent of women. Her conduct is beyond reproach."

"Do you have the letter with you, Mr. Gillsworth?" father asked.

The poet groaned. "I destroyed it," he said. "And the envelope it came in. I hoped it might be a single incident, and I had no wish that Lydia would ever find and read that piece of filth. So I burned it."

Then we sat in silence. Gillsworth had his head averted, and I was able to study him a moment. He was a tall, extremely thin man with a bony face split by a nose that ranked halfway between Cyrano and Jimmy Durante.

He was wearing a short-sleeved leisure suit of black linen. With his mighty beak, scrawny arms, and flapping gestures he looked more bird than bard. I wondered what a young coed had seen in the poet that persuaded her to plight her troth. But it's hopeless to try to imagine what spouses find in each other. It's better to accept Ursi Olson's philosophy. She just shrugs and says, "There's a cover for every pot."

The silence stretched, and when the seigneur didn't ask the question that had to be asked, I did.

"But you've received another letter?" I prompted Gillsworth.

He nodded, and the stare he gave me seemed dazed, as if he could not quite comprehend the inexplicable misfortune that had befallen him and his wife. "Yes," he said in a voice that lacked firmness. "Two days ago. Lydia is home now, and she opened the letter, read it, showed it to me. I thought it even more disgusting and frightening than the first. Again it said that she must die for what she was doing, and it described her murder in horrendous and obscene detail. Obviously the work of a homicidal maniac."

"How did your wife react to the letter?" my father asked gently.

Gillsworth shifted uncomfortably in his wing chair. "First," he said, "I must give you a little background. My wife has always been interested in the occult and in psychic phenomena. She believes in supernatural forces, the existence of spirits, ESP, and that sort of thing." He paused.

I was curious and asked, "Do you also believe in those things, sir?"

He made one of his floppy gestures. "I don't believe and I don't disbelieve. Quite frankly, the supernatural is of minor interest to me. My work is concerned with the conflict between the finite expression of the human psyche and the Ur-reality concealed within. I call it the Divine Dichotomy."

My father and I nodded thoughtfully. What else could we do?

"To answer your question, Mr. McNally," Gillsworth continued, addressing mein papa, "my wife reacted to the letter with complete serenity. You may find it remarkable—I certainly do—but she has absolutely no fear of death, no matter how painful or horrid its coming. She believes death is but another form of existence, that we pass from one state to another with no loss, no diminution of our powers, but rather with increased wisdom and added strength. This belief—which she holds quite sincerely, I assure you—

enables her to face her own death with equanimity. And so that letter failed to frighten her—if that was its purpose. But it frightens *me,* I can tell you that. I suggested to Lydia that it might be wise if she returned to Rhode Island for an extended visit until this whole matter can be cleared up."

"Yes," father said, "I think that would be prudent."

"She refused," Gillsworth said. "I then suggested both of us take a trip, perhaps go abroad for a long tour. Again she refused. She will not allow the ravings of a lunatic to alter her life. And she is quite insistent that the matter not be referred to the police. She accepts the entire situation with a sangfroid that amazes me. I cannot take it so lightly. I finally won her permission to seek your counsel with the understanding that you will make no unauthorized disclosure of this nasty business to the police or anyone else."

"You may depend on it," my father said gravely.

"Good," the poet said. "Would you care to see the second letter?"

"By all means."

Gillsworth rose and took a white envelope from his outside jacket pocket. He strode across the room and handed it to my father.

"Just a moment, please," I said. "Mr. Gillsworth, I presume only you and your wife have touched the letter since it was received."

"That's correct."

"Father," I said, "I suggest you handle it carefully, perhaps by the corners. The time may come when we might wish to have it dusted for fingerprints."

He nodded and lifted the flap of the opened envelope with the tip of a steel letter opener taken from his desk. He used the same implement to tease out the letter and unfold it on his desktop. He adjusted the green glass shade of his brass student lamp and began to read. I moved behind his shoulder and peered but, without my reading glasses, saw nothing but a blur.

Father finished his perusal and looked up at the man standing before his desk. "You did not exaggerate, Mr. Gillsworth," he said, his voice tight.

"Would you read it aloud, sir?" I asked him. "I'm afraid I left my glasses upstairs."

He read it in unemotional tones that did nothing to lessen the shock of those words. I shall not repeat the letter lest I offend your sensibilities. Suffice to say it was as odious as Gillsworth had said: a naked threat of vicious murder. The letter was triple-distilled hatred.

Father concluded his reading. The client and I returned to our chairs. The three of us, shaken by hearing those despicable words spoken aloud, sat in silence. The pater looked at me, and I knew what he was thinking. But he'd never say it, never dent my ego in the presence of a third person. That's why I loved him, the old badger. So I said it for him.

"Mr. Gillsworth," I said as earnestly as I could, "I must tell you in all honesty that although I appreciate your confidence in me, I am beyond my depth on this. It requires an investigation by the local police, post office inspectors, and possibly the FBI. Sending a threat of physical harm through the mail is a federal offense. The letter should be analyzed by experts: the typewriter used, the paper, psychological profile of the writer, and so forth. It's possible that similar letters have been received by other Palm Beach residents, and yours may provide a vital lead to the person responsible. I urge you to take this to the proper authorities as soon as you can."

My father looked at me approvingly. "I fully concur with Archy's opinion," he said to Gillsworth. "This is a matter for the police."

"No," the poet said stonily. "Impossible. Lydia has expressly forbidden it, and I cannot flout her wishes."

Now my father's glance at me was despairing. I knew he was close to rejecting Gillsworth's appeal for help, even if it meant losing a client.

"Mr. Gillsworth," I said, leaning toward him, "would you be willing to do this: Allow me to meet and talk with your wife. Let me try to convince her how seriously my father and I take this threat. Perhaps I can persuade her that it really would be best to ask the authorities for help."

He stared at me an excessively long time. "Very well," he said finally. "I don't think it will do a damned bit of good, but it's worth a try."

"Archy can be very persuasive," my father said dryly. "May we keep the letter, Mr. Gillsworth?"

The poet nodded and rose to leave. Handshakes all around. My father carefully slid the opened letter into a clean manila file folder and handed it to me. Then he walked Roderick Gillsworth out to his car. I carried the folder up to my cave and flipped on the desk lamp.

I put on my glasses and read the letter. It was just *awful* stuff. But that wasn't what stunned me. I saw it was on good quality paper, had been written with a word processor, and had an even right-hand margin.

How does that grab you?

Chapter 3

I went to sleep that evening convinced that the Peaches letter and the Gillsworth letter had been written on the same machine, if not by the same miscreant. But what the snatching of a cranky cat had to do with a murderous threat against a poet's wife, the deponent kneweth not.

I awoke the next morning full of p. and v., eager to devote a day to detecting and sorry I lacked a meerschaum pipe and deerstalker cap. Unfortunately I also awoke an hour late, and by the time I traipsed downstairs my father had left for the office in his Lexus and mother and Ursi had taken the Ford to go provisioning. Jamie Olson was seated in the kitchen, slurping from a mug of black coffee.

We exchanged matutinal greetings, and Jamie—our houseman and Ursi's husband—asked if I wanted a "solid" breakfast. Jamie is a septuagenarian with a teenager's appetite. His idea of a "solid" breakfast is four eggs over with home fries, pork sausages, a deck of rye toast, and a quart of black coffee—with maybe a dram of aquavit added for flavor. I settled for a glass of OJ, buttered bagel, and a cup of his coffee—strong enough to numb one's tonsils.

"Jamie," I said, sitting across the table from him, "do you know Leon Medallion, the Willigans' butler?"

"Uh-huh," he said.

Our Swedish-born houseman was so laconic he made Gary Cooper sound like a chatterbox. But Jamie had an encyclopedic knowledge of local scandals—past, present, and those likely to occur. Most of his information came from the corps of Palm Beach servants, who enjoyed trading tidbits of gossip about their employers. It was partial recompense for tedious hours spent shining the master's polo boots or polishing milady's gems.

"You ever hear anything freaky about Leon?" I asked. "Like he might be inclined to pinch a few pennies from Mrs. Willigan's purse or perhaps take a kickback from their butcher?"

"Nope."

"How about the cook and the maid? Also straight?"

Jamie nodded.

"I know Harry Willigan strays from the hearth," I said. "Everyone knows that. What about his missus? Does she ever kick over the traces?"

The houseman slowly packed and lighted his pipe, an old discolored briar, the stem wound with adhesive tape. "Mebbe," he said. "I heard some hints."

"Well, if you learn anything definite, pass it along to me, please. Their cat's been swiped."

"I know."

"Have you heard anything about the Gillsworths, the poet and his wife?"

"She's got the money," Jamie said.

"That I know."

"And she's tight. He's on an allowance."

"What about their personal lives? Either or both seeking recreation elsewhere?"

"Haven't heard."

"Ask around, will you?" I urged. "Just in a casual way."

"Uh-huh," Jamie said. "The Miata could use a good wash. Get the salt off. You going to be around this morning?"

"No," I said, "I have to hit the road. But I should be back late this afternoon. I'd appreciate it if you could get to it then."

"Sure," he said and accepted with a nod the tenner I slipped him. I wasn't supposed to do that, and my father would be outraged if he knew. But Jamie and I understood the pourboire was for the information he provided, not a domestic chore. The Olsons were amply paid for managing the McNally household.

I drove southward to the Willigans' hacienda. That ominous message sent to Lydia Gillsworth had given new urgency to my search for Peaches' abductors. It didn't seem incredible to me that the two cases might be connected; I had learned to accept the bizarreness of life.

Leon Medallion opened the door to my ring, and if it wasn't so early in the morning I would have sworn the fellow was smashed. His pale blue eyes were bleary and his greeting was slurred, as if he had breakfasted on a beaker of the old nasty.

He must have seen my astonishment because he said, "I ain't hammered, Mr. McNally. I got my allergies back again. I been sneezing up a storm and now I'm stuffed with antihistamines."

"So it wasn't the cat after all?"

"I guess not," he said mournfully. "But this place has enough molds and pollens to keep my peepers leaking for the rest of my life. You find Peaches?"

"Not yet, Leon. That's why I stopped by—to talk to you and the rest of the staff. Is Mrs. Willigan home?"

"Nah, she took off about a half-hour ago."

"And Miss Trumble?"

"In the pool doing her laps. The woman's a bloomin' fish. You want to talk to all us peons together?"

"Might as well," I said. "No use repeating the same questions three times."

We assembled in the big kitchen: Leon; Ruby Jackson, the cook-housekeeper; the maid, Julie Blessington; and me. Ruby was a tiny, oldish woman who looked too frail to hammer a scaloppine of veal. Julie was younger, larger, and exceedingly plain. Trust Laverne not to employ a skivvy who might light her husband's fuse.

I questioned the three of them for about twenty minutes and got precisely nowhere. Only Julie and Leon had been in the house the afternoon Peaches disappeared. They swore the back door of the screened patio had been securely closed. There were no holes in the screening through which the cat might have vamoosed.

None of the three had seen strangers hanging about recently. No one lurking in the shrubbery; nothing like that. And none could even hazard a guess as to who might have shanghaied Peaches. They all testified to Harry Willigan's mad infatuation for his pet and hinted they'd all be happy to endure the permanent loss of that irascible feline. I could understand that.

I hadn't expected to learn anything new and I didn't. I thanked them for their cooperation and wandered out to the back lawn. Meg Trumble was still slicing back and forth in the pool, wearing the shiny black maillot that looked like a body painting. She saw me approach, paused to wave, then continued her disciplined swim. I moved a sling chair into the shade and waited.

She finished her workout in about five minutes. I loved the way she got out of the pool. No ladder for her. She simply placed her hands flat on the tiled coping and in one rhythmic surge heaved up and out, a bent leg raised for a foothold. It was a joy to see, and I never could have done it in a million years.

She came padding to me across the lawn, dripping and using her palms to scrape water from hair, face, arms. "Good morning, Archy," she said, smiling. "Isn't it a lovely day?"

"Scrumptious," I said, staring at her admiringly. She really was an artfully constructed young lady. "Would you care to have dinner with me tonight?"

"What?" she said, startled.

"Dinner. Tonight. You. Me."

"I don't—" she said, confused. "I shouldn't— I better— Perhaps if—"

I waited patiently.

"May I pay my own way?" she asked finally.

"Keep talking that way," I said, "and you'll be asked to resign from the female sex. No, you may not pay your own way. I'm inviting you to have dinner with me. Ergo, you will be my guest."

"All right," she said faintly. "What shall I wear?"

I was able to repress the reply that came immediately to mind. "Something informal," I said instead. "A flannel muumuu in a Black Watch tartan might be nice."

"Are you insane?" she said.

"Totally," I assured her. "Pick you up around seven."

I left hastily before she had second thoughts. I walked through the house, down that long corridor lined with antique weapons. They made me wonder if someone might, at that very moment, be taking a scimitar to Peaches. I do believe the plight of that offensive beast was beginning to concern me.

I exited and closed the front door behind me. Took two strides toward the Miata and stopped. Turned around and rang the bell again. Eventually the butler reappeared.

"Sorry to bother you, Leon," I said, "but a question occurred to me that I neglected to ask before. Was Peaches ever taken to the vet?"

"Oh sure," he said. "Once a year for her shots, but more often than that for a bath and to have her teeth and ears cleaned. And once when she got a tapeworm."

"How was she taken? Do you have a carrier—one of those suitcase things with air holes and maybe wire mesh at one end?"

"Yeah, we got a carrier."

"Could I take a look at it, please?"

"I'll dig it out," he said and departed, leaving me standing in the foyer.

I waited. And waited. And waited. It must have been at least ten minutes before he returned. He looked flummoxed.

"Can't find the damned thing," he reported. "It's always been kept in the utility room, but it's not there now. It's probably around here somewhere."

"Sure it is," I said, knowing it wasn't. "Give me a call when you find it, will you."

I drove officeward, not pondering so much on the significance of the missing cat carrier as wondering what inspired me to ask about it in the first place. Frequently, during the course of an investigation, I get these utterly meshuga ideas. Most of them turn out to be Looney Tunes, but occasionally they lead to something important. I had a creepy feeling this particular brainstorm would prove a winner.

My office in the McNally Building had the spaciousness and ambience of a split-level coffin. I suspected my father had condemned me to that closet to prove to the other employees there was no nepotism in his establishment. But allowing me one miserable window would hardly be evidence of filial favoritism, would it? All I had was an air-conditioning vent.

So it was understandable that I rarely occupied my cubby, using it mainly as a message drop. On those rare occasions when I was forced to write a business letter, my father's private secretary, Mrs. Trelawney, typed it for me and provided a stamp. She also informed me when my salary check was available, the dear lady.

On that morning a telephone message placed precisely in the middle of my pristine desk blotter requested that I call Mrs. Lydia Gillsworth. I lighted and smoked my first cigarette of the day while planning what I might say to a woman who had received a dreadful prediction of her doom.

Actually, when I phoned, she could not have been more gracious and lighthearted. She inquired as to my health and that of my parents. She expressed regret that she did not see the McNallys more often. She said she had brought a small Eyelash begonia back from Rhode Island especially for my mother, and as soon as it recovered from jet lag, she would send it over. I thanked her.

"Now then, Archy," she said, "Roderick says you'd like to talk to me about that silly letter I received."

"If I may, please," I said. "I really don't think it should be taken lightly."

"Much ado about nothing," she said firmly. "People who mail letters like that exhaust all their hostility by writing. They never *do* anything."

"I would like to believe you're correct, Mrs. Gillsworth," I said. "But surely it will do no harm if I look into it a bit."

"Rod said you thought the police should be consulted. I will not allow that. I don't wish this matter to become public knowledge and perhaps find its way into the tabloids."

She spoke so decisively that I knew it would be hopeless to plead with her, but I reckoned her command could be finessed. I have sometimes been called "devious"; I much prefer "adroit." It calls up the image of a skilled fencer and a murmured "Touché."

"No police," I agreed. "Just a private, low-key investigation."

"Very well then," she said. "Can you come over at two o'clock this afternoon?"

"With pleasure," I said. "Thank you."

"And I'll take another look at the Eyelash begonia," she added. "If it seems fit to travel, perhaps you can carry it back to your mother."

"Delighted," I said bravely.

After she hung up, I took the box of English Ovals from my jacket, stared at it a moment, then returned it unopened to my pocket. I was attempting to renounce the things and was at the point where denying myself a cigarette yielded almost as much satisfaction as smoking one. Almost—but not quite.

I phoned Sgt. Al Rogoff at the Palm Beach Police Department. Al was a compadre of many years, and we had worked together on several cases, usually to our mutual benefit.

"Sergeant Rogoff," he answered.

"Archy McNally," I said. "How was the vacation?"

"Great," he said. "I spent a week bonefishing off the Keys."

"Liar," I said. "You spent a week in Manhattan and went to the ballet every night."

"Shhh," he said, "not so loud. If that got around, you know what a ribbing I'd take from the Joe Sixpacks?"

"Your secret is safe with me," I said. "How about lunch in an hour?"

"Nope," he said promptly. "I could make it but I'm not going to."

"Al!" I said, shocked. "Since when do you turn down a decent lunch? I'll pay the bill."

"You'll pay the bill for the food," he said, "but every time I have lunch with you I end up paying a lot more—like more work, more stress, more headaches. No, thanks. You solve your own problems."

"I have no problems," I protested. "I'm not working a case. I merely wanted to have a pleasant social get-together."

"Oh sure," he said. "When shrimp fly. I appreciate the invitation, but I'll pass."

"Well, will you at least answer one little question for me?"

"Trot it out and I'll let you know."

"Has the Department had any complaints lately from people receiving poison-pen letters? Vicious stuff. Threats of murder."

"I knew it!" Rogoff said, almost shouting. "I knew you'd never feed me without getting me involved in one of your cockamamy investigations. Who got the letter?"

"I can't tell you that," I said. "Client confidentiality. And I'm not trying to get you involved. I just want to know if it's part of a local pattern."

"Not to my knowledge," he said. "I'll ask around but I haven't heard of any similar squeals."

"Al," I said, "the crazies who mail filth like that—do they ever do what they threaten?"

"Sometimes they do," he said, "and sometimes they don't."

"Thank you very much," I said. "That's a big help."

"We're here to serve," he said. Then, gruffly, "Keep me up to speed on this, Archy. I don't like the sound of it."

"I don't either," said I, and we hung up.

I drove home for lunch reflecting that Sgt. Rogoff was right; sooner or later I'd have to get him involved. I needed professional help on the Willigan and Gillsworth letters: analysis of the paper and the printing machine used, perhaps a psychological profile of the writer. I laughed aloud at what Al's reaction would be when he learned I wanted his assistance to recover an abducted pussycat.

It was not, after all, a major criminal act. In fact, considering Peaches' personality, I didn't think it was a crime at all. I remembered *The Ransom of Red Chief,* and wondered if the case might end with the catnappers paying Harry Willigan to take back his disagreeable pet.

My mother had departed for the monthly meeting of her garden club so I lunched in the kitchen with Ursi and Jamie Olson. We had a big platter of cold cuts, a bowl of German potato salad, and the marvelous sour rye Ursi bakes once a week. We all made sandwiches, of course, with a hairy mustard and cold bottles of St. Pauli Girl to cool the fire.

It was all so satisfying that I went up to my digs for a short nap. I had a demented dream that involved Peaches wearing pajamas in convict stripes. The pj's then turned into a sleek black maillot. Can you help me, Dr. Freud?

I awoke in time to freshen up, smoke a cigarette (No. 2), and vault into the freshly washed Miata for my trip to the Gillsworth home. I was looking forward to my conversation with Lydia, a lovely woman.

She was younger than her husband by about ten years, which would put her in my age bracket. But I always thought of her as a married woman and that made her seem older. I can't explain it. Why do married people strike one as older than singles of the same age? I must puzzle that out one of these days.

Physiognomically Lydia Gillsworth was unique—at least in my experience. She had an overbite so extreme that I once heard it cruelly remarked that she was the only woman in Palm Beach who could eat corn on the cob through a picket fence. But to compensate for this anomaly she had the county's most wonderful eyes. They used to be called bedroom eyes: large, deep-set, luminous. It was almost impossible to turn one's gaze away from those seductive orbs.

And charm? A plentitude! She had the rare faculty of making you believe she thought you the most fascinating creature on God's green earth. She listened intently, she asked pertinent questions, she expressed sympathy when needed. All with integrity and dignity. Can a woman be a mensch—or is that a term reserved for honorable men? If it is, then Lydia was a menschess.

I knew the Gillsworths had no staff of live-in servants but employed a Haitian housekeeper who worked thrice a week. So I wasn't surprised when the mistress herself opened the door in answer to my knock. She drew me inside in a half-embrace and kissed my cheek.

"Archy!" she cried. "This *is* nice! Guess what I have for you."

"An autographed photo of Thelma Todd?"

"No," she said, laughing, "a pitcher of pink lemonade. Let's go out on the patio. It's a super day."

She led the way through the Gillsworth home. It was decorated in the French Country style: everything light, airy, in muted colors. Fresh flowers were abundant, and the high-ceilinged rooms seemed to float in the afternoon sunlight. Overhead fans billowed gossamer curtains, and the uncarpeted floor, random-planked and waxed to a high gloss, reflected the antique bestiary prints framed on the whitewashed walls.

The patio was small but trig. It faced west but a striped awning shielded it from the glare of the setting sun. We sat at a glass-topped table and drank iced pink lemonade from pilsners engraved with a vine design.

She wasted no time with small talk. "Archy," she said, "I do wish Roderick hadn't consulted your father and you about that letter." She was as close to petulance as I had ever seen her. "It's so embarrassing."

"Embarrassing? Mrs. Gillsworth, through no fault of yours, you have received a very venomous message. I could understand your being concerned, but why should you be embarrassed?"

"Because I seem to be causing such a foofaraw. Isn't that a lovely word? I've wanted to use it for ages. The letter doesn't bother me; it's such a stupid thing. But I am upset by the disturbance it's causing. Poor Rod hasn't been able to write a line since it arrived, and now you've been dragooned into trying to find the writer when I'm sure there are a dozen other things you'd rather be doing. That's why I'm embarrassed—because I'm causing so much trouble."

"One," I said, "I wasn't dragooned; I volunteered. Two, there is nothing I'd rather be doing than getting to the bottom of this thing. Three, your welfare is important to your husband and to McNally and Son. None of us take the matter lightly. Speaking for my father and myself, we would be derelict in our duty if we did not make every effort possible to identify the sender. And only you can help."

"I don't see how I can, Archy," she said, pouring us more lemonade. "I haven't the faintest idea who might want to murder me."

"Have you ever been threatened in person?"

"No."

"Have you had any recent arguments with anyone?"

"No."

"What about some event in your past? Can you think of anyone who might have harbored a grudge, even for years and years?"

"No."

"Have you, however unintentionally, given anyone cause to believe he or she has been injured by you, insulted, offended, or even slighted?"

"No."

I sighed. "Mrs. Gillsworth, the writer of that piece of filth is obviously not playing with a full deck. Please think hard. Is there anyone amongst your friends and acquaintances you have felt, occasionally or often, might be emotionally or mentally off the wall?"

She was silent a moment, and I hoped she was obeying my adjuration to "think hard."

"No," she said finally, "I know of no one like that."

"What about a chance meeting with someone unknown to you? A clerk in a store, for example. A parking attendant. A waiter. Have you had any problems at all with people who serve the public? Any disagreements, no matter how trivial? Complaints you've made?"

"No, I can't recall anything like that."

I could not believe this woman was deliberately lying, but I found it hard to believe her denial of any altercation whatsoever with clerk, waiter, or bureaucrat. The world being what it is, we all have occasional disputes with those being paid to serve us.

I finished my lemonade. It was a bit sweetish for my taste. Lydia attempted to fill my glass again, but I shook my head, held a palm over the glass.

"Delicious," I told her, "but I'm fighting a losing war against calories. Mrs. Gillsworth, do you know of anyone who envies you?"

She was startled, then looked at me with a wry smile. "What an odd question to ask."

"Not so odd," I said. "You are an attractive, charming lady. Everyone in Palm Beach knows you are well-to-do, if not wealthy. You are happily married to an intelligent, creative man. Your life seems to be serene and trouble-free. You have a lovely home and you dress beautifully. It appears to me that there are many reasons why you might be envied."

That discomposed her and she showed her perturbation by standing suddenly to lower the patio awning farther so that we sat in warm shade.

"You know, Archy," she said, frowning, "it has never occurred to me that I might be envied. But when you list my blessings in that fashion, I can understand why I might be. But I assure you I have never heard anyone express anything that could be construed as envy. Oh, I've had compliments on my gowns or on the house, but those were just conventional social remarks. Nothing that suggested the speaker was jealous."

Then we sat in silence a moment. I was depressed by all her negative reactions to my questions. She had given me nothing, not a hint of a lead that might give direction to my discreet inquiries. She caught my mood, because she leaned forward and placed a hand lightly on my arm.

"I'm sorry, Archy," she said softly. "I really think you should drop it."

"No, ma'am," I said stubbornly, "I won't do that. The letter you received frightens me."

She gave me a smile that surprised me. It was an amused smile, as if she appreciated my concern but thought my determination excessive.

"Let me try to explain how I feel," she said. "And give you the reason why that letter doesn't terrify me. I don't know whether or not my husband spoke to you about my faith, but I believe deeply that life is but one form of existence and what we call death is another. I believe that when we die, we pass into another world as viable as this one but much more wonderful because it is inhabited by all those who have gone before. The soul never dies. Never! So corporeal existence is just a temporary state. When we give it up, voluntarily or not, we pass to a higher spiritual plane, just as a butterfly emerges from a cocoon. I am not trying to convert you, Archy; really I'm not! I'm just trying to explain why death holds no terrors for me."

I abstained from reminding her that the death promised by the poison-pen letter involved torture and agony; it would not be a peaceful passing to her higher spiritual plane. But I was curious. "Tell me, Mrs. Gillsworth, are there many people, do you think, who share your beliefs?"

She laughed. "Many more than you think, I assure you. I call them 'kindred souls.' That's a nice, old-fashioned phrase, isn't it? Oh yes, there are many who feel as I do. Right here in Palm Beach, as a matter of fact. A number of us meet frequently to discuss out-of-body experiences and attempt to communicate with those who have already passed over."

I hoped she didn't notice, but I came to attention like a gun dog on point. "Oh?" I said, as casually as I could. "These gatherings—something like a club, are they? You meet at members' homes?"

"Not exactly," she said, seemingly gratified by my interest. "They're orchestrated by our psychic adviser and held in her home. Mrs. Gloriana. A wonderful woman. So sensitive."

"That *is* fascinating," I said, and it *was* because I now had a name. "Is she a medium? A seer?"

"*Not* a seer," Lydia said definitely. "Hertha doesn't attempt to predict the future or tell your fortune or any claptrap like that. But I suppose you might call her a medium. We prefer to think of her as a channel, our means of communication to the great beyond."

She spoke so simply and sincerely that I had no inclination to snicker. I am something of an infidel myself but I never scorn belief. If you are convinced the earth is flat, that's okay with me as long as it gives you comfort.

"And this is Mrs. Gloriana's profession?" I asked. "I mean, she does it for a living?"

"Oh yes. But don't get the idea that it's some kind of a con game. Hertha is licensed and bonded."

"But she does charge for her services?" I said gently.

"Of course she does," Mrs. Gillsworth said. "And why shouldn't she, since her talents are so special. But her fees are quite reasonable and she takes credit cards."

"Uh-huh," I said. "And these meetings—sort of like séances, are they?"

"Well . . ." she said hesitantly, "somewhat. But there are no blobs of protoplasm floating in space or weird noises. We meet in a well-lighted room, sit in a circle around a table, and hold hands. To increase our psychic power, you see. Then Mrs. Gloriana tries to communicate with the other world. Her contact is a Mayan shaman who passed over hundreds of years ago. His name is Xatyl. Through him, Hertha attempts to reach people her clients wish to question. Sometimes they are famous people but usually they are relatives. I've spoken to my great-grandmother many times."

"And communication with the, ah, deceased is made through Xatyl via Mrs. Gloriana?"

"Not always," Lydia said sharply. "The contact fails as often as it succeeds. Sometimes the departed person requested is not available, or the line of communication is too faint to produce results because our combined psychic power that particular night is simply not strong enough to allow Mrs. Gloriana to get through to Xatyl."

"Incredible," I said, shaking my head, "and positively entrancing. Does Mrs. Gloriana provide private, uh, consultations?"

"Of course she does. But she'll warn you that the chances of a successful contact are less for an individual than for a group. Because the psychic power is usually not sufficient, you see. A gathering of believers with linked hands generates much more energy than one person."

That seemed reasonable to me. If you accepted the original premise, it even sounded *logical.*

"Tell me something else," I said, "and this is just idle curiosity on my part, but has your husband ever attended the meetings with Mrs. Gloriana?"

"Oh, Rod came to three or four," she said lightly, "but then he just drifted away. He never scoffed, but he never accepted the concept wholeheartedly. Rod's interests are more intellectual than spiritual. And he's uncomfortable in groups. He needs solitude to create."

"I can appreciate that," I said. "He has his work to do, and very important work it is, too." I stood up. "Mrs. Gillsworth, I thank you for your time and hospitality."

"You intend to continue your investigation?"

I nodded. "I can't promise success, but I must try."

"I haven't been much help, have I?"

"I'm sure you've provided all the information you possibly can."

"And you promise not to take this ridiculous matter to the police? It's really of no consequence."

I made no reply. She conducted me back through the house, then suddenly stopped and put a hand on my arm.

"Wait just a moment, Archy," she said. "I must show you something I brought back from Rhode Island for Rod's collection. I found it at a country shop near Woonsocket."

Roderick Gillsworth collected antique canes and walking sticks. In fact, collecting was an absolute frenzy in Palm Beach, and the more outré the collectibles, the stronger the passion. I myself had succumbed to the madness and was buying up every crystal shotglass I could find. The star of my collection was an etched Lalique jigger.

I had seen Gillsworth's collection before, and he had some beauts, including several sword canes, one that concealed a dagger, a walking stick that held a half-pint of whiskey, and a formal evening stick which, when one peered through a small hole in the handle, revealed a tiny photo of a billowy maiden wearing nothing but long black stockings and a coy smile.

The cane Lydia had brought her husband from Rhode Island was a polished, tapered cone of ash topped with a heavy head of sterling silver in the shape of a unicorn. It really was an impressive piece, probably about two hundred years old, and I longed to know what it cost—but didn't ask, of course.

I complimented Mrs. Gillsworth on her purchase and thanked her again for the pink lemonade. But I was not to escape so easily. She brought me that Eyelash begonia intended for my mother. I thought it should have been called a Godzilla begonia but thanked Lydia once again and lugged it out to the Miata. I drove home slowly, mulling over everything I had just learned. I am an amateur muller. I get that from my father, who is a world-class muller and has been known to ponder for two minutes trying to decide whether or not to salt a radish.

Mother was still absent when I arrived home so I left the monstrous plant on her workbench in the potting shed. I had plenty of time for my ocean swim before the family cocktail hour. It was while plowing through the murky sea that I had an idea which was absolutely bonkers. What if Mrs. Lydia Gillsworth had written the poison-pen letter herself and mailed it to herself?

I could think of several possible motives. (1) She wished to elicit sympathy from friends. (2) She wanted attention from her husband, who apparently spent most of his time cuddling with his muse. (3) She yearned for a little drama in a life that had become hopelessly humdrum. (4) She herself was around the bend and was now subject to irrational impulses.

A case could be made for suspecting Lydia as the culprit, but it fell apart when I remembered the similarly printed ransom note delivered to the Willigans. I doubted if Mrs. Gillsworth even *knew* the Willigans, and it was absurd to believe her guilty of swiping their cat.

I showered and dressed carefully for my date with Meg Trumble. I was in a Bulldog Drummond mood and wore total black: raw silk jacket, jeans, turtleneck, socks, and loafers. My father took one look, elevated an eyebrow, and commented, "You look like a shadow." But of course his taste in male attire is stultified. He thinks my tasseled loafers are twee. I think of him as the Prince of Wingtips.

We sipped our martinis, and mother told us how delighted she was with Lydia Gillsworth's gift. The pater asked offhandedly if I had made any progress with the "Gillsworth matter," and I said I had not.

"And the Willigans' missing cat?" he added.

"Negative," I said, and was tempted to tell him I was convinced the two cases were connected. But I didn't, fearing he might have me certified.

We finished our drinks, and my parents went downstairs to dine. I went out to the Miata and sat long enough to smoke my third English Oval of the day, knowing that in Meg Trumble's company I would have to forgo nicotine.

Then I drove down to the Willigans' home, ruminating on where I could take Meg for dinner. It had to be someplace so distant that my presence with another woman might escape the notice of Consuela Garcia's corps of informants. I finally decided to make the journey to Fort Lauderdale.

I was familiar with W. Scott's warning about tangled webs. But I wasn't really practicing to deceive Connie.

Was I?

Chapter 4

I had suggested to Meg that she dress informally and so she did: Bermuda shorts of blue silk, a tank top the color of sea foam, and a jacket in a muted shepherd's plaid that she wore over her shoulders cape-fashion. All undoubtedly informal, but so elegantly slender was her figure and so erect her carriage that she made even casual duds look as formal as a Givenchy ball gown.

"Smashing," I told her. "Have you ever modeled?"

"I tried once," she said, "but I don't photograph well. I come out all edges and sharp corners. The photographer said I looked like a stack of slates."

"Stupid photographer," I grumbled. "He probably prefers cheeseburgers to veal piccata."

Meg laughed. "Is that the way you think of me? As veal piccata?"

"It's a splendid classic dish," I said.

I turned southward and she asked where we were going. I told her I knew a fine restaurant in Fort Lauderdale, and would she mind traveling for about an hour?

"Couldn't care less," she said. "I'm so happy to get out of that house."

"Oh?" I said. "Problems?"

"My brother-in-law," she said. "I can't stand the way he treats Laverne. The man is really a mouthy lout. I don't know how my sister puts up with him."

"Maybe she loves him," I said mildly.

Meg hooted. "Laverne loves the perks of being Mrs. Harry Willigan. But she's paying her dues. I'd never do it. If a man screamed at me the way Harry does, I'd clean his clock."

"I'll remember that."

"See that you do," she said, so solemnly that I couldn't decide if she was serious or putting me on.

I had hoped it would be a pure night, the air crystal, the sky glittering like a Cartier ad in *Town & Country*. But it was not to be. That murky ocean should have warned me; there was a squall brewing offshore, and the cloud cover was thickening.

"I think it's going to rain," Meg said.

"It wouldn't dare," I said. "I planned a romantic evening, and it's hard to be romantic when you're sopping wet."

"Oh, I don't know," she said thoughtfully, which convinced me this woman had *depths*.

Her prediction was accurate; rain began to spatter when we hit Deerfield

Beach, south of Boca Raton. I didn't think it would last long—summer squalls rarely did—but it could be a brief vertical tsunami.

"We can stop and put up the top," I told Meg, "and then continue on to Lauderdale. Or we can take potluck and stop at the first restaurant we see that offers shelter for the car. Which shall it be?"

"You call it," she said.

So we continued on, the Miata hatless and the rain becoming more determined. Then, at Lighthouse Point, I spotted a Tex-Mex joint that had a portico out front. We pulled under just in time to avoid a Niagara that would have left us bobbing in a filled bathtub.

"Good choice," Meg said. "I love chili."

Marvelous woman! Not the slightest complaint that her jacket was semi-sodden and her short hair wetly plastered to her skull. We scampered inside the restaurant, laughing, and at that moment I really didn't care if the Miata floated away in our absence.

It was not the Oak Room at the Plaza. More of a Formica Room with paper roses stuck in empty olive jars on every table. It was crowded, which I took as a good omen. We grabbed the only empty booth available and slid in. Paper napkins were jammed in a steel dispenser, and the cutlery looked like Army surplus. But the glassware was clean, and there was a bowl of pickled tomatoes, mushrooms, and jalapenos, with tortilla chips, for noshing until we ordered.

The menu, taped to the wall, was a dream come true. We studied the offerings with little moans of delight. Dishes ranged from piquant to incendiary, and I reckoned that we might have been wise to wear sweats.

The stumpy waiter who came bustling to take our order had a long white apron cinched under his armpits. He also had a mustache that Pancho Villa might have envied.

"Tonight's spassel," he announced proudly, "is pork loin basted with red *mole* sauce and served with black bean relish in a tortilla with roast tomato chili sauce. Ver' nice."

"Mild?" I asked him.

"You crazy?" he said.

But we skipped the spassel. Meg relaxed her stricture against red meat to order an appetizer of Kick-Ass Venison Chili. (I am not making it up; that's what it was called.) Her entree was Cajun Seafood Jambalaya (including crawdads) in a hot Creole sauce with garlicky sausage rice.

I went for an appetizer of Swamp Wings (fried frog legs with pepper sauce) and, for a main course, Sirloin Fajita. It was described on the menu as a grilled marinated steak basted with Jack Daniel's and served with sautéed peppers and onions and a lot of other swell stuff, all inflammatory. Meg asked for a diet cola and I ordered a bottle of Corona beer.

"And a stomach pump for two," I was tempted to add, but didn't.

I shall not attempt to describe the actual consumption of that combustible meal. Suffice to say that it was accompanied by gasps, brow-mopping, and frequent gulps of cold diet cola and Mexican beer. Our tonsils did not actually shriek in protest, but my stomach began to glow with an incandescent heat, presaging an insomniac night.

Of more importance to this narrative was our conversation that evening, for it included tidbits of information that would have aided my investigation—if I had had the wit to recognize clues in Meg's casual remarks. But I was too busy gnawing fried frog legs and swilling Corona to pay close attention. Do you suppose S. Holmes ever neglected a case because Mrs. Hudson brought him a plump mutton chop?

"Good news," Meg said, working on her chili. "I found an apartment. I already have the keys. I'm moving in tomorrow."

"Wonderful!" I said. "Where?"

"Riviera Beach. It's just a small place and I only have it till October. But the off-season rent is reasonable. I'm going to fly back to Pennsylvania, pack up more clothes and things, and then drive my Toyota back. Now I'll be able to stop freeloading on my sister."

"And get away from Harry," I added.

"That's the best part," she said. "I'll still see Laverne, of course, but not in that house."

We discussed her hope of becoming a personal trainer to Palm Beach residents seeking eternal youth through diet and exercise. I offered to supply a list of friends and acquaintances who might be potential clients.

"That would be a big help, Archy," she said gratefully. "Laverne has already given me some names, but I need more prospects. How about you?"

I laughed. "I'm really not the disciplined grunt-and-groan type. I try to do a daily swim, as I told you, and I play tennis and golf occasionally. I admit I'm hardly in fighting trim, but regular workouts are not my cup of sake. Too lazy, I suspect. I'm surprised you're willing to accept men as clients. I thought you'd limit your efforts to reducing female flab."

"Oh no," she said. "I'll be happy to train men. As a matter of fact, Harry Willigan has already volunteered to be my first client. But he's not interested in improving his health and fitness."

"No?" I said. "What is he interested in?"

I knew the answer to that, and it was just what I expected.

"Me," Meg Trumble said.

Our entrees arrived and we plunged in.

"I hope your sister isn't aware of her husband's interest," I said.

"Of course she's aware. She trusts me, but secretly she'll probably be relieved to have me out of the house."

That amused me. "If there was anything going on between you and Harry, your moving out wouldn't end it. Facilitate it more likely."

"Well, there's nothing going on," she said crossly, "and never will be. I told you what I think of that man."

"I share your opinion," I assured her. "He can be grim. It's amazing that Laverne puts up with his nonsense."

"Oh, she ignores him as much as she can. And she has other interests. She's taking tennis lessons, and she's very active in local clubs. She's at meetings two or three nights a week. But enough about Laverne and Harry. How are you making out on finding Peaches?"

"Not very well," I said. "No progress at all, except for one oddity that needs looking into."

I thought it would do no harm to tell her about the missing cat carrier. I thought it would surprise her, and that she'd immediately guess what I had already assumed: someone in the Willigan household had stuffed Peaches in the carrier and hauled her away.

But Meg kept her head lowered, picked through the jambalaya for shrimp, and said only: "Oh, I'm sure it will turn up somewhere around the house."

We finished our dinner with scoops of lemon sherbet, which helped diminish the conflagration—but not enough.

"Everything hokay?" the mustachioed waiter asked.

"Fine," I said. "If you don't mind a charred epiglottis."

I paid the tab with plastic and we went out to the Miata. I took along a handful of paper napkins and wiped the seats reasonably dry. The squall had passed, the night air was freshening, and there were even a few stars peeking out from behind drifting clouds.

"Yummy dinner," Meg said. "Thank you. I really enjoyed it."

"We must dine there again," I said. "Perhaps after the turn of the century."

The drive home was a delight. We sang "It Ain't Gonna Rain No Mo' " and several other songs of a more recent vintage. Meg had a throaty alto, and I thought we harmonized beautifully. Then, like an idiot, I suggested we do "Always," and she started weeping again. Not heaving sobs; just a quiet cry.

"Sorry," I said.

"Not your fault," she said, sniffling. "It's memories. I'll get over it."

"Of course you will," I said, not all that sure.

But she shook off the brief attack of the megrims and, spirits restored, began describing her new apartment. Suddenly she stopped.

"Hey, Archy," she said, "would you like to see it? It's not too late, is it?"

"Not late at all," I said, "and I'd like to see it."

It took a good hour to get back to Riviera Beach, but the weather improved as we drove. It became mellow with a salty breeze, palm fronds rustling, the sea providing a fine background of whispering surf. It turned out to be the pure night I had hoped for. I wish I could say the same for my thoughts.

Meg now had her own private pad; that was provocative. Even more stimulating was the fact that it was in Riviera Beach, as distant from Connie Garcia's espionage network as I could reasonably hope. The McNally luck seemed to be holding, and I resolved not to waste it. Luck is such a precious commodity, is it not? Especially on a voluptuous night in the company of a young woman whose clavicles drove me mad with longing.

I lied gamely and told Meg how attractive her apartment was. In truth, I found it utterly without charm. It had obviously been furnished as a rental property; everything was utilitarian and designed to withstand rough usage. Nondescript pictures were bolted to the walls and the dinnerware on the open kitchen shelves was white plastic and looked as if it might bounce if dropped.

"Of course it's a little bleak right now," Meg admitted. "It needs some personal things scattered about. But the air conditioner works fine and there's even a dishwasher. I can stand it till October. By that time I hope to have something better lined up."

"I'm sure you will," I said. "Is the phone connected?"

"Not yet. I'll have that done when I return. After I get settled in and fill up the fridge, I hope you'll come over for dinner."

"Love to," I said. "We'll have a housewarming."

She looked at me speculatively. "We could have one right now," she said. "It's a king-sized bed."

"I like to be treated royally," I said.

I feared she might be a white-bread lover. You know: spongy and bland. Men and women who devote all their energies to body-building and no-smoke, no-drink discipline are sometimes incapable of the kinder, gentler arts, like lovemaking.

I needn't have worried about Meg Trumble. Rather than white bread, she was pumpernickel, robust and zesty. She never used her strength to dominate, but I was always aware that her complaisance was voluntary, and so vigorous was her response to my efforts that I reckoned she could, if she wished, twist me into a pretzel.

It is generally thought that highly spiced foods act as aphrodisiacs. But I do not believe our behavior that night on coarse, motel-type sheets can be credited to Kick-Ass Venison Chili and Swamp Wings. I think Meg's fervor was partly inspired by her determination to banish aching memories, and my excitement fed on her passion.

Depleted (temporarily), we stared at each other with pleased recognition: two strangers who had discovered they spoke the same language.

"And you said you weren't in fighting trim," Meg scoffed. "You didn't mention loving trim."

"It was your doing," I told her. "Your beauty and joie de vivre. I rose to the occasion and, with your assistance, shall do so again."

"By all means," she said, moving closer.

It was a bit after midnight when we departed from Riviera Beach and headed homeward. We had tarried in her new apartment long enough to bathe together in a delightfully cramped shower stall, using a sliver of soap as thin as a potato chip. The towels had all the absorbency of alençon, but by that time nothing could lessen our beaming felicity.

I pulled into the driveway of the Willigan estate, crawled out of the car, and went around to open Meg's door. I held out a hand to assist her.

"Thank you for a lovely evening, Miss Trumble," I said, completely po-faced. "The pleasure of your company at dinner was exceeded only by the kindness of your hospitality."

"Thank you, Mr. McNally," she said, just as deadpan. "I trust our paths may cross again."

"A consummation devoutly to be wished," I said, and then we both dissolved and kissed. Lingeringly.

Science defines a kiss as the close juxtaposition of two or more orbicular muscles in a state of contraction. Science has a lot to learn.

I drove home in an ecstatic mood, knowing there would be no insomnia and no nightmares that night. And there weren't. I slept the sleep of the just.

Just exhausted and just content.

I awoke the next morning infected with a galloping case of joie de vivre I had obviously contracted from my companion of the night before. At breakfast, mother commented on my good humor and sought the cause.

"Did you have a pleasant dinner engagement, Archy?" she asked.

"Very."

"Connie?"

"No," I said. "Margaret Trumble, sister of Laverne Willigan. I think I may be in love."

My father uttered a single syllable that sounded suspiciously like "Humph."

I told him I would not be driving to the office with him that morning, as I sometimes did, but would be busy with discreet inquiries.

"Oh?" he said. "The cat?"

"No, sir," I said. "The Gillsworth letter."

He nodded. "The more important of the two. Do you have a lead?"

"Anorexic," I said. "But it's all I have."

He left for the office, mother went out to the greenhouse to bid good morning to her begonias, and I went upstairs to my den. I brought my journal up to date, which didn't take long, and then made a phone call.

"Lady Cynthia Horowitz's residence," she recited. "Consuela Garcia speaking."

"Hi, Connie," I said. "Archy. How about lunch today?"

"Love to," she said, "but can't. I'm working on the madam's Fourth of July bash, and I'm having lunch with the fireworks people."

Her friendly tone was gratifying. Obviously she had not been informed of my dinner date the previous night. And since we had agreed on an open relationship, I saw absolutely no reason to feel guilty. So why did I feel guilty?

"Another time then," I said breezily.

"When?" she asked.

Meg Trumble had said she planned to fly back to King of Prussia, so that romance would be on hold until her return. It seemed an ideal time to reassure Connie that our attachment remained intact.

"Dinner tonight?" I suggested.

"You're on," she said. "How about Tex-Mex food?" For a brief instant my world tottered, but then she went on: "There's a new place in Lantana that's supposed to have great chili. Want to try it?"

"Sounds good to me," I said bravely. "Pick you up around seven?"

"I'll be ready."

"Oh, Connie, one more thing: Did you ever hear of a woman named Mrs. Hertha Gloriana?"

"The séance lady? Of course I've heard of her. A lot of people swear she's a whiz."

"You don't happen to have her address and phone number, do you?"

"No, but I think she's listed in the Yellow Pages."

"The Yellow Pages!"

"Sure. Under Psychic Advisers. Why are you laughing?"

"I don't know," I said. "It just seems odd to have Psychic Advisers listed in the Yellow Pages. I mean, if you had a tumor, would you look in the Yellow Pages for Brain Surgeons?"

"You know, Archy," she said, "you have a freaky sense of humor."

"I guess," I said, sighing. "Thanks, Connie. See you tonight."

I went downstairs to my father's study. All his telephone directories had leather slipcovers. Stodgy? I agree. But you must understand that, to my knowledge, he was the only man in South Florida who wore rubbers when it rained.

There she was in the Yellow Pages, listed under Psychic Advisers: a two-column display ad that stated Mrs. Hertha Gloriana was licensed, bonded, provided "advice and direction," and accepted all major credit cards. It didn't say if she was a Freudian, Jungian, or W. C. Fieldsian.

I decided a personal encounter was preferable to a phone call, so I boarded the Miata and headed for West Palm Beach. That city has seven times the population of the Town of Palm Beach and, as this is written, is in the process of shedding its image as a poor country cousin and enjoying a long overdue rejuvenation.

Mrs. Hertha Gloriana's address was on Clematis Street in an area that was now awash with new office buildings, pricey boutiques, and quaint shoppes of all kinds. It would never be Worth Avenue, of course, but what will?

I had imagined the haunt of a medium would resemble one of those Dracula castles in the cartoons of Charles Addams. But Mrs. Gloriana had a fourth-floor suite in one of the new glass and stainless steel buildings.

Her office was impressive, the large, airy waiting room decorated in mauve and aqua. There was a man seated behind the receptionist's desk. He was idly leafing through a copy of *Vanity Fair* and didn't look up when I entered. He was about my age, a handsome devil in a dark, saturnine kind of way. And he was dressed beautifully. As you may have gathered, I fancy myself something of a Beau Brummell, but this dude made me look like Bozo the Clown.

He was wearing a suit of dove gray flannel that didn't come off a plain pipe rack. His shirt had white French cuffs and a collar wide enough to accommodate a knitted black silk cravat tied in a Windsor knot. The body of the shirt was striped horizontally with lavender bands. What a dandy he was!

He finally looked up. "May I help you, sir?" he inquired pleasantly enough.

"May I speak to Mrs. Gloriana, please."

He smiled. "Do you have an appointment?"

"Afraid not."

"Mrs. Gloriana prefers appointments. Would you care to set a date?"

"No possibility of seeing her now?"

He pursed his lips and appeared to be giving my request serious consideration. "Mrs. Gloriana is busy with a client at the moment. May I ask how you learned of us?"

I didn't believe mentioning the Yellow Pages would cut much ice. A personal recommendation might prove more efficacious.

"Mrs. Lydia Gillsworth suggested I consult Mrs. Gloriana."

He brightened immediately. "Mrs. Gillsworth. Of course. A charming lady."

He stood and came from behind the desk. He was a tall one and lean as a fencer. He was wearing, I noted, a heavy ring of Navaho silver set with a large turquoise in the expensive sky-blue shade.

"I'm Frank Gloriana," he said. "Hertha's husband."

We shook hands. He had a hard, bony grip.

"Archibald McNally," I said. "Happy to meet you."

He stared at me a moment. "McNally?" he repeated. "The law firm across the lake?"

"That's correct," I said. "McNally and Son. I'm the son."

His smile was cool. "I've heard excellent things about your outfit. As a matter of fact, I may need some legal advice shortly, and McNally and Son heads a short list of possibles I have drawn up."

"Glad to hear it," I said. "We have a number of specialized divisions, and I'm sure we can provide the services you require."

"I'm sure you can. Your visit here today—it concerns some legal business of your firm?"

"Oh no," I said hastily, "nothing like that. It's a personal thing, and I'm afraid you'll find it rather silly."

"Try me," he said.

"A close friend has lost his cat," I said earnestly. "Lost, strayed, or stolen. He really loves the animal and has been worried sick since it's been gone. He's advertised but with no results. It occurred to me that Mrs. Gloriana might possibly be able to give me some hints or suggestions as to where his pet can be found."

"It's possible," he said immediately. "Hertha has had remarkable success in visualizing where missing objects or people might be located. I don't believe she's ever worked on an animal before, but I see no reason why she couldn't. She once enabled a builder in Atlanta to find his missing bulldozer."

"Wonderful," I said. "Where was it?"

"In his foreman's garage," Gloriana said with a slightly sardonic smile. "Listen, why don't you make yourself comfortable out here, and I'll go in and see how much longer Hertha will be. Perhaps she'll have time to fit you in before her next appointment."

"I'd appreciate that," I said.

He departed through an inner door, closing it carefully behind him. I flopped into a mauve-and-aqua armchair alongside a glass cocktail table. It held a selection of thin books and magazines, most of them dealing with astrology, channeling, crystals, mysticism, and occult philosophies of the Far East.

There was also a stack of fliers, advertising circulars that looked as if they had been designed for mailing. A small sign read TAKE ONE—so I did. It stated that Mrs. Hertha Gloriana, a licensed and bonded adviser, would prepare a "psychic profile" for anyone providing her with the exact time, date, and place of birth, names of parents and grandparents, and a snapshot or personal possession of the sender.

The cost of the psychic profile was a hundred dollars in U.S. funds, payable in advance.

I was stuffing a copy of this intriguing offer into my jacket pocket when Frank Gloriana returned. He saw at once what I was doing.

"Our new project," he said. "What do you think?"

"It makes no promises," I observed.

"Oh no," he said quickly, "no promises. The profile merely analyzes and suggests directions the subject might wish to take that could possibly enrich their lives. It is a serious attempt to provide psychic counseling. I assure you it is not a bunko scheme."

"I never thought for a moment it was."

"We've just started," he said, "but the response to newspaper and magazine ads has encouraged me to plan a direct-mail campaign. I think it could turn out to be a very successful enterprise, and that's the reason I may need legal advice on setting up a separate business venture." He paused and laughed: a thin, toneless ha-ha. "But you didn't come to listen to my business problems. Hertha is available now. Follow me, please."

He led the way through that inner portal, down a short hallway to an interior room. The door stood open, and I could see the chamber was furnished more as a residential sitting room than a commercial office. A young woman—younger than Frank Gloriana by at least five years, I guessed—rose from a high-backed mauve-and-aqua wing chair as we entered.

"Dear," he said, "this gentleman is Archibald McNally. Mr. McNally, my wife, Hertha. I'll leave you two alone."

And he left us, closing the hall door softly behind him.

She floated to me and offered a hand so soft and tender I feared I might crush it in my sinewy paw.

"Mrs. Gloriana," I said, "this *is* a pleasure."

I had always imagined a medium as an older woman, heavy through the bosom and hips, with dyed and frizzled hair, caked makeup, a frowsy appearance, and perhaps the overwhelming scent of patchouli. In this case, all wrong. Hertha Gloriana was, if you will pardon the wordplay, a very rare medium indeed.

She was definitely a Pre-Raphaelite type, with a nimbus of chestnut hair, skin as white and smooth as wax, and features so classic they might have graced a coin. There was something ethereal in her beauty, I thought, and something delicate and unworldly in her manner. She moved slowly with a languid ease, and if she had suddenly levitated to the ceiling, I wouldn't have been a bit surprised. She was so insubstantial, you see.

"Mr. McNally," she murmured, voice low and breathy, "Frank has told me why you are here. Perhaps I can help. *Perhaps*. But I cannot promise. You do understand that, don't you?"

"Of course," I said, trying to determine the exact shade of her eyes. Periwinkle blue, I finally decided. "I would appreciate your trying."

"What is the cat's name?"

"Peaches."

"Female?"

"Yes."

"What breed?"

"Persian, I believe."

"Describe her, please."

"Plump. Silver-gray with tabby markings."

"How old?"

"I don't really know," I confessed. "Perhaps five years."

"Affectionate?"

"Not really. Not with strangers."

She nodded. "Please leave your address and phone number with my husband. If I'm able to do anything, he will contact you."

Apparently our consultation was at an end, but she continued to stare at me. Our eyes were locked, and her gaze was so intent and unblinking that I wanted to look away but could not.

She came close. She was wearing a light floral scent. She put a hand gently on my arm. "You are troubled," she said.

"About the cat? Well, yes. This close friend of mine is very—"

"No," she interrupted, "not the cat. You, personally, are troubled."

"Not really," I said, my short laugh sounding nervous to me. "Nothing I can't handle."

She continued to stare. "Two women, two loves," she said. "That is troubling you."

I wasn't impressed; it smacked too much of a fortune teller on a carnival midway. Many men—at least many I know—are frequently involved with more than one woman. It's hardly a unique situation, is it? Mrs. Gloriana was not demonstrating any special clairvoyant talent.

She stepped back and smiled: a tremulous smile, very vulnerable. "Do not worry," she told me. "The problem will eventually be solved."

"Glad to hear it," I said.

"But not by you," she added. "It was nice meeting you, Mr. McNally. I'll do my best to get a message about Peaches."

"Thank you," I said and turned away. I was at the door when I looked back. I hadn't heard her move but she was seated again in the high-backed wing chair, regarding me gravely. I made up my mind.

"Mrs. Gloriana," I said, "Lydia Gillsworth has told me of the meetings she attends during which you are sometimes able to contact those who are—who are—"

"Dead," she said.

"Yes," I said. "I was wondering if I might possibly sit in at one of your gatherings. I find the whole concept fascinating."

Her stare never wavered. "Very well," she said softly. "Ask Lydia to bring you to our next session. She knows the time and place."

"Thank you," I said again and left her sitting there, distant and complete.

There was a middle-aged couple in the waiting room, holding hands. And Frank Gloriana was seated behind the desk, impassive and doing nothing.

"Your wife said she'd let me know if she is able to help," I told him and handed over my card.

He glanced at it. "You wish to be billed at your office, Mr. McNally?"

All business, this lad.

"Please," I said. "Thank you for your assistance."

I went out into the corridor. I had a lot of impressions I needed to sort out, but there was something I wanted to do first.

When I had entered the office, Frank Gloriana had stalled me by saying the medium was busy with a client. Then, after a period of time, he reported she was now available. But I had seen no client leave the office.

That was understandable if there was another exit from the Gloriana suite. Psychiatrists frequently have such an arrangement to protect the privacy of their analysands. I mean, it would be a bit off-putting, would it not, to enter a shrink's office and bump into your spouse, lover, or boss coming out.

So, before I pushed the elevator button, I roamed the fourth-floor corridor looking for another doorway to the Gloriana offices. There was none. Which probably meant that Hertha had not been busy with another client when I arrived.

There were several innocent explanations. Frank Gloriana's prevarication might mean nothing.

Or it might mean something.

Chapter 5

On my way back to the McNally Building I stopped at Harry Willigan's office. He was in his usual vile mood, and I wondered if he got his disposition from Peaches or if the cat had learned how to be nasty from her master.

He demanded to know what progress I was making in the search for his beloved pet. Very little, I told him, but my investigation would be aided if he'd let me have a photocopy of the ransom note.

"What the hell for?" he screamed at me.

I explained as patiently as I could that I wanted the letter analyzed by an expert. The vocabulary and grammar might enable the specialist to make some shrewd guesses as to the education, occupation, nationality, and social status of the writer. That wasn't total kaka, of course; there are analysts who can glean such information from the language of a document.

Finally, Willigan had his receptionist make a photocopy for me. I folded it carefully and tucked it into my jacket pocket along with the Gloriana flier. Then I left as quickly as I could, with Willigan shouting obscene threats of the mayhem he'd wreak if he ever got his hands on those effing catnappers. I believed him.

Back in my office, I found a message on my desk asking me to call Connie Garcia as soon as possible.

"Archy," she wailed, "about tonight—Lady Horowitz wants me to come back here after dinner and go over the budget for the Fourth of July shindig with her."

"Aw," I said, "that's too bad. Want to postpone our date?"

"No," she said definitely. "I haven't seen you in ages. Instead of driving to Lantana for chili, we'll grab a bite at the Pelican Club and you can get me back here by eight-thirty or so. Okay?"

"Sure," I said, much relieved that I wouldn't have to incinerate my uvula two nights in a row. "But I guess that means no fun and games later. I'm disappointed."

"Me, too," she confessed. "It's been so long that every time I sneeze, dust comes out my ears."

"We'll have to do something about that," I said.

Long pause. Then, suspiciously:

"You haven't been making nice-nice with that Meg Trumble, have you, Archy?"

"Who?"

She sighed. "Now it's coming out *your* ears, and it's not dust. If I discover you've been cheating, you know what'll happen to you, don't you?"

"I'll be singing soprano?"

"You've got it, son," she said. "See you tonight."

She hung up, and I sat there a few minutes remembering that her Latin temper was not to be trifled with. Once, during our initial liaison, she had caught me dining with another young lady and had dumped a bowl of linguine Bolognese on my head. Took me a week of shampoos to get rid of all those damned chicken livers.

It was a dangerous game I was playing, I reflected mournfully, and wondered if a vow of celibacy might be the answer. But then I recalled Hertha Gloriana's prediction: my problem would eventually be solved, and not by me. A welcome thought. I had enough bad habits without adding chastity.

I took the Gloriana flier from my pocket and reread it. Mommy didn't raise her boy to be an idiot, and my first reaction was that the offer of individualized psychic profiles was a scoundrelly con game. I figured the Glori-anas had printed up a standard profile they mailed back to all the suckers, similar to those canned horoscopes you can buy at newsstands.

But, despite my cynicism, I found it hard to believe Hertha Gloriana was an out-and-out swindler. Husband Frank—the business manager—could be a flimflam artist capable of cutting a shady deal. But not Hertha, not that soft, vulnerable waif. Her eyes were too blue. How's that for logical deduction?

But there was a way I could test Hertha's bona fides, and I resolved to launch my mini-plot that evening. I was certain Connie Garcia would coop-erate. She'd think it was a hoot.

Musing about the Glorianas and the apparently thriving business they owned, I realized how little I knew about parapsychology. I decided it was time I learned more about what I was investigating. I phoned Lydia Gillsworth. It was then almost noon.

"Oh, Archy," she said after an exchange of cordial greetings, "I do hope this isn't about that stupid letter I received."

"Not at all," I said, lying valiantly. "This call includes a confession and a request. I was so interested in what you told me about Hertha Gloriana the other day that I went to see her this morning. I used your name shamelessly. I hope you don't object."

"Of course not. Isn't she a remarkable woman?"

"She is that," I said. "And lovely."

"Careful, Archy," Mrs. Gillsworth said, laughing. "Hertha is happily married, and Frank carries a gun."

That shook me. "Why on earth would he do that?"

"He says it's just a precaution. Sometimes they have to deal with irra-tional or deeply disturbed people."

"I can imagine," I said. "The lunatic fringe."

"Exactly," she said. "If you don't mind my asking, why did you consult Hertha?"

I told her my loopy story about the close friend whose beloved cat was missing and how I had asked Mrs. Gloriana to visualize the pet's present whereabouts. Lydia didn't think my request unusual at all.

"I'm sure Hertha will be able to help," she said. "She's very good at lo-cating lost things. She told Laverne Willigan where to find her pearl ear-rings."

I suspect that if I had been wearing dentures they might have popped out at that moment. I know my jaw flopped open and I stared about wildly to make certain the world was still there.

"And where were the earrings?" I asked hoarsely.

"Behind her dresser drawer. They had caught on the inside molding."

"I know Mrs. Willigan," I said as casually as I could. "Her husband is a client of ours. Does Laverne attend those séances Mrs. Gloriana holds?"

"Oh yes, she never misses a session."

I didn't want to push it any farther.

"That's another part of my confession, Mrs. Gillsworth," I said. "I asked

Hertha if I might sit in on one of your meetings. She said I could, and have you bring me to the next gathering."

"Of course," she said. "As a matter of fact, there's one tonight at seven o'clock."

"Ah, what a shame," I said. "I have a dinner date I dare not break. Well, I'll make certain I'm at the next one, with your kind assistance. And now the request: I'd like to learn more about spiritualism, and I wondered if you had any books on the subject you'd be willing to lend me. Return guaranteed. I'm especially intrigued about the possibility of contacting those who have, uh, departed this life for existence on another plane."

"Oh, Archy, I have a whole library of books on the subject. You'll find them fascinating, I'm sure. Suppose I select three or four that will give you the basic information on our beliefs."

"I'd certainly appreciate that. When may I pick them up?"

"Let me see . . . I have a little shopping to do, but I should be back around two o'clock. Can you stop by then?"

"Love to. Thank you so much for all your help, Mrs. Gillsworth."

I drove home for lunch and found I had the McNally manse to myself. Mother and the Olsons had departed on a shopping safari to replenish our larder, but a note left on the kitchen table informed me that a Caesar salad, heavy on the garlic, had been prepared for my pleasure and was chilling in the fridge.

I had a glass of California chablis with the salad and popped a few fresh strawberries for dessert. Then I trudged upstairs to my digs, donned my reading specs, and placed the photocopy of Peaches' ransom note next to the poison-pen letter sent to Lydia Gillsworth. I compared them carefully, and to my inexpert eye they definitely appeared to have been composed on the same machine.

Even more telling, both documents included the word "horrendous." That is not an adjective commonly used in written communications. What could I think but that both letters had quite likely been written by the same person? It was not hard evidence, I admit, but I was more convinced than ever that the catnapping and the threats against Mrs. Gillsworth were somehow connected.

I started to scrawl notes in my journal about the morning encounter with Hertha and Frank Gloriana, but I tossed my gold Mont Blanc aside, unable to concentrate.

What was confounding me was Laverne Willigan's apparent interest in spiritualism. She always seemed to me such a *physical* woman, whose main enthusiasms were chocolate eclairs, tanning her hide, and amassing expensive baubles. It came as a shock to hear she attended séances.

It was obvious I had misjudged Laverne; she was more than a feather-brain with a zoftig bod. It made me wonder if my opinions of other actors in this drama were similarly in error. Perhaps Harry Willigan, beneath his bluster, was a devotee of macramé, and Frank Gloriana a keen student of the bass lute. Anything, I concluded glumly, was possible.

But my sour mood dissipated as I drove southward to my meeting with Lydia Gillsworth. Now there was a woman who harbored no hidden passions or guilts; I was ready to swear to that. She was complete and without artifice.

She was waiting for me in a sitting room that was an aquarium of light. She had just purchased several twig baskets of dried flowers, and their presence made the room seem like a country garden. She took such an innocent joy in the hydrangea, pepper-berries, and love-in-a-mist that her pleasure was infectious. I requested and received a pink strawflower to place in the buttonhole of my Technicolor jacket.

She had three books ready for me, neatly stacked in a small Saks shopping bag.

"Now, Archy," she said, "you must promise to read these slowly and completely."

"I promise," I vowed.

"Your first reaction," she went on, "will be laughter. You'll say to yourself, 'What nonsense this is!' But if you open your mind and heart to these ideas you'll find yourself wondering if the whole concept might not be true. Do try to wonder, Archy."

"I shall."

"You must not think about spiritualism in a logical manner," she said severely. "It is not a philosophy; it is a faith. So don't try to analyze. Just let the belief enter into you and see if it doesn't answer a lot of questions you've always asked."

She was so sincere and earnest that I was more impressed by her than by her words. Mr. Webster defines "nice" as, among other things, "well bred, virtuous, respectable." Lydia Gillsworth was all of that, I thought, and observing her eager efforts to set me on the right path, I felt great affection for her.

Among the zillion problems I've never been able to solve is whether there can ever be a true friendship between a man and a woman if sexual attraction is totally lacking. I'm just not sure. But at that moment, in Mrs. Gillsworth's sunlit country garden, listening to her quiet voice and gazing into her limpid eyes, I did feel a kinship that I believed came near to love.

I thanked her for the books and rose to leave. She came close and held me by the shoulders. She gave me a smile of surpassing warmth.

"Be prepared, Archy," she said, almost mischievously. "These books may change your life."

"Any change would be an improvement," I said, and she laughed and leaned forward to kiss my cheek.

I returned home thinking what a *sweet* woman she was. I felt empathy for the terror those dreadful letters aroused in Roderick Gillsworth. It may sound odd to you, but I now considered threats against Lydia's life an act of blasphemy; that's how convinced I was of her goodness.

Back in my cave, I did little more than glance at the books she had loaned me. I read the introductions and scanned the chapter headings, then tossed the volumes aside. Oh, I planned to read them in their entirety eventually, but I knew it would be heavy going.

I went for my ocean swim, dutifully attended the family cocktail hour, and at seven o'clock that evening I was waiting in the driveway of the Lady Cynthia Horowitz estate, having announced my arrival to the housekeeper. Ten minutes later Consuela Garcia came scampering out, slid into the Miata, and away we went.

I don't care how exacting your standards may be, I assure you, male or female, that if you ever saw Connie you'd think me a dolt for casting a libidinous eye at any other woman. She is not beautiful in a conventional way, but she is certainly attractive and so sparkling that she could persuade a golem to dance a gavotte.

She is rather shortish and plumpish, but she sports a year-round tan and usually lets her long, glossy black hair float free. I think I mentioned previously that I once saw her in a string bikini. More impressive than Mount Rushmore, I assure you.

That evening she was wearing a white silk shirt with white denim jeans. Atop her head was a jaunty straw boater with a cerise silk band. It had once been my hat, and it still rankled that it looked better on her than it had on me. All in all, she looked so fetching that once again I lamented my philandering. I suspect it may be due to a defective gene.

I was happy to see the Pelican Club was not too mobbed when we arrived. Priscilla was able to seat us at a corner table in the dining area.

"Just right for lovebirds," she said, and looked at me. "Or should I say one lovebird and one cuckoo."

"What sass!" I said. Then to Connie: "It's so hard to get good help these days."

"Watch yourself, Simon Legree," Priscilla said, "or I'll tell pop to slip a Mickey in your margarita."

"In that case I'll have a vodka gimlet," I said. "Connie?"

"Ditto," she said. "Pris, what's Leroy pushing tonight?"

"Yellowtail with saffron rice and an endive salad."

That's what we both ordered, and after our drinks were brought, I wasted no time in broaching my nefarious plot. I handed Connie the Glorianas' flier advertising individualized psychic profiles. She read it swiftly and then looked up at me.

"A swindle?" she asked.

"I think so," I said. "I'd like to prove it, and you can help. Have you ever met Hertha or Frank Gloriana?"

"Nope."

"Do you think they've ever heard of you?"

"I doubt it."

"Good," I said. "Now here's what I'd like you to do: Answer the ad in your own name from your home address. But make up a completely phony woman. Fake the date and place of birth. Fake the names of parents and grandparents. Buy some cheap gimcrack and send it along as this nonexistent woman's personal possession. I want to see what kind of a psychic profile you'll get for an imaginary person."

Connie laughed. "You're a tricky boyo, you know that? You really think the Glorianas will provide an analysis of a make-believe woman?"

"For a hundred bucks they will," I said. "I'll bet on it. Send a personal check along with your letter, and I'll make sure you get reimbursed. Will you do it?"

"Of course," she said. "It'll be fun. But why are you going to so much trouble, Archy?"

I had a con ready.

"An elderly gent is addicted to the mumbo jumbo the Glorianas are peddling. He's spending a fortune on private séances, fake demonstrations of telepathy and psychokinesis, and similar stuff. His grown children, our clients, are furious, figuring the old man is wasting their inheritance. They think the Glorianas are frauds. My father told me to investigate."

Connie bought it.

"Okay," she said, "I'll order a psychic profile for a woman who doesn't exist. Ah, here's our food. Now shut up and let me eat."

"Yes, ma'am," I said.

We finished dinner in record time, stopped at the bar for ponies of Frangelico, and then I drove Connie back to the Horowitz mansion.

"Sorry you have to work late," I said. "Next time we'll make a night of it."

"We better," she said. "Archy, tell the truth. Have you been faithful to me?"

I avoided a direct lie, as is my wont. Subterfuge is the name of the game.

"Connie," I said somberly, "I must be honest. Last week I flipped through a *Playboy* in the barbershop, and I confess I had lust in my heart."

She tried not to laugh but failed. "Just make sure it stays in your heart," she said, "and doesn't migrate southward. Thanks for the dinner, luv."

She gave me a very nice kiss, slid out of the Miata, and stalked back to her office. I waited until she was safely inside, and then I drove home singing "If You Knew Susie—Like I Know Susie." Actually, I've never met a woman named Susie, but one never knows, do one?

When I pulled into our driveway I saw Roderick Gillsworth's gray Bentley parked on the turnaround. The windows of my father's study were lighted, and he came out into the hallway when I entered.

"Archy," he said, "Gillsworth just arrived with bad news. Join us, please."

The poet was slumped in a leather club chair, biting at a thumbnail. The governor went behind his massive desk and I pulled up a straight chair.

"Another letter arrived today," my father said grimly and gestured toward a foolscap lying on the desk blotter. "Even more despicable than the others. And more frightening."

I hardly heard his final comments. I was thinking of "Another letter arrived today" and wondering why Lydia Gillsworth hadn't mentioned it. But perhaps she had. I recalled that during our telephone conversation, she had said, "I hope this isn't about that stupid letter I received." I had assumed she was speaking about the previous letter, not referring to a new one.

"Well, Archy?" father demanded impatiently, and I realized he had asked me something that simply hadn't registered.

"I beg your pardon, sir," I said. "Would you repeat the question?"

He stared at me, obviously saddened by the imbecile he had sired. "I asked if you had made any progress at all in identifying the writer of this filth."

"No, sir," I said, and let it go at that.

Gillsworth groaned. "What are we going to *do?*" he said, his last word rising to a falsetto.

I had never seen the man more distraught. In addition to the nail biting, he was blinking furiously and seemed unable to control a curious tremor of his jaw; it looked as if he was chewing rapidly.

"Mr. Gillsworth," I said, "I really think the police should be brought in. Or if your wife continues to forbid it, then private security guards should be hired. Round-the-clock. It will be costly, but I feel it's necessary until the perpetrator can be found."

The seigneur fell into one of those semi-trances that signified he was giving my proposal heavy thought, examining the pros and cons, and considering all the options in-between.

"Yes," he said finally, "I think that would be wise. Mr. Gillsworth, we have dealt several times in the past with a security service that provides personal guards. We have always found their personnel trustworthy and reliable. May I have permission to employ guards for your wife, twenty-four hours a day?"

"Oh God, yes!" Gillsworth cried, his skinny arms flapping. "Just the thing! Why didn't I think of it?"

"Where is Mrs. Gillsworth at the moment?" I asked.

"She went to a séance this evening," he said. "She should be home by now. May I use your phone?"

"Of course," father said.

Gillsworth stood, walked rather shakily to the desk phone, and dialed his number. He held the receiver clamped tightly to his head. While we all waited, I noted how he was perspiring. His face was sheened with sweat, and there was even a drop trembling at the tip of his avian honker. Poor devil, I thought; I knew exactly how he felt.

Finally he hung up. "She's not home," he said hollowly.

"No cause for alarm," my father said. "She may have stayed a few extra moments at the séance. She drove her own car?"

"Yes," the poet said. "A Caprice. I don't understand why she isn't home. She's rarely late."

"She may be delayed by traffic. Try again in five or ten minutes. Meanwhile, I suggest we all have a brandy. Archy, will you do the honors?"

I welcomed the assignment. In truth, I had caught Gillsworth's fear and needed a bit of Dutch courage. I went to the marble-topped sideboard and poured generous tots into three snifters. I served the poet and father.

Gillsworth finished half of his drink in one gulp and gasped. "Yes," he said, "that helps. Thank you."

"Father," I said, "when you talk to the security people about personal guards, I think it might be smart to ask that female operatives be assigned. I believe Mrs. Gillsworth might be more inclined to accept the constant presence of women rather than men."

"Yes, yes!" Gillsworth said, animated by the cognac and flapping his arms again. "You're quite right. A capital idea!"

The senior McNally nodded. "Good thinking, Archy," he said, and I felt I had been pardoned for my earlier inattention. "Mr. Gillsworth, would you have any objection if the female guard or guards actually moved into your home? Temporarily, of course."

"None at all," the poet said. "We have extra bedrooms. I'd welcome the presence of someone who'll watch over Lydia every minute I'm not with her. May I use the phone again?"

"Naturally," father said.

He called, and a moment later I saw his entire body relax and he actually grinned.

"You're home, Lydia," he said heartily. "All safe and sound? Good. Doors and windows locked? Glad to hear it. I'm at the McNallys', dear, and I should be home in fifteen minutes or so. See you soon."

He hung up and rubbed his palms together briskly. "All's well," he reported. "I'll stay with her until your security people arrive. When do you think that will be?"

"Probably early in the morning," father told him. "I'll call the night supervisor, and he can get things started. I'll request a female guard be sent to your home early tomorrow. Will that be satisfactory?"

"Eminently," Gillsworth said, and finished his brandy. "I feel a lot better now. I'm going to tell Lydia I insist the guards remain until this whole horrible mess is cleared up. Thank you for your help, Mr. McNally—and you too, Archy. I better go now."

"I'll see you to your car," my father said. "Please wait here for me, Archy."

He went out with the client, and I sneaked another quick cognac. Just a small one.

My father returned and regained his throne. "Personal guards are an excellent idea," he said. "I only hope Mrs. Gillsworth doesn't refuse them."

"I don't believe she will, sir," I said. "Especially if it's explained that their assignment will not be made public. But I still think the police should be informed of the letters. Granted they cannot provide round-the-clock surveillance, but they might be able to trace the source of the paper used and identify the make of the printing machine that was used."

Father looked at me steadily. "Then you were telling the truth? You've made no progress at all?"

"That's not completely accurate," I admitted, "but what I have is so slight that I didn't want to mention it in Gillsworth's presence."

Then I told him of Hertha and Frank Gloriana, who might or might not be frauds, and how Lydia attended their séances. I said nothing about Laverne Willigan's connection with the Glorianas, nor did I mention that I believed the poison-pen letters and Peaches' ransom note had been composed on the same word processor by the same author.

Why didn't I tell my father these things? Because they were very thin gruel indeed, vague hypotheses that would probably make no sense to anyone but me. Also, I must admit, I didn't want to tell the pater everything I knew because he was so learned, so wise, so far my intellectual superior. What I was implying by my reticence was "I know something you don't know!" Childish? You bet.

He looked at me, somewhat bewildered. "You think the Glorianas are responsible for the threatening letters?"

"I just don't know, sir. But Mrs. Gillsworth gave me no other names. Apparently she's convinced that no one in her social circle—relatives, friends, acquaintances—could possibly be capable of anything like that. So Hertha Gloriana is the only lead I have."

"It's not much," he said.

"No," I agreed, "it's not. But they do say the medium is the message."

He gave me a sour smile. "Well, stay on it," he commanded, "and keep me informed. Now I must call the security—"

But just then his phone rang.

He broke off speaking and stared at it a moment.

"Now who on earth can that be?" he said and picked it up.

"Prescott McNally," he said crisply. Then:

"What? *What?* Oh my God. Yes. Yes, of course. We'll be there immediately."

He hung up slowly and turned a bleak face to me.

"Lydia Gillsworth is dead," he said. "Murdered."

I don't often weep but I did that night.

Chapter 6

We later learned that Roderick Gillsworth had called 911 before phoning my father. By the time we arrived at the poet's home, the police were there and we were not allowed inside. I was glad to see Sgt. Al Rogoff was the senior officer present and apparently in charge of the investigation.

Father and I sat in the Lexus and waited as patiently as we could. I don't believe we exchanged a dozen words; we were both stunned by the tragedy.

His face was closed, and I stared unseeing at the starry sky and hoped Lydia Gillsworth had passed to a higher plane.

Finally, close to midnight, Rogoff came out of the house and lumbered over to the Lexus. Al played the good ol' boy because he thought it would further his career. But I happened to know he was a closet intellectual and a ballet maven. Other Florida cops might enjoy discussing the methods of Fred Bundy; the sergeant preferred talking about the technique of Rudolf Nureyev.

"Mr. McNally," he said, addressing my father, "we're about to tape a voluntary statement by Roderick Gillsworth. He'd like you to be present. So would I, just to make sure everything is kosher."

"Of course," father said, climbing out of the car. "Thank you for suggesting it."

"Al—" I started.

"You stay out here, Archy," he commanded in his official voice. "We've already got a mob scene in there."

"I have something important to tell you," I said desperately.

"Later," he said, and he and my father marched into the Gillsworth home.

So I sat alone for another hour, watching police officers and technicians from a fire-rescue truck search the grounds with flashlights and big lanterns. Finally Rogoff came out of the house alone and stood by my open window peeling the cellophane wrapper from one of his big cigars.

"Your father is going to stay the night," he reported. "With Gillsworth. He says to tell you to drive home. He'll phone when he wants to be picked up."

I was shocked. "You mean Gillsworth wants to sleep in this house tonight? We could put him up or he could go to a hotel."

"Your father suggested it, but Gillsworth wants to stay here. It's okay; I'll leave a couple of men on the premises."

Then we were silent, watching as a wheeled stretcher was brought out of the house. The body was covered with a black rubber sheet. The stretcher was slid into the back of a police ambulance, the door slammed. The vehicle pulled slowly away, the siren beginning to moan.

"Al," I said as steadily as I could, "how was she killed?"

"Hit on the head repeatedly with a walking stick. It had a heavy silver spike for a handle. Pierced her skull."

"Don't tell me it was in the shape of a unicorn."

He stared at me. "How did you know?"

"She showed it to me. She brought it back from up north as a gift for her husband. He collected antique canes."

"Yeah, I saw his collection. Is that what you wanted to tell me?"

"No. Something else. Remember my asking you about poison-pen letters? Lydia Gillsworth was the person getting them."

"Son of a bitch," the sergeant said bitterly. "Why didn't you tell me?"

"Because she refused to let us take it to the police. And if we had, would you have provided twenty-four-hour protection?"

"Probably not," he conceded. "Where are the letters now?"

"At home."

"How's about you drive me there and hand them over. Then drive me back here. Okay? You weren't planning to get to bed early, were you?"

"Not tonight," I said. "Let's go."

I drove, and Al sat beside me juicing up his cigar.

"Tell me what happened," I asked him.

"Not a lot to tell," he said. "Gillsworth was at your place, talked to his wife on the phone, told her he'd see her soon. He says he drove directly home. Says he found the front door open although she had told him all doors and windows were locked. She was facedown in the sitting room. Signs of a violent struggle. Spatters of blood everywhere. Baskets of flowers knocked to the floor. A grandfather clock tipped over. It had stopped about ten minutes before Gillsworth arrived."

"My God," I said, "he almost walked in on a killing."

"Uh-huh."

"Did he see anyone when he drove up?"

"Says not."

"Anything stolen?"

"Doesn't look like it. He can't spot anything missing."

"How's he taking it?"

"Hard. He's trying to do the stiff-upper-lip bit, but it's not working."

"She was a lovely woman, Al."

"She's not now," he said in the flat tones he used when he wanted to conceal his emotions.

When we entered the house, mother was waiting in the hallway. She wore a nightgown under a tatty flannel robe, and her feet were thrust into fluffy pink mules. She glanced at Sgt. Rogoff in his uniform, then put a hand against the wall to steady herself.

"Archy," she said, "what's wrong? Where is father? Has he been hurt?"

"He's all right," I said. "He's at the Gillsworth home. Mother, I'm sorry to tell you that Lydia has been killed."

She closed her eyes and swayed. I stepped close and gripped her arm.

"A car accident?" she asked weakly.

I didn't answer that. One shock at a time.

"Father will be staying with Gillsworth tonight," I said. "I came back with the sergeant to pick up some papers."

She didn't respond. Her eyes remained closed and I could feel her trembling under my hand.

"Mother," I said, "it's been a bad night, and the sergeant and I could use a cup of black coffee. Would you make it for us?"

I hoped that giving her a task would help, and it did. She opened her eyes and straightened.

"Of course," she said. "I'll put the kettle on right away. Would you like a sandwich, sergeant?"

"Thank you, no, ma'am," he said gently. "The coffee will do me fine."

Mother bustled into the kitchen, and I led Rogoff into my father's study. The letter was still lying on the desk blotter.

"There it is," I told Al. "Both the Gillsworths handled it but not my father and not me. Maybe you'll be able to bring up some usable prints."

"Fat chance," he growled, sat down behind the desk, and leaned forward to read.

"That was the third letter received," I said. "The first was destroyed by Gillsworth. The second is upstairs in my rooms. I'll get it for you."

A few moments later I returned with the second letter in the manila folder. I did not bring along the photocopy of Peaches' ransom note. Willigan had told us, "No cops!" And he was paying the hourly rate.

Rogoff had his cigar burning and was leaning back in my father's chair. He read the second letter and tossed the folder onto the desk.

"Ugly stuff," he said.

"A psycho?" I suggested.

"Maybe," he said. "Maybe someone trying to make us think they were written by a psycho."

"What will you do with the letters?"

"Send them to the FBI lab. Try to find out the make of machine used, the paper, the ink, and so forth. See if they've got any similar letters in their files."

"Even right-hand margins," I pointed out.

"Oh, you noticed that, did you? Got to be a word processor or electronic typewriter. We'll see. How about that coffee?"

When we entered the kitchen, mother was filling our cups. And she had put out a plate of Ursi Olson's chocolate-chip cookies, bless her.

"The coffee is instant," she said anxiously to Rogoff. "Is that all right?"

"The only kind I drink," he said, smiling at her. "Thank you for your trouble, Mrs. McNally."

"No trouble at all," she assured him. "I'll leave you men alone now."

We sat opposite each other at the kitchen table, hunching over our coffee and nibbling cookies.

"You suspect the husband, don't you?" I said.

The sergeant shrugged. "I've got to, Archy. Seventy-five percent of homicides are committed by the spouse, a relative, a friend, or acquaintance. These cookies are great."

"She was alive when he left here, Al," I reminded him. "He talked to her on the phone. You think he drove home and killed her?"

"Doesn't seem likely, does it?" he said slowly. "But what really helps him is that there were no bloodstains on his clothes. I told you that place looked like a slaughterhouse. Blood everywhere. The killer had to get splashed. What was Gillsworth wearing when he left here?"

I thought a moment. "White linen sports jacket, pale blue polo shirt, light gray flannel slacks."

Rogoff nodded. "That's what he was wearing when we got there. And he looked fresh as a daisy. His clothes, I mean. Absolutely unstained. And he sure didn't have enough time to change into identical duds. Also, we searched the house. No bloodstained clothes anywhere."

We sipped our coffee, ate more cookies. The sergeant relighted his cold cigar.

"So Gillsworth is off the hook?" I asked.

"I didn't say that. He's probably clean, but I've got to check out the timing. A lot depends on that. How long did it take him to drive from here to his place? Also, what time did the victim leave the séance? How long would it take her to drive home? What time did she arrive? Was someone waiting for her? There's a lot I don't know. After I find out, maybe Gillsworth will be off the hook. Right now he's all I've got."

I stared at him. "Al, is there something you're not telling me?"

"Would I do that?"

"Sure you would," I said. "Look, I know this is your case. You wear the badge; you're the law. You can order me to butt out. You're entitled to do that. But I'm telling you now I'm not going to do it. That woman meant a lot to me. So no matter what you say, I'm going to keep digging."

He looked at me strangely. "That's okay," he said. "You stay on it. Just keep me up to speed—all right?"

We finished our coffee, went to the study where Rogoff collected the letters. When we came out into the hallway mother was waiting with a small overnight bag.

"I packed father's pajamas, robe, and slippers," she said. "And his shaving gear and a fresh shirt for tomorrow morning."

I'll never cease to be amazed at how *practical* women can be, even under stress. I imagine that when the flood came and Noah was herding everyone aboard the ark, Mrs. Noah plucked at his sleeve and asked, "Did you remember to empty the pan under the icebox?"

Rogoff took the little valise and promised to deliver it to father. This time I drove the open Miata; after inhaling Al's cigar, I wanted fresh air—lots of it.

We didn't speak on the trip back to the Gillsworth home. But when we arrived and the sergeant climbed out, he paused a moment.

"Archy, I know Roderick Gillsworth was your father's client. Was Mrs. Gillsworth?"

"Yes, she was."

"I hear she had plenty of money. Did your father draw her will?"

"I don't know, Al. Probably."

"Who inherits?"

"I don't know that either. Ask my father."

Then I drove back to the McNally fiefdom for the final time that night. I feared I'd have trouble getting to sleep but I didn't. First I recited a brief prayer for a noble lady. I consider myself an agnostic—but just in case . . .

The weekend had started badly and didn't improve. The weather was no help; Saturday morning was dull and logy—just the way I felt when I awoke.

I had an OJ, cinnamon bun, and coffee with Jamie Olson in the kitchen. He was wrapping a fresh Band-Aid around the cracked stem of his ancient briar. I had given him a gold-banded Dupont for Christmas, but he saved it for Sunday smoking.

"Heard about Mrs. Gillsworth," he said in a low voice. "Too bad."

"Yes," I said. "It was in the papers?"

"Uh-huh. And on the TV."

"Jamie, if you hear anything about enemies she may have had, or maybe an argument with someone, I wish you'd let me know."

"Sure," he said. "You asked about that Mrs. Willigan."

"So I did. What about her?"

"She's got a guy."

"Oh?" I said and took a gulp of my coffee. "Where did you hear that?"

"Around."

"Know who it is?"

"Nope. No one knows."

"Then how do they know she's got a guy?"

He looked up at me. "The women know," he said, and added sagely, "They always know."

"I guess," I said and sighed.

I went back upstairs to work on my journal. It was a slow, gloomy morning, and I couldn't seem to get the McNally noodle into gear. I was stuck in neutral and all I could think about was pink lemonade and strawflowers in twig baskets. It wasn't the first time a friend had died, but never so suddenly and so violently. It made me want to telephone every friend I had and say, "I love you." I knew that was goofy but that's the way I felt.

My phone rang about ten-thirty, and I thought it would be my father asking me to come fetch him. But it was Leon Medallion, the Willigans' houseman.

"Hiya, Mr. McNally," he said breezily. "Soupy weather—right?"

"Right," I said. "What's up, Leon?"

"Remember asking me about the cat carrier? Well, I found it. It was in the utility room, where it's supposed to be. I guess I missed it the first time I looked."

"That's probably what happened," I said. "Thanks for calling, Leon."

I hung up and the old cerebrum slipped into gear. Not for a moment did I think Medallion had missed spotting Peaches' carrier on his first search of the utility room. Then it was gone. Now it had been returned. Puzzling. And even more intriguing was the fact that I had mentioned the carrier's disappearance to Meg Trumble.

I was still diddling with that nonplus when my phone rang again. This time it was my father, announcing he was ready to return. He specifically requested that I drive the Lexus. He didn't have to say that; I knew very well he thought riding in my red two-seater dented his dignity.

He was waiting outside when I arrived at the Gillsworth home. He placed his overnight bag in the back and motioned for me to slide over to the passenger side so he could get behind the wheel. He thinks I drive too fast. But then he thinks motorized wheelchairs go too fast.

"I'm going to drop you at home, Archy," he said, "and then go to the office. Gillsworth wants me to inform his wife's relatives."

"Shouldn't he be doing that, sir?"

"He should but he's still considerably shaken and asked me to handle it. Not a task I welcome. Also, I want to review Lydia's will."

"Did Sergeant Rogoff question you about that?"

"He did, and Gillsworth had no objection to full disclosure. To the best of my recollection, she left several specific bequests to nieces, nephews, an aunt, and her alma mater. But the bulk of her estate goes to her husband."

"Hefty?" I asked.

"Quite," he said. "I told the sergeant all that, and he asked for the names and addresses of the beneficiaries. He is a very thorough man."

"Yes, sir," I agreed, "he is that. He wants me to continue my investigation of the poison-pen letters."

"So he said. I also want you to, Archy. Lydia was a fine lady, and I would not care to see this crime go unsolved or her murderer unpunished."

"Nor would I, father. Do you know where Rogoff is now?"

"He came to the Gillsworth home early this morning. He was driving his pickup, and with Roderick's permission he loaded the grandfather clock into the truck and drove off with it."

"The clock that was tipped over during the assault?"

"Yes."

"What on earth does Al want with that?"

"He didn't say. Here we are. Please take my overnight bag inside and tell mother I'll be at the office. I'll phone her later."

I followed his instructions and then went into his study and used his phone to call the Glorianas' office. I wasn't certain mediums worked on Saturdays, but Frank Gloriana answered, and I identified myself.

"Ah, yes, Mr. McNally," he said. "About the missing cat . . . I intended to contact you on Monday."

"Then you have news for me?"

"My wife has news," he corrected me. "When might you be able to stop by?"

"Now," I said. "If that's all right."

"Just let me check the appointment book," he said so smoothly that I was convinced he was scamming me again. "Well, I see we have a very busy afternoon ahead of us, but if you can arrive within the hour I'm sure we can fit you in."

"Thank you so much," I said, playing Uriah Heep. "I'll be there."

Mother wanted me to stay for lunch, but I had no appetite at all. And besides, I had recently noted that the waistbands of my slacks were shrinking alarmingly. So I went upstairs and pulled on a silver-gray Ultrasuede sport jacket over my violet polo shirt. Then I went outside and jumped into the Miata for the trip to West Palm Beach.

As I've mentioned before, basically I'm a cheery sort of chap, and that black cloud that had been hovering over my head since I heard of Lydia Gillsworth's death began to lift as I drove westward. That doesn't mean I ceased to mourn, of course, or that I was any less determined to avenge her. But the world continues to spin, and one must continue to spin along with it or step off. And I wasn't ready to do that.

Actually, I hadn't called the Glorianas to inquire about Peaches. The fate of that miserable felid was small spuds compared to finding the killer of Lydia Gillsworth. But I reckoned the cat's disappearance would serve as a good excuse for seeing the medium again. Not only did I want to learn more about her relationship to Lydia, but the woman herself fascinated me.

When I entered the Glorianas' suite there was no crush of clients Frank had forecast during our phone conversation. In fact, he was alone in that mauve and aqua office, listlessly turning the pages of a magazine and looking bored out of his skull. He glanced up as I came in, put the magazine aside, and rose to greet me.

He was wearing an Armani double-breasted in taupe gabardine and sporting a regimental tie. It happened to be the stripe of the Royal Glasgow Yeomanry, a regiment of which I doubted he had ever been a member. We shook hands, and he reached to stroke the sleeve of my Ultrasuede jacket.

"Nice," he said. "Would you mind telling me what it cost?"

I knew then he was no gentleman. "I don't know," I said. "It was a gift." I think he guessed I was lying, but I didn't care.

He nodded and turned back to his desk. "I'll tell Hertha you're here," he said, then paused with his hand on the phone. "We heard about Lydia Gillsworth," he said. "Dreadful thing."

"Yes," I said, "wasn't it."

He pushed a button, spoke softly into the phone, and hung up. "She's ready for you," he reported. "This way, please."

He again conducted me down the hallway to his wife's chamber. There were two other closed doors in that corridor but they were unmarked, and I had no idea what lay behind them. Gloriana ushered me into the medium's sanctum, then withdrew.

She was standing alongside her high-backed chair, and when the door closed she came floating forward to place her hands on my shoulders. I marveled at how petite she was: a very small wraith indeed, and seemingly fragile.

"Lydia has gone over," she said in that muted voice, "and you are desolated."

"It was a shock," I agreed. "I still find it hard to accept."

She nodded, led me to her wing chair, and insisted I sit there. She remained standing before me. I thought it an awkward position for a conversation, but it didn't seem to trouble her.

"Did Lydia tell you how she felt about physical death?" she asked.

"Yes, she did."

"Then you must believe the spirit we both knew still exists. This is not the only world, you know."

She said that with such conviction that I could not doubt her sincerity. But I thought her a world-class fruitcake. Strangely, her feyness made her more attractive to me. I'm a foursquare hedonist myself, but I've always been intrigued by otherworldly types. They live as if they're collecting Frequent Flier points for a one-way trip to the hereafter.

"Mrs. Gloriana," I started, but she held up a soft palm.

"Please," she said, "call me Hertha. I feel a great kinship with you. May I call you Archy?"

"Of course," I said, pleased. "Hertha, Lydia promised to bring me to one of your séances. In fact, she suggested the meeting last evening, but I was unable to make it. Perhaps if I had, things might have turned out differently."

"No," she said, staring at me, "nothing would have changed. Do not blame yourself."

I hadn't, but it was sweet of her to comfort me.

"I would still like to attend one of your gatherings. Would that be possible?"

She was silent for a long moment, and I wondered if I was to be rejected.

"There will be no more sessions until October, Archy," she said finally. "So many people have gone north for the summer."

The off-season seemed a curious reason to halt spirit communication, but I supposed the medium charged per communicant, so there was a good commercial justification for it.

"Do you ever hold private séances?" I asked. "Could that be arranged?"

She turned and began to move back and forth, hugging her elbows. She was wearing a flowered dress of some gossamer stuff, and it wafted as she paced.

"Perhaps," she said. "But the chances of success would be lessened. The psychic power of a circle of believers is naturally much stronger than that of an individual. I could ask Frank and his mother to join us. Would that be acceptable?"

"Of course."

"And do you have a friend or two you could bring along? Individuals who are sympathetic to spiritualism even if they are not yet firm believers?"

"Yes, I think I could provide at least one person like that."

"Very well," she said. "I'll plan a session and let you know when arrangements have been finalized."

Her language surprised me. She spoke as if she was scheduling a corporate teleconference.

"Fine," I said. "I'm looking forward to it. And now about Peaches . . . Have you received any messages on the cat's whereabouts?"

She stopped moving and turned to face me. But instead of the intent gaze I expected, her eyes slowly closed.

"Faint and indistinct," she said, and now her wispy voice took on what I can only call a singsong quality. "The cat is alive and healthy. I see it in a very plain room. It's just a single room with bed, dresser, small desk, armchair." Her eyes opened. "I am sorry. Archy, but that is all I have. I cannot see where this room is located. But if you wish, I will keep trying."

"Please do," I urged. "I think you've done wonders so far."

She didn't reply, and I had nothing more to ask about Peaches. I rose, moved toward the door, then paused.

"Hertha," I said, "when we have our séance, do you think we could contact Lydia Gillsworth?"

She looked at me gravely. "It might be possible."

"Could we ask her the name of her murderer?"

"Yes," she said, "we will ask."

"Thank you," I said. "Please let me know when the session will be held."

She nodded and then moved close to me. Very close. She lifted up on her toes and kissed me full on the mouth. It was not a kiss of commiseration between two fellow mourners. It was a physical kiss, sensual and stirring. Her lips were soft and warm. So much for my vision of her as a wraith. Ghosts don't kiss, do they?

She pulled away and must have seen my shock, for she smiled, opened the door, and gently pushed me out.

There was no one in the reception room. The place seemed deserted.

I drove home in a State of Utter: utterly startled, utterly confused, utterly flummoxed. I confess it wasn't the catnapping or murder that inspired my mental muddle; it was that carnal kiss bestowed by Ms. Gloriana. What did she *mean* by it? Kisses usually have meaning, do they not? They can signal a promise, serve as a lure, demonstrate a passion—any number of swell things.

Hertha's kiss was an enigma I could not solve. It *had* to be significant, but where the import lay I could not decide. As you may have guessed, my ego is not fragile, but I could not believe the lady had suddenly been overwhelmed by my beauty and brio. I am no Godzilla, but I am no young Tyrone Power either. I mean women are not repelled by my appearance, but neither do they swoon in my presence or feel an irresistible desire to nibble my lips.

I was still trying to puzzle out the mystery of that inexplicable kiss when I arrived home just as my father was garaging his Lexus. We paced back and forth together on the graveled turnaround before going inside.

"Have you heard from Sergeant Rogoff?" he asked.

"No, father. I expect he's busy."

"Have you made any progress?"

I was tempted to reply, "Yes, sir. I was smooched by a medium." But I said, "No, sir. Nothing of importance. Was Lydia's will as you remembered it?"

He nodded. "Roderick is the main beneficiary—which causes a problem. We also drew his will: a simple document since his estate is hardly extensive. He leaves what little cash he has and his personal effects to his wife. He bequeaths the original manuscripts of his poems to the Library of Congress."

"They'll be delighted," I said.

"Don't be nasty, Archy," he said sharply. "You and I may feel they are nonsense; others may see considerable literary merit."

I said nothing.

"The problem," my father continued, "is that Roderick is now a wealthy man. It is imperative that he revise his will as soon as possible. As things stand, the bulk of Lydia's estate is in a kind of legal limbo. If Gillsworth should die before dictating a new will, the estate might be tied up for years. I'd like to suggest to him that a new testament is necessary, but the man is so emotionally disturbed at the moment that I hesitate to broach the subject. I invited him to dine with us tonight, but he begged off. Too upset, he said. That's understandable."

"Yes, sir," I said. "I don't suppose he's quite realized the enormity of what's happened. Do you think he is aware of his wife's will?"

"I know he is. He was present when I discussed the terms with Lydia. Let's go in now. Considering recent events, I think we might schedule the family cocktail hour a bit earlier today."

"Second the motion," I said.

But despite the preprandial drinks and a fine dinner (duckling with cherry sauce), it was a lugubrious evening. Conversation faltered; the death of our neighbor seemed to make a mockery of good food and excellent wine. I think we all felt guilty, as if we should be fasting to show respect. Ridiculous, of course. An Irish wake makes much more sense.

After dinner I retired to my nest and worked on my journal awhile. Then I tried to read those books on spiritualism Mrs. Gillsworth had lent me. Heavy going. But I began to understand the basic appeal of the faith. It does promise a kind of immortality, does it not? But then so does every other religious belief, offering heaven, paradise, nirvana—whatever one wishes to call it.

It was all awfully serious stuff, and as I've stated on more than one occasion, I am not a serious johnny. In fact, my vision of the final beatitude is of a place resembling the Pelican Club where all drinks are on the house.

So I tossed the books aside and went back to wondering about the motive for Hertha Gloriana's kiss. I came to no conclusion except to resolve that if there was an encore I would respond in a more manful and determined fashion.

Only to further the investigation, of course.

Chapter 7

The most noteworthy happening of the following Sunday was that I accompanied my parents to church. I am not an avid churchgoer. As a matter of fact, I had not attended services since a buxom contralto in the choir with whom I had been consorting married a naval aviator and moved to Pensacola. After that, my faith dwindled.

But that morning I sat in the McNally pew, sang hymns, and stayed awake throughout the sermon, which was based on the dictum that it is more blessed to give than to receive. I supposed that included a stiff bop on the snoot. But the final prayer was devoted to Lydia Gillsworth, a former member of the congregation. The short eulogy was touching, and I was glad I was there to hear it.

We returned home to find a police car parked outside our back door. Sgt. Al Rogoff, in civvies, was in the kitchen drinking coffee with the Olsons. He stood up when we entered and apologized for his presence on a Sunday.

"But there are some things to talk about," he said to my father. "Including funeral arrangements. The Medical Examiner will release the . . ." He glanced at mother, and his voice trailed off.

"Of course, sergeant," Père McNally said. "Suppose you come into the study. I'll phone Gillsworth and find out what his wishes are."

"Fine," Al said, then looked at me before he followed my father. "You going to be around awhile?" he asked.

"I can be," I said.

"Do try, Archy," Rogoff said with that heavy sarcasm he sometimes affects. "I want to talk to you."

"I'm on the third floor," I told him. "Come up when you and father have finished."

I trudged upstairs, took off my Sunday-go-to-meeting costume, and pulled on flannel bags and a fuchsia Lacoste. I was wondering if I had time to nip downstairs for a tub of ice cubes when there was a knock on the door.

It was the first time the sergeant had been in my rooms, and he looked about with interest.

"Not bad," he said.

"The best thing about it is the rent."

He laughed. "Zilch?" he asked.

"You got it," I said. "Al, would you like a wee bit of the old nasty?"

"What's available?"

"Marc."

"What the hell is that?"

"Brandy made from wine sludge."

"I'm game. But just a small one."

I poured two tots, and Al sampled his. He gasped and squinched his eyes.

"That'll take the tartar off my teeth," he said.

I had few accommodations for visitors, so the sergeant sat in the swivel chair behind my desk while I pulled up a rather tatty leather ottoman.

"How did you and father make out with Gillsworth?"

"Okay. He's going to take the casket up north. Apparently there's a family plot in a Rhode Island cemetery. She'll be buried there."

We sipped our minuscule drinks slowly. There is no other way to imbibe marc and survive.

"Al," I said, "I understand you hauled away the grandfather clock from the murder scene."

"That's right. It's a nice antique. Bleached pine case."

"What was the reason for taking it?"

"I wanted to find out if it was in working order before it was toppled."

"And was it?"

"Yep, according to the expert who examined it. When it was knocked over, one of the gears jolted loose and the clock stopped."

"So the time it showed was the time of the murder?"

"Seems like it, doesn't it."

I sighed. "You're not giving anything away, are you? Have you finally decided Gillsworth is clean?"

"He appears to be," Rogoff said grudgingly. "The time it takes to drive from here to his place at a legal speed checks out. Ordinarily his wife would have been home earlier from the séance, but she stayed awhile to talk with one of the women."

"Who told you that?"

"The woman."

"This is like pulling teeth," I said. "Would you mind telling me the woman's name, sergeant?"

"Mrs. Irma Gloriana, the mother-in-law of the medium. You know her?"

"Mrs. Irma Gloriana?" I said carefully. "No, I've never met the lady. What's she like?"

"A tough broad," Al said, then paused and cast his eyes heavenward. "Forgive me, Susan B. Anthony," he said. "I meant to say that she's a strong-willed individual of the female gender."

"That's better," I said approvingly. "Otherwise I might have to charge you with PI—Political Incorrectness. Did you meet the medium?"

"Nope. She and her husband weren't home. I'll catch up with them tomorrow, along with all the others who were at the séance. I have their names."

"Where was the séance held?"

"At the Glorianas' condo. It's in a high-rise near Currie Park."

"A luxury high-rise?"

"Not very," Rogoff said. "In fact, I thought it was a ratty place. I guess communing with the dear departed doesn't pay as well as selling pizzas."

"Guess not," I said. "How did you get on to this Mrs. Irma Gloriana?"

"Gillsworth gave me her name. He had been to three or four séances with his wife and knew where they were held. But after a while he stopped going. Says the whole idea of spiritualism just doesn't grab him."

"Uh-huh. Did you time how long it would take Lydia to drive home from the séance?"

"That was the whole point, wasn't it? Of course I timed it. If Lydia left when the mother-in-law says she did, then she would have arrived home about when her husband talked to her from your father's study."

"So everything fits and Gillsworth is cleared?"

"I guess so," Rogoff said dolefully. "Could I have another shot of that battery acid? A tiny one. Just enough to dampen the glass."

I poured and said, "Al, what's bothering you? You don't seem to be convinced."

He drew a heavy breath and blew it out. "As you said, 'Everything fits.' Whenever that happens, I get antsy and start wondering if I've missed something. What's chewing me is that I've only got the statement of one witness as to the time the victim went home. I'd prefer to have several. But all the others who attended the séance had already left, and the medium and her husband had gone out to dinner. So only Mrs. Irma Gloriana can say when Lydia started home."

"You think she's lying?"

He stirred restlessly in the swivel chair. "Why the hell should she? What could possibly be her motive for lying? No, she's probably telling the truth. Now what about you? What have you been up to?"

"Not a great deal," I said, all innocence. I had been pondering how much to tell him. Not everything, of course, because I was certain he wasn't telling me everything. In the past we had cooperated on several investigations to our mutual benefit, but I always reckoned—and I think Rogoff did, too—that part of our success was due to the fact that we were as much competitors as partners. I believe we both enjoyed it. Nothing like rivalry to put a little Dijon on the sandwich. Adds zest, *n'est-ce pas?*

It was at that precise moment that the McNally talent for improv showed its mettle.

"Al," I said earnestly, "I just had an idea I think you'll like."

"Try me."

"Until you get the FBI report on those poison-pen letters, the séance and everyone connected with it represents our best lead—right?"

"Not necessarily," he argued. "Archy, we're just starting on this thing. We'll have to identify and question all the victim's neighbors, friends, and acquaintances, and establish their whereabouts at the time of the homicide."

"Agreed," I said. "A lot of legwork. But while you're doing that, why don't I zero in on the Glorianas? What I had in mind was going to them, passing myself off as a half-assed spiritualist, and setting up a séance with the medium. I'm not suggesting you ignore them entirely, but let me go at them from the angle of an eager client."

He stared at me thoughtfully. "Why do I have the feeling I'm being euchred?"

"You're *not* being euchred," I said heatedly. "The more I think of it, the better it sounds. I can be Mr. Inside and you can be Mr. Outside. The Glorianas will never know we're working together. They won't even realize we know each other. But between us, we should be able to get a complete picture of their operation."

He was silent a long time, and I feared I had lost him. But finally he sighed, finished his drink, and stood up.

"All right," he said. "I can't see where it will do any harm. You set up a séance and try to get close to the medium."

"I'll try," I said.

"And you'll keep me informed of anything you turn up?"

"Absolutely," I said. "And you'll keep me informed on your progress?"

"Positively," he said, and we smiled at each other.

After he left, I sat in the swivel chair, finished my marc, and licked the rim of the snifter. I was satisfied with the plot I had hatched. I wasn't deceiving Al, exactly, but now I had an official imprimatur for doing something I had already done. It's called finagling.

I jotted a few notes in my journal, trying to recall everything the sergeant had told me. One contradiction immediately apparent was his description of the Glorianas' condo as "ratty" while their glittering offices in a new building indicated a profitable enterprise. But their mauve and aqua suite, I decided, could be a flash front. During my two visits I certainly hadn't seen hordes of clients clamoring for psychic counsel. And despite Frank's elegant duds, I thought him something of a sleaze.

The weather was still blah, but being the sternly disciplined bloke I am, I went for my ocean swim nonetheless. Surprisingly, the sea was calm as the proverbial millpond, so as I plowed along I was able to think about the coming séance and plan a course of action.

When Hertha Gloriana suggested I provide a friend who might join the circle of believers and augment its psychic powers, I had intended to ask Consuela Garcia to accompany me. Connie was a go-for-broke kiddo and she'd think the whole thing an adventure she could gossip about for weeks.

But then I remembered I had asked Connie to answer the Glorianas' ad for a "personalized psychic profile." The risk was too great that they would recognize her name, and that might eliminate whatever chance I had of proving their mail order project a fraud. I decided that instead of Connie, I'd ask Meg Trumble to attend the séance with me.

What a fateful decision that turned out to be!

I returned from my swim in time to dress for the family cocktail hour—my third change of apparel that day. It was while dispensing our first martini that my father delivered unexpected news.

"Roderick Gillsworth would like to see you, Archy," he said.

I blinked. "What on earth for?"

"He didn't say. He suggested you come over this evening after dinner. I think perhaps you better phone first."

"All right," I said doubtfully. "Rather odd, wouldn't you say, sir?"

"I would. But I'd like you to take advantage of your meeting, if you feel the time is opportune, to mention the necessity of his drafting a new will. Just refer to it casually, of course. It may serve to start him thinking of his financial responsibilities."

"I'll do what I can," I said. "But I really can't imagine why he should want to talk with me."

Mother looked up. "Perhaps he's lonely," she said quietly.

Sunday dinner was a more relaxed occasion than that of the previous night. I think my parents and I were determined not to let our sorrow at

Lydia Gillsworth's death affect the serenity of our household. What a cliché it is to say that life goes on, so I shall say it: "Life goes on." And Ursi Olson's mixed grill (lamb chops, tournedos, medaillons of veal) was a splendid reminder.

We finished our key lime mousse and coffee a little after eight-thirty. I phoned Gillsworth, and he asked if I could arrive around nine. He sounded steady enough. I said I'd be there and inquired if there was anything he needed that I might bring along. First he thanked me and said there was not. But then, after a pause, he asked timidly if the McNallys could spare a bottle of vodka. His supply was kaput and he would repay as soon as he could get to a liquor store.

I saw nothing unusual in this request, but I feared it might trouble my father. (Tabloid headline: "Grieving Hubby Drinks Himself into Insensibility on Attorney's Booze.") So I sneaked a liter of Sterling from our reserve in the utility room and hustled it out to the Miata without being caught.

Crime scene tape was still in place around the Gillsworth home, but there were no police cars in sight. Roderick himself answered my knock and greeted me with a wan smile. He said he was alone, finally, and thanked me for bringing the plasma.

"Have the reporters been a nuisance?" I asked as he led me to his study. (I was happy he hadn't selected the sitting room where the body was found.)

"Not too bad," he said. "Your father handled most of them, and I refused to grant television interviews. Make yourself comfortable while I fetch some ice cubes. Would you like a mix?"

"Water will be fine," I said, and when he left, I settled into a threadbare armchair and looked about with interest.

I had never before been in a poet's den, and it was something of a disappointment: just a small book-lined room with worn desk, battered file cabinet, an unpainted worktable laden with reference books and a typewriter. It was an ancient Remington, not electronic and definitely not a word processor. I don't know what I expected to find in this poet's sanctum sanctorum— perhaps a framed photograph of Longfellow or a Styrofoam bust of Joyce Kilmer. But there were no decorative touches. That drab room could easily be the office of any homeowner: a nook too cramped and depressing to be used for anything but answering threats from the IRS.

He returned with a bucket of ice cubes, a flask of water, and two highball glasses. He placed them on the table alongside my bottle of Sterling.

"I'm a miserable bartender," he confessed. "Would you mix your own?"

"Certainly, sir," I said.

"That's another thing," he added. "Your 'sir' and 'Mr. Gillsworth,' while appreciated, really aren't necessary. I've always addressed you as Archy. If you called me Rod, my ego would not be irretrievably damaged."

"Force of habit," I said. "Or rather force of training. I may be the last son in America who addresses his father as 'sir.' "

"Your father's different."

"Yes," I said, sighing, "he is that."

I built my own drink: a little vodka, a lot of water. He mixed his own: a lot of vodka, a little water. I took the armchair again, and he lowered himself into a creaky swivel chair behind his desk.

"Rod," I said, beginning to recite a short speech I had rehearsed, "I haven't had a chance to express my condolences on the death of your wife. It was a terrible tragedy that saddened my parents and me. We shall always remember Lydia as a good neighbor and a gracious lady."

"Yes," he said, "she was. Thank you."

I sipped, but he gulped, and I wondered if he swilled in that fashion to make certain he'd sleep that night.

"It makes my poems seems so meaningless," he mused, staring into his glass. "So futile."

"It shouldn't have that effect," I said. "Surely your wife's tragic death could provide inspiration for poetry in an elegiac mood."

"Perhaps," he said. "In time. At the moment my mind is empty of everything but sorrow. I hope you're right. I hope that eventually I'll be able to express my bereavement and by writing about it exorcise my pain and regain some semblance of emotional tranquility."

I thought that rather much. In fact it sounded like a speech *he* had rehearsed. But perhaps poets talked that way. Or at least this poet.

He took another heavy swallow of his drink and slumped in his chair. His eyes were reddened, as if from weeping, and his entire face seemed droopy. I fancied that even his long nose had sagged since I last saw him. He was now a very gloomy bird indeed.

"Archy," he said, "I understand that you will continue investigating the poison-pen letters."

"That's correct."

"You'll be working with Sergeant Rogoff?"

I nodded.

"What do you think of him? Is he competent?"

"More than competent," I said. "Al is a very expert and talented police officer."

Gillsworth made a small sound I think he intended as a laugh. "I believe he suspects me."

"That's his job, Rod," I explained. "The investigation is just beginning. The sergeant must suspect everyone connected with Mrs. Gillsworth until their whereabouts at the time the crime was committed can definitely be established."

"Well, my whereabouts have definitely been established. I was with you and your father."

"Rogoff understands that," I said as soothingly as I could. "But he can take nothing for granted. Every alibi must be verified."

He finished his drink and poured himself another, as massive as the first.

"What angers me the most," he said, "is that he won't give me any information. I ask him what is being done to find the maniac who killed my wife, and he just mutters, 'We're working on it.' I don't consider that adequate."

"At this stage I doubt if there is anything to tell you. And even when progress is made, the police are very cautious about revealing it. They don't want to risk raising false hopes, and they are wary about identifying any person as being under suspicion until his or her guilt can be proved."

Gillsworth shook his head. "It's maddening. Now I've got to accompany Lydia's casket up north for the funeral. Her family is sure to ask what is being done to find the killer, and all I'll be able to tell them is that the police are working on it."

"I know it's frustrating," I said sympathetically. "It's difficult to be patient, but you must remember the police have had the case for only forty-eight hours."

"How long do you think it will take to solve it?"

"Rod, there is absolutely no way to predict that. It could be days, weeks, months, years."

He groaned.

"But there is no statute of limitations on homicide," I said. "The police will keep at it as long as it takes—and so will I."

"Thank you for that," he said. "I see you need a refill. Please help yourself." While I was doing exactly that, he said, "Archy, will you be exchanging information with Rogoff?"

"I hope so."

"While I'm up north for Lydia's funeral, may I phone you to ask if any progress has been made? I don't want to call Rogoff; he'll tell me nothing."

"Of course you can phone me," I said. I was about to add that naturally I'd be unable to reveal anything without Rogoff's permission. But Gillsworth's animus toward the sergeant seemed evident, and not wanting to exacerbate it, I said no more.

"I'll really appreciate it if you can keep me informed."

"How long will you be gone, Rod?"

"Two or three days. I'd like to give you a set of house keys before you leave tonight. Would you be kind enough to look in once or twice while I'm gone?"

"I'd be glad to."

"Thank you. Our cleaning lady, Marita, has been given two weeks off, so she won't be around. And I have handed over a set of keys to the police. I don't know why they wanted them, but that sergeant grunted something about security. Oh God, what a mess this whole thing is."

"Rod, I hate to add to your burdens, but my father asked me to mention something to you. It is imperative that you make out a new will. Unfortunately, circumstances have changed, and your present will is simply inadequate."

His head snapped up as if I had slapped him.

"I hope I haven't offended you by referring to it," I said hastily.

"No, no," he said. "That's all right. I was just shocked that it hadn't even occurred to me. Your father is correct, as usual. As you probably know, Lydia inherited a great deal of money, and now I suppose it comes to me. What a filthy way to get rich."

"It was her wish," I reminded him.

"I know, but still . . . Very well, you can tell your father that I'll certainly give it a lot of thought, and when I return from the funeral I'll get together with him."

"Good," I said. "A will isn't something that should be delayed."

He looked at me with a twisted smile. "A legal acknowledgment of one's mortality," he said. "Isn't that what a will is?"

"I suppose so," I said. "But for a man in your position it's a necessity."

He poured himself another drink with a hand that trembled slightly. I wondered how many more of those bombs he'd be able to gulp without falling on his face. I wanted to caution him but it wasn't my place.

He must have guessed what I was thinking because he grinned foolishly and said, "I'll sleep tonight."

"That you will."

"You know, these are the first drinks I've had since Lydia died. I wanted a drink desperately while waiting for the police to arrive, but it seemed shameful to need alcohol to give me courage to see it through. But now I don't care. I need peace even if it comes from a bottle and even if it's only temporary. Can you understand that?"

"Of course," I said. "As long as you have no intention of leaving the house tonight."

"No intention," he mumbled, his voice beginning to slur. "Positively no intention."

"That's wise," I said, finished my drink, and stood up. I had no desire to witness this stricken man's collapse. "Then if you'll give me your house keys, I'll be on my way."

He rooted in the top drawer of his desk and finally handed me three keys strung on an oversized paperclip. "Front door, back door, and garage," he said.

"I'll look in while you're gone," I promised. "And may I tell father you'll consult him about a new will when you return?"

"Yes," he said. "New will. I'll think about it."

He didn't stagger when he accompanied me to the front door, but he moved very, very slowly and once he placed a palm against the wall for support. He turned to face me at the entrance. I couldn't read his expression.

"Archy," he said, "do you like me? Do you?"

"Of course I like you," I said.

He grabbed my hand and clasped it tightly between both of his. "Good man," he said thickly. "Good man."

I gently drew my hand away. "Rod, be sure to lock up and put the chain on."

Outside, the door closed, I listened until I heard the sounds of the lock being turned and the chain fumbled into place. Then I took a deep breath of the cool night air and drove home.

I garaged the Miata and saw lights in my father's study. His door was open, which I took as an invitation to enter. He was seated in the leather club chair, a glass of port at his elbow. He was reading one of the volumes from his leather-bound set of Dickens. The book was hefty, and I guessed it to be *Dombey and Son.* He was stolidly reading his way through the entire Dickens oeuvre, and I admired his perseverance. Even more amazing, he remembered all the plots. I don't think even Dickens could do that.

He looked up as I entered. "Archy," he said, "you're home. You saw Gillsworth?"

"Yes, sir. He gave me a set of his house keys and asked that I look in once or twice while he's up north at the funeral."

I was waiting for him to ask me to sit down and have a glass of something, but he didn't.

"You brought up the subject of the will?"

"I did. He said he'd give it some thought and consult you when he returned."

"I suppose that's the best that can be hoped for. What condition is he in?"

"When I left him, he was half in the bag and still drinking."

One of father's eyebrows ascended. "That's not like Gillsworth. I've never known him to overindulge."

"Emotional strain," I suggested.

"No excuse," the lord of the manor pronounced and went back to his Dickens.

I climbed the stairs to my perch, thinking of what an uncompromising man my father was. And as I well knew, his bite was worse than his bark.

I undressed, showered, and scrubbed my choppers. Then I pulled on a silk robe I had recently purchased at a fancy-schmancy men's boutique on Worth Avenue. It bore a design of multicolored parrots carousing in a jungle setting. One of those crazy birds had a startling resemblance to Roderick Gillsworth.

I treated myself to a dram of marc and lighted an English Oval—my first cigarette of the day! I slouched in the padded swivel chair, put my bare feet up on the desk, and ruminated on why the poet had asked if I liked him. His question was as perplexing as Hertha Gloriana's kiss.

I didn't think it was the vodka talking; Gillsworth was seeking reassurance. But of what—and why from me? I could only conclude that his wife's death had left him so bereft that he had reached out to make contact with another human being. I happened to be handy.

But that explanation was not completely satisfying. Sgt. Rogoff has often accused me of having a taste for complexity, of searching for hidden motives and unconscious desires when I'd do better to accept the obvious. Al could be right, and mother was correct in suggesting that Gillsworth was simply lonely. But I was not totally convinced.

Take as a case in point the recent behavior of yrs. truly. When the poet had asked, "Do you like me?" I had automatically replied, "Of course I like you." That was the polite and proper response to an intimate query from a man who was apparently suffering and needed, for whatever reason, a boost to his morale. And I had duly provided it.

But if the truth be known, I didn't like him. I didn't *dis*like him; I just felt nothing for him at all. That was my secret, and hardly something I'd reveal to him. I mention it now merely as an illustration of how the obvious frequently masks reality.

I was still musing gloomily on the strangeness of human nature when my phone rang. It was then almost midnight, and a call at that hour was not calculated to lift the McNally spirits. My first thought was: Now who's died?

"H'lo?" I said warily.

"Archy?" A woman's voice I could not immediately identify.

"Yes. To whom am I speaking?"

"Such elegant grammar! Meg Trumble."

Relief was better than a schooner of marc.

"Meg!" I practically shouted. "How *are* you?"

"Very well, thank you. I didn't wake you up, did I?"

"Of course not. It's the shank of the evening."

"Well, I did call earlier, but I guess you were out. Behaving yourself, I hope."

"Unfortunately. You're calling from King of Prussia?"

"Yes, but I'm leaving early tomorrow morning, and I do mean early. I should be in Florida by Tuesday."

"Can't wait," I said. "Listen, if you arrive in time, give me a call and we'll have dinner. You'll be ready to unwind after all that driving."

"I was hoping you'd say that," she said. "I'm not even telling Laverne when I expect to arrive, but I'll phone you as soon as I get in. See you Tuesday night."

"Good-o," I said. She hung up, and I sat there grinning like an idiot at the dead phone.

It was incredible what a goose that phone call gave to my dismal mood. I was immediately convinced I would rescue Peaches, find the killer of Lydia Gillsworth, the sun would shine full force on the morrow, and I would lose at least five pounds.

When A. Pope wrote about hope springing eternal, he obviously had A. McNally in mind.

Chapter 8

I don't believe I've ever mentioned my peculiar infatuation with hats. I love hats. When I was attending Yale Law (briefly), I wore suede and tweed caps, fedoras, bowlers, and once, in a moment of madness, a fez. But all that head-gear was a mite heavy for South Florida, so when I returned to Palm Beach I opted for mesh caps, panamas, and a marvelous planter's sombrero with a five-inch brim.

Recently I had written to a custom hat maker in Danbury, Conn., and had ordered three linen berets in white, puce, and emerald green. They arrived on Monday morning, and I was highly pleased. They were soft enough to roll up and tuck in a hip pocket, yet when they were donned and the full-ness pulled rakishly over to one side, I felt they gave me a certain devil-may-care look.

I went down to a late breakfast wearing my new puce beret. Fortunately my father had already departed for the office so I didn't have to endure his incredulous stare. Mother took one look, laughed delightedly, and clapped her hands.

"Archy," she said, "that beret is *you!*"

I was so gratified by her reaction that I wore the cap while breakfasting on fresh grapefruit juice, three slices of Ursi Olson's marvelous French toast with honey-apricot preserve, and a pot of black coffee. I was finishing my sec-ond cup when mater remarked casually, "Oh, by the way, Archy, Harry Willi-gan phoned just before you came down. He'd like you to call him as soon as possible. He sounded in a dreadful temper."

Dear mother! She made certain I had a nourishing breakfast before breaking the bad news. I went into father's study and called the Willigan home. Julie Blessington, the maid, answered the phone. I identified myself and asked to speak to the master. In a moment our splenetic client came on the line and began screaming at me.

He was spluttering and shouting so loudly that it was difficult to grasp the reason for his rancorous outburst. I finally determined that a second ran-som note had been found that morning, slid under the Willigans' front door.

"When was it found?" I asked.

"I told you already—this morning."

"How early this morning?"

"Very early. When Ruby Jackson came down to make breakfast."

"You think it was delivered last night?"

"Who the hell knows? You're the detective, aincha?"

"Plain white envelope?"

"Yeah, same as before."

"Who in your house has handled it?"

"Ruby handled the envelope. I handled the envelope and the letter inside."

"Don't let anyone else touch it, Mr. Willigan. What does the letter say?"

"Peaches is crying a lot. Poor Sweetums. She misses me."

"Uh-huh," I said. "What else?"

"They want me to put together a bundle of fifty thousand dollars. Used bills, unmarked, no numbers in sequence, nothing over a hundred."

"Any instructions for delivery?"

"Nah. I should just have the cash ready. They'll tell me when and how to get it to them."

"I better come over and pick up the letter," I said. "Will you be there, sir?"

"No, I won't be here," he said aggrievedly. "I got a meeting I'm late for already. I'll leave the letter with Laverne. You get it from her."

"Please tell her not to handle it."

"All right, all right," he said angrily, "I'll tell her. Listen, Archy, you've got to work harder on this thing. As far as I can see, you're spinning your wheels."

"Not exactly," I said. "I have a very important lead I can't discuss on the phone."

"Yeah?" he said. "Well, it better pan out or I'm hiring me a *professional* private eye. And I might even pull my business from McNally and Son unless I get some results."

And with that naked threat he slammed down the phone before I had a chance to reply. The response I had ready would have shocked my father. He believes a soft answer turneth away wrath. Sometimes it does. And sometimes a knuckle sandwich is required.

I went upstairs to exchange my puce beret for the white one because I feared the puce would clash with a flag-red Miata. (Genius is in the details.) Then I drove toward the Willigans' estate. My spasm of fury at our client's insulting treatment ebbed as I noted the sun was shining brightly and the sky looked as if it had just come from the tumble-dry cycle. A splendid day!

The door of the Willigan hacienda was opened by Leon Medallion, glum of countenance, eyes bleared by whatever allergy was affecting him that morning.

"Another ransom note, Leon," I said.

He nodded gloomily. "The old man was in a ferocious temper. When he starts shouting up a storm like that, I disappear. He can be mean."

"I'm supposed to pick up the letter from Mrs. Willigan. Is she here?"

"Out by the pool toasting her buns. You can find your way, can't you? I'm still polishing the effing silver, trying to get the tarnish off. This climate is murder on silverware, brass, and copper."

"Maybe we should all switch to plastic," I suggested.

He brightened. "Fair dinkum, mate," he said.

It hadn't been an exaggeration to say Laverne was toasting her buns. She was lying prone on a padded chaise pulled into the sunlight. She was wearing a thong bikini, and I was immediately reminded of a Parker House roll. She raised her head as I approached. It was wise of her not to rise farther since she had unhooked her bra strap.

"Hi, Archy," she said breezily. "Love your tam."

"Beret," I corrected, "and I thank you. I hope you're using a sunscreen."

"Baby oil," she said.

"You won't roast," I told her, "you'll fry. May I pull up a chair?"

"Sure," she said. "And if you're a good boy I'll let you oil my back."

She was at it again, and I decided she was a lady who enjoyed playing the tease. There is a coarse epithet for women like that—but I shall not offend by repeating it.

I placed a canvas director's chair close to her chaise, but not within oiling distance, and sat where I could see her face.

"Another letter from the catnappers," I said.

"That's right. Harry said to give it to you. It's on the taboret in the hallway. They want him to get the cash ready."

"So I understand. I imagine the next letter will give instruction for delivery."

"Archy, do you have any notion of who might have swiped Peaches?"

"A few frail leads," I said, "but nothing really definite. Laverne, I have a fantastic idea I'd like to try out on you. Do you know what a psychic is?"

Her face was half-buried in the padding, and I couldn't observe her reaction.

"Sure," she said, voice muffled. "People who are supposed to have second sight. They claim they can predict the future and things like that."

"Things like locating missing persons and objects," I said. "My idea is to contact some local psychic and see if he or she can get a vision of where Peaches is now."

Laverne raised her head to stare at me with an expression I could not decipher. "That's the nuttiest idea I've ever heard," she said. "You don't believe that voodoo stuff, do you?"

"I don't believe and I don't disbelieve. But it's worth trying, wouldn't you say?"

"No, I would not say," she said with what seemed to me an excess of vehemence. "It's crazy. Don't do it, Archy. If Harry finds out you've gone to someone who reads tea leaves or whatever it is they do, he'll fire both you and your father."

"Yes," I said regretfully, "I guess you're right. As I said, it was just a wild idea. I better forget it."

"That's smart," she said, settling down again. "By the way, I heard from Meg. She'll be back sometime this week. She's got her own apartment now in Riviera Beach. Will you be glad to see her again, Archy?"

"Of course. She's a very attractive lady."

Her head came up again, and this time she grinned at me. "I think you ought to make a move there," she said. "I think Meg is ready."

I was happy to learn that Meg didn't tell Laverne *everything*.

"Laverne!" I said as if shocked. "She's your sister!"

"That's why I want her to have fun. Give her a break, darling. It doesn't have to be heavy. Just for laughs."

"I don't know," I said doubtfully. "I'm not sure she has eyes for me."

"Try it," Laverne urged. "It would do her a world of good. I realize she's a skinny one, but remember: the nearer the bone, the sweeter the meat."

Yes, she *did* say that. Was there a more vulgar woman in Palm Beach? If there was, I hadn't met her and had no desire to.

"I'll take it under advisement," I said and stood up. "I better pick up that letter and see if it's any help in finding the catnappers."

"And you'll forget all about going to a psychic?"

The first two rules of successful deception are keep it short and never repeat. Ask me; I know. Laverne was obviously an amateur at deceit.

"I've already forgotten," I assured her. "Don't get too much sun or you might start peeling."

Her reply is unprintable in an account that may possibly be read by impressionable youngsters and innocent oldsters.

I found the second ransom note on the taboret in the hallway. I handled it carefully by the corners and slipped it into my jacket pocket. No one was about so I let myself out and drove home, still smiling at Laverne's final comment and wondering why she felt it necessary to conceal her acquaintance with the Glorianas.

At home, I went immediately to my rooms, sat at the desk, shoved on my reading specs. I unfolded the second ransom note carefully and examined it. It appeared to be printed in the same font as the first and the missives sent to Lydia Gillsworth. The right-hand margin was justified. The ink and paper stock seemed identical in all the letters.

The message itself was as Harry Willigan had stated. I was amused by the casual mention of Peaches being in good health but crying a lot. That was clearly intended to pierce the heart of the cat's owner who might have the personality of a Komodo dragon but was obviously sappy with love for his obnoxious pet.

I added the second ransom note to my photocopy of the first, slid both into a manila envelope, and started out again. This time I left my new beret at home but took along my reading glasses tucked into a handsome petit point case that mother had made and given to me on my 36th birthday.

Before leaving, I phoned Mrs. Trelawney, my father's private secretary. I asked if she could persuade the boss to grant me at least fifteen minutes from his rigidly structured daily schedule. I was put on hold while she went to inquire. She came back on the line to tell me His Majesty had graciously acceded to my request if I arrived promptly at eleven-thirty.

"On my way," I promised.

The McNally Building on Royal Palm Way is a stark edifice of glass and stainless steel—so modern it makes my teeth ache. But it's undeniably impressive—which was why my father had approved the architect's design even though I knew he would have preferred a faux Georgian mansion.

But the esquire had drawn a line at his private office. *That* was oak paneled and furnished in a style that would have earned the approbation of Oliver Wendell Holmes. The main attraction was an enormous rolltop desk—an original, not a reproduction—that had, by actual count, thirty-six cubbyholes and four concealed compartments that I knew about.

Father was standing in front of this handsome antique when I entered, looking like a handsome antique himself. He glowered at me, and I was happy I had left the linen beret at home.

"This couldn't have waited?" he demanded.

"No, sir," I said. "In my judgment it is a matter that brooks no delay."

Don't ask why, but in his presence I sometimes began to speak like a character from his beloved Dickens. I knew it but couldn't help myself. We sounded like a couple of barristers discussing *Jarndyce vs. Jarndyce*.

"Harry Willigan received a second ransom letter from the catnappers," I told him.

"I am aware of that," he said testily. "Willigan phoned me this morning. In a vile temper, as usual."

"Yes, sir," I said, "but I don't believe you've seen the two letters. I've brought them along. The first is a photocopy, the second is the original. Please take a look, father."

I spread them on his desk. Still standing, he bent over to examine them. It didn't take him long to catch it. I heard his sharp intake of breath, and he straightened to stare at me.

"They appear to resemble the poison-pen letters received by the late Lydia Gillsworth," he said stonily.

"More than resemble," I said. "Same type font. Justified right-hand margins. Apparently the same ink and the same paper."

He drew a deep breath and thrust his hands into his trouser pockets. "Where are the Gillsworth letters now?"

"Sergeant Rogoff has them. He's sending them to the FBI lab for analysis."

"Does he know about these letters?"

"Not to my knowledge. I've told him nothing about the disappearance of Peaches."

Hands still in pockets, he began to pace slowly about the office. "I see the problem," he said. "The client has specifically forbidden us to bring the catnapping to the attention of the police."

"And we are obligated to respect our client's wishes and follow his instructions," I added. "But by so doing, are we not impeding an official homicide investigation? That's assuming all the letters were produced on the same word processor or electronic typewriter, as I believe they were."

He stopped his pacing to face me. "And do you also believe they were all composed by the same person?"

"I think it quite possible."

He was silent a moment. Then: "I don't like this, Archy; I don't like it at all. As an officer of the court I don't relish being put in a position where I might fairly be accused of withholding evidence."

"Possibly vital evidence," I said. "In the investigation of a particularly heinous crime."

He took one hand from his pocket and began to tug at his thick mustache, a sure sign of his perturbation. When he's in a mellow mood, he strokes it.

"May I make a suggestion, father?"

"You may."

"I think civic and moral duty outweigh ethical considerations in this case. I believe the police *must* be told of the Willigan letters. Perhaps they have nothing to do with the Gillsworth murder, but we can't take that chance. Let me show them to Sergeant Rogoff, for his eyes only. I'll impress upon him the need for absolute discretion on his part. Al is certainly no blabbermouth. I think we can safely gamble that Willigan will never learn we have told the police about the catnapping."

"It's not so much Willigan I'm concerned about, it's the catnappers. If they learn the police have been informed, it's quite possible they will carry out their threat to kill Peaches. And then McNally and Son may well be the target of a malpractice suit brought by our contentious client. It would be difficult to defend our conduct: a clear breach of confidentiality."

We were both silent then, pondering all the ramifications of the problem. The decision was not mine to make, of course. It was my father who might have to take the flak, and it would be presumptuous of me to urge him to any particular course of conduct.

"Very well," he said at last. "Show the Willigan letters to Sergeant Rogoff, explain the circumstances of the catnapping, and try to convince him that the future of Peaches depends on his circumspection." He paused to smile wryly. "To say nothing of the future of McNally and Son."

"I'll convince him," I said, gathering up the letters. "I think you've made the right decision, father."

"Thank you, Archy," he said gravely. "I am happy you approve."

I think he meant it. Irony is not the governor's strong suit.

I was exiting through the outer office when Mrs. Trelawney beckoned me to her desk. My father's secretary is one of my favorite people, a charming beldame with an ill-fitting gray wig and a penchant for naughty jokes. She was the first to tell me the one about the American, the Englishman, and the Frenchman who visit a—but I digress.

"What have you been up to, young McNally?" she said accusingly. "Romancing married women, are you? And if you are, why wasn't I first on your list?"

"I am not," I assured her, "but if I were, you would certainly be first, last, and always. Also, my dear, just what, exactly, are you talking about?"

She looked down at a note she had jotted on a telephone message form. "While you were with your father, you received a call from a Mrs. Irma Gloriana, who demanded to speak to you personally. From her voice I would judge her to be of what is termed a 'certain age.' She insists you phone her immediately. What's going on, Archy?"

"A professional relationship," I said haughtily. "The lady happens to be my acupuncturist."

Mrs. Trelawney laughed and handed me the message. "I'm glad someone's giving you the needle," she said.

I had intended to phone Sgt. Rogoff the moment I was in my office, but this call from Mrs. Irma Gloriana seemed more important and more intriguing. I sat at my desk and punched out the phone number. It was not, I noted, the number of the Glorianas' office on Clematis Street.

My call was answered on the second ring.

"The Glorianas' residence," a woman said sharply. A deep voice, very strong, with a rough timbre. Almost a longshoreman's voice.

"This is Archibald McNally," I said. "Am I speaking to Mrs. Irma Gloriana?"

"You are, Mr. McNally," she said, the tone now softened a bit. "Thank you for returning my call so promptly. Hertha has informed me that you wish to arrange a private séance."

"That's correct," I said. "My understanding is that it would be attended by Hertha, her husband, you, myself, and a friend who accompanies me. Will that be satisfactory?"

"Mr. McNally," she said, and I marveled at that voice so deep it was almost a rumble, "I prefer to meet personally with new clients before making plans. You must understand that many people who apply to us simply cannot be helped by Hertha's unique talents. It saves us a great deal of time— and would-be clients a great deal of money, of course—if we might have an interview during which I describe exactly what happens at our séances, what we hope to achieve, and what we cannot do. I must know what you hope to accomplish. I trust this preliminary screening doesn't offend you, Mr. McNally."

"Not at all," I said. "I can understand why—"

"You see," she interrupted, "we are sometimes approached by people who seek the impossible or who are motivated by idle curiosity and have no real interest in sharing the truth of spiritualism."

"That seems to be a—"

"And there are those who come just to mock," she said darkly. "My daughter-in-law is much too sensitive and vulnerable to be forced to cope with stupid and arrogant disbelief."

"I assure you that—"

"When may I expect you, Mr. McNally?" she demanded.

"I can come over now, Mrs. Gloriana," I said. "I could be there in a half-hour."

"That will be satisfactory," she said crisply. "Please make a note of this address. You should also be aware that smoking is not permitted in our home."

So I made a note of her address, hung up, and immediately lighted a cigarette. I smoked it down before venturing out to meet this termagant with the
foghorn voice.

On the drive across the bridge to West Palm Beach I tried to make sense
of what Mrs. Irma Gloriana had told me. Her insistence on a preliminary
screening of would-be clients seemed suspect. Why should the medium and
her entourage question the motives of potential customers? Their ability to
pay the tariff demanded would seem to be the only necessary requirement.

But then I realized there might indeed be method to this madness. Mrs.
Gloriana wanted to know what I hoped to accomplish at the séance. Suppose
I told her I wished to contact the spirit of Sir Thomas Crapper. Thus fore-
warned, Irma, Frank, and Hertha could easily discover that the gentleman in
question was the inventor of the water closet, and they could call up a ghost
familiar with the workings of that justly famed device.

Similarly, these preliminary interviews could reveal names, dates, even intimate personal details that would be of value in convincing a séance attendee
that the medium possessed extraordinary psychic gifts.

This was, I admit, a very jaundiced view of extrasensory powers. But at
that stage of the investigation I believed a healthy dollop of cynicism was justified. "Innocent until proven guilty" is the cornerstone of our law. But most
detectives, myself included, prefer the dictum "Guilty until proven innocent."
That's how crimes are solved.

The building in which the Glorianas' condo was located was not as
"ratty" as Al Rogoff had described, but it was surely no Trump Plaza either.
It had an air of faded elegance, with cooking odors in the hallways and fraz-
zled carpeting.

The matron who opened the door of Apt. 1102 was as I had imagined
her: tall, heavy through the hips, but more muscular than plump. There was
a solid massiveness about her: a large head held erect on a strong neck. Definitely a dominant woman.

But what I had not been prepared for was her sensuousness, so overt it
was almost a scent. It was conveyed, I thought, by her full red lips, glossy
black hair as tangled as a basket of snakes, ample bosom, and a certain loose-
ness about the way she moved. It was easy to fantasize that she might be
naked beneath her shift, a voluminous gown of flowered nylon.

She shook my hand firmly, got me seated in an armchair covered in a
worn brocade. She asked if I would care for an iced tea. I said that would be
welcome, and while she was gone I had an opportunity to inspect the apartment—or at least the living room in which I was seated.

It was a dreary place, colors drab, furniture lumpy. It was difficult to believe this was the home of the forthright Irma, the dapper Frank, the delicate
Hertha. There was nothing that bespoke luxury, or even comfort. They were
ambitious people; this dingy apartment had to be a temporary residence to be
endured until something better came along.

Mrs. Gloriana returned with my iced tea—nothing for her—and sat in the
middle of a raddled couch, facing me. She wasted no time on preliminaries.

"You believe in spiritualism, Mr. McNally?" she asked.

I took a sip of my tea. It had a hint of mint and was quite good. "Really more of a student," I confessed. "I'm reading as much about it as I can."

"Oh? And what are you reading?"

I mentioned the titles of two of the books Mrs. Gillsworth had lent me.

"Very good," Irma Gloriana said approvingly. "But you must realize they are only instructional. True belief must come from the heart and the soul."

"I understand that," I said, fearing I was about to be proselytized and dreading the prospect. But she dropped the subject of my conversion.

"Hertha tells me you have asked her assistance in finding your missing cat."

"A friend's cat."

"She may be able to help. My daughter-in-law has amazing psychic powers. And did you wish to ask about the cat during the séance?"

"No," I said, "something else. I hope to receive a message from Lydia Gillsworth. I'm sure you knew her and have heard what happened to her."

Her expression didn't change. "Of course I knew Lydia. A sensitive soul. She attended a session here the evening she was killed. A brutal, senseless death."

"Yes," I said, "it was. Do you think there's a possibility that Hertha may be able to contact the spirit of Lydia Gillsworth?"

"There is always a possibility," she said, then added firmly, "But naturally we can offer no guarantees. You wish to ask Lydia the identity of her murderer?"

"Yes, that is what I intended."

"It is worth trying," she said thoughtfully. "Hertha has assisted in many police investigations in the past. With some success, I might add. Our standard fee for a séance is five hundred dollars, Mr. McNally. But that is usually divided amongst several participants. Since only you and your friend will attend, I believe a fee of two hundred dollars will be more equitable. Is that satisfactory?"

"Completely," I said. "And you do accept credit cards?"

"Oh yes. This friend who will accompany you—a man or a woman?"

"A woman."

"Could you tell me her name, please? Numerology is a particular interest of mine, and I enjoy converting names to numerical equivalents and developing psychic profiles."

"Her name is Margaret Trumble."

"A resident of this area?"

Then I was certain she was prying—no doubt about it.

"She is a new resident," I said.

"So many refugees from the north, aren't there?"

If she expected me to divulge Meg Trumble's hometown, she was disappointed; I merely nodded.

"My son tells me you work for a law firm, Mr. McNally."

"Yes, McNally and Son. My father is the attorney."

"But you are not?"

"Regretfully, no," I said, unable to cease staring at her bare neck, the skin seemingly so flawless and tender that it might be bruised by a kiss.

"And what is it you do at McNally and Son?"

It wasn't exactly a third degree. Call it a second degree.

"Research, mostly," I told her. "Usually very dull stuff."

I finished my iced tea, but she didn't offer a refill.

"Did you know Lydia Gillsworth a long time?" she asked.

"Several years. She and her husband were clients. And neighbors as well."

"I have met Roderick Gillsworth. He attended a few of our sessions with his wife. His late wife, I should say. I found him a very intelligent, creative man. A poet, you know."

"Yes, I know."

"He was kind enough to give me autographed volumes of his poems. Have you read his work, Mr. McNally?"

"Some," I said cautiously.

"What is your opinion of his poetry?"

"Ah," I said. Then: "Very cerebral."

"It is that," she said, her deep voice resonating. "But I believe he is more than an intellectual. In his poems I sense a wild, primitive spirit struggling to be free."

"You may be right," I said diplomatically, thinking I had never heard such twaddle. Roderick Gillsworth a wild, primitive spirit? Sure. And I am Vlad the Impaler.

She rose to her feet, a boneless uncoiling. "I'll try to arrange your séance for later this week, Mr. McNally. I'll give you at least a day's notice. Will that be sufficient?"

"Of course," I said. "I may be speaking to your daughter-in-law before that if she is able to receive additional information about Peaches."

"Peaches?"

"The missing cat."

Unexpectedly she smiled, a mischievous smile that made her seem younger. And more attractive, I might add.

I hesitate to use the adjective "seductive" to describe any woman, but I can think of none more fitting for Irma Gloriana. I don't wish to imply her manner was deliberately designed to entice, but I could not believe she was totally unconscious of her physical allure. But perhaps she was. In any event, she projected a strong and smouldering sexuality impossible to ignore.

"Peaches," she repeated. "A charming name. Is the cat charming?"

"The cat is a horror," I said, and this time she laughed aloud, a booming laugh. "But my friend loves her," I added.

"Love," she said, suddenly serious. "Such an inexplicable emotion, is it not, Mr. McNally?"

"It is indeed," I said, and her final handclasp was soft and warm, quite different from the hard, cool handshake with which she had greeted me.

I drove back to the office trying to sort out my impressions of Mrs. Irma Gloriana. Al Rogoff had initially dubbed her a "tough broad," and I could understand his reaction. But I thought her more than that: a very deep lady whose contradictions I could not immediately ken. I had a sense that she was playing a role, but what the script might be I had no idea.

The first thing I did on my return to the McNally Building was to phone Sgt. Rogoff. He wasn't in, so I left my name and number, requesting he call me as soon as possible.

I then clattered down the back stairs to our real estate department on the second floor. This section of our legal supermarket advises clients on the purchase and sale of commercial properties and raw land. It also assists on negotiations for private homes, helps arrange mortgages, and represents clients at closings.

The chief of the department was Mrs. Evelyn Sharif, a jovial lady married to a Lebanese who sold Oriental rugs on Worth Avenue. But Evelyn was absent on maternity leave (twins expected!), so I spoke to her assistant, Timothy Hogan, an Irishman who wore Italian suits, English shirts, French cravats, and Spanish shoes. The man was a walking United Nations.

I explained to Tim what I needed: all the skinny he could dig up on the Glorianas' Clematis Street office and their condo near Currie Park. That would include rent, length of lease, maintenance, purchase price of the apartment if they indeed owned it rather than renting, and the references they had furnished.

"Are you sure you don't want the name of their dentist?" Hogan asked.

"I know it's a lot of work, Tim," I said, "but see what you can do, will you?"

"What's in it for me?" he asked.

"I won't tell the old man you're peddling Irish Sweepstakes tickets on company time."

"That's called extortion," he said.

"It is?" I said. "I could have sworn it was blackmail. Whatever, do your best, Tim."

Back in my private closet, I got busy on the phone calling a number of contacts at banks, brokerage houses, and credit rating agencies. Most of the people I buzzed were fellow members of the Pelican Club, and the only price I had to pay for the financial lowdown I sought on the Glorianas was the promise of a dinner at the Pelican.

It was late in the afternoon before I finished my calls, and a subdued growl from the brisket reminded me that other than breakfast the only nourishment I had had all day was a glass of iced tea and a cigarette. I was heading out the door for a pit stop at the nearest watering hole when a jangling phone brought me back to my desk. It was Sgt. Rogoff.

"I'm phoning from the airport," he said. "I just checked with the station and they told me you called."

"What are you doing at the airport?" I asked. "Leaving for Pago Pago?"

"Don't I wish," he said. "Actually I wanted to make sure Roderick Gillsworth made his flight. He's taking the casket up north."

"And he did?"

"Yeah, he's gone. I'm a little antsy about letting him go, but he swears he'll be back in a couple of days. He better be or I'll look like a first-class schmuck for letting him go."

"Al, don't tell me you still suspect him?"

"No, but he's a material witness, isn't he?"

"What kind of condition was he in?"

"It's my guess he was nursing a hangover."

"Shrewd guess," I said. "When I left him last night he was sopping up the sauce like Prohibition was just around the corner. Listen, Al, I've got to talk to you."

"That's what we're doing."

I sighed. "You want me to be precise? Very well, I shall be precise. It is extremely urgent that I meet personally with you, Sergeant Rogoff, since there are certain letters I wish to show you that may prove to be of some importance in your current homicide investigation. There, how's that?"

"What letters?" he demanded.

"Al," I said, "you're going to kill me."

"Cheerfully," he said.

Chapter 9

Al told me he wanted to drive back to the Gillsworth home to make certain the poet had locked up when he left. I said I'd meet him in an hour.

"Take your time," he said. "I'll be there awhile."

I thought that an odd thing to say but made no comment. I grabbed the envelope with the Willigan letters and rode the elevator down to our underground garage. I waved to the security guard and mounted the Miata for the canter home.

No one was about in the McNally castle so I hustled into the kitchen and slapped together a fat sandwich of salami on sour rye, slathered with a mustard hairy enough to bring tears to your baby blues. I cooled the fire with a chilled can of Buckler non-alcoholic beer, then ran upstairs to get Gillsworth's house keys in case I arrived before Rogoff.

But when I got there, a police car was parked in the driveway and the front door of the house was open. I walked in and called, "Al?"

"In here," he yelled, and I found him sprawled in a flowered armchair in the sitting room where Lydia had been murdered. He hadn't taken off his cap, and he was smoking one of his big cigars.

"Make yourself at home," I said.

"I already have," he said. "Let's see those cockamamy letters you were talking about."

I tossed him the envelope. "Photocopy of the first received by Harry Willigan. The second is the original. Handle it with care; it might have prints."

He read both letters slowly while I lounged on a wicker couch and lighted an English Oval. Then he looked up at me.

"Same paper," he said. "Looks like the same ink, same typeface, same even right-hand margins."

"That's right," I said. "The reason I haven't shown them to you before is that the client forbade it. You know Willigan?"

"I know him," he said grimly. "A peerless horse's ass."

"I concur," I said. "And if he ever finds out I've told you about the cat-napping, he'll be an ex-client and probably sue McNally and Son for malpractice. Al, will you please keep a lid on this? My father knows I'm showing you the letters; it was his decision. All we ask in return is your discretion."

"Sure," he said, "I'm good at that. What have you done so far about finding the damned cat?"

"Not a great deal," I said. "One thing I did do—and this will probably give you a laugh: I went to Hertha Gloriana, the psychic, and asked her help in locating Peaches."

But he didn't laugh. "Not so dumb," he said. "Cops hate to admit it, but psychics and mediums are consulted more often than you think. Mostly in missing person cases. What did she say?"

I repeated Hertha's description of the room where she envisioned Peaches was being held prisoner. "She couldn't give me a definite location but said she'll keep trying. Do you think these ransom notes have anything to do with the Gillsworth homicide?"

"Definitely," he said. "Too many similarities in the letters to call it coincidence. I'll get these off to the FBI and ask for a comparison. I'm betting they were all printed on the same machine."

"So what do we do now?"

"Nothing, until we get the FBI report. If Willigan gets instructions on delivering the fifty thousand, let me know and we'll try to set up a snare. I wonder if there's anything to drink in this place."

"Let me take a look," I said. "I'm a neighbor; Gillsworth won't mind if I chisel a drink or two."

I went into the kitchen and found my bottle of Sterling vodka in the freezer. It was still a third full. I brought that and two glasses into the sitting room, then made another trip to bring out a bowl of ice cubes and a pitcher of water.

"Help yourself," I said to Rogoff. "It's McNally booze; I loaned it to Gillsworth last night when he ran dry."

We built drinks for ourselves and settled back. It was really a very attractive, comfortable room—if you didn't look at the bloodstains that had not yet been scrubbed away or painted over.

"That cane that killed her," the sergeant, said. "You told me Mrs. Gillsworth showed it to you."

"That's right."

"Did you touch it?"

"No, she held it while she was telling me about it."

"The shank has a lot of prints," Al said. "Hers, Gillsworth's, some other."

"Probably the antique dealer who sold it to her."

"Probably, and any other customers who picked it up in his shop. But it also has some interesting partials. Our print expert says they were made by someone wearing latex gloves."

"The killer?"

"Seems likely, doesn't it? The latex prints were over the old ones, so I've got to figure they were the last to be made."

"Where does that leave you?"

"Out in left field—unless you spot a guy in the Pelican Club wearing latex gloves."

"Surgeons use them."

"And house painters, window washers, people who scrub floors, dentists, and your friendly neighborhood proctologist. How are you doing with the Glorianas?"

"They're setting up a private séance for me this week. Irma is handling it."

"So you met that bimbo. Did she come on to you?"

"I don't think she's a bimbo, Al, and she didn't come on to me."

He looked at me quizzically. "But didn't you get the feeling that if you hit on her she wouldn't be insulted?"

"Maybe," I said warily. "But I think she's a very complex woman."

"You and your complexities," he said disgustedly. "You can't call a spade a spade. To you it's a sharp-edged implement used for digging that can be inserted into the ground with the aid of foot pressure. To me Irma Gloriana is a hard case with a bottom-line mentality."

I let it go. Al thinks like a policeman. I think like an aged preppy.

"I know you've checked the Glorianas through records," I said. "Anything?"

"No outstanding warrants," he reported. "I've got a lot of queries out and I'm waiting to hear. Something may turn up—but don't hold your breath."

I told him about the inquiries I had made to determine the Glorianas' financial status.

"Good going," he said. "I'm betting they're on their uppers—but that's just a guess. Elegant vodka, Archy."

"It's all yours," I said, finishing my drink and rising. "I've got to get home for the family cocktail hour or mommy and daddy will send out the bloodhounds. Something you should be aware of, Al: You're not Roderick Gillsworth's favorite police officer."

"Tell me something I don't know. And you think I lose sleep over it?"

"He asked if he could phone me from up north and get a report on the investigation. He thinks you're holding out on him."

"I am," Rogoff said with a hard smile. "Do me a favor, will you? If he calls you, tell him I've been acting very mysteriously and you think I've got a hot lead I'm not talking about."

"Do you? Have a hot lead?"

"No."

"Then why should I tell him that?"

"Just to stir him up, keep him off balance."

"Is your middle name Machiavelli or Borgia?"

"It happens to be Irving, but don't tell anyone."

I laughed and started out, then paused. "You're staying?" I asked him.

"For a while. I thought I'd look around the house."

"What for?"

"One never knows, do one?"

"Hey," I protested, "that's my line."

"So it is," Al said, "and you're welcome to it."

He was pouring himself another shot of Sterling when I left.

I started the Miata and drove up Via Del Lago toward the beach. As I did, a car turned off Ocean Boulevard and came toward me. I recognized that clunker, an ancient Chevy that needed an IV. And as it passed I recognized the driver from her carroty hair. It was Marita, the Gillsworths' Haitian housekeeper who, according to Roderick, had been given two weeks off. I pulled to the curb, stopped, and watched in my side mirror.

Marita parked next to the police car, not at all daunted, got out, and went into the house. She was a tubby little woman who walked with a rolling gait. And there was no mistaking that dyed hair.

I started up again and drove homeward. I never doubted for a moment that she had been summoned by Sgt. Rogoff. Their meeting was prearranged, but for what purpose I couldn't even guess. Obviously Al wasn't telling me everything about his investigation. But then I wasn't telling him everything about mine: e.g., the relationship between Laverne Willigan and the Glorianas.

There was something else I hadn't told him, something I hadn't really told myself, for it wasn't a fact or even an idea; it was just a vague notion. And I have no intention of telling you what it was at this juncture. You'd only laugh.

The family cocktail hour and dinner went off with no untoward incidents that evening. After coffee, mother went to her television in the second-floor sitting room, father retired to Dickens in his study, and I trotted upstairs and got to work on my journal.

I was interrupted that night by two phone calls. The first was from Connie Garcia.

"You swine," she started. "Why haven't you called?"

"Busy, busy, busy," I said. "I *do* have a job, you know, and I work hard at it. I'm not just another pretty face."

She giggled. "I'll testify to *that*. Have you been seeing Meg Trumble lately?"

"Haven't seen her in days," I said, feeling virtuous because I could be honest. "She may have gone back up north."

"I hope she stays there," Connie said. "Listen, I have a family thing for tomorrow night—a bridal shower for one of my cousins—but I'm available for lunch. Make me an offer."

"Connie, would you care to have lunch with me tomorrow?"

"What a splendid idea! I'd love to. Pick me up around noon—okay?"

"You betcha. I have a new hat to show you—a puce beret."

"Oh God," she said.

I went back to my journal, scribbling along at a lively clip until I started on an account of my meeting with Irma Gloriana. Then I paused to lean back and stare at the stained ceiling, trying to bring her into sharper focus.

I had thought Frank Gloriana functioned as Hertha's business manager. But Irma's role in setting up the séance and her authoritative manner led me to believe that perhaps she was the CEO of the Gloriana menage.

If the Glorianas were engaged in hanky-panky, as I was beginning to think they were, then Irma was the Ma Barker of the gang, a very robust and attractive chieftain. That would make son Frank her foppish henchman. But what part was Hertha playing? I could not believe that sweet, limpid innocent could be guilty of any wrongdoing. Her lips were too soft and warm for a criminal. (I know that is a ridiculous non sequitur; you don't have to tell me.)

My musings were interrupted by the second phone call, this one from Roderick Gillsworth in Rhode Island.

"How are you getting along, Rod?" I asked.

"As well as can be expected," he said. "Isn't that what doctors say when the patient is in extremis? The funeral is scheduled for tomorrow after a church service at noon. Then I am expected to attend a buffet dinner at the home of an elderly aunt. I fear she may serve dandelion wine or chamomile tea so I shall be well fortified beforehand, I assure you. I'll get through it somehow."

"Of course you will. When are you returning?"

"I have a flight on Wednesday morning. Tell me, Archy, is there anything new on the investigation?"

I hesitated, long enough for him to say, "Well?"

"Nothing definite, no," I said. "But I spoke to Sergeant Rogoff today and he was rather mystifying. He seemed quite pleased with himself, as if he had uncovered something important. But when I asked questions, all he'd do was wink."

"Dreadful man," Gillsworth said. "If I can't get any satisfaction from him when I return on Wednesday, I intend to go directly to his superior and demand to be told what's going on."

I made no reply to that. "I stopped by your home early this evening, Rod," I said. "Just to make certain it was locked up. Everything is fine."

"Thank you, Archy," he said. "I may call you again tomorrow to ask if you have learned anything new."

"Of course."

"I appreciate all that you and your father have done for me. You might tell him that I've been thinking about my new will. I'll probably have the terms roughed out by the time I return."

"Good," I said. "He'll be happy to hear that."

I hung up, having lied as requested by Al Rogoff and wondering what the sergeant really wanted to accomplish by giving Gillsworth false hopes that the murder of his wife was nearing solution. Sometimes Al moves in mysterious ways.

It was almost midnight before I finished my journal entries. I decided I didn't want to smoke, drink, or listen to Robert Johnson singing "Kindhearted Woman Blues." So I went to bed and thought happily of Meg Trumble arriving on the morrow. I hoped she would be kindhearted and I would have no cause to sing the blues.

I was awakened early Tuesday morning by the growling of what sounded like a brigade of power mowers. I stumbled to the window and looked down to see our landscape gardener's crew hard at work. They showed up periodically to mow the lawn, trim shrubbery, and spray everything in sight.

They were making such a racket that I knew it would be futile to try resuming my dreamless slumber—which explains why I was showered, shaved, and dressed in time to breakfast with my parents in the dining room. It was such a rare occurrence that they looked at me in astonishment and mother asked anxiously, "Are you ill, Archy?"

I proved to her I was in fine fettle by consuming a herculean portion of eggs scrambled with onions and smoked salmon. Over coffee, I told my father about Gillsworth's call the previous evening, and that the poet would be returning on Wednesday ready to draw up a new will.

He looked up from *The Wall Street Journal* long enough to nod. I then informed him I expected a hectic day so I would drive to the office in my own car rather than accompany him in the Lexus. That earned me a second nod before he went back to his paper. The master doesn't like to be interrupted while he's checking the current value of his treasury bonds.

I ran upstairs to collect a fresh box of English Ovals, my reading glasses, and the puce beret, which I rolled up and tucked into a jacket pocket. I wore my madras that day, a nifty number gaudy enough to enrage any passing bull.

I arrived at my miniature office just in time to receive a phone call from Mrs. Irma Gloriana.

"Good morning, Mr. McNally," she said crisply and didn't wait for a return greeting. "I have arranged a private séance for you and your companion tomorrow evening at nine o'clock. Will that be satisfactory?"

"Completely," I said. "Shall we—"

"It will be held here in the apartment," she continued. "We have found that an informal, homey setting is more likely to result in a successful session than a meeting held in a commercial office."

"I can—"

"Please be prompt," she went on, and I despaired of contributing to the conversation. "As you can imagine, these sittings are quite a strain on Hertha, and if they are delayed it only adds to her spiritual tension."

"We'll be on time," I said hurriedly and just did get it out before she hung up.

What a peremptory woman she was! I wondered what had happened to her husband. Had he died of frustration because he couldn't get a word in edgewise? Or had he divorced her for a more docile woman who welcomed small talk and could schmooze for hours about his gastritis and her bunions? My own guess was that Irma's husband went out to buy a loaf of bread, vamoosed, and was now employed as a tobacco auctioneer.

I worked fitfully on my expense account that morning, a monthly task that challenged my creativity. My labors were interrupted by three phone calls from informants I had queried about the Glorianas' financial status and credit rating.

By the time I had to leave for my luncheon date with Connie Garcia, I was convinced Al Rogoff had been right: the Glorianas were on their uppers. They weren't candidates for welfare—far from it—but their bank balances were distressingly low, and they had an unenviable reputation for bouncing checks. They always made good, eventually, but rubber checks make bankers break out in a rash, and they usually suggest chronic paperhangers take their business elsewhere.

I drove back to the beach to pick up Connie, reflecting on the Glorianas' impecunious state and dreaming up all kinds of fanciful scenarios to link their dreaded ailment, lackamoola, to the catnapping of Peaches. The connection seemed obvious; proving it was another kettle of flounder entirely.

When Ms. Garcia came bouncing out of her office in Lady Horowitz's mansion, I was lounging nonchalantly alongside the Miata, my new beret atop my dome and tilted dashingly to one side. Connie took a long, open-mouthed look and then bent almost double in a paroxysm of mirth.

"Please!" she gasped. "Archy, *please* take it off. I can't *stand* it! My ribs ache."

Much affronted, I crammed the cap back in my pocket. *Ut quod ali cibus est allis fuat acre venenum.* Translation: One's puce beret is another's aching ribs.

But your hero's generosity of spirit is sufficient to pardon a lapse of taste, and Connie's insult to my headgear was soon forgiven as we headed for the Pelican Club.

There was a goodly crowd at the bar but surprisingly few members were seated in the dining area. We got our favorite corner table, and Priscilla strutted over to take our order.

"Archy," Connie said, "show Pris your new hat."

Obediently I dug the beret from my jacket pocket and tugged it on at a rakish tilt. Priscilla stared, aghast.

"You know, Connie," she said, "the man really should be committed. It's obvious his elevator doesn't go to the top floor."

"What's obvious," I said, removing the beret, "is that the two of you are fashion's slaves but have no appreciation of style. Believe me, linen berets are the coming thing."

"If they're coming," Priscilla said, "I'm going. You folks want to sit here arguing about goofy hats or do you want to order?"

Connie and I had vodka gimlets to start, and we both went for Leroy's special of the day: a grilled grouper sandwich with spicy french fries, served with a salad of Bibb lettuce, red onions, and a vinaigrette sauce. A winner.

Connie attacked her food with enthusiasm and didn't mention a word about proteins, cholesterol, or fat, for which I was thankful. Nutrition nuts are the world's most boring dining companions. They make every bite a guilt trip, which forces me to gorge to prove my disdain for calories. I mean, if God had wanted us to nibble, He wouldn't have created veal cordon bleu.

"By the way," Connie said, looking up from her salad, "I sent in that application to the Glorianas, asking for a psychic profile."

"Good for you," I said. "Thank you, Connie. I hope you didn't make it too ridiculous."

"Nope. I just invented all the vital statistics, birthplace, names of parents, and so forth. And I bought a little red plastic heart at a gift shop and sent it along as my beloved personal possession. You really think the Glorianas will send me a phony profile?"

"As phony as your letter," I assured her. "Let me know as soon as you receive a reply. Meanwhile I'll get you a check from McNally and Son for services rendered."

"I'm not worried," she said. "But don't leave town."

We both laughed. She really was a jolly woman, and there was no side to her; what you saw was what you got. I think our problem—or rather *my* problem—was that we had become so familiar over the years that mystery was lacking; we knew each other too well. We were really more buddies than lovers, more contented than passionate. But content is never enough, is it? Which is why men and women cheat on each other, I suppose.

Thoughts like that saddened me, and I resolved to buy Connie a diamond tennis bracelet. Remorse can be costly—right?

I signed the tab for lunch, and Connie preceded me from the dining room and through the bar area. It was gratifying to see how many male noggins turned in her direction and to note the longing looks. She even drew appreciative glances from several of the females present, for Connie was an enormously attractive lady who radiated a buoyant delight in being alive, young, and full of fire.

I knew well that I was a fool to be unfaithful to her. But that knowledge didn't deter me. I consoled myself with the thought that if we all acted in an intelligent, disciplined manner, what a dull world it would be. I'm sure Napoleon thought the same thing as he staggered home from Moscow.

We returned to the Horowitz estate and sat in the car a few moments before Connie went back to work. She turned sideways to look directly at me, her expression set.

"Archy," she said in a firm voice, "*you* don't want to break up again, do you?"

"Break up?" I cried. "Of course I don't want to break up. What kind of nonsense is that?"

"You've been acting so strangely lately, so distant."

"I told you how busy I've been. I know you've heard about Lydia Gillsworth being killed. Well, she was our client, and father wants me to assist the police in finding the murderer. We were both very deeply affected by her death."

"I can understand that, but surely you're not busy twenty-four hours a day. We haven't had a night together for ages."

"That's not all my fault," I pointed out. "We did have a small bacchanalia planned, but then you had to work late. You do recall that, don't you?"

She nodded. "But that doesn't mean we can't plan another mini-orgy. Archy, remember the time we went skinny-dipping in the ocean at midnight?"

"A memory I shall retain forever," I said. "I got stung by a Portuguese man-of-war."

"A very small sting."

"On a very embarrassing portion of my anatomy. But you're right, Connie; it has been a long time since we two were one."

"Tomorrow night?" she suggested.

"Ah," I said, the old neurons and dendrites working at blinding speed, "regretfully I cannot. I have a meeting with Sergeant Al Rogoff to help prepare a statement to the press on the investigation. How about the weekend? Perhaps Saturday night?"

"Sounds good," she said. "I'll plan on it. Don't disappoint me, Archy."

"Have I ever?"

She gave me a rueful smile. "I better not answer that." She leaned forward to kiss my cheek. "Thanks for the lunch, luv. See you Saturday night. But do try to phone me before that—okay?"

"Of course," I said. "Absolutely."

She scampered into her office, and I drove home terrified that on some future date all the women I had wronged might hold a convention, compare grievances, and decide a prompt lynching of yrs. truly would be justified. I even imagined myself swinging from a palm tree, clad in nothing but my silk briefs imprinted with an image of Pan tootling his syrinx to a bevy of naked dryads.

I had no idea when Meg Trumble might call to announce her arrival, so I decided to stick close to the phone, even forgoing my ocean swim so I wouldn't miss her. I went directly to my quarters and switched the air conditioner to High Cool. It wasn't all that hot, but it was oppressively muggy, and I stripped to my skivvies before setting to work.

I remembered I had promised Meg a list of friends and acquaintances who might be interested in employing a personal trainer. Consulting my address book, I compiled a choice selection of men and women, concentrating on the suety and notorious couch potatoes. At the end, just for a giggle, I added the name of Al Rogoff.

It came time to dress for the family cocktail hour, and I still hadn't heard from Meg. It was quite possible she was delayed on the road for one reason or another, so I thought it best to dine at home with my parents. If she called after I had eaten, I could still take her to dinner but limit my own intake to fresh fruit, like a wedge of lime in a frozen daiquiri.

Actually, she didn't phone until a little after nine o'clock. She was all apologies; heavy traffic and road construction had thrown her schedule out of kilter.

"I hope you went ahead and had dinner, Archy," she said. "I'd hate to think you were starving because of me."

"As a matter of fact I have eaten," I confessed. "But that doesn't mean we can't keep our dinner date."

"You don't have to do that," she protested. "I'll just run out for a snack and we can make it another time. Perhaps tomorrow night, if you're free."

"That's what I want to talk to you about," I said. "Listen, suppose we do this: I'll pick up a pizza and something to drink and hustle it over to your place while the pie is still warm. Or you can heat it up in your oven. How does that sound?"

"Marvelous—if you're sure you want to do it."

"I do," I said. "Be there within the hour."

Recently a new pizzeria had opened on Federal Highway south of the Port of Palm Beach. It offered "designer pizzas" to be consumed on the premises or taken out in insulated boxes. I had tried it a few times and found the fare rather exotic. But then I'm strictly a pepperoni addict.

I drove to the pizza boutique to purchase a pie for Meg. I selected one consisting of eggplant, sun-dried tomatoes, and Gorgonzola on a thin crust. I was reminded of the time Peaches had barfed on my lavender loafers, but I was certain the vegetarian Ms. Trumble would love it. I also bought a six-pack of Diet Pepsi, my dream of a frozen daiquiri vanishing.

Meg opened the door for me with a broad smile and a cheek kiss, on the same spot favored by Connie Garcia not too many hours previously. As Willy Loman pointed out, it's important to be well-liked.

Meg looked smashing. She had obviously just showered; her spiky hair was still damp and her face was shiny. She was wearing white duck short-shorts and a skimpy knitted top that left her midriff bare. I swear that rib cage was designed by Brancusi.

Also, she smelled good.

Her apartment was crowded with unpacked suitcases, cartons, and bulging shopping bags. She cleared a space on a clunky cocktail table for the pizza box and brought us both iced Pepsis. She didn't bother heating up the pie but immediately began wolfing it down, occasionally rolling her eyes and uttering, "Yum!"

"Good lord," I said, "didn't you have anything to eat today?"

"A country breakfast at seven this morning," she said. "I'm really famished."

"I should think so. Meg, did you call me from your phone here?"

She shook her head. "From a gas station. But my phone will be connected in the morning. They promised."

"Fine," I said. "I may need to call. About tomorrow night, Meg—how would you like to go to a séance with me?"

I was afraid she might refuse or think the whole idea so hysterically off-the-wall that I wouldn't be able to introduce her to the Glorianas as a serious student of spiritualism. But she surprised me.

"Love to," she said promptly. "Laverne and I used to go to them all the time. I didn't know you were interested in New Age things."

"Oh yes," I lied brazenly. "I'm deep into crystals, ESP, telepathy, and all that. I've arranged a private séance with a local medium, her husband, and mother-in-law for tomorrow evening. The psychic is supposed to be very gifted. I've never attended a séance before, so I'm looking forward to it. You'll go with me then?"

"Of course. What time?"

"Nine o'clock. I thought we'd have dinner first. Suppose I pick you up at seven."

"I'll be ready," she said. She licked her fingers, crossed her sleek legs, settled back with her drink. She had demolished the entire pizza. But of course it was only the eight-inch size.

"That was delicious," she proclaimed. "Thank you, Archy; you saved my life. I wish I had something stronger than Pepsi to offer you. I'm going to load up the fridge tomorrow, get this place organized, and then start looking for clients."

"I'm glad you mentioned that," I said and handed her the list of potential customers I had prepared.

"Wonderful," she said, scanning the names. "I'm so glad you didn't forget. How can I ever thank you?"

I gave her my Groucho Marx leer. "I'll think of something," I said.

She laughed. "Oh, Archy," she said, "what a clown you are. Would you mind awfully if we skipped tonight? Right now I want to get unpacked and catch a million Zs."

"Of course," I said, upper lip stiffening. "You must be exhausted after all that driving." I stood up to leave. "I'll see you at seven tomorrow night, Meg."

She came close and hugged me tightly. I was breathlessly aware of her muscled arms. "Tomorrow will be different," she whispered. "I promise."

"Sleep well," I said as lightly as I could. I drove home thinking there really should be an over-the-counter remedy that cures habitual hoping.

Roderick Gillsworth didn't call that night—for which I was grateful.

Chapter 10

Why do men's jackets and shirts button left over right while women's button right over left? I have asked this question of people at cocktail parties, and they invariably give me a frozen smile and move away.

But I'm sure there is an explanation for this buttoning conundrum that is at once profound and simple. I felt the same way about the disappearance of Peaches and the murder of Lydia Gillsworth. Those twin mysteries had a logical and satisfying solution if I could but find it.

I spent Wednesday morning slowly going over my journal, reading every entry twice. I found nothing that even hinted at some devilish plot that would account for a missing *Felis domestica* and the death of a poet's wife. All my diary contained was a jumble of facts and impressions. I could only pray that the séance that evening would yield a spectral suggestion that might inspire me.

I drove to the office and found on my desk, sealed in an envelope, a memo from Tim Hogan, temporary chief of our real estate section. It concerned the Glorianas' office and condo.

The commercial suite on Clematis Street had been leased for a year. The Glorianas had put up two months' rent as security but were currently a month behind in their payments. Similarly, their apartment had not been purchased but was rented on a month-to-month basis. At the moment, the Glorianas were current on their rent.

In both cases the references given were a bank and individuals in Atlanta. Hogan had thoughtfully provided names and addresses, but mentioned he could find no record of the references ever having been checked. That was unusual but not unheard of in the freewheeling world of South Florida real estate.

I called Sgt. Rogoff and told him what I had.

"Why don't you check them out, Al?" I suggested. "Just for the fun of it."

"Yeah," he said, "I will. But first I think I'll contact the Atlanta cops. Just in case."

"Do that," I urged. "It's the first real lead we've had on where the Glorianas operated before they arrived here."

I gave him the names and addresses of the Glorianas' references, and he promised to get back to me as soon as he had something. At that point I had no idea of where I might turn next in my discreet inquiries, so I decided to drive over to Worth Avenue and see if I could buy a tennis bracelet for Connie at a price that wouldn't land me in debtors' prison.

Then fate took a beneficent hand in the investigation—which proves that if you are pure of heart and eat your Wheaties, good things can happen to you.

I went down to the garage to board the Miata for the short drive over to Worth. Herb, our lumbering security guard, had come out of his glass cubicle and was leaning down to stroke the head of a cat rubbing against his shins. I strolled over.

"Got a new friend, Herb?" I asked.

He looked up at me. "A stray, Mr. McNally," he said. "He just came wandering down the ramp."

That had to be the longest, skinniest cat I had ever seen. It was a dusty black with a dirty-white blaze on its chest. One ear was hanging limply and looked bloodied. And the poor animal obviously hadn't had a decent table d'hôte in weeks; its ribs and pelvic bones were poking.

But despite its miserable condition, it seemed to be in a lighthearted mood. It purred loudly under Herb's caresses, then came over to sniff at my shoes. I leaned to scratch under the chin. It liked that.

"Looks hungry, Herb," I said.

"Sure does," he said. "Maybe I'll run up to the cafeteria and get it something to eat."

"*Our* cafeteria?" I said. "You're liable to be arrested for cruelty to animals. Are you going to adopt it?"

"Mebbe," he said. "But if I take it home with me, it's liable to get into my tropical fish tanks. You think it would be all right if I kept it around here? I'll bet it's a great mouser."

"It's okay with me," I said, "if you're willing to take care of it."

"I think I should take it to the vet first," he said worriedly. "I'll have that ear fixed up and get it a bath."

I stared down at the stray, and I swear it grinned at me. That was one devil-may-care cat. It looked a little like Errol Flynn in *The Charge of the Light Brigade*.

"You're going to be okay," the guard said, addressing his new pal. "The vet'll fix you up like new."

That's when it hit me. I clapped Herb on the shoulder. "God bless you," I said hoarsely, and he probably thought I was approving his kindness to a wounded and homeless beast.

I immediately returned to my office and dug out the Yellow Pages for what Southern Bell called Greater West Palm Beach. I turned to the listings for Veterinarians.

This was my reasoning: Suppose Peaches got sick while she was in the custody of the catnappers. That was possible, wasn't it? In fact, it was likely when the irascible animal found herself being held prisoner by strangers in unfamiliar surroundings. The thieves wouldn't want to risk the health of their fifty-grand hostage, so they'd hustle her to a vet. All I had to do was contact local veterinarians and ask if they had recently treated a fat, silver-gray Persian with a mean disposition.

It was a long shot, I admitted, but at the moment I didn't have any short shots.

But my brainstorm fizzled when I took a look at the Veterinarian listings in the Yellow Pages. There were pages and pages of them, seemingly hundreds of DVMs. It would take S. Holmes and a regiment of the Baker Street Irregulars a month of Sundays to check out all those names and addresses. Good idea, I decided, but imdamnedpossible to carry out.

But then my roving eye fell on a short section headed Veterinarian Emergency Service and listed animal clinics and hospitals open twenty-four hours a day. The roster contained only fifteen names and addresses, some as far afield as Boynton Beach. It seemed reasonable to guess that if Peaches became ill, her captors would rush her to the nearest emergency facility.

I was back in business again!

I scissored out the vital section and with my gold Mont Blanc I carefully circled the animal emergency wards in the West Palm Beach area. There were seven of them. I estimated I could visit all seven in two days, or perhaps more if I became bored with routine snooping.

Now the only problem that remained was devising a scenario that would insure cooperation at all those infirmaries for ailing faunas. I mean I couldn't just barge in, describe Peaches, and demand to know if they had treated a cat like that lately. The medicos would call the gendarmes for sure and tell them to bring a large butterfly net.

No, what I needed was an imaginary tale that would arouse interest and eager response. In other words, a twenty-four-karat scam. Here is what I came up with:

"Good morning! My name is Archibald McNally and here is my business card. I have a problem I hope you will be able to help me with. I returned from a business trip last night and found on my answering machine a message from a close friend, a lady friend, who apparently had arrived in West Palm Beach during my absence. The message was frantic. Her cat—she always travels with her beloved Peaches—had suddenly become ill and she was rushing it to an emergency animal hospital. But the poor dear was so hysterical that she neglected to inform me where she was staying or to which clinic she was taking her sick pet. I wonder if you could tell me if you have treated such an animal recently and have the address of the owner. It would help me enormously."

I would then describe Peaches.

It seemed to me a plea that would be hard to resist. Naturally I didn't know if the catnapper was male or female, but I planned to put in that bit about a "lady friend" to suggest a romantic attachment that might evoke sympathy. Emerson said all mankind love a lover—but of course he never met Fatty Arbuckle.

Anyway, that's how I spent Wednesday afternoon—driving to four animal hospitals and putting on my act. In all four the receptionist was a young woman, and I would bestow upon her my most winning 100-watt smile and launch into my spiel. The results? Nil.

But I was not discouraged. In fact, as I drove back to the beach for my ocean swim, I was delighted that my monologue had been readily accepted at all four facilities I visited. Although none of them had treated a feline of Peaches' description, all were cooperative in searching their records and sorrowful when they could not provide the assistance requested.

I had my swim and returned to my chambers to prepare for the family cocktail hour, my dinner with Meg Trumble, and the séance with the Glorianas that was to follow. I decided to dress soberly, if not somberly: navy tropical worsted suit, white shirt, maroon tie. But examining myself in the full-length mirror, I realized I looked a bit too much like a mortician, so I exchanged the maroon cravat for a silk jacquard number with a hand-painted design of oriental lilies. Much better.

Over martinis that evening, mother remarked that I looked "very smart." Father took one glance at the lilies, and a single eyebrow shot up in a conditioned reflex. But all he said was, "Gillsworth has returned. He phoned me late this afternoon."

"Is he ready to execute a new will?" I asked.

The patriarch frowned. "He said he would call me next week and set up an appointment. I would have preferred an earlier date—tomorrow, if possible—and told him so. But he said he hadn't yet decided on specific bequests and needed more time. I do believe the man was stalling, but for what purpose I cannot conceive."

"Prescott," mother said softly, "some people find it very difficult to make out a will. It can be a wrenching emotional experience."

"Nonsense," he said. "We're all going to die and it's only prudent to prepare for it. I wrote out my first holographic will at the age of nine."

I laughed. "What possessions did you have to leave at that age, father?"

"All my marbles," he declared.

A derisive comment on that admission was obvious, but I didn't have the courage to utter it.

Later, as I drove northward to Riviera Beach, the problem of Roderick Gillsworth's last will and testament was eclipsed by a more immediate quandary; to wit, where was I going to take Meg Trumble for dinner?

It had to be close enough so that we could arrive at the séance at the time dictated by Mrs. Irma Gloriana. And yet it had to be distant enough and relatively secluded so I had a fighting chance of not being seen in Meg's company by Connie Garcia or any of her corps de snitches.

I finally decided on a Middle Eastern restaurant on 45th Street not far from an area known as Mangonia Park. It was a very small bistro, only six booths, but I had been there once before and thought the food superb, if you liked grape leaves. However, it did have one drawback: it had no bar; only beer and wine were served. But, paraphrasing the Good Book, I consoled myself with the thought that man doth not live by vodka alone.

Meg was ready when I arrived, which was a pleasant surprise. Another was her appearance. She wore a short-sleeved dress of silk crepe divided into two panels of solid color, fuchsia and orange. Sounds awful, I know, but it looked great. It had a jewel neckline, but her only accessories were gold sea-horse earrings. Meg still had most of her Florida tan, and she looked so slender, vibrant, and healthy that I immediately resolved to lose weight, grow muscles, and drink nothing but seltzer on the rocks.

I whisked her to the Cafe Istanbul, assuring her that although it might appear funky, it had become the *in* place for discriminating gourmets. That wasn't a *big* lie, just a slight exaggeration to increase her enjoyment of dining in a joint that had nothing but belly dance music on the jukebox.

It turned out that Meg was fascinated by the place and relaxed her vegetarian discipline sufficiently to order moussaka. I had rotisseried lamb on curried rice. We shared a big salad that was mostly black olives that really were the pits and pickled cauliflower buds. I also ordered a half-bottle of chilled retsina. Meg tried one small sip, then opted for a Coke, so I was forced, *forced,* to drink the entire bottle myself.

It was over the honey-drenched baklava that I finally got around to the séance we were about to attend.

"I didn't know you and your sister were interested in spiritualism," I said as casually as I could.

"Laverne more than me," Meg said. "She's into all that stuff. I think she's had her horoscope done by a dozen astrologers, and she always sleeps with a crystal under her pillow."

"I wonder if she knows Hertha Gloriana, the medium we're going to visit tonight."

"I've never heard her mention the name, but that's understandable. Harry goes into orbit if anyone brings up the subject of parapsychology. He thinks it's all a great big swindle. Do you, Archy?"

The direct question troubled me. "I just don't know," I confessed. "That's one of the reasons I'm looking forward to the session tonight. Meg, do you believe it's possible to communicate with ghosts?"

"Of course," she said promptly. "I went to a séance once and talked to my grandmother. I never knew her; she's been dead for fifty years. But her spirit knew things about our family that were true and that the medium couldn't possibly have known."

"Did your grandmother's spirit tell you where she was?"

"In Heaven," Meg said simply, and I finished the retsina.

We arrived at the Glorianas' residence ten minutes before the appointed hour. The family was assembled in that rather shoddy living room, and I introduced Meg. The greetings of Irma and Frank were courteous enough, although not heavy on the cordiality. But Hertha welcomed Meg warmly, held her hand a moment while gazing deeply into her eyes.

"An Aries," she said. "Aren't you?"

"Why, yes," Meg said. "How did you know?"

Hertha only smiled and turned to me. "And how are you tonight, Pisces?" she asked.

She was right again. But of course she could easily have researched my birthday. In all modesty, I must admit my vital statistics are listed in a thin booklet titled: *Palm Beach's Most Eligible Bachelors*. And I could guess how she knew Meg's natal date.

Hertha was wearing a long, flowing gown of lavender georgette which I thought more suitable for a garden party than a séance. Irma Gloriana wore a black, wide-shouldered pantsuit with a mannish shirt and paisley ascot. Son Frank, that fop, flaunted a double-breasted Burberry blazer in white wool with gold buttons. He made me look like an IRS auditor, damn him.

No refreshments were offered, and no preparatory instructions or explanations given. We all moved into a dimly lighted dining room. There, leaves had been removed from an oval oak table, converting it to a round that accommodated the five of us comfortably. The chairs were straightbacked, the seats thinly padded.

I was placed between Irma and Frank. He held Hertha's left hand while Meg grasped her right. From the top of the table, moving clockwise, we were Hertha, Frank, Archy, Irma, Meg. An odd seating arrangement, I thought: the two men side-by-side, and the three women. But perhaps there was a reason for it.

Hertha looked around the circle slowly with that intent, unblinking gaze of hers. And she spoke slowly, too, in her low, breathy voice.

"Please, everyone," she said, "clasp hands tightly. Close your eyes and turn your thoughts to Xatyl, the Mayan shaman who is my channel to the hereafter. With all your spiritual strength try to *will* Xatyl to appear to me."

At first, eyes firmly shut, all I was conscious of was Frank's muscular handclasp and the softer, warmer, moister hand of his mother. But then I tried to think of Xatyl. I had no idea of what a Mayan shaman looked like—certainly not like any member of the Pelican Club—so I concentrated on the name, silently repeating Xatyl, Xatyl, Xatyl, like a mantra.

I thought five soundless minutes must have passed before I heard Hertha speak again in a voice that had become a flat drone.

"Xatyl appears," she reported. "Dimly. From the mists. Greetings, Xatyl, from your supplicants."

The next words I heard were a shock. Not their meaning as much as the tone in which they were uttered. It was the frail, cracked voice of an old man, a worn voice that quavered and sometimes paused weakly.

"Greetings from the beyond," Xatyl said. "I bring you love from a high priest of the Mayan people."

I opened my eyes to stare at Hertha. The words were issuing from her mouth, no doubt of it, but I could scarcely believe that ancient, tremulous voice was hers. I shut my eyes again, grateful for the handholds of Irma and Frank to anchor me to reality.

"Who wishes to contact one of the departed?" Hertha asked in her normal voice.

"I do," Meg Trumble said at once. "I would like to speak to my father, John Trumble, who passed on eight years ago."

"I have heard," the Xatyl voice said. "Be patient, my child."

We waited in silence several long moments. I must tell you honestly that

I didn't know what to make of all this. But I confess I was moved by what was going on and had absolutely no inclination to laugh.

"Meg," a man said, "is it you?"

Now the voice was virile, almost booming, and I opened my eyes just wide enough to see that the words were being spoken by Hertha.

I heard Meg's sudden, sharp intake of breath. "Yes, dad," she said, "I am here. Are you all right?"

"I am contented since mother joined me last year. Now we are together again as we had prayed. Meg, are you still doing your exercises?"

"Oh yes, dad," she said with a sobbing laugh. "I'm still at it. How is your arthritis?"

"There is no pain here, daughter," John Trumble said. "We are free of your world's suffering. Have you married, Meg?"

"No, father, not yet."

"You must marry," he said gently. "Your mother and I want you to be as happy as we were and are. I must go now, Meg. If you need me, I am here, I am here."

The voice trailed away, and I could hear Meg's quiet weeping.

"Please," Hertha whispered, "do not let our psychic power weaken. Clasp hands firmly and think only of the other world."

There was silence a few moments, then I heard again the trembling voice of Xatyl.

"There is one among you who is deeply troubled," he said. "Let him speak out now."

"Yes," I said impulsively, hiding behind my closed eyes. "My name is Archibald McNally. I wish to contact Lydia Gillsworth, a friend. She passed over a few days ago."

"I will summon her," Xatyl said. "Be patient, my son."

Once again we waited several minutes. I found myself gripping the hands of Irma and Frank so tightly that my fingers ached, and I was conscious of hyperventilating.

"Archy?" a woman's voice asked. "Is that you?"

After I heard my name I opened my eyes to verify that it was Hertha speaking, but I swear, I *swear* it was Lydia Gillsworth's sweet, peaceful voice. So dulcet.

"It is I, Lydia," I found myself saying, almost choking on the words. "Are you well?"

"Oh yes, Archy," she said, a hint of laughter in her voice. "It is as I told you it would be. Have you read the books I loaned you?"

"Some. Not all."

"You must read *all* of them, dear. The truth is there, Archy."

"Lydia," I said, eager to ask *the* question, "you must tell me another truth: Who killed you?"

There was no answer. Just silence. I tried again.

"Please tell me," I implored. "I can never rest until I know. Who murdered you, Lydia?"

What happened next shocked and galvanized us.

"Caprice!" Lydia Gillsworth's voice shrieked. "Caprice!"

Handclasps were loosened, four of us rose, stared at Hertha. She was still seated, head thrown back, bare throat straining. And she continued to scream, "Caprice! Caprice! Caprice!" But now it was her voice, not Lydia's.

Meg Trumble got to her first, held her arms, spoke soothing words. We all clustered around, and gradually those piercing screams diminished. Hertha opened her eyes, looked about wildly. She was ashen, shivering uncontrollably.

Frank left hastily and came back in a moment with a shot glass of what appeared to be brandy. Meg took it from him and held it gently to the medium's lips. Hertha took a small sip, coughed, stared at us and her surroundings as if finally realizing where she was. She took the glass from Meg's fingers and gulped greedily.

We stayed in the dining room until Hertha's color had returned and she was able to stand, somewhat shakily. She gave us a small, apologetic smile, and then we all moved back to the living room.

Frank had the decency to bring us ponies of brandy, and since Meg wouldn't touch hers, I had a double—and needed it. I sat in one corner with Irma and Frank. Across the room, on the couch, Meg Trumble comforted the medium, her muscled arm around the other woman's shoulders. She spoke to her and stroked her hair.

"What on earth happened?" I asked Irma.

She shrugged. "Hertha heard or saw something that terrified her. And she became hysterical. It's happened a few times before. I told you she is a very sensitive and vulnerable spirit."

"Caprice," Frank said, looking at me. "That's what she was screaming. Does that mean anything to you, Mr. McNally?"

I shook my head. "A caprice is a whim, an unplanned action. Perhaps Lydia Gillsworth was trying to tell us that the killer acted on a sudden impulse, and her murder was totally unpremeditated."

"Yes," Irma said, "I'm sure that was it."

"I'm sorry now that I asked the question," I said. "I didn't mean to frighten Hertha. But I did inform you that I intended to ask."

"No one blames you," Irma said. "There are many things in this world and the next that are beyond our understanding."

Hamlet said it better, but I didn't remind her of that. "You're so right, Mrs. Gloriana," I said.

She nodded. "Did you bring your credit card, Mr. McNally?"

I handed it over; she and Frank left the room to prepare my bill. I remained seated, finishing Meg's brandy and watching the two women on the couch. Hertha seemed fully recovered now. She and Meg were close together, holding hands and giggling like schoolgirls. I found it a bit off-putting.

Irma returned with my bill. I signed it, reclaimed my plastic, and took my receipt.

"I'm sorry the séance ended the way it did," she said. "But I would not call it a total failure, would you?"

"Far from it," I said. "Meg was able to speak to her father and I made contact with Mrs. Gillsworth. I'm perfectly satisfied."

"Good," she said. "Then perhaps you'd like to arrange another private session."

"Of course I would. Let me check my schedule and speak to Meg about a date that will be suitable for her. You'll be here all summer?"

"Oh yes. We have many activities to keep us busy."

"Then you'll be hearing from me."

"When?" she asked.

A demon saleswoman, this one.

"Soon," I said, stood up, and motioned to Meg.

I shook hands with all the Glorianas before we left. Meg did the same, but then Hertha embraced her, kissed her on the lips, clung to her a moment. In gratitude for Meg's sympathetic ministrations. No doubt.

On the drive back to Riviera Beach Meg was so voluble that I could scarcely believe this was the same woman who had been so reticent on our first ride together.

"What a *wonderful* medium she is, Archy," she burbled. "So *gifted*. She knew so *many* things about me. And it was so *great* to talk to dad. Wasn't it *incredible* to hear all those voices coming from *her*? And guess what: I told her I hope to become a personal trainer, and she *insisted* on being my first client. Isn't that *marvelous*?"

"Yes."

"And she's going to do my horoscope for *free!* It must be *scary* having the talent to see into the beyond. She said she usually refuses to predict the future, but after she does my horoscope she'll tell me what she sees ahead for me. Isn't that *fantastic*?"

I didn't want to rain on her parade, so I neither voiced my doubts nor cautioned her against relying on the predictions of a seer. It seemed unnecessarily cruel to tell her my own reactions to what we had just experienced. Being essentially without faith myself, I think it rather infra dig to mock the faith of others.

We arrived outside Meg's apartment, and now her initial ebullience had faded and she was speaking calmly and seriously of spirituality and how she had neglected that side of her nature and really should start seeking answers to what she termed the "big questions." I presumed they included Life, Death, and why only one sock got lost in the laundry.

Somehow it didn't seem the right moment to remind her of her carnal promise of the previous evening. So, rather than risk rejection, I said:

"Meg, would you mind awfully if I didn't come in? I feel totally shattered by what happened tonight—hearing Lydia Gillsworth's voice and all that. I think I better go home and try to figure things out."

She promptly agreed—so promptly that she severely bruised the ego of A. McNally, who may or may not be suffering from a Don Juan complex.

"I think that would be best, dear," she said in the kindliest way imaginable, patting my hand. "I'm as emotionally wired as you. We'll make it another time, Archy."

So I drove home alone, howling curses at a full moon and wondering why Hertha Gloriana had granted Meg a farewell kiss and not the laughing cavalier who had picked up the tab. Did the medium bestow her osculations freely without regard for sex, age, race, color, or national origin? Was she, in fact, an Equal Opportunity kisser?

I went directly to my rooms when I arrived home. I stripped off the dull costume I was wearing and donned my favorite kimono, a jaunty silk number printed with an overall pattern of leaping gazelles. Then I put on reading glasses, sat at my desk, and went to work.

I was determined to play the devil's advocate, to view the evening's events as a cynic who completely disbelieved in alleged manifestations of the occult and had a perfectly rational explanation for what others might consider evidence of the supernatural.

I scribbled furiously, and this is what I came up with:

Hertha's knowledge of Meg Trumble:

Meg's sister, Laverne, was a client of the Glorianas and quite likely had her horoscope prepared by the medium. Hertha could easily be aware of Meg's birthdate, the death of her parents, Meg's interest in physical exercise.

The voices:

Of course no one was familiar with the voice of Xatyl, the Mayan shaman, and it would be relatively simple for an actress with a gift of mimicry to imitate the speech of an old man. The voice of John Trumble might offer a problem, but the man had been dead for eight years, and it was doubtful if Meg remembered the exact sound of his voice. More importantly, she *wanted* to believe and was eager to accept any masculine voice as that of her departed father.

Lydia Gillsworth's voice would be easy for Hertha to reproduce since Lydia had been present at several séances and was well known to the medium.

Hertha's knowledge of Archy McNally:

I have already speculated on how my date of birth might have been learned by the Glorianas. And I had mentioned to Irma at our first meeting that I had been reading books on spiritualism. I hadn't revealed that they had been loaned to me by Mrs. Gillsworth, but Lydia had attended her final séance *after* lending me the books and could have casually mentioned that she was assisting me.

I read over what I had written. I didn't claim that all my explanations and suppositions were one hundred percent accurate. But they *could* be. And they certainly had as much or more claim to the truth than ascribing all the revelations made by the medium to paranormal powers. If you had to bet, where would you put *your* money?

But acting the disbeliever and applying cold logic to the occurrences at the séance failed in one vital and bewildering instance. That was the medium's screams "Caprice! Caprice!" in answer to my query as to the identity of the murderer of Lydia Gillsworth. Those shocking screams had been uttered in the voices of both Lydia and Hertha.

I had told Irma and Frank Gloriana that the outburst probably meant that the killer had acted on a whim, a sudden impulse, and the murder was unpremeditated. That was pure malarkey, of course. I thought I knew what that shrieked "Caprice! Caprice!" really signified.

It was the car in which Lydia Gillsworth had driven home to her death.

Chapter 11

I set out detecting on Thursday morning sans beret—which was certainly more socially acceptable than setting out sans culotte. It was my intention to visit the remaining three animal hospitals on my list, and I feared outré headgear might tarnish the image I wished to project: a worried swain seeking his lost love and her ailing cat.

But first I had a small chore to perform and phoned Roderick Gillsworth.

"Good morning, Rod," I said. "Archy McNally. Welcome home."

"Thank you, Archy," he said. "You have no idea how wonderful it is to be home."

"Rough time?" I inquired.

"Rough enough," he said. "I meant to call you Tuesday night after the funeral, but I had a duel with a bottle of California brandy. The bottle won."

"That's all right," I said. "There was nothing new to report anyway. Rod, I'd like to return your house keys. Will you be home this morning?"

Short pause. Then: "Only for another half-hour. I have some errands to run—supermarket shopping and all that. Including a liquor store so I can return your vodka."

"Don't worry about that. Could I pop over now? It'll just take a minute; I won't linger."

"Sure," he said, "come ahead."

When I arrived at the Gillsworth home, his gray Bentley was parked on the bricked driveway. I admired that vehicle. Subdued elegance. A bit staid for my taste but undeniably handsome.

I rang the bell, Rod opened the door, and I blinked. He usually wore solid blues, whites, and blacks, nothing flashy. But that morning he was clad in lime-green slacks with yellow patent leather loafers, complete with fringed tongues. And over a pink polo shirt was a Lilly Pulitzer sport jacket.

I don't know if you're familiar with that garment, but about twenty years ago it was de rigueur for the young bloods of Palm Beach. Ms. Pulitzer doted on flower prints, and a jacket of her fabric made every dude a walking hothouse. Rod's was a bouquet of daisies, mini carnations, and Dolores roses.

He saw my surprise and gave me an embarrassed smile. "A transformation," he said. "What?"

"Quite," I said.

"Lydia found the jacket in a thrift shop," he said. "A perfect fit, but I never had the courage to wear it. I'm wearing it now for her. You understand?"

I nodded, thinking that chintzy jacket had to be the world's strangest memorial.

"Come on in, Archy," he said. "Too early in the morning to offer you an eye-opener, I suppose."

"By about two hours," I said. "But thanks for the thought."

I moved inside and we stood talking in the hallway.

"Here are the keys, Rod," I said, handing them over. "Everything all right in the house when you returned?"

"Shipshape. Thank you for your trouble. And you've learned nothing new about the investigation from Sergeant Rogoff?"

"Not a word. The poison-pen letters Lydia received have been sent to the FBI lab for analysis. Rogoff should be getting a report soon."

"Do you think he'll tell you what the report says?"

"Probably."

"Then I wish you'd tell me," he said, and added testily, "That man simply refuses to let me know what's going on."

I had no desire to listen again to his complaints against Al, so I changed the subject. "By the way, Rod," I remarked, "I had an unusual experience last night. I attended a séance at the Glorianas'."

His face twisted into a tight smile. "Did you now? Good lord, I haven't been to one of those things in ages. I didn't know you were interested in spiritualism."

"Curiosity mostly," I said. "And the Glorianas are fascinating people."

He considered a moment. "Yes," he said finally, "I suppose you could call them fascinating. Lydia always said that the medium had a genuine psychic gift. Did Hertha tell you anything?"

"Nothing I didn't already know," I said. Then a question occurred to me. "Incidentally, Rod, do you happen to know if Irma, the mother-in-law, is widowed, divorced—or what? I was wondering and of course I didn't want to ask her directly. It would have sounded too much like prying."

Again he paused a moment before answering. Then: "I believe Lydia mentioned that Irma is a widow. Yes, now I recall; her husband was an army officer, killed in the Korean War."

"A strong woman," I opined. "Domineering."

"Do you really think so?" he said. "That's a bit extreme, isn't it? Dominant perhaps, but not domineering."

"You poets," I said, smiling. "You make a nice distinction between adjectives."

"I hate adjectives," he said. "And adverbs. They're so weak and floppy. Don't you agree?"

"Indubitably," I said, and we both laughed.

Your hero drove away wondering and happy. Wondering why the bird had suddenly transmogrified from crow to peacock, and happy that I had picked up another item to add to my journal: Mrs. Irma Gloriana was a widow.

I tooled over to West Palm Beach and started my search. It would add immeasurably to the dramatic impact of this narrative if I could detail fruitless visits to two emergency animal clinics and then conclude triumphantly by telling you I struck paydirt at the last on my list. But I have resolved to make this account as honest as is humanly possible, so I must confess that I succeeded at the first hospital I canvassed.

I performed my song and dance for the receptionist, a comely young miss. She seemed sympathetic and spoke into an intercom. In a moment a veterinarian exited from an inner office and accosted me. He was wearing a long white doctors' jacket with five—count 'em, five!—ballpoint pens clipped to a plastic shield in his breast pocket. He was a short, twitchy character who appeared to be of nerdish extraction.

I repeated my fictional plea, and he blinked furiously at me from behind smudged spectacles. I returned his flickering stare with a look I tried to make as honest and sincere as possible.

Apparently it worked, for he said in a reedy voice, "I have recently treated a female cat such as you describe, but a man brought her in, not a lady."

"A man?" I said thoughtfully. "That was undoubtedly her uncle. He frequently travels with her to prevent her being propositioned by uncouth strangers. She is an extremely attractive young woman. Could you describe the man, please, doctor?"

"Tall," he said. "Reddish hair. Broad-shouldered. Very well-dressed in a conservative way. About sixty-five or so, I'd guess."

"Her uncle to a T," I cried. "I'm enormously relieved. And was Peaches seriously ill?"

"I cannot divulge that information," he said sternly. "Medical ethics."

"Of course," I said hastily. "Completely understandable. Would you be willing to give me their address, sir? I'm eager to offer them what assistance I can."

He went back into his office and returned a few minutes later to hand me a scribbled Post-It note.

"The man's name is Charles Girard," he said. "On Federal Highway. A strange address for someone as prosperous as he seemed to be."

"A temporary residence, I'm sure," I said. "I believe Mr. Girard and his niece are on their way to the Lesser Antilles. Thank you so much for your cooperation, doctor."

I had noticed a glass jar on the receptionist's desk. It bore a label requesting contributions for the feeding and rehabilitation of stray felines. The jar was half-filled with coins. I extracted a twenty-dollar bill from my wallet and stuffed it into the jar.

"For the hungry kitties," I said piously.

The vet blinked even more rapidly. "You are very generous," he commented.

"My pleasure," I said, and meant it.

I boogied out to the Miata. I was very, *very* pleased with the triumph of my charade. Surely you recall Danton's prescription for victory: "Audacity, more audacity, always audacity." How true, how true!

The veterinarian had been correct about the address given him by Charles Girard: it *was* a strange neighborhood. The buildings on that stretch of Federal Highway appeared to have been erected fifty years ago and never painted since. They were mostly one- and two-story commercial structures housing a boggling variety of businesses: taverns, used car lots, fast-food joints, and a depressing plethora of stores selling sickroom equipment and supplies.

But there were many vacant shops with For Rent signs in their dusty windows. There was something inexpressibly forlorn and defeated about the entire area, as if the Florida of shining malls and gleaming plazas had passed it by, leaving it to crumble away in the hot sun and salt wind.

I found the address the vet had provided. It proved to be a motel, and when I tell you it consisted of a dozen individual cabins, you can estimate when it was built. I guessed the late 1940s. I drove past and left the Miata in a small parking area beside a seemingly deserted enterprise that sold plastic lawn and patio furniture.

I walked slowly back to the Jo-Jean Motel and entered the office. It was not air conditioned, but a wood-bladed ceiling fan revolved lazily. A large, florid lady was perched on a stool behind the counter, bending over one of those supermarket newspapers that everyone denies reading and which sells about five million copies a week. She didn't look up when I came in.

"I beg your pardon," I said loudly, "but I'm looking for Mr. Charles Girard."

"South row, Cabin Four," she said, still perusing her tabloid. I could read the big headline upside down. It said: "Baby Born Whistling 'Dixie.' "

I went out into that searing sunlight again, found the south row of cabins. Then I stopped, stared, turned around, and walked hastily back to my Miata.

Parked alongside Cabin Four was Roderick Gillsworth's gray Bentley.

I headed back to the McNally Building, reflecting that I had refused Gillsworth's offer of an eye-opener that morning, but he had certainly provided one now. I was totally flummoxed. I couldn't conjure up even the most fantastic scenario to account for the poet visiting a man who apparently had catnapped Harry Willigan's pride and joy. It made absolutely no sense to me whatsoever.

And that turned out to be a mistake. I was looking for rationality in a plot that might have been devised by the Three Stooges.

I was making a turn off Federal when it suddenly occurred to me that the

Pelican Club was only a few minutes' drive away. The sun was inching toward the yardarm, and I decided that refreshment, liquid and solid, in a cool, dim haven was needed to clear my muddleheadedness and get the old ganglia vibrating again.

I lunched alone, waited upon by the saucy Priscilla. Ordinarily we'd have had a bout of chivying, but Pris recognized my mood, and after taking my order left me alone with my problems. I scarfed determinedly through a giant cheeseburger and a bowl of cold potato salad, and by the time I started on my second schooner of Heineken draft, the McNally spirits were bubbling once again. I finished lunch by devouring a wedge of key lime pie while silently reciting those fatuous lines from Henley's "Invictus," although I wasn't positive I was the captain of my soul. More like a Private First Class.

I paid my bill at the bar. Simon Pettibone was wearing a striped shirt with sleeve garters and a small black leather bow tie. With his square spectacles and tight helmet of gray hair, he radiated the wisdom and understanding of an upright publican familiar with all the world's enigmas.

"Mr. Pettibone," I said, "I need your advice."

"No charge, Mr. McNally," he said.

"I have a small puzzle I'm trying to solve. There are two men utterly dissimilar in occupation and probably education and personal wealth. Now what could those two men possibly have in common?"

Mr. Pettibone stared at me a moment. *"Cherchez la femme,"* he said.

I could have hugged him! I was convinced he had it exactly right, and I was determined to follow his counsel. Unfortunately, as events later proved, I cherchezed the wrong femme.

I stopped briefly at the office, hoping Al Rogoff might have left a message to call him. I wanted to learn if the FBI report had been received and what it contained. I also needed to know if he had spoken to the Atlanta PD about the Glorianas. But there was no message from the sergeant, so I phoned him. He was not available and I left my own message.

Then, acting on Mr. Pettibone's advice, I drove over to Ocean Boulevard and headed south for the Willigans' home. I decided it was time to play the heavy with Laverne, to lean on her enough to discover her relationship with Hertha, the kissing medium.

The lady was home, but Leon Medallion informed me she was having her "bawth" and he'd ask the maid when Mrs. Willigan would be receiving. All very upper class and impressive until you remembered the lord of the manor was a lout. So I cooled my heels in the tiled foyer until the butler returned and notified me I had been granted an audience with milady.

I found Laverne in the master suite, which looked like it had been decorated by someone who specialized in Persian bordellos. I've never seen such a profusion of silken draperies, porcelain knick-knacks, and embroidered pillows. Instead of Laverne, it should have been Theda Bara reclining on that pink satin chaise longue, swaddled in a robe of purple brocade so voluminous it seemed to go around her three times.

"Hiya, Archy," the siren sang. "What's up?"

"Why didn't you tell me you knew Hertha Gloriana?" I demanded, figuring it would stun her.

But she wasn't at all discombobulated. "Because I was afraid you'd tell Harry," she said calmly. "I already told you how he hates all that stuff. He calls it 'fortune-telling bullshit.' If he knew I was going to the Glorianas' séances, he'd break my face."

"Did you go to the one Lydia Gillsworth attended on the night she was killed?"

"No," she said, looking at me wide-eyed. "I had to go to a builders' association dinner with Harry that night. If you don't believe me, ask the Glorianas; they'll tell you I wasn't there. But why all the sudden interest in spiritualism?"

"Because I asked Hertha's help in finding Peaches."

I thought she'd be furious because I had ignored her instructions, but she seemed unperturbed.

"Oh?" she said. "And what did Hertha tell you?"

"Not very much. She saw Peaches in a single room, but she didn't know the location."

Laverne examined the chartreuse polish on her fingernails. "Well, Hertha is very gifted but she can't win them all. No medium can."

"Did she ever do your horoscope?"

"Sure she did. So what?"

"Did you tell her details about your personal life, about Meg and your parents?"

"Of course. Hertha has to know those things to draw your psychic profile."

"Uh-huh. Laverne, do you know a man named Charles Girard?"

"Nope," she said promptly. "Never heard of him. Who is he?"

"He may be one of the catnappers."

"No kidding?" she said. "How did you get on to him?"

"Any genius could have done it. Did you ever hear your husband mention him?"

"Not that I recall. You better ask Harry."

"I shall. Laverne, how long have you known the Glorianas?"

"Oh, months and months. I guess it must be almost a year now."

"Where are they from—do you know?"

"Chicago, I think."

"Is Mrs. Irma Gloriana widowed or divorced?"

"Divorced. She said her ex lives in California somewhere with their daughter. Frank went with his mother, and the daughter lives with their father."

"How long have Hertha and Frank been married?"

"I think they said four years. Why all these questions about the Glorianas, Archy?"

I shrugged. "I find them interesting people. Mysterious."

"Mysterious?" She laughed. "Not very. They're just trying to grab the brass ring like everyone else."

"You grabbed it," I said boldly.

She wasn't offended. She looked around that scented chamber with satisfaction, then stroked the raised gold and silver design on her robe. "You bet your sweet ass I grabbed it," she said. "But I've paid my dues. By the way, Meg is back in town. She phoned me this morning. You going to see her again?"

From which I deduced that Meg hadn't told her sister about the séance she attended with me. Initially I was thankful for that, but then I realized that Laverne would probably learn about it from the Glorianas.

"Yes, I'd like to see her again," I said.

"Good boy," she said approvingly. "She has to learn that not all men are shitheads. Most, but not all."

I had been standing throughout this interview because Laverne hadn't invited me to sit down. I was weary of standing in one position and couldn't think of any additional questions to ask.

"Thank you for your help," I said. "I'll phone Harry and ask him if he knows Charles Girard."

"Where does Girard live?" she said casually. "Do you know?"

She shouldn't have asked that. I had suspected she might be lying when she denied knowing Charles Girard. Her question convinced me she knew very well who he was and now she was trying to discover how much I knew of him.

"Haven't the slightest idea," I said, furrowing the old brow. "But eventually I'll find him. And Peaches."

"Don't strain yourself, Archy," she advised. "What difference does it really make? Harry can easily afford the fifty grand they're asking."

"Laverne!" I protested. "Don't let your husband hear you say that. He wants his pet back without paying and he wants the catnappers strung up by their thumbs—or whatever other bodily appendages are handy."

"My husband," she repeated darkly. "What he wants and what he gets are two different things."

I figured that was a good moment to make my farewell, so I did. I drove home thinking that Laverne Willigan had more than ozone between her ears. She had lied glibly and shrewdly, I was certain of that, but what her motives were I wasn't yet sure.

And in addition to the Charles Girard business, she had given me another puzzle. Roderick Gillsworth had said Irma Gloriana was widowed. Laverne had just told me she was divorced. I couldn't believe Irma would give varying accounts of her background to different people; she was too clever for that.

Which meant that Gillsworth was lying or Laverne was lying.

Or both.

I used the phone in my father's study to call Harry Willigan. He greeted me with screams, and I had to wait until he ran out of breath before I could get in my question about Charles Girard.

"Never heard of the bozo," he bellowed and took up his ranting again.

I hung up softly, hoping he might continue for another five minutes before he realized he was raving into a dead phone.

I went upstairs and scribbled in my journal for more than an hour. The dossier on the Peaches-Gillsworth case was bulking up nicely, but I still could not see any pattern in all those disparate tidbits of information. Where was Xatyl now that I needed him?

I had returned from my ocean swim and was dressing for the evening when Al Rogoff called. He wasted no time on preliminaries.

"I've got some news for you," he said. "Interesting stuff."

"And I have a few choice morsels for you," I said. "When and where can we meet?"

"I'm up to my pipik in paperwork," he said. "I probably won't be able to get away until late. How about you coming over to my wagon around nine-thirty or so."

"Sounds good to me," I said. "Can I bring something to lubricate your tonsils?"

"Nah," he said, "I have a bottle of wine I'll pop. It's a naive domestic burgundy without any breeding, but I think you'll be amused by its presumption."

"Thank you, Mr. Thurber," I said. "See you tonight."

That evening Ursi Olson served a Florida dinner of conch chowder, grilled swordfish and plantains with a mango salsa and hearts of palm salad. My father relented, and instead of a jug chablis he brought out a vintage muscadet, flinty hard.

I returned to my rooms after dinner and added a few more notes to my journal. Then I phoned Information and asked if they had a new listing for Margaret Trumble in Riviera Beach. They gave me the number and I called. I let it ring seven times before I hung up, wondering where she was. I don't know why I felt uneasy, but I did.

Then I grabbed up a golf jacket and went trotting out to the Miata. It was a super evening, clear and cool enough to sleep without air conditioning. But that night I didn't get much chance.

What Al Rogoff called his "wagon" was actually a mobile home set on a sturdy foundation in a park of similar dwellings off Belvedere Road. It was a pleasant place—lots of lawns and palm trees, a small swimming pool and a smaller recreation room.

Most of the residents were retirees, and I always suspected Al got a discount on his maintenance because the owner of the park liked the idea of having a cop on the premises. I mean if any villain got the idea of ripping off one of the mobile homes—and they didn't provide much security—he might think twice if he spotted a guardian of the law strolling around with a howitzer strapped to his hip.

Al's home was trim outside and snug inside. He had a living room, bedroom, kitchen, and bath, all in a row, like a railroad flat. He had decorated the place himself, and though nothing was lavish or even expensive, I thought it a very attractive and comfortable bachelor's pad—the kind of place where you could kick off your shoes and mellow out.

He had a bottle of wine chilled and uncorked when I arrived. But it wasn't a burgundy, it was an '87 Sterling cabernet. If you think it blasphemous to cool a good red like that, I must tell you that Floridians customarily refrigerate even the most costly Bordeaux. We dine alfresco a great deal of the time, and if the wine isn't chilled, you're slurping soup.

We sat in padded captain's chairs at an oak dining table tucked into one corner of the living room. I sampled the wine, and it was just right.

"Who goes first?" Al asked.

"You start," I said. "My amazing revelations can wait."

He got up to fetch his notebook. He was wearing tan jeans and a T-shirt. He was unshod but his meaty feet were stuffed into white athletic socks. I noticed he was getting a belly, not gross but nascent. Most cops don't eat very well. They think a balanced diet is an anchovy pizza and a can of Dr Pepper.

"Okay," the sergeant said, hunching over his notebook, "here's what I got from Atlanta. Those people the Glorianas named as references just don't exist at the addresses given. The Atlanta bank they named was a savings and loan that folded three years ago."

"Beautiful," I said.

"Then I got through to a detective in the Atlanta PD who knew all about the Glorianas. Jerry Weingarter. A nice guy. He's a cigar smoker, like me. He was a big help so maybe I'll send him a box of the best."

"McNally and Son will pick up the tab," I said.

Al grinned. "That's what I figured," he said. "Anyway, this Weingarter told me that Irma Gloriana and her husband were—"

"Whoa," I said, holding up a hand. "You mean Irma is married?"

He looked at me. "Sure she's married. What did you think?"

"I didn't know what to think," I said honestly. "Is her husband still living?"

"He was about six months ago when he got out of the clink. His name is Otto. Otto Gloriana. Got a nice sound to it, doesn't it? Drink your wine; there's another bottle cooling. Irma and Otto were running what my dear old granddaddy used to call a house of ill repute. It wasn't a sleazy crib; the Glorianas had a high-class joint. All their girls were young and beautiful. The johns paid anywhere from a hundred to five hundred, depending on what they wanted. Irma was the madam, Otto the business manager. They had been in business four or five years and had a nice thing going with a well-heeled clientele of uppercrust citizens. The law got on to it when one of their girls OD'd on heroin."

I finished my glass of wine and poured myself another. "A pretty picture," I said. "And what part did the son, Frank, play in all this?"

"He was like a bouncer, providing muscle if any of the johns got out of line."

"And Hertha?"

"Apparently she had no connection with the cat-house. Weingarter says she had her own racket, doing what she does now: holding séances and doing horoscopes. He also said she's a crackerjack psychic. Once she helped the Atlanta cops find a lost kid. Weingarter doesn't know how she did it, but the lead she gave them was right on the money."

He paused to refill his glass, and I had a moment to reflect on what he had told me. I think I was more saddened than shocked.

"What happened after the cops closed them down?" I asked.

"Otto cut a deal. He'd take the rap if his wife and son got suspended sentences and promised to leave town."

"Very noble of Otto," I said. "How long did he get?"

"He drew three-to-five, did a year and a half, and was released about six months ago. No probation. Present whereabouts unknown."

I gazed up at the ceiling fans. "Al," I said, almost dreamily, "do you have a physical description of Otto?"

"Yeah," he said, flipping pages of his notebook, "I've got it somewhere. Here it is. He's—"

I interrupted him. "He's tall," I said. "Reddish hair. Broad-shouldered. Very well-dressed in a conservative way. About sixty-five or so."

The sergeant stared at me. "What the hell," he said hoarsely. "You been taking psychic lessons from Hertha or something?"

"Did I get it right?" I asked.

"You got it right," he acknowledged. "Now tell me how."

"He's down here," I said. "Using the name Charles Girard."

Then I gave Rogoff an account of how I figured Peaches might get sick, how the catnappers would seek medical help, how I canvassed emergency animal hospitals with a flapdoodle story, how I finally found a veterinarian who remembered treating Peaches and gave me the name and address of the man who brought her in.

Al looked at me and shook his head in wonderment. "You know," he said, "you have the testicles of a brazen simian. You also have more luck than you deserve. Where is Otto living?"

"In a fleabag motel on Federal Highway. But I haven't told you the punch line, Al. I went out there this morning to pay a visit to Charles Girard, or, if he wasn't present, to see if Peaches was on the premises and could be rescued. But I took one look and departed forthwith. Roderick Gillsworth's gray Bentley was parked outside Otto's cabin."

The sergeant stared and slowly his face changed. I thought I saw vindictiveness there and perhaps malevolence.

"Gillsworth," he repeated, and it was almost a hiss. "I knew that—"

But I wasn't fated to learn what it was the sergeant knew, for the phone rang at that instant, startlingly loud.

Al waited until the third ring, then hauled himself to his feet. "I'll take it on the bedroom extension," he said.

He went inside and closed the door. I wasn't offended. If it was official business, he had every right to his privacy. And if it was that schoolteacher he dated occasionally, he had every right to his privacy.

He seemed to be in there a long time, long enough for me to finish what was left of the cabernet. Finally he came out. He had pulled on a pair of scuffed Reeboks, the laces flapping, and a khaki nylon jacket. He was affixing his badge to the epaulette of the jacket. After he did that, he took his gunbelt with all its accoutrements from a closet shelf and buckled it about his waist with some difficulty.

Then he looked at me. I could read absolutely nothing in his expression, because there wasn't one; his face was stone.

"There was a fire at Roderick Gillsworth's place," he reported tonelessly. "A grease fire in the kitchen. The neighbors spotted it. The firemen had to break down the door to get in. They put out the fire and went looking for Gillsworth. They found him in the bathtub. His wrists were slit."

I gulped. "Dead?" I asked, hearing the quaver in my own voice.

"Very," Al said.

"Can I come with you?"

"No," he said. "You'd just have to wait outside. I'll phone you as soon as I learn more."

"Al, there's something else I've got to tell you," I said desperately.

"It'll have to wait. Go home, Archy. You better tell your father about this."

"Yes," I said. "Thanks for the wine."

"What?" he said. "Oh. Yeah."

We both went outside and paused while Al locked up. Then he got in his pickup and took off. I stayed right there, smoking a cigarette and looking up at the star-spangled sky. Another spirit had passed over. Another ghost. It had never occurred to me before that the living were a minority.

Chapter 12

The door to my father's study was open. He was seated at his desk working on a stack of correspondence brought home from the office. He looked up when I entered.

"I'm busy, Archy," he said irritably.

"Yes, sir," I said, "but I have news I think you should hear immediately. Not good news."

He sighed and tossed down his pen. "It's been that kind of day," he said. "Very well, what is it?"

I repeated what Al Rogoff had told me and, like the sergeant's, his face became stone.

"Yes," he said in a quiet voice, "I heard the fire engines go by earlier this evening. The man has definitely expired?"

"According to Rogoff. He promised to phone me when he learns more about it."

"Does the sergeant believe it was suicide?"

"He didn't say, father."

"Do *you* think it was?"

"No, sir," I said, and told him of my early morning meeting with the poet. "He seemed very up, as if he was happy Lydia's funeral was over and he could get on with his life. He said he had some errands to do today, shopping and so forth. A man planning suicide doesn't go to a supermarket first, does he?"

"He was sober, I presume."

"As far as I could tell. He did offer me an eye-opener but in a joking way. Yes, I'd say he was completely sober."

My father drew a deep breath. "And now all my fears come true. As things stand, he leaves all his worldly goods, except for his original manuscripts, to a wife who predeceased him. As far as I know, he has no immediate survivors."

"None?" I said, shocked. "Siblings? Cousins? Aunts? Uncles? No one at all?"

"Not to my knowledge. Would you pour us a port, please, Archy. I believe we both could use it."

I did the honors, and the sire gestured me to the armchair alongside his desk. He sipped his wine thoughtfully.

"If an investigation proves I am correct and he had no survivors, then I imagine Lydia's aunt and cousins will have a claim on the bulk of her estate inherited by Roderick."

"A mess," I offered.

"Yes," he said, "it is that." Suddenly he was angered. "Why the devil the idiot didn't make out a new will immediately after his wife's death I'll never know."

"You tried to persuade him, father," I said, hoping to mollify him.

"I should have been more insistent," he said, and I realized his fury was directed as much at himself as at Gillsworth.

"You couldn't have anticipated what happened," I pointed out.

"I should have," he said, refusing to be assuaged. "I learned long ago that in legal matters it's necessary always to prepare for a worst-case scenario. This time I neglected to do that, and the worst happened. You say Sergeant Rogoff will call you when he learns the details of Roderick's death?"

"He said he would."

"Please let me know as soon as you hear from him."

"It may be very late, father. After midnight."

"Then wake me up," he said sharply. "Is that understood?"

"Yes, sir," I said, drained my glass of port, and left him alone with his anger. The old man likes things tidy, and this affair was anything but.

I went upstairs but I didn't undress, figuring it was possible Al might want to meet me somewhere else. I sat in my swivel chair, put my feet up on the desk, and tried to make some sense, *any* sense, out of Gillsworth's death.

Despite the corpse's slit wrists, no one was going to convince me the poet was a suicide. If I tell you why I refused to accept that, you'll think me an ass, but it's how my mind works: I could never believe that a man with the joie de vivre to wear a Lilly Pulitzer sport jacket in the morning could kill himself in the evening. Unless, of course, he had suffered a cataclysmic defeat during the day, and so far there was no evidence of that.

Do you recall my mentioning that I had a vaporish notion of what had gone down and was still going down? It was so vague that I couldn't put it into words. But now Gillsworth's death made a difference. I'm not saying all the mists had cleared, but I began to see a dim outline that had shape if not substance.

I obviously dozed off because when the phone rang I discovered my head was down on the desktop, cradled in my forearms. I roused and glanced at my Mickey Mouse watch: almost two-thirty A.M.

"Rogoff," he said. "Why should you be sleeping when I'm not?"

"You still at Gillsworth's house, Al?"

"Still here. If I take a breather and run up to your place, do you think you could buy me a cup of coffee?"

"You bet. How about a sandwich?"

"Nope, but thanks. Just the coffee, hot and black. I won't stay long."

I went down to my parents' bedroom and knocked softly. Father opened the door so quickly that I guessed he hadn't been sleeping, even though he was wearing Irish linen pajamas: long-sleeved jacket and drawstring pants.

"The sergeant called," I said in a low voice, hoping not to disturb mother. "He's coming for a cup of coffee."

"May I join you?" the pater asked.

That was so *like* him. I mean it was his home, he was the boss, he could have said, "I'll join you." But he had to couch it as a polite request to sustain his image of himself as a courtly gentleman. He's something, he is.

"Of course," I said. "Decaf for you?"

He nodded and I went on down to the kitchen. I put the kettle on and set out three cups and saucers, cream and sugar, spoons. In less than ten minutes I heard tires on our graveled turnaround and looked out the window to see Rogoff's pickup.

He came in a moment later, looking weary and defeated. He collapsed onto one of the chairs without saying a word. He put a heaping teaspoon of regular instant into his cup and I poured boiling water over it.

Then my father came in. He had changed to slacks, open-necked shirt, an old cardigan, and older carpet slippers. The sergeant stood up when he entered. I admired him for that. The two men shook hands, wordlessly, and we all sat down. Father and I had instant decaf with cream, no sugar.

"He *is* dead, sergeant?" the senior asked.

"No doubt about that, sir," Rogoff said. "The exact cause will have to wait for the autopsy. I'm no medic, but I'd say it was loss of blood that finished him."

"Exsanguination," I remarked.

Al looked at me. "Thank you, Mr. Webster," he said. "Well, there was enough of it in the tub."

"How do you interpret it?" father asked.

"I don't," Rogoff said. "Not yet. There are too many questions and not enough answers. Let me set the scene for you. The people next door were having a barbecue on their patio. One of the guests spotted flames behind the window of Gillsworth's kitchen. The men ran over there but the back door was locked. Meanwhile the women called nine-one-one. When the firemen arrived, they had to break down the back door. It was locked, bolted, and chained. They also broke through the front door of the house. That was closed with a spring lock but not bolted or chained."

He paused to blow on his coffee and then sipped cautiously. It wasn't too hot for him, and he took a deep gulp. Father and I sampled ours.

"That's significant," I said. "Don't you think? The front door on a spring lock but not bolted or chained?"

"Maybe," Rogoff said. "Maybe not. Anyway it wasn't much of a fire. There was a big frying pan on the range. The pan had grease in it—butter or oil, it hasn't been determined yet. But it caught fire and spattered, igniting the curtains and cafe drapes. The range coil was still on High when the firemen got there."

"Then he was preparing dinner," my father said, a statement not a question.

"It sure looked like it, sir. There was a plate of six big crab cakes on the countertop, ready for frying. And in the fridge was a huge bowl of salad, already mixed."

"Any booze?" I asked.

"Yeah, an open liter of gin on the countertop, about two slugs gone. Also a highball glass still half-full. Looked like a gin and tonic. It had a slice of lime in it. And there was a six-pack of quinine water in the cabinet under the sink. One of the bottles was half-empty."

I shook my head. "That doesn't compute. A man is making dinner. He has a drink, mixes a salad. He gets ready to sauté his crab cakes. Then he decides to slit his wrists instead. Do you buy that, Al?"

"Right now I'm not buying anything. Could I have another cup of coffee? I'm not going to get any sleep tonight anyway."

I fixed him another regular and another decaf for myself after my father put his palm over his cup.

"Please continue, sergeant," he said. "How was Gillsworth found?"

"The firemen figured things didn't look kosher and went searching for him. They found him in the tub of the downstairs bathroom, the one next to his den. He was fully clothed. There was a bloody single-edge razor blade on the bath mat alongside the tub. Both his wrists were slashed."

"Both?" I said. "If you slit one wrist, do you then have enough strength in that hand to grip a razor blade and slit the other wrist?"

"Don't ask me," Rogoff said. "I've never tried it. We're going to need a forensic pathologist on this one."

"Did the body show any other wounds?" father asked.

The sergeant looked at him admiringly. "Yes, sir, it did," he said. "On the back of the head, high up. The hair was matted with blood. But after he slashed his wrists he could have slipped down in the tub and cracked his head on the rim. In fact, there's a bloody mark on the rim that looks like he did exactly that. It's one of the questions the ME will have to answer."

"What's your guess, Al?" I said. "Suicide or homicide? I'm not asking what you're absolutely certain about, but what's your *guess?*"

He hesitated for just a brief instant, then he said, "Homicide."

"Of course!" I said triumphantly. "No one is going to slit his wrists in the middle of preparing dinner—unless he finds worms in the crab cakes."

"That's not my main reason for calling it homicide," Rogoff said. "Suicides sometimes do goofy things before they work up their courage to take the final exit. No, it's something else that makes me think someone cut Gillsworth's wrists for him. Archy, do me a favor. Show me how you'd slit your wrists if you were determined to shuffle off to Buffalo."

I stared at him. "You want me to pretend to slash my wrists?"

He nodded. "Use your spoon."

I picked up the spoon from my saucer. I held it in my right hand, gripping it by the bowl, the handle extended. I held out my left forearm and turned it palm upward. I was wearing a short-sleeved polo shirt; my arm was bare.

"I feel like a perfect fool," I said.

"Nobody's perfect," Al said, "but you come close. Go ahead, slit your wrists."

As my father and the sergeant watched intently, I drew the spoon handle swiftly across my left wrist, just hard enough to depress the skin. Then I transferred the spoon to my left hand and made the same slashing motion down across my right wrist. I admit the playacting gave me the heebie-jeebies.

"Uh-huh," Rogoff said. "That's what I figured."

"*What* did you figure?"

"You cut from the outside of your wrist down to the inside. You did it on both wrists."

I looked at my forearms and then tried slashing with the spoon handle from the underside of each wrist up to the top.

"Of course I did," I said. "It wouldn't be impossible to cut in the other direction, but it's awkward and you wouldn't be able to apply as much force. It would be like a backhand tennis stroke versus a forehand."

"For sure," Rogoff said, nodding. "I've seen slit wrists before, on suicides and would-be suicides. The slash is always made from top to bottom. But the cuts on Gillsworth's wrists looked like they had been made from the underside of the wrist to the top. That was my impression anyhow, but I admit I could be wrong. But there's another thing: Gillsworth's wrists showed no hesitation marks. Those are scratches and shallow cuts a suicide sometimes makes before he finally decides to go for broke. Gillsworth's wrists had single deep slashes. Hey, I've got to get back. Thanks for the coffee, it juiced me up."

"Thank *you*, sergeant," father said, "for being so forthcoming. I assure you that Archy and I will keep what you've told us in strictest confidence."

"Yeah," Rogoff said, "I'd appreciate that."

They shook hands, and I accompanied Al out to his pickup.

"Got just a few more minutes?" I asked him.

He looked at me a sec, then grinned. "Something you didn't want your father to hear?"

"That's right," I said. "Or he'd have me committed."

"Sure, I got a few minutes," Al said. "Gillsworth isn't leaving town."

I climbed into the cab of the pickup with him. He pulled out a cigar and I pulled out a cigarette. We got our weeds burning, and I turned to face him.

"Remember before you took off from your place last evening I said I had something important to tell you? Well, I went to a séance at the Glorianas' on Wednesday night."

He didn't seem surprised. "So? Did you talk to your old friend Epicurus?"

"No, but I talked to Lydia Gillsworth. The medium contacted her through Xatyl, a Mayan shaman. He's Hertha's channel to the spirit world."

"Uh-huh. Makes sense to me."

"It does? Anyway, Al, I heard Lydia talking. I know the words were being spoken by Hertha, but I could have sworn it was Lydia. But Hertha knew her well, and if the medium has a gift for mimicry, which she obviously has, she could have imitated Lydia's voice."

"That *does* make sense. What did you and Lydia talk about? Did you ask who offed her?"

"Of course."

"And what did she say?"

"She became hysterical. She screamed, 'Caprice! Caprice!' over and over again."

That shook him. He turned his head slowly to look at me, and his expression was a puzzlement.

"You're sure that's what she said?"

"I'm sure. First it was screamed in Lydia's voice, then Hertha kept shrieking 'Caprice!' in her own voice. You know what she meant, don't you?"

"Yeah, I know. Mrs. Gillsworth's car was a Caprice. She drove it from the séance to her home the night she was murdered."

"That's right. How do you figure it?"

Al was silent a long time. He turned away to stare fixedly through the windshield.

"I'll tell you something, Archy: I suspected Roderick Gillsworth might have killed his wife. He says he talked to her from your place, was told she had just arrived, and immediately drove home to find her dead. He called nine-one-one, and I got there about fifteen minutes later. Tops. After I heard his story, I went out to the garage and felt the engine block on her Caprice. I didn't think it was as hot as it should have been if she had just driven home from the séance. But that was a subjective judgment. Also, she was killed on a warm night, and no one in South Florida drives around in late June without turning on the air conditioning. The interior of Lydia's Caprice wasn't as cool as it should have been if she had just arrived home—another personal judgment. It was nothing I could take to the State Attorney, but I began to wonder about Roderick Gillsworth."

"What about the grandfather clock that was toppled and stopped at the time of death?"

"Doesn't mean a thing, Archy. Anyone could have set the clock at any time desired and then pushed it over to stop it ticking. An easy alibi to fake."

"So far, so good," I said. "But he *did* call his wife from my father's study."

"I know he did," Al said almost mournfully. "There's no getting around that. And then, last night, Roderick gets iced—if it *was* homicide, and I think it was. That helps eliminate him as a suspect, wouldn't you say? It looks like someone, for whatever reason, crazy or not, wanted to wipe out the entire Gillsworth family, wife and husband. But now you tell me the psychic, speaking in the murdered woman's voice, yelled, 'Caprice! Caprice!' So I've got to start thinking again if Lydia's car really does provide a clue to her killer. Maybe I was right in the first place about the lack of engine heat and no air conditioning inside the car. Listen, Archy, I've really got to get back to the Gillsworth place. There's still a lot to do."

"Sure," I said and started to climb from the truck cab. But he reached out a hand to stop me.

"I'm going to be tied up with this thing for the next few days at least. Will you check on Otto Gloriana and the catnapping?"

"I intend to."

"Good. One more thing: that Atlanta detective said Otto is a nasty piece of work."

I was indignant. "And what do you think I am—Little Lord Fauntleroy?"

"Just watch your step," he warned.

I went back into the house, locked up, and climbed the stairs to bed. I tried to sleep but my mind was a kaleidoscope of scary images, and it must have been five A.M. before I finally conked out. I awoke a little before noon, and I was under the shower, all soaped up, when, in accordance with tradition, my phone rang.

I went dashing out uttering a mild oath—something like "Sheesh!"—and grabbed up the phone only to have it drop to the floor from my slippery grasp. I retrieved it after much fumbling and finally cupped it in both hands.

"H'lo?" I said.

"What the hell's going on?" Harry Willigan demanded. "You drunk or something?"

I started to explain, but he had no time or inclination to listen. He said he was about to leave on a flight to Chicago for a business meeting. He would be gone until Tuesday, and if I had any news about Peaches I was to phone Laverne; she knew where he could be reached. He hung up before I could tell him I was hot on the trail of his beloved.

I finished my shower, dressed, and phoned Meg Trumble again. Again there was no answer. Very frustrating. I went downstairs for breakfast-lunch and found Jamie Olson seated at the kitchen table. He was munching on a thick sandwich that seemed to be mostly slices of raw Spanish onion between slabs of sour rye. It looked good to me so I built one for myself, heavy on the mayo. I sluiced it down with a bottle of Buckler beer (non-alcoholic, if you must know).

"Jamie," I said, "remember my asking if Laverne Willigan had a little something on the side? You said there was talk she was putting horns on dear old Harry."

"Yuh."

"Hear any more on the grapevine about who he is?"

"A dude."

"A dude? That's all? Just a dude?"

"Yuh. Dresses sharp."

"But no name?"

"Nope."

"So all you heard is that Laverne's Consenting Adult or Significant Other is a dude—correct?"

"Tall."

"Ah-ha, a tall dude! Now we're making progress. Young? Old?"

"Half-and-half."

"About my age, you think?"

"Mebbe."

"Better and better. Now we've got a tall, half-and-half dude. Slender or fat?"

"Thin."

"Dark or fair?"

"Darkish."

"Handsome?"

"Mebbe, I guess she thinks so."

"Excellent," I said. I now had a tall, half-and-half, thin, darkish, handsome dude. There were many men in the Palm Beach area answering that description, including you-know-who.

I slipped Jamie a tenner for his enthusiastic cooperation. Then I went into my father's study and looked up the number of the Jo-Jean Motel on Federal Highway. I phoned and was greeted by a woman's voice.

"Jo-Jean," she said, and I wondered which one she was.

"May I speak to Mr. Charles Girard?" I asked. "South row, Cabin Four."

"I know where he is," she said crossly.

There was a clicking, the connection went through, and the ringing started. Nine times, I counted, before the phone was picked up.

"Yeh?" A man's voice, deep and thick.

"Mr. Charles Girard?"

"Yeh. Who's this?"

"Mr. Girard, this is the veterinarian who recently provided medical care for your cat. It is my custom to make follow-up calls regarding the animals I have treated to make certain they have recovered satisfactorily. No charge, of course. Let's see, your cat's name is, ah, Gertrude?"

"Peaches," he said.

"Of course," I said. "It slipped my mind. And how is Peaches feeling, Mr. Girard?"

"She's okay."

"Glad to hear it. Well, remember we're here to serve and ready to provide emergency medical care for your pet should it ever be needed. Thank you, Mr. Girard, and have a nice day."

"Yeh," he said and hung up.

I was enormously pleased with the results of my discreet inquiries that morning. I reckoned that if my good luck continued, before nightfall I might find Judge Crater and identify Jack the Ripper.

I boarded the Miata and started my journey to Federal Highway. I drove slowly, for I meant to beard Otto Gloriana in his den at the Jo-Jean Motel and needed to cobble up a believable scenario to justify my appearing on his doorstep. But I could think of no scam that wasn't sheer lunacy. I decided to trust my modest talent for improvisation.

I parked in the same area I had used before and walked back to the Jo-Jean office through the midday heat. The same woman I had spoken to previously was perched on the same high stool behind the same counter, bending over a newspaper. But at least the tabloid was different. The headline was "Chef Slays Six With Spatula."

"I beg your pardon," I said, "but is Mr. Girard in?"

"You just missed him," she said, not looking up. "Him and the missus drove out a coupla minutes ago."

"Drat!" I said. "He told me he was staying here. I haven't seen him in ages, and I came all the way from Fort Lauderdale hoping to surprise him. Is he still driving his Lincoln Continental?"

"Chrysler Imperial."

"Ah, he must have traded in the Lincoln. And is his wife still the same tall, striking blonde?"

"Brunette. Chunky. Built like a bulldog."

"Oh my!" I said, laughing merrily. "Then I guess old Charlie traded in his first wife too. Did he say when he'd be back?"

"Nope."

"Perhaps I'll just drive around awhile, see the sights, and return later. Thank you for your help."

I thought I had been devilishly clever, but suddenly, without looking up, she said, "You got a lot of information for free, didn't you?"

I sighed, took a twenty from my billfold, and placed it on the countertop. She plucked it away so swiftly that I swear the visage of Old Hickory seemed shocked.

I went out into the hot sunlight and wandered down to Cabin Four, south row. It was larger than I had imagined, but it was surely a decrepit structure, badly in need of painting—or a hand grenade. A rusty air conditioner wheezed away in one window, and there was a dented deck chair on the sagging porch, the plastic webbing broken and hanging.

I stepped up to the door and knocked softly. No one opened it, but I heard a single plaintive meow. I put my lips close to the jamb and whispered, "Do not despair, Peaches. The cavalry is on the way."

Then I returned home, realizing that events were moving so rapidly that I needed to update my journal to make sure nothing was forgotten or ignored, no matter how trivial. But first I phoned Meg Trumble again, and this time she answered.

"Meg!" I said. "Where on earth have you been? I've been trying to reach you for ages. I was beginning to get concerned."

"Oh, Archy," she said, her voice positively bubbling, "I've been so busy. That list of names you gave me was a godsend. I've already visited four of them, and two are really interested in having a personal trainer. Isn't that wonderful!"

"Absolutely," I said. "How about dinner tonight?"

"Love to," she said promptly. "As a matter of fact, I called Laverne just minutes ago to ask if she'd like to eat with me tonight, but she has a meeting of the Current Affairs Society. Now I'm glad she couldn't make it; I'd much rather we have dinner together."

"Ditto," I said. "Pick you up around seven?"

"Super," she said. "Can we go back to that Cafe Istanbul again? I loved it. 'Bye!"

I sat there a moment, adding two and two and coming up with five. To wit: Harry Willigan was out of town. His wife had a lover lurking in the wings. And Laverne couldn't join Meg for dinner because she had a meeting of the Current Affairs Society. Hah!

That Society is a Palm Beach association of men and women, mostly elderly, who meet once a month to hear a lecture on current affairs by a congressman, political science professor, repentant Communist, or the deposed dictator of a banana republic. The lecture would be followed by a Q&A period, and the meeting concluded with the serving of coffee and oatmeal cookies. My mother was a faithful member and had once served as sergeant at arms.

I went galloping downstairs and found the mater in the greenhouse, chatting to her begonias.

"I know it's hot," she was saying, "but it's summer, and you must keep your spirits up."

"Hallo, luv," I said, swooping to kiss her velvety cheek. "And how is mommy baby feeling today?"

"Oh my," she said, "you *are* in a chipper mood. Are you in love again, Archy?"

"Quite possibly," I acknowledged. "I do feel strange stirrings about the heart, but of course it could be the onion sandwich I had for lunch. Listen, Mrs. McNally, do you have a meeting of the Current Affairs Society tonight?"

She paused, sprinkling can in hand, to look at me, puzzled. "Why, no," she said. "The next meeting isn't until July fifteenth. Why do you ask?"

"Just confused," I said. "As usual. See you for cocktails, but I have a dinner date tonight."

"Good for you," she said, beaming. "Someone nice, I hope."

"I hope so too," I said.

I went back upstairs convinced that the only current affair Laverne Willigan would attend to that night was her own. There seems to be a lot of adultery going around these days. I suspect it may be contagious.

I worked on my journal for the remainder of the afternoon, jotting down all the information I had learned about Roderick Gillsworth's death. I added the family history of the Glorianas as related by Al Rogoff, and what I had discovered that day of Otto's probable involvement in the catnapping of Peaches, aka Sweetums. I finished with an account of Laverne Willigan's apparent infidelity and her clumsy attempt to conceal it with a feeble falsehood.

Satisfied with my day's labors and the way in which the Gillsworth-Peaches case was slowly revealing its secrets, I closed up shop and went for my daily swim. I returned to shower and dress with particular care. I intended to dazzle Meg Trumble with sartorial splendor, which was why I selected a knitted shirt of plum-colored Sea Island cotton and a linen sport jacket of British racing green. Slacks of fawn silk. Cordovan loafers. No socks.

I displayed this costume at the family cocktail hour.

"Good God!" my father gasped.

I prayed Meg would be more favorably impressed by my imitation of a male bower bird. I was convinced I had been working dreadfully hard and needed a quiet evening to unwind, with no violent deaths, no catnappings, no shocking messages from the beyond. I imagined Meg and I would spend prime time together smiling and murmuring.

And later, surfeited with moussaka and overcome by gemütlichkeit, she would grant me a session of catch-as-catch-can intimacy. Just the two of us. Alone in the world.

I rang her bell, quivering with eagerness like a gun dog on point. Meg greeted me with a winning smile. And behind her, seated in the living room, was Hertha Gloriana, who gave me a smile just as winning.

"Hertha is going to join us," Meg said happily. "Isn't that marvelous?"

Chapter 13

I had dined with two women before, of course—most lads have—and I usually found it a pleasurable experience. To be honest, it gives one a pasha-like feeling: entertaining two from the harem, or perhaps interviewing wannabes. Male self-esteem, always in need of a lift, is given an injection of helium by the presence and flattering attention of not one but two (count 'em!) attractive ladies.

Having said all that, I must tell you from the outset that the evening was a disaster. Never have I felt so extraneous, so *foreign*. I began to wonder if men and women are not merely two different genders but are actually two different species.

It started when we arrived at the Cafe Istanbul. I selected a booth, Meg and Hertha preferred another, although as far as I could see the booths were identical. I expected to sit alongside Meg, with Hertha, the third wheel, placed across the table from us. But the women insisted on dining side by side, so I sat alone, facing them.

Nothing so far to elevate a chap's dander, you say—and right you are. But it was only the beginning.

Hertha and Meg seemed to vie with each other in casting snide references to the conjunction of colors I was wearing. Even worse, the medium suggested I'd do well to ask her husband for tips on how to coordinate hues and fabrics in order to present a pleasing appearance.

"It's an idea," I said with a glassy smile, hoping the gnashing of my teeth was not audible. "And where is Frank this evening?"

My innocent question resulted in a convulsion of laughter by both, and it continued until our salad was served and the wine uncorked. I never did receive a reply to my query, though it was obvious that both my dinner partners knew the answer. Is there anything more maddening than an inside joke to which one is neither privy nor offered an explanation?

My essays at light-hearted conversation were similarly rejected. Both women remained po-faced in response to the truly hilarious tale of how Binky Watrous and I, somewhat in our cups, stole a garbage truck and drove it to Boca Raton. Nor did they seem interested in my favorite anecdote about Ferdy Attenborough, a member of the Pelican Club, who was debagged by his cronies and thrust into the ballroom during a formal dance at The Breakers.

As a matter of fact, the ladies didn't seem interested in me at all. But they spent a great deal of time whispering to each other—a shocking breach of good manners—and I recalled my uneasy feeling when I saw them sitting close and holding hands after the séance on Wednesday night. I began to get a disconcerting picture of who the third wheel really was.

Eventually that calamitous dinner came to an end, and I definitely did not suggest we go on to a nightclub for a bottle of bubbly and a spot of dancing. At the moment I felt biodegradable and ready for a New Jersey landfill.

We went back to Meg's apartment, with Hertha sitting on Meg's lap as she had before. I had no desire to linger, since it was painfully obvious that my presence was lending nothing to the festivities. And so, pleading an early morning engagement with my periodontist, I made my escape. The protests of the two women at my early departure were perfunctory, their farewells just as mechanical.

I drove away more thoughtful than angry. You may find this difficult to believe, but there are times, many of them, when my duties as chief of discreet inquiries for McNally & Son take precedence over the *Sturm und Drang* of my personal affairs.

So, in the wake of that discomfiting evening, I pondered less on the outrageous behavior of my two dining companions than on the present whereabouts and activities of Frank Gloriana. I didn't have to be Monsieur C. Auguste Dupin to deduce that Frank and Laverne Willigan had what Jamie Olson once referred to as a "rappaport."

To test my theory I decided to make a quick return trip to the Jo-Jean Motel on Federal Highway. This time I pulled into the motel area just long enough to confirm that Laverne's pink Porsche was parked outside Cabin Four.

Then I drove home, deriving some amusement from imagining Harry Willigan's reaction if he was to learn of his wife's involvement in the catnapping of Peaches. I had no intention of snitching on her, of course. It was simply not something a gentleman would do.

I arrived at my burrow to find a scrawled message slipped under the door. It was from Ursi Olson and stated that Sgt. Al Rogoff had phoned early in the evening and requested I call him back.

I tried him first at police headquarters but was told he had left for the night. I then phoned him at his mobile home, and he picked up after the third ring.

"McNally," I said.

"You're home so early?" he said. "What happened—the girlfriend kick you out of bed?"

"You're close," I said. "What's happening, Al?"

"A lot. I finally got the FBI report on the Gillsworth and Willigan letters."

"Printed on the same machine?"

"Yep. I also have a preliminary report from the Medical Examiner and some stuff from the lab. There are more tests to be made, but things are beginning to get sorted out. We better meet."

"Fine," I said. "I have something to tell you, too. I know who swiped the cat."

"Don't tell me it was Willie Sutton."

"No," I said, laughing. "Even better. When do you want to make it?"

"Tomorrow morning at ten," he said. "At Gillsworth's house."

"Why there?"

"We're going to reenact the murder. You get to play the victim."

"My favorite role," I said. "I rehearsed this evening."

"What?"

"Nothing," I said. "See you tomorrow."

I poured myself a small marc and spent a few hours reviewing my journal, paying particular attention to the entries dealing with Laverne Willigan, her feelings about her husband, her reactions to the snatching of Peaches, and the gossip Jamie had relayed about her alleged lover.

I poured a second marc and lighted a cigarette. Absorbing alcohol and inhaling nicotine with carefree abandon, I mused on Laverne's motive for assisting in the catnapping, for I was certain she was involved up to her toasted buns. I scribbled a few notes:

1. Laverne is a sensual young woman with a jumbo appetite for the pleasures of the good life.

2. She is married to Harry, an ill-natured dolt much older than she but with the gelt to provide the aforementioned delights.

3. She meets a rakishly handsome immoralist, Frank Gloriana. He is married to the psychic, Hertha, but has no scruples about cheating on his wife, especially when the possibility of a payoff exists. (Or perhaps the medium is aware of his infidelity and couldn't care less, being as amoral as he.)

4. Laverne and Frank become intimate, enjoying each other's company with absolutely no intention of leaving their respective spouses.

5. But Frank suffers from a bad case of the shorts. (Bounced checks, etc.)

6. Question: Did Laverne or Frank dream up the idea of swiping Peaches for a good chunk of walking-around money?

7. Answer: My guess is that it was Frank's scam, but Laverne merrily goes along since it causes distress to her boorish husband, he can easily afford the bite, and *not* to aid Frank might result in her losing him.

8. She sneaks the cat out of the Willigan home in its carrier and delivers it to Cabin Four.

9. Frank slides the ransom notes under the Willigans' front door.

10. Laverne returns the carrier when she learns from her sister that I have noted its absence.

11. All that remains to be done is the glomming of the ransom and the return of Peaches to her hearth.

12. Everyone lives happily ever after.

I reread these notes, and everything seemed logical to me—and so banal I wanted to weep. I went to bed reflecting that there are really no new ways to sin.

If you discover any, I wish you'd let me know.

Saturday morning brought brilliant sunshine and a resurgence of the customary McNally confidence. This high lasted all of forty-five minutes until, while lathering my chops preparatory to shaving, I received a phone call from Consuela Garcia.

"Archy," she wailed, "our orgy tonight—it's off!"

The bright new day immediately dimmed. I had consoled myself, in typical masculine fashion, that despite my rejection by Meg Trumble on Friday night, there was always Connie awaiting me on Saturday. I had envisioned a debauch so profligate that it might even include our reciting in unison the limerick beginning, "There was a young man from Rangoon." But apparently it was not to be.

"Connie," I said, voice choked with frustration, "why ever not?"

"Because," she said, "I got a call from my cousin Lola in Miami. She and Max, her husband, are driving up to Disney World and want to stop off and spend the night in my place."

"Ridiculous!"

"I know, but I've *got* to let them, Archy, because I spent a weekend with them at Christmastime."

I sighed. "At least we can all have dinner together, can't we?"

"Archy," she said, "Max wears Bermuda shorts with white ankle socks and laced black shoes."

"No dinner," I said firmly.

"But I want to see you," she cried. "Can't the two of us have lunch even if there's no tiddledywinks later?"

"Of course we can," I said gamely. "Meet you at the Club noonish."

"You are an admirable man," she proclaimed.

"I concur," I said.

A zingy breakfast did wonders for my morale. Being of Scandinavian origin, the Olsons had a thing for herring. Ursi kept a variety on hand, and that was my morning repast: herring in wine, in mustard sauce, in dilled cream, and one lone kipper. I wolfed all this with schwarzbrot and sweet butter. I know iced vodka is the wash of choice with a feast of herring, but it was too early in the morning; I settled for black coffee.

Much refreshed and happy I had been blessed with a robust gut, I tooled the Miata southward to meet Sergeant Al. It was a splendid day, clear and soft. If you're going to reenact a murder, that was the weather for it. The glory of sun, sea, and sky made homicide seem a lark. No one could possibly die on a day like that.

Rogoff was waiting for me in the flowered sitting room of the Gillsworth manse. I thought his meaty face was sagging with weariness, and I made sympathetic noises about his strenuous labors and obvious lack of sufficient sleep.

He shrugged. "Comes with the territory," he growled. "How to be a successful cop: Work your ass off, be patient, and pray that you're lucky. You smell of fish. What did you have for breakfast?"

"Herring."

"I shouldn't complain," he said. "I had a hot pastrami sandwich and a kosher dill. Tell me about the crazy cat."

We sat in facing armchairs, and I recited all the evidence leading to my conclusion that Laverne Willigan and Frank Gloriana had conspired in the catnapping.

Al listened intently and grinned when I finished. "Yeah," he said, "I'll buy it: the two of them making nice-nice and cooking up a plot to swipe the old coot's pet for fifty grand. I love it, just love it. You figure the cat is still out at the motel?"

"There's *a* cat in Cabin Four," I said. "I heard it mewing. I can't swear it's Peaches, but I'd make book on it."

He thought a moment. Then: "It might make our job easier when push comes to shove. That Cabin Four sounds like the combat center of everything that's going down. Otto Gloriana is staying there, and that's where you saw Gillsworth's Bentley and Laverne's Porsche."

"And heard the cat," I reminded him. "And also, the lady in the office said Otto drove off with a woman who could be Irma."

"Probably was."

"You want to raid the place, Al?"

"Not yet," he said. "The cat isn't as important as the homicides. I'd hate to tip our hand and send all the cockroaches scurrying back in the woodwork. But I think I'll put an undercover guy in one of the other cabins, just to keep an eye on things."

"All right," I said, "you play it your way. Now tell me about the FBI report."

He took out his notebook and flipped pages until he got to the section he wanted. Then he paused to light a cigar. I waited patiently until he had it drawing to his satisfaction. Then he started reading.

"The machine is a Smith Corona PWP 100C personal word processor with pica type. Paper is Southworth DeLuxe Four Star. Smith Corona ribbon used throughout. All letters written on same machine, probably by same operator."

"Interesting," I said, "but what good is it? What do we do with it?"

He smiled at me. "Archy, you've got to start thinking like a cop. I just had a rookie assigned to me. What I'll do is have the guy go through the Yellow Pages and make a list of all the companies in the area that sell and service office machines. He hits every one of them and makes his own list of those that handle the Smith Corona PWP 100C. Then he gets the names and addresses of customers who have bought that machine or had it serviced. It's a lot of legwork, I admit, but it's got to be done, and I think it'll pay off."

I thought a moment. "That's one way of doing it," I said. "The hard way."

Al looked at me, a little miffed. "Oh?" he said. "And what's the easy way, sherlock?"

"Give your rookie a twenty-minute crash course on word processors. Tell him to get a business card from a legitimate company. Send him to call on Frank Gloriana at their office on Clematis Street. The rookie is wearing civvies. He tries to sell Frank a Smith Corona PWP 100C. I'm betting Frank will say, 'Sorry, we've already got one.'"

The sergeant burst out laughing and slapped his thigh. "What a scamster you are!" he said. "Thank God you're on our side or you'd end up owning Florida. Yeah, that's a great swindle, and we'll try it before the rookie starts pounding the pavement. You really think the letters are coming out of the Glorianas' office?"

"A good bet," I said. "There are some doors up there leading to closed-off rooms I didn't see. It's worth a go."

"It sure is," Rogoff said. "Thanks for the suggestion."

"You're quite welcome," I said. "Al, are you serious about reenacting the murder?"

"Sure I'm serious. Look, we picked up some odds and ends of physical evidence. None of them are heavy by themselves, but taken together they add up to a possible homicide planned to look like a suicide. I'll explain as we go along. Now I want you to go back to the kitchen. I'll go outside and pretend I'm the perp. You try to act like you think Gillsworth did in the few minutes before his death."

I went to the kitchen, which still showed blackened scars from the grease fire. In a moment I heard the front doorbell ring. I paused a moment and then returned to the entrance. I peered through the judas window. The sergeant was standing there. I opened the door.

"All right," Rogoff said, "the victim probably does the same thing: glances through the window, sees someone he knows, and lets him in."

"*Him?*" I said. "Not a woman? Or maybe two people?"

"Possible," he said. He stepped inside, closed the door behind him. "Now the perp is inside but doesn't know Gillsworth has left a pan of oil heating on the range. And before the victim can tell him, the killer does this . . ."

He leveled a forefinger at me thumb up, other fingers clenched.

"Why the gun?" I asked him.

"Because the killer wants to get Gillsworth into the bathtub so he can fake a suicide. A polite invitation just isn't going to do it. Now put your hands in the air and turn around."

I followed orders. In a few seconds I felt a light slap on the back of my skull.

"What was that?" I asked.

"The guy—or lady if you insist—slugs Gillsworth on the back of the noggin. The docs found it: a forcible blow caused by the famous blunt instrument. Could have been a gun butt. Heavy enough to render the victim unconscious. Now fall backward. Don't worry; I'll catch you."

Somewhat nervously I toppled. Al caught me under the arms.

"My God," he said, "what do you weigh?"

"One-seventy."

"Bullshit."

"Well, maybe a little more."

"Yeah, twenty pounds more," he said. "Gillsworth weighed about one-fifty."

"That figures," I said. "He was a scrawny bird."

"And a lot easier to drag than you," Al said, moving backward down the corridor toward the bathroom, pulling me along with him.

"We know it was done like this," the sergeant said, "because the victim's heels made furrows in the carpet. Photographed and the fibers analyzed. And guess what we found in the parallel tracks."

"What?"

"Cat hairs."

"Oh-oh. The motel."

"You got it. So we went upstairs and vacuumed Gillsworth's other clothes and shoes. More cat hair. He must have spent a lot of time in Cabin Four. The hair was silver-gray."

"Peaches," I said. "Definitely."

He made no comment, trying not to huff and puff as he dragged me past the poet's den and through the door of the bathroom.

"Okay," he said, "you can stand up now. I'm not going to put you in the tub; it hasn't been washed out yet." He assisted me to my feet and glanced at his watch. "Less than three minutes from front door to bathroom. Then I figure the killer tugged Gillsworth over the edge of the tub and let him fall. That's when the victim cracked his head on the rim. He had two separate and distinct wounds on the back of his skull: one from the gun butt, the other made when he was dumped in the tub and smashed his head. You can still see the mark on the rim."

I stood erect and gazed down into the tub. Blood had dried and caked on the bottom and inner surfaces of the walls.

"Was the drain closed?" I asked.

"No," Rogoff said. "But Gillsworth was wearing a crazy jacket. The tail blocked the drain enough so the blood didn't run out freely. Now the victim is lying in the tub, face up, unconscious. The killer takes a single-edge razor blade and slashes both his wrists."

"In the wrong direction?"

"Correct. And drops the blade on the bath mat to make it look like Gillsworth had let it fall there."

"Any prints on the blade?"

"Nothing usable."

"Where did it come from? Did Gillsworth shave with single-edge blades?"

"Ah-ha," Rogoff said. "The beauty part. I wanted to make sure this wasn't a burglary-homicide, so I called Marita to come over and check out the house. She said nothing was missing. She also said they had no single-edge blades; Gillsworth used an electric shaver. We found it in the upstairs bathroom. So the killer brought the blade with him. Which means the fake suicide was planned. It would make a nice headline: 'Heartbroken Poet Takes Own Life After Tragic Death of Beloved Wife.' "

"Uh-huh," I said. "And your mention of Marita reminds me of something. The last time you and I met in this house—that was right after Lydia Gillsworth was killed—I saw Marita drive up. What was she doing here?"

Al gave me a look. "You don't miss much, do you? Well, after his wife was murdered, I asked Roderick to check out the house and see if anything was missing. He did and said nothing was gone as far as he could tell. But I called in Marita to double-check, figuring a housekeeper would know better whether or not anything was missing."

"And was it?"

"Yeah," Al said, staring at me. "A pair of latex gloves. Marita kept them under the sink to use when she scoured pots."

"Latex gloves," I repeated. "Lovely. The final prints on the walking stick that killed Lydia were made with latex gloves, weren't they?"

"That's right."

I took a deep breath. "How do you compute it, Al?"

"I don't," he said, almost angrily. "It makes absolutely no sense that a stranger breaks into the house and goes looking for latex gloves before he kills. I've got that mystery on hold. But meanwhile, what do you think of my scenario on Gillsworth's murder and the faked suicide?"

"Plausible," I said. "There's only one thing wrong with it."

"What's that?"

"You've provided a believable exegesis on *how* it happened, but you haven't said a word about *why*."

"*Why?*" he said disgustedly. "Why does a chicken cross the road?"

"For the same reason a fireman wears red suspenders," I said. "Let's get the hell out of here, Al. A bloody bathtub is not the most fitting dessert for a herring breakfast."

But he said he wanted to stay, and mumbled something about taking additional measurements. I didn't believe that. Al Rogoff, despite his cop's practicality, is something of a romantic. I reckoned that he wanted to wander through that doomed house for a while, reflect on the two sanguinary murders that had happened within its walls, try to absorb the aura of the place, listen for ghosts, and perhaps conceive a reason for the seemingly senseless killings.

All I wanted was blue sky, hot sunshine, and uncontaminated air to breathe. Evil has a scent all its own, not only sickening but frightening.

I drove directly to the Pelican Club. I was a bit early for my date with Connie Garcia, but having spent the morning impersonating a corpse, I was badly in need of a transfusion. I was certain a frozen daiquiri would bring roses back to the McNally cheeks.

The luncheon crowd had not yet assembled, but Simon Pettibone was on duty behind the bar, reading *Barron's* through his Ben Franklin glasses. He put the financial pages aside long enough to mix my drink, an ambrosial concoction with just a wee bit of Cointreau added.

Mr. Pettibone went back to his stock indices, and I nursed my plasma, savoring the quiet, cool, dim ambience of my favorite watering hole. A few members wandered in, but it was a pleasant Saturday afternoon and most Pelicanites were in pools or the ocean, on fairways and courts, or perhaps astride a polo pony out at Wellington. Life is undoubtedly unfair and one would be a fool not to enjoy one's good fortune.

Connie showed up a few minutes after noon. She was wearing stone-washed denim overalls atop a tie-dyed T-shirt. Her long black hair was gathered with a yellow ribbon, and there were leather strap sandals on her bare feet. She looked—oh, maybe sixteen years old, and I told her she might have to show her ID to get a drink.

We went back to the empty dining area, and a yawning Priscilla showed us to our favorite corner table. Connie ordered a white zin and I had a repeat of my daiquiri.

"Sorry about tonight, Archy," she said, "but there was just no way I could turn Lola and Max away; they *are* family."

"No problem," I said. "After they've gone, we'll make up for lost time."

She reached across the table to clasp my hand. "Promise?" she said.

"I swear by Zeus," I said. "And a McNally does not take an oath to Zeus lightly."

"Who's Zeus?" she asked.

"A Greek who owns a luncheonette up near Jupiter," I said.

I was spared further explanation when Pris brought our drinks and rattled off the specials of the day. Connie and I both opted for the mixed seafood salad (scallops, shrimp, Florida lobster) with a loaf of garlic toast.

"I've got news for you," Connie said after we ordered, "and you're not going to like it."

"You're pregnant?"

"No, dammit," she said. "I'd love to have kids, wouldn't you?"

"I can't," I said. "Being of the male gender."

"You know what I mean," she said, laughing. "Anyway, the bad news is this: I was turned down by that medium."

"What!?"

She nodded. "I got a letter from Hertha Gloriana, a very cold letter. She said it was obvious to her that the person I described doesn't actually exist, and therefore she could not provide a psychic profile and was returning my check. She also told me not to apply again unless I told her the truth."

"I'll be damned."

"Archy, how did she know my letter was a phony? There was nothing in it that might tip her off it was a scam."

I shook my head. "I can't figure how she knew. But what's even more puzzling is that she returned your money. If the Glorianas have a swindle going, as I thought, Hertha would have cobbled up a fictitious profile and cashed your check."

"Perhaps she really is clairvoyant and knew at once that my letter was a trick."

"Perhaps."

Our lunch was served, and we talked of other things as we devoured our salads. Connie gave me a long account of her trials and tribulations in planning Lady Horowitz's Fourth of July bash, but I hardly listened; I couldn't stop brooding about Hertha's reaction to the fake letter. How *did* she know?

Connie didn't want any dessert and said she had to get back to her houseguests. I told her I was going to loll around the Club awhile and would phone her on Sunday. I escorted her out to her little Subaru.

"Thanks for the lunch, Archy," she said, "and I'm sorry I depressed you with the bad news about the medium's letter."

"You didn't depress me."

"Sure I did. You've hardly said a word since I told you, and when Archy McNally doesn't chatter, he's depressed."

"I think I'm more mystified than anything else. Connie, you don't happen to have that letter you received from the Glorianas, do you?"

"Yep," she said, fishing in the hip pocket of her overalls. "I'm glad you reminded me; I thought you might want it for your files. Don't forget to call me tomorrow, sweet."

She handed me a folded envelope, kissed my cheek, and hopped into her dinky car. I waved as she drove away. Then I unfolded the envelope, took out the letter, and read it in the bright sunlight. It was coldly phrased and stated pretty much what Connie had already told me. There were no surprises.

But what shocked was that it had an even right-hand margin and had obviously been written on the same word processor as the Gillsworth letters and Peaches' ransom notes.

I went back into the Pelican Club and used the public phone in the rear of the bar area. I called Al Rogoff but he wasn't in his office, and they refused to tell me where he was. On a hunch, I then phoned Roderick Gillsworth's home and got results.

"Sergeant Rogoff," he said.

"McNally," I said. "You're still there? What on earth are you doing?"

"Reading poetry."

"Gillsworth's? Awful dreck, isn't it?"

"Oh, I don't know," Al said. "Erotic stuff."

"You've got to be kidding," I said. "Gillsworth's poetry is about as erotic as the Corn Laws of England. Which book of his are you reading?"

"I'm not reading a book. I'm going through unpublished poems I found in a locked drawer in his desk. I picked the lock. A piece of cheese. Inside was a file of finished poems. They're dated and all appear to have been written in the past six months or so. And I'm telling you they're hot stuff."

I was flabbergasted. "I don't dig that at all," I told Al. "I've dipped into some of his published things, and believe me they're dull, dull, dull."

"Well, the stuff I've been reading is steamy enough to add a new chapter to *Psychopathia Sexualis*. Maybe he decided to change his style."

"Maybe," I said. "We can talk about that later. Right now I've got something more important."

I told him how the Glorianas were selling psychic profiles by mail, how I tried to prove it a scam by having Consuela Garcia send in a trumped-up letter from a nonexistent woman, how Hertha rejected the fake application, and how her missive was identical in format to the Gillsworth-Willigan letters.

"That does it," Rogoff said decisively. "I'll send the rookie to the Glorianas' office to see if he can confirm that they own a Smith Corona word processor. And instead of one undercover cop, I'll plant a couple, man and woman, out at the Jo-Jean Motel and put round-the-clock surveillance on Cabin Four. And if the brass will give me the warm bodies, I'll stake out the Glorianas' apartment."

"That should do it," I said. "Al, Frank Gloriana carries a gun. Lydia Gillsworth told me."

"Thanks for the tip. Tell me, Archy, how do you figure the medium knew the letter you sent her was a phony?"

"I don't know," I said. "I just don't know."

I went back to the bar to sign the tab for lunch.

"Mr. Pettibone," I said abruptly, "do you believe in ghosts?"

He stared at me a moment through his square specs. "Why, yes, Mr. McNally," he said finally. "As a matter of fact, I do."

"Surely not the Halloween variety," I said. "The kind who wear white sheets and go 'Whooo! Whooo!' "

"Well, perhaps not those," he admitted. "But I do believe some of the departed return as spirits and are able to communicate with the living."

I had always considered the Pelican Club's majordomo to be the most practical and realistic of men, so it was startling to learn he accepted the existence of disembodied beings. "Have you ever spoken to the spirit of a deceased person?" I asked him.

"I have indeed, Mr. McNally," he said readily. "As you know, I am an active investor in the stock market. On several occasions the spirit of Mr. Bernard Baruch, the successful financier, has appeared to me. We meet on a park bench and he gives me advice on which stocks to buy and what to sell."

"And do you follow the ghost's advice?"

"Frequently."

"Do you win or lose?"

"Invariably I profit. But Mr. Baruch's spirit has a tendency to sell too soon."

"Thank you for the information, Mr. Pettibone," I said gravely and left him a handsome tip.

I drove home, garaged the Miata, and entered the house through the kitchen. Ursi and Jamie Olson were both working on a rack of lamb dinner we were to have that evening. They looked up as I came in.

"Ursi," I said without preamble, "do you believe in ghosts?"

"I do, Mister Archy," she said at once. "I frequently speak to my dear departed mother. She's very happy."

"Uh-huh," I said and turned to Jamie. "And how about you?" I asked. "Do you believe in ghosts?"

"Some," he said.

That evening during the family cocktail hour I asked my mother the same question.

"Oh my, yes," she said airily. "I have never seen them myself, but I have been told by people whose opinion I respect that spirits do exist. Mercedes Blair's husband died last year, you know, and she says that ever since he passed, their house has been haunted by his ghost. She knows because she always finds the toilet seat up. No matter how many times she puts the cover down, she always finds the seat up when she returns. She says it must be her dead husband's spirit."

I looked to my father. His hirsute eyebrows were jiggling up and down, a sure sign that he was stifling his mirth. But when he spoke, his voice was gentle and measured.

"Mother," he said, "I would not accept the testimony of Mrs. Blair as proof positive of the existence of disembodied spirits. It's similar to saying, 'I saw a ghost last night. It ran down the alley and jumped over a fence. And if you don't believe me, there's the fence.' "

I asked: "Then you don't believe the spirits of the departed return to earth and communicate with the living?"

He answered carefully. "I think when people report seeing a ghost or talking to a spirit, they sincerely believe they are telling the truth. But I suggest what they are actually reporting is a dream, a fantasy, and the spirit they allegedly see is a memory, a very intense memory, of a loved one who is deceased."

"But what if the spirit they claim to see is a historical character, someone they couldn't possibly have known?"

"Then they are talking rubbish," my father said forthrightly. "Utter and complete rubbish."

I retired to my lair after dinner to add entries to my journal, which was beginning to rival the girth of *War and Peace,* and to sort out the day's confused impressions.

I consider myself a fairly lucid chap. Oh, I admit I might exhibit a few moments of pure lunacy now and then, but generally the McNally hooves are solidly planted on terra firma. But now I was faced with a mystery that baffled me. How *did* Hertha Gloriana know Connie's letter was a hoax? And how was the medium, speaking in the voice of Lydia Gillsworth, able to shriek "Caprice!" and identify a clue that had already intrigued Sgt. Al Rogoff?

It was possible that Hertha had a genuine psychic gift. But if you admitted the existence of such a specialized talent, then you had to allow that the actuality of spirits was also conceivable, communication with the dead tenable, and all the other phenomena of the psi factor similarly capable of realization, including ESP, psychokinesis, telepathy, precognition, and perhaps, eventually, discussing the International Monetary Fund with dolphins.

That afternoon I had discovered that several perfectly normal citizens believed in ghosts and by extension, I supposed, in other manifestations of the supernatural. Could they be right and my father's cogent disbelief wrong?

I went to bed that night and with my eyes firmly shut I willed with all my strength for the appearance of Carole Lombard's ghost.

She never showed up.

Chapter 14

Like most people I consider Monday the first day of the week. It is actually the second, of course, but Sunday is usually observed as a day of rest, a faux holiday, a twenty-four-hour vacation to be devoted to worship, a big midday meal, and just lollygagging about and recharging one's batteries.

But that particular Sunday turned out to be something entirely different. It deepened my confusion and increased my suspicion that events were moving so swiftly it was impossible to cope. Men who have been in battle have described it to me as disorder in the nth degree. Before that Sunday concluded, I felt I deserved a combat ribbon.

It began when I overslept and went downstairs to find that my parents had already departed for church. And the Olsons had left for *their* church. So I fixed my own matutinal meal, succeeding in dropping a buttered English muffin onto the floor. Butter-side down, inevitably—another puzzle I've never solved. I also knocked over a full cup of coffee. That brunch did not augur a successful Sabbath.

The phone rang as I was mopping up the spilt coffee and I really didn't want to answer, thinking it was sure to be calamitous news. But I girded my loins (how on earth does one gird a loin?) and picked up after the sixth ring.

"The McNally residence," I said.

"Archy?" Meg Trumble said. "Good morning!"

You could have knocked me over with a palm frond. "Good morning, Meg," I said. "What a pleasant surprise."

"What are you doing?" she asked.

"If you must know, I'm wiping up spilled coffee."

She laughed. "That doesn't sound like much fun. Archy, Hertha Gloriana is with me, and she'd like to speak to you."

"Sure," I said. "Put her on."

"No, no. Not on the telephone. Can you come over to my place?"

"Now?"

"Please. We're going to do some aerobics, and then we plan to go to the beach. Could you make it soon, Archy? It's important."

"All right," I said. "Half an hour or so."

The day was muddling up nicely, and as I spun the Miata toward Riviera Beach I didn't even want to imagine what lay ahead. I knew only that it would add to my flummoxization—and if there isn't such a word, there should be.

I walked into quite a scene for an early Sunday afternoon. The two women were wearing exercise costumes of skin-tight gleaming spandex; Meg in a cat-suit of silver and Hertha in a purple leotard and pink biking shorts. Apparently they had finished their workout, for both were sheened with sweat and still panting slightly. And they were sipping glasses of orange sludge.

"Carrot juice, Archy?" Meg asked.

I fought nausea valiantly. "Thank you, no," I replied. "I have no desire to see in the dark."

"A cold beer?"

"Thank you, yes."

Hertha patted the couch cushion beside her, and I sat there, a bit gingerly I admit. I had an uneasy feeling of having intruded into a ladies' locker room. I had been invited but couldn't rid myself of feeling an interloper.

Meg brought me a popped can of Bud Light, which I accepted gratefully.

"Hertha," she said commandingly, "tell him."

The medium turned to me. She seemed uncommonly attractive at that moment, her fair skin flushed from exercise and something in her eyes I had never seen before. It was more than happiness, I thought; it was triumph.

"It's about Peaches," she said to me. "I had another vision. Remember I told you I saw her in a plain room? It's in a small building, like a cabin. I think it may be at an old-fashioned motel."

I took a gulp of my beer. "That's interesting," I said. "Did you see where the motel is located?"

"I'm sure it's in the West Palm Beach area."

"Tell him what else you saw, Hertha," Meg ordered.

The medium hesitated a second. "Perhaps I shouldn't be revealing this," she said, "but it troubles me and you did ask for my help. I hope you will keep it confidential."

"Of course."

"I saw my husband, Frank, in the room with the cat."

The two women looked at me expectantly. That they were attempting to manipulate me I had no doubt. There was no alternative but to play along. I'm good at acting the simp; it just seems to come naturally.

"That *is* a shocker," I said. "What on earth do you suppose he was doing there?"

"I don't know," she wide-eyed me. "Do you suppose he had anything to do with the catnapping?"

The greatest actress since Duse.

"Why don't you ask him?" I suggested.

"I've got to be completely honest with you, Archy," she started—and my antennae stiffened. When people say that to you it's time to button your hip pocket to make certain your wallet is secure. "Frank has an awful temper," she went on. "I'm afraid of angering him. He can become quite physical."

"The brute beats her," Meg said wrathfully.

"Not exactly," Hertha said. "But he has struck me on occasion."

I was terribly tempted to remark that if she was truly a seeress she would foreknow the blows in time to duck. I said nothing of the sort of course. I said, "Dreadful."

"So you see I can't ask Frank about it," the medium said sorrowfully. "But I hope it may help you recover the cat."

"I'm sure it will," I said. "And I thank you for being so cooperative."

I finished my beer (sadly, only an 8-oz. can) and bid the ladies adieu. They were both looking at me thoughtfully when I left the apartment.

I drove home slowly, reflecting on what I had just been told. It was obvious the two women had compared notes, and Hertha now knew the original reason I had given her for wanting to find Peaches was false. She was aware the cat had been snatched and I had been employed to find it. That much was clear.

What wasn't quite so apparent was how she knew the missing feline was presently incarcerated in a motel cabin. Either she was telling the truth and had seen the cat and Frank in a psychic vision or she had overheard conversation at home revealing the cat's whereabouts and Frank's guilt.

But then I realized *how* she knew was unimportant. What was vital was that she was intent on implicating her husband. The story of the physical abuse she suffered at his hands might or might not be true. But I felt Hertha had a deeper motive for wanting her spouse apprehended and perhaps tucked away for an appreciable period in the clink.

I was still pondering the medium's motive for snitching when I arrived home, saw the Lexus in the garage, and knew my parents had returned from church. When I entered the house, my father was standing in the open doorway of his study.

"Are you acquainted with a woman named Mrs. Irma Gloriana?" he demanded. It was almost an accusation.

"Yes, sir, I am," I replied.

He nodded, beckoned, led the way into his study, and closed the door. He sat behind his desk and motioned me to an armchair.

"I think you better tell me about her," he said.

"It's a long story, father."

"Dinner will not be served for another hour," he said dryly. "Surely that will be sufficient time."

Usually mein papa does not question me about details of my discreet inquiries. I think he suspects I cut ethical corners—which I do—and he'd rather not have knowledge of my modi operandi. Successful results are really all that concern him.

But since he wanted to know about Mrs. Irma Gloriana, I told him. And not only Irma, but husband Otto, son Frank, and daughter-in-law Hertha. I also gave him an account of the séance I had attended and related how I had managed to locate Peaches in Cabin Four of the Jo-Jean Motel. I concluded with a brief report on my most recent meeting with Hertha Gloriana and Meg Trumble. In fact, I told him everything you already know.

He listened closely and never once interrupted. When I had finished, he rose and walked slowly to the sideboard where he carefully packed one of his silver-mounted Upshall pipes. I took that as permission to light up an English Oval. He regained his swivel chair and held his loaded pipe a moment before flaming it.

"Then I gather you and Sergeant Rogoff believe the Glorianas are guilty of criminal behavior," he pronounced.

"I cannot speak for the sergeant," I said, "but I am convinced that Frank Gloriana connived with Laverne Willigan to steal the cat and hold it for ransom. I also think Otto Gloriana, probably Irma, and possibly Frank were involved in the murders of Lydia and Roderick Gillsworth. But I have no idea as to their motive."

He finally lighted his pipe. When he had it drawing freely without a gurgle, he blew a plume of smoke at the coffered ceiling. "Perhaps we'll learn tomorrow," he remarked.

I was astonished. "Tomorrow, father?" I said.

He nodded. "Shortly after returning from church, I received a phone call from Mrs. Irma Gloriana. A very forceful woman."

"Yes, sir, she is that."

"She wishes to see me tomorrow. She said it was an important matter concerning Roderick Gillsworth. I thought it best to listen to what she has to say. We're meeting in my office at ten o'clock. I'd like you to be present, Archy."

"Of course," I said, grinning. "Absolutely. Looking forward to it, sir. May I tell Sergeant Rogoff about the meeting?"

He considered that request a long, long time. I had learned to wait patiently, knowing that eventually his mulling would end and he'd come to a decision.

"Yes," he said at last, "you may tell the sergeant. And he will be informed as to the results of the meeting if circumstances and ethics allow. It may possibly aid his investigation. You say this woman was formerly the madam of a brothel?"

"Yes, sir. According to the Atlanta police."

"A coarse woman?"

"No, sir, I would not say that—although Al Rogoff might possibly disagree. As you said, she is a forceful woman. I find her almost domineering. Very sure of herself, very heavy in the willpower department. I see her as the Chief Executive Officer of the Gloriana family, the dynamo, with perhaps a tendency to tyrannize." I hesitated a second. Then: "There is something else. In my opinion she is a disturbing woman. Physically, that is. She exudes a certain sensuality. I believe she is aware of it and uses it. I put her age at close to sixty, but there has certainly been no diminution of her sexual attractiveness."

One of my father's hairy eyebrows slowly ascended. But all he said was, "Interesting."

But then, as I rose to leave, he added, "I usually find your reaction to people very perceptive, Archy."

Praise! How sweet it was.

That evening I called Al Rogoff, reported on my meeting with Hertha

Gloriana, and informed him of my father's Monday morning appointment with Mrs. Irma Gloriana.

"Oh boy," Al said. "I have a feeling the lady is about to drop a bomb. Keep me up to speed on what happens, Archy."

"Did you get your spies into the Jo-Jean Motel?"

"Yep. Man and woman in Cabin Five, right next to Otto's pad. They've already reported by radio. He's had two visitors so far. I make them as Frank and Irma. Be sure to call me tomorrow after your father's meeting."

"Wait a minute," I cried. "Don't hang up. Those erotic poems Gillsworth wrote—did he mention any names?"

"No one you know," Rogoff said.

"Come on, Al," I said, "don't play games. What names did he mention?"

"Just one. Astarte. I looked it up. Goddess of fertility and sexual love."

"I know her well," I said. "She lives in Miami Beach."

Then he did hang up.

But that long, aggravating day had not yet ended. Later that evening I was in my sanctum, working on my journal, when Laverne Willigan phoned.

"Another ransom note, Archy," she told me. "It was slipped under the front door sometime tonight."

"Uh-huh," I said. "Will you read it to me, please?"

She did. The letter commanded Harry Willigan to assemble fifty thousand dollars in fifty-dollar bills, unmarked with no numbers in sequence. Then he or his representative would deliver the money to a messenger. That was the term used: "Messenger." He would be waiting in the parking area of a twenty-four-hour convenience store on Federal Highway at midnight on Monday. The address given, I judged, was about a mile from the Jo-Jean Motel.

After the ransom had been handed over, the messenger would leave, but Willigan or his representative was ordered to remain in the parking area. When the fifty thousand had been counted and the bills examined and approved, Peaches would be delivered, hale and hearty.

Laverne continued: "It also says if the messenger sees or suspects the presence of the police, Harry will never see his pet alive again."

"I don't like the setup," I said immediately. "What if the fifty thousand is handed over to the messenger, he disappears, and Peaches is never produced? It seems to me they're asking Harry to take a horrendous risk."

"He doesn't have much choice, does he?" Laverne said. "Not if he wants to rub noses with Sweetums again. I called Harry in Chicago and told him what the letter said. He cursed a blue streak but finally said he'll play ball. He's going to phone his Palm Beach bank in the morning and tell them to get the cash together. The bank will call me when it's ready. Then I'll phone you. Harry wants you to deliver the money and get Peaches back. Will you do it, Archy?"

"Of course," I said. "It's the least I can do after failing to locate the cat-nappers. Let me know when the bank has the cash ready. I'll pick it up from them. And sometime tomorrow I'll stop by your place and get the letter. If you're going out, leave it with Leon."

"Thank you, Archy," she said briskly. "I'm sure everything will work out just fine."

"I think so, too," I said. "Harry will be back on Tuesday?"

"Yes. Early in the morning. By that time you should have Peaches."

After she hung up I phoned Al Rogoff again to alert him to this new development. But I was unable to locate him and decided it could wait until the morning. Then we'd devise a plan to thwart the villains.

Monday was shaping up as a hellacious day. I only hoped I'd live to see Tuesday.

Chapter 15

I awoke Monday morning with a dread feeling of having forgotten to do something I should have done. I recognized my lapse while scraping my jowls, and if it hadn't been a safety razor I might have nicked the old jug, I was that mortified. What I had disremembered was to phone Connie Garcia on Sunday as I had promised. Not for the first time did I wonder why I treated that dear woman with such thoughtless neglect. I suppose it was because I knew she was *there*.

I had roused in time to breakfast with my parents in the dining room. While scarfing my way through a stack of buckwheat pancakes, I informed the governor of Laverne Willigan's phone call the previous night.

He glanced up from *The Wall Street Journal* long enough to gaze at me speculatively. "You actually intend to deliver the money to the catnappers yourself, Archy?"

"Yes, sir. I expect Sergeant Rogoff will come up with a plan for a trap."

He nodded. "When you receive the fifty thousand at the bank," he advised, "count it before you sign a receipt."

I sighed. "Yes, father," I said. Sometimes he treated me as if I were the village idiot. I do have a brain, you know, even though occasionally I choose not to use it.

Before leaving for the Willigan hacienda, I phoned Al Rogoff at his office and found him in a surprisingly lively mood.

"What are you so chirpy about?" I asked him.

"It's all coming together, old buddy. I'll fill you in later. What's up?"

I repeated what Laverne Willigan had told me of the catnappers' letter and the instructions as to how the ransom was to be paid.

"I don't like it," Al said at once. "Too much risk of a double X."

"I told Laverne that but she said Harry has no choice and is willing to shell out the fifty grand."

"Which makes her and the boyfriend happy—right? Okay, Archy, I'll start working on a snare for midnight tonight."

"After I collect the money from the bank, do you want to mark the bills?"

"Haven't got time," he said. "And too dangerous if they've got a lamp to read the markings. We'll make a list of the serial numbers; that'll hold up in court. Stay in touch; it's going to be a rackety day."

"Tell me about it. Al, do you think you'll be able to keep Laverne Willigan out of it?"

He was silent a moment. Then he said, "It depends," and I had to be satisfied with that.

Then I buzzed down to the Willigan manse. Leon told me the lady of the house was busy with her pedicurist, but he handed me the latest ransom note in its white envelope.

"I guess Peaches is coming home," he said.

"Looks like it," I agreed.

"And I start sneezing again," he said mournfully.

"If you don't like cats," I said, "why don't you buy yourself a koala or a wallaby? Just to remind you of down under."

"I've been down *and* under since I got here," he complained. "Florida is the outback with oranges."

Have you ever noticed that some people aren't happy unless they're unhappy?

Then I scooted for the McNally Building somewhat in excess of the legal speed limit. I arrived in time to smoke a cigarette before joining my father. I noted my hands weren't exactly shaking, but I would not have selected that moment to thread a needle. It was amazing how the prospect of a meeting with Mrs. Irma Gloriana rasped my nerves.

I went up to my father's office a few minutes before ten o'clock.

"I think it best, Archy," he said, "if you serve as a witness, a silent witness. Please let me ask the questions. If you are addressed directly, of course, you may respond. But I would prefer the conversation be limited to Mrs. Gloriana and myself."

"I'll be a fly on the wall," I assured him.

"Exactly," he said with his wintry smile.

His phone rang, and he glanced at the antique railroad clock on the wall over his rolltop desk. "The lady is prompt," he said. He picked up the phone. "Yes, show her in, please."

Mrs. Trelawney opened the door and stood aside to allow Mrs. Irma Gloriana to enter. Then the secretary closed the door softly.

Father was standing at his desk and I was across the room next to the bottle-green leather chesterfield. Irma took two steps into the office, her eyes on my father. Then she became aware of my presence, stared at me for a beat or two, and turned back to father.

"What is he doing here?" she demanded.

"I am Prescott McNally," he said in a plummy voice, "and I presume you are Mrs. Irma Gloriana. Since you are already acquainted with my son, I have asked him to attend this meeting as witness and adviser. You may be assured of his discretion."

Irma shook her head angrily. "It won't do," she said. "I don't need a witness and I don't need an adviser. I insist on a private, confidential conversation between you and me."

"In that case," my father said, "I suggest this meeting be terminated forthwith. Good day, madam." (He accented the "madam" ever so slightly.)

How I admired his tactics! Not only was he establishing his command of the situation but he was determining her anxiety level. If she marched out, then she felt she held a winning hand. If she remained, then her role was that of a supplicant, anxious to cut a deal.

She stood a moment in silence, and I reflected it was the first time I had seen her irresolute.

She was wearing a tailored suit of pale pink linen with a high-necked blouse. It was certainly a conservative costume, but not even a chador could conceal that woman's sexual radiance, and I wondered if my father was aware of it. I suspected he was. He might be stodgy but he was not torpid.

We waited.

"Very well," Mrs. Gloriana said finally. "If you wish . . ."

Father gestured toward an armchair upholstered in the same leather as the chesterfield. He sat in his swivel chair, turned to face his visitor. I remained standing in a position where I could observe them both without making like a fan at a tennis match.

"Mr. McNally," she said crisply, "I understand you were the attorney for the late Roderick Gillsworth."

"That is correct."

"Then I suppose you're handling his estate?"

He inclined his head, and she took that for assent. In addition to a black calfskin handbag she was carrying a zippered envelope of beige suede, large enough to hold legal documents. She opened the three-sided zipper with one swift motion and withdrew two sheets of white paper stapled together.

"I have here," she began (and I marveled at how assertive her voice was), "a photocopy of a handwritten last will and testament executed by Roderick Gillsworth approximately a month ago. It has been properly prepared, dated, and witnessed. Attached is a photocopy of an affidavit signed by the testator and both witnesses in the presence of a notary public and so certified. I believe the affidavit makes Mr. Gillsworth's will self-proving, and it may be admitted to probate without further testimony by the witnesses."

She leaned forward to proffer the documents. My father bent forward to accept them. He remained in that position a moment, staring at her expressionlessly. Then he leaned back and began to read. He perused the two sheets slowly, then read them again. He turned his swivel chair a bit to face me.

"Archy," he said, his voice dry, "this purportedly holographic will, al-

legedly signed by Roderick Gillsworth and witnessed by Irma Gloriana and
Frank Gloriana, states that the original manuscripts of the testator's poems
shall be given to the Library of Congress. Other than that, the total assets of
Roderick Gillsworth at the time of his death are bequeathed to Irma Gloriana."

Al Rogoff had been right; the bomb had been dropped.

My father's aplomb was something to see. He showed absolutely no sign
of the turmoil I knew must be racking him. The face he turned to Mrs. Gloriana was peaceable, and when he spoke, his voice and manner were pleas-
antness personified.

"You were a friend of the late Mr. Gillsworth?" he inquired.

"A close personal friend," she said defiantly, lifting her chin. "Especially
after his dear wife passed over. I believe my family and I provided him with
spiritual comfort."

"My son tells me your daughter-in-law is a medium."

"She is. And very gifted, I might add."

"Did Mr. Gillsworth attend the séances I understand are held at your
home?"

"Occasionally. He attended with his wife."

Father nodded and seemed to relax. He looked down at the papers he
was holding, rolled them into a loose tube, tapped them gently on his knee.
He didn't speak, and his silence obviously perturbed Mrs. Gloriana.

"Is there any reason why this will cannot be filed for probate immediately?" she said. "It is absolutely authentic."

"Well, naturally that must be determined," he said smoothly. "The testator's signature must be verified, as well as that of the certifying notary public. A search must be conducted to locate immediate survivors—family
members—if such exist. In addition, I wish to review the statutes of the State
of Florida dealing with holographic wills."

That last, of course, was complete nonsense. My father knew Florida law
as well or better than any attorney practicing in the State. He knew the music,
knew the lyrics, and could sing you verse and refrain. He was simply stalling
this would-be client.

"How long will you need?" Irma asked. "I know that probating a will
takes months, so I want to get it started as soon as possible."

"Very understandable," he said. "And I shall attempt to expedite the
process as much as possible. Where are the originals of these documents now?"

"In my safe deposit box."

He nodded. "And do you have any evidence, Mrs. Gloriana—personal
letters from Mr. Gillsworth, for instance—that might attest to your friendship
with the testator?"

"Why should that be necessary?" she asked indignantly. "Take my word
for it, we were close friends."

"Oh, I do take your word," he said. "But sometimes probate judges make
inquiries to establish to their own satisfaction the relationship between testator and beneficiary."

"Well, yes," she admitted, "I do have some letters from Rod. And a few unpublished poems he sent to me. And autographed copies of two of his books."

"Excellent. And where is this material at present?"

"Also in my safe deposit box."

"I suggest you have photocopies made of anything that relates to your friendship with Mr. Gillsworth and have the copies delivered to my office."

"Must I do all that?"

"I strongly urge it. It is my duty to anticipate any questions the presiding judge might have and be prepared to answer them. Do you have any notion of the size of Mr. Gillsworth's estate, madam?"

That last was asked suddenly in a sharp voice, and I could see it flustered her for a brief moment.

"Why, no," she said. "Not exactly. At the time Rod wrote out his will, he said he didn't have much."

That at least, I acknowledged, was the truth.

"And did he give you any reason why he was making a holographic will rather than coming to me, his attorney of record, to have his last testament revised?"

She was obviously ready for that query; her answer was immediate and glib: "He said that because you also represented his wife, he didn't want to run the risk of Lydia learning he had changed his will."

That implied Prescott McNally might be guilty of unethical conduct, but father voiced no objection. He stood and waited until she had gathered up handbag and suede envelope.

"Thank you for coming in, Mrs. Gloriana," he said cordially. "If you will supply me with copies of the personal correspondence in your safe deposit box, I will start preparing an application for probate as well as initiating those other inquiries I mentioned. Please feel free to phone me if you have any further questions or desire a progress report."

She nodded coolly. I wondered if they would shake hands on parting. They didn't. He opened the office door for her and she swept through, head high, indomitable.

Father returned to his swivel chair, and I collapsed onto the couch, weary from standing erect for so long.

"As you said, Archy," the sire remarked with a wry smile, "a disturbing woman."

"Sir," I said, "is a handwritten will legal in Florida?"

"Oh yes," he said, "if it is properly prepared, as this one apparently is. In addition, the attached affidavit serves as self-proof of the authenticity of the will."

"And is a witness allowed to inherit?"

"Yes, a witness to a last will and testament may also be a beneficiary, under Florida law. Archy, methinks the lady and Gillsworth had the assistance of an attorney in preparing this will and the accompanying affidavit. Some of the language she used was legalese, borrowed from the lawyer I'm certain she consulted. The question then arises: Why did she come to me? The will I prepared for Gillsworth has been superseded by this holographic will. And, in effect, I have been superseded. Mrs. Gloriana could just as easily have retained the attorney who assisted her and asked him to file for probate. But she came to me. Why?"

"Father, I think she figured that by retaining you she would eliminate the possibility of your asking embarrassing questions, causing trouble, delaying her receiving what she considers her rightful due. And if you raise too many objections, she'll offer to cut you in on her inheritance."

He looked at me thoughtfully. "Yes," he said, "I do believe you may be correct. The lady is using me, and I don't relish it."

We sat in a moody silence awhile, chewing our mental cud, and then my father drew a deep breath.

"Archy," he said, "yesterday you told me you thought the Glorianas were involved in the murders of Lydia and Roderick Gillsworth but you had no idea as to their motive." He held up the copy of the holographic will. "Now you have a motive."

I rose to my feet. "I better call Sergeant Rogoff," I said. "Interesting morning, sir."

"Wasn't it," he agreed.

On my way through the outer office Mrs. Trelawney took one look at my expression and evidently decided not to crack any jokes or make any reference to our recent visitor. Instead she silently handed me a message: Mrs. Laverne Willigan had phoned and I was to call her as soon as possible.

I returned to my closet, phoned the Willigan house, spoke to Leon, and eventually Laverne came on the line. She told me she had heard from the bank, the fifty thousand was ready, and I could pick it up anytime. I thanked her and hung up at once, fearing she might ask questions about plans for delivery of the ransom.

Then I phoned Sgt. Rogoff.

"Al," I said, "I'm in my office. Irma Gloriana just left, and you were right. But that bomb she dropped was a blockbuster. Can you come over?"

"On my way," he said. "Fifteen minutes."

He was as good as his word. He came barging in and plumped down in the uncomfortable steel chair alongside my desk. He lighted a cigar and took out his notebook. "All right," he said, "let's have it."

I gave him a complete account of what had transpired in my father's office. When I started, he tried to keep up by scribbling notes, but then he became so entranced by my report that he left off writing, let his cigar go out, and just listened, bending forward intently.

I finished, and he leaned back, relighted the cold cigar and stared at me. I lighted a cigarette, and within minutes my tiny office was fuggy.

"A handwritten will is legal?" he asked finally.

"My father says so. And a witness can be a beneficiary."

"And Irma gets everything?"

"Everything but the original manuscripts."

He made a grimace of disgust. "Why did the idiot do it?"

"That's obvious," I said. "Sexual obsession."

"I love the way you talk," he said. "You mean he had the hots for her."

"That's exactly what I mean," I said.

Then, when we both grasped the implications of the poet's folly, I think we became excited—hunters on a fresh spoor. We couldn't talk fast enough.

"Look, Al," I said. "Lydia was a lovely woman but something of a blue-stocking. The gossip in Palm Beach was that the Gillsworths had a marriage in name only."

"Then Roderick goes to one of those cockamamy séances with his wife and meets Mrs. Irma Gloriana. Snap, crackle, and pop!"

"Irma was everything Lydia wasn't: voluptuous, dominant, and a wanton when it suited her purpose."

"And as rapacious as a shrike."

"So they have an affair. Rod learns there's more to life than iambic pentameters, and Irma calculates this besotted fool might be the answer to her family's money problems. Do you buy all that?"

"Every word of it," Rogoff said. "That's why he began writing those erotic poems; the poor devil couldn't control his glands. It happens to all of us sooner or later."

"But not many of us end up dead because of it."

"Thank God."

"You think Gillsworth knew Otto was Irma's husband?"

"I doubt that. I think she passed him off as her brother or a friend."

"You're probably right," I said. "How's this scenario: Irma learns that Rod is practically penniless but his wife is loaded."

"And if she dies, her husband inherits the bulk of her estate."

"Who do you think made the first fatal suggestion?"

"The husband," Al said promptly. "If that was the price he had to pay to keep enjoying Irma, he was willing."

"Maybe Irma promised to marry him once Lydia was out of the picture. That's assuming he didn't know she was already married."

"And I'm betting Irma told him he wouldn't have to do the dirty deed himself; her so-called brother or friend would take care of Lydia—for a price, of course."

"Maybe the price was Gillsworth writing out that holographic will, leaving everything to Irma. A lovely quid pro quo. But why the poison-pen letters, Al?"

"Just to send the cops galloping off in all directions looking for a psycho who didn't exist. By the way, I sent that rookie up to the Glorianas' office to try to sell Frank a Smith Corona word processor. You were right; Frank already owns a model PWP 100C."

"You think he was in on the plot to murder the Gillsworths?"

Rogoff pondered a moment. "I doubt it," he said finally. "He obviously knew about it—he witnessed the will, didn't he?—but I don't think he was a partner. Frankie boy had his own plot in the works: the catnapping of Peaches with the loving assistance of Laverne Willigan."

"Who he probably met at a séance. Those séances are beginning to resemble the bawdyhouse the Glorianas operated in Atlanta."

"Archy, you figure the medium knew what was going down?"

"Hertha? I don't think she knew about the murder plan. She knew her
husband was nuzzling Laverne Willigan, but she just didn't care. Hertha isn't
guilty of any crimes, Al."

He looked at me, amused. "How about conduct that violates the ethical
code of psychics?"

"Well, yes, she may possibly be guilty of that."

He laughed. "Listen, let's go through the whole megillah one more time
from the top and see if we can spot any holes."

So we reviewed our entire scenario, starting with Roderick Gillsworth
meeting Irma Gloriana and falling in love—or whatever he fell into. It seemed
a reasonable script with only a few minor questions to be answered, such as
the date Otto Gloriana arrived in Greater West Palm Beach, where Irma and
Rod consummated their illicit union, and why Lydia Gillsworth had opened
her locked door to allow her murderer to enter.

"We'll clear those things up," the sergeant said confidently. "Now that
we've got a logical hypothesis, we'll know what evidence to look for and
what's just garbage."

"Whoa!" I said. "I hope you're not going to discard facts simply because
they don't fit our theory. That's ridiculous—and dangerous."

"It's not a question of discarding facts," he argued. "It's a matter of interpretation. Let me give you a for-instance. When Gillsworth's body was
found, there was a big meal he had been preparing in the kitchen: six huge
crab cakes and an enormous salad. Now there were three interpretations of
that humongous meal. One: He was famished and was going to eat the whole
thing himself. Two: He was making enough food so he could have a leftover
dinner the next day. And three: He was expecting a guest and was preparing
dinner for two people. According to our theory, the third supposition is the
most likely. He was expecting Irma Gloriana to join him for dinner. The doorbell rings, he looks through the judas window, sees her, and unlocks the door.
Otto is standing to one side, out of sight, and the moment the door is open,
he comes barreling in with his single-edge razor blade. Doesn't that sound
right to you? It's what I mean by interpreting facts. They don't become evidence until you can establish their significance. If you don't have a reasonable
supposition, you can drown in facts."

"Thank you, professor," I said. "I've enjoyed your lecture enormously.
Of course it's based on the belief that our scenario is accurate."

"You believe that, don't you?"

"I do," I said. "It seems to me the only plausible explanation of what
happened."

But that wasn't the whole truth. Do you recall my mentioning a vague no-
tion I had early on, something so tenuous that I couldn't put it into words?
Then, as more was learned about the homicides, I began to see an outline.
Now, with the most recent revelations, the outline was filling in and taking

on substance. If it proved valid, it would radically alter the script Sgt. Rogoff had adopted so enthusiastically. But I didn't tell him that.

"Al," I said, "the bank has the ransom money ready. Will you go with me to pick it up? You're the man with the gun."

"Sure," he agreed readily. "Then I want you to come back to headquarters with me. We've got to go over the program for tonight's payoff."

"I hope you've devised an effective plan."

"It should work," he said.

I sighed. "Can't you be more positive than that? After all, it's my neck that's at risk."

"Well . . ." he said doubtfully, "maybe you better not buy any green bananas."

Then he laughed. I didn't.

Chapter 16

I spent that entire afternoon with Sgt. Rogoff and an ad hoc squad of uniformed officers assigned to him. As the night's action was outlined to me, and my own role described, I realized Al had done a remarkable job of organizing a complex operation in a short time.

Of course, in accordance with Murphy's Law, some things were bound to go wrong, and we spent much of our time brainstorming possible contingencies and planning how they might best be handled. I was satisfied that the overall plan was workable and, with a little bit o'luck, would achieve its objectives.

I wanted to leave the ransom money with Rogoff, but he was loath to accept the responsibility. He did keep a copy of the list of serial numbers the bank had thoughtfully provided. But when I left the Palm Beach police headquarters, which looks like a Mediterranean villa, I was lugging fifty thousand dollars in fifty-dollar bills. The bank had supplied a K-Mart shopping bag as a carrier. Why do all the great dramas of my life contain the elements of farce?

Naturally my mother had not been informed that her dear little boy was engaged in a perilous enterprise that might involve violence. Father and I tried to make our family cocktail hour and dinner that night no different from the umpteen that had gone before. We talked, we laughed, we each devoured a half-dozen delightful quail, and I don't believe mother had an inkling that I was—well, I won't say I was scared out of my wits, but I admit my trepidation level was high.

After dinner, she left us to go upstairs to her television program, and I resisted the temptation to kiss her farewell. I mean I wasn't going off to the Battle of Blenheim, was I? It was really just a small piece of law enforcement business from which I was certain to emerge with all my limited faculties intact. I told myself that. Several times.

My self-induced euphoria was rather diminished when father invited me into his study for a cognac. I knew he meant well, but I considered offering me a brandy was somewhat akin to being supplied with a blindfold and final cigarette. But at least he didn't say, "Be careful." He did say, "Call me as soon as it's over."

Then I went upstairs to change. Al Rogoff had suggested I dress in black, and when I had asked why, he replied, "You'll make a harder target." The other cops on his special squad thought that uproariously funny, but I considered their levity in poor taste.

About nine o'clock I came downstairs, dressed completely in black and carrying my shopping bag of cash. I went out to the Miata and paused to look about. It was a warm night, the dark sky swirled with horsetail clouds. Stars were there, a pale moon and, as I stared heavenward, an airliner droned overhead, going north. I wished I was on it.

I drove directly to police headquarters. Sgt. Rogoff and his cohorts were donning bulletproof vests and inspecting their weapons which, I noted, included shotguns and tear gas and smoke grenades and launchers. There was also a variety of electronic gizmos being tested. I wasn't certain of their function and intended use.

I stripped to the waist and a technician "wired" me, an unpleasant experience involving what seemed to be yards of adhesive tape. When he finished, I was equipped with microphone, battery pack, and transmitter. I put on shirt and jacket again, and we moved outside to test my efficacy as a mobile radio station.

The sergeant instructed me to move a hundred feet away, turn on the power switch, and say something. I did as ordered, activated myself and recited the "Tomorrow, and tomorrow . . ." speech from *Macbeth*. Rogoff waved me to return. "Loud and clear," he said. "Let's get this show on the road."

It was a veritable parade. This was a joint operation, and we had cars and personnel from the police departments of the Town of Palm Beach, the City of West Palm Beach, and the Sheriffs Office of Palm Beach County. All for Peaches! The three jurisdictions were cooperating under a long-standing system Sgt. Rogoff described as "Share the glory and spread the blame."

And in the middle of this procession was a flag-red open convertible sports car inhabited by yr. humble servant, Archibald McNally.

I soon cut out and let the armada proceed without me. The script called for my arrival at the parking area of the convenience store on Federal Highway at 11:45 P.M. I was right on schedule and pulled into a parking slot that provided a good view of the storefront. I switched on my transmitter.

"McNally on station," I reported in a normal voice.

I watched, and in a moment the policewoman in civvies, planted in the store by Rogoff, came to the front window and began to fuss with a display of junk foods: the signal that she was receiving my transmission and would relay it to the task force via her more powerful radio.

I settled down, lighted an English Oval, and wondered why I hadn't relieved myself before setting out on this adventure. All my anxiety and discomfort, I realized, resulted from my trying to assist that fatheaded Willigan, and I was trying to recall lines from *Henry V:* "Unto the breach, lads, for Harry and . . ." when an old Chrysler Imperial pulled slowly into the lighted parking area and stopped in a space about twenty feet away from me.

"I think he's here," I said aloud. "Black Chrysler Imperial. Man getting out and walking toward me."

Rogoff and I had agreed that the messenger was not likely to be Frank Gloriana; he would have no desire to be identified by me as the catnapper. The logical choice for collector would be Otto Gloriana, Frank's daddy.

And as he came closer, I had no doubt whatsoever that this tall, reddish-haired, broad-shouldered man of about sixty-five was indeed Otto Gloriana, aka Charles Girard, former bordello owner and the ex-con described by Atlanta police as "a nasty piece of work." What surprised me was how handsome he was.

He was wearing a rumpled seersucker suit, and his hands were thrust deep into the jacket pockets. He came near, almost pressing against my door. That was fine with me; it brought him closer to my concealed microphone.

"You from Harry Willigan?" he asked in a resonant baritone.

"That's correct," I said.

"You have the fifty thousand?"

"Right here," I said and started to lift the shopping bag from the passenger seat to hand it to him. But he moved back one step.

"Get out of the car," he said. "Carry the money."

I was astonished. "Why should I do that?" I said.

"Because if you don't," he said pleasantly, "I'll kill you."

He withdrew his right hand from his jacket pocket far enough to reveal that he was gripping a short-barreled revolver that appeared to be a .38 Special. His back was to the window of the convenience store, and there was no one nearby. I was certain his action was unobserved.

"You have a gun?" I said in a tone of disbelief, praying this conversation was being received "loud and clear" by the officer inside the store. "That's not necessary. Just take the money and bring the cat back."

He sighed. "You're not very swift, are you? I'll say it just once more, and if you don't do what I say, you'll have three eyes. Now get out of this baby carriage slowly. Carry the money. Walk to my car. I'll be right behind you."

I did as ordered, thinking sadly that we had prepared for every possible contingency except my being taken hostage. At least that's what I hoped was happening. I had no wish to meet my Maker in the parking lot of a store that sold Twinkies and diet root beer.

We came up to the Chrysler and the rear door was opened from within by the man sitting behind the wheel.

"Get in," Otto commanded.

I did, swinging the bag of cash onto the floor. I sat back in one corner and got a look at the driver.

"Why, Frank Gloriana," I said in a loud voice. "What a surprise!"

"Shut your face," the older Gloriana said to me. And to his son, "Drive."

We pulled out and headed south on Federal Highway. I reckoned we were out of range of the receiver in the store, but just in case, I said, "Going to the Jo-Jean Motel, are we?"

Otto took the revolver from his pocket and rapped the side of my skull with the steel barrel. What can I tell you? It hurt.

"I told you to keep your yap shut," my captor said. "I'll do all the talking."

So I remained silent and tried to calculate the odds against my ever playing the harpsichord again. Rather heavy, I concluded. The fact that I had been allowed to witness Frank's involvement in this caper boded ill for my future. It seemed highly unlikely that I would be allowed to live, even if I vowed to keep my yap permanently sealed.

We turned into the driveway of the Jo-Jean Motel. I knew there were two police officers in Cabin Five and two more in the back room of the motel office. They had been stationed there with the enthusiastic cooperation of the owner who probably hoped the Jo-Jean would rival the O.K. Corral, and she'd be featured on the front page of her favorite tabloid.

But I saw no police cars and no signs that snipers had been deployed to hold Cabin Four in their sights. I could only have faith that Sgt. Rogoff was aware of my plight and was feverishly revising his plans to give my safety precedence over that of Peaches'.

We pulled up alongside Cabin Four and Otto nudged my ribs with his weapon. "Out," he said. "Take the money. Walk around to the front door. Frank, you go first and unlock."

Within moments we were all inside, the door closed, a floor lamp lighted. I looked about. It was a simple room, exactly like the one Hertha had claimed to see in her vision. There was also a pan of cat litter, a bowl of water, and a plate of cat food.

"Where is Peaches?" I inquired.

"At the movies," Frank sniggered, the first words he had spoken. He needn't have bothered.

"Count the money," his father ordered.

Frank dumped the contents of the bag onto the bed, stacked the bundles of banded bills. Otto and I remained standing. Nothing was said until Frank finished.

"All here," he said. "The bills look legit."

"They got the numbers," Otto growled, "but so what? Where we'll pass them no one looks at numbers."

"May I take the cat now?" I asked, figuring I had nothing to lose.

Otto looked at me somberly. "I finally figured how you found Charles Girard," he said. "It was the vet, wasn't it? At the animal hospital. That was cute."

For a minute or two I couldn't comprehend how he knew I had identified him. Then I remembered I had mentioned the name Charles Girard to Laverne. She had undoubtedly told Frank and he, in turn, had reported to his father that Archy McNally, a blabbermouthed gumshoe, was on his trail.

"So now you know about me," Otto said. "And you know about Frank. We don't have much choice, do we?"

His meaning was clear and more chilling than a brutal threat.

"It's no big deal," I pointed out. "Catnapping is hardly a capital crime. How heavy a sentence can you possibly get?"

"When you've been inside," he said darkly, "one more day is too much."

He stared at me, and I knew it wasn't only a charge of catnapping that concerned him. He wouldn't kill for that. But he was calculating how much I might know or guess about his other activities, including the vicious murders of the Gillsworths. Finally I could see that he had made up his mind, and his fatal decision seemed to relax him.

"Put the money back in the bag," he told his son. "Shove the bag under the bed. Then get the cat. We'll do them both at the same time. I spotted a good place. A deserted canal."

It was all I could do to keep from crying, "But I can't swim!" and laughing hysterically. Somehow I restrained myself.

Frank hid the money, went into the bathroom, and came out carrying a large cardboard carton that had once held bottles of Jim Beam. It was tied shut with heavy twine, and air holes had been cut in the sides. I heard a few faint meows and the box rocked a bit as Peaches moved.

"Let's go," Otto said.

Up to that point the motel cabin had been illuminated by a single floor lamp with a low-wattage bulb. But now, suddenly, the interior was flooded with a hard white glare. Beams of bright spotlights came stabbing through the front and side windows of the cabin.

"What the hell!" Frank yelped.

Otto moved swiftly. He stood behind the wooden door and leaned to peer cautiously out the corner of the front window.

"Police cars," he reported tonelessly. "Four or five at least. And an army of cops."

"Oh God," Frank said despairingly.

Then I heard Sgt. Rogoff. The bullhorn made him sound harsh and metallic, but there was no mistaking his voice.

"Cabin Four," he boomed. "Everyone come out the front door with your hands raised. Now!"

Frank appealed to his father. "What should we do?" he asked nervously.

Otto went into the bathroom, stood on the closed toilet lid, and glanced out the small window. He returned to the main room. "No good," he said. "The back is covered."

"Please," I said. "Give yourselves up. It's only a charge of catnapping. It's not worth a shoot-out."

"He's right," Frank said. "Let's do what they want."

His father looked at him with disgust. "You do what you like," he said. "I'm getting out. I'm not taking a fall for you again."

He reached under the bed, jerked out the bag of cash. He removed several bundles and stuffed them into his pockets. Then he leveled his revolver at me.

"Turn around," he said. "You and I are going out of here together. You first."

"Cabin Four!" Rogoffs voice came crashing. "Come out the front door, hands raised. You have exactly one minute."

Otto Gloriana stepped up close behind me. He put a heavy hand on my left shoulder. He pressed the muzzle of his weapon behind my right ear.

"Nothing cute," he warned. "Or you're dead. You understand?"

"Yes," I said.

"Now open the door. Slowly. Step out slowly. Move to the Chrysler. Everything nice and slow."

I did as he ordered. We moved out onto the porch almost in lockstep.

"Hold your fire!" Al screamed. "Hold your fire!"

The spotlights half-blinded me. I could see nothing but the dark bulk of the cars. I walked as slowly as I could toward the Chrysler.

We were alongside the car when the bullhorn barked: "Otto! Otto!" But Rogoff didn't pronounce it "Oddo." He split the name into two distinct syllables: "Ot-to! Ot-to!"

Gloriana was so shocked that the police knew his real name that his grip loosened, his left hand slid from my shoulder. The pressure of the gun behind my ear lessened. I was vaguely aware that he had turned slightly toward the source of that raucous shout.

Then I did something that anyone with an IQ greater than their waistline would have done: I fell down.

Sounds simple, does it? Well, it isn't. I am not a tumbler or circus clown trained to fall without risk of injury. I just let myself go and crumpled, bruising shoulders, elbows, rump.

I hoped Al Rogoff and his troops would have the wit to take advantage of my sudden collapse. They did. I was on the ground and Otto Gloriana was still standing, stunned, when there was an ear-cracking fusillade. I cowered.

I heard Otto grunt, and he was driven back. His body went slack and he flopped to his knees. Then, as the firing continued, his head bowed and he seemed to stretch out prone onto the earth.

"Cease firing!" the sergeant bawled. "Cease firing!"

The silence was deafening. I lay where I had fallen, knowing I was alive but fearing to move my limbs lest broken bones come poking through the skin. I was still shaken by the gunfire and trying to determine what bullets flying overhead sounded like. They did not whine, hum, or whistle. I finally decided the sound was like a sheet of good rag paper being ripped.

I raised my head cautiously. Sgt. Rogoff and two officers were standing next to Gloriana. One of them plucked away the revolver. The other knelt and turned Otto's head to peer at his face.

"He's gone, sarge," he said.

"Yeah," Al said. "A clear case of lead poisoning. Call for the meat wagon." He turned and gently assisted me to my feet. I stood shakily. "You okay?" he asked anxiously.

"I've got to get to a john," I said.

He laughed, and we started for the cabin door. Two officers came out gripping Frank Gloriana by the arms. He was limp and his feet were dragging. As they hauled him away he raised his head and glanced at me.

"Glad you're alive," he mumbled. "Really."

"Thank you," I said.

He didn't look at the corpse of his father.

We went into the cabin. Al started to pack the spilled money back into the shopping bag. I headed directly for the bathroom. When I came out, Rogoff had gone. The cardboard carton was still sitting in the middle of the floor.

I leaned down and untied the twine. I lifted the flaps warily. I feared that Peaches, thinking I was one of the miscreants, might leap at my throat and try to wrench out my Adam's apple with her teeth. But she hopped out of the box and began rubbing against my shins, purring like a maniac.

"Why, Peaches," I said, "you know a hero when you smell one, don't you?"

When Rogoff returned, I was seated on the bed and the cat was lying on her back next to me, all four paws raised in the air. I was scratching her stomach, and her eyes were closed in ecstasy.

Al said, "That's the most sickening sight I've ever witnessed in my life."

"You're just jealous," I said, "because no one does it for you."

"What makes you so sure?" he said.

"Al, can I return Peaches to Harry Willigan?"

"Yep. Tell him we'll have to hang on to his fifty grand for a while. Evidence. He'll get it back eventually. Come on, I'll give you a lift back to your car."

"I have to call the old man first. I promised."

I used the phone in the motel office. Father answered so promptly that I knew he hadn't been sleeping. It was then about two A.M.

"Archy, sir," I said. "I'm fine, and the cat has been rescued."

"Glad to hear it," he said. "Tell me about it tomorrow." Then he added precisely, "Or I should say later today."

Rogoff drove me back to the convenience store in a squad car. I had left the cardboard carton in Cabin Four and held Peaches on my lap. She was content.

"What about Irma?" I asked.

"We picked her up at midnight. She's acting the haughty, insulted grande dame and won't say a word until she sees a lawyer."

"And Hertha?"

"She wasn't in the apartment. Neighbors say they haven't seen her around for two or three days. They don't know where she is."

I could guess, but said nothing to the sergeant.

When I got out to transfer to the Miata, he said casually, "Nice work tonight, Archy."

"Thank you," I said. "You behaved admirably yourself. I'll call you after I get some sleep. Al, I don't believe Frank Gloriana is a strong character. Sweat him."

"I intend to," he said grimly.

I drove with Peaches curled up in the passenger bucket. When we arrived home I thought she might be hungry and offered her a slice of pastrami from the fridge. She ate it with obvious enjoyment. Smart cat.

She slept at the foot of my bed for the rest of the night. When I awoke around eight o'clock I discovered she had upchucked the pastrami onto the cover of my journal.

You can't win 'em all.

Chapter 17

I breakfasted with my parents on Tuesday morning. Peaches sat patiently alongside the dining room table, and when I gave her a hunk of brioche, she nibbled it daintily, a perfect lady. Mother was delighted with her. We had had no animal in the family since Max, our golden retriever, died, and I wondered aloud if we might invite a pup, perhaps a Dandie Dinmont, to join our menage. Father promised to consider the suggestion.

After breakfast I drew him aside and gave him an abbreviated account of the police action the previous night.

"Then Otto is dead?" he asked when I had finished.

"Definitely."

"And the son is in custody?"

"That's correct, sir. And also Mrs. Irma Gloriana. I expect Al Rogoff will be questioning them today."

He nodded. "I'd like to speak to the sergeant," he said. "Do you think he could come over this evening?"

"I'm sure he's awfully busy, father, but he might be ready for a break by tonight."

"Ask him," he said. "Tell him it concerns Roderick Gillsworth's holographic will and may possibly affect his investigation."

I knew it would be useless to ask questions, so I told him I'd try to reach Rogoff. Then he departed for the office in his Lexus, and I lifted Peaches into my Miata and headed for the Willigan home. The cat sat upright in her bucket seat, sniffed the morning air, and looked about rather grandly.

I carried her up the Willigans' stoop, but before I had a chance to ring, the door was flung open and Harry rushed out, arms outflung. "Peaches!" he screamed. "Peaches is home!" I swear there were tears in the poor goof's eyes.

He reached for his pet, but the cat had other ideas. She leaped from my arms, darted through the opened door, and went scampering down the long corridor. Willigan lumbered after her, shouting, "Sweetums! Sweetums baby! Papa is here! Come to papa, darling!"

Gruesome.

They disappeared, and I entered the house, closing the door behind me. I wandered down the hallway and out onto the back lawn. Laverne was lying supine on a chaise, wearing a hot-pink French-cut bikini. She also had a plastic shield over her eyes.

"Good morning, Laverne," I called as I approached.

She lifted the shield long enough to glance at me, then replaced it. "Hi, Archy," she said in a flat voice.

"I just returned Peaches," I said. "She was recovered last night."

"I know," she said tonelessly. "We heard it on the radio this morning."

"Will you please tell Harry the police have his fifty thousand? They're holding it temporarily as evidence. He'll get it back eventually."

"I'll tell him," she said.

I don't know why I felt sorry for her. One has to pay for one's stupidity in this world—ask me; I know!—and Laverne had certainly behaved stupidly. But I supposed she had her reasons and obviously they were sufficient for her.

"I'll try to keep you out of it," I said, "but I'm not sure it can be done."

"Out of what?" she said in a dead voice.

"Laverne, please," I said. "The police are holding Frank Gloriana. I don't know how much he'll tell them."

"What are you talking about?" she said listlessly.

I sighed and started away. I was almost at the screen door when she called, "Archy," and I turned back. Now she was sitting on the chaise, hunched over, head bowed. She was twirling the eye shield in nervous fingers.

"You really think you can keep my name out of it?" she asked, looking up at me.

"Laverne," I said, "let me be frank . . ." Then I caught myself. "Oh lordy," I said, "don't let me be Frank!"

She smiled for the first time.

"Look," I said, "Frank is not a stand-up guy. He's liable to tell the police you talked him into it, that he went along because he was in love with you."

Then she frowned. "That's crazy. How could he say that? The ransom notes were written on his word processor."

"The police already know that. But you did sneak Peaches out of here in her carrier, didn't you?"

"It was a laugh," she said. "Frank needed money, and Harry has plenty. As for Frank being in love with me, that's bullshit. It was just a game with us."

"It's gone sour, Laverne. If Harry finds out, you know what'll happen to you, don't you?"

"Yeah," she said dolefully. "Out on my can. With no pre-nup."

"You took an awful risk," I marveled.

"A girl gets bored," she said, shrugging. "Listen, Archy, if you can keep me out of it, I'll make it worth your while."

And she put her hands behind her, leaned back, crossed her legs. She looked up at me, smiling again. There was a lot of her.

I laughed. "Laverne," I said, "you're incorrigible."

She licked her glossed lips, still smiling. "Think about it," she said.

I got out of there as hastily as I could. I don't care how macho a man claims to be, when a woman says Yes, his first reaction is not desire, it's fear.

I drove away with the feeling that this was going to be Dénouement Day with all current problems solved and complexities unraveled. It didn't turn out *quite* that way, but it came close.

There was a question I wanted to ask Hertha Gloriana, and I thought I knew exactly where to find her. I guided the Miata up to Riviera Beach and within a half-hour I was tapping on the door of Meg Trumble's apartment.

"Why, Archy," she said, "what a pleasant surprise."

The "surprise" I could buy; the "pleasant" was iffy. But she allowed me to enter and, sure enough, Hertha was curled up on the couch. There was a box of Kleenex on the cushion beside her, and she was dabbing at her eyes.

Despite the medium's tears and Meg's rather frosty demeanor, both women looked extraordinarily attractive to me. They were wearing identical short-shorts of white twill with men's work-shirts, the tails knotted about their waists to reveal a few inches of midriff. And they displayed a quartet of splendidly tanned legs.

"Did you hear the news?" Meg demanded. "About Hertha's husband and her in-laws?"

"I heard," I said, nodding. "Have you been to the police, Hertha?"

She shook her head.

"I really think you should," I said gently. "They may want to question you. Ask to speak to Sergeant Rogoff."

"Hertha knows nothing about that cat," Meg said angrily. "I don't see why she should get involved."

I sighed. "Meg," I said, "she *is* involved. Her husband and mother-in-law have been arrested and her father-in-law shot dead. If she doesn't go to the police, they'll start looking for her. Sooner or later they're sure to find her, and then they'll want to know why she didn't come forward."

"Perhaps I should talk to them," Hertha said timidly. "Meg, will you come with me?"

Meg sat down beside her, put an arm about her shoulders. "Of course I will, darling," she said in a soothing voice. "We'll go together. Who did you say to ask for, Archy?"

"Sergeant Al Rogoff. He's a friend of mine, and I suggest you tell him that you already spoke to me. You'll find him very sympathetic."

"What do you think he'll ask me?" Hertha said.

It was a perfect opportunity to pose my own question. "He'll probably want to know if Roderick Gillsworth came to your office frequently."

The medium looked at me with widened eyes. "What an odd question."

"Well, did he?" I persisted. "Did Gillsworth come to your office and talk to Frank?"

"Several times," she said, nodding. "But they always went into the room where we did our mailings. I don't know what they talked about."

"Just tell Sergeant Rogoff that," I advised. "I'm sure he'll be interested. Hertha, will you be staying here?"

"Of course she will," Meg said definitely. "As long as she wants. Forever, I hope."

The medium turned and embraced the other woman tightly, kissing her on the lips. "Oh sweetheart," she cried, "what would I ever do without you?"

The two were hugging and whispering to each other when I left. I headed for the Pelican Club, hoping a wee bit of the old nasty might help restore my sanity. As I drove, I reflected on the strange convolutions of human behavior.

I could understand Meg's decision. After all, she had been betrayed by a man in a particularly cruel and humiliating manner. But Hertha's actions puzzled me. The married medium who dispensed her kisses so freely seemed a contradiction: she was a very *physical* spiritualist.

But that, I realized, was occupational stereotyping. Most of us are guilty of it.

For instance, librarians are generally thought to be sexless, dried-up biddies who affect a pince-nez and don rubber gloves before shaking hands with a man. I know from personal experience that this image is totally, *totally* false. (I wonder what Nancy is doing now?)

So it was really not too surprising to learn that being a psychic did not preclude Hertha from having urges of a more corporeal sort. A horny medium? Well, why not? And if she was subject to nymphomaniacal twinges, who was I, a hapless lothario, to condemn her? And if her nature included a predilection for sapphic relationships, so be it.

When I walked into the Pelican Club, the radio behind the bar was on, and Vikki Carr was singing "It Must Be Him." It was just too much, and I burst out laughing.

"You seem in a happy mood today, Mr. McNally," Simon Pettibone said.

"Pondering life's ironies, Mr. Pettibone," I said. "It is indeed a mad, mad world."

"But the only one we have," he reminded me.

"A frozen daiquiri, please," I responded.

I left the bar to use the public phone. Of course I called Rogoff, and of course he was unavailable. I slowly sipped my way through two daiquiris, called the sergeant every ten minutes with no results, and finally got through to him on my fifth call. He was brusque, obviously under pressure, and I hurriedly blurted out an invitation to stop by the McNally home that night at nine. "Okay," he said and hung up abruptly.

I had lunch while seated at the bar. Priscilla brought me a jumbo cheese-burger with side orders of french fries and coleslaw. I wolfed this Cholesterol Special with great enjoyment and had an iced Galliano for dessert. I suspected my arteries might soon require the services of a Roto-Rooter man.

I drove back to Worth Avenue to take up a project I had started days ago and never completed: buying a tennis bracelet for Consuela Garcia. The need for a gift seemed more important now than when the idea had first occurred to me, for I had neglected that marvelous woman shamefully. The morning's encounters with Laverne Willigan, Meg Trumble, and Hertha Gloriana made me realize how important Connie was to me. Vital, one might even say, and I do say it.

I visited four jewelry shops before I found a bracelet that appealed to me: two-carat, cushion-cut diamonds set in 18K gold. It was horribly expensive, but I handed over my plastic gaily, following McNally's First Law of Shopping: If you can afford it, it's not worth buying.

I went directly home, stripped to the buff, and fell into bed for a nap, for I had enjoyed only five hours of shuteye the previous night. Before sleep claimed me, I thought again of my experiences that morning and laughed aloud. I simply could not take them seriously.

It is my conviction that solemnity is the curse of civilization. Think of all the earnest people who have sacrificed themselves for gods now forgotten or wasted their lives on causes no one remembers. Laughter is our only salvation. Pray with a giggle and mourn with a smile. And if you happen to believe, as I do, that women are nature's noblest work, know ye that long face ne'er won fair lady.

Thus endeth the scripture according to St. Archy.

Chapter 18

It had been a sunny day with a scattering of popcorn clouds, but when I awoke from my nap around six P.M., a dark overhang had moved in from the east and rain had started. There was no wind, so the drizzle fell vertically and soon became a steady downpour that threatened to drive us all to the rooftops.

I wondered if Al Rogoff would show up in that drencher, and by nine o'clock I was waiting in the kitchen, peering out the window and ready to go out with my big golfing umbrella if he arrived. He plowed up in his pickup only fifteen minutes late, parked close to our back door, and came rushing in before I had a chance to unfurl my bumbershoot.

He looked godawful. His features were slack with weariness and there were puddles of shadow under his eyes. Even worse, he seemed harried and uncertain, as if he was faced with momentous decisions and didn't know which way to jump. I took his dripping slicker, hung it away to dry, and led him to the study.

Father was waiting for us, took one look at the sergeant, and immediately broke out his bottle of Rémy Martin XO. He reserved this superb cognac, he said, for "special occasions." To my knowledge there had been two in the past ten years.

Rogoff flopped into a club chair, accepted his glass gratefully, and took a deep pull. Then he sucked in a long breath, exhaled noisily, and said, "Manna."

"Sorry to bring you out on a night like this, sergeant," father said. "It could have waited."

"No, sir," Al said, "I don't think so. Things are moving too quickly. Right now it's all a big mishmash, and I'm hoping you can help make some sense out of what we know and what we guess."

I had poured tots of brandy for father and myself. He was enthroned behind his desk, as usual, and I took an armchair to one side, facing both of them. Rogoff fished a cigar from an inside pocket and looked at the old man questioningly.

"Of course," father said. "Light up. Are you hungry? We can supply combat rations."

"No, thanks, counselor," he said. "I had an anchovy pizza an hour ago. I'm just stressed-out. The cognac will do fine."

"How are things going, Al?" I asked. "Making any progress?"

He flipped a palm back and forth. "*Comme ci, comme ca*. Right now I'm working with an Assistant State Attorney, a brainy lady, and we're trying to get a handle on our options and figure out the best deal we can make."

"Is Frank Gloriana talking?"

"Some. We've got him cold on the catnapping. The ransom notes were written on his word processor and he was found with the money. But he claims it was all Laverne Willigan's idea, and she was the one who snatched the cat. He says he played along because he's madly in love with her."

"Oh sure," I said. "I was afraid he'd pull something like that. Any chance at all of keeping Laverne's name out of it?"

"Very thin," Al said. "We're trying to work a deal with his lawyer. If Frank tells us what he knows about his parents' murder plot, charges may be reduced and he could get off with a fine and suspended sentence."

My father spoke up. "As you know, sergeant, I represent Harry Willigan, and I'm just as eager as Archy to keep Mrs. Willigan out of any court proceedings. I presume everything said here tonight is *entre nous*."

"If that means will I keep my mouth shut, the answer is yes."

"Good. Is this Frank Gloriana a man of means?"

"He's stone-broke. His lawyer will probably end up with Frank's office furniture as his fee."

"I see," father said thoughtfully. "Archy, to your knowledge, does Laverne have any liquid assets?"

"I don't know about her bank balance, father, but I do know she's got a heavy collection of jewelry. Gifts from Harry. Expensive things."

"Better and better. Perhaps, sergeant, you might suggest to Frank Gloriana's attorney that he have a confidential talk with Laverne Willigan. She might be willing to pawn or sell enough of her gems to provide funds for Frank's legal defense. In return, of course, he would avoid mentioning her name. But this arrangement, I strongly urge, should be approved only after Frank tells you what he knows of his parents' involvement in the Gillsworth homicides. Frank might be disinclined to agree to that but if you explain the deal thoroughly to his attorney, I expect he'll recommend that Frank accept it. Especially if the ASA promises to do what she can to have charges reduced."

"Yeah," Al said slowly, "that plot might work. We clear up a catnapping and Frank gives us what he has on the murders. He gets off with a slap on the wrist. His lawyer gets paid. And Laverne keeps her name out of it. Everyone wins. A slick plan, Mr. McNally. I'll bring it up with the ASA."

I saw that his cognac was gone and my glass was getting low. I rose and refilled our snifters without asking permission. My father made no objection although he had barely touched his drink.

"Okay, Al," I said, "so much for the catnapping. Now what's happening with the homicides?"

He sighed deeply. "This is where things get sticky. First of all, you've got to know the whole thing started with Roderick Gillsworth's obsession with Irma Gloriana. We're trying to get a court order to open her safe deposit box, but even without the letters he wrote her, we have the evidence of his holographic will and the erotic poems he started writing after he met her. It's obvious the guy was nuts about her. I'm not saying he was temporarily insane; let's just say that after meeting Irma he became mentally disadvantaged."

"But penniless," I observed.

"Right," Rogoff said. "Which wasn't the way to win Irma's heart. The lady is Queen of the Bottom Line. So Roderick, knowing he was slated to inherit most of his wife's estate, suggested Lydia be knocked off. Irma said she could get it done if Roderick would sign over his inherited wealth to her."

"Wait just a minute, please," my father interrupted. "That doesn't quite compute. Why did Roderick make Irma his beneficiary? The fee for the murder was going to someone else."

"I admit it's fuzzy," the sergeant said. "But I figure Roderick wanted to marry Irma after Lydia was dead. He didn't know Irma was already married. And she agreed to marry him when he was a widower only if he made her the sole beneficiary of his estate. I think Roderick executed that handwritten will and signed it cheerfully because he knew that if Irma reneged, he could cancel out the holographic will at any time by writing a more recent will that superseded it. Am I correct, counselor?"

"Yes," father said slowly, "that's generally true. The most recently executed will at the time of death takes precedence."

But he and I looked at each other. I know we were both troubled by the

sergeant's tortuous explanation of why Roderick had made Irma his beneficiary.

"There is something you should know about that holographic will, sergeant," father said. "It was executed about a month ago. At that time Lydia
Gillsworth was still alive. Florida statutes provide that the surviving spouse
of a decedent has a right to thirty percent of the decedent's estate regardless
of the provisions of the decedent's will."

Rogoff was startled. "You mean Gillsworth's holographic will was null
and void when it was written?"

"Not necessarily," father replied. "But if Roderick had predeceased Lydia
and had left a sizable estate, Lydia could either let his will stand or 'elect
against the will,' as it's called, and claim her rightful thirty percent. But the
whole question is moot because Lydia died before Roderick, and if he had
predeceased her, he had no estate to leave."

Al and I exchanged a brief glance. I knew what he was thinking: If the
whole matter was moot, why had Prescott McNally mentioned it? I could
have told him: If there was a nit to be picked, my father would be the first to
volunteer.

"Well," Rogoff said, shaking his head, "all I know is that when Roderick signed that handwritten will he signed his own death warrant. I figure
Irma and Otto had it worked out from the start, but Roderick was too pussy-
whipped to suspect it. First, they knocked off Lydia. That made Roderick a
rich man. Then Roderick was snuffed. And that was supposed to make Irma
wealthy according to the terms of his last will and testament."

"You're probably right, sergeant," father said, nodding. "It's a likely scenario. But how much of it can you prove?"

"That Otto bashed in Lydia's skull with a walking stick? Not sufficient
evidence to make a case. But things are different with the murder of Roderick, framed to look like a suicide. The most important piece of hard evidence
is that we found a package of single-edge razor blades in Cabin Four of the
Jo-Jean Motel. Otto Gloriana shaved with them. The same brand was left on
the bath mat beside Roderick Gillsworth's corpse."

Father was obviously disappointed. "Hardly conclusive evidence," he
said.

"I agree, sir. But we have something much better. Irma Gloriana states she
was with her husband when he entered Gillsworth's house to kill him. She
claims she didn't witness the actual murder but that Otto announced his intention to kill the poet beforehand and bragged about it afterward."

Both my father and I were astounded. "Why on earth would she admit
that?" I said. "It makes her an accessory."

"Why?" Rogoff said disgustedly. "Because she thinks it'll get her off the
hook. Otto is dead. He can't refute what she says or defend himself in any
way, shape, or form. So his widow now says he was the sole killer. His motive, according to Irma, was to kill the man having an affair with his wife. He
was aware of it, Irma says, and vowed revenge. He knew she had a dinner
date at Gillsworth's home, put a gun to her head, and forced her to ring the

doorbell so he could gain entrance to slit Roderick's wrists. She says she was in deathly fear of Otto, a man known to have a violent temper and who had already served time in prison. But she was totally innocent of complicity in Gillsworth's death, she claims. She was coerced, in fear of her life. But since she played no voluntary role in the homicide, she is free to walk and inherit Roderick's estate. A load of kaka—right? The only problem is that she may get away with it. It's the kind of story a jury just might buy if she ever comes to trial. And she's got an awfully smart lawyer who's probably charging her a nice hunk of Gillsworth's estate."

Father and I were silent. Rogoff was correct. Irma Gloriana had concocted a defense that just might work. If she told her story to judge and jury with all the sincere forcefulness of which I knew she was capable, she had a better than fifty-fifty chance of strolling out of the courtroom a free woman with no worries other than how long it might take to probate Roderick's will and collect his millions.

"It stinks," I said wrathfully and stood to refill our glasses.

"Counselor," Rogoff said, "isn't it true that under Florida law a murderer can't inherit anything from the victim?"

Father nodded. "Anyone who unlawfully and intentionally kills or participates in procuring the death of a decedent is not entitled to any benefits from the decedent's estate whatsoever."

"Then somehow," Al said determinedly, "I don't know how, but *somehow* I'm going to nail that lady. She's guilty as hell, and I don't want to see her getting one thin dime."

As I had listened to all the foregoing, my originally dim vision that had gained an outline and then taken on substance now suddenly snapped into sharp focus, and I knew it was time to display the McNally genius. If, in what follows, you feel I acted like a hambone, you must realize it was my Big Dramatic Moment. I could not let it pass without exhibiting my histrionic gifts, inherited, no doubt, from my grandfather, the famed burlesque comic.

I was still standing and addressed both men. "There is something you should know," I said portentously, "and I believe it may help the cause of justice. Otto didn't kill Lydia Gillsworth. And Irma didn't. Roderick murdered his wife."

Their jaws didn't sag, but Rogoff spluttered brandy and father looked at me sadly as if he finally realized his Number One (and only) son had gone completely bonkers.

"Impossible, Archy," he said hoarsely. "You and I sat in this room and heard Roderick talk to his wife. She was alive when he left here."

I made a great pretense of looking at my watch. "Damn!" I said. "It's getting late, and I promised Binky Watrous I'd call. May I use your phone, father?"

He glared at me. "You wish to make a personal call at this moment? Can't it wait?"

"No, sir," I said. "It's important."

"Very well," he said huffily. "Make it short."

I used the phone on his desk, punched out a number, waited half a mo.

"Binky?" I said. "Archy McNally here. How are you feeling? Glad to hear it. Listen, how about dinner tomorrow night at the Pelican Club. Great! About eightish? Good-o. See you then, Binky."

I hung up and turned to the others. "Who did I just speak to?" I asked them.

They looked at each other, silent a moment, then Rogoff said, "All right, I'll play your little game. You talked to a guy named Binky."

"Binky Watrous is in Portofino," I said gently. "He's been there for the past two weeks and expects to stay another two. I was talking to a dead phone."

They caught it immediately, of course. The sergeant smote his forehead with a palm, then rose and began to walk in agitated circles. "Snookered," he said, his voice a gargle. My father groaned once, then shook his head in wonderment—at his own credulity, I suspect.

"Father," I said, "you and I didn't hear Roderick speak to his wife; we heard him talking, and that's all we heard. We just assumed his wife was alive and conversing with him."

He sighed heavily. "All my professional life I've sought never to assume *anything,* and yet I allowed myself to be deceived by Gillsworth. The man was a consummate actor."

"He had to be," I pointed out. "His fate depended on it. I reckon he killed his wife about an hour before he showed up here. He deliberately murdered her so he could inherit her wealth and marry Irma, just as the sergeant suggested. He set the grandfather clock an hour ahead and pushed it over to stop it. Then he put on fresh clothes and came to our house."

"Wait a minute," Rogoff said, sitting down again. "If you've got it right, then Lydia arrived home an hour before Roderick told you she did. But Irma Gloriana told me that Lydia had stayed late at the séance."

"That's easy," I said. "Irma lied to you. She was setting up an alibi for Roderick. And her price for lying was the holographic will. She made him pay in advance."

"Yes," my father said, "that's credible."

Rogoff swore a horrible oath. "I suspected that guy from the start," he said wrathfully. "The spouse is always the first choice in a homicide case. But I couldn't get around that phone call he made from here. How did you get on to the dead phone trick, Archy?"

"I really don't know," I confessed. "Maybe it's because I'm such a scamster myself—only when the occasion demands it, you understand."

"We were used," my father said angrily. "Roderick Gillsworth *used* us."

"That's right, sir," I agreed. "His attorney and his attorney's son—perfect witnesses to confirm his alibi. We were an important part of his plot."

Rogoff had been reflecting on my reconstruction of the murder. "Hold on," he said suddenly. "You say Roderick killed his wife and then changed his clothes. I'll buy that because his clean duds helped convince me he was innocent. But what did he do with the bloodstained clothes? We searched his entire house the moment we got there. No bloody clothes. He didn't have time to burn them or dump them somewhere. So what did he do with them?"

I didn't know then and if I live a millennium I don't think I'll ever know why I said what I did.

"Caprice!" I almost shouted. "Did you search Lydia's car, Al?"

He stared at me. "I told you I felt the engine block to test the heat, and I stuck my head inside the car to see how long the air conditioning had been off. But I didn't search the trunk." He stood up abruptly. "I think I'll do it right now. I've still got the keys to the house and garage. It's just possible . . ."

"I'll come along," I said.

"May I join you?" my father asked.

Al pulled on his slicker and went out to his pickup. I took my big multi-colored umbrella. My father donned his rain jacket. He and I ran out to the Lexus, and we followed Rogoff's truck southward to the Gillsworth home. We went slowly, for the roads were hubcap deep, and the rain showed no sign of lessening.

We pulled into the Gillsworth driveway, got out, and I opened my umbrella. Before it became soaked through, the sergeant had unlocked the garage door and lifted it up. We all crowded in, and Al switched on the light. The gray Bentley nestled close to the white Caprice. There was something ineffably sad about those two silent, empty cars, their owners slain.

Rogoff examined the lock on the trunk of the Caprice. "I can't pick that," he said. "This calls for surgery."

He went out to his pickup and came back with a two-foot crowbar. "Look the other way, gents," he said with heavy jocularity. "Then you can't testify against me." But we watched as, with some difficulty, he jammed the wedge end into the trunk's seal and then leaned all his weight onto the crowbar. The lock popped with a screech of metal. Al lifted the lid and we all pressed close.

It was in plain sight alongside the spare: a blue plastic garbage bag.

"Bingo," Rogoff said softly.

He used the crowbar to pry open the mouth of the bag, then hooked out the contents. We saw skivvies, T-shirt, khaki slacks. And a wadded pair of latex gloves. Everything was darkly blotched with blood.

"He didn't wear much," I observed.

"Did you expect him to put on soup and fish to snuff his wife?" Al said. "It's plenty." He closed the trunk lid with the bag of clothing inside. "I'll use the phone in the house. I need lab technicians on this stuff. I think it'll make the case."

"Sure it will," I said. "The clothes will be identified as Roderick's from the laundrymarks, and the blood will be identified as Lydia's. The holographic will and those letters he wrote to Irma will establish motive. Hertha Gloriana told me that Roderick came to the office frequently, and he and Frank would go into a back room to confer. Frank will probably testify that Roderick composed and mailed the threatening letters to his wife. You've got a strong case, Al."

"I concur," my father said. "I believe that when presented with the evidence Archy detailed, the court will make a determination that Roderick Gillsworth murdered his wife. Congratulations, sergeant. You get your wish."

Al was puzzled. "What wish?"

"You didn't want Irma Gloriana to get one thin dime. If it's determined that Roderick did indeed kill his wife, then he is not entitled to any benefits from her estate. And so, even if Irma manages to go free, she will inherit nothing from Roderick."

The sergeant walked out of the garage and turned his face up to the streaming heavens.

"Thank you, God," he said.

Chapter 19

I have frequently heard northerners denigrate South Florida because, they say, we have no seasons, meaning there are no radical weather changes from January through December. Actually, Palm Beach has two: the *in* season and the off-season. Many of our citizens are in residence only from October through May. Then, to escape summer heat and humidity and avoid hurricanes, they scatter to their villas in Antibes, Monte Carlo, St. Tropez, and the Costa del Sol.

But some of us, gainfully employed or not, are content to enjoy the island year-round. I will not claim Palm Beach is a paradise, but it does have its unique charms. Where else in the world would a Rolls-Royce Silver Shadow be dropped in the ocean to provide an artificial reef for fish?

So Lady Cynthia Horowitz's Fourth of July party was attended by more than a hundred distinguished permanent residents, most of whom knew each other and were linked by their off-season loyalty to this spit of sand that could be submerged by a thirty-foot storm surge.

It was a black-tie affair, and the ladies welcomed the opportunity to step out of their old tennis togs and into new evening gowns purchased at designer boutiques on Worth Avenue. I had never seen such a profusion of billowing summer silks, and the rainbow of sequins out-glittered the stars.

It was a stupendous bash that was talked about for weeks afterward. In the pool area behind the Horowitz mansion, three service bars had been set up, a six-piece dance band played, and the buffet tables were so heavily laden with exotic (and sclerotic) viands that they were not groaning boards; they whimpered.

This extravaganza had been planned and was overseen by Consuela Garcia, Lady C.'s social secretary, and shortly after the McNally family arrived,

I deserted my parents, grabbed a Bellini from the nearest bar, and went looking for Connie. Tucked into the pocket of my dinner jacket was the tennis bracelet. It was, I had decided, a night to make amends.

I found her reading the riot act to the caterer who apparently had failed to provide Amaretto-flavored gâteau as promised. I waited until Connie's tirade was completed, and the poor fellow had slunk away in disgrace, his professional competence belittled and his ancestry questioned. Then I approached.

Connie looked absolutely stunning. She was wearing a silver tank dress of metallic knit, and with her long black hair and glorious suntan she presented a vision that made me question my own sanity for giving other women even a glance.

The glance she gave me I can only describe as scathing.

"I do not wish to speak to you," she said coldly.

"Connie, I—"

"Never once did you call."

"Connie, I—"

"You didn't care if I was alive or dead."

"Connie, I—"

"I never want to see you again. Never, never, never!"

"Connie, ai-yi-yi!" I cried. I plucked the gift-wrapped package from my pocket and held it out to her, speaking earnestly and rapidly to forestall interruption. "Nothing you can say to me is worse than what I've told myself. I have acted in a cruel, heartless fashion, and I am ashamed of it. I want you to have this. I know it won't make up for my atrocious conduct, but it is a small symbol of the way I truly feel about you."

She accepted the gift gingerly, looking at me with a slight softening. Then: "This isn't going to make everything right between us. You know that, don't you?"

"Of course," I said. "It is intended as a plea to let me prove to you, by my future actions, how sincerely I regret my past neglect and my resolve to treat you henceforth with the respect and love you so richly deserve. Open it."

She tore the wrapping away, lifted the lid and tissue paper. I saw her lustrous eyes widen. She was so overwhelmed she lapsed into her mother tongue.

"*Por Dios*" she shouted. "*Magnífico!*"

A warm *abrazo* was my reward.

She insisted on wearing the bracelet immediately. It needed adjustment, but she pushed it up almost to her elbow and vowed she would never remove it. Never, never, never!

Then we discussed plans. She would have to remain after the fireworks display, scheduled for midnight. In fact, her presence was required until most of the guests had departed and the debris cleaned up.

"I probably won't be able to get away until two in the morning," she said. "Can you wait for me, Archy?"

"I can," I said. "Gladly. But I fear I won't be able to resist those pitchers of Bellinis. By two A.M. I may be comatose."

"We can't have that," she said. "Tonight I want you alert and loving and in full possession of your powers. Suppose we do this: I'll give you my house keys, and you go to my place whenever you like and wait for me. You can even take a nap if you want to. I'll be along as soon as I can get away."

So that's what we did. I left the party, bright-eyed and bushy-tailed, even before the fireworks started. I drove to Connie's condo in a high-rise facing Lake Worth. The balcony of her apartment, on the fourteenth floor, overlooked the lake and provided a fine view of the Flagler Memorial Bridge and all the yacht clubs and marinas on the far shore.

I made myself at home, for I had been there many times before and knew where she kept the Absolut—in the freezer. I went out onto the balcony with a small vodka and watched fireworks being lofted from West Palm Beach. I knew I had a few hours before Connie arrived, and I vowed to drink moderately and stay sober.

And this solitary wait gave me an opportunity to muse on everything that had happened during the past fortnight.

On that rainy Tuesday, after father and I had driven home from the Gillsworths' garage, we went into his study for a nightcap. We discussed the end of the investigations into the catnapping and the homicides, and we exchanged platitudes on the unpredictability of human behavior.

Then father looked at me with a quirky smile. "Archy," said he, "I suppose you believe Lydia's ghost came back to haunt Roderick."

"Yes, sir," said I. "Something like that."

"Nonsense," said he.

But now, sitting on the balcony, sipping vodka, and watching fireworks, I wondered if there really might be a supernatural world beyond reason and logic. Hertha had known the letter she received from Connie was a fake, and she had accurately visualized the room in which Peaches was being held prisoner. There might be reasonable explanations of both those insights. But there was certainly no logical way to account for Hertha's shriek of "Caprice! Caprice!" in the voice of Lydia Gillsworth during the séance. And was that the reason I so promptly shouted "Caprice!" when Rogoff had asked where the murderer's bloody clothes might be hidden?

I brooded about that a long time, thinking of Hertha's psychic gifts, the existence of ghosts, and all the other mind-numbing manifestations of the paranormal I had recently witnessed.

The display of fireworks ended at the same time I came to the conclusion that I shall never know the truth.

Nor shall you.

But then I realized the whole subject came perilously close to being *serious,* and I resolutely reminded myself that life is just a bowl of kiwis. And so when Connie finally arrived, glowing, I rushed to embrace her, eager for a larky interlude of laughter and delight.

McNALLY'S RISK

Chapter 1

Occasionally my behavior reminded me of that famous apothegm of the theatre: "Good acting demands absolute sincerity—and if you can fake that you've got it made."

What brought on that introspective twitch was that at the moment I was perched on the edge of a lumpy armchair, leaning forward attentively, alert as a bird dog, exhibiting every evidence of sympathetic interest, including clucking—and bored out of my gourd.

I was listening to a lecture by Mrs. Gertrude Smythe-Hersforth, a large, imperious lady who may have been the best bridge player in the Town of Palm Beach, but whose conversation had once been described to me as "a diarrhea of words and a constipation of ideas."

Mrs. Smythe-Hersforth was expounding on the importance of family tradition and bloodlines, and how in the current mongrelized (her word) Palm Beach society it was more important than ever that people of breeding circle the wagons to defend their world against the determined assault of lesser beings, many of whom didn't have a single hyphen to their name.

"After all, Archy," quoth she, "one must have pride in one's family."

Don't you just love it? This overstuffed matron was implying that if your name was Smith, DiCicco, or Rabinowitz, you were incapable of pride and probably bought your Jockey shorts at K-Mart. In Britain, family determines class. But in America, it's money. I could have explained that to her, but what was the use?

The reason I was listening to Mrs. Smythe-Hersforth's rubbish with dissembled fascination was that she was an old and valued client of McNally & Son, Attorney-at-Law. (My father is the Attorney; I am the Son.) We had inherited Gertrude after her husband, Reginald, dropped dead from cardiac arrest after missing a ten-inch putt on the fourth green at his club. It is now reverently referred to as Reggie's Hole, in his honor.

I am not an attorney myself, having been expelled from Yale Law for a minor contretemps. During a performance by the New York Philharmonic, I had streaked across the stage, naked except for a Richard M. Nixon mask. To this day it is of some satisfaction that I garnered more applause than Shostakovich's Symphony No. 9 in E-flat Major.

After I returned in disgrace from New Haven to Palm Beach, my father provided me with gainful employment by creating a section in his law firm yclept the Department of Discreet Inquiries. I was the sole member, and it was my task to conduct investigations requested by our moneyed clients who didn't wish to consult law enforcement agencies and possibly see their personal problems emblazoned on the covers of those tabloids stacked next to sliced salami in supermarkets.

This particular inquiry had been initiated with iron determination by the aforementioned Mrs. Gertrude Smythe-Hersforth. Her son, unmarried, had apparently become enamored of a local lady fifteen years his junior, and he wished to plight his troth. In other words, Chauncey Wilson Smythe-Hersforth yearned to get hitched, and to a woman whose surname of Johnson seemed to his mother distressingly plebeian and therefore suspect.

In view of mommy's prejudices, you would think, wouldn't you, that the Smythe-Hersforths rated at least a page in Burke's Peerage? *Au contraire.*

I happened to know that Lemuel Smythe had founded the family fortune by selling moldy bread to Union forces during the Civil War and had subsequently tripled his net worth by marrying Abagail Hersforth, the only child of Isaac Hersforth, who had made *his* pile in the slave trade. So much for our client's family tradition. It couldn't hold a candle stub to my own pride in my paternal grandfather, who was known as Ready Freddy McNally and was one of the most popular burlesque comics on the old Minsky Circuit.

I promised Mrs. Smythe-Hersforth I would conduct a discreet but thorough investigation into the antecedents and character of Miss Theodosia Johnson, the young woman who had snared her son's heart.

"I wouldn't be surprised if she was just a common fortune hunter," Mrs. S-H said darkly.

That was the tip-off, of course. The old biddy was less interested in protecting the family's name than in protecting the family's bucks, which, according to gossip I had heard, amounted to Gettysburg Address millions: four score and seven. A tidy sum, to be sure, but petty cash compared to the wealth of some of her neighbors on Ocean Boulevard.

I was happy to depart the Smythe-Hersforth manse. The interior looked as if it had been decorated in the Avocado Green–Harvest Gold era of the 1950s and hadn't been dusted since. I emerged into bright August sunshine, the sea glittering and a sweet sky dotted with popcorn clouds. I vaulted into my fire-engine-red Miata and headed for the Pelican Club, desperately in need of a liquid buck-up. An hour spent with Mrs. Gertrude Smythe-Hersforth was an affront to the Eighth Amendment, the one dealing with cruel and unusual punishment.

As I tooled westward I reflected that this was not the first time I had been handed the job of establishing the bona fides of a prospective bride or groom. I recalled that on my initial assignment of this type I had expressed some misgivings. I am essentially a romantic cove—and something of a featherbrain, my father might add—and it seemed rather infra dig to investigate the personal history, bank balance, and private kinks of a potential mate with whom one is madly in love.

"Archy," the squire explained in his stodgy way, "you must understand that marriage is a legal contract, presumably for life. Would you sign a contract with a party of the second part without first making an inquiry into his or her trustworthiness? Would you sign a mortgage without inspecting the property and perhaps having it evaluated by an independent appraiser? Would you make a loan without first establishing the financial resources of the borrower? If you would do any of those things, then you are a mindless ass."

I had to acknowledge the logic of his argument, and so I surrendered and accepted the task. I must confess I am not a bloke of strong convictions, other than hot English mustard is splendid on broiled calves' liver.

The Pelican Club is a private dining and drinking establishment housed in a rather decrepit freestanding building out near the airport. It is my favorite watering hole and a popular home-away-from-home for many golden lads and lasses in the Palm Beach area. I was one of the founding members and am proud to say I helped create its most famous annual event, the Running of the Lambs—more fun than Pamplona with considerably less possibility of being gored.

It was not quite noon and the luncheon crowd had not yet come galloping in. The sole occupant of the bar area was Mr. Simon Pettibone, an elderly and dignified gentleman of color who served as club manager and bartender. At the moment, he was watching the screen of a TV set showing a running tape of stock quotations.

I swung aboard a barstool. "Is the market up or down, Mr. Pettibone?" I inquired.

"Sideways, Mr. McNally," he said. "Frozen daiquiri?"

"Excellent suggestion," I said, and watched him prepare it with the deft movements of a practiced mixologist.

"Mr. Pettibone," I said, "are you by any chance acquainted with the Smythe-Hersforth family?"

"Somewhat," he said warily. "When the mister was alive I worked a few of their soirées."

"And what was your impression?"

He chuffed a short laugh. "You could see up their nostrils," he said.

I smiled at his description of nose-in-the-air snoots. "I know the son," I mentioned. "Chauncey Wilson Smythe-Hersforth. He belongs to my golf club. I played a round with him once. Just once. He's an awful duffer. He likes to be called CW—for Chauncey Wilson, you know. So we oblige. He hasn't yet caught on that most of us mean the Chinless Wonder."

"He is that," Mr. Pettibone agreed. "I would call him a young codger."

"Well put," I said. "He must be—what would you say—about forty-five?"

"About."

"And never married?"

"Not to my knowledge. What woman would want a mama's boy?"

"Not even a rich mama's boy?" I asked.

Mr. Pettibone paused to consider that. "Um," he said finally.

I sipped my plasma and considered what might be the wisest next move in my investigation of CW's intended. I had never met the lady, never heard of her prior to that morning, knew absolutely nothing about her. I mention this because it was so unusual. Palm Beach is a small town, especially in the off-season, and everybody knows everybody. But Ms. Theodosia Johnson was, as far as I was concerned, Ms. Terra Incognita.

Ordinarily, I would have immediately consulted Consuela Garcia. She is social secretary to Lady Cynthia Horowitz, one of Palm Beach's wealthiest chatelaines. Connie is plugged in to *all* our town's gossip, rumors, and scandals. She would surely have some poop to contribute on the subject of Theodosia Johnson.

But Connie is also my light-o'-love, and has been for several years. She is a Marielito and an absolutely smashing senorita to whom I have been, I must regretfully confess, unfaithful on more than one occasion.

If Connie has one failing, it's that the green-eyed monster seems permanently perched on her soft, tanned shoulder. We have vowed, many times, to maintain an open relationship, both of us free to consort with whomever she (Connie) or he (me) chooses. I have faithfully hewed to this agreement, but occasionally Connie has been overwhelmed by her fiery Latin blood.

For instance, not too long ago I escorted a charming miss to Testa's for Sunday brunch. We entered the dining room and I immediately espied Connie alone at a distant table. Unfortunately she spotted me and my companion at the same time. She gave me a look I don't wish to describe. She rose immediately and, carrying her brunch plate, marched up to us. I attempted an awkward introduction but to no avail. Connie pulled open the waistband of my lime green linen slacks and slipped in two eggs Benedict. Then she stalked out. It is not a memory I cherish.

So, in view of that recent confrontation, I thought it best not to request Connie's assistance in investigating a nubile young woman. Instead, I went to the rear of the Pelican Club's bar area and used the public phone to call Lolly Spindrift, the social reporter for one of our local gazettes. His popular column is called "Hither and Yon," which I presume refers to the Island of Palm Beach and West Palm Beach across Lake Worth.

"Lol?" I said. "Archy McNally here."

"You swine!" he shrieked. "You don't write, you don't call. How could I possibly have offended? I've never written a word about your vulgar dalliances, although the evidence occupies a full file drawer. And did I not mention your name—spelled correctly, incidentally—in my scoop on the Gillsworth homicides? A word of thanks from you? Hah! Stony silence has been my reward. Watch your step, bucko, or I may add you to my annual list of the Island's most noxious bachelors."

"Slow down a mo, Lol," I begged, "and have lunch with me."

"Where?" he demanded.

"The Pelican Club?" I suggested hopefully.

"Surely you jest," he said. "I wouldn't dine there if I was suffering from a terminal case of malnutrition. Try again."

"The Cafe L'Europe?"

"You're on, darling," he said promptly. "But only if I can have Krug with my beluga. You obviously want something from me, and it's going to cost you, sweetie. Meet you at the bar in a half-hour."

But it was two hours later that I was finally able to muffle his volubility long enough to broach the reason for this extravagant feast. By that time we were on our second bottle of bubbly. Not smashed, you understand, but not whimpering with pain either. Lolly was a sparrow of a man, all dash and chatter. Despite his small size, his capacity for food and drink is legendary. Once, at a party, I saw him consume an entire roast chicken, belch delicately, and head for the broiled lobster.

"Theodosia Johnson," I said to him. "About thirty years old, I think. The chosen of Chauncey Wilson Smythe-Hersforth. What do you know about her?"

Spindrift looked at me sorrowfully. "Oh dear," he said, "I fear I have been dining under false pretenses. There is very little I can tell you about the lady. I like to think of her as Madam X."

"Surely you must know *something* about her," I urged. "She lives in Palm Beach? On the acceptable side of the water?"

"She does indeed. In a rented condo. With her father."

"Single? Divorced? Widowed?"

"Part of the mystery," Lol said, filling our glasses again. "She's been in residence about a year. Seems to be well-heeled. Becoming more active in local charities. That's how she met the Chinless Wonder. At a black-tie bash to save the whales or dolphins or manatees—whatever. You've never met her?"

"Never heard of her until this morning."

He gave me a pitying glance. "Be prepared to have your timbers shivered, m'lad."

"Oh?" I said. "Why is that?"

"Beautiful!" he said enthusiastically. "A corker, believe me. If I was of a different religion, I would definitely be attracted. She's half-Garbo, half-Dietrich. Careful, darling. One look and you'll lose that prune you call your heart."

"An intriguing prospect," I said, pouring the remainder of the second bottle into our glasses. "How do you suggest I might meet this lalapalooza?"

"Easiest thing in the world," he told me. "Tonight the Pristine Gallery is having an exhibit of Silas Hawkin's portraits. You know him?"

"I've met him," I said. "I think he's an idiot."

"More oaf than idiot," Lolly said. "And a *rich* oaf. You know what they say about him, don't you? As a portrait painter he's the best plastic surgeon in Palm Beach. He charges thirty grand and up—mostly up—for a genuine oil portrait of our wealthier beldames. And every matron he's painted has her bosom lifted, wattles excised, and her gin-dulled stare replaced with a youthful sparkle. The man is really a genius at pleasing his clients. Anyway, at the to-do tonight, the gallery is going to show his latest masterpiece: a portrait of Theodosia Johnson. How does that grab you? Madam X herself is sure to be there. Why don't you pop by?"

"Thank you, Lol," I said gratefully. "I think I'll do exactly that."

Eventually we tottered outside and stood in the afternoon heat grinning foolishly at each other.

"Another luncheon like that," I said, "and I'll have a liver as big as the Ritz."

"Nonsense, darling," Spindrift said, gently swaying back and forth. "It was a yummy spread, and I'm pickled tink you asked me."

He gave me a careless wave and wandered away, leaving me to wonder if his "pickled tink" was deliberate or a lurch of a champagne-loosened tongue. I stood rooted, knowing I should return to my miniature office in the McNally Building and begin an inquiry into the creditworthiness of Madam X, including bank balances, net worth, source of income, and all that. But I feared my Krugged brain might not be capable of the task.

During my brief sojourn at Yale Law I had learned an effective method of determining whether one was or was not plotched. You recited aloud the following:

"Amidst the mists and coldest frosts, with stoutest wrists and loudest boasts, he thrusts his fists against the posts and still insists he sees the ghosts."

If you can say that without slobbering all over your chin, you are definitely *not* hors de combat. So I declaimed it aloud on Worth Avenue, attracting wary glances from passing tourists. I was delighted to discover my lower mandible remained bone-dry; the McNally medulla oblongata had not lost its keen edge.

But it was then threeish or fourish, much too late to return to the salt mines. So I drove home, slowly and cautiously, and took a nap.

I roused an hour later, full of p&v, and went for my daily swim. The Atlantic is just across Ocean Boulevard from the McNally digs, and I try to do two miles each day, chugging along parallel to the shore and hoping no Portuguese man-of-war is lurking nearby, licking its chops. I returned home in time to dress and attend the cocktail hour, a family ceremony. That evening, as usual, my father did the honors, stirring up a pitcher of traditional dry martinis.

My mother, Madelaine, is one of the ditsiest of all mommies, but a lovely gentlewoman who talks to her begonias. She also drinks sauterne with meat and fish courses and is very concerned about the ozone layer, without quite knowing what ozone *is*.

My father, Prescott McNally, has been playing the part of landed gentry so long that he has become exactly that: a squire, rectitudinous attorney, and possibly the most hidebound man I know. He has a wide Guardsman's mustache, tangled as the Amazon rain forest, and I like to visualize him wearing a busby, planted outside Buckingham Palace, staring fixedly into space.

I don't wish to imply that my parents are "characters." They, and I, would be offended by that designation. They are just very decent, loving, and lovable human beings. They have their oddities—but who does not? I happen to believe I do a marvelous imitation of Humphrey Bogart, though friends assure me I sound more like Donald Duck.

What I'm trying to convey is that I love my parents. Of course. But just as important, I *enjoy* them. How many sons and daughters can say that?

That evening I was wearing the palest of pink linen suits with a deep lavender polo shirt of Sea Island cotton. Tasseled white loafers with no socks, of course. My father raised one eyebrow (a trick I've never been able to master), and I hastened to explain the glad rags.

"I'm attending an exhibit at the Pristine Gallery tonight," I said. "Silas Hawkin's paintings. I understand the showpiece will be his latest work, a portrait of Theodosia Johnson."

"Ah," the guv said.

Mother looked up. "I've met her father," she declared. "Hector Johnson. A very fine gentleman."

The pater and I exchanged glances.

"How did you happen to meet him, Maddie?" he asked.

"Why, he joined our garden club," she said. "He's only been in South Florida a short while—about a year I think he said—and he's into orchids. He seems very knowledgeable."

"How old is he, mother?" I inquired.

"Oh, I don't know, Archy," she answered. "Mid-sixties perhaps. Shall I ask him?"

McNally père smiled. "I don't think that will be necessary," he said. "A civilized man?"

"Charming," mother said, "just charming! He said my 'Iron Cross' was the healthiest begonia he had ever seen."

Father gulped the remainder of his martini. "That was very kind of him," he said, absolutely deadpan. "Shall we go down to dinner?"

I remember well the menu that night, the way I imagine the condemned might savor their last meal before the unknown. Ursi Olson, our cook-housekeeper, had sautéed red snapper with white wine and shallots. And husband Jamie, our houseman, served the dessert: chocolate torte with cappuccino ice cream. Any wonder why the waistbands of my slacks continue to shrink?

Before departing for the Pristine Gallery I climbed to the third floor of the McNally faux Tudor manor. There, under a leaking copper roof, I had my own aerie, a rather dilapidated but snug suite: sitting room, bedroom, bath. Not luxurious, you understand, but you couldn't beat the rent. Zip.

Since becoming chief of Discreet Inquiries at McNally & Son, I had kept a private journal in which I recorded the details of my investigations. It was an invaluable aid in keeping track of things, especially when I had two or more cases running concurrently. I jotted down facts, impressions, bits of actual dialogue, and whatever else I thought might be of value. Most of my scribblings turned out to be of no value whatsoever. But one never knows, do one?

That night I hurriedly made brief notes on my interview with Mrs. Gertrude Smythe-Hersforth, the chat with Simon Pettibone, the information learned at that bibulous luncheon with Lolly Spindrift, and what mother had mentioned about Hector, Theodosia Johnson's father. Finished, I read over what I had written and found absolutely zilch in the way of inspiration. So I closed up shop, clattered downstairs, and went to meet my fate.

It was a still, cloudless night but hot and humid as a sauna. As I drove back to Worth Avenue I hoped the owner of the Pristine Gallery, Ivan Duvalnik, would have the decency to serve something refreshing. He did: a Chilean chardonnay so cold it made my fillings ache.

It turned out to be a hugger-mugger evening, the gallery overcrowded, chatter too loud, paintings almost hidden by the billows of chiffon gown (f.) and the sheen of silk sport jackets (m.). I knew most of the guests and mingled determinedly, working my way toward the pièce de résistance: the portrait of Theodosia Johnson.

When I finally stood before it, I was simultaneously rapt and unwrapped. I mean I was totally engrossed and at the same time felt a sag of the knees and a horrible need to let my jaw droop and just gawk. Spindrift had not exaggerated; the lady was a corker. What beauty! But not of the plastic variety one sees so often in fashion ads and centerfolds. Again, Lolly had it right: she was half-Garbo, half-Dietrich, with all the mystery and promise in those two mesmerizing faces.

I am not an expert on paintings, figuring one man's "September Morn" is another man's "Les Demoiselles d'Avignon." But I defy any hot-blodded yute to look at that portrait of Madam X without saying to himself, "I *must* meet her."

I was filling my eyes when a voice at my elbow interrupted my fantasies by stating, "Awfully good, am I right, Archy? Si has caught her expression perfectly, and the colors are striking. Don't you agree?"

I turned, and there was the Chinless Wonder himself, Chauncey Wilson Smythe-Hersforth, wearing a midnight blue dinner jacket and looking like the groom on a wedding cake. His pushbroom mustache was meticulously trimmed and he was exuding a fruity cologne. That was a surprise. CW was known as a nebbishy sort of chap. Palm Beach gossips (the total population) claimed he wore a helmet while pedaling his Exercycle.

"You couldn't be righter, CW," I said. "Or more right—whichever comes first. Hawkin has done a marvelous job, and the lady is beautiful."

"My fiancée," he said with a fatuous grin. "Or soon to be."

"Congratulations!" I said, smiling, and recalling that "one may smile and smile, and be a villain."

"Well, it's not exactly official yet," he said in that pontifical way he had of speaking. "But it soon will be, I assure you."

"I'd like to meet the lucky lady," I said, perking his ego. "Is she here this evening?"

"Somewhere," he said vaguely, looking about the mobbed gallery. "Just find the biggest crowd, and she's sure to be the center."

Then he drifted away, obviously having no desire to introduce me personally. Quite understandable.

I glanced around and saw in one corner a jammed circle of men surrounding someone I presumed to be the star of the evening. Rather than join the adoring throng, I eased my way to the bar to replenish my supply of that excellent chardonnay. And there I bumped into Silas Hawkin, the famous portraitist and plastic surgeon himself.

"Hi, Si," I said, thinking how silly that sounded.

He stared. "Do I know you?" he demanded.

We had met several times; he knew very well who I was. But feigning ignorance was his particular brand of one-upmanship.

"Archy McNally," I said, as equably as I could.

"Oh yeah," he said. "The lawyer feller. Didn't know you were interested in fine art."

"Oh my yes," I said. "I have a lovely collection of Bugs Bunny cels. Good show tonight."

"I think so," he said complacently. "People know quality when they see it. You caught my latest? The portrait of Theodosia Johnson?"

"Extraordinary," I said.

"It is that," he agreed. "Took me a week to do her lips."

A ribald reply leaped to mind, but I squelched it. "By the way, Si," I said, "may I give you a call? It concerns a silly inquiry I'm making. Nothing of any great importance."

"Sure," he said casually, his eyes roving. "Anytime."

Then we were jostled away from the bar and separated. I finally decided I had to make my move—win or lose. So I joined the ring of admirers, and sure enough Theodosia Johnson was at the center, flushed but poised and accepting compliments with the graciousness of E. II. I slowly inched forward until I was standing directly in front of Madam X herself.

"Archy McNally," I said, giving her the 150-watt smile I call my Jumbocharmer.

"Theo Johnson," she said, and reached out a hand to shake. It was one of the hardest decisions of my life to let go.

"A fantastic portrait, Miss Johnson," I told her. "But it doesn't do you justice."

"Thank you," she murmured, and gave me the full blaze of azure eyes. "You're very kind."

Naturally I wanted to say more, but I was elbowed away by other victims, and regretfully departed with the feeling that I had been privileged to be in the presence of great, almost supernal beauty. For the third time, Lolly Spindrift had been right: my timbers had been shivered and I was in love.

Again.

I left the gallery and drove home singing one of my favorite songs: "When It's Apple Blossom Time in Orange, New Jersey, We'll Make a Peach of a Pair."

Chapter 2

I awoke the next morning with the conviction that if Johnny Keats was right—"Beauty is truth, truth beauty."—then Mrs. Smythe-Hersforth had no reason to worry about the motives of Ms. Theodosia Johnson. How could a paragon with that mass of shimmering chestnut hair, those burning eyes, that Limoges complexion ever be guilty of even the teeniest deceit? Ridiculous! As far as I was concerned, my investigation could be canceled forthwith.

But I knew if I dared suggest such a thing to my father, he wouldn't say a word. He would merely glare at me from under those snarled eyebrows, and that would be my answer. So, sighing, I started the second day of what I later came to call The Affair of Madam X.

I was late getting downstairs, as usual, and so I breakfasted in the kitchen, served by Jamie Olson. He was working on what was probably his third mug of black coffee to which, I was sure, he had added a splash of aquavit.

Jamie is seventyish, semi-wizened, and a taciturn bloke. He is also privy to all the backstairs gossip in Palm Beach, stuff even Lolly Spindrift isn't aware of since it's shared only by the servants of the Island's nabobs. And the things these maids, chauffeurs, valets, housekeeps, and butlers know or suspect would make a platoon of tabloid editors moan with delight.

"Jamie," I said, after I had smeared my toasted onion bagel with salmon mousse, "have you ever heard of Theodosia Johnson?"

"Yep," he said. "A looker."

"She is that," I agreed. "I understand she's been here about a year. Lives with her father, Hector, in a rented condo. Do they have any staff?"

"Don't know."

"Could you find out?"

"Mebbe."

"What about the Smythe-Hersforths? Hear any talk?"

"Tight."

"Tight? You mean stingy?"

"Uh-huh."

I seemed to be making little progress with Jamie, but I had learned from past experience that patience frequently paid off. He really was a remarkable fount of inside info. Turning on the tap was the problem.

"I can believe the gammer might have miserly tendencies," I said. "What about the son, Chauncey Wilson? I know he's got a good job with a local bank. All title and no work. Is he also a penny-pincher?"

"Yep," Jamie said.

"Blood will tell," I said, and poured myself another cup of coffee that had been laced with chicory. "One more: How about the painter, Silas Hawkin? Know him?"

He nodded.

"How many in his ménage?"

"Ménage?"

"Household."

"Him, wife, daughter. One live-in."

"Everything harmonious there? All peace and goodwill?"

"Nope," Jamie said.

I woke up. "What seems to be the problem?" I asked.

"Him."

"I can understand that," I said. "The man's a dolt. Know any details?"

He shook his head.

"Ask around, will you, Jamie? About Theodosia and her father, and the reason for discord in Si Hawkin's not-so-happy home."

He nodded.

I slipped him a tenner before I left. The lord of the manor would be outraged to learn that I customarily gave Jamie a pourboire for information. The Olsons drew a handsome stipend to keep the McNally family comfortable and well-nourished, but I felt revealing inside skinny to yrs. truly was not included in domestic chores and deserved an extra quid now and then.

I went into my father's study and sat in the big armchair behind his desk, feeling like a fraudulent dauphin. I used his local telephone directory that had been bound in a leather slipcover. I swear, he would put a calfskin cozy on a teapot. I looked up the number and pecked it out.

"The Hawkins' residence," a chirpy female voice answered. I presumed this was the live-in.

"May I speak to Mr. Hawkin, please," I said. "Archy McNally calling."

"Just a moment, please, sir," she said.

It was more than a moment, more like three or four, before he came on the line.

"Yeah?" he said. It was practically a grunt.

"Good morning, Si," I said, giving him a heavy dose of the McNally cheer. "That was a wonderful show last night."

"It went okay," he said. "Ivan Duvalnik called earlier and claims we got two new clients out of it and four possibles."

"Congratulations!" I cried. "Due to that marvelous portrait of Theo Johnson, no doubt. Listen, may I pop over this morning and ask a few questions? That silly inquiry I mentioned to you last night. It won't take long."

"Well . . . all right," he said, "if you keep it short. I've got a lot of work to do."

"Just take a few minutes," I promised. "I'm on my way."

They lived in an imitation Mizner on the Intracoastal down toward South Palm Beach, and when I saw the house, really a villa, I guessed a million five. Then I saw the guest house and changed my estimate to two million five. That detached, two-story edifice looked like an enormous Nebraska barn painted white, but the upper floor seemed entirely enclosed in glass, and I mean big, openable picture windows. It had to be the artist's studio—or a solarium devoted to sunbathing in the buff.

I was greeted at the front door of the main house by the chirpy-voiced domestic who had answered the phone. I had envisioned her as young, small, lissome. She was old, large, creaky.

"Archy McNally," I said. "To see Mr. Hawkin."

"Of course," she said, and her smile won me over. "Do come in."

I followed this pleasant woman into a home decorated in what is called the Mediterranean Style, but whether that means Marseille or Beirut I've never been able to figure out. Anyway, I thought it a strident interior with a lot of rattan, jangling patterns, acidic hues, and the skins of endangered species. On the walls, to my surprise, were seascapes and paintings of Lake Worth by Silas Hawkin. I had no idea he did that kind of thing, but there was no mistaking his style; the man *was* a superb colorist.

There were two women seated in the Florida room, leafing through slick magazines, and it was the older who rose to greet me.

"You must be Archy McNally," she said, holding out a hand. "I do believe I've met your parents. I am Louise Hawkin."

"A pleasure to make your acquaintance, ma'am," I said, pressing dry, bony fingers.

"And this is my daughter, Marcia," she added.

"*Step*daughter," the younger woman said in a Freon voice, not looking up from her copy of *Vogue*.

Mrs. Hawkin made a small moue as if she had suffered that correction before.

"Glad to meet you, Miss Hawkin," I said, and was rewarded with a nod. One.

"Would you care for something to drink?" Mrs. Hawkin asked. "Coffee perhaps? Or anything else?"

"Thank you, no," I replied. "I promised your husband I'd only stay a few minutes. I know how busy he must be."

"Oh yes," she said airily, "he's always busy."

I heard a sound from the stepdaughter. It might have been a short, scornful laugh. Or maybe she was only clearing her throat.

"He's in the studio now," Louise Hawkin said. "Through that door and along the walkway. He's on the second floor."

"Thank you," I said. "I hope to meet you ladies again."

Neither replied and I left in silence. Happy to leave, as a matter of fact. Bad vibes in that room. Something bilious about the relationship between the two women. But perhaps they had merely had an early morning squabble ("Aren't you finished with the *Vogue* yet?" "No, I am *not* finished with it!"), and I thought no more about it.

The walkway to the guest house was roofed with slates. A nice touch, I acknowledged, but not very practical if you got a blowy squall coming in from the sea. The door to the Nebraska barn was oak and etched frosted glass. It was horribly scarred, and I judged it had been purchased from one of those antique shops that specialize in old saloon furnishings.

I pushed in and found myself in an enormous space that had indeed been designed for sleep-over guests: bedroom area, conversation pit, kitchenette. But it did have all the comforts of home: fridge, TV set, VCR, and what appeared to be a well-stocked bar. Everything was precisely arranged, new and unused, awaiting guests who never arrived.

I climbed a cast-iron staircase to the second story and entered the studio, as large and open as the floor below. But this area was cluttered with all the paraphernalia and detritus a working artist might accumulate: easels, taborets, palettes, tubes of oil, stretched blank canvases, stacks of finished paintings leaning against the outside walls, innumerable cans of turps and who knows what.

There was a dais decorated like a stage set, the floor carpeted, maroon drapes, an ornate armchair alongside a delicate tea table. I remembered seeing those drapes and that tea table in the painting of Theodosia Johnson, and had little doubt that the artist used the same props in all his portraits of Palm Beach matrons.

Oh yes, one more thing: In a far corner was a battered sleigh bed that might have been a charming antique at one time but was now in such a dreadful state of disrepair that it had all the compelling grace of an army cot. It was covered with rumpled sheets, and the wadded pillow looked as if it had been used to smother palmetto bugs.

The artist himself was seated at a shockingly dilapidated desk, smoking a morning cigar and apparently making entries in a ledger. He slapped it shut when I entered. He rose and came forward to meet me, viewing with some distaste the madras blazer and electric blue slacks I was wearing. He made no offer to shake hands.

"Found me, did you?" he said. "Pull up a chair. That one over there. It looks ready to collapse, but it won't. You met my wife and daughter?"

"I did," I said, seating myself rather gingerly on the spindly kitchen chair he had indicated. "Lovely ladies."

"Yeah," he said, going back behind his desk. "Now what's all this bullshit about an inquiry and questions?"

It *was* bs, but it was a scam I had used before with some success, and I saw no reason why it wouldn't work on this crude man. He might have been a talented artist, but he was also, in my opinion, a vulgar pig. There. I said it and I'm glad.

"It's a project dreamed up by the Real Estate Department of McNally and Son," I said earnestly. (Hey, I can do earnest.) "We are agents for perhaps a dozen mansions in the Palm Beach area, ranging from two million to twelve. Asking price, of course. What we're planning to do is put together a list of potential buyers, people with sufficient resources to afford one of these magnificent estates. Before we send them a very expensive four-color brochure, we'd like to do a little research and make certain they're completely trustworthy and capable of making such a hefty investment. One of the names on the list is Hector Johnson, and I hoped you'd be willing to tell me a little about him. Strictly *entre nous,* of course."

He looked at me. I could see he didn't believe and he didn't *dis*believe. He finally decided to give me the benefit of the doubt. People are continually doing that—until they learn better.

Let me tell you something about Silas Hawkin. He suffered from what I called the Hemingway Syndrome—very prevalent in South Florida and particularly in the Keys. Bulky, middle-aged men cultivate a grizzled beard, wear a long-billed fishing cap, and drink nothing but Myers's Dark rum. Some go so far as to sport a small gold ring in one ear or even a ponytail. None wear bifocals or a hearing aid in public.

Hawkin was a charter member of this macho cult. I didn't know whether or not he was an obsessed fisherman, but I would have bet a farthing that he had the cap and drank rum. I could see he had the requisite pepper-and-salt beard, for at the moment he was combing it with his fingers and regarding me with a mixture of hostility and suspicion.

"Hector Johnson," he repeated. "Theo's father. I've only met the guy a couple of times. He seems okay. Knows a lot about art. Good taste."

Which meant, I presumed, that Hector said he admired Hawkin's work.

"Seems to have bucks, does he?" I asked.

The artist shrugged. "I get the feeling he ain't hurting."

"Paid your bill on time?" I pressed.

He took that badly. "None of your damned business," he snapped angrily. "As a matter of fact, I haven't sent in my bill yet."

"I have no desire to pry unnecessarily," I hastily assured him. "I'm just trying to get a handle on the man. Do you know anything about his background? What he did before he and his daughter moved to South Florida?"

"I don't really know. I think he said he was a professor."

"Oh?" I said. "Biology?"

"Biology?" He was puzzled. "Why do you say that?"

"I heard he was an expert on orchids."

"Nah," the artist said. "Maybe he knows orchids, but I think he taught electronics or computer stuff—something like that. Look, I've really got to get back to work."

"Of course," I said, rising. "Before I go I must tell you again that I think your portrait of Theodosia Johnson is the best thing you've ever done."

"Yeah," he agreed, "but I couldn't miss with a model like that. Beautifully proportioned. Classic. Incredible skin tone. That hair! And carries herself like a duchess. A complete woman. I'll never find another like her."

I was somewhat surprised by his excessive praise but made no comment—mostly because I concurred with everything he had said. Before I departed I proffered my business card.

"If you come across anything that might help my inquiry," I said, "pro or con, I'd appreciate it if you'd give me a call."

"Sure," he said, tossing my card into the litter on his desk.

And that was that. I tramped downstairs wondering what I had learned. Not much. I reached the ground level, glanced in, and there was Mrs. Louise Hawkin, a winsome lady, seated on one of the couches in the conversation pit. She beckoned, and I obeyed. Good boy! Now *heel.*

"I'm having a vodka gimlet," she said. "There's a pitcher in the fridge. Would you like one?"

I considered this invitation for a long time—possibly three seconds. "Yes," I said, "thank you."

It was an excellent gimlet, not so tart that it puckered one's lips but sharp and energizing. Mrs. Hawkin patted the cushion beside her and I obediently took my place. Good boy! Now sit up and beg.

"How did you make out with Si?" she inquired lazily, her drawl obviously an attempt to conceal a real curiosity.

"Fine," I said. "I only had a few questions. Your husband was very cooperative."

"He was?" she said, mildly astonished. "Questions about what?"

"Whom," I said. "A mutual acquaintance." I hoped she wouldn't push it. She didn't.

"You're a lawyer?" she asked suddenly.

"No, ma'am," I said. "My father is an attorney but I am not."

"Does he do divorce work? A friend of mine is looking for a good divorce lawyer and asked if I could recommend someone."

"Sorry," I said. "McNally and Son doesn't handle divorces. But if you like, I can ask my father. I'm sure he can suggest someone who would be willing to talk to your friend. Shall I do that?"

"Yes. Let me know as soon as possible."

"Of course," I said.

She sipped her gimlet, stared at the high ceiling, and ignored me. Good boy! Now lie down and play dead.

She was a heavy-bodied woman with an attractive mastiff face: very strong, very determined. I decided I would rather have her for a friend than an enemy. That may sound simple, but there are some people, men and women, of whom you are instinctively wary, knowing they could be trouble.

I finished my drink, rose, and expressed thanks for her hospitality. She gazed at me thoughtfully but made no reply. So I slunk away, grateful to be out of her presence. I can't explain exactly why. Just that I was conscious of a very deep anger there with which I could not cope, and had no desire to.

I retraced my route and entered the main house through the door to the Florida room. I could have circled around and reclaimed my Miata on the bricked driveway, but I wanted to learn the name of the pleasant, chirpy-voiced maid who had ushered me in.

Instead, I found Marcia Hawkin wandering about, hugging her elbows. I was about to bid her a polite farewell when she accosted me—and accosted is a mild word for her attitude. She was in my face.

"Did you go to daddy's show last night?" she demanded.

"Why, yes, Miss Hawkin," I said as softly as I could. "I did attend the exhibit."

"It was a circus, wasn't it?" she challenged. "A bloody circus."

"Not really," I said cautiously. "Not much different from a hundred other similar affairs."

"And I suppose *she* was there," she said bitterly.

Complete confusion. Did she mean Mrs. Hawkin or the cynosure of the evening?

"*She?*" I repeated. "Your stepmother or Theodosia Johnson?"

"You know who I mean," she said darkly. "The *whore!*"

That was rough stuff that not only shocked but left me as flummoxed as before. To whom was she referring? All I could do at the moment was stare at her, utterly bewildered.

I cannot say she was an unattractive woman. Quite young. Tall and attenuated. But there was a brittleness about her I found a mite off-putting. She seemed assembled of piano wire and glass, ready to snap or shatter at any moment.

She stalked away from me and stood staring through an open window at her father's studio. I judged it would be wise to make a quiet and unobtrusive exit. To tell you the truth, I had enough of naked human passions for one morning. I felt like I had been wrung out hard and hung up wet. I murmured a courteous goodbye and slipped away. I don't believe she was even aware of my going.

I loitered in the entrance hallway a moment, hoping to have a few words with the live-in domestic. I was rewarded when she came bustling forward to show me out.

"You've been very kind," I told her, "and I thank you for it. You know, I must confess that I don't know your name. You know mine, and I don't know yours. That's not fair!"

She gave me that radiant smile again. "Mrs. Jane Folsby," she said.

"Mrs. Folsby," I said, reaching to shake her hand, "it's been a pleasure to meet you. Have you been with the Hawkins long?"

The smile faded. "Too long," she said.

I left that acorn academy and turned to see if there was a nameplate over the front door. Some Palm Beach mansions have cutesy titles such as "Last Resort" and "Wit's End." But the Hawkins' manse boasted no legend. I thought "Villa Bile" might be fitting.

But I'm a sunny-tempered johnny, and even the events of that gruesome morning didn't drag me down for long. I wasn't quite certain if what I had heard from the Hawkin family had anything at all to do with Theodosia Johnson, the intended bride of the Chinless Wonder.

It was time, I concluded, to inject some joy and innocent delight into my life. So as I drove northward I used my new cellular phone to call Consuela Garcia at Lady Cynthia Horowitz's mansion.

"Miss Garcia," I said formally, "this is Archy McNally speaking. I wish to apologize for my recent behavior and beg your forgiveness. I also wish to invite you to lunch at twelve-thirty at the Pelican Club."

"Okay," Connie said cheerfully.

Divine woman! Why I continually fall in love with others of the female persuasion is beyond me. If it isn't a genetic defect, it must be a compulsive-obsessive disorder. I really should read up on it, and I fully intend to—one of these days.

Chapter 3

The Pelican Club was cranking with the noonday crowd when I entered, but fortunately most of the Pelicanites were seated at tables in the bar area or dining room. I was able to find an unoccupied barstool, and Simon Pettibone came ambling over to ask my pleasure.

Ordinarily, my favorite summer potion is a frozen daiquiri, but recently I had been browsing through a secondhand bookstore and had come across a bartender's guide published in the mid-1930s, shortly after Prohibition was repealed. (Bless you, FDR!)

Naturally I purchased this fascinating compendium and spent many enjoyable hours studying the recipes of cocktails now lost and forgotten. Of course it included such classics as Manhattan, Bronx, Rob Roy, and Sazerac. But it also listed the ingredients of such obscure mixed drinks as Sweet Patootie, Seventh Heaven, and Arise My Love. (I kid you not.)

Much to my astonishment, I discovered our publican knew, he actually *knew,* how to mix many of these antique libations. It had become a game to test his expertise, and he succeeded more often than he failed.

"Today, Mr. Pettibone," I said, "I would like a Soul Kiss." It was a request that drew a few startled glances from nearby bar patrons.

"Soul Kiss," he repeated thoughtfully, cast his eyes upward and reflected. "Ah, yes," he said finally. "Orange juice, Dubonnet, dry vermouth, and bourbon."

"Bravo!" I cried. "You've got it—and I hope to get it as soon as possible." He set to work.

I was sipping my Soul Kiss, wondering how long it might take to work my way through the 1000-plus drinks listed in the guide, when Consuela Garcia came bouncing into the Club. She immediately looked toward the bar, spotted me, and waved. I stood up and beamed happily.

Connie is as toothsome as a charlotte russe, but that is hardly the limit of her appeal. She has a sharp wit, is extremely clever at her job, and is just naturally a jolly lady. There are those who wonder why I don't marry the girl.

The answer is simple: cowardice. Not fear of Connie so much as fear of matrimony itself.

I see wedded bliss as a kind of surrender—which I agree is an immature attitude. But I think of myself as an honorable chap, and if I were married it would mean that never again could I look at a dishy woman with lust in my heart. That is what scares me: that I would be incapable of resisting temptation, and so my self-esteem would evaporate, let alone the trust of my mate.

You may possibly feel all that is blarney, and my sole reason for remaining a bachelor is that I relish the life of a rake. You may possibly be right.

Connie and I had Leroy's special hamburgers, a beef-veal-pork combination mixed with chilies. We shared a big side order of extra-thick potato chips and drank Buckler, which is a non-alcoholic beer that tastes swell but doesn't do a thing for you except quench your thirst.

Connie chattered on about a reception Lady Horowitz was planning for a visiting Russian ballerina and didn't mention a word about L'Affaire d'Oeufs Benedict, for which I was thankful. She was excited about her arrangements for the party, and it showed in her features: snappy eyes, laughing mouth, squinched-up nose to express displeasure.

Charming, no doubt about it. But different from Theodosia Johnson's beauty. Not inferior or superior, just different. Connie was earthy, open, solid. Madam X was an unsolved riddle. So far.

"Hey," Connie said over coffee, "I've been yakking up a storm and haven't asked about you. What mischief are you up to these days, Archy?"

"Oh, this and that," I said. "Nothing heavy. Right now I'm running a credit check on a man named Hector Johnson. Ever hear of him?"

"Of course," she said promptly. "He sent in a nice check for Lady Cynthia's latest project, to install Art Nouveau pissoirs on Worth Avenue. Can you imagine? Anyway, the boss asked him over for cocktails. What a doll! He's got charm coming out his ears."

"Uh-huh," I said. "Retired, is he?"

"Semi, I guess. He said he used to work for the government. He didn't say doing what, but I got the feeling it was the CIA."

"Connie, whatever gave you that idea?"

"Because he was so mysterious about it. I suppose I could have asked straight out, but I didn't want to pry. Who cares if he was a spy? He's nice and that's all that counts."

"Sure," I said.

She looked at her Swatch. "Oh, lordy, I have to get my rear in gear. Sorry to eat and run, luv, but I've got a zillion things to do. Okay?"

"Of course," I said. "You go ahead. I think I'll dawdle a bit."

She swooped to kiss my cheek, gathered up handbag and scarf, and sashayed out. I wasn't the only man, or woman, in the dining room who watched her leave. Connie radiates a healthy vigor that even strangers admire. With her robust figure and long black hair flying, she could model for the hood ornament on a turbo-charged sports coupe.

I finished a second cup of coffee, signed my tab at the bar, and wandered out. I was musing about Hector Johnson, a man who apparently was knowledgeable about orchids, had been a professor of electronics or computer stuff, and had worked for the U.S. of A., possibly as a spy. Curiouser and curiouser. I had been enlisted to investigate Theo Johnson, but now I found myself concentrating on daddy. Because, to paraphrase Willie Sutton, that's where the money was, I supposed.

I went back to my cubicle in the McNally Building on Royal Palm Way. It is a squarish structure of glass and stainless steel, so stark and modern it makes you yearn to see a Chick Sales just once more before you die.

My office was a joke: a tiny windowless room as confining as a Pullman berth. I am convinced my father banished me there to prove to other employees that there would be no nepotism at McNally & Son. But at least I had an air-conditioner vent, and I lighted my first English Oval of the day as I set to work gathering the financial skinny on Hector Johnson and his wondrous daughter.

I phoned contacts at local banks, promising my pals a dinner at the Pelican if they would reveal whatever they had on the enigmatic Hector. Then I prepared a letter to be faxed to national credit agencies to which we subscribed. Those snoops could usually deliver everything from an individual's date of birth and Social Security number to current Zip Code, hat size, and passionate preferences, such as an inordinate fondness for sun-dried tomatoes. Privacy? It doesn't exist anymore. Not even if you're lucky enough to be dead.

I finished the letter and was about to take it upstairs to Mrs. Trelawney, my father's private secretary, and have her fax it out, when my phone rang. That was such an unusual occurrence that I stared at it a moment before picking up. I was sure it would be an automatic marketing machine working through every possible telephone number in sequence and delivering a recorded spiel on the wonderful opportunity I had been granted to invest in a rhinestone mine.

"H'lo?" I said cautiously.

"Archy McNally?"

I thought I recognized that whiny voice but hoped I was wrong.

"Yes," I said. "Speaking."

"This is Chauncey Wilson Smythe-Hersforth," he said, reeling off the four names like a sergeant selecting a latrine detail.

"Hello, CW," I said, resolving to get rid of this world-class bore as fast as humanly possible.

"Archy," he said, and I thought I detected a note of desperation, "I've got to see you as soon as possible."

"Oh?" I said. "Concerning what?"

"Well . . ." he started, stopped, gave me a few "Uh's" and "Um's," and finally said, "It's a legal matter."

"Then you better speak to my father," I told him. "As you know, I am not an attorney. Would you like me to set up an appointment?"

"No!" he cried. "No, no, no! I know your father is an estimable man, but he scares me."

"Well . . . yes," I conceded. "At times he can be rather daunting. But if you need legal advice, CW, I'm just not your man."

"It's not really a legal thing," he stammered on. "It is and it isn't. And I'd rather talk about it to you. *Please,* Archy."

Now I was intrigued; the Chinless Wonder, with an ego as big as all outdoors, was pleading for help. And it just might have something to do with the trustworthiness of Theodosia Johnson.

"All right, CW," I said. "Would you like to pop over to the office?"

"Oh no," he said immediately. "I'd probably be seen, the word would get back to mother, and she'd demand to know why I was seeing our lawyer."

"Very well. Then how about the Pelican Club? Cafe L'Europe? Testa's? Perhaps a Pizza Hut?"

"Won't do," he said despairingly. "I can't be seen huddling with you in public. You know how people talk."

"CW," I said, more than a little miffed, "you ask to meet me to discuss what is apparently a personal matter of some importance, and then you reject all my suggestions for a rendezvous. Here is my final offer, and I do mean final: The McNally Building has an underground garage. If you will drive down there, I will be pleased to meet with you, and we will have a cozy tête-à-tête."

"Is that the best you can do?" he said, the whine becoming a drone.

The McNally temper, though rarely displayed, is not totally nonexistent. "Not only the best," I said with some asperity, "but the only. Either be there within fifteen minutes or forget about the whole thing."

"All right," he said faintly.

I dropped my letter off in Mrs. Trelawney's office, asked her to fax it out, and went down to the garage. After that goofy exchange with CW, I was far from being gruntled, so I merely waved at Herb, our security guard, and lighted my second cigarette of the day. I leaned against a concrete pillar, puffed away, and awaited the arrival of the Chinless Wonder.

About ten minutes later his black Mercedes came rolling slowly down the ramp. He pulled into an empty parking slot, and I went over and slid in next to him.

"Are you certain no one will see us?" he asked nervously.

"No, I am not certain," I answered. "But the odds against it are worth a wager. Now what's this all about?"

"Mother told me she asked you to investigate Theodosia."

"That's correct."

"Well, I'm sure you'll find she's true-blue."

"I'm sure I shall. So what's the problem?"

He hesitated. "This is embarrassing," he said.

"Not for me," I said. "What is it?"

"Well . . ." he started, and I got another dose of "Uh's" and "Um's." "You see, Archy, before I met Theo, I had a, ah, fling with another young woman."

"Hardly a mortal sin, CW."

"Well, after I met Theo, I realized she was the genuine article. I fell completely in love and decided I wanted to marry her. So I broke off with the previous young woman—or attempted to."

"Oh-ho," I said, "I'm beginning to get the picture. The previous lady has raised objections?"

"Loud and clear," he said miserably. "She claims I had promised to marry *her*, and she threatens to sue me."

I laughed. "Breach of Promise? Forget it, CW. That's as common as Contempt of Congress. Everyone's guilty. The lady has no case."

"Well, uh," he continued, "she may not have a *legal* case, but there's more to it than that. I wrote her letters."

I looked at him. "You actually wrote letters to her? Promising marriage?"

"Yes."

"Told her how much you adored her, did you?"

"Yes."

"That you would be faithful for a lifetime?"

"Yes."

"That you desire no girl in the world but her?"

"Yes."

"CW, you're a fool."

"Yes," he said. "And now she's threatening to sell my letters to a tabloid. They're, um, somewhat passionate."

It was difficult to believe this lump could compose passionate prose, but I let it go. "How much does she want?" I asked.

"She doesn't mention money," he said. "She keeps saying that all she wants is to marry me."

"Who is she? What's her name? What does she do for a living besides collect letters from brainless bachelors?"

He swallowed the insult. "Her name is Shirley Feebling, and she works in a topless car wash down near Lauderdale. That's how I met her."

I wasn't surprised. Florida is the home of the topless car wash, topless restaurants, topless maid service, topless coffee shops. It is only a matter of time before we have topless funeral homes.

"And what is it you wish me to do?" I asked.

"Talk to her," he begged. "Persuade her to turn over the letters and keep quiet. If she wants money, I'll pay. Within reason, of course. Archy, if she carries out her threat, she could ruin me. Mother would disown me, Theo would give me the broom. You've got to do *something!*"

I didn't know why I should, but then the thought occurred to me that someday I might be in a similar fix myself. And after all, he was a client—or at least the son of a wealthy client.

"All right," I said finally, "I'll see what I can do. Give me her name, address, and telephone number."

He reached into his inside jacket pocket and withdrew a ballpoint pen. Typical Chinless Wonder: He drove a Mercedes and carried a Bic. He tore a page from a pocket notebook and jotted down all the vital info.

I tucked it away, started to get out of the car, then paused.

"By the way, CW," I said, "I imagine you've met Hector Johnson many times. What is your impression of him?"

"A great fellow!" he said enthusiastically. "Never knew a man who understands as much about banking as old Heck. He used to own a bank somewhere out West, you know."

"Uh-huh," I said, and started to leave again. This time he stopped me.

"Listen, Archy," he said, the whine rising in pitch, "I hope you won't mention anything about my problem to your father. I mean it's just between us, isn't it? Confidential and all that?"

"Of course," I said. "My lips are sealed."

"Good man," he said.

So that evening, after my ocean swim, the family cocktail hour and dinner, I followed the sire to his study.

"Father," I said, "may I have a word with you?"

"Can't it wait?" he said testily.

I knew what irked him; I was delaying his nighttime routine. He was looking forward to having one or more glasses of port while he continued slogging his way through the entire oeuvre of Charles Dickens. I think he was currently deep in the complexities of *Martin Chuzzlewit* but it might have been *Little Dorrit*. The amazing thing was that he stayed awake while reading.

"It'll just take a few minutes," I promised.

"Oh, very well," he said. "Come on in."

He stood erect behind his massive desk and I stood in front. As I delivered a report on my recent conversation with Chauncey Wilson Smythe-Hersforth, his face twisted with distaste.

"A tawdry business," he pronounced when I had finished.

"Yes, sir," I said, "but troubling. Was I correct in telling him that the woman had no legal grounds for a suit against him for Breach of Promise?"

"You were quite right," he said. "Breach of Promise actions were abolished by the Florida legislature in 1945. In fact, lawmakers had such an abhorrence of the practice that they decreed that anyone initiating such a suit would be guilty of a misdemeanor in the second degree. Shortly after the statute was passed, a law review published an article on the subject entitled 'No More Torts for Tarts.'"

"Not bad," I said. "But now the question is how to handle CWs problem. I imagine the complainant will accept a cash settlement."

"A reasonable assumption," father said dryly. "But that doesn't necessarily mean the end of the affair. I can draw up a release she will be required to sign before she hands over the letters and gets paid. But a release never completely eliminates the possibility of her making another claim at some future date, especially if she's shrewd enough to keep photocopies of the letters. It could go on and on. It's really blackmail, Archy, and blackmailers rarely give up after one payoff."

"I concur," I said. "I think I better meet the young woman, get a take on

her, and perhaps a rough idea of how much she expects for the letters. After
that, we can decide how to deal with it."

My father was silent, mulling over my suggestion. He was a champion
muller; I have seen him spend three minutes deciding whether to furl his golf
umbrella clockwise or counterclockwise.

"Yes," he said finally, "I think that would be best. Interview the lady, appear to be sympathetic and understanding, and find out exactly what she
wants. Then report to me, and we'll take it from there."

"Yes, sir," I said, resisting an urge to salute.

I trudged upstairs to my nest, put on the reading specs, and set to work
recording the details of that eventful day. I paused while I was scribbling a
précis of the Chinless Wonder's remarks about Hector Johnson: "Knows
banking. Owned a Western bank." Let's see, I recapped, that made Theodosia's father an expert on orchids, electronics and/or computer stuff, government service (possibly espionage), and banking. Why, the man was a
veritable polymath, and I wouldn't be a bit surprised if my next interviewee
claimed that Hector was a master bialy maker.

I finished my labors, closed my journal, and was preparing to relax by
sipping a dram of marc and listening to a Patricia Kaas cassette when my
blasted phone blasted. I glanced at my Mickey Mouse watch (an original, not
a reproduction) and saw it was almost ten-thirty.

"Archy McNally," I said, expecting the worst. It was close.

"Ah-ha!" Sgt. Al Rogoff, PBPD, said in his heavy rumble. "I have tracked
the sherlock of Palm Beach to his elegant lair. How you doing, old buddy?"

"Up to my nates in drudgery," I said. "And you?"

"Likewise," he said. "But enough of this idle chitchat. You know the
painter Silas Hawkin?"

I hesitated for just the briefest. "Yes, I know him," I said. "Matter of fact,
I visited him at his studio this morning."

"Interesting," Al said. "I think you better wheel your baby carriage back
to his studio. Right now."

"Why on earth should I do that?"

"Because the maid just found Silas with a knife stuck in his neck."

I swallowed. "Dead?"

"Couldn't be deader," Rogoff said cheerfully.

"But why pick on me, Al?"

"Because your business card was on his desk. You coming or do I have
to send a SWAT team after you?"

"On my way," I said.

I paused long enough to take one sip of marc (a gulp would have demolished me) and bounced downstairs. I trotted out to the garage to board my
pride and joy. It had been a sparkling day, and the night was still dulcet. As
I drove, I admired Mother Nature while I pondered who might have stuck a
shiv in the throat of Father Hawkin.

People acquainted with my investigative career sometimes ask, "What
was your first case?" To which I invariably reply, "A 1986 Haut Brion." Ac-

tually, my first Discreet Inquiry that involved criminal behavior turned out to be a debacle because I hadn't yet learned that in addition to lust, we all have murder in our hearts—or if not murder, at least larceny.

So now I could easily come up with a Cast of Characters who might have put down Silas Hawkin, including wife, daughter, maid, gallery agent, and any of his clients. But, as in any homicide investigation, the prime question was *Cui bono?* Or who benefited from the artist's death?

When I arrived at the Villa Bile the studio building had already been festooned with crime scene tape. The bricked driveway was crowded with official vehicles including an ambulance, indicating they had not yet removed what Al Rogoff enjoys referring to as the corpus delicious.

There was a uniformed officer standing guard at the studio door, inspecting the heavens and dreaming, no doubt, of Madonna.

"Archy McNally," I reported to this stalwart. "Sergeant Rogoff asked me to come over."

"Yeah?" he said, not very interested. "You stay here and I'll go see."

I waited patiently, and in a few minutes the sergeant himself came trundling out, a cold cigar jutting from his meaty face. Al is built like an M1-A1 tank, and when he moves I always expect to hear the clanking of treads.

"What were you doing here this morning?" he demanded, wasting no time on preliminaries.

"Good evening, Al," I said.

"Good evening," he said. "What were you doing here this morning? The maid, wife, and daughter don't know—or maybe they do and aren't saying."

"I'm doing a credit check on a man Hawkin knew," I said. "I stopped by to get his opinion on the subject."

"And who is the subject?"

I had calculated how much I could tell him and how much, in good conscience, I could withhold.

"Hector Johnson," I told him. "The father of one of the late artist's customers."

"And why are you doing a credit check on him?"

"At the request of a client of McNally and Son."

"What client?"

"Nope," I said. "Unethical. Confidentiality."

He looked at me. "You're no lawyer and you know it."

"But I represent my father who *is* an attorney," I pointed out. "And I can't divulge the information you request without his permission."

"Son," Al said heavily, "you've got more crap than a Christmas goose. All right, I won't push it—for now. Let's go up."

We entered through that oak and etched glass door. I glanced into the ground floor area. Mrs. Louise Hawkin was slumped at one end of a sailcloth-covered couch and Marcia Hawkin was at the other end, both as far apart as ever. We tramped up the cast-iron staircase and walked into the studio. The techs were busy.

Rogoff stopped me. "Wife was out playing bridge. Daughter went to a movie. They say. Silas didn't go over to the main house for dinner, but everyone says that wasn't unusual. When his work was going good he hated to stop. Finally, around nine o'clock, the maid called him to ask if he was coming over to eat or if he wanted her to bring him a plate. No answer. But she could see the lights on up here. So she came over and found him. Let's go take a look."

He was lying supine, naked on that tattered sleigh bed. His eyes were still open. The knife was still in his throat. An assistant from the ME's office was fussing over him. I knew the man. Thomas Bunion. One of the few people I've ever met who are simultaneously cantankerous and timid.

I stared down at the remains of Silas Hawkin. There was an ocean of blood. An *ocean*. I am not a total stranger to violent death and thought I had learned to view a corpse with some dispassion, without needing to scurry away and upchuck in private. But I admit I was spooked by the sight of the murdered artist. So pale. For some reason his beard looked fake, as if it had been spirit-gummed to his face.

A wooden handle protruded from his neck.

"It looks like a palette knife," I said, trying to keep my voice steady.

"Uh-huh," Rogoff said. "We already figured that."

"But a palette knife doesn't have a cutting edge," I said. "And the blade is usually thin and pliable, something like a spatula. It's difficult to believe it was driven in so deeply and killed him."

"Well, it did," Bunion said crossly. "Looks like an artery was severed, but we won't know for sure until we get him on a slab. Thin blade or not, it was a lucky hit."

"Not for Silas," Al said.

"Poor devil," I muttered, turned away, and took a deep breath.

The sergeant inspected me. "Want to go outside, Archy?" he asked quietly.

"No, I'm fine," I told him. "But thanks." I looked around the studio. A plainclothesman was seated behind the decrepit desk, slowly turning pages of the ledger Si had slammed shut when I visited him that morning.

"What is he doing?" I asked.

Rogoff answered: "Hawkin may have been a nutsy artist, but he was a helluva businessman. He kept a record of every painting he did: date started, date finished, and disposition. If it was sold, he wrote down the size of the painting, name and address of the buyer, and the price paid. What we'll do is check his ledger against those finished works stacked against the wall and see if anything is missing."

"That makes sense," I said, but then I thought about it. "Al, are you figuring Hawkin was sleeping naked on that ugly bed and a burglar broke in to grab something he could fence? Then the artist wakes up and the crook grabs the nearest deadly weapon, a palette knife, and shoves it into the victim's throat to keep him quiet?"

He shrugged. "The wife and daughter were away. The maid was in the kitchen at the far side of the maid house with her radio going full blast. She couldn't have heard or seen an intruder. The door to the studio building was unlocked. It could have been a grab-and-run scumbag. Maybe a junkie."

"Do you really believe that?" I asked him.

"No," he said.

We went downstairs together. "Excuse me a moment," I said to the sergeant. I went over to the couch where wife and daughter were still sitting, isolated from each other. "May I express my sympathy and my deepest sorrow at this horrible tragedy," I said. It came out more floridly than I had intended.

Only Mrs. Louise Hawkin looked up. "Thank you," she said faintly.

Al and I moved outside. He used a wooden kitchen match to light his cold cigar and I borrowed the flame for my third cigarette of the day, resolving it would be the last.

Rogoff jerked a thumb over his shoulder at the ground floor of the studio building. "Not much love lost there," he said.

"No," I agreed, "not much. It was a sex scene, wasn't it, Al?"

He nodded. "That's the way I see it. The guy's in bed with someone, woman or man. There's an argument. She or he grabs up the nearest tool, the palette knife. I think it was a spur-of-the-moment thing. Not planned. They started out making love and then things went sour."

"Where do you go from here?"

"Check his inventory of paintings. Check the alibis of wife, daughter, maid, agent, clients, friends, enemies, and everyone connected with him."

"When did it happen—do you know that?"

"Tom Bunion figures it was about an hour before we got the squeal. That would put the time of death around nine o'clock, give or take."

"I was home," I told him. "Upstairs in my rooms. I had just talked with my father in his study."

"We'll check it out," he said with ponderous good humor. Then, suddenly serious, he added, "You got any wild ideas?"

"Not at the moment," I said. "Except that it must have required a great deal of strength to drive a blunt blade into Hawkin's throat. That would suggest a male assailant."

"Yeah," the sergeant said. "Or a furious woman."

"One never knows, do one?"

"There you go again," he said.

I returned home that night to find the house darkened except for the bulb burning over the rear entrance. I went directly to my quarters and finished that marc I had started aeons ago. Also my fourth English Oval. Then I went to bed hoping I wouldn't have nightmares involving palette knives and oceans of blood. I didn't. Instead I had a dotty dream about Zasu Pitts. Don't ask me why.

Chapter 4

I glanced at local newspapers the next morning and watched a few TV news programs. I learned nothing about the homicide I didn't already know.

But after reading the obits on Silas Hawkin, I was surprised to discover that Louise was his third wife, and Marcia his daughter by his first. She was his only child. Wife No. 1 had died of cancer. Divorce had ended Marriage No. 2.

I was even more startled to read of the professional career of the artist. He had studied at prestigious academics in New York and Paris. His work was owned and exhibited by several museums. He had been honored with awards from artists' guilds. In other words, the man had been far from a hack. I had underestimated his talents because I thought him a dunce. But then the creative juices have no relation to intelligence, personality, or character, do they?

Finally, a little before noon, I decided I needed a change of subject and a change of venue. So I determined to wheel down to Fort Lauderdale and have a chat with Shirley Feebling, the young woman who was causing Chauncey Wilson Smythe-Hersforth to suffer an acute attack of the fantods.

In my innocence it never occurred to me the two investigations might be connected. But as A. Pope remarked, "Fools rush in . . ." Right on, Alex!

Less than two hours later I was in a mini-mall north of Ft. Liquordale, staring with some bemusement at a large sign that advertised in block letters: TOPLESS CAR WASH. And below, in a chaste script: "No touching allowed." The activities within were hidden from prurient passers-by by a canvas curtain slit down the middle. Customers' cars were driven through the curtain to the interior, where vehicles and drivers were presumably rejuvenated.

I decided my flag-red Miata convertible would be abashed by such intimate attention, so I parked nearby and returned on foot to push my way through the slit curtain. I was confronted by a woolly mammoth, who appeared to be either the manager or a hired sentinel assigned to halt sightseers who didn't arrive on wheels.

"I'd like to speak to Miss Shirley Feebling, please," I said.

"Yeah?" he said belligerently. "Who're you?"

"Andrew Jackson," I said, proffering a twenty-dollar bill. "Here is my business card."

"Oh yeah," he said, grabbing it. "I thought I recognized you. She's over there washing down the Tuchas."

I turned to look. "Taurus," I said.

"Whatever," he said, shrugging.

I was a bit taken aback by my first sight of Ms. Feebling. I suppose I had expected a brazen hussy and instead I saw a small, demure brunet who looked rather sweet and vulnerable. There was a waifish innocence about her that made her costume even more outré. She was wearing the bottom section of a pink thong bikini, and she was indeed topless.

It would be indelicate to describe those gifts that qualified her for employment in a topless car wash. Suffice to say that she was well-qualified.

I waited until she finished wiping the Taurus dry and had been handed what appeared to be a generous tip by the pop-eyed driver. Then I approached and offered her my business card, a legitimate one this time.

"My name is Archibald McNally," I said with a restrained 100-watt smile. "My law firm represents Mr. Smythe-Hersforth. I was hoping to have a friendly talk with you so that we might arrive at some mutually beneficial solution of your misunderstanding with our client."

"There's no misunderstanding," she said, inspecting my card. "Chauncey said he'd marry me, and I've got the letters to prove it."

"Of course," I said, "but I hope you'll be willing to discuss it. I drove down from Palm Beach specifically to meet you and learn your side of this disagreement. Could we go somewhere reasonably private where we can chat? I would be more than willing to recompense you or your employer for the time you are absent from work."

She looked up at me. "Will you buy me a pizza?" she asked.

"Delighted," I told her.

"Then I'll ask Jake," she said. She went over to the woolly mammoth, talked a moment, then came back. "He wants fifty for an hour. Okay?"

"Certainly," I said, imagining my father's reaction when he saw this item on my expense account.

"That's neat," she said, and her smile sparkled. "I'll go get dressed. Just take a minute."

She went through an unmarked door that I presumed led to a dressing room, or rather an undressing room. I thought she would don a voluminous coverup, but when she reappeared she had added only a T-shirt that had PEACE printed on the front, an affirmation to which I heartily subscribed. But unfortunately—or fortunately, depending on the state of one's hormones—the T-shirt appeared to be sodden, and it clung. Lucky T-shirt.

"The pizza joint is just two doors away," she said. "All us girls go there. The owner don't mind as long as our boobs are covered."

A few moments later we were seated in the pizza joint, a fancy palace with real Formica-topped tables and real paper lace doilies under the plates. We decided we would share a Ponderosa Delight, which, the menu claimed, came "with everything." Shirley ordered a Diet Cherry Coke. I asked for a Pepsi since a 1982 Mumm's Cordon Rouge was not available.

"Miss Feebling—" I started, but she interrupted.

"You can call me Shirl," she said. "Everyone in the world calls me Shirl."

"And so shall I," I said, "if you'll call me Archy. Shirl, I know that Chauncey said he loved you, but people do fall out of love, you know."

"I haven't," she promptly replied. "I still love him and want to marry him like he promised in his letters. He's such a wonderful guy."

I was about to ask if she didn't find CW somewhat dim. But I refrained, reflecting that Shirley herself might be somewhat dim and had found a soul mate in the Chinless Wonder.

"Shirl," I said, "you seem to me a very sensitive and intelligent young lady."

"Thank you, sir," she said coyly.

"And I am sure you want only the best for yourself—and for Chauncey, too, of course. He has informed you that he wishes to wed another?"

She nodded.

"I know you want him to be happy," I pleaded, "even though it might mean your own unhappiness. But a generous cash settlement would help you endure a temporary sorrow."

"Oh, I don't want any money," she said brightly. "I just want to marry Chauncey."

"Shirl, it's impossible for me to believe that a young lady of your outstanding attributes hasn't had and doesn't have the opportunity to marry any of a dozen eager young men."

"Oh sure, I've had the chance," she said, almost dreamily. "But no one like Chauncey."

That I could believe. But then our Ponderosa Delight and drinks were served, and I postponed further attempts to convince her to reach an equitable compromise.

She was starting on her second wedge of pizza when I noted she was casting furtive glances over my shoulder.

"Something wrong?" I asked.

She leaned forward across the table to speak in a low voice. "There's a man over there who keeps staring at me."

"Quite understandable," I said cheerily. "You're worth staring at, Shirl, and I'm sure you're aware of it."

"But I don't like the way he keeps smiling with a smirky grin. Like he knows something secret about me."

"Have you ever seen him before?"

"No, I'm sure I haven't."

"Shall I go over and ask him to stop smirking at you?"

"Oh no," she said quickly, "don't do that. I don't want to cause no trouble."

We finished the pizza, and I tried again to persuade her to accept cash in return for CW's mash notes. But she was adamant; she wanted only to marry the man as he had promised, not once but many times, and if he reneged she would have no choice but to make his letters public.

She was explaining all this, determinedly and with some passion, when she suddenly broke off and said, "Here he comes."

A man halted alongside our table. I looked up to see a tall, saturnine bloke in raw black silk with a white Izod. He stared down at my companion, and I could agree with what she had said: It *was* a smirky grin. He didn't even glance at me.

"Hiya, Shirl," he said in a raspy baritone. "Having a good time?"

Then he sauntered away, paid his bill at the front counter, and went outside. I noted that he had a profile like a cleaver. I watched him get into a gunmetal Cadillac de Ville and pull away. I turned back to Shirley.

"You don't know him?" I asked.

She shook her head.

"He knew your name."

"I don't know how," she said, obviously troubled.

"Perhaps he was a customer," I suggested.

"No," she insisted. "I'd have remembered. I don't like his looks. He scares me."

"Nothing to be scared about," I assured her. "I doubt if you'll ever see him again."

But I couldn't comfort her. Her bouncy mood had vanished; she seemed subdued. "Listen," she said finally, "I've got to get to work."

I paid our tab and walked her back. I gave her fifty dollars, wondering how much would go to Jake and how much she'd be allowed to keep.

"Shirl," I said, "it's been a pleasure meeting you. I'll relay what you've told me to our client. But I still hope a mutually satisfactory solution to this impasse can be arranged."

"Sure it can," she said, "if he marries me."

"Uh-huh," I said. "May I come back and talk to you again if it proves necessary?"

"Of course," she said. Then: "You're nice," she added, and stretched up to kiss my cheek. "Thanks for the pizza."

She marched through the slit canvas curtain, providing me with a final glimpse of her thong bikini, also called a shoestring bikini in South Florida, and sometimes a flosser.

I drove back to Palm Beach in a reflective mood. It had not been a totally profitless trip, although CW might think so. But I had, at least to my own satisfaction, learned something about Shirley Feebling and could guess at what might be motivating her demands. There were three possibilities, none of which would bring a gleeful smile to the puss of our distraught client.

1. My discussion with Shirl had been the opening round of what would prove to be lengthy and difficult negotiations. In other words, the lady was hanging tough in order to up the ante.

2. She was shrewd enough to forgo an immediate cash settlement, no matter how generous, in hopes of marrying the Chinless Wonder and becoming the wife of a man who would inherit millions when his mommy passed to that bourn from which no traveler returns.

3. And this was the most disquieting: Shirley Feebling was totally sincere and honest. She really did love the simp, wanted to marry him, and was determined to become a loving helpmate. His present or potential wealth had no influence on her decision.

Very disturbing. I don't pretend to understand True Love. I don't know what it is or how it works. Oh, I know all about affection, attachment, admiration—stuff like that. But True Love stumps me. I am not only ignorant of its nature but suspicious of its effects because whenever I have observed it in others, it has always seemed to me infernally *serious*. And since my life has been sedulously devoted to triviality, I find the seriousness of True Love to be a fatal flaw.

Still, although I know no more about TL than I do about Babylonian cuneiform, I cannot ignore the testimony of poets and Tin Pan Alley tunesmiths. It is obvious that True Love *does* exist, and I reckoned Ms. Feebling might very well be infected with a particularly virulent strain. If so, it did not bode well for the Chinless Wonder.

Which led me to musing about his intended fiancée, Theodosia Johnson, and wondering if my own reactions to that stellar lady might be True Love or merely gonadal twinges. I just didn't know and decided that only another personal meeting with the radiant Theo might provide the answer.

I was then approaching South Palm Beach and on a sudden whim (*the* guiding principle in my life) resolved to stop at the Hawkin residence. You may ask, and justly so, what on earth I thought I was doing since I was not part of the official homicide investigation and my assistance had not been requested.

The answer to your question is simple: I am nosy. I admit it and don't give a tinker's damn—or dam, depending on your erudition—who knows it. Also, there were several puzzling aspects about the murder that piqued my curiosity. I could have asked Sgt. Al Rogoff, of course, but would he have told me? Fat chance.

Al is a closemouthed gent, even when he doesn't have to be. He and I worked several cases together in the past, to our mutual benefit, but he never tells me *everything* he knows any more than I Reveal All to him. I think that in addition to our friendship we keep the scimitar of competitiveness keenly honed, sensing that it contributes to our success.

The crime scene tape still surrounded the studio building, and there was a sole uniformed officer on guard. But the main house appeared to be open to all comers. I rang the chimes, expecting they would be answered by Mrs. Jane Folsby, the live-in servant I hoped to question.

And she indeed opened the door, recognized me, and smiled warmly. "Good afternoon, Mr. McNally," she said. "It's good to see you again."

"And it's a pleasure to see you, Mrs. Folsby," I said. "I can imagine what you've been going through. You have my sympathy, I assure you. What a shock it must have been."

She stood aside to allow me to enter, then closed the door.

"It *was* a shock," she said in a low voice. "I found him, you know."

"So I heard. A horrifying experience."

She sighed deeply. "He had his faults," she said, "but don't we all? But he wasn't a mean man, and no one should have to die like that."

"No," I agreed, "no one should. Mrs. Folsby, I'd like to ask you a few questions. But first I want you to know I am not part of the police investigation, and it's entirely up to you whether or not you choose to answer."

She looked at me steadily. "Questions about the murder?"

"Yes," I said. "That and other things."

"Why do you want to ask?"

"Because your answers possibly, just possibly, might have some bearing on a private inquiry I am making: a credit check on a person Mr. Hawkin knew."

She considered a long time. "Very well," she said finally, "you ask your questions and then I'll decide whether or not to answer them."

"Excellent," I said. "Sergeant Rogoff, a friend of mine, told me you went to the studio after you phoned your employer and received no reply. Is that correct?"

She nodded. "The wife and daughter were out, and he hadn't come over for dinner. So I called to ask if he wanted me to bring him a plate. I did that sometimes when he was working late. He didn't answer, but I could see the studio lights were on, and I got concerned."

"Of course."

"So I went over to see if everything was all right. To tell you the truth, I thought maybe he had fallen asleep. Or passed out."

"Passed out? He was a heavy drinker?"

"He did his share," she said wryly. "Rum, mostly."

"Uh-huh. Tell me this if you will, Mrs. Folsby, when you entered the studio, did you see anything that might lead you to believe that he had been working? For instance, was there an unfinished painting on one of his easels?"

She thought a moment. "No," she said, "there was nothing on the big easel. That was the one he liked to use for his portraits. And nothing on the two smaller ones either."

I was disappointed. "So you saw absolutely no evidence that he had been working in the hours prior to his death?"

She closed her eyes briefly as if trying to recall details of that frightful scene. "Now that you mention it," she said hesitantly, "there was something odd. On the taboret next to the big easel was Mr. Hawkin's palette and the paints on it were still wet. I could see them glistening under the lights. Also, there was a long-handled brush alongside the palette, and that had wet paint, a kind of creamy crimson, on the bristles. That wasn't like him at all because he was very finicky about cleaning his brushes and palette when he wasn't working."

"But you saw no evidence of what he might have been working on?"

She shook her head.

"Curious," I said, "but I suppose there's a very obvious explanation for it." (I didn't suppose anything of the sort, of course.) "Another question, Mrs. Folsby: When Mr. Hawkin was doing a portrait, did he ever allow anyone else in the studio other than the sitter?"

"Never," she said definitely. "He was very strict about that. He said the presence of an observer would distract the model and destroy his rapport with whomever he was painting."

"I expect most portrait artists feel that way. A final question, please. You know how people in Palm Beach love to gossip. I've heard rumors there was serious discord in the Hawkin family, an atmosphere of hostility in this house. Would you care to comment on that?"

"No," she said stonily.

I persisted. "You mean no discord or no, you don't wish to comment?"

"I don't wish to comment."

I admired her. There was loyalty up. I hoped there would be loyalty down.

"Perfectly understandable," I said, nodding, "and I wish to thank you for your patience and cooperation. You have been very helpful."

"I have?" she said, mildly surprised.

I bid her good-bye and left the house. Marcia Hawkin was coming up the walk carrying one of those miniature Tiffany's shopping bags. She saw me and stopped suddenly.

"What are you doing here?" she demanded.

"I stopped by for just a moment to express my sympathy to Mrs. Folsby on the death of your father."

She made a sound. I believe she intended it to be a sardonic laugh, but I thought it more a honk.

"My father was a goat," she said. "A *goat!*"

Then she strode into the house and slammed the door. The Villa Bile indeed.

I drove directly home, looking forward to an ocean swim that would slosh away, even temporarily, all the clotted human emotions I had dealt with that day. But it was not to be. I was just tugging on my new, shocking pink Speedo when my phone shrilled.

"What were you doing at the Hawkin place?" Sgt. Al Rogoff said in that gritty voice he uses when he's ready to chew nails.

I sighed. "Who squealed on me, Al? Mrs. Folsby? Marcia Hawkin?"

"Neither," he said. "That guard I parked outside the studio had orders to watch for visitors. He just reported seeing a guy wearing purple slacks and driving a maroon Miata. Who could that be but Monsieur Archibald McNally?"

"The slacks were lilac," I protested, "and the car is screaming red."

"What were you doing there?" he repeated. "Nosing around?"

"Of course," I said. "Any objections?"

"Not if you don't get in my way," he said. "Learn anything?"

"Al, is it trade-off time?"

"Run it by me first."

I related what Mrs. Folsby had told me: When she entered the scene of the crime she saw no painting on the easel but had noted wet pigments on Silas Hawkin's palette and brush.

Rogoff was silent a moment. "How do you figure it?" he asked finally.

"I don't," I said. "But it's intriguing, isn't it?"

"Your favorite word," he said grumpily. "You find things intriguing that I find a pain in the ass. If the guy was working on a painting before he was offed, where is it?"

"A puzzlement. Did you check Si's ledger? Is anything missing?"

He replied with a question of his own. "That guy you said you were doing a credit check on, Hector Johnson, is he related to Theodosia Johnson?"

"Her father."

"Uh-huh. Well, she's in the ledger. Hawkin did an oil portrait of her."

"I know, Al. I saw it at the Pristine Gallery. It may still be on display. Positively enchanting."

"Yeah? I'll have to go take a look. But the thing is—and I know you're going to find this intriguing—right after her portrait is listed in Hawkin's ledger another painting is noted. It's just called 'Untitled.' "

"That's odd."

"Not half so odd as the fact that we can't find it. All the other paintings in the studio have titles and are recorded in the ledger. The widow, the daughter, and the maid say they know nothing about 'Untitled,' don't know what it is, never heard Hawkin mention a word about it."

"And now you're guessing the same thing I'm guessing, aren't you, sergeant? That 'Untitled' was the painting Si was working on before he was murdered."

"Could be," Rogoff said. "And the killer walked off with it. Listen, Archy, are you still checking out this Hector Johnson?"

"Oh yes."

"And his daughter, too?"

"Definitely."

"Have you met them?"

"I've met her briefly, but I haven't met Hector."

"Keep on it, will you?" Al said. "Maybe Silas told them something about that untitled painting."

"I'll be happy to ask," I said. "It gives me an excuse to see her again."

"Oh-ho. A winner, is she?"

"Divine is an understatement," I assured him. "I think I'm in love."

"So what else is new?" he said.

I finally got him off the phone after promising to report on my meeting with Theodosia and Hector Johnson. It was then too late for a dip in the Atlantic. So I peeled off my snazzy Speedo, showered, and dressed in time to attend the family cocktail hour and dinner.

I then retired to my one-man dormitory to bring my journal au courant with the day's events. After reading over what I had scribbled, I was dismayed to see how my initial inquiry into the trustworthiness of Theo Johnson appeared to be interacting with the investigation into the murder of Silas Hawkin.

I simply refused to believe that the beautiful Madam X could possibly be involved in that heinous crime. But then Lucrezia Borgia was hardly a gorgon, and neither was Lizzie Borden. It was all enough to make one ponder the advantages of celibacy.

Which I did, and finally decided there were none.

Chapter 5

A weekend intruded here, and a very welcome intrusion it was. For two sunspangled days I was able to enact my favorite role of blade-about-town. On Saturday morning I played tennis with Binky Watrous on his private court—and lost. I treated Connie Garcia to lunch at the Pelican Club, challenged her to a game of darts—and lost. In the evening I played poker with a group of intemperate cronies—and lost.

I was more successful on Sunday. I spent most of the afternoon gamboling on the beach with Connie and a Frisbee, and demolishing a bottle of a chilled Soave I had never tried before. Tangy is the word. Then we picked up two slabs of ribs barbecued with a Cajun sauce and returned to Connie's digs with a cold six-pack of Heineken. A pleasant time was had by all. I was home and in bed by ten o'clock and asleep by 10:05, sunburned, slightly squiffed, exhausted, and oh so content.

I overslept on Monday morning, as usual, and found a deserted kitchen when I bounced downstairs. I fixed myself a mug of instant black, and built an interracial sandwich: ham on bagel.

I used the kitchen phone to call the office. I asked Mrs. Trelawney if the honcho could spare me a few moments that morning. She put me on hold, and I listened to wallpaper music a few minutes while she went to check. She returned to tell me His Majesty would grant me ten minutes at precisely eleven o'clock.

"Thank you, Mrs. T.," I said. "Tell me, have you ever cooked a goose—or vice versa?"

"Why, no," she said. "But I once took a tramp in the woods."

She hung up cackling, and I trotted out to my chariot, much refreshed by that silly exchange of ancient corn.

Twenty minutes later I was in my crypt at the McNally Building and lighted my first English Oval of the day, considering it a reward for having spent the entire weekend without a gasper. On my desk was a sheaf of faxed replies to my inquiries to national credit agencies regarding the financial status of Theodosia and Hector Johnson.

I read them all slowly and carefully, and, to put it succinctly, my flabber was gasted. It was not that they contained derogatory information about the Johnsons; they contained no information at all.

If those reports were to be believed, Theo and Hector had never had a credit card, never had a charge account, never bought anything on time, never made a loan or had a mortgage, never purchased anything from a mail order catalogue, never received a government check for whatever reason, had no insurance, owned no assets such as real estate, stocks, bonds, or other securities, and had never filed a tax return.

Improbable, would you say? Nay, dear reader. Utterly impossible! In our society even a toddler of three has already left a paper trail, carefully recorded on a computer somewhere. I refused to believe that two adults had no financial background whatsoever. Even if they scrupulously paid cash for all their purchases, what was the source of the cash and why was there no mention of bank accounts, checking and savings, and no record of having paid federal, state, and local taxes?

They had names and Social Security numbers. And that's all their dossiers revealed.

I tried to puzzle it out, resisting the urge to light another cigarette. The more I gnawed at it, the more ridiculous it seemed to me that the Johnsons could be totally without a financial history. There must be a logical explanation for it, but whatever it might be I could not imagine. I hoped my Palm Beach contacts would help solve the riddle.

It was then pushing eleven o'clock, and I rushed upstairs to my father's office, for if I was even one minute late he was quite capable of canceling the appointment.

Prescott McNally, Esq., was standing solidly planted before his antique rolltop desk, and in his three-button, double-breasted suit of nubby cheviot, looking somewhat of a relic himself. He cast a baleful glance at my awning-striped seersucker jacket and didn't invite me to be seated.

I recited a condensed account of my interview with Shirley Feebling in Fort Lauderdale and finished by suggesting the lady might be sincere in professing love for Chauncey Wilson Smythe-Hersforth.

"She seemed totally uninterested in a cash settlement, sir," I remarked.

"Nonsense," father said sharply. "Did you make a specific offer?"

"No, I did not."

"That was a mistake, Archy," he said. "The mention of dollars would have concentrated her mind wonderfully. I'm afraid the lady bamboozled you. Her protestations of love were merely a bargaining ploy. And even if she is smitten, as you seem to believe, how can she possibly profit from an unrequited love? She can't force that young fool to marry her, you know."

"No, sir, but she can carry out her threat to sell his letters to a tabloid."

"Don't be so certain of that," he admonished me. "I would have to research relevant law, but it might be claimed the letters are his property since he created them, and if so ruled, the sale and publication could be legally enjoined. But before we go to that trouble, I suggest you consult with Smythe-Hersforth. Obtain his approval of your returning to Fort Lauderdale and making a definite offer to this woman. I believe the proposal of an actual cash payment will persuade her to talk business."

I was doubtful but made no demur. "How much do you think we should offer?"

He went into his mulling trance, and I waited patiently for his decision.

"I reckon a thousand dollars would be adequate," he finally said.

I was startled. "Isn't that rather mingy, sir?"

"Of course it is," he said testily, "and I expect the woman will reject it immediately. But it will serve as an opening move to begin bargaining. It will require her to reveal what she believes she should receive, and eventually, I trust, an equitable compromise can be agreed upon. The important thing is to shift negotiations away from discussion of her alleged emotional injury to the realm of a hard cash settlement. Do you understand?"

"Yes, father, and I'll attempt to explain it to CW, though he is not the swiftest man in the world."

"When you speak to him you might also ascertain how high he is willing to go. Five thousand? Ten? Or more? The decision must be his. Now is there anything else?"

"Just one more thing," I said hastily. "I had occasion to speak to Mrs. Louise Hawkin prior to the death of her husband. She said a friend was seeking a divorce lawyer and asked if we might recommend someone."

Father stared at me. "Do you really believe she was asking on behalf of a friend?"

"No, sir."

"Nor do I. And now that Mrs. Hawkin is a widow I doubt very much that she will inquire again about a divorce attorney. Your ten minutes are up."

I returned to my broom closet, slumped behind my steel desk, and silently groused. I was frustrated by that conversation with the senior. I thought he was totally mistaken about Ms. Shirley Feebling—but then I had met the lady and he had not. I really didn't believe she would accept a cash settlement, no matter how generous.

Still, I had no wish to flaunt my father's advice. His experience had been so much more extensive than mine, I simply had to defer to his judgment. But I am, as you may have guessed, an incurable romantic, and I mournfully reflected that if mein papa was correct and Shirley accepted money in lieu of love, I would be horribly disappointed and possibly take up the lute to express my weltschmerz in musical form.

Meanwhile, I had a job to do and when duty calls, yrs. truly can never be accused of shlumpery. I called Information and obtained the phone number of Hector Johnson. I had prepared a scam that, I felt, included sufficient truth to convince the most worldly-wise pigeon.

"The Johnson residence," a man's voice answered. Deep and resonant. A very slight accent. Midwestern, I guessed.

"Mr. Hector Johnson, please," I said.

"Speaking. Who is this calling?"

"Mr. Johnson, my name is Archibald McNally, and I am associated with McNally and Son, a law firm located on Royal Palm Way. I had the pleasure of meeting your lovely daughter during a recent art exhibit at the Pristine Gallery."

"Ah, yes," he said. "I'm afraid Theo is busy at the moment."

"No, no," I said. "It is you I'd like to talk to. Mr. Johnson, I am assigned to the real estate section of McNally and Son, and we have a number of very attractive properties for sale or lease in the Palm Beach area. Rather than deluge you with brochures and listings, I am taking the liberty of calling to ask if you have any interest in a Palm Beach estate, either as a residence or an investment."

"Not right now, thank you," he said. "But quite possibly at some time in the near future."

"In that case," I said, continuing to act the role of a pushy real estate hustler, "could I meet with you personally and perhaps get some idea of what you might be looking for? We have properties that range in asking price from a half-million to twelve, with financing readily available, I assure you. They are located on the beachfront, inland, and with Waterway frontages. Rather than try to sell you a particular offering, I'd much rather learn what you prefer, either now or, as you say, in the near future."

"That makes sense," he said. "You say your name is Archibald McNally?"

"That's correct, sir. Everyone calls me Archy."

He laughed. "Don't complain. Everyone calls me Heck. Who put you on to me, Archy?"

"Lady Cynthia Horowitz suggested I call," I said boldly. "She was quite impressed by your contribution to her latest effort at civic beautification."

I was hoping he would be impressed, and he was. "I was happy to help," he said. "And if you're a friend of Lady Horowitz I'll be glad to meet with you. When would you care to make it?"

"At your convenience, sir."

There was a brief pause. Then: "Well, I have an appointment with a business associate at three this afternoon, but if you could come by at, say, two o'clock, we should be able to get to know each other in an hour's time. How does that sound?"

"Splendid," I said. "I'm looking forward to it, and I promise you, no high-powered sales pitch."

"I'll hold you to that," he said, laughing again. "See you at two, Archy."

"Thank you, Heck," I said.

He gave me his address, and we hung up. I sat a moment staring at the dead phone and thinking of what a personable guy he was, how he projected warmth, confidence, good humor. Some people sound like duds when their voices come over the wire. Hector Johnson sounded like a political candidate who is absolutely certain he's going to win.

My second phone call was to CW's office. His secretary informed me that Mr. Smythe-Hersforth had departed that morning for a bankers' convention in New Orleans and was not expected back until Thursday morning. I thanked her, grateful that I could postpone for three days another go-around with a man silly enough to certify a proposal of marriage in writing.

I had time to buzz home and change into a costume more befitting a sober, industrious, and sincere real estate agent. I bounced down to the kitchen for a spot of lunch and found Ursi Olson preparing a Florida bouillabaisse that was to be our dinner that evening. But she paused long enough to make me an open sandwich of Norwegian brisling sardines with slices of beefsteak tomato and shavings of red onion on her home-baked sour rye. Life *can* be beautiful.

I found the Johnsons' condo to be on ground level and smallish. I figured if you stood on a chair and peered out the kitchen window to your left you might catch a glimpse of Lake Worth. But it was located in a decent neighborhood, the landscaping was well-groomed, and if the building didn't shout big bucks, there was really nothing to apologize for.

What suddenly made me think it a place of magical charm was that Theodosia Johnson opened the door when I rang, and my knees buckled. She gave me a smile as inflammatory as a nuclear meltdown, and I was immediately convinced that True Love did exist and I was its latest willing victim.

I saw her clothed in golden gossamer, though actually she was wearing white linen shorts and a man's rugby shirt the same color as her sky-blue eyes. Her long chestnut hair was bound up in a braid and piled atop her head. No queen ever wore a lovelier crown.

She addressed me as Archy, and I was so grateful I wanted to roll on my back on the floor and beg to have my stomach scratched. But instead I followed her through a short foyer to the living room, where she invited me to be seated and asked if I'd care for a drink.

My tongue seemed swollen to unmanageable proportions, and all I could do was shake my head. I simply could not stop staring at her. I know the room was decorated and contained furniture, but don't ask me to describe it; I only had eyes for Madam X, and the rest of the universe faded away.

"You heard about Si Hawkin?" she asked sorrowfully.

I nodded. "Dreadful," I said, not believing that croaky voice was mine.

"I wept for hours," she said. "He was *such* a good friend. And a major talent, don't you think?"

"Major," I repeated, wondering how I could stop my head from bobbing up and down like one of those crazy little birds that sips water perpetually from a glass.

"It must have been awful for his family," she went on.

She was trying her best to make conversation, poor dear, but I was so overwhelmed by her beauty that I could contribute nothing. I, Archy McNally, sometimes known to his confreres as Mighty Mouth, sat there like a perfect clod, and if my jaw was agape I wouldn't have been a bit surprised.

"Father will be along in a minute," Theo said, "and then I'll leave you two alone to talk business."

The possibility of her disappearing from view shocked me back to volubility. "Please don't do that," I beseeched. "I hope to speak to your father about your purchasing or leasing another property, and I'd be happy to hear your requirements as well as his. It's been my experience that women are much more knowledgeable than men in the planning or selection of a livable home."

"I do have some very definite ideas about what I'd like to have," she said. "For instance, daddy knows absolutely nothing about gardens."

I wasn't so stunned by her loveliness that I didn't pick up on that. I thought it exceedingly odd that a man who claimed to be an expert on orchids—according to my mother—would know absolutely nothing about gardens. Possible but highly unlikely.

Theo was speaking of her dream of someday having a home with a private gym when a beefy, thick-necked linebacker came striding energetically into the room.

"Heck Johnson," he shouted, thrusting out his hand.

"Archy McNally," I said, rising to my feet and shaking that big paw. His grip wasn't exactly a bone-crusher, but you knew it was there.

"What's this?" he demanded, looking about. "No drinks? Theo, you're neglecting your duties as a hostess."

"I did ask, dad, but Archy turned me down." She smiled. She had one dimple. Left cheek. Oh, lord! I was a goner.

"Nonsense," he said, and turned to me. "I'm having a vodka gimlet. Theo gets it just right. How about it?"

"Thank you, Heck, I will."

"Of course," he said. "Theo, be a darling and mix two of your specials."

"Three," she said, and left the room.

He waved me back to my wicker armchair and sat in the middle of a couch facing me. He crossed his legs and carefully adjusted the crease in his trousers.

I fancy myself something of a minor league Beau Brummell, but Hector Johnson belonged in the Hall of Fame. He was wearing a trig suit of lightweight taupe wool, a shirt striped in pale lavender with French cuffs, and a wide-spread white collar closed with a knitted black silk cravat tied in a Windsor knot. A fashion plate!

I guessed him to be about sixty, but his age was difficult to estimate since it was obvious that he was no stranger to facials, manicures, and massages. What was most impressive was his air of assurance. This was a man, I decided, who never had a doubt in the world. It was rather daunting to a goof like me whose theme song could be "What's It All About, Archy?"

We chatted casually for a few minutes and, without my asking, he remarked that he was semi-retired and that he and his daughter were so impressed by Palm Beach they were determined to make it their permanent home.

"Y'see, Archy," he said, "we've lived all over the world. As a mining engineer I was forced to travel a great deal, and I think we're both ready to settle down."

I nodded understandingly, mentally adding mining engineer to his growing list of former occupations.

Our conversation was interrupted when Theo returned with our drinks. Hector had been exactly right; she *did* have a way with a gimlet: not too tart, not too heavy on the vodka, and with a delightful slice of fresh lime in each glass.

We toasted each other, sipped appreciatively and, again without my asking, he began to describe the type of dwelling he and his daughter would like to inhabit.

"On Ocean Boulevard," he said definitely, "or close to it. A view of the sea, if possible, or at least a short stroll to the beach. Three bedrooms at a minimum. Florida room, of course. A pool is not necessary, but I would like a nice piece of lawn, front and back. Wouldn't you say, Theo?"

"Room for a gazebo," she replied, almost dreamily. "A flower garden. Perhaps a small greenhouse. My private gym, of course. And an enormous kitchen."

Hector laughed. "Perfection is not for this world, sweet," he said, "but perhaps we can find a reasonable facsimile."

"I'm sure you can," I said. "Let me go through our listings, talk to colleagues, and bring you a very limited selection for your consideration."

"We're not ready to buy," he said. "I warned you about that."

"Of course," I said. "I understand completely. It sometimes takes a year, or even more, of viewing, evaluating, and finally making a decision. After all, you're choosing a home you'll probably live in for the rest of your lives, and you want it to be *right*. Believe me, I'm not going to pressure you. I have one client who's been debating a final choice for almost three years."

"You're a very patient man, Archy," Theo said.

"Yes," I agreed, "I am."

"Are you an attorney?" Heck asked suddenly.

"No, I am not," I said. "But my father is. His law firm represents some of the most reputable people in Palm Beach." (And a few disreputable, I was tempted to add.) "I do hope you'll ask friends and neighbors about McNally and Son. We're proud of our reputation."

They smiled at me encouragingly. They were seated close together on the couch, a rather hideous number covered with flowered cretonne. I could see little resemblance between father and daughter, and I wanted to ask about the missing Mrs. Johnson but naturally I didn't. Not quite comme il faut, y'know.

Our glasses were almost empty when I saw Hector peek at his watch. I would have expected it to be a gold Rolex, but from where I sat it appeared to be an old, clunky digital, which surprised me.

I finished my drink and rose. "I know you have another appointment, Heck," I said, "and I don't want to take up more of your time. Thank you for seeing me and for your kind hospitality. The gimlet was splendid!"

"Our pleasure, Archy," he said, standing. "When you have something special you think we should see, do give us a call."

"I'll certainly do that," I said. "And thank you again."

"I'll walk you to your car," Theo said, and I could have screamed with delight.

We went outside, she preceding me, and I saw how her tanned legs gleamed in the sunlight. As an experienced aesthetician I notice such things.

She laughed when she saw my red Miata. "What a little beauty!" she said.

"Isn't it?" I said, happy that she approved of my wheels. "They're producing new models in black and British racing green. I may trade it in."

"Don't you dare," she said, patting the hood. "This one is *you*. Where do you live, Archy?"

"Ocean Boulevard. The Atlantic is practically lapping at our doorstep."

"How wonderful," she said. "I'd love to see your home."

"Of course," I said, almost spluttering with pleasure. "Whenever you like." I handed her a business card. "Do give me a call."

"I shall," she said, looking at me thoughtfully. "Perhaps we could make an afternoon of it. There are so many places in the Palm Beach area I'd love to see and haven't had the chance."

"I'd be happy to serve as your cicerone," I said warmly. "Perhaps we might start with lunch."

"That *would* be fun," she said.

The thought then occurred to me that maybe the Chinless Wonder was bonkers in describing Theodosia as his soon-to-be fiancée. That might be his fantasy, but the way this Lorelei was coming on, it certainly didn't seem to be hers.

"Theo," I said, "there is something I'd like to ask and I do hope it won't upset you. I'm acquainted with Silas Hawkin's widow and daughter, and in his ledger they found a notation of a painting he had been working on at the time of his death. It's listed merely as 'Untitled.' They can't find the painting and have no idea what the subject matter might be. They requested I ask you if Si ever discussed it while he was doing your portrait."

She shook her head. "No, Si never mentioned anything else he was working on. I have no idea what 'Untitled' might be."

"I didn't think you would," I assured her, "but I promised to ask. Thank you so much for welcoming me to your home. I do appreciate it."

"I'm looking forward to that lunch," she said lightly.

She shook my hand, turned, and walked back to her condo. I watched her stroll away. An entrancing sight.

I sat a moment on the hot cushions of the Miata, trying to cool off and calm down. Madam X was fascinating, no doubt about it.

I had confused impressions of both the Johnsons. Despite his air of surety Hector struck me as the type of man who constantly has to reassure himself by exaggerating his wealth, accomplishments, and prospects. Not exactly bragging, you understand, but just keeping his illusions about himself intact.

As for Theo, I ruefully admitted I may have made an initial error by equating her beauty with sweetness, purity, modesty, innocence—all that swell stuff. Now I began to wonder if there might not be a darker side to her nature, including unbridled hedonism, willfulness, cold ambition, and other attitudes that added up to a self-centered young lady with an eye out for the main chance.

Maybe, just maybe, the suspicions of crabby Mrs. Gertrude Smythe-Hersforth were justified.

Musing on the complexities of human temperament I started up the Miata and headed slowly out of the parking area. As I did, another car entered. I glanced, drove on a few yards, stopped, and made a great show of lighting a cigarette while I watched in the rearview mirror.

The newcomer stopped in front of the Johnsons' town house. The driver alighted, rang the doorbell, and was immediately admitted. Apparently Hector's expected business associate.

The car he was driving was a gunmetal Cadillac de Ville. And he was a saturnine bloke with a profile like a cleaver. Undoubtedly the gink who had spoken so familiarly to Shirley Feebling in Fort Lauderdale.

I sat there, shaken, and looked up to the heavens for revelation.

Nothing.

I returned to the McNally Building and found on my desk a message requesting that I call Sgt. Rogoff immediately. I did, finding him at police headquarters, an edifice the sergeant called the Palace but which looks to me as if it should be in the hills overlooking the Cote d'Azur.

"What's cooking, Al?" I asked.

"Me," he replied. "Murphy's Law is in action. Whatever can go wrong *is* going wrong."

"Laddy," I said, "you do sound gloomy."

"I am gloomy," he said. "It's this Hawkin kill. You know if you don't break a homicide in the first forty-eight hours, the clearance rate drops like a stone. And I'm no closer to figuring it out than I was when the squeal came in. Listen, did you talk to the Johnsons?"

"About an hour ago. I didn't ask Hector, but Theodosia says she knows nothing about a Hawkin painting called 'Untitled.' "

He sighed. "Another long shot that ran out of the money. Archy, you've spoken to the widow and daughter a couple of times. Do you get the feeling there's hostility there?"

"You better believe it."

"Got any idea what it's all about?"

"Nope," I said. "I even asked Mrs. Folsby, the maid, but she's not talking."

"Yeah," he said, "I struck out with her, too. Well, it probably has nothing to do with Silas getting iced. Keep in touch, pal."

"Al, before you hang up," I said hastily, "did Hawkin have sex just before he died?"

"Why do you ask that?"

"Idle curiosity."

"As a matter of fact he did. Satisfied?"

"No," I said, "but I hope he was."

After the luscious bouillabaisse that evening, I scampered up to my cave to record the day's happenings in my journal. There was a lot to set down, but I found myself getting all bollixed up when it came to analyzing Theo Johnson's behavior and how it affected your humble servant.

Despite my revised opinion of her—I now believed her to be as much sinner as saint—she continued to quicken me, and probably for that very reason. Obviously she was not an ingenue but I could not begin to unravel her mysteries. Lolly Spindrift's title for her, Madam X, was perfect.

I had the impression that she thought me a lightweight. That was all right. I can be a bubblehead, sometimes naturally and sometimes deliberately when I mean to profit by it. I was content to have Theo consider me a twit. My reputation for deviousness is not totally undeserved.

All this brooding about Another Woman gave me a slight attack of the guilts, and so I phoned Connie Garcia. She sounded happy to hear from me.

"Connie," I said, "have you been trying to call me?"

"Why, no," she said, "I haven't."

"Well, my phone hasn't rung all evening, and I thought it might be you."

Silence.

Finally: "Archy," she said, "I think you need professional help."

We chatted casually of this and that, made a tentative dinner date for later in the week, and disconnected after mutual declarations of affection. My stirrings of culpability had been neatly assuaged.

Do you condemn me for infidelity? Might as well blame me because I lack wings and cannot fly. I mean it's all genetics, is it not? You examine any chap's DNA and it'll show that sooner or later he'll have athlete's foot and cheat on his mate. It's simply the nature of the beast.

Chapter 6

I had several extremely important tasks scheduled for Tuesday morning: get a haircut, visit my friendly periodontist for my quarterly scraping, and drop by my favorite men's boutique on Worth Avenue to see if they had anything new in the way of headgear. I am a hat freak, and that morning I was delighted to find and purchase a woven straw trilby. Cocked over one eye it gave me a dashing appearance—something like a Palermo pimp.

I eventually found my way back to the McNally Building, slowed by the lassitude that affects all citizens of South Florida in midsummer. Denizens of the north are fond of remarking, "It's not the heat, it's the humidity." In our semi-tropical paradise we prefer, "It's the heat *and* the humidity."

So I welcomed the return to my itsy-bitsy office where the air-conditioning was going full blast and the ambient temperature approximated that of Queen Maud Land in Antarctica.

Since the affair of the Chinless Wonder vs. Ms. Shirley Feebling was on temporary hold, I was free to concentrate on the investigation into the background and financial probity of Theodosia Johnson and her father. I spent a half-hour phoning my contacts at local banks, following up on my initial inquiries.

I had hoped that what I would learn might solve the riddle of those anorexic dossiers I had received from national credit agencies. But what I heard only deepened the mystery. Apparently a year ago Hector Johnson had opened a checking account at a Royal Palm Way bank with a cashier's check drawn on a bank in Troy, Mich. The identification offered had been a Michigan driver's license. He had submitted the names of two Fort Lauderdale residents as references. He had made no additional deposits, and his current balance was slightly less than $50,000.

I thought about that for a while and realized that if the Johnsons were hardly nudging poverty they soon might be if their level of spending continued and no additional funds became available. Perhaps that was the reason for Hector's business meeting with the cold-faced gent who had accosted Shirley Feebling in the pizza joint.

Another puzzle was why, with limited resources, the Johnsons had commissioned Silas Hawkin to do a portrait of Theo. Si had told me he had not yet billed for the painting, but according to Lolly Spindrift the artist charged thirty grand and up for portraits. Quite a hefty bite, wouldn't you say, from a bank balance of less than fifty?

Sighing, I donned my jacket and my new lid and ventured out again into the sauna enveloping the Palm Beach area. Walking slowly and trying to keep in the shade, I made my way to the Pristine Gallery on Worth Avenue. The portrait of Theodosia Johnson was prominently displayed in the front window with a card chastely lettered: *The Last Painting by Silas Hawkin*. Rather a macabre touch, wouldn't you say?

The gallery appeared empty when I entered, but a bell jangled merrily as the door opened, and Ivan Duvalnik, the corpulent owner, appeared from an inner room. I had met him when I purchased a charming watercolor of begonias in bloom as a Christmas present for my mother. Momsy had been delighted with the gift, and the painting now hung over the mantel in our second-floor sitting room.

"Mr. McNally," he said, holding out a plump hand. "A pleasure to see you again, sir."

"It's good to see you, Mr. Duvalnik," I said, briefly pressing his damp flipper. "I'm dreadfully sorry about Si Hawkin."

"He was my shining star," Ivan said dramatically. "I shall not see his like again."

"I notice you're still showing the portrait of Theo Johnson."

His mouth twitched. "An irritation," he said. "The painting has not yet been paid for. As a matter of fact, Si asked me to hold off billing for it. So now the painting is part of his estate, and I suppose I shall have to represent his widow. It's a valuable work."

"That I can believe," I said. "I'm surprised the Johnsons haven't claimed it."

He was mildly astonished. "The Johnsons?" he said. "But it isn't their legal property. The portrait was commissioned by Chauncey Smythe-Hersforth. I thought everyone knew that. He certainly made no secret of it. He intended it to be his engagement gift to Theo."

"Of course," I said. "And speaking of gifts, I was hoping to ask Hawkin to do a small portrait of my mother as a birthday present for her. Although I doubt if I could have afforded him."

"He *was* pricey," Duvalnik admitted. "I wanted to charge a minimum of thirty thousand for the Johnson portrait but, as I say, I could never get a firm number from Si. I think perhaps he hated to see that painting go. It was his best work and he knew it. A few fine artists are like that; they do something special and they want to hang on to it. But I represent a number of other gifted portraitists if you're really interested in a present for your mother. First let me get you something to wet your whistle."

He brought me a glass of white wine. No Chilean chardonnay this time. It was dreadful plonk, but I smacked my lips gamely and told him how splendid it was. He showed me Polaroids and color slides of the works of several other artists, none of whom had Hawkin's talent. Prices ranged from twenty-five hundred to ten thousand.

"Let me think about it," I said. "If it's to be a surprise birthday gift I can hardly ask mother to sit for a portrait. I presume some of these people can do a painting from photographs."

"Naturally," he said. "No problem at all. Si Hawkin refused to work that way; he insisted on several sittings. He was a real pro."

"Was he working on anything new at the time of his death?" I asked casually.

"Not to my knowledge," the gallery owner said sadly. "Like the card in the window says, that portrait of Theo Johnson was Hawkin's final work."

"What a shame," I said. "Thank you for your help, Mr. Duvalnik. You'll be hearing from me."

And I tramped back to the McNally Building through parboiled streets, having picked up a few more tidbits of information that might prove valuable or might turn out to be the drossiest of dross. My investigations usually depend on the amassing of minor facts rather than major leaps of inspiration. When it comes to tortoise versus hare, I'm no cottontail.

It took a few minutes in my gloriously chilled office for my temperature, pulse, and respiratory rate to regain some semblance of normality. Then I phoned Lolly Spindrift at his newspaper, hoping to add a few truffles to my collection of bonbons.

"Hi, darling," Spindrift said in his high-pitched lilt. "Have you called to invite me to another lunch of champagne and caviar?"

"You mock," I said. "I haven't yet recovered from the last one."

"Wasn't that a kick?" he said. "We were talking about Silas Hawkin, and the next day the man is defunct. Let that be a lesson to you. Gather ye rosebuds while ye may, laddie."

"I fully intend to," I said. "Lol, I need some information."

"So do I," he replied. "Every day, constantly. My lifestyle depends on it. You've heard of quid pro quo, haven't you, darling? English translation: You scratch my back and I'll scratch yours. Not literally, of course, since we're of different religions. But if you've got nothing for me, I've got nothing for you."

"I have a little nosh that may interest you," I said. "You will, of course, refuse to reveal your source?"

"Don't I always?" he demanded. "Jail before dishonor. What have you got?"

"Si Hawkin had sex just before he was killed."

I heard Lol's swift intake of breath.

"Beautiful," he said. "*That* I can use. Can I depend on it?"

"Would I deceive you?" I asked. "With your authenticated file on the peccadilloes of Archy McNally?"

"Okay," he said, "I'll run with it. Now what do you want?"

"Have you heard any rumors that Silas Hawkin may have had, ah, intimate relations with any of the women whose portraits he painted?"

His laughter exploded. "*Any* of the women?" he said, gasping. "You mean *all* of the women! Darling, the man was a stallion, a veritable *stallion*."

"Odd you should say that. I recently heard him described as a goat."

"More of a ram," Spindrift said. "Absotively, posilutely insatiable."

"Thank you, Lol," I said. "Keep fighting for the public's right to know."

"And up yours as well, dearie," he said before he hung up.

And that, I decided, was enough detecting for one morning. I reclaimed my horseless carriage in our underground garage and drove directly to the Pelican Club to replenish my energy. I might even have something to eat.

And so I did. I sat at the bar, ordered a Coors Light from Mr. Pettibone, and asked daughter Priscilla to bring me a double cheeseburger with home fries and a side order of coleslaw. She spread this harvest before me and shook her head wonderingly.

"On a diet, Archy?" she inquired.

"None of your sass," I said. "I have been engaged in debilitating physical labor and require nourishment."

She shrugged. "They're your arteries," she said.

As I made my way through all that yummy cholesterol I pondered the murder of Silas Hawkin and wondered if one of his clients with whom he had been cozy had slid that palette knife into his gullet. I could imagine several motives: jealousy, revenge, fury at being jilted for another woman.

If it was my case, and it wasn't, I would concentrate on the missing painting. Find "Untitled," I thought, and you'd probably find the killer. I had enough faith in Sgt. Al Rogoff's expertise to reckon he was on the same track.

But why would the murderer risk making off with the painting? It couldn't be sold, at least not locally, and if it was unfinished, as it apparently was, it would be of little value anywhere. The only logical conclusion was that the importance of "Untitled" lay in its subject matter. The killer didn't want it to be seen by anyone.

But if that was true, why wasn't the painting destroyed on the spot? After slaying the artist it would have taken the assassin only a few minutes to slash "Untitled" to ribbons, or even douse it with one of the inflammables in the studio and set it afire. But instead, "Untitled" was carried away.

Which led me to reflect on the size of the painting. The portrait of Theo Johnson, I estimated, was approximately 3½ ft. tall by 2½ wide. If "Untitled" had the same dimensions it was hardly something one could tuck under one's arm and then saunter away, particularly if the painting was still wet. A puzzlement.

I knew that art supply stores carried blank canvases already framed. But I also knew that most fine artists preferred to stretch their own canvas, buying the quality desired in bolts and cutting off the piece required for a planned endeavor. It would then be tacked to a wooden frame.

Still, it might be worthwhile to check the store where Silas bought his supplies. It was just barely possible he had recently purchased a stretched canvas that was to become "Untitled." And so, after I had consumed that cornucopia of calories in toto, I inserted myself behind the wheel of the Miata with some difficulty and set out for the Hawkin residence.

As I said, it was not my case, but it was of interest to me because of the peripheral involvement of Theo and Hector Johnson.

Also, I had nothing better to do on that sultry afternoon.

It had been my intention to ask the housekeeper for the information I sought, but when I rang the chimes at the main house the door was opened by Mrs. Louise Hawkin.

"Oh," I said, somewhat startled. "Good afternoon, Mrs. Hawkin. May I speak to Mrs. Folsby for a moment?"

"She is no longer with us," she said in a tone that didn't invite further inquiries.

But I persisted. "Sorry to hear it," I said. "Could you tell me where I might be able to contact her?"

"No," she said shortly. Then: "What did you want to talk to her about?"

"I just wanted to ask if your late husband used prepared canvases or if he stretched his own."

She stared at me. "Why on earth would you want to know that?"

I have a small talent for improv. "A young friend of mine is a wannabe artist," I told her. "He is a great admirer of Mr. Hawkin's technique and requested I ask."

She bought it. "My husband stretched his own canvas," she said. "A very good grade of linen. Good day, Mr. McNally."

And she shut the door. What I should have said was, "No more interest in a divorce lawyer, Mrs. Hawkin?" But I knew the answer to that.

I glanced toward the studio building. It seemed to be unguarded, and the crime scene tape drooped in the heat. I wandered over and tried the scarred oak and etched glass door, but it was locked. I turned away, then heard a "Psst!" that whirled me back. Marcia Hawkin was standing in the opened doorway, beckoning to me.

She drew me inside, then locked the door after us.

"What did she tell you?" she said fiercely.

Bewilderment time. "Who?" I asked.

"Her," she said, jerking a thumb in the direction of the main house. "Did she say anything about me?"

"Not a word," I assured her. "We had a very brief conversation about your father's work."

She clutched my arm and pulled me into the sitting area on the ground level. She leaned close and almost whispered. "She's a dreadful woman. Dreadful! Don't believe anything she says. Do you want a drink?"

"I think I better," I said, and she went into the kitchenette. I watched with horror as she poured me a tumbler of warm vodka.

"Miss Hawkin," I said, "if I drink that I'll be non compos mentis. Please let me do it."

I moved to the sink and mixed myself a mild vodka and water with plenty of ice. Meanwhile Marcia had thrown herself on the couch and lay sprawled, biting furiously at a fingernail. An Ophelia, I decided.

It would be difficult to describe her costume in detail without sounding indecent. I shall merely say that she wore an oversized white singlet, soiled and possibly belonging to her dead father, and denim shorts chopped off so radically that they hardly constituted a loincloth. But her lanky semi-nakedness made her seem more helpless than seductive. She was long and loose-jointed; a puppeteer had cut her strings.

"My stepmother is a bitch," she declared. "You know what that means, don't you?"

"I've heard the word," I acknowledged.

"What am I going to do?" she cried despairingly. "What *am* I going to do?"

Never let it be said that A. McNally failed to respond to a damsel in distress. But when the damsel in question appears to be a certifiable loony—well, it does give one pause, does it not?

"What seems to be the problem, Miss Hawkin?" I asked, speaking as slowly and softly as possible.

My soothing manner had the desired effect. She suddenly began talking rationally and with some good sense.

"Money," she said. "Isn't that always the problem?"

"Not always," I said, "but frequently. Surely your father left you well-provided for."

"I have a trust fund," she admitted, "but I can't touch it until I turn twenty-one."

That was a shocker. I had guessed her to be in the mid-twenties. "How old are you, Miss Hawkin?" I asked gently.

"Nineteen," she said. "I look older, don't I?"

"Not at all," I said gallantly.

"I know I do," she said defiantly. "But you don't know what my life has been like. When daddy was alive, money made no difference. He was very generous. Anything I wanted. But now I'm totally dependent on *her*. My food, the house, spending money—*everything*. It just kills me."

"Surely you have relatives or friends who'd be willing to help out."

She shook her head. "No one. I'm on my own, and I'm frightened, I admit it."

"Don't be frightened," I counseled her, "because then you won't be able to think clearly. You must keep your nerve and review your options calmly and logically as if you were called upon to advise someone else."

She looked at me queerly. "Yes," she said, "you're right. If I have the courage to act I can solve my own problems, can't I?"

"Of course. Courage and energy: That's what it takes."

She laughed. I didn't like that laugh. It came perilously close to being a hysterical giggle.

"Thank you, Archy," she said. "I may call you Archy, mayn't I?"

"I'd be delighted."

"And you must call me Squirrel," she said. "That's what daddy always called me."

"What an unusual nickname," I said, smiling.

"You think so?" she challenged, and abruptly she was back in her manic mood again. "I see nothing unusual about it. You just don't understand. No one can ever understand. I think you better go now."

My first impression had been correct: definitely an Ophelia.

I finished my drink hastily, bid her a polite farewell, and left her still sprawled, starting on another fingernail. I was thankful to be going. Those moments with her were too intense, too charged with things unsaid, furies suppressed and threatening to break loose.

I drove away without a backward glance. The master of that home might be deceased but it was still the Villa Bile.

When I arrived at the McNally digs, a *much* happier household, I found Jamie Olson in the garage hosing down my mother's antique wood-bodied Ford station wagon. He was smoking one of his ancient briars, the one with the cracked shank wrapped with a Band-Aid.

"Jamie," I said, "Mrs. Jane Folsby was the live-in at Silas Hawkin's residence, but she has suddenly left their employ. Do you think you can find out where she's gone?"

"Mebbe," he said.

"Try," I urged. "She's a nice lady, and I'd like to talk to her."

I had a pleasant ocean swim, the family cocktail hour that followed was just as enjoyable, and dinner that night capped my pleasure. Mother went upstairs for an evening of television in the sitting room, father retired to his study to continue his wrestle with Dickens, and I climbed to my suite to update my journal, sip a small marc, and listen to a tape of Hoagy Carmichael singing "Star Dust."

It was a normal evening at the McNally manse, all quiet, peaceful, content. But just when you start believing the drawbridge is up, the castle is inviolate, and the rude world can't possibly intrude, along comes leering fate to deliver a swift kick to your gluteus maximus.

On that particular evening the boot came at approximately 9:30 P.M. in the form of a phone call from Sgt. Al Rogoff. He spent no time on greetings.

"I'm beginning to wonder about you," he said.

"Are you?" I said, thinking he was joshing. "Wonder about what?"

"Do you know a guy named Chauncey Smythe-Hersforth? Lives in Palm Beach."

"Of course I know him," I said. "He and his mother are clients of McNally and Son."

"Uh-huh. And do you know a woman named Shirley Feebling? In Fort Lauderdale."

"I don't *know* her," I said warily, beginning to get antsy about this conversation. "I met her once for an hour. Why the third degree, Al?"

"Son," he said, "you're just too free with your business cards. About an hour ago I got a call from a dick I know who works out of Lauderdale Homicide. This afternoon they found Shirley Feebling in her condo shot through the back of her head. Much dead. They also found your business card and a batch of hot letters from this Smythe-Hersforth character."

I closed my eyes. Her T-shirt had been lettered PEACE. What a way to find it.

"Your father still awake?" Rogoff asked.

"Of course he's still awake. It's only nine-thirty."

"I think I better come over," he said. "Okay?"

"Don't tell me I'm a suspect," I said with a shaky laugh.

"Right now you and Smythe-Hersforth are the only leads that Lauderdale's got. I promised to check you out, both of you. Makes sense, doesn't it?"

"I guess," I said, sighing. "The second time my business card has landed me in the soup. You're correct, Al; I've got to stop handing them out. Sure, come on over."

"Be there in fifteen minutes," he said and hung up.

I sat there a few moments remembering that ingenuous and not too bright young woman with her firm belief in True Love and a sunny future. It didn't take long for sadness and regret to become anger and a seething desire for vengeance. The murder of Shirley Feebling affected me more keenly than the killing of Silas Hawkin. I could conceive that his actions might have led to his demise. But hers, I was convinced, was the death of an innocent.

I prepared to go downstairs and alert father to the arrival of Sgt. Rogoff. I glanced nervously at the darkness outside my window. Our snug home no longer seemed secure.

Chapter 7

Al had the look of an exhausted beagle. He sat in front of my father's magisterial desk and in a toneless voice recited what little he knew of the murder of Shirley Feebling.

She did not show up for work at the topless car wash on Tuesday morning. The boss was not concerned; his employees were usually late and frequently absent for a day or two simply because they had better things to do than lave insect-spattered vehicles driven by the curious and/or lubricious.

But when there was no word from Shirl by noon, and her phone wasn't answered, a friend and co-worker with the unlikely name of Pinky Schatz became alarmed and stopped by her place after work. The door of Ms. Feebling's condo was unlocked, and inside Pinky discovered the sanguinary corpse. After a single scream, she dialed 911.

The homicide detective to whom Rogoff had spoken had revealed only that my business card and the letters of Chauncey Wilson Smythe-Hersforth had been found during the initial search. If any additional significant evidence was discovered, he just wasn't saying.

"And that's all I've got," the sergeant concluded. He turned to me. "What have *you* got?"

I glanced at mon père. He was the attorney; it was his responsibility to decide how much to reveal and how much to keep undisclosed in the name of client confidentiality. Al and I waited patiently while Prescott McNally went through his mulling routine, a process that endured long enough to calculate the square root of 2. Finally the guru spoke.

"Discretion?" he demanded, looking sternly at Rogoff.

"As usual," Al said.

Father then described the letters Smythe-Hersforth had written Shirley Feebling during a time the two apparently had been enjoying a steamy affair. Later the client had a change of heart, but the woman insisted he honor the proposal of marriage he had made in writing. If not, she vowed to sell his letters to any interested tabloid.

"Uh-huh," Rogoff said. "How much was she asking?"

"Archy?" papa said. "You take it from here."

"I went down to Lauderdale to see her," I told the sergeant. "I had just the single meeting and left my business card. She absolutely refused to discuss a cash settlement. She wanted to marry him and that was that."

"Where is the guy now—do you know?"

"His office says he left Monday morning for a bankers' convention in New Orleans and won't be back until Thursday."

Al had been making brief notes on all this in a fat little notebook he carried. Now he slapped the cover closed and bound it with a wide rubber band. He said casually, "Archy, you got any idea who might have clobbered the woman?"

I had learned to lie convincingly by age four. "Not a glimmer," I said.

"Sergeant," father said, "if inquiries by the Fort Lauderdale authorities prove—as I am certain they will—that Smythe-Hersforth was in New Orleans at the time of this unfortunate woman's death, I will deeply appreciate any assistance you may provide in retrieving our client's personal letters since they obviously will be of no further interest or import in the official investigation."

All that was said in one sentence. It's the way my old man talks.

"I'll see what I can do, sir," Rogoff said, rising, and the two men shook hands.

The sergeant was driving a police car that night, not his personal pickup truck, and I walked him outside. He paused to light a cigar and blow a plume of smoke toward the cloudless sky.

"Nice weather," he observed.

"You don't find it a trifle warm?"

"Nah," he said. "I like the heat. It keeps the juices flowing."

"And how are they flowing on the Hawkin homicide?"

"They ain't," he admitted. "We're going through the drill, talking to everyone. It's what I call an NKN case: nobody knows nothing."

"A double negative," I pointed out.

"The story of my life," he said. Then suddenly: "How about you? You got anything?"

"A crumb," I said. "Mrs. Jane Folsby has left the Hawkins' employ. For reasons the deponent knoweth not."

"Yeah?" he said. "Can't say I blame her for getting out of that nuthouse. Go to bed, sonny boy; I only wish I could. And remember what I said about your business cards. Will you, for God's sake, stop passing them out? Every time you do, someone gets whacked and I have to put in more overtime."

I watched him drive away, reflecting that his warning came too late. The last card I had distributed went to Theodosia Johnson. It was not a comforting thought. I went back inside. The door to father's study was shut, which meant he was deep in Dickens and port. So I trudged upstairs, finished scribbling in my journal, and prepared to crawl into the sack.

I cannot say my mood was melancholy, but neither was it chockablock with joie de vivre. I have never been a victim of presentiments, but that evening I must confess I had a sense of impending doom.

The only way I could calm my quaking spirits was to remind myself firmly that seriousness is a sin. I happen to believe that our Maker is the greatest farceur in the universe. And so sleep came only with the blessed remembrance of the sentiment: "Long live the sun! And down with the night!"

I thought it might be Pushkin. But then it might have been just Archy McNally. No matter. I slept.

And awoke on Wednesday morning revivified, alert, and wondering why

I had been in such a funk the previous night. After all, I was alive, reasonably young, in full possession of my faculties (others might disagree), and inhabiting a world that offered such glories as lamb shanks braised in wine and tiramisu with zabaglione sauce. There was absolutely no reason to despair.

I knew exactly what I must do, but of course I had overslept and didn't arrive at my office in the McNally Building until a bit after ten o'clock. Oversleeping, I realized, was becoming a habit I seemed unable to break, and it occurred to me that I might have contracted trypanosomiasis. I have never been to Africa, but a chum of mine, Binky Watrous, had recently spent a weekend in Marrakech, and it was quite possible that, unknowingly of course, he had brought a tsetse fly home with him. It was troubling.

The moment I was behind my ugly desk I phoned Jack DuBois, my pal at the Royal Palm Way bank handling Hector Johnson's checking account.

"Jack," I said, "you told me that when Johnson made his initial deposit with a cashier's check from Troy, Michigan, he presented a driver's license as ID and supplied the names of two Fort Lauderdale residents as references."

"That's right."

"Could I have the names and addresses of the references, please?"

He groaned. "Archy, it seems to me I'm doing all your work for you."

"Jack, there's no such thing as a free lunch."

"Lunch?" he cried indignantly. "You promised me a dinner."

"I was speaking metaphorically," I soothed him. "You shall have your dinner complete with appetizer, soup, entrée, dessert, and whatever else your ravenous hunger and thirst demand. Now let's have the names of Johnson's references."

"Wait a sec while I call them up on my screen," he said. "We've got new software and it's a doozy. When are you going to get a computer, Archy?"

"Give me a break," I pleaded. "I can't even operate a battery-powered swizzle stick."

Eventually I received the information requested. Hector Johnson's two references were J.P. Lordsley and Reuben Hagler. I studied their addresses and reckoned that if I left immediately, I could manage a relaxed drive to Fort Lauderdale, enjoy a leisurely snack, check out both individuals, and be back in time for my daily dunk in the sea.

But it did not happen. My phone jangled ere I could depart, and a feminine voice inquired, "Archy McNally?"

I recognized that coo, and my heart leaped like an inflamed gazelle. "Theo!" I said. "How nice to hear from you."

"I do hope I'm not interrupting," she said. "I know how busy you must be."

"Work—" I said. "It's a four-letter word and I try to avoid it."

"Let me help," she said, her voice positively burbling. "You did offer to show me your home, you know, and it's such a lovely day I was hoping to persuade you to take a few hours off."

"Splendid idea!" I practically shouted. "And as I recall, lunch was also mentioned. Still on?"

"Of course. Daddy is using our car this afternoon, so could you pick me up?"

"Delighted," I said. "Half an hour? How does that sound?"

"I'll be waiting for you, Archy," she said softly and hung up, leaving me to interpret her final words in several ways, not all of them honorable.

I was happy I had worn dove gray slacks and my navy blue blazer adorned with the Pelican Club patch: a pelican rampant on a field of dead mullet. I also sported tasseled cordovan loafers (no socks) and a mauve cashmere polo shirt, the cost of which had made a severe dent in my net worth.

Thankfully the heat and humidity of the previous day had dissipated and it was a brilliant noontime with a cerulean sky brushed with horsetail clouds, and a sweet ocean breeze moving the palm fronds. I should have been elated by the anticipation of spending a few enchanting hours with Madam X, but I must admit two questions dampened my euphoria.

One: If the Chinless Wonder was correct in stating that he was to become the fiancé of Theodosia Johnson—and commissioning her portrait certainly proved the sincerity of his intent—why did she seem so eager to enjoy a luncheon with yrs. truly? She had to be aware that Chauncey was out of town, and her cozying up to another man in his absence was a mite offputting.

I was not accusing her of blatant infidelity, mind you, and I had no desire to make a moral judgment. Not me, who believes "connubial bliss" is an oxymoron. But her conduct *was* a puzzle. I concluded she had a motive I could not ken.

The second question was where in the world was I going to take Madam X to lunch. You must understand that Connie Garcia, partly due to her position as social secretary to Lady Horowitz, maintains a network of spies, snitches, close friends, and catty enemies who like nothing better than to relate the behavior of Archy McNally, particularly when I am observed in activities sure to ignite Connie's Latin temper. If I was seen lunching with the nubile Ms. Johnson, it would undoubtedly be reported to the lady with whom I was intimate, and I didn't wish to imagine what her reaction would be. Incendiary, I was certain, and possibly damaging to the McNally corpus.

But all my uncertainties and hesitancies vanished when I rang the bell of the Johnsons' condo and the door was opened by Theo. A vision! Physical beauty, the eggheads tell us, is ephemeral, of no lasting value, and we must admire only the inner virtues. I much prefer a swan-like neck.

She was wearing a slip dress of tangerine silk. With her apricot-tanned shoulders and peachy complexion she was a veritable fruit salad of delight. Once again her beauty had the effect of answering all my questions and banishing all my doubts. Suspect this woman of chicanery? Nonsense! Might as well accuse the Venus de Milo of being a pickpocket.

"Archy!" she said, clasping my hand. "You look smashing. What is that crest on your jacket?"

"The Pelican Club. A private dining and drinking establishment."

"Wonderful. Are we going there for lunch?"

"No, no," I said hastily. "It's a comfortable spot, but regretfully the cuisine is something less than haute. We'll find a place with a more enticing menu. But first let me show you the McNally home."

What a pleasure it was to have that paragon seated alongside me in the Miata as we zipped over to Ocean Boulevard and gazed on the glimmering sea.

Theo was wide-eyed as she glimpsed the mansions fronting the Atlantic. "The money!" she said.

"Playpen of the idle rich," I admitted blithely. "But not all of us. The McNallys, for instance. We work, we're hardly multis, and our spread is relatively modest. My father had the great good sense to buy years and years ago before real estate prices rocketed into the wild blue yonder."

I parked on the graveled turnaround at our three-car garage and led my guest on a stroll through our smallish estate.

"We employ a live-in couple who have their own apartment over the garage," I said. "The greenhouse is my mother's domain. No pool, you'll notice. What's the point with the ocean a short trot away? The doghouse belonged to Max, our golden retriever, but he's gone to the great kennel in the sky. Let's see if mother is at work."

We found her in the potting shed. She stripped off a rubber glove to shake hands with our visitor.

"How nice to meet you, Miss Johnson," she said brightly. "I've already met your father at our garden club. What a charming man he is."

"Thank you, Mrs. McNally. Your home is lovely."

"But you haven't seen the inside yet," I protested. "It's nothing but bare walls and a few hammocks."

"Don't believe a word he says," mum advised.

"I don't," Theo said with more conviction than I liked.

"Archy, will you and Miss Johnson be staying for lunch?"

"Not today, darling," I told her. "We want to see some of the local scenery."

"Well, do come back," she urged Theo. "Perhaps you and your father might visit some evening."

"I'd love that, Mrs. McNally. Thank you so much."

We walked toward the house. "She's beautiful," Theo said. "And so—so *motherly*."

"Isn't she," I agreed. "I just adore sitting on her lap."

"You're a nut," she said, laughing.

"And now for the fifty-cent tour," I said. "Let's make it fast because the pangs of hunger are beginning to gnaw."

I showed her everything: kitchen, father's study, living and dining rooms, second-floor sitting room, master and guest bedrooms, and my own little suite on the third floor. All the furnishings were of good quality but obviously mellowed. The interior looked as if everything had been inherited, which was exactly the ambience my father had striven to create when he moved up from Miami.

"It's all so handsome," Theo said, suitably impressed. "So solid and warm and comfy."

I didn't tell her the truth, that everything in the place had been purchased in the past thirty years from decorators, galleries, and antique shops. Our home was a stage set. But it was convincing.

We reboarded the Miata, and I had what I fancied was a minor stroke of genius.

"You know," I said thoughtfully, "there are many fine restaurants in Palm Beach, but it's such a scrumptious day, why don't we take a drive down to Boca Raton along A1A. I know a marvelous place in Boca where we can lunch alfresco."

"Sounds divine," Theo said.

So having reduced the possibility of being spotted by one of Connie Garcia's spies to an absolute minimum, I turned southward. We followed the corniche, and my companion never stopped exclaiming at the glory of the vistas and the wealth displayed by the private mansions and luxury condominiums along the way.

I drove directly to Mizner Park, my favorite mini-mall in South Florida. There we entrusted the Miata to a valet and secured an umbrella table at the Bistro L'Europe. Outdoor dining at Mizner is a charming way to enjoy anything from a boutique pizza to a five-course banquet. But, of course, the main attraction is people-watching.

I cannot recall the exact details of our lunch. I have a vague recollection of sharing an enormous Caesar salad with Theo after we had demolished a duck terrine. I do remember very well that everything I consumed was ambrosial. That may have been due to the full bottle of Beaujolais we finished, but I prefer to believe my pleasure was heightened by being in the company of such a ravishing dining partner.

"Archy," she said, nibbling on a garlic crouton, "why have you never married?"

I had an oft-repeated response to that. "I am very prone to allergies," I told her. "Research has shown that more than half of all divorces are caused by one spouse becoming allergic to the other. I just can't take the chance."

That sinfully entrancing dimple appeared and she shook her head hopelessly. "You're a devil," she said.

"That wounds," I said. "All I wish to be is your guardian angel. Where are you from, Theo?"

"Michigan," she said promptly. "Isn't everyone?"

"During the tourist season one might think so. I understand Michiganders refer to Florida as the Lower Peninsula. Tell me, if a man is a Michigander, is a woman a Michigoose?"

She ignored that antiquated wheeze—and rightly so. "Where are *you* from?" she asked.

"Right here. One of the few residents actually born in Florida."

"You don't sound like a native Floridian."

"I went to prep school up north and then later to Yale."

I told her the story of why I was booted out of Yale Law and she was mightily amused. "You *are* a devil," she said, "and I really shouldn't be associating with you."

"Perhaps you shouldn't," I said boldly. "I understand you're soon to be affianced."

She lifted her chin and looked at me coolly. "Maybe," she said, "and maybe not. I haven't yet decided. Do you know Chauncey Smythe-Hersforth?"

"Yes."

"And his mother?"

"I am acquainted with the lady."

"Then surely you know why I am postponing a decision."

I said nothing.

"Meanwhile," she went on, "I am living the way I want to live. I'm an independent cuss. Does my behavior shock you?"

"No, it does not. But it puzzles me."

"You feel I should leap at the chance of marrying Chauncey?"

"You could do much worse. Me, for instance."

"Let me be the judge of that," she said.

"May I ask how old you are, Theo?"

"You may ask but I shan't answer. Older than you think, I'm sure."

"Another personal question you may or may not wish to answer: Is your mother living?"

"Yes. My parents are divorced. My mother has remarried and is presently living in San Diego. And now I have a personal question for you: Do you have a ladyfriend?"

"I do."

"But you're not faithful to her."

"Is that a question or a statement?"

She laughed. "A statement. I do believe you're as selfish as I am."

"Quite possibly," I acknowledged. "Theo, would you care for dessert?"

"Yes," she said decisively, staring at me. "You."

I sought to quell a slight tremor.

She discussed the logistics of our assignation as calmly as if she were making an appointment for a pedicure. Daddy had driven down to Fort Lauderdale that morning. It was a business trip and daddy would be gone all day. And daddy had promised to phone before he started back to Palm Beach so they could make dinner plans.

In addition, both condos adjoining the Johnsons' were unoccupied, the owners having gone north for the summer.

"So you see," Theo concluded, "we'll have all the privacy we could possibly want."

"Yes," I said, tempted to add, "But God will be watching." I didn't, of course, since it verged on blasphemy.

We didn't converse on our return trip to Palm Beach although there were a few occasions when I suspected she was humming. I was simply amazed at her insouciance. She sat upright, smiling straight ahead, shining hair whipping back in the breeze. She looked as if she owned the world, or at least that part of it she coveted.

We arrived at the Johnsons' condo, and I suggested that since the blood-red Miata was such a noticeable vehicle, it might be more discreet if I parked some distance away. But Theo would have none of that, insisted I park at her doorstep, and led the way inside. And instead of inviting me into a bedroom, she rushed to that hideous cretonne-covered couch in the living room and beckoned. I scurried to her side.

She undressed with frantic and unseemly haste, and all I could think of was a cannibal preparing for a feast of a succulent missionary.

I shall not attempt to describe the rapture of that afternoon. It is not that I lack the vocabulary—you know me better than that—but it is because some events in one's life are so private that it is painful to disclose them, even if they are pleasurable.

I can only permit myself to record that Theodosia Johnson was all women. Not all woman but all women. She reduced the plural to the singular, multiplicity to one. After knowing her, there seemed no need for another. She was the Eternal Female, capitalized, and at the moment I was bewitched. Not bothered and bewildered—just bewitched.

There was one intimate detail I am forced to reveal because it has a bearing on what was to follow. Theo had a small tattoo of a blue butterfly on the left of her tanned abdomen, almost in the crease of her thigh. It was, to the best of my recollection, the first time I had ever kissed a butterfly.

I returned home too late for my ocean swim—a mercy since I hadn't the strength—but in time to shower and dress for the family cocktail hour and dinner. My thoughts, needless to say, were awhirl, but I believe I hid my perturbation from my parents. The only discomposing moment came during our preprandial martinis when I eagerly asked my mother, "What did you think of Theo Johnson?"

The mater gave me her sweet smile. "She's not for you, Archy," she said.

It was cataclysm time. "Why on earth not?" I demanded.

Her shrug was tiny. "Just a feeling," she said.

I was subdued at dinner and retired to my quarters as soon as decently possible. I wanted to note the day's adventures in my journal but was unable. I merely sat rigidly, counting the walls (there were four), and tried to solve the riddle of Madam X.

I was still in this semi-catatonic state when Connie Garcia phoned. Her first words—"Hi, honey!"—were an enormous relief since they signified she had not yet learned of my hegira to Mizner Park with Theo Johnson.

"Listen," she went on, "seems to me you gabbled about a dinner date this week. When? Put up or shut up."

"Let me consult my social calendar," I said. "My presence has been requested at so many—"

"Cut the bs," she interrupted. "It's on for tomorrow night at the Pelican Club. I called and Leroy is planning to roast a whole suckling pig. How does that sound?"

"Gruesome," I said. "I *am* a suckling pig."

"As well I know," Connie said. "Around eight o'clock—okay?"

"Fine," I said. "I'll even change my socks."

I realized, after hanging up, that perhaps an evening with the open, forth-right, and completely honest Ms. Garcia was exactly what I needed. After an afternoon spent with the disquieting and inexplicable Ms. Johnson, it would be like popping a tranquilizer. Of course after dinner Connie would expect me to expend some energy in her Lake Worth condo, but that prospect didn't daunt me. I hustled to the medicine cabinet in my bathroom and slid two B-12 sublingual tablets under my tongue.

Wasn't it John Barrymore who said, "So many women, so little time"? If he didn't say it, he should have.

Chapter 8

Chauncey Wilson Smythe-Hersforth returned from New Orleans on Thursday morning, and at eleven o'clock he and his mother had a conference with my father. I was not invited to attend. But after it ended the Chinless Wonder came down to my office wearing a grin so smarmy I wanted to kick his shins.

"This is your *office?*" he said, glancing around. "My walk-in closet at home is bigger than this."

"Most of my work is done on the outside," I said frostily. "Like going down to Fort Lauderdale to interview Shirley Feebling on your behalf."

He immediately composed his features into a theatrical expression of sorrow. "That was a terrible thing," he said, shaking his fat head. "Just terrible. She was a nice girl, Archy. I really liked her."

I made no response.

"What's the world coming to?" he demanded rhetorically. "Violence everywhere. Silas Hawkin murdered and now this. A decent citizen isn't safe on the street anymore."

I had enough of his profundities. "What's happening with your letters?" I asked.

The smarmy grin returned. "Your father is going to pull every string he can to get them back from the Lauderdale police. They're of no use to them, are they? I mean I have a perfect alibi; a hundred people saw me at the convention. Listen, Archy, how much money did Shirley want?"

"She didn't want any. She just wanted to marry you."

"She should have known that was impossible," he blustered, running a finger between collar and neck. "The difference in our class and all that . . ."

"Uh-huh," I said. "And what was your mother's reaction to your pro-posing marriage to Shirley?"

That deflated him. "Well, uh, in your father's office she just said, 'Boys will be boys.' But when I get home tonight I expect she'll have more to say on the subject."

"Yes, I expect she will," I said with some satisfaction. "Tell me, CW, did Shirl ever say anything about someone threatening her or following her or annoying her?"

"No, she never mentioned anything like that. I think it was a druggie who broke in to rob her. She caught him at it and he killed her."

"Could be," I said, waiting for him to say, "She was just in the wrong place at the wrong time."

"She was just in the wrong place at the wrong time," he said, keeping his reputation for fatuousness intact. "Well, it was an awful thing, but in all honesty it's a load off my mind to have that business about the letters cleared up."

Which I thought was somewhat akin to the classic question: "But other than that, Mrs. Lincoln, how did you enjoy the show?"

"I can't wait to tell Theo Johnson," he went on. "She'll be so relieved."

I was as aghast at hearing that as I'm sure you are in reading it. "Good lord, CW," I said, "don't tell me you informed your intended fiancée about Shirley Feebling?"

"Of course I did," he said, stroking that ridiculous pushbroom mustache. "Theo and I promised to be completely frank and honest. No secrets. We tell each other absolutely everything."

If that were true, I reflected, I better leave for Hong Kong immediately.

I finally got rid of him with a keener appreciation of why Ms. Johnson was postponing her decision to become affianced. The man was a pompous ass, and Theo had the wit to recognize it.

It was then noonish and time to saddle up if I expected to make that delayed trip to Fort Lauderdale. So I grabbed my notes on Hector Johnson's bank references and went down to our underground garage to embark. It was probably a fool's errand, I glumly reckoned, and if so I was just the man for the job.

The Miata was cranky on that drive and I realized my darling was badly in need of a tune-up and perhaps a new set of tires. So I didn't pretend I was competing in the Daytona 500 but took it easy and arrived in Lauderdale a bit after two o'clock. I stopped at a Tex-Mex joint for a bowl of chili hot enough to scorch my uvula and a chilled bottle of Corona. Then I headed for the address of the first reference.

It was easy to find. J.P. Lordsley was a men's clothier on Federal Highway south of Oakland Park Boulevard. It seemed to be a hip-elegant shop where Hector might have purchased his fancy duds. I admired his chutzpah in supplying the name of a clothing store as a bank reference. I didn't even bother going in the place.

The second required a little more time to locate. The address of Reuben Hagler was on Copans Road and I drove past twice before I realized it was a hole-in-the-wall tucked into a rather decrepit strip mall half-hidden by dusty palms and tattered billboards. I parked and found a narrow door bearing a sign: REUBEN HAGLER, INVESTMENT ADVISER. It was squeezed between the office of a chiropodist and a store selling raunchy T-shirts.

I didn't enter. Because sitting out front was a gunmetal Cadillac De Ville, and I was certain Mr. Hagler would have a profile like a cleaver. The Caddie had Michigan plates, and I remembered the number long enough to jot it down on a matchbook cover with my gold Mont Blanc when I returned to the Miata.

I drove even more sedately on the trip back to Palm Beach. I had a lot to ponder. And the result of all my intense ratiocination? Zilch. I needed help.

I had hoped to keep Sgt. Al Rogoff out of this nonsense. After all, I was engaged in nothing more than a credit investigation, and it was really none of his business. But conviction was growing that possibly, just possibly, Hector Johnson might be involved in the Shirley Feebling homicide.

I drove directly home, garaged the Miata, and went looking for my mother. I found her in the greenhouse, sprinkling can in hand, murmuring to her plants.

"See here, Mrs. McN.," I said, "last night you said Theo Johnson wasn't for me and ascribed that opinion to a vague feeling. Couldn't you be a bit more specific?"

She paused and stared at me thoughtfully. "Archy, I just thought her a little too determined, a little too aggressive."

"Certainly nothing she said."

"Oh no. She was quite polite. It was her manner, the way she carried herself. I suppose you think I'm being foolish."

I swooped to kiss her cheek. "Not at all," I said valiantly. "I think you're a very wise lady."

"She's after you, Archy," mother said, nodding, and that's all she'd say.

Ordinarily, after hearing that a woman was "after me," I might preen. But as I left the greenhouse a cobweb drifted across my forehead, and as I wiped it away I thought of those female spiders who, after the ecstasy of the bedchamber, devoured their mates. I imagine the poor chaps might seek their fate with a curious mixture of passion and helplessness. Just like me.

I went into the main house and was heading upstairs when Jamie Olson stopped me in the hallway.

"That Mrs. Jane Folsby," he said. "Used to be the Hawkins' live-in."

I nodded.

He handed me a grimy slip of paper. "Got her phone number," he said. "No address, but I hear she's staying with her sister in West Palm Beach."

"Thank you, Jamie," I said gratefully and slipped him a sawbuck. Then I continued up to my nest, stripped off my travel-wrinkled jacket, and phoned Al Rogoff at headquarters.

"Can you give me an hour?" I asked him.

"Five minutes," he said.

"Then I'll talk fast," I promised. "I've got two names and one license plate. I'd like you to check them out with the gendarmes of Troy, Michigan."

"And why should I do that?"

"I would prefer not to say."

"Then I would prefer to reject your request," he said puckishly.

Silence.

"Tell you what," he said finally, "I'm going to make you an offer you can't refuse. I'll do your digging for you, but if and when I get the skinny I won't turn it over until you tell me why you want it. Okay?"

"You drive a hard bargain."

"No, I don't," he said. "I drive a sensible bargain."

"You have a point," I agreed. "Very well, it's a deal."

I gave him the two names, Hector Johnson and Reuben Hagler, and the latter's license tag.

"Johnson?" the sergeant repeated, and I could hear interest quickening in his voice. "Isn't he the guy you're running a credit trace on?"

"That's correct."

"And his daughter was the model for Hawkin's last painting?"

"Yes," I said. "Except for 'Untitled.' "

"Uh-huh," Al said. "All right, I'll see what I can do. Don't expect a report tomorrow, Archy. These things take time. But eventually I'll get back to you."

"A consummation devoutly to be wished," I said.

"When are you going to learn to talk like a human being?" he demanded and hung up.

I showered and dressed informally for my dinner at the Pelican Club with Connie Garcia that evening. I thought I looked rather posh in a jacket of carmine houndstooth check and slacks in what I considered a muted olive plaid. But during the cocktail hour the guy commented that I looked like a sideshow barker, which I thought unnecessarily cruel. But then the old man considers an ascot an affectation so his sartorial opinions really can't be taken seriously.

I arrived early at the Club and put Mr. Pettibone to the test by ordering an Emerald Isle. Again I failed to stump him. He just nodded and said, "Gin, green crème de menthe, bitters," and set to work. The result was quite tasty but packed such a wallop I thought it best to switch to Labatt's Ale, and I was sipping that when Connie arrived.

She looked delicious, as usual, but that woman would be ravishing in a cast-iron muumuu. Fortunately she was wearing a silk jacket and shorts in a sea foam shade that complemented her suntan perfectly. Her long black hair was up in a chignon, and she was the cynosure of all eyes—including mine. We moved immediately to the dining room before Leroy's whole suckling pig was reduced to a glistening skeleton.

Glancing around at the crowd of famished diners I was happy to see that Americans were finally getting off their pernicious health kick. I mean there was a time when, scared silly by nutritionists, everyone seemed to believe that if they limited their diet to oats, turnips, and other goopy stuff, they'd live forever. Rubbish! Man does not live by tofu alone. Go for it, America!

We had roasted pork chops and sweet-and-sour sauce, minted noodles, and a salad of arugula and endive with blue cheese dressing. Crusty pumpernickel baguettes. Dessert was a passion fruit tart served with fresh pineapple ice cream. If all that doesn't put your gastric juices in full flood, go back to your yogurt and see if I care.

Connie was in a bright, chatty mood that evening. As we gourmandized and steadily emptied our bottle of cab, she prattled on about Lady Cynthia Horowitz's activities and the latest Palm Beach scandals, real and alleged. It was during dessert that she asked, "Want to hear the latest rumor?"

"Of course," I said. "Gossip is mother's milk to me."

"Remember your asking me about Hector Johnson? Well, the talk is that he's taking a close interest in Silas Hawkin's widow. In fact, from what I hear, the two of them are what used to be called an item."

"No kidding?" I said, feigning a mild but not excessive interest. "He's pitching her, is he?"

"Apparently," Connie went on. "It started the day after Silas was killed. Now Johnson is at her house almost every day, and they've been seen together all over the place."

"Comforting the bereaved, no doubt."

"Oh sure," she scoffed. "Louise Hawkin also happens to be a well-put-together lady and probably stands to inherit a bundle. Johnson just moved faster than the other middle-aged bachelors in Palm Beach."

"I wonder what the daughter thinks of it."

"Marcia? Oh, she's a ding-a-ling; everyone knows that. About a year ago she was picked up at midnight wandering stark naked down Ocean Boulevard."

"I never heard that one," I said. "Drunk? Or stoned?"

"I don't think so," Connie said. "Just a crazy, mixed-up kid."

"Aren't we all?" I said lightly. "You know what I'd like at the bar?"

"A stomach pump?" she suggested.

"Slivovitz," I said. "To settle the old tumtum."

"Oh God," she said. "I hope you won't start howling at the moon again."

"I've never done that," I protested. "Have I?"

"Yes," Connie said.

She had recently purchased a new car, a white Ford Escort. Not enough pizzazz for my taste, but Connie loved it. She led the way back to her place and I followed in the Miata.

Connie lives in a high-rise condo on the east shore of Lake Worth. Her one-bedroom apartment is small but trig, and the view from her little balcony is tremendous. It's not really my home-away-from-home, but I had been there many, many times and knew where she kept the Absolut (in the freezer) and that you had to jiggle the handle of the toilet to stop it flushing.

We sprawled on her rattan couch, shoes off, and just relaxed awhile after that humongous meal. We were so comfortable with each other that we weren't bothered by long silences. Connie put on a Spanish tape and we listened to a great chantootsie sobbing. I think her songs were all about love betrayed but my Spanish isn't all that good.

The tape ended and Connie didn't flip it, for which I was thankful. She rose and held out her hand. I clasped it and trailed after her into the bedroom. It was a very feminine boudoir with lace ruffles on the bedspread and French dolls propped on the pillows. Over the bed was a framed poster of the movie *Casablanca*. Connie has a thing for Bogart.

We undressed as slowly and unconcernedly as an old married couple while we wondered if that passion fruit tart might not have been better with pistachio ice cream. Very domestic. Then we slid into bed, and those B-12s didn't let me down.

Connie was a languid lover that night, and it surprised me; she's usually quite kinetic. But I was grateful; I was more in the mood for violins than electric guitars. So it was sweet to hear murmurs rather than yelps and to embrace softly rather than jounce.

Then I think we both may have drowsed a bit because when I glanced at her illuminated bedside clock it was close to two A.M.

"I think I better hit the road," I said in a low voice.

Connie opened her eyes. "Yes," she said. "Super evening, Archy. Thank you."

"Thank *you*," I said. "And happy dreams."

She watched me dress. "Who is she, Archy?" she asked quietly.

I paused with one leg in my slacks and one leg out, an awkward posture as any guilty lad will tell you. "Who is whom?" I inquired, expecting the worst and getting it.

"That woman you had lunch with at Mizner Park yesterday."

I resumed getting into my trousers. "I suppose it would be fruitless to deny it," I said.

"Yes," she said steadily, "it would."

"What if I told you she was my cousin?" I said hopefully.

"Then by actual count she would be the seventeenth female cousin you've claimed."

I decided to be absolutely honest—a dreadful mistake. "The lady in question," I said, "is Theodosia Johnson, daughter of Hector. Chauncey Wilson Smythe-Hersforth hopes she will become his fiancée. McNally and Son have been requested by Chauncey's mother to investigate Theodosia's credentials and make certain she is worthy of becoming a member of the Smythe-Hersforth clan."

"And part of your investigation included taking her to lunch in Boca Raton?"

"There is no adequate substitute for a personal interview," I said piously.

Connie turned her head away from me and stared at the wall. "Son," she said, "it's coming out your ears."

I finished dressing and got my pale pink shirttail caught in the zipper of my slacks. I tried to free it to no avail. The tail hanging out looked like—well, you know what it looked like. Connie turned back to watch my struggle. She began to giggle.

"I hope you have to go home like that," she said. "Serves you right."

"Listen," I said furiously, "my luncheon with Miss Johnson was strictly in the line of business. We went to Mizner Park because she had heard of it and wanted to see it. It was a simple business luncheon, and that's all it was. I don't expect you to believe that, but I'd like to remind you that some time ago you and I vowed to have an open relationship. Both of us could see and consort with whomever we wished. Isn't that correct?"

Unexpectedly she amiably agreed. "You're right, Archy. My first reaction, after Mercedes Blair told me of seeing you at the Bistro L'Europe—she was having a pizza at Baci—was to hire a hit man and have you blown away. But that, I decided, was a childish reaction. Archy, I have made up my mind. From now on you are completely free to share lunch or dinner or anything else with whomever you please. And I promise not to be jealous or to attack you physically in retaliation."

"Well put," I said enthusiastically.

"And in return, I expect the same consideration from you."

"Granted," I said. "And gladly."

"Good," she said. "Because tomorrow night I'm having dinner at the Ocean Grand with Binky Watrous."

Outrage detonated. "Binky Watrous!" I cried. "But he's a close friend of mine!"

"I know," Connie said calmly. "And I do believe he hopes to become a close friend of *mine*."

"I should warn you," I said darkly, "his table manners are not of the most delicate. He's been known to suck his teeth while slurping a beef ragout."

"I think I can endure it," she said, "after seeing you manhandle a stuffed avocado. And on Saturday night I have a movie date with Ferdy Attenborough."

"Ferdy?" I almost shouted. "Another old buddy! Connie, how can you possibly be seen in public with that man? He has an Adam's apple that looks like he swallowed an elbow."

"I think he's charming," she said. "In any event, the choice is mine, is it not?"

"Yes, yes," I said irascibly, finally getting my shirttail freed from the zipper. "But I question your choice. I fear you are doomed to grievous disappointment."

"No problem," she said cheerfully. "There are plenty of others waiting in the wings. Surely you have no objections, do you?"

"Of course not," I said, stiff-upperlipping it.

"As Shakespeare said, all's fair in love and war."

"It was Smedley," I said, "but you're quite right. I hope you have a merry time."

"I intend to," she said evenly.

I did not kiss her a fond good-night.

I drove home in a tumultuous mood. Binky Watrous! Ferdy Attenborough! And perhaps scores of unnamed others waiting in the wings. I was shocked, *shocked*. Naturally I wished Consuela Garcia all the happiness in the world, but the thought of her sharing her felicity with other johnnies was a tad discombobulating. More than a tad if you must know the truth.

I entered my home through the kitchen, making certain to relock the back door. I paused a moment in the kitchen to pick up a cold bottle of St. Pauli Girl from the fridge. I toted it upstairs, moving as quietly as I could on our creaky staircase. Then I was alone in my own chambers—no French dolls on the pillows—but in no mood for sleep. I believe I mentioned previously that I was bewitched by Theo Johnson's conduct. Connie's revelations completed the triumvirate; I was now also bothered and bewildered.

Binky and Ferdy? Good pals, of course, but birdbrains! I found Ms. Garcia's declaration of her intentions totally incomprehensible. I mean we had enjoyed so many jolly times together that I saw no reason for her to seek male companionship elsewhere. How could she possibly find another chap who can match my repertoire of ribald limericks?

I opened my bottle of beer and sat behind my desk. I was still fully clothed and still broody. It just seemed so unfair of Connie, so unjust, so un-everything. Oh, I may have a few minor faults; I admit I am not a perfect swain—but then what man is?

But after a few swigs of brew I began to regain that cool detachment I have always proudly considered an integral part of my character. I frankly acknowledged I was suffering a twinge, a *wee* twinge, of jealousy, which I had heretofore believed myself incapable of feeling.

Even worse, I realized, I was guilty of an unconscionable possessiveness. I expected fidelity from Connie, with no desire to provide faithfulness in return. A rank injustice, obviously, and moreover a distressing breach of civilized behavior. I should be ashamed.

But I wasn't. Because I recognized too clearly my limitations. I mean I could not soar like a condor, could I? Nor play "Turkey in the Straw" on a zither. Nor remain loyal to one woman. In other words, without the vilest form of hypocrisy, I could not be what I was not. It was a quandary.

Amidst all this muzzy meditation I slid a cassette of Cole Porter tunes into my player, clamping earphones to my noggin so as not to disturb my parents whose bedroom was directly below. And as I listened to all that evocative music I tried to distinguish between True Love, romantic love, and affection. Precise definitions escaped me.

And so the night dwindled down as I sat alone, sipping beer, and brooding about love and women and my own incapacity to make a permanent commitment. After a time I realized the poignant songs I was hearing impinged on my perplexities.

How about "Just One of Those Things"?

Or "From This Moment On"?

But the one that summed up my private philosophy most accurately, I mournfully concluded, was "Anything Goes."

Chapter 9

I awoke late on Friday morning, as you may have surmised, and after a comforting breakfast of kippers and scrambled eggs I arrived at the office a little before noon. I resolutely shelved my personal problems for the nonce. When duty calls, McNally is not one to cup his ear and mutter, "Eh?"

I called the phone number of Mrs. Jane Folsby, provided by Jamie Olson, and waited for seven rings. I was about to hang up when a woman said, somewhat breathlessly, "Hello, hello, hello?"

It was a rich voice, totally unlike Mrs. Folsby's chirp, and I guessed it might be her sister.

"Could I speak to Mrs. Jane Folsby, please?" I said.

"May I ask who's calling?"

When I hear that I'm always tempted to say, "Yes, you may," and then wait. But it didn't seem a ripe time for fraternity house humor, so I merely said, "Archy McNally," and hoped for the best.

"Just a minute," she said.

It was more than a minute but I used the time profitably to light my first English Oval of the day, and what a treat it was. Finally the chirper came on the line.

"Mr. McNally!" she said. "How nice to hear from you. How on earth did you find me?"

"My spies are everywhere," I said. "How are you, Mrs. Folsby?"

"Couldn't be better."

"Glad to hear it. I was sorry to learn you had left the Hawkins."

"Sorry?" she said. "No need for that because I'm not. After Mr. Hawkin passed I knew it was time for me to go."

I waited for more but she didn't seem inclined to offer any additional information.

"Mrs. Folsby," I said, "I have a question I hope you may be able to answer. Do you happen to know where Silas Hawkin purchased his art supplies?"

"Why, certainly," she answered. "He bought all his canvas and paints and things from Grabow's right here in West Palm Beach."

"Grabow's," I repeated. "That's a big help. Thank you so much." I hesitated a moment, wondering if I dared push her. I decided to take the chance. "Tell me, Mrs. Folsby," I said as sympathetically as I could, "what was your reason for leaving the Hawkins? I hope there was no unpleasantness."

"Mr. McNally," she said sharply, "there are certain things a lady doesn't talk about."

I could not, for the life of me, imagine what those things might possibly be. But then I consoled myself with the thought that perhaps I had been associating with an abnormal breed of ladies.

"I understand completely," I said, although I didn't. "Thank you again for your assistance and I wish you the best of good fortune in the future."

"Thank you," she said faintly.

I hung up and finished my cigarette, still mired in the stygian as to what happened at the Hawkin ménage that a lady couldn't or wouldn't talk about. Mrs. Folsby was no mossback, and if she refused to utter a word or even drop a teeny hint it had to be something truly horrendous. To say my curiosity was piqued is putting it mildly.

I looked up Grabow's Art Supplies in the Yellow Pages and made a note of the address, telephone number, and proprietor's name, Luther Grabow. I grabbed up the white linen golf cap I was sporting that day and went downstairs to the Miata, with absolutely no idea why I was jaunting to West Palm to talk to Mr. Grabow. I could claim it was "gut instinct"—that favorite cliché of authors of detective novels. Actually, I had nothing better to do.

I found Grabow's Art Supplies in a freestanding building off Dixie Highway. It looked as big as a warehouse and the interior gave the same impression: row after row of steel racks holding an incredible assortment of everything from Crayolas to jointed six-ft. mannequins of polished wood that could be adjusted to any possible position including, I presumed, obscene.

The man behind the sales counter was seated on a high stool. He was reading a paperback, and I was bemused to note it was a Western. It seemed an odd choice for a clerk in an art supply emporium. He looked up when I approached.

"Could I speak to Mr. Luther Grabow, please," I said.

He inspected me. "I'm Luther Grabow," he said, "but I'm not buying."

"And I'm not selling," I said. "Mr. Grabow, I understand the late Silas Hawkin was a customer of yours."

He continued to stare. "Who told you that?" he demanded.

"His widow," I said, lying without hesitation.

He softened. "Yeah," he said, "he was a customer. That was a helluva thing, him getting knocked off like that. I don't say it just because he was a regular customer but because I admired the guy. He was a real professional and knew exactly what he wanted. Never settled for anything but the best. And a good painter. Not great, mind you, but one of the best around."

"Mrs. Hawkin told me he stretched his own canvases."

"That's right. The most expensive linen I carry."

"Did you sell him the wooden frames?"

"Assembled? Nah. He bought what we call sticks, the wood sides, top and bottom. Dovetail joints. You put together the size and shape you want. Hey, what's your interest in all this?"

He was a wizened little fellow, almost emaciated, with a Vandyke so jetty it looked dyed, and no larger than a merkin. The eyes behind wire-rimmed specs were alert and suspicious.

I handed him a business card and after he had examined it I plucked it away, remembering Sgt. Rogoff's warning. "My firm is settling Mr. Hawkin's estate," I glibly explained. "We have made a very careful inventory of his unsold works, using his own ledger. The one item we've been unable to locate is a painting he was apparently working on at the time of his death. It is carried in his ledger simply as 'Untitled,' but there is no indication of its size or subject matter. We were hoping you might be able to help."

His stare was owlish. "He was working on it when he was killed?"

"The police believe so."

"And it's missing?"

"That's correct."

"Do the cops think the killer took it?"

"A possibility."

He was silent for such a long time I had almost given up hope of gleaning any additional information when he suddenly sighed and began to speak.

"I guess there's no reason I shouldn't tell you," he said, "as long as you keep my name out of it. I don't want to get involved. Okay?"

"Certainly," I said.

"About a month ago Hawkin came in and told me he wanted to try acrylic on wood. It was a technique he had learned in Europe years ago, but then he decided to concentrate on watercolors and oil on canvas. Anyway, he wanted a whole palette of acrylics and a nice piece of wood. I had the primer and colors in stock, but I had to special order the panel from a guy in Boston."

"That's interesting," I said. "What kind of wood was it?"

"Seasoned oak. A beautiful plank. Just perfect. Hawkin was happy."

"Do you recall the dimensions?"

"Sure. Half-inch thick. Eighteen inches by twenty-four inches."

"That's not very large," I commented. "Most of his oil paintings were much larger."

"That's right," he agreed. "But where are you going to get a huge plank of oak that hasn't got a flaw? Not to mention what the damned thing would weigh."

"Yes," I said, "that would be a consideration. So the size Hawkin bought could easily be carried?"

He nodded. "No problem."

"Did Hawkin say anything at all about what he intended to do with it? The subject matter of the painting?"

Owl eyes flickered. "Why, no," he said finally. "He never mentioned a word about it, and I never asked."

I knew he was lying, but there wasn't a thing I could do about it. I thanked him for his kind cooperation and walked out. I was not too displeased with the interview. If Hawkin had painted "Untitled" on that wood panel, his killer could easily have tucked it under one arm and strolled away. I knew Al Rogoff would be interested in what I had learned but decided not to inform him pro tem, figuring I might need it in the future for a bargaining chip. Such are the ways of the world.

I drove back to the McNally Building, and my train of thought (really a trolley car) was curious. It may have been due to seeing all those artists' supplies, but I suddenly recalled Sargent's portrait of Madam X. Totally unlike Theodosia Johnson, of course, but I could visualize her in that black velvet gown with the marvelous décolletage.

Do you think I need professional help?

I am attempting to make this account as honest as possible so I must confess that after I returned to my office I had contemplated taking a short nap. But it was not to be, for propped against my stained coffee mug (POVERTY SUCKS) was a message stating that Mrs. Louise Hawkin had phoned and desired I return her call, which I did.

"Mr. McNally," she said briskly, "Hector Johnson, a good friend, tells me you are a real estate agent."

"Not a licensed broker," I said hastily, "but I do work closely with our Real Estate Department." That was true enough; I went to all their parties and frequently participated in their office pools.

"Since Si died," she went on, "I have decided to put our property here on the market, and I'd like to discuss it with you."

"Of course," I said, having little doubt I could sustain my impersonation of a realtor. "What time would be convenient for you?"

"Why, right now if you can make it," she said. "I intend to be in all afternoon."

"Excellent," I said. "Be there within the hour. Thank you for calling, Mrs. Hawkin."

Ordinarily the Real Estate Department of McNally & Son does not handle residential properties but is limited to recommending to our clients the purchase or sale of commercial parcels and raw land. But occasionally they were called upon to broker the sale of the homes of Palm Beach residents who had gone to the great Gold Coast in the sky, and so they had all the printed forms required for listing.

I picked up a file of the necessary bumf and headed southward in the Miata, ruminating on Mrs. Hawkin's mention of Hector Johnson as "a good friend." That certainly gave credence to what Connie Garcia had told me about Louise and Hector being an "item." The pot was beginning to boil, I reflected, and the bubbling delighted me. I enjoy the mess *other* people make of their lives, don't you?

And when I pealed the chimes at the Hawkin home, who should open the door but Hector Johnson himself. Surprise! He looked as elegantly jaunty as he had the first time we met and his hearty assurance hadn't deserted him.

"Archy!" he shouted, grasping my hand and pulling me into the house. "Glad you could make it! Good to see you again!"

In contrast to that enthusiasm, my response must have sounded like a mumble but, in any event, I don't believe he was listening. He led me into the Florida room where Louise Hawkin was half-reclining on a white wicker couch. She was wearing lounging pajamas in a garish flowered pattern, and since she was gripping a tall drink I didn't offer to shake hands.

"Mrs. Hawkin," I said, "I'm happy we meet again. I hope you're well, ma'am."

She gave me a glazed smile. "Tip-top," she said.

Not completely smashed, I reckoned, but about halfway there. I mean she spoke intelligently but slowly and carefully as if fearful of slurring. And her movements were also slow, careful, and seemingly planned beforehand as if she might suddenly spill her drink or knock over a lamp.

"Darling," Hector Johnson said, and I chalked that up, "you and I are indulging. Surely we can offer our guest the same opportunity. Archy, we're working on gin and tonics. How does that sound?"

"Just right," I said.

"Shall I mix it?" Hector asked the hostess.

"I'll get it," she said thickly, set her glass aside, and lurched to her feet. "Besides," she added, "I have to make wee-wee."

Johnson laughed uproariously. I managed a strained smile. She walked from the room in slow motion, and Hector and I sat facing each other in matching armchairs. Then he launched into one of the strangest conversational gambits I had ever heard.

"What do you think about luck?" he demanded.

I blinked, then stared at him, wondering if he might be attempting an elaborate joke. But he was quite serious. "Nice to have," I said lamely.

"When you need it," he continued, "*desperately* need it, it's gone. When you don't give a damn—win or lose, who cares?—there it is. Funny thing, huh?"

"Yes," I said, thinking, what's *with* this man?

"Real estate agents get six percent from the seller," he said, looking at me thoughtfully. "Am I correct?"

"Generally," I said. "But on commercial properties and undeveloped land it's usually ten percent."

"Uh-huh," he said, still looking at me. "I was the one who told Louise to give you a call."

There was no mistaking his meaning, but I wasn't going to help him. Let him spell it out.

"You ever pay a finder's fee?" he asked casually.

"It's not unheard-of," I said.

"Didn't think it was," he said with a wolfish grin, then concluded swiftly with, "Keep it in mind," as Louise Hawkin came back into the room carrying my drink.

I sampled it cautiously. Heavy on the gin, light on the tonic. If she had been drinking those bombs all afternoon it was no wonder her smile was glazed.

"Mrs. Hawkin," I said, "I presume the property will not be legally yours until your late husband's will is settled."

"No," she said, "it's mine now. The title is in my name."

"Louise is a lady of property," Johnson put in. "But that doesn't pay for the liverwurst, does it, darling? Land-poor is what it's called."

No matter how impeccably he was dressed, it was a louche thing to say, was it not? I mean his words and tone seemed calculated to belittle the widow, reduce her to the role of a hapless mendicant.

"Did you have a specific asking price in mind?" I asked her.

She glanced at Hector Johnson.

"Two million five," he said promptly. "For everything."

"Suppose I send out a professional appraiser," I suggested. "No cost to you. He or she will know the value of comparable parcels in the neighborhood and will be able to make an informed estimate of how your property should be priced to sell quickly."

"Two million five," Johnson repeated. "Asking, of course. Louise will be willing to negotiate. Won't you, sweetie?"

"What?" she said. "Oh, sure. Negotiate."

"Suppose I leave these listing applications," I said, placing my folder on an end table. "Have your attorney review them before you sign. They're standard boilerplate by which you grant McNally and Son the right to represent you in the sale of your home for a specified period of time at a specified percentage of the selling price."

"Honey," Louise Hawkin said anxiously, "what do you think?"

"Sounds legit," he told her. "I'll take a look at the contract."

"Mrs. Hawkin," I said, "if your home is sold, do you intend to remain in the Palm Beach area?"

"Of course she's going to stay," Hector answered. "Get rid of this white elephant, use part of the proceeds to buy or lease a smaller place, maybe on the beach, and have enough left over to invest in something that'll provide her with a guaranteed income. Doesn't that make sense?"

The moment he used the phrase "guaranteed income," my opinion of his financial acumen plunged to subzero. Dear old dad had taught me years ago that there is no such thing as a guaranteed income. As pop said, "Who guarantees the guarantor?" Scary, huh?

"Whatever Mrs. Hawkin wishes," I said. "It's her future happiness that's at stake, and she must decide how it best may be achieved."

"Dear Hector," she said, gazing at him blearily, "I don't know what I'd do without your advice."

He rose, porky face glowing, and seated himself on the couch next to her. He picked up her hand and kissed the knuckles. "Just like Archy said, baby," he crooned, "your happiness is all that counts."

I must tell you I felt acutely uncomfortable. I was invited, but I had the impression of having barged into an intimate and probably semi-drunken tête-à-tête. I was certain that after I departed they would dance the horizontal hula-hula.

That was hardly my business or my concern. What did trouble me was the role of Svengali that Hector Johnson seemed to have assumed. It was hard to believe that in the short period since her husband's murder Louise Hawkin had succumbed to the man's forceful charm and blandishments.

Unless, of course, their affair had started before Silas Hawkin's death.

That could be easily explained. Hector's daughter had posed for the artist. It would not be extraordinary if he had met and become friendly with the Hawkin family. Perhaps what I had just witnessed was a relationship that had existed not for days but for months. One never knows, do one?

By then I'd had just about enough of the Hawkin and Johnson families for one day, thank you, and was looking forward to a quiet evening at home. I intended to retire to my digs after dinner and play my favorite Al Jolson cassette while bringing my journal up to date. I might even have a small marc to help me forget that as I labored, Connie Garcia and Binky Watrous were dining together. I hoped their raspberry soufflé would collapse. A savage desire, I admit, but surely understandable.

Unfortunately I was no sooner ensconced behind my desk, marc in fist and Jolson singing "Swanee," than my phone buzzed. When it's an outside call it rings; when it's an interior call it buzzes. Don't ask me why. The caller was Jamie Olson downstairs in the kitchen.

"Woman parked outside," he reported. "Wants to talk to you."

"What woman?"

"Won't say."

"Did you ask her to come in?"

"Won't come in."

"What's she driving?" I asked, dreaming it might be Connie's white Ford Escort and that she had had a squabble with Binky and had sought me out for comforting. I would, I decided, provide it generously.

"A black Jeep Cherokee," Jamie Olson said.

I sighed. "I'll be right down."

It was parked on the graveled turnaround in front of our garage. The door on the passenger side was opened as I approached. I peered within. Marcia Hawkin. She was wearing a soiled cotton trench coat buttoned up to the neck. I wondered what she wore underneath—if anything. Right about then, I figured, Jolson was singing "I'm Sitting on Top of the World." I wasn't.

"Marcia," I said. "How nice. Won't you come in?"

"No," she said and beckoned.

I slid in but left the door ajar a few inches in case I had to make a hasty exit. If she was as dotty as Connie had implied, a fast retreat might become necessary. I know there are times when my father is convinced he spawned a dunderhead, but there are also times when I have the wit to calculate possible dangers and take the proper precautions.

She didn't turn to look at me but stared straight ahead through the windshield. "She's selling our home," she announced. "The studio. Everything. Even my bed. Can she do that?"

I thought it best to feign ignorance, hoping she was not aware of my visit that afternoon.

"Your mother?" I asked.

"Stepmother," she corrected me angrily. "Can she sell the house?"

"Is the title in her name?"

"Yes."

"Then she can dispose of it any way she wishes."

"Shit!" she said furiously. "I love that place. Where am I going to live?"

"Surely she'll buy or lease another dwelling. Perhaps smaller but just as attractive and comfortable."

"I don't want another," she said. "I'm not going to live with her anymore. Never, never, never!"

She seemed so distraught I hesitated to say anything but felt I had to express sympathy for her plight. "Do you have family or friends you could stay with?" I asked.

"I told you I have no one. It's all his fault."

"Whose fault?"

"Hector Johnson. That bitch's father."

The word didn't shock me so much as her tone. Pure venom.

"Marcia," I said quietly, "sometimes things happen we feel are outrageous. The best thing to do is accept with resignation and as much grace as we can muster."

Finally she turned to look at me. "That's bullshit," she said. "I'm not going to meekly accept what's happening. I've done that all my life—accept. But I'm not going to do it anymore. Believe me, I know what's going on."

"What's going on?" I asked her.

"That's for me to know and you to find out," she answered, a response so childish I felt like weeping. "You know that saying: Don't get mad, get even? That's what I'm going to do—get even."

"I hope you won't do anything foolish," I ventured.

Her laugh was a cackle. "They're the fools," she said. "Not me. They'd like to put me away—did you know that?"

I was overwhelmed by her mysteries. "Who wants to put you away? For what? And where?"

"I'm as normal as you are," she said hotly, which I thought was an artless comparison. "You're sure she can sell the house?"

"She can," I repeated, "if the title is in her name."

"That's all I wanted to know," she said. "You can go now."

This abrupt, impolite dismissal was a minor affront from an obviously disturbed young woman, and I was happy to make my escape. I started to climb out of the Jeep when she suddenly yanked me back and kissed me on the lips, her tongue darting.

"There!" she cried. "See?"

I got out and before I could turn and close the door she had started up and pulled away with engine roar and a spurt of gravel. I stood there and watched the Cherokee make a wild turn onto Ocean Boulevard and speed away.

I went back upstairs to finish my marc and hear Jolson singing "Baby Face." I worked steadily on my journal until eleven-thirty. Then I closed up shop and, feeling brain dead, prepared for bed. But the aggravations of that wretched day had not yet ended.

My phone rang. Not buzzed but rang.

"Hi, luv," Connie Garcia said cheerily. "I'm home safe and sound. All locked up, bolted, and chained. I knew you'd want to know."

"Yes," I said.

"I hate to tell you this, Archy, but I had a wonderful time tonight."

"Why should you hate to tell me?" I said, gritting the old bicuspids. "I'm happy you enjoyed yourself."

"And Binky," she said, giggling. "I also enjoyed him."

It was too much.

"He's such good company," she prattled on. "Why didn't you tell me he can do birdcalls."

"Oh yes," I said. "His imitation of a loon is especially realistic."

"And tomorrow night it's Ferdy Attenborough," she went on blithely. "We're going to La Vieille Maison in Boca."

"How nice," I said stiffly. "Do try the quail with grapes."

"I intend to," she said. "It'll be a welcome change from cheeseburgers at the Pelican Club. Actually, I called to tell you that you were exactly right. You and I should become more socially active. Separately. I mean we should both date other people. Our relationship was becoming much too restrictive. Don't you agree?"

It was impossible to disagree since I had been warbling that tune for years. "As long as you're happy," I said.

"Oh, I am," she said. "Deliriously. I hope you don't mind, Archy."

"Mind?" I said loftily. "Of course not. Why on earth should I mind?"

"I'm glad to hear you say that. On Monday Wes Trumbaugh is taking me to a dinner-dance at his club."

"Wes Trumbaugh?" I screamed. "Connie, that man is the biggest lecher in Palm Beach!"

"Ooooo," she said, "that does sound fascinating. Good-night, Archy, and sleep well."

She hung up. Sleep well? Hah! I fiercely punched my pillows twice, once for Binky, once for Ferdy. Then I added a third for Wes Trumbaugh.

Chapter 10

I would prefer not to write about that weekend. I would prefer it never happened. I would prefer the world went directly from Friday night to Monday morning.

But unfortunately it did occur: two ghastly days during which I made a complete ass of myself and am still apologizing for my abominable conduct.

I shall not detail all my disgraceful actions during those forty-eight hours.

Suffice to say that I ate too much, drank too much, smoked too much, laughed too loudly, and told pointless jokes. My most shameful memory is standing on a table at the Pelican Club at two A.M. trying to recite "When Lilacs Last in the Dooryard Bloom'd" to a jeering audience as hammered as I.

I awoke on Monday wondering if it might be possible to commit hara-kiri with my Swiss Army knife. An ax-murderer, having dispatched wife, children, in-laws, and the family dog, always tells the police, "The devil made me do it." I would have liked to make that defense but my pride would not allow it. No, my beastly behavior was completely the fault of yrs. truly, Archibald McNally.

I usually scrape my jowls with a conventional single-edged razor but that morning, being somewhat unsteady, I opted for an electric shaver, fearing I might nick the old jugular. It was only after drinking a quart of cold water and a pint of hot coffee that I started to regain a slight semblance of normality.

I arrived at the office before noon, determined that henceforth I would forswear cigarettes, strong drink, and ham hocks. I sat at my desk, absent-mindedly lighted an English Oval, and jumpstarted my groggy cerebrum. The result of my lucubrations? The murder of Silas Hawkin was really none of my business. The murder of Shirley Feebling was really none of my business. My job was merely to investigate the bona fides of Theodosia Johnson.

Yet I could not ignore a conviction that the two homicides and my assignment were inextricably mixed. One loose end that might lead to untangling this snarl was Reuben Hagler, the self-styled investment adviser of Fort Lauderdale. Another was Marcia Hawkin's fury and implied threats. A third was the don't-give-a-damn attitude of Madam X. And the fourth was her father's patent attempt to cozy up to the Widow Hawkin.

This logical recap included all of my questions but provided none of the answers. So I decided to forgo logic, do a bit of improv riffing and see what happened. Hey, if you can't get a little fun from your job, seek employment elsewhere. Thus spaketh A. McNally.

Pinky Schatz. Do you remember the name?

She was the confidante of Shirley Feebling and had the misfortune of finding that poor woman's corpse. I was sure Pinky had been interrogated by the Fort Lauderdale police, but sometimes a material witness doesn't tell the cops everything he or she knows, not in an effort to impede the investigation but because of a personal motive. Or the witness doesn't fully comprehend what observations and/or knowledge are germane. In any event, I reckoned it might help my own inquiry if I met Ms. Schatz and heard her story personally.

She was not listed in the Fort Lauderdale or Pompano Beach telephone directories. She and Shirl had been co-workers so I called the topless car wash. The man who answered had a growly voice, and I guessed him to be Jake, the woolly mammoth.

"Yeah?" he said.

"Could I speak to Pinky Schatz, please."

"She don't work here no more."

"Do you have her present home address?" I asked. "This is the McNally Insurance Company. We have a check for her in payment for damages her car suffered in a recent collision, but our letter was returned to us marked 'Not at this address.' I imagine she's moved and neglected to inform us."

"I don't know where she's living," he said. "Try the Leopard Club on Federal. She's dancing there."

He hung up before I could thank him.

I had heard of the Leopard Club. It was said to be an upscale and pricey nude dancing establishment where the performers mingled freely with the patrons, most of whom were suits carrying calfskin attaché cases. I had never been tempted to visit since the idea of sipping an overpriced aperitif while a naked young woman gyrated on my table seemed to me a betrayal of Western Civilization.

However, I resolutely conquered my squeamishness and set out to find Pinky Schatz. But first I drove the Miata to my garage in West Palm Beach where I left it for a tune-up, eschewing new tires until my checking account was off life-support and breathing normally. I was given a loaner, a black three-year-old Buick LeSabre. It was rather sedate for my taste but certainly less noticeable and less likely to be remembered than my jazzy little chariot.

Two hours later I entered the Leopard Club, after passing a tenner to the muscular sentry at the door. A score of men, mostly middle-aged and solemn of mien, sat at small tables and watched nude dancers on a brightly lighted stage oscillating more or less in rhythm to music from overhead loudspeakers.

There were a half-dozen dancers, each au naturel except for a single garter about one thigh. Tucked into the elastic strip were folded bills: ones, fives, tens, a few twenties: tips from appreciative customers. When the music ended, the dancers left the stage and came down to cajole patrons into paying an added fee for a solo dance atop their table. Meanwhile the music started again, and a new set of dancers pranced onto the stage and began to demonstrate their flexibility.

I had been approached by a surly waitress, fully clothed, who took my order for a bottle of Heineken. She brought it almost immediately along with a tab for ten dollars I was apparently expected to pay instanter. But before I did, I asked if Pinky Schatz was present.

"Yeah," the waitress said, "the fatso redhead on the stage. You want I should send her over when the set ends?"

"Please," I said, paid for the beer, gave her a five-dollar tip, and glanced sorrowfully at my rapidly shrinking wallet.

The music paused briefly, the dancers left the stage, a new squad took over. The "fatso redhead" came sashaying toward my table. She had the loveliest silicone I've ever seen.

"Hi, honey," she said, beaming. "You asked for me?"

"If you're Pinky Schatz."

She nodded. "That's right, and I bet you want a table dance. It's my specialty,"

"No, no," I said hastily. "Just a little conversation."

"Oh-ho," she said. "Well, that's okay, too. You can tell me how your wife doesn't understand you. Can I have a drink?"

"Of course. Whatever you want."

"Hey, Mabel," she called to the waitress. "My usual." Then she leaned to me. "They'll charge you for booze," she whispered, "but it's just iced tea."

I liked her. She was a large, vital woman with a ready smile and a hearty laugh. Marvelous skin tone. Also, she had a tattoo of an American flag on her left bicep, and that reminded me of you know who.

Her drink was served and we lifted our glasses to each other.

"You're a tall one," she said. "I like that. How come you asked for me?"

"You were a close friend of Shirley Feebling, weren't you?"

Her face hardened and she started to rise. I put out a hand to stop her.

"Please don't leave," I begged. "I'm not a cop, and this is very important to me."

She sat down slowly. It was odd conversing at a minuscule table with a rosy, naked woman, but I swear to you I wasn't distracted. Charmed, as a matter of fact, but not unduly aroused.

"Who are you?" she demanded.

I had devised a scam on the drive down from Palm Beach. It was a cruel deception but I could think of no alternative.

"My name is Chauncey Smythe-Hersforth," I said. "Did Shirl ever mention me?"

Her big eyes grew even bigger. "Oh gawd," she said. "You're the guy who wanted to marry her."

I nodded.

Her hand fell softly on my arm. "I'm sorry, Chauncey," she said. "Really sorry."

"Thank you," I said. "Listen, I need your help. The police seem to be getting nowhere on this, and I want the guy who did it found and sent to the chair. You can understand that, can't you?"

"Sure," she said. "Me, too. Shirl was my best friend, and a sweeter girl never lived."

"Did she ever say anything about someone following her or annoying her or making threatening phone calls? Anything like that?"

"I told the cops. She said that for the last few days—this was before she was killed—she kept seeing this Cadillac. It was around all the time while she was at work and at home and when she went shopping."

"A Cadillac? Did she describe the model and color?"

"Not the model. She said it was a funny color, like bronzy."

"Did she get a look at the driver?"

"Not a good clear look. She said he had a hatchet face. She said she thought she had seen him before in the pizza joint near the car wash."

"Pinky, have you any idea who she was talking about? Did you ever meet a hatchet-faced man who drives a car like that?"

She looked at me steadily, her stare unwavering, unblinking. It shocked me because when people are about to lie, they put on a look like that. It is not true that liars are shifty-eyed, blink frequently, or turn their gaze away. Experienced liars hope to prove their honesty by a steady, wide-eyed look expressing complete probity.

"Why, no," Pinky Schatz said. "I never met a man like that. I have no idea who he could be. That's what I told the cops."

I thanked her, slipped her fifty dollars, and left the Leopard Club. I was depressed. Not so much by the sadness of that joint—lonely, longing men and bored, contemptuous women—but by what I considered the blatant falsehoods of Pinky Schatz. It wasn't difficult to imagine the motive for her lies. It was fear.

It was latish when I arrived back in Palm Beach and it seemed silly to return to my office and stare at the walls. So I went for a swim, removed the ocean's residue with a hot shower and loofah glove, and dressed for what I devoutly hoped would be an uneventful evening.

And it was until about nine-thirty. I had gone up to my lair after dinner and was recording in my journal the mise-en-scène at the Leopard Club when my phone did what phones are supposed to do. I wasn't sure I wanted to pick it up, fearing it might be Connie calling to tell me what a frabjous evening she was having with Wes Trumbaugh.

But I answered. It wasn't Connie. It was Theodosia Johnson.

"Hey, Archy," she said, "how would you like to buy a girl a drink?"

"Love to," I said. "Do you have any particular girl in mind?"

"Yes," she said, laughing, "this girl. Daddy is using the car tonight so you'll have to come get me."

I hesitated. It was a rather dicey situation. After all, she was practically betrothed to the Smythe-Hersforth scion and he *was* a client of McNally & Son. I decided to express my fears.

"What about Chauncey?" I asked her. "Mightn't he object?"

"He doesn't *own* me," she said coldly. "Besides he just dropped me off after dinner and is on his way home to mommy."

"Be there in a half-hour," I said. "Will casual rags be acceptable?"

"Pj's will be acceptable," she said.

What a sterling woman!

I pulled on a silvery Ultrasuede sport jacket over a pinkish Izod and flannel bags, thrust my bare feet into black penny mocs, and paused long enough to swab the phiz with Obsession. Then I dashed.

I pulled up outside the Johnsons' condo and Theo exited immediately, pausing just long enough to double-lock her door. Then she came bouncing down to the LeSabre.

"Archy," she said, "how many cars do you own?"

"Just one. But the Miata's in the garage for an enema. Theo, you look smashing!"

It was the truth. She was dressed to the tens in honey-colored silk jacket and pantaloons. Her only jewelry was a choker of braided gold, and if the Chinless Wonder had donated that he had more taste than I had given him credit for.

"Thank you, dear," she said and leaned forward to kiss my cheek. "Yummy," she said. "Obsession?"

"Correct, supernose," I said. "You know everything, and it's scary. We're going to the Pelican Club. Nothing fancy, but the drinks are huge and if you want to sing 'Mother Machree' no one will call the cops."

"Great," she said. "My kind of joint."

That phrase she used—"My kind of joint"—jangled the old neurons. It sounded like something Pinky Schatz might say. But from the soon-to-be fiancée of Chauncey Wilson Smythe-Hersforth?

I mean we all make critical judgments, usually immediate, of people we meet, based on their appearance, speech, behavior. We instantly decide: He's a nudnick. She's a cipher. And so forth. Sometimes these initial impressions are modified or even totally revised after closer acquaintance, but it's amazing how often first reactions prove to be accurate.

I had thought Theo Johnson to be a well-bred young lady, independent, emancipated, and rather freewheeling in the morality department. But her saying "My kind of joint" made me wonder if there was a coarser side to her nature I had not heretofore recognized. Does that make me a snob? I thought you had already determined that.

In any event, my confusion grew. I simply could not categorize this woman; she was truly Madam X. Her taste in clothes and makeup, her table manners and social graces seemed faultless. And, of course, her physical beauty was nonpareil. I think perhaps what I found most inexplicable was her tattoo. It was like finding a hickey on the neck of the Mona Lisa.

"Where did you and Chauncey dine?" I asked as we sped westward.

"Cafe L'Europe."

"Excellent. I hope you had the veal."

"I did," she said. "Archy, I think you and I enjoy the same things. Don't you agree?"

"Oh yes!" I said. "Yes, yes, yes!" And she laughed.

Jolly Pandemonium was the leitmotiv of the Pelican Club that night. It was at its noisiest and smokiest. Dart players were darting, table-hoppers were hopping, and everyone was guzzling happily and laughing up a typhoon.

"Uh-huh," Theo said, glancing around, "I belong here. Is Chauncey a member?"

" 'Fraid not."

"Didn't think so," she said with a wry-crisp smile. "Not his scene. He's such a fuddy-duddy. I mean he still reads newspapers. Can you believe it?"

I made no comment but led her into the dining area. Lights were dimmed, dinner was no longer being served, but there were a few couples lingering, holding hands across tables and looking into each other's eyes for promise. I claimed my favorite corner spot, and we were no sooner seated than Priscilla came sauntering over.

"You know the reputation of this man?" she asked Theo.

Madam X actually giggled. "I can imagine," she said.

"No, you can't," Pris said. "Whenever there's a full moon he gets long hair on the backs of his hands."

"Love it," Theo said, tilted her head back and bayed a long "Wooooo!" at the ceiling.

"Just what I need," Priscilla said. "A couple of loonies."

"Enough of your sass," I said. "We may be loonies but we're thirsty loonies. Theo?"

"Wine," she said promptly.

"Pinot Grigio?"

"Just right."

"A bottle, please," I said to Pris. "And try not to crumble the cork."

"Keep it up, buster," she said, "and I'll crumble *your* cork."

She strolled into the bar area, and Theo laughed. "You've known her a long time, Archy?"

"Years. Her family runs the place. Brother Leroy is our chef. Daddy Simon is bartender-manager. And her mom Jasmine is our housekeeper and den-mother. The Pettibones made the Pelican Club a winner. We were going down the drain before they took over."

"I hope you'll ask me here again."

I didn't quite know how to reply to that, but I was saved by Priscilla serving our wine. Chilled just right and with a slight flowery aroma.

Theo sipped. "Loverly," she said. "Thank you for coming to my rescue. I was in the doldrums."

"I've visited the doldrums," I said. "Miserable place. It's near the pits, isn't it?"

"Too near," she said, not smiling.

We drank our wine slowly, comfortable with each other. What a selfish delight it was to be in the company of such a beautiful woman. I tried not to stare at her but it was difficult to resist. "Feasting your eyes" is the cliché, and mine were famished.

"I know so little about you," I mentioned casually, trying not to sound like a Nosy Parker. "Tell me."

"Not a lot to tell," she said just as casually. "Besides, I hate to look back, don't you? The past is such a drag. The future is much more exciting."

She had neatly finessed me, and I feared that if I asked specific questions she'd think me a goof.

"All right," I said, "let's talk about your future. Have you decided to become Chauncey's one-and-only?"

She gave me a mocking half-smile. "Let's talk about it later," she said. "Right now I'm with you."

"For which I give thanks to Aphrodite," I said. "A.k.a. Venus. The goddess of love and beauty."

"It's skin-deep," she said.

"Beauty?" I asked. "Or love?"

"Both."

That seemed to me a rather harsh judgment, but I had no desire to argue.

"And what about your lady?" she asked me.

"We have an open relationship. Tonight she's at a dinner-dance with an-other chap."

"And you're jealous?"

"Of course not."

"Liar, liar, pants on fire!" she said with a boomy laugh. "Tell me, Archy, what do you do when you're not real-estating."

"Eat, drink, smoke, swim in the ocean, play tennis, golf, and poker, watch polo, read trash, listen to pop singers, occasionally attend the theatre, opera, ballet, charity bashes, and private shindigs, buy clothes and trinkets, write to old friends, party with new friends, and sleep. I think that about cov-ers it."

"Not quite," she said. "You didn't mention sex."

"I didn't want to offend your sensibilities."

"What makes you think I have any?" And before I could come up with a saucy rejoinder, she said, "You know what I'd like to do after we finish this bottle of wine?"

"Have another?"

"No," she said, "take a walk on the beach. Could we do that?"

"Of course," I said. "Sorry I can't provide a full moon to prove my hands don't grow hair. There's just a sliver."

"It'll be enough. Can I take off my sandals, roll up my pants, and wade in the surf?"

"Whatever turns you on."

She looked at me with a crooked smile. "I asked Chauncey the same thing earlier this evening. He said the water might be too cold, I might cut my bare feet on shells, and the Beach Patrol might pick us up for loitering."

"Well, yes," I said. "All those things could happen."

"But you don't care, do you, Archy?"

"Not much."

She reached across the table to clasp my hand. "I told you how alike we are," she said. "I wish you were the marrying kind."

"What kind is that?"

"Chauncey," she said, almost bitterly. "Let's finish this divine wine and go."

And so we did. When I signed the tab, Priscilla looked about to make sure Theo was out of earshot and then whispered, "You're asking for trouble, son."

"What do you mean by that?" I demanded.

"I just *know*," she said and moved swiftly away.

I drove back to the shore and parked the Buick in the McNally driveway. Hand in hand, Theo and I trotted across Ocean Boulevard and stepped down the rickety wooden stairway to the sea. That splinter of moon was obscured by clouds, and an easterly breeze was warm and clammy. We didn't care. It was the wine, I suppose, and the joy of being alone on the beach at midnight.

Theo kicked off her sandals, rolled the cuffs of her pantaloons above her knees, and strode into the milky surf, kicking her way through. I stood on dry land, bemused, and watched her cavort. She seemed suddenly released, laughing, bending to scrub her face with cupped handfuls of saltwater. I wouldn't have been a bit surprised if she stripped starkers and plunged in. But she didn't.

I walked back to the wall, sat on the sand, lighted a cigarette. I had finished it before she came gamboling out, flicking glittery droplets from her fingertips and caroling, "Super, super, super!" She plumped down beside me and asked for my handkerchief to dry sodden strands of her chestnut hair. There wasn't much moonglow, but I could see her face was shining.

"Was that what you wanted?" I asked.

"It was what I needed," she said, and then gestured toward the dark, rolling sea. "What's out there, Archy?"

"Water. Lots of it."

"No, I mean eventually."

"Eventually? Africa. Around Morocco, I'd guess."

"Let's go."

"Tonight?"

"Whenever."

Her voice was light but I felt she was serious. Certainly half-serious.

She turned, took my face between her cool palms, kissed me, drew away. She leaned forward, hugged her knees. "Do I scare you?" she said.

"Of course not," I lied valiantly, because to tell you the truth she did. A little. There was a wildness in her, a willfulness that was daunting.

"Do you think I'm pretty?" she asked suddenly.

"More than pretty," I said. "Lovely. Beautiful."

"Yes," she said, nodding, "I know. And I thought it would bring me happiness but it hasn't. Like an actress who knows, just *knows* she has a special talent. But she can't get an acting job so it doesn't do her a damned bit of good. Just goes to waste. Do you understand what I'm saying, Archy?"

"Yes."

"I've got the looks and the body," she went on. "It's not conceit; I just know. But things didn't work out the way I thought they would. Bad luck, I guess."

"Your father spoke to me about luck," I told her. "He said, in effect, that when you need it desperately, it doesn't appear. But when you don't give a damn you have all the luck in the world."

"Did daddy say that? Well, he should know. Take off your clothes."

"What?"

"Take off your clothes," she repeated, unbuttoning her jacket.

"All right," I said.

I must inform you that anyone who attempts to make love on a sandy beach soon learns the meaning of true grit. But we managed, and we were so enthusiastic, so joyously *vocal* that I suspect both of us were tempted to wonder "Was it as good for me as it was for you?"

I shall not fully describe the scene—dying moon, scudding clouds, sultry wind—because I've always felt love scenes are best played on bare stages. There may be scenery artfully arranged but it becomes invisible when the butterfly flutters—as it did that night.

And then, triumphant, we both laughed. At our own madness, I imagine. It was a sweet moment, but brief. Because as we nakedly embraced, Theo murmured, "Tonight at dinner I told Chauncey I'd marry him. That's why he hurried home, to tell mommy the news."

"Oh," I said, which I admit was not a very cogent reaction. But I was stunned.

"Do you blame me?" she asked softly.

"Blame?" I said. "Of course not. What right do I have to blame you? It's your life and you must live it in whatever fashion you decide. Believe me, darling, I wish you all the happiness in the world."

She made no reply but rolled away from me and slowly began to dress. I did the same, and we made ourselves presentable in silence. Finally I stood shakily and helped her to her feet. We hugged tightly a moment. I was affected, thinking it a final farewell.

"Thank you for tonight," I said huskily. "The only word for it is memorable. I know we shan't be seeing much of each other from now on."

She drew away far enough to tap my cheek lightly with her fingertips. "Silly boy," she said.

I don't believe we exchanged a dozen words during the drive back to her condo. When we arrived I saw a white Lincoln Town Car parked outside, next to a gunmetal Cadillac De Ville.

"Daddy's home," Theo announced. "The Lincoln is ours. The Caddie belongs to a friend."

"Oh?" I said. "He's got Michigan plates. Down for a visit?"

"No, he moved here recently. Just hasn't switched to a Florida license yet." I didn't push it.

She gave me a parting kiss. "Thank you, Archy," she said. "Fabulous night." She whisked out of the car. I waited until she was safely inside, then I headed homeward. I was not as fatigued as you might expect. I wasn't eager to dance a polka, but I was more replete than exhausted.

It was too late to shower since the gurgling of the drain would disturb my parents. I did my best with a washcloth to capture the vagrant grains of sand that remained on my carcass. Then I brushed the old choppers and donned a pair of silk pajama shorts emblazoned with multicolored crowns and scepters. Fitting, for I felt like royalty that night. Don't ask me why.

I waited patiently for sleep to come, knowing it would not take long. Meanwhile I did some heavy brooding on The Case of Madam X. I was not so concerned with the murders of Silas Hawkin and Shirley Feebling as I was with the unaccountable personality of the lady herself. I simply could not solve her.

Did I know any more about her than I did when our evening began? Yes, I did, but what I had learned was disquieting. Her character seemed so complex, with nooks and crannies I had not yet glimpsed, let alone explored.

Surely you've seen matryoska. (I think that's the correct spelling.) They're Russian nesting dolls. Remove the top half of the largest wooden doll and within is a smaller. Remove the top of that one and an even smaller doll is within. This continues for five or six dolls. You finally come to the last, which is solid wood and no larger than an unshelled peanut.

That's how I thought of Theodosia Johnson. She was a series of nesting women, and I had hardly begun to get down to the solid core. I was slowly unlayering her, and the awful thought occurred to me that when I finally uncovered the penultimate woman, there might be nothing within.

I could not forget her final comment on the beach after I had suggested our just completed coupling would be the last. "Silly boy," she said, an obvious implication that her affiancing to Chauncey Wilson Smythe-Hersforth, or even her marriage to that bubblehead, need not bring our fun and games to a screeching halt. A very amoral attitude, and it disturbed me.

I mean I am not a holier-than-thou johnny. Far from it. But her insouciance was startling. I have always been a hopeful romantic, but it was still something of an epiphany to learn that a woman of ethereal beauty could have earthy desires.

Or if not earthy, at least sandy. As well I knew.

Chapter 11

I awoke on Tuesday morning in time to breakfast with my parents in the dining room. Ursi served paper-thin latkes with little pork sausages and apple sauce, and a big wedge of casaba with a crisp winy flavor.

The boss wanted to know if I required a lift to the office, his not-so-subtle way of telling me it would be nice if I got to work on time for a change. I explained I had to return the Buick and pick up my rejuvenated Miata. He accepted that without comment and took off alone in his black Lexus 400.

I drove over to West Palm Beach and reclaimed my little beauty, sparkling after a bath and wax job. Then I returned to the McNally Building around ten-thirty to find on my desk two telephone messages, both asking me to call. The name Hector Johnson was familiar, of course, but I stared at the other, Luther Grabow, and at first it meant nothing.

Then a lightbulb flashed above my head just as it does in comic strips. Luther Grabow. Ah-ha. The owner of the store where Silas Hawkin bought his art supplies. Intrigued, I phoned immediately and identified myself.

"Oh yeah," he said. "Listen, your firm is settling Si Hawkin's estate—am I right?"

"That's correct, Mr. Grabow." The experienced liar always remembers his falsehoods.

"And you told me one painting is gone. Is it still missing?"

"It is. It's listed in his ledger as 'Untitled,' but we haven't been able to locate it."

"The paintings you did find—were they on canvas?"

"All of them."

"So the chances are good that the missing work is the one he did on that wood panel I told you about. You agree with me?"

"Completely," I said. "There were no paintings on woods in Mr. Hawkin's inventory."

Long pause. Then he sighed. "I've been thinking about it," he said, "and I decided there's no reason I shouldn't tell you. The reason I didn't before was that I thought it might make the widow unhappy. You know? But when you sell off his stuff, she's going to get all the proceeds—am I right?"

"Oh yes," I said, padding my deception. "Mrs. Hawkin is the sole beneficiary."

"Then I might as well tell you. When Hawkin ordered the oak panel and said he was going to try acrylics, I asked him what he had in mind and he said he was planning to do a nude."

I may have gulped. "A nude?"

"That's what he said. He told me he had done some nudes when he was young, but then he found out there was more money to be made doing portraits."

"Did he tell you who the model would be?"

"Nah. He just said it was going to be a nude."

"Thank you very much for your cooperation, Mr. Grabow," I said. "I appreciate it and will make certain you are adequately recompensed for your professional assistance."

"That would be nice," he said.

I hung up, lighted a cigarette, and stared at the ceiling. A nude? I wondered if Silas Hawkin had met Pinky Schatz. Ridiculous. Or was it?

My second call, to Hector Johnson, was just as puzzling.

"Hiya, Arch," he said breezily. "How're you doing?"

I don't object to the diminutive Archy for Archibald, but I have an intense aversion to being called Arch. Too much like an adjective.

"Fine," I said. "And you?"

"Couldn't be better. I want to buy you lunch today. How about it?"

"Sounds great," I said.

It didn't. To be candid, Hector Johnson and men like him dismay me. They know all about professional football, they understand baccarat, and they can cure an arthritic septic tank. I mean they're so *practical*. I know little about such things. But then, on the other hand, if you're seeking an apt quotation from Publius Vergilius Maro, I'm your man.

"Do you like tongue?" Hector asked. I could think of a dozen snappy retorts to that query, some of them printable, but he plunged ahead before I could reply. "Nothing like a tongue sandwich on rye with hot mustard and a cold beer. You know Toojay's Deli on U.S. One, up near Jupiter?"

"Yes, I know it," I said, wondering why he was picking such a distant spot. Tongue sandwiches were available closer to home. His home, for instance.

"Meet you at twelve-thirty," he said briskly. "Okay?"

"I'll be there."

"My treat," he said, and hung up.

Toojay's is an excellent deli, no doubt about it, but hardly the place for a quiet, intimate luncheon even in midsummer when the tourists are absent. I could only conclude that Hector didn't want to be seen conferring with me in more familiar Palm Beach haunts. But what his reasons might be I could not fathom.

I arrived at Toojay's fashionably late, and it was as crowded and clamorous as I expected. I looked around for Hector and spotted him sitting at a table for four. With him was a gent with a profile like a cleaver and the body of a very tall jockey. I had absolutely no doubt that he drove a gunmetal Cadillac De Ville and his name was Reuben Hagler.

I made my way to their table, dodging the scurrying waitresses. By the time I arrived I had what I hoped was an unctuous smile pasted on my puss. Johnson rose to greet me, but the other man remained seated.

"Heck," I said, shaking his hand, "good to see you again."

"Likewise," he said. "Arch, I want you to meet Reuben Hagler, an old buddy of mine. Rube, this is Archy McNally, the dude I told you about."

The old buddy didn't rise or offer his hand, but he did grant me a glacial nod. I gave him one in return and sat down next to Hector, across from Hagler. The two men had glasses of beer but no food. Johnson snapped his fingers at a passing waitress, a habit I detest.

"How about it?" our host asked. "Tongue sandwiches all around with fries and slaw? And a beer for you, Arch?"

There were no objections, and that's what he ordered. Hector glanced at his wristwatch but it wasn't the old digital he had been wearing the first time we met. Now it was a gold Rolex, and I wondered if it might have been a gift from Louise Hawkin.

"Don't want to rush you, Arch," he said, "but Rube and I have an important business meeting in about an hour so we'll have to eat and run."

"No problem," I said and looked at the man sitting opposite. "What business are you in, Mr. Hagler?"

"Investments," he said. "Interested?"

"Sorry," I said. "At the moment I'm teetering on the edge of abject poverty."

Hector laughed but not Reuben. He didn't strike me as the kind of man who laughed often, if at all.

"If you change your mind," he said, "look me up. I'm in Lauderdale. I can promise you a twenty percent return with no risk."

When pigs fly, I thought, but didn't say it.

Our luncheons were served. They were enormous sandwiches with what I estimated was a half-pound of tongue between two slabs of sour rye. We set to work, but gluttonizing didn't bring our conversation to a halt.

"Arch," Hector said, "I got something to ask you, but first I want you to know you can talk in front of Reuben here. We've been friends a long time, and we got no secrets from each other. Right, Rube?"

"Right," the other man said.

"And he knows how to keep his mouth shut," Johnson added.

"I don't blab," Hagler agreed.

"Now tell me," Hector went on, "you work in the real estate department of your daddy's law firm. Is that correct?"

"Usually," I said cautiously, "but not all the time. Occasionally my father gives me other assignments. Things that require special handling."

"Well, I'm glad to hear that," he said, "because it's been bothering me. I couldn't figure out how you got involved if all you did was real estate."

"I don't understand," I said, understanding very well. "Involved in what?"

"That's what I like," Hector said, addressing the other man. "A close-mouthed guy. Archy don't blab either. Well, a few days ago this Chauncey Smythe-whatever, a fellow my daughter has been dating, comes to me and says he wants to marry Theo and he wants my approval. Can you top that? In this day and age he wants the father's permission before he pops the question. Is that nutsy or what?"

He looked at me to gauge my astonishment.

"Amazing," I said.

"Yeah," he said. "This Chauncey—hey, Arch, what in hell kind of a name is Chauncey?"

"I believe it's of French derivation."

"No kidding? Well, this Chauncey works in a bank and I guess he's got mucho dinero. You know anything about that?"

He was, I decided, one brash lad. "I don't believe the Smythe-Hersforth family is hurting," I said carefully.

"Uh-huh," he said, shoveling in more coleslaw, "that's what I thought. Well, that's all to the good; every father wants to see his little girl well-provided for. But from what he said I figure his mama holds the purse strings. Am I right? Hey, let's have another round of beers."

And without waiting for our acquiescence he did his finger-snapping shtick again. I was glad he did because it gave me time to frame a discreet answer to the question about who controlled the Smythe-Hersforth millions. But I needn't have bothered; Hector didn't pause for a reply.

"The reason I figured that," he continued, "is because this guy who wants to be my son-in-law told me his mother asked her lawyers to investigate my daughter. Is that right, Arch?"

If the Chinless Wonder had been there at that moment I could have cheerfully throttled the numskull, possibly by force-feeding him a dozen of those colossal tongue sandwiches.

I realized I had no choice but to tell the truth, even though it is foreign to my nature. "That's correct, Heck," I said. "I have been assigned the job of gathering information about your daughter."

Unexpectedly he accepted it quite good-naturedly. "I can understand that," he said. "Can't you, Rube? The old lady's got a lot of loot and she doesn't want her sonny boy falling into the hands of a gold digger. Isn't that about it?"

"Something like that," I agreed, taking a deep swallow of my beer.

"Sure," Reuben Hagler put in. "If I was the old lady, I'd be doing the same time. Smart—know what I mean?"

"Absolutely," Johnson said. "She's protecting her own, and who can blame her for that? So I went to Theo and asked her if she really liked this guy. And she—"

"Wait a minute," I interrupted, suddenly horrified. "You didn't tell Theo I was investigating her, did you?"

"Hell, no!" Hector said, drowning his remaining fries in catsup. "Positively not! Because that girl's got a lot of pride, and if she knew she was being tracked she'd have dumped that Chauncey so fast he wouldn't know what hit him. No, I didn't tell her, Arch; I just asked if she wanted to marry Chauncey, and she said she did. So I phoned him and gave him the go-ahead."

Both men looked at me, and I wondered what they were expecting me to say. All I could manage was a weak, "You gave him permission to propose to Theo?"

"That's right," Hector went on. "He seems like an okay guy. Maybe not too swift, if you know what I mean, but solid. You agree, Arch?"

"Oh yes," I said, wanting to add "especially between the ears," but didn't.

"So now," Hector said, "the only thing standing in the way of these two swell kids getting hitched, as far as I can see, is the report you deliver to Chauncey's mommy. When I first told Rube about all this, he said I should offer you, you know, like a nice tip. But that's how Rube thinks—always dollars and cents."

"It's my way," Hagler said tonelessly.

"But I told him if I did that you'd be insulted. Was I right?"

I couldn't believe this totally inane conversation was taking place. Larry, Moe, and Curly were gobbling tongue sandwiches and discussing the fate of a lovely young woman. Where were Abbott and Costello when they were so sorely needed? And who's on first?

"You were quite right," I told Hector. "I would have been insulted."

"Sure you would. Because you're a straight arrow; I knew that from the start. You haven't heard anything bad about Theo, have you?"

"Not a word," I said. "No gossip. Not a hint of scandal. Nothing."

"And you won't find anything," he assured me. "That girl is true-blue, believe me. So that's what you'll tell old lady Smythe-whatshername?"

"If I had to report today," I said, "that's what I'd tell her."

If he caught my tergiversation he gave no sign of it. "That's great!" he enthused. "Listen, Rube and I have got to run. But I want to thank you from the bottom of my heart for having a nosh so we could clear the air. I'm happy to know you're on our side."

We finished our beers and rose to depart. I noticed that not Hector Johnson but Reuben Hagler paid for lunch, and with a hundred-dollar bill. We walked outside into the afternoon sunshine. We all shook hands. Hagler's grip was cool and surprisingly boneless. I thanked them for lunch and we all agreed to do it again real soon.

I paused to light a cigarette. I watched them get into Johnson's white Lincoln and jazz away. Those two, I reflected, were definitely not gentlemen. But then, on occasion, neither am I.

I drove back to Palm Beach in a fractious mood. I was furious with the Chinless Wonder for telling his prospective father-in-law that the bride-to-be was being investigated. How dense can you get? But then I sighed and acknowledged the man was what he was—a brainless twit—and there was no point in getting angry at what God hath wrought. As Groucho Marx said, "Why wax wroth; let Roth wax you for a change."

Still reviewing that crazy luncheon, I concluded it was a clear case of attempted manipulation. If I was naive, which I trust I am not, I would have said Hector Johnson was simply a concerned father who wanted only the best for his "little girl" and would do whatever he could to insure her happiness.

But I could not believe his motives were as innocent as that. For instance, his mentioning that Reuben Hagler had suggested I be offered a "tip" for a favorable opinion on Theo was surely a trial balloon to test my mendacity. If I had expressed even a mild interest, I'm sure our conversation would immediately have degenerated into vulgar haggling. To wit: How much did I want to turn in an A-plus report card on his daughter?

The whole thing was a jeroboam of annelids. What had begun as a simple investigation of the character of a young woman had become as complex as an inquiry into the causes of the Seven Years' War. And I was certain more surprises awaited me.

Sure enough, one was awaiting when I drove into the underground garage of the McNally Building. The moment I dismounted from the Miata, Herb, our porcine security guard, came bustling over, his huge revolver in its dogleg holster slapping against his thigh.

"You got a visitor, Mr. McNally," he said. "Been waiting a long time."

"Oh?" I said. "Where? In my office? The reception room?"

"Nah," he said, jerking a thumb. "Over there."

I turned to look. A black Jeep Cherokee. Marcia Hawkin. "Oh lordy," I said aloud and stared about wildly for an escape route. But I was doomed. The Cherokee door swung open, a white arm beckoned. I shuffled over, dreading another go-around with that young lady. And her greeting did nothing to relieve my angst.

"Where have you been?" she demanded angrily.

I wished I had my father's gift of raising one eyebrow. "Luncheon," I said. "People do have them, you know."

"Get in," she commanded imperiously.

I got in, wondering how I could possibly connive to drop off this spacey child at the nearest day-care center.

And she looked like a child, wearing a navy middy piped with white and a pleated skirt of creamy silk. Her face was scrubbed, and she seemed young enough to roll a hoop or engage in an exciting game of jacks. But she was smoking a joint; that muddied the picture.

"How are you, Squirrel?" I asked.

That pleased her. "You remembered my name!"

"Of course."

"You're my very best friend," she said. "Really."

I was as much saddened as startled. I had met her—what? Twice? Thrice? And now I was her very best friend. I was aware of her hostility toward her stepmother and reckoned she had adopted me as a confidant since the death of her daddy. I had never before served as a father figure and it made me a mite uneasy.

"I know how much you miss him," I murmured.

"My father?" she said. "He was the most wonderful and the most horriblest person in the world."

I looked at her. "Horriblest? Marcia, I'm not sure there is such a word."

"Well, you know what I mean. A devil. He was a devil." She offered me the roach. "Would you like a toke?" she asked.

"No, thank you."

She pinched it out carefully, wrapped the stub in a facial tissue, and tucked it into her purse. It was an ugly thing: red plastic with a tarnished chain handle. It looked like something from a garage sale.

"Listen, Archy," she said, "I want you to do me a favor."

I was immediately wary. If she asked me to assassinate her stepmother or blow up Fort Knox I wouldn't be a bit surprised.

"If I can," I said cautiously.

She took a white envelope from that awful purse and handed it to me. "Keep this," she said. "But you must promise not to open it unless something happens to me."

I inspected the envelope, sealed and with no writing on the outside. "Marcia, what do you think is going to happen to you?"

"I don't know," she said. "But if something does, then you can open the letter. It explains everything."

I sighed. "You're being very mysterious," I told her.

"Screw that," the child said. "All I want you to do is promise not to open the envelope unless something happens to me. If nothing happens, then you give the letter back to me."

"Nope," I said, "I won't do it. You're too vague. What if you decide to go to the Bahamas for a week. Do I open the envelope? What if you get appendicitis and they pop you in a hospital. Do I open the envelope? What if you're busted on a shoplifting charge. Do I open the envelope? What I'm trying to tell you, Squirrel, is that you've got to be more specific. Just saying 'If something happens to me' doesn't cut the mustard."

She thought about that, gnawing on the lower lip with her upper incisors.

"All right," she said finally, "I'll be more specific. You must promise not to open the envelope and read the letter unless I die. Okay?"

"You're not going to die," I said.

She flipped out. "Stop arguing!" she screamed at me. "Stop treating me like a stupid kid! Just do what I asked you! Promise me this instant!"

I put a hand on her arm. "Take it easy," I said as softly as I could. "Of course I promise to do what you ask. I'll keep the envelope and won't open it until you die. And you can have it back, unopened, whenever you like. Is that satisfactory?"

"Yeah," she said, beginning to sniffle, "that's fine." She took another tissue and wiped her nose. "I'm sorry I blasted you, Archy, but people have been pushing me around and I can't take it anymore. But everything's going to get better. You'll see. My money worries will be over and I'll be able to live my life the way I want to."

"Glad to hear it," I said, suspecting she was handing me a lot of hooey.

"Oh yes," she said and smiled for the first time. "Things are going to change. I'm in the driver's seat now and certain people are going to do things my way if they know what's good for them. They think they're so smart but I'm smarter."

I hadn't the slightest idea of what she was talking about, of course, but her words sounded to me like a threat against a person or persons unknown, and that worried me.

"Marcia," I said, "I don't wish to pry. I know nothing about your personal affairs and have no desire to know. But if you're in a sticky situation and would like advice, assistance, or just encouragement, I'd be happy to help."

"I don't need help," she said disdainfully. "From you or anyone else. Daddy is dead and can't tell me what to do. No one can tell me what to do. I'm in control of my own life now. For the first time. And I know how to do it."

I was convinced she didn't. She wasn't a child, she was an infant, an impetuous, disturbed, and possibly violent infant. I saw no way to aid her without becoming immersed in the same madness that was obviously engulfing her. So I did nothing. Save yourself. It's a hard and sometimes cruel dictum. But it's the first law of survival.

"I wish you the best, Squirrel," I said. "I hope all your plans succeed." I opened the door of the Cherokee, holding that damned white envelope. "Please let me know how you make out."

"Sure," she said with an elfin grin that broke my heart.

I stood there and watched her gun up the ramp and out of the garage. I was in no mood to return to my claustrophobic office, so I remounted the Miata and headed for home. I needed a long, slow ocean swim, the family cocktail hour, and a merry dinner with my parents to reassure me that God was in his heaven and all was right with the world.

And it worked—for a while. I arose from the table feeling content and full of beans (actually they were haricots verts with slivered almonds), but then my father summoned me to his study. I followed him with the premonition that my serene mood was soon to evaporate.

"Glass of port, Archy?" he inquired.

That cinched it. When the patriarch invites me to have a postprandial libation it usually means he's going to give me a world-class migraine in the form of an unwelcome assignment. The proffered drink is his a priori apology.

He did the pouring, from one of his crystal decanters into Waterford goblets. He seated himself behind his massive desk and I took the nearest leather club chair. We sipped our wine. I thought it rather musty but I didn't tell him that.

"Anything new on Chauncey Smythe-Hersforth's young lady?" he asked.

"No, sir," I replied. "Nothing definite."

"His mother came in today. Apparently her son has proposed and the woman in question has accepted. Were you aware of that, Archy?"

"Yes, sir."

"I wish you had informed me."

"I learned of it only last night, father."

He accepted that. "Mrs. Smythe-Hersforth was quite upset. Perhaps indignant would be more accurate."

"I can imagine."

"However, I think she is reconciled to the fact that her son is determined to marry. Unless, of course, your investigation should prove the lady to be completely unsuitable."

"I've uncovered nothing to date that would disqualify her, sir." Naturally I said nothing of uncovering the lady herself.

"But you're continuing your investigation?"

"Yes, father, I am."

"Good. But our client has raised another objection. Before she gives her final blessing to the match she is determined to retrieve her son's letters to that unfortunate woman in Fort Lauderdale—what was her name?"

"Shirley Feebling."

"Yes. Mrs. Smythe-Hersforth fears that if she gives her approval, it's possible that before, during, or shortly after the marriage those embarrassing letters might surface as a cover story in one of our more lurid tabloids."

"She has a point."

"Indeed she does, Archy. I told her of the efforts I have made, with the assistance of Sergeant Rogoff, to seek the return of the letters from the Lauderdale police, to no avail. Their position is that they can release no evidence, particularly that found at the murder scene, until the case is cleared."

"That's understandable, father."

"Of course it is," he said crossly. "They're entirely in the right, even though Chauncey is not a suspect. So apparently his letters will remain in their possession until the homicide of Miss Feebling is solved."

He looked at me intently, knuckling his Brillo mustache. I knew what he wanted me to say and I said it.

"Let me look into it, father."

"Yes, Archy," he said gratefully, "you do that. Nothing illegal, of course. Do not, in any way, shape, or form, interfere with the official investigation. But though I admire your ingenuity, I must tell you I doubt you will succeed where, to date, the police have failed. However, I want to be able to assure our client that McNally and Son has done its best to accede to her wishes." He paused a moment and gave me a wry smile. "Also," he added, "your investigation should result in a large number of billable hours."

I laughed. "I expect it will, father," I said.

He finished his glass of wine and stood up. It was my dismissal. The moment I left he would pack and light one of his James Upshall pipes, pour another port, and get back to Dickens. I wondered if he had started *The Mystery of Edwin Drood.*

"Kindly keep me informed of the progress of your investigation," he said. Very patrician. I admired him. He had the intonation just right.

I nodded, left his study, and started upstairs. I paused at the second-floor sitting room, where mother was watching a rerun of "The Honeymooners." I kissed her good-night and she patted my cheek while laughing delightedly at Ralph Kramden. I continued up to my own cloister.

It had been a long, arduous day, and instead of a shower I opted for a bath. I frothed the water with a mildly scented oil and launched a squadron of rubber duckies Connie had given me as a gag. Then I slid in with a moan of contentment.

An hour later I was dried and had donned one of my favorite kimonos, the one printed with images of Elmer Fudd at play. I sat at my desk and worked hard at my journal, recording everything that had happened since the last entry. I do work hard, you know, though I suspect you may think I'm just another pretty face.

I remembered to jot notes on what Luther Grabow had told me of Silas Hawkin's intention to paint a nude on wood; the insane luncheon with Hector Johnson and Reuben Hagler; and the even madder conversation with Marcia Hawkin in an underground garage.

That last item reminded me to take the white envelope from my jacket pocket and slip it into the top desk drawer. But before I did that, I held it up to the strong light of my student lamp. Unfortunately it appeared to be a security envelope— one of those with an overall pattern printed on the inside— and I could decipher nothing of what Squirrel might have written on the letter within. Frustrating, but I swear I was not tempted to steam it open. Subsequent events made me wish to hell I had.

Finished with my scribbling, I reviewed everything I had written since my initial interview with Mrs. Gertrude Smythe-Hersforth. Even more frustrating, for it seemed to me I had compiled a compendium of disparate facts and fancies. If there was a pattern, a design no matter how bizarre, I simply could not see it. Mishmash would be an apt description.

And now there was another spud in the stew: my father's request that I investigate the murder of Shirley Feebling. I could understand his doubts that

I would succeed where, so far, the Lauderdale homicide detectives had failed. But neither the squire nor the police, as far as I knew, were aware of the existence of Reuben Hagler, the "old buddy" of Hector Johnson, father of the woman I had been assigned to dissect.

There were connections, I was convinced, but they were so tenuous as to be ungraspable. (There is such a word; you can look it up.) After a long bout of jumbled pondering I decided I had no choice but to engineer another meeting with Pinky Schatz, close friend of the slain Shirl Feebling. I could not forget my impression that the bouncy Ms. Schatz had lied to me because of fear. But fear of whom I could not imagine. Unless he drove a gunmetal Cadillac.

All this Sturm und Drang was so depressing. I really don't know how psychiatrists do it. I mean they listen to woeful confessions of ridden people every day. All they hear is weeping, wailing, and the gnashing of teeth: stories of hate, abuse, greed, lust, violence, and other swell stuff. Who could blame the shrinks if they went home at night and, to survive, read fairy tales—or anything that ends "And they lived happily ever after."

I suppose I was in that mood when I determined to call Connie Garcia. I needed a dose of normality. It was close to midnight, and I let her phone ring and ring. But she did not answer.

I went to bed. I was not gruntled.

Chapter 12

I might have slept forever on Wednesday morning but I was gradually nudged awake by the persistent ringing of my bedside phone. I opened one eye wide enough to see the clock dimly. It was either 9:05 A.M. or a quarter to one P.M. But since a low sun was striking through my bedroom window I judged a new day had just begun.

"H'lo?" I said in the middle of a jaw-cracking yawn.

"Don't you ever get to your office on time?" Sgt. Al Rogoff complained.

"That's why you called?" I said sleepily. "To comment on my working habits?"

"Wake up," he said sternly, "and try to listen. Have you seen Marcia Hawkin lately?"

I woke up. I saw no reason to prevaricate. "Yesterday afternoon," I told him. "At the McNally Building. We had a talk."

"About what?"

"Pure craziness. She was off the wall."

"That I can believe," Al said. "We've got a sheet on that young lady. Picked up for strolling naked on Ocean Boulevard at midnight. Picked up for throwing rocks at seagulls. Picked up for setting off illegal fireworks. Nothing serious. No charges. But the girl is a total fruitcake. What was she wearing when you talked to her?"

I tried to recall. "Uh, blue middy blouse with white piping, pleated silk skirt, scuffed running shoes."

"Uh-huh," Rogoff said. "That tallies. She have wheels?"

"Black Jeep Cherokee. Al, what's this all about?"

"Her mother called this morning. The kid didn't come home last night. She's gone and so is the Cherokee. We usually wait forty-eight hours on things like this. People stay overnight at a friend's house or pull off the road to grab some sleep. But since the Silas Hawkin homicide is still open, I got interested and decided to give you a call. Did she say anything about leaving home?"

"No."

"Meeting someone?"

"No."

"Going somewhere in particular?"

"No."

"Thank you for your kind assistance," the sergeant said with his heavy irony. "Would you care to make a wild guess as to where this loony might be?"

"Haven't the slightest," I said. "Al, did you hear anything from Michigan on those two names I gave you?"

"*Nada.* I told you these things take time. When I do hear, you'll be the first to know—after you tell me why you want the skinny. Archy, if you hear from Marcia Hawkin give me a shout."

"Sure I will," I said.

I hung up and crawled out of bed. It was just what I needed—a moral dilemma first thing in the morning. Should I open that cursed envelope or shouldn't I? Recalling my promise to Marcia, I decided not to. Only if she died, not if she was merely missing. I told myself she was sure to show up. Told but not convinced.

There was no one in the kitchen when I clattered downstairs, so I fixed my own breakfast: a large GJ, instant black coffee, and two toasted English muffin sandwiches with fillings of brisling sardines in olive oil. Look, you eat what you want for breakfast; don't give me a hard time.

I should have enjoyed that mini-meal but I didn't. Because the tickling of guilt continued. Had I been as sympathetic with Squirrel as I could have been? Might I have expressed more forcibly my willingness to help her? In other words, had I failed another human being in trouble? But then I am neither Dr. Schweitzer nor Mother Teresa. Looking for a saint, are you? Ta-ta.

I futzed about the house till noontime. I prepared my laundry and dry cleaning for the weekly pickup. I scanned several personal letters I had received which I had intended to answer but now were so dated there was no point. I tore them up. I clipped my fingernails. I examined my tongue in the bathroom mirror. Yuck.

Actually, as I well knew, I was delaying what I had to do: drive to Fort

Lauderdale and confront Pinky Schatz. I didn't relish another visit to the Leopard Club; all those juicy dancers and desiccated spectators seemed unbearably dreary. I mean when it comes to nudity, public revelation is in reverse ratio to private stimulation. Or something like that.

But when duty's bugle blares, yrs. truly is ready to lead the charge. Also, I consoled myself with the opportunities the trip offered to jigger my expense account. And so I set off whistling a merry tune and reflecting that if one strove to maintain a positive attitude, life could be a bowl of *pasta con fagioli*.

There had been reports of potential hurricanes heading our way, departing the coast of Africa and boiling westward. You'd never know it from that day's sky. Pellucid is the word. About the same shade of blue, I decided, as the wings on Theo Johnson's butterfly tattoo. But I digress.

I parked outside the Leopard Club and approached the guarded portal. The sentinel on duty was not the same chappie I had previously encountered. This one had the head of a bald eagle and the body of an insurance salesman.

"Is Pinky Schatz dancing today?" I inquired politely.

"Nah," he said. "She called in sick."

"Sick?" I cried. "Good heavens, I must bring the poor girl some chicken soup or calf's-foot jelly. Do you happen to know where she lives?"

The griffin looked at me. "Yeah," he said, "I know. But you don't."

"True enough," I said, taking out my wallet. "A Jackson?"

"A Grant," he said firmly.

Sighing, I handed over a fifty. He consulted a tattered notebook he extracted from his hip pocket. He gave me Pinky's address, and I was startled. I knew the building: an elegant high-rise condo on the Galt Ocean Mile.

"Fancy," I commented.

"What else?" he said. "If you got it, flaunt it. And Pinky's got it."

"How true, how true," I agreed.

It took another twenty minutes to drive down to the Galt Ocean Mile. On that stretch of beach a row of huge high-rise condos forms a concrete wall that effectively prevents the peasants from viewing the seascape. Life is unfair; even tykes know that.

I found Pinky's building and pulled into the Guest Parking area. I neglected to eyeball the other cars. That was an error because when I started to open the lobby door Reuben Hagler was about to exit. We both halted, shocked, and exchanged stares.

"Hey, Mr. Hagler," I said, my voice ripe with false joviality, "imagine meeting you here."

"Yeah," he said. "Small world."

"A friend is coming down from New York," I explained, "and wants to rent for a year. I understand they have some attractive rentals in this building."

"I'd guess so," he said. "One of my investors lives here, and he's got a lush pad. Have a nice day."

"You, too," I said, and we traded puny smiles.

I paused to light a cigarette slowly, long enough to observe him get into that gunmetal De Ville I should have spotted. He drove away and I discovered I was suffering a mild attack of the heebie-jeebies. Did you ever catch Bela Lugosi in *Dracula?* That was Reuben Hagler. He looked as if he had just yawned, stretched, and climbed out of his coffin.

Of course Hagler could have been telling the truth and had just visited a male client rather than Pinky Schatz. And if you believe that, I told myself, leave an extracted molar under your pillow and expect the Truth Fairy to arrive.

I sauntered over to the security desk, where a uniformed stalwart (armed) was on duty.

"To see Miss Pinky Schatz, please," I said.

"Name?" he demanded.

I remembered who I was just in time. "Chauncey Wilson Smythe-Hersforth," I told him.

"What was that?" he said.

"Just announce me as Chauncey," I advised.

He looked up her number in a ledger, stabbed his phone, and murmured. "Okay," he said to me. "Apartment Nineteen-ten. First elevator on your right."

"Thank you," I said. "Attractive building. Do you have any security problems here?"

"Do dogs have fleas?" he asked, reasonably enough.

I rode a silent, Formica-paneled elevator to the nineteenth floor. The corridor was ceramic tile. Impressive, but the color was off-putting: a sort of pasty pink. I remembered how my tongue had looked that morning.

Ms. Schatz opened the door wearing a diaphanous peignoir. I was aware of it but all I could see was her face. Ah, bejaysus, but she was sporting a fine mouse under her left eye. It was of recent vintage and I knew that within an hour it would be rainbowed. Raw steak or leeches wouldn't help. Pancake makeup might.

"Good lord," I said, "what happened to you?"

"An accident," she said dully. "Come on in."

It was a one-bedroom condo decorated in a style I call Florida Glitz. That includes veined mirrors, patterned tiles, silver foil wallpaper, a glass cocktail table on a base of driftwood and, of course, the requisite six-ft. ficus tree made of silk. I mean the place shrieked. But the glitter was dimmed by an overall scruffiness; everything needed an industrial-strength douche.

"I wasn't going to let you in," she said. "I don't feel so hot."

"Would you like me to go?" I asked.

"Nah," she said, "you can stay. I was about to have a wallop. Would you like one, Chauncey?"

"A wallop of what?"

"All I got is gin. I like to mix it with diet cream soda. How about it?"

"I think not," I said hastily. "But a splash of gin on the rocks would be nice."

I watched her mince into the kitchen. She may have been injured but she still jiggled. She returned a few moments later with our drinks. She had given me more than a splash of gin but that was all right; I needed it; deceit makes me thirsty.

She lolled on an enormous couch covered with greasy cerise velvet. I sat in an overstuffed armchair big enough to accommodate King Kong. I looked at her but she didn't look at me. She was busy feeling that discoloration under her eye.

"Hurt?" I said.

"I've been hurt before," she said defiantly. "The story of my life. How did you find out where I live, Chauncey?"

"Fifty bucks."

Her smile was sour. "That Ernie," she said. "He'd sell his sister if anyone wanted to buy, which no one does. How come you looked me up?"

"I just want to find the man who killed Shirley Feebling."

"Yeah?" she said, and gave me a cruel, knowing glance. "You sure you're not looking for a replacement? Like me?"

Sad, sad, sad.

"Pinky," I said, "can we stop playing games? Please. I'm certain you know more about Shirl's murder than you've told the police."

She said nothing, just sipped her noxious drink and kept touching her bruise.

"I thought she was your best friend," I continued.

"I got a lot of best friends," she said. "Women and men both."

"I can promise you protection," I told her.

"No, you can't," she said. "Not total. I don't mind getting hurt occasionally; that comes with the territory. But I don't want to end up like Shirl, with my brains splattered."

"You won't. If you're willing to tell what you know, the cops will pick him up and shove him behind bars. You have nothing to fear."

"What are you talking about?" she said. "Who is *him?*"

I decided I might as well go for broke. "Reuben Hagler," I said. "The man who just gave you that black eye. Drives a Cadillac with Michigan plates. You knew he was tailing Shirley. And you know or suspect he was the one who put her down."

"You're nuts," she said, affectedly bored.

"How did he get to you?" I went on. "Threats of what might happen if you talked? Or a payoff?"

She suddenly stood up. "You get out of here," she screamed at me. "Right now!"

"But then again," I said thoughtfully, "maybe you weren't just an innocent witness. Maybe you were in on it from the start, an accomplice who helped that creep knock off your best friend."

She collapsed back onto the couch. The glass fell from her hand and shattered on the tile floor. Gin and diet cream soda made an ugly pool, the color of old blood. She began wailing, her face muffled in the cushions.

"Leave me alone," I heard her say. "Just leave me alone. I can't take any-more. Please, just leave me alone."

I rose, finished my gin, and departed. I left her sobbing on the couch. It was not one of my proudest moments. But you comprehend the reason for my cruelty, do you not? I reckoned she would report my visit to Reuben Ha-gler. And he would be forced to react. If he was guiltless, he would seek me out and denounce me for vile slander. And if he was involved in the murder of Shirley Feebling, he would seek me out and . . . I didn't want to envision what he might do.

I don't wish to imply that I was acting heroically, offering myself as a sac-rificial lamb in order to snag an assassin. But Shirl's death continued to haunt me, and my personal safety seemed of minor import compared to finding and bringing her murderer to justice. Lofty, huh? Well, I do have a moral code. A bit skewed, I admit, but it's *mine*.

Look, at that point all I had was a suspicion that Reuben Hagler had stalked her. I had no proof and couldn't conceive what his motive might have been. So I had no choice but to force events. I thought of my actions as a lighted fuse. If I was correct, there would be a stupendous KA-BOOM! If I was mistaken, there would be a mild sizzle as the fuse burned out.

I was engaged in this mental nattering on the drive back to Palm Beach. I believe I was just leaving Boca Raton on A1A when my cellular phone sounded. It was lying on the passenger seat and its harsh ring startled me be-cause I rarely get calls when I'm on the road. I suspected it would be a wrong number but it wasn't; Sgt. Al Rogoff was calling.

"Where are you now, Archy?" he asked in that sepulchral voice he uses when he's about to announce the world is coming to an end in fourteen min-utes.

"North of Boca," I reported. "Heading home. What's up, doc?"

"Did you tell me Marcia Hawkin was driving a black Jeep Cherokee when you saw her yesterday?"

"That's right."

"Uh-huh," he said. "Well, right now there's a black Cherokee in the lake. It's upside down and the divers say there's a woman inside."

I was silent.

"You there?" he said.

"I'm here. Where is it, Al?"

"Off Banyan Road. You know it?"

"Yes."

"We're trying to get a cable on the car to haul it out. You want to stop by?"

I didn't. "Yes," I said, "I'll stop by."

By the time I arrived there was a crowd of spectators, perhaps twenty or thirty, many in bathing suits. Two gendarmes were herding them back from the scene of operations.

There was a short wooden pier extending out into Lake Worth. It looked relatively new and mounted on one side was a steel gantry with canvas slings for lifting small boats out of the water. The police tow truck had backed up alongside the pier, the cable from its winch stretched taut into the lake.

I joined the rubbernecks, spotted Rogoff, and yelled to him. He waved and came over to escort me past the guards. He was wearing khaki slacks and scuffed loafers. His shield was clipped to the shoulder of his white T-shirt.

"I was on a forty-eight," he explained. "Then they called me to come in to honcho this mess."

"Who found the car?"

"Some kid who was snorkeling. Just chance. It could have laid there for days, weeks, or months without being spotted. We got a hook on it, but like I told you, it's upside down and it's a tough haul."

We walked down to the shoreline. The winch was whining and the cable was retracting very, very slowly. We stood silently and watched the Jeep come skidding out of the lake. The winch stopped when the car was in the shallows. Then four huskies, two uniformed cops, and two wet-suited divers began turning it over. It was a muscle job, and it took five tries before they got the Cherokee onto its wheels.

"Rather them than me," Al said. "Instant hernia."

The winch started up again, not straining now, and the car was pulled up onto the beach. Water streamed from it and strands of seaweed were clinging to the windshield. We moved forward for a closer look. The door on the driver's side was open and the window was shattered.

"Take a look," Rogoff said.

I peered within. Marcia Hawkin was lying face up in the back. Her eyes were wide. She stared at nothing. She was still wearing the middy blouse and silk skirt but one shoe was off. That single bare foot—small, pale, limp—affected me most.

"Squirrel," I said softly.

"What?" Al said.

"Squirrel," I repeated. "Her nickname. Her father called her that."

"Then he knew," Al said roughly. "She was a real wacko."

Thomas Bunion, the Assistant ME, was there and directed the removal of the body after photographs and a video had been taken of the car's interior.

"What's that?" I asked Rogoff, pointing through a back window.

He shielded his eyes from the rays of the lowering sun. "Looks like a sheet," he said. "All wadded up. Stained. Could be blood. Or maybe stuff in the water. I'll leave it to the wonks."

"Al," I said, "did you drive your pickup here?"

"Sure," he said. "It's parked up near the road. Why?"

"Want to follow me back to my place?"

He looked at me. "Now why should I do that?"

"Because," I said, "I have something I think you better see."

And I told him how Marcia Hawkin had given me a letter to be opened only in the event of her death. The sergeant listened intently.

"You haven't opened it, Archy?" he asked when I had finished.

"Of course not. I promised her."

"I wish you had told me this morning when we talked about her."

"Why should I have done that, Al? She had just been reported missing. And you told me yourself that the Department would take no action for forty-eight hours."

"Yeah, but if I had known she left you a letter it might have changed things."

"How so?"

"Because it meant she figured she could die—and soon. Most young kids think they're going to live forever. Where is the letter now?"

"In my desk at home."

"Let's go," he said.

We were at the Chez McNally in less than an hour. I stopped in the kitchen to pluck a bottle of Sterling vodka from the freezer and fill a plastic bowl with cubes from the ice tray. Then we tramped upstairs to my barrack.

Al likes to claim he's inured to the sight of violent death. He's lying, of course, because he's a sensitive man. I don't even try to pretend. That bare foot of the dead Marcia Hawkin had spooked me. The sergeant made no objection when I poured us heavy vodka-rocks. We both gulped and sighed.

I sat behind my desk, took out Squirrel's white envelope, and held it out to him.

"Don't you want to open it, Archy?" Rogoff said. "After all, the girl gave the letter to *you*."

I shook my head. "It's totally irrational," I admitted, "but I just can't. You do it."

I handed him my opener, which looks like a miniature Persian dagger. He slit the flap of the envelope carefully and shook out the contents, a single sheet of white notepaper, and unfolded it with the tip of the dagger. He bent over my desk to read.

"Well?" I said impatiently. "What does it say?"

He chuffed a dry laugh. "Written in ink, addressed 'To Whom It May Concern.' How does that grab you? And it's signed Marcia Hawkin."

"All right, all right!" I cried. "But what does it *say*?"

He looked up at me with a queer expression. "One sentence," he said. "It says 'I murdered my father.' "

Chapter 13

That evening, during the cocktail hour, I informed my parents of the death of Marcia Hawkin. They were as much bewildered as shocked, for the sudden and brutal loss of two lives in one family seemed totally inexplicable. Mother, I believe, was ready to ascribe it to a cruel vagary of fate. But father, I knew, suspected dark mischief was afoot. He is instinctively suspicious of linked events others might term a coincidence.

"Was the young woman a suicide, Archy?" he inquired.

"I really don't know, sir," I answered. "Sergeant Rogoff promised to tell me what he can after the cause of death has been established."

"She was a friend of yours?" he asked, busying himself with the martini pitcher.

"She thought so," I said defensively, "although I had spoken to her only three or four times. She seemed quite disturbed."

"How awful," the mater said. "Perhaps her father's murder was the reason. I must send Louise a letter of condolence."

"No need, mother," I said, "I intend to call on her tomorrow, and I'll express our sympathy."

"Oh yes, Archy," she said, "that would be nice. And be sure to ask if there is anything we can do to help."

And we left it at that. I mentioned nothing of the final letter Marcia had entrusted to my care. Rogoff and I had decided to keep that dreadful message from public knowledge until its authenticity could be determined. As Al said, she was such a scatty kid she might have imagined the patricide.

"Or protecting someone else," I suggested. "The actual killer."

"Yeah," the sergeant said. "That, too."

Dinner that evening was baked salmon with a heavenly crust of dill. I knew it was a magnificent dish, but it was one of the rare occasions in my life when my appetite faltered, and I refused a third helping. As soon as decently possible, I excused myself and retired to my aerie.

There I poured myself a marc and opened a fresh packet of English Ovals. Wasn't it Mark Twain who said, "It's easy to stop smoking; I've done it a dozen times." If it wasn't Mr. Clemens, it might have been Fred Allen. No matter; I had no intention that evening of even trying. I lighted up, sipped my brandy, and thought of Marcia Hawkin. Squirrel.

I tried to recall everything she had said during our final conversation. Then I consulted my journal, which offered some assistance but no actual quotations. She had spoken of taking control of her own life, of solving her money worries, of outsmarting persons unknown who were apparently treating her with contempt.

I did remember exactly one thing she had said, and in light of what I had witnessed that afternoon it was so poignant I drained my drink and poured another. She had said, "I'm in the driver's seat now." But the last time I saw her, she wasn't in the driver's seat at all, was she? She was crumpled in the rear of a sodden car, one pale, dead foot dangling.

I endured that aching memory as long as I could, and then I phoned Consuela Garcia. I had to talk to a young woman who was still alive. After what had happened to Shirley Feebling and Marcia Hawkin I was beginning to fear I had become a Jonah and all the ladies of my acquaintance were doomed.

"Hiya, Archy," Connie said warmly. "I'm glad you called. Did you hear what happened to Marcia Hawkin? It was on TV."

"Yes," I said, "I heard."

"Sounds like suicide to me," she said. "The poor kid. Maybe her father's murder pushed her over the edge."

"Maybe. What have you been up to, Connie?"

"Oh, this and that. Lady Horowitz is running me ragged. Right now we're planning a buffet dinner for fifty. The McNallys are on the A-list. Isn't that nice?"

"Splendiferous," I said, delighted she wasn't going to give me a blow-by-blow account of her date with Wes Trumbaugh. "What are you serving the serfs?"

"Cold seafood. Lobster, shrimp, crabmeat, scallops, oysters, periwinkles, calamari, and lots of other swell stuff."

My appetite returned with a jolt. "I'll starve myself for two days to prepare for that feast," I promised. "Plenty of flinty white wine?"

"Of course."

"Wonderful. When can I see you again, Connie?"

"Soon," she said. "Give me a buzz on Friday, Archy. Okay?"

"Will do," I said happily. "Get a good night's sleep."

"I'm already in bed."

"Under that poster of Bogart? 'Here's looking at you, kid.' "

She giggled and hung up.

I went in for my shower, but my mopes had already been sluiced away. I had a prof at Yale who was something of a misogynist and was fond of paraphrasing Thoreau by remarking, "Most women lead lives of noisy desperation."

Not Connie Garcia. She is a bubbler and always inflates my spirits except, of course, when she is dumping a bowl of linguine on my head as punishment for a real or fancied infidelity. But other than her occasional physical assaults, she really is a 24-karat woman.

Lacking only a blue butterfly tattoo.

That was my last lubricious thought before Morpheus and I embraced. Away we went. I awoke on Thursday morning ready to slay dragons. I donned a somber costume, for I had decided that my first port of call would be the Hawkin home, an obligatory visit of condolence I hoped to make as brief as possible.

It was a 3-H day in South Florida: hot, humid, hazy. I wondered, not for the first time, if I wouldn't have been wiser to opt for roofed transportation rather than a convertible. But surrendering my dashing Miata would destroy my self-image of a damn-the-torpedoes buckler of swashes. I wasn't quite ready to do that. Sometimes egoism demands sacrifices.

When I turned into the Hawkins' driveway I saw, parked at the front door, the white Lincoln Town Car belonging to Hector Johnson. My first reaction was to turn and flee, but then I thought why should I. His presence might even be an assist in my expressing the McNally family's sympathies as quickly as possible, and then leaving him to provide additional solace to the twice-bereaved Louise.

But it was Theodosia Johnson who opened the door. Madam X was wearing a longish dress of aubergine silk, and she seemed preternaturally pale, features composed but drawn. It was the face of a woman who had suffered a sleepless night—completely understandable if the Hawkins and Johnsons had been as intimate as I imagined.

"Archy," she said, clasping my hand and drawing me inside, "it's good of you to come."

"How is Mrs. Hawkin?" I asked.

"Surviving," she said. "But just barely."

She led me into the Florida room. Louise and Hector were seated close together on the couch. He was holding her hand, gazing at her with an expression of sorrowful concern. On the cocktail table before them was a silver coffee service, three cups and saucers, and a bottle of California brandy. Johnson glanced up as I entered, and Mrs. Hawkin gave me a befuddled stare as if not quite certain of my identity.

"Ma'am," I said, beginning to recite my rehearsed speech, "I'd like to extend the condolences of myself and my parents. It is a terrible tragedy. If there is any way we can help, please let us know."

"Thank you," she said in the wispiest of voices.

"Hey, Arch, how about a cuppa jamoke?" Hector asked in his brutish way. "With a slug of the old nasty to put lead in your pencil."

"Oh, father," Theo said in a tone of disgust that expressed my own.

"Thank you, no," I said. "I just stopped by for a moment to offer the sympathy of the McNally family. Mrs. Hawkin, is there anything at all we can do to assist you?"

She looked at Johnson. "Nah," he said to me. "It's damned decent of you, but Theo and I are going to take care of our Louise. And she's going to be just fine. Aren't you, hon?"

She nodded and reached for a coffee cup with a trembling hand. But before she could lift it to her lips he slopped in a dollop of brandy.

"Father," Theo said sharply, "that's enough."

"Not yet," he said. "She's got a lot of grief to forget and this is the best medicine."

His daughter sat down abruptly in a rattan armchair, crossed her legs, and immediately one foot began to jerk up and down in vexation. I remained standing, knowing I should depart but enthralled by this unpleasant scene that was threatening to become a high-octane confrontation.

"Louise," Theo said, "wouldn't you like to lie down for a while? Take a pill and get some rest."

"She doesn't need a pill," Hector said. "Those things are poison. Just leave her alone; she'll get through it."

"The woman needs sleep," Theo said angrily. "Can't you see that?"

I was bemused by the way they spoke, as if Mrs. Hawkin was not present. But I don't believe the poor woman was even aware of the contention swirling around her. She sipped her brandy-laced coffee and stared vacantly into space.

"Just mind your own business, kid," Hector said. "I know what I'm doing."

"Since when?" Theo said. "She just lost her husband and stepdaughter. Give her a break."

He looked at her coldly. "Keep it up and you'll get a break," he said.

There was no mistaking the menace in his voice, and I suddenly realized this was more than a family squabble. Their conflict was fascinating, but I had no desire to be a witness to violence. Chivalrous heroism comes rather far down on my list of virtues.

"Theo," I said, "I wonder if I might have a glass of water."

She glared at me, furious that I was interrupting the wrangle. But then she softened, her taut body relaxed; she recognized my effort to end an unseemly shindy in a house of sorrow.

"Sure, Archy," she said, rising. "Come with me."

She led the way without hesitation as if it was her home and there was no need to ask permission from the owner. But once we were in the tiled kitchen her wrath returned.

"That crude son of a bitch," she said, leaning close so I could hear her low voice. "Couth? He never heard the word. He just bulls his way through life, all fists and elbows. He'll get his one of these days. Do you really want a drink of water?"

"Yes, please."

She took it from the tap on the refrigerator door, and I drained the glass gratefully.

She reached to stroke my hair. "You look very handsome this morning, Archy," she said. "Dressed so formally. But I prefer you in something more casual. Or nothing at all."

Her brazenness shocked me and she must have seen it in my face because she laughed delightedly and pressed her body against mine. "Don't worry, darling," she said, "I'm not going to be a problem. I'm going to marry Chauncey and become a nice little hausfrau."

"You may find you enjoy it," I told her.

"Do you really believe that?" she asked.

"No," I said, and she kissed me.

I drew regretfully away. Her flesh felt glossy under that silk, and she was wearing a scent I could not identify, although I suspected cantharides might have been one of the ingredients.

We moved back to the Florida room, and I made a respectful farewell, which Louise Hawkin and Hector Johnson barely acknowledged. Madam X gave me a wave and a devilish smile, and I left the Villa Bile. My original label for that house now seemed more apt than ever.

I exited to find Sgt. Al Rogoff leaning against the fender of his parked pickup. He was wearing civvies—a suit of khaki poplin, white shirt, black knitted tie—and puffing one of his fat cigars.

"I thought you were on a forty-eight," I said to him.

"Still am," he said. "And still working my tail to the bone. Who's inside besides Mrs. Hawkin?"

"Theodosia and Hector Johnson."

"I'll wait till they leave. I'd like to talk to the widow alone."

"You may have to wait until Hades has a cold snap," I informed him. "The Johnsons have taken over."

"Oh-ho," he said. "It's like that, is it?"

"Apparently."

He gestured toward the white Lincoln. "Is that his?"

"Yep."

"Nice," Rogoff said. "Do you know what he did before he moved down here?"

"You name it, Al, and he's done it. I've heard a dozen different versions of his former occupation."

"Yeah?" the sergeant said, grinning. "I know what it was."

I stared at him for a few beats before I caught it. "You swine!" I cried. "You heard from Michigan."

"That's right," he said. "I was going to give you a call. Want to come to my place tonight? We can talk about it then."

"Can't you tell me now?"

"No. I want to go inside and brace Mrs. Hawkin."

"Forget it," I advised. "The lady is half in the bag. Hector has been invigorating her morning coffee with California brandy."

"All to the good. *In vino veritas.* Come over to my wagon around nine o'clock. Okay?"

"I'll be there," I promised. "Is the scoop on Johnson and Hagler interesting?"

"Very," he said. He tossed away the stub of his cigar, straightened his jacket, began striding up to the door.

"Al," I called, and he turned back. "About Marcia Hawkin," I said. "Was it suicide?"

He smiled grimly. "Not unless she managed to wring her own neck."

What a curtain line that was! I drove back to the McNally Building with my thoughts awhirl. The Miata had just had a tune-up and I wished my brain could get the same. I mean I simply could not make sense of what was happening: three homicides and the seemingly irrational behavior of the people involved.

Oh, I could concoct several scenarios but all were too bizarre to convince even a fantasist like me. I kept trying to rein in my supercharged imagination and remind myself that usually the most complex evils are the result of the most prosaic of motives: greed and revenge, for instance. But even concentrating on the basics of crime detection yielded no hint as to the connection between the murders of Silas Hawkin, Shirley Feebling, and Marcia Hawkin. If there was a solution to that conundrum, it eluded me.

Only temporarily, of course. I assure you I shall not end this account by confessing failure. You'd never speak to me again.

I had hoped to spend the remainder of that morning sitting quietly in my office composing my expense account. Quiet was necessary since my monthly swindle sheet demands intense creativity. I will not claim it is *totally* factual but it is *based* on fact. The theme is exaggeration rather than prevarication. To quote an historic American epigram, "I am not a crook."

But peace was not to be mine. I found on my desk a message from our receptionist stating that Mrs. Jane Folsby had phoned and requested I return her call. I immediately did so and let the phone ring seven times but received no reply. I put the message aside and began assembling the bills, memos, vouchers, and receipts that were to provide evidence, however flimsy, for my claimed reimbursement.

I had hardly started when my phone rang and I hoped it might be Mrs. Folsby. No such luck. I recognized that whiny voice at once.

"Archy?" he said.

"Chauncey," I said, "how are you?"

"All right," he said. "I guess."

"I understand congratulations are in order."

"What? Oh, you mean me and Theodosia. Well, sure, thanks."

"You must be a very happy man."

"Uh, not completely. Archy, I have a problem. I'd like to talk to you about it. Get your input."

"CW," I said, "if it's legal input you require, I suggest you consult my father. I'm just a rank amateur."

"Well, uh, it's not really legal input," he whined. "At least not at this stage. It's more friendly input I need."

By this time the input madness was sending me right up the wall. But I was determined not to be the first to surrender. "Well, I can provide that," I told the Chinless Wonder. "I presume you're speaking of personal input."

"That's right," he said eagerly. "Intimate input."

"Confidential input?"

"Correct! Top secret input."

Then I knew I was never going to win the Great Input War. "Chauncey," I said, sighing, "what exactly is it you want?"

"Can you come over to my office?"

"At the bank? Now?"

He had the decency to say, "Please."

"You wouldn't care to chat over lunch? At Bice perhaps?"

"Oh no," he said hastily. "No, no, no. Someone might overhear. My office would be best."

"Better than my garage," I said, alluding to our previous meeting. "Very well, CW, I'll come at once."

"Thank you," he said, and the whine had an overtone of piteousness.

I walked to his bank, only a short distance on Royal Palm Way. The building was definitely *not* Florida. It looked like a Vermont relic of the 1920s: heavy granite exterior, towering pillars, a marbled, high-ceilinged ulterior, brass-barred cages for the tellers. And a funereal silence. Even the antiquated clients spoke in whispers.

And the private office of Vice-president Chauncey Wilson Smythe-Hersforth was more of the same. It was huge, oak desk unlittered, furnishings in grave good taste. No file cabinets, no computer terminals, no indication that any business at all was conducted in that somber chamber. And it probably wasn't. CW's sinecure was due to mommy's wealth being invested with the private banking division. If she ever pulled her bucks, the Chinless Wonder might find himself flipping burgers at McDonalds.

"What's this all about?" I asked after he got me planted in a leather wing chair alongside his desk.

Before he replied he made certain his door was firmly closed and locked. Then he returned to the calfskin throne behind his desk.

"It's confidential, Archy," he said portentously. "I trust that's understood."

I looked at him. I was about to make an impudent remark, but then I saw the poor dolt was truly disturbed. As he had cause to be, having been cuckolded before he was married. And I was the lad who had put the horns on him. Levity on my part would have been rather pitiless, wouldn't you say?

"Of course," I said solemnly. "What seems to be the problem?"

He drew a deep breath. "Well, uh, Theo Johnson has agreed to marry me. I first asked her father for permission, of course."

"Of course," I said, wondering if he had fallen to one knee while making his proposal to Madam X.

"And mother has given her conditional approval to our union," he added. Yes, he actually said "our union."

"Then things seem to be going swimmingly," I commented.

"Uh, not quite," he said, not looking at me. "Theo wants me to sign a paper."

I must admit the lower mandible dropped a bit. "Oh?" I said. "What kind of a paper, CW?"

"A sort of a contract," he confessed, fiddling with a letter opener on his desk.

"Are you talking about a prenuptial agreement?" I asked. "A contract that spells out the property rights of both spouses—and their children, if any—in the event of separation, divorce, or death?"

"I guess that's what it is," he said miserably.

"Uh-huh," I said. "And how much is the lady asking?"

He looked up at the ceiling—anywhere but at me. "Five million," he said.

I am proud to say I did not whistle or emit any other rude noise. "Rather hefty," I observed.

"Oh, it's not the sum that bothers me," he said. "Because, of course, Theo and I would never separate or divorce, and we're both in good health. In any event, I'd leave her well-provided for in case I should die. No, the money isn't an issue. The problem is that if I inform mother of this—what did you call it?"

"Prenuptial agreement."

"Yes. Well, uh, if I tell mom about it, she might change her mind about Theo. You understand? In fact, she might become so furious that she'd rewrite her will. And then where would I be?"

"You're her only child, are you not? And the closest family member. I doubt very much if she could disinherit you completely."

"Maybe not," he said worriedly, "but she could cut me down to the bare minimum, couldn't she? And then would I have enough to promise Theo the five million she wants?"

"Ah," I said, "you do have a problem. I presume your mother has been introduced to your fiancée."

"Yes, they've met. Once."

"And how did they get along?"

"Well, uh, they didn't exactly become instant pals."

I nodded, recalling my mother's reaction to Madam X. Maybe the matrons saw something neither Chauncey nor I recognized. Or perhaps it was merely maternal possessiveness. ("No one's good enough for my boy!")

"What is it you'd like me to do, CW?"

He stroked his bushy mustache with a knuckle. "I don't know," he admitted. "But everyone says you're so clever. I thought maybe you could give me a tip on how to handle this situation in a clever way."

"I'd like to help you," I told him. "But I can't come up with an instant solution this moment. Let me think about it awhile."

"Well, all right," he said grudgingly. "But not too long, Archy. I mean I don't want Theo to think I'm stalling her. You know?"

"Of course," I said, rising. "It's obvious you're very intent on marrying this woman."

"Oh God, yes!" he said with more fervor than I had believed him capable of. "I must have her!"

"Quite understandable," I said. "But meanwhile, CW, do not sign any paper, agreement, or contract. Is that clear?"

"If you say so."

"I do say so. Sign nothing!"

We shook hands and exchanged wan smiles. He unlocked his door, and I departed. I ambled back to the McNally Building suffused with a warm feeling of schadenfreude. But that, I admitted, was unkind and unworthy of the McNally Code of Honor, the main principle of which is never to kick a man when he's down. Unless, of course, he deserves it.

When I returned to my own office, which, after an hour spent in Chauncey's cathedral, had all the ambience of a paint locker, the first thing I did was phone Mrs. Jane Folsby again. This time she came on the line.

"Oh, Mr. McNally," she said, "I'm so glad you called. I know you've heard about Marcia Hawkin."

"I have," I said. "Sorrowful."

"Terrible," she said with some vehemence. "Just terrible. She had her faults as we all do, but she didn't deserve to die like that. It wasn't suicide, was it?"

"I really don't know the details," I said cautiously.

"I know it wasn't," she said decisively. "And I have my suspicions. That's what I want to talk to you about."

"Mrs. Folsby, if you know anything relating to Marcia's death, don't you think you should speak to the police? Sergeant Al Rogoff is handling the case. You've met him."

"No," she said determinedly. "This is something I don't want to tell the police. Because then they'll want a sworn statement and I'll get all involved and might even be forced to testify in court. And I really don't have any proof. But I know what I know, and I've got to tell someone. Please, Mr. McNally. I'll feel a lot better if I tell you, and then you can do whatever you think best. At least my conscience will be clear."

"This sounds serious," I said.

"It *is* serious. Will you meet with me?"

"Of course. Would you care to have lunch someplace or come to my office?"

"Oh no," she said immediately, "that won't do at all. Could you possibly come over here to my sisters home in West Palm Beach?"

"Be glad to," I told her, and she gave me the address. We agreed to meet at eleven o'clock on Friday morning.

"Thank you so much," she said, and the chirp came back into her voice. "You don't know what a relief it will be to tell someone. I haven't been able to sleep a wink since Marcia died."

And she hung up. Al Rogoff accuses me of overusing the word "intriguing." But at that moment I couldn't think of a better one.

I had absolutely no idea of what Mrs. Jane Folsby wished to reveal to me, so I discarded that topic instanter. I would learn on the morrow.

As for CW's admission that his marriage depended upon his signing a five-million-dollar agreement with his bride-to-be, I could only conclude that Mrs. Gertrude Smythe-Hersforth might not be as witless as I had assumed. And further, the senior McNally had been his usual omniscient self when he had described marriage as a contractual obligation.

What was perhaps most astonishing to me was my own ingenuousness. When I first met Theodosia Johnson I was convinced her nature *had* to be as pure as her beauty. Then, after I had been privileged to view that blue butterfly, I became aware of her fiercely independent willfulness. And now third thoughts had superseded the second; she was apparently a young lady with a shrewd instinct for the bottom line.

But then my musing veered from the relations of Madam X with the Chinless Wonder to her relations with yrs. truly. It occurred to me that Theo had been aware from the start that I had been assigned to investigate her bona fides. During that demented deli luncheon, her father had denied she knew of my role. But Hector, I now reckoned, was as consummate a liar as I.

And if Theo was cognizant of what I was about, perhaps the granting of her favors (with the promise of more to come) was her astute method of insuring my willing cooperation in her endeavor to snare the heir to the Smythe-Hersforth fortune. It's possible that was her motive, was it not? Naturally I preferred to believe she had succumbed to the McNally charm. But I could not delude myself by completely rejecting the notion that she had been the seductress and I the object of her Machiavellian plotting.

I simply did not know. And so I left immediately for the Pelican Club bar, seeking inspiration.

Chapter 14

My parents were not present that evening, having been invited to dinner at the home of octogenarian friends celebrating the birth of their first great-grandchild. And so I dined in the kitchen with the Olsons, and a jolly time was had by all. Ursi served a mountainous platter of one of her specialties: miniature pizzas (two bites per) with a variety of toppings. Romaine salad with vinaigrette dressing. Raspberry sorbet on fresh peaches for dessert. (Please don't drool on this page.)

That delightful dinner numbed me, but I was able to work on my journal in lackadaisical fashion until it became time to depart for my meeting with Sgt. Rogoff. Obeying my mother's dictum—"Never visit without bringing a gift."—I stopped en route to pick up a cold six-pack of Corona. It is one of Al's favorites, but I must admit that when it comes to beers he has no animosities that I'm aware of.

Rogoff's "wagon" is a double mobile home set on a concrete foundation and furnished in a fashion that would make any bachelor sigh with content. Comfort is the theme, and everything is worn and shabby enough so you feel no restraint against kicking off your shoes.

The barefoot host was wearing jeans and a snug T-shirt, and when he uncapped the beer I had brought he put out a large can of honey-roasted peanuts. I said, "Al, I speak more as friend than critic, but your waistline is obviously expanding exponentially. To put it crudely, pal, you're cultivating a king-sized gut."

"So what?" he said. "I've noticed you're no longer the thin-as-a-rail bucko you once were."

"Touché," I said, "and I hope it will be the last of the evening. I've been meaning to ask, did you ever get to see that portrait of Theodosia Johnson by Silas Hawkin in the Pristine Gallery?"

We were sprawled in oak captain's chairs at the sergeant's round dining table. He had put on a cassette of the original cast recording of "Annie Get Your Gun," and what a delight it was to hear Ethel Merman belt out those wonderful tunes, even if the volume was turned down low.

"Oh yeah," Rogoff said, "I saw it. Great painting. And a great model. She's a knockout."

"My sentiments exactly," I said.

He looked at me quizzically. "Taken with the lady, are you?"

"Somewhat."

"You're asking for trouble."

"Odd you should say that, Al. Priscilla Pettibone at the Pelican Club told me the same thing."

"Smart girl," he said. "But I don't expect you to take her advice or mine. You're a hopeless victim of your glands. But enough of this brilliant chitchat. I've got the skinny on Hector Johnson and Reuben Hagler. The agreement was that you tell me why you want it before I deliver. So let's hear."

"It's a long story."

He shrugged. "And it's a long night. We've got your six-pack and another of Molson in the fridge. Get started."

I told him everything relevant: my first glimpse of Hagler while I was with Shirley Feebling; learning that Hagler was one of Hector Johnson's bank references; his hole-in-the-wall office as an investment adviser; my luncheon with the two men; and my accidental meeting with Hagler when I had traveled to Fort Lauderdale to question Pinky Schatz.

"My, my," Rogoff said when I finished, "you have been a busy little snoop, haven't you. You figure these two guys are close?"

"Peas in a pod."

"And you think Hagler shot Shirley Feebling?"

"That's my guess."

"Motive?"

"Haven't the slightest," I admitted. "Pinky Schatz might know, but she's not talking. At least not to me."

"How did you get chummy with her in the first place?"

"Told her I was Chauncey Smythe-Hersforth."

The sergeant laughed. "What a scammer you are! If you ever turn your talents to crime, Florida will be in deeeep shit. Well, it's not my case but I'll give Lauderdale Homicide a call and tell them about this Reuben Hagler. I don't think I've ever seen the guy. What's he like?"

"Dracula."

"That sweet, huh? And what was the name of the woman you talked to?"

"Pinky Schatz. She's a nude dancer at the Leopard Club."

"Your new hangout?" he said. "Well, I guess it's better than collecting stamps."

"Oh, shut up," I said. "Now tell me what you learned from Michigan."

"Hector Johnson used to be a stockbroker. Racked up for securities fraud. He was fined, made restitution, and was banned from the securities business for life. He never did hard time but apparently while he was in jail for a few weeks he met Reuben Hagler. This Hagler has a nasty file: attempted robbery, felonious assault, stuff like that. He's done prison time: three years for rape. He was also suspected of being an enforcer for local loan sharks."

"Sounds like he'd be capable of killing Shirley Feebling."

"I'd say so," Rogoff agreed. "And now he's an investment adviser in Fort Lauderdale?"

"That's what the sign on his office claims. But in view of Johnson's history, Hagler might be a front and Hector is calling the shots."

"Wouldn't be a bit surprised. What do you suppose Johnson's angle is on all this?"

I shook my head. "Can't figure it." I confessed, "but there's obviously frigging in the rigging."

We sat in silence awhile, trying to imagine scenarios that made some loopy kind of sense. But neither of us had any suggestions to offer.

"Al," I said, "how did you make out this morning when you talked to Louise Hawkin?"

"You were right," he said. "The lady was totally befuddled. And you know what? I think Hector Johnson means to keep her that way."

I will not say his comment was the key to the whole meshugass. But it did start me thinking in a new direction. I began to get a vague notion of what might be going on.

"Do you believe that letter Marcia Hawkin gave me?" I asked the sergeant. "Do you think she really did kill her father?"

He shrugged. "Beats me. Maybe yes, maybe no. If he had given her motive, I'd be more certain one way or the other."

"Me, too," I said. "Any word yet on that stained sheet or whatever it was we saw in the back of her Cherokee?"

"Nothing yet. These tests take time; you know that."

I stared at him a moment, then decided to put my vague notion to the test. "Are you a betting man, Al?"

"I've been known to place a small wager now and then."

"Tell you what," I said. "I'll bet you ten bucks I can tell you what those stains on the sheet are even before the tests are completed."

"They're not blood," he said. "I told you she was strangled."

"I know they're not blood. But I know what they are. Is it a bet?"

"Okay," he said. "For ten bucks. What are they?"

"Acrylic paint."

He took a swig of his beer. "How the hell did you come up with that?"

"A swami told me."

"If you turn out to be right, tell the swami there's a job waiting for him in the PBPD."

"I think I'm right," I said, "but I don't want your ten dollars. I want a favor instead."

He groaned. "I'd rather pay the ten."

"A simple favor," I said. "Get back to your Michigan contact and ask if they've got anything on Theodosia Johnson, Hector's daughter. The last name may be different but 'Theodosia' is probably for real. What woman would use that as an alias? And you met her this morning, you can describe her accurately. Or send Michigan a photo of that Silas Hawkin portrait."

He looked at me a long time. "She's involved?" he asked.

"I would prefer to think not."

"Screw what you'd prefer," he said roughly. "Do you figure she is?"

"As you just said about Marcia Hawkin, maybe yes, maybe no. This is one way to find out."

"I guess," he said, sighing. "All right. I'll play your little game. I'll query Michigan just for the fun of it. But our sawbuck bet is still on."

I finished my beer, grabbed a fistful of peanuts, and stood up. "I'm going home," I declared. "It's been a long, tumultuous day, and bed beckons."

"Yeah," Rogoff said, "I could do with some shut-eye myself. Thanks for the beer."

"And thank you for the peanuts," I said politely. "Al, let me know if anything turns up."

"Sure," he said. "And Archy . . ."

"Yes."

"That Reuben Hagler sounds like a foursquare wrongo. Watch your back."

"I always do," I said blithely.

By the time I returned home my parents had retired. I ascended to my seventh heaven and prepared for bed. I had had quite enough mental stimulation for one day and decided to postpone adding recent revelations to my journal.

I awoke on Friday morning ready for a fight or a frolic—or perhaps both simultaneously. Again I had overslept and was forced to construct my own breakfast. It consisted of leftover mini-pizzas from dinner the previous evening.

Before leaving home I remembered to phone Consuela Garcia as I had promised. She was at work in her office and was already in a snit trying to answer the demands of Lady Horowitz. I was hoping for a lazy, affectionate chat, but Connie made it short and sweet. Well . . . not exactly. Just short. But she did agree to meet me for dinner that evening at the Pelican Club.

I then tooled over to the McNally Building to check my messages (none) and incoming correspondence (none). My business day was starting auspiciously. I finished my inventive expense account, signed it with a flourish, and dropped the completed document on the desk of Ray Gelding, the firm's treasurer. He glanced at the total.

"You've got to be kidding," he said.

I treated that remark with the silent contempt it so richly deserved, bounced downstairs, and vaulted into the Miata for a drive to West Palm Beach and my appointment with Mrs. Jane Folsby.

Her sister's home was located in a neighborhood I can only term bucolic and was more bungalow than South Florida split-level ranch. Rose bushes were plentiful and the front yard boasted two orchid trees that would have elicited gasps of awe from my mother. The house itself was freshly painted and had a semicircular stained-glass window over the front door. Very nice.

Mrs. Folsby answered my knock and seemed pleased to see me. She led the way to a small, brightly furnished living room in the rear with windows mercifully facing north. Everything was flowered chintz but not overpowering, and the white wicker armchair I sat in was comfortable enough.

She insisted on serving minted iced tea. I told her how delicious it was—which wasn't *quite* the truth. Then we agreed that South Florida was, indeed, hot in midsummer. We also concurred that crime rates were too high and youngsters today had little respect for their elders.

Then there was a pause in this brilliant conversation. "About Marcia Hawkin . . ." I promoted.

"Yes," she said, looking down and moving a gold wedding band around and around on her finger. "I don't know how to say this, Mr. McNally."

"Take your time," I said encouragingly. "I am not a policeman, you know, although Sergeant Al Rogoff is a close friend. But if you wish this conversation to remain confidential, I shall certainly respect your wishes."

"That's for you to decide," she said. "The only reason I'm telling you is that a crime has been committed, and someone should be punished."

I have previously described her as "old, large, creaky," and with a chirpy voice. But now I saw something in her I had not recognized before: strong will and stiff determination. Not a woman to be trifled with, and I wondered how she had endured the disorder of the Hawkin ménage. Economic reasons, I supposed; she needed the money.

"I hadn't been with the Hawkins long," she started, "before I realized something was going on."

Again there was a short lull. I didn't want to spur her with questions, feeling it best to let her tell the story at her own pace.

"Mrs. Louise Hawkin and Marcia . . ." she finally continued. "Always at each other. I thought it was because Louise was a stepmother. Sometimes daughters resent it. And her drinking so much," she added. "The missus, that is."

I nodded.

"But it was more than that," she went on. "I don't know how to tell this and I wouldn't blame you if you didn't believe me, but I've got to say it."

I waited.

She looked away from me. "Silas Hawkin," she said, and her voice was dry, "the mister, he was bedding his daughter. I know that for a fact."

I took a gulp of my iced tea. "You're certain of this, Mrs. Folsby?"

"I am," she said firmly. "There is no doubt in my mind. I don't know how long it had been going on. Years, I'd guess. Before Silas married Louise. She was his third wife."

"So I read in his obituary."

"And Marcia was his daughter by the first. Yes, I think it had been going on for a long time."

I drew a deep breath. "Marcia was very disturbed," I commented.

"She had every right to be," Mrs. Folsby said angrily. "What her life must have been like! So naturally Louise was her enemy."

"Naturally," I said.

"I can't tell you how poisonous they were to each other. They had a fight once. And I mean a *fight* with slapping and kicking. The mister broke it up."

"Dreadful," I said.

"They hated each other," she said sadly. "Jealous, you see. Louise knew what was going on. Marcia was her rival. And Marcia saw Louise as *her* rival. All because of that awful man. He came on to me once. Can you believe it?"

"Yes," I said. "I can believe it."

"So that's why I think she did it."

It took me a moment to sort that out. "Mrs. Folsby," I said, "are you suggesting that Louise may have murdered her stepdaughter?"

"It does not behoove me to accuse her," she said primly. "But I think the matter should be looked into."

"It shall be," I assured her. "May I have your permission to relay what you've told me to the authorities?"

"Will you give them my name?"

"Not if you don't wish it."

"I do not," she said sharply. "But if you want to tell them the other things—well, that's up to you. I've done all I can do."

"I understand completely," I said, "and I thank you for your honesty. And for your hospitality."

I finished that wretched iced tea and rose to leave. She accompanied me to the front door. Just before I departed I said, "Mrs. Folsby, do you think Marcia Hawkin killed her father?"

"No," she said, shaking her head, "she loved him too much."

I drove back to the Island in a broody mood. I figured that conversation with Mrs. Folsby had yielded one Yes, one No, and one Maybe.

The Yes was the information that Silas Hawkin was having an incestuous relationship with Marcia. After what Lolly Spindrift had told me of the man's sexual proclivities, I could believe it. And probably, as Mrs. Folsby had guessed, for many years.

The No was her accusation—or suggestion—that Louise Hawkin had killed her stepdaughter. That I could not believe. Marcia had been strangled, and that is very, *very* rarely the modus operandi of a murderess. Also, I did not think Louise had the strength—to be crude, it takes muscle to wring a human neck—and what could possibly be her motive since Silas, the reason for the two women's enmity, had been eliminated.

The Maybe was Mrs. Folsby's stout declaration that Marcia didn't murder her father because she loved him too much. Perhaps. But that unhinged child had also described daddy to me as the "horribilest" person in the world. Theirs could have been a love-hate affair in which the second verb finally triumphed over the first.

It was then a bit past noon and I lunched alone at Bice, ordering a hearts-of-palm salad and a single glass of sauvignon blanc. Feeling justifiably virtuous at having put a choke collar on my appetite, I returned to the McNally Building and phoned Mrs. Trelawney. I asked if the seigneur might be available for a short conference. She was absent a moment and then returned to tell me I had been granted a ten-minute audience before the boss departed for lunch with a client.

I scampered up to the sanctum and found him at his antique rolltop desk filling a briefcase with blue-bound documents.

"Can't it wait, Archy?" he said irascibly.

"Just take a moment, sir," I said. "It's something I think you should be aware of."

I related exactly what Chauncey Smythe-Hersforth had told me of the prenuptial agreement demanded by Theodosia Johnson. The sire halted his packing to listen closely. And when I mentioned the amount requested, five million dollars, one of his tangled eyebrows rose slowly as I knew it would.

"A tidy sum," he remarked wryly when I had finished. "I am not too familiar with the precedents of prenuptial agreements, but I shall certainly research the subject. Why didn't Chauncey consult me on this matter?"

"Father," I said gently, "I think he's afraid of you."

He actually snorted. "Nonsense," he said. "Am I an ogre?"

"No, sir."

"Of course not. And he obviously requires legal counsel. I suspect Chauncey's actual fear is having to inform his mother of what his fiancée has requested."

"I'd say that's close to the mark," I agreed.

He pondered a moment. "That young man does have a problem," he finally declared. "He's of age, of course, and can marry whomever he chooses without his mother's permission. But I can understand his not wishing to endanger his inheritance of the Smythe-Hersforth estate in toto. Any suggestions, Archy?"

"Yes, sir," I said. "Let me stall him as long as I can. A few things have turned up in my investigation that lead me to believe the question of a prenuptial agreement may become moot."

He stared at me. "Are you suggesting the young lady may prove to be unsuitable? Persona non grata, so to sneak?"

"Possibly," I acknowledged. "But not so much as her father."

He nodded. "In that case I concur with your recommendation. Delay Chauncey's decision as best you can and redouble your efforts to bring this rather distasteful business to a successful conclusion."

"Yes, father," I said, resisting an impulse to tug my forelock.

I left his office and returned home for my ocean swim, then labored on my journal. I showered, dressed, attended the family cocktail hour, and departed for my dinner date with Connie Garcia.

And, you know, during all that time I do not believe there was a single moment when I ceased glooming about Marcia Hawkin, her life and her death. The things we do to each other! Sometimes I think I'd rather be a cocker spaniel or even a hamster rather than a human being. But I did not choose my species and so I must learn to deal with it. And it would be nice if I could become a nobler example of Homo sapiens. But I know better than to hope.

When I arrived at the Pelican Club that evening Connie was already standing at the bar surrounded by a ring of eager young studs.

She was wearing a jumpsuit of burgundy velvet with an industrial zipper from neck to pipik. Her long black hair swung free and oversized golden hoops dangled from her lobes.

But I knew it was mostly her warm vivacity that attracted that pack of hopefuls. Connie is a vibrant young woman with physical energy to spare and a spirit that seems continually effervescing. Add to that a roguish smile and Rabelaisian wit and you have a complete woman who, on a scale of 1 to 10, rates at least a 15.

She saw me standing there like a forlorn bumpkin, excused herself, and came bopping over to grant me a half-hug and an air kiss.

"Hiya, hon," she said cheerily. "I was early so I had a spritzer at the bar."

"And why not?" I said. "You look glorious tonight, Connie."

"You like?" she asked, twirling for my inspection. "The tush isn't too noticeable?"

"Not *too*," I said. "Never *too*."

"Let's go eat," she said. "I'm starving."

I wish I could tell you the evening was an unalloyed delight, but I must confess that dinner was something less than a joyful occasion.

It wasn't the food because chef Leroy Pettibone scored with a marvelous special of fried rabbit in a cranberry-orange sauce. And it wasn't Connie's fault because she was her usual bubbling self.

No, the fault was totally mine. I knew it and was utterly incapable of summoning up the McNally esprit. I seemed unable to utter anything but banalities—mercifully brief banalities—and I realized I was behaving like a zombie on barbiturates.

Finally Connie's chatter faded away, and she reached across the table to squeeze my hand. "Archy," she said, "what's wrong with you tonight?"

"Nothing."

"Don't shuck me, sonny boy," she said angrily. "I know you too well. Is it because I've been dating other men, including your close friends?"

"Of course not. Positively not. We agreed that we can see whomever we please."

"Then what is it?"

I never ever talk to anyone but my father and Sgt. Al Rogoff about details of my investigations. I mean I head the Department of Discreet Inquiries at McNally & Son, and how discreet can they be if I blab? No, I am a close-mouthed lad and fully intend to remain so.

But at that moment I had to tell someone. I think it was because I needed to share the awful burden. I could understand why Mrs. Folsby had to tell me. It was just too much for one person to bear alone.

"Connie," I said, "I know you love to gossip and so do I. I want to tell you something. I *need* to tell you, but I want your cross-my-heart-and-hope-to-die promise that you won't repeat it to anyone."

"Archy," she said, suddenly solemn, "do you trust me? I mean really trust me?"

"Of course I do."

"Then I swear to you that whatever you tell me will go no farther."

I nodded. "I believe you," I said, and I meant it. "Well, you've heard about Marcia Hawkin's death, haven't you?"

"Of course. Now the police say she was murdered."

"That's correct. But today I heard something else and it's been tearing me apart."

I told her Silas Hawkin had been intimate with his daughter, probably for many years, beginning when she was quite young.

Connie stared at me, her lustrous eyes widening. Suddenly she began weeping. Silently, but the tears flowed.

"Oh God," I said helplessly. "I shouldn't have told you."

She shook her head and held her napkin up to her face. Her shoulders continued to shudder and I knew she was sobbing soundlessly. I could do nothing but wait and curse myself for shattering her.

Finally she calmed, dabbed at her swollen eyes, blinked. Her mouth still quivered and I feared the lacrimation might begin again.

"The poor child," she said in an anguished voice. "The poor, poor child."

"Yes," I said. "Can we move to the bar now and have a brandy? I think we both could use a buckup."

We sat close together at the bar, held hands, and sipped our Remy Martins without speaking. I admit that telling Connie of the Hawkins' incestuous relationship afforded me a small measure of relief. Do you believe that sorrow is lessened by sharing? It must be so because old wisdom declares that misery loves company.

What is amazing is that the pain seems to diminish slightly as it is transferred to another. I had no doubt that eventually, when Marcia's murder was solved, her secret would become known to the public. Then the distress, shared by millions, would dwindle away to become just another of the daily outrages we read about and eventually forget because to remember them all would be too painful to suffer.

After a while we agreed it was time to leave. Connie didn't suggest I accompany her home, nor did I. Before we separated, we stood alongside her car locked in a tight embrace. There was nothing passionate about it. It was the trembling hug of two mourners surviving in a world that sometimes seems too cruel to be endured.

Chapter 15

I awoke on Saturday and discovered my morosity had evaporated with the morning sun. What a relief that was! I don't mean to suggest I had totally forgotten Marcia Hawkin—I am not the froth-head my father seems to believe—but now I was able to accept her tragedy without reviling the human race or cursing fate.

The new day helped, of course. The sky was lucent, a sweet sea breeze billowed our curtains, the birds and my mother were twittering and, all in all, it seemed a lucky gift to be animate. I celebrated by eating eight blueberry pancakes—count 'em: *eight!*—at breakfast.

Then father departed for his customary Saturday morning foursome at his club, mother and Ursi went grocery shopping in our old Ford station wagon, and Jamie Olson disappeared somewhere on the grounds, muttering about the depredations of a rogue opossum he was determined to slay. And so I had the McNally manse to myself.

I went into my father's study and sat in his chair behind his desk. Anyone spotting me there might have thought I was contemplating a regicide so I could inherit the throne. Actually, all I wanted to do was use His Majesty's telephone directory. I phoned Lolly Spindrift's newspaper, knowing he worked Saturdays to meet his deadline for the Sunday edition.

"Lol?" I said. "Archy McNally here."

"Can't talk," he said shortly. "Busy."

"Too bad," I said. "And I have something so choice."

"Never too busy to chat," he said merrily. "What have you got for me, darling?"

"What are you working on?" I temporized. "Marcia Hawkin's death?"

"Of course. It's the murder de jour. All of Palm Beach is nattering about it. And now I'll give you a freebie, only because it will be in my column tomorrow morning. Did you know the unfortunate victim had twice attempted suicide?"

"No, I didn't know," I said slowly, "but I can't say I'm surprised. Where did you hear that?"

"Oh please," he said. "You know I protect my sources. Now what do you have for me?"

"I went first last time," I reminded him. "It's your turn."

He sighed. "What a scoundrel you are. Very well, what do you want?"

"About Theodosia Johnson, your Madam X . . . She's been in Palm Beach about a year. But only recently has she become the one-and-only of Chauncey Smythe-Hersforth. Do you know if she dated other men before meeting Chauncey?"

His laugh was a bellow. "Oh, laddie, laddie," he said, "do you think she sat home knitting antimacassars? Of course she saw other men. A horde. A multitude. *Very* popular, our Theodosia. I have the names of all her swains in my file and, frankly, sweets, I'm amazed that you're not included."

"I am, too."

"Perhaps it was because her taste seemed to run to older men of wealth. That would remove you from her list of eligibles, would it not?"

"Effectively," I said.

"And now that I've paid my dues," he went on, "what delicacy do you have for me? Tit for tat, you know—although my personal preference is somewhat different."

"I don't know how you can use this, Lol," I said, "but I'm sure you'll find a way. It concerns Hector Johnson, father of the beauteous Theo. He was racked up for securities fraud in Michigan. Spent some time in the local clink, paid a fine, made restitution, and was banned from the securities business for life."

"Love it!" Lolly shrieked. "Just love it! Yes, I expect I shall find an occasion to use that gem one of these days. Ta-ta, luv, and keep in touch."

I sat at father's desk a few moments longer, reflecting on what Spindrift had told me of Theo's social activities prior to her meeting Chauncey. It was easy to believe. A young woman of her multifarious charms would attract scads of beaux: single, married, divorced, or lonely in widowerhood. I was certain she had many opportunities to form a lasting relationship. But she had chosen Chauncey Wilson Smythe-Hersforth. Her selection of that noodle, I thought, was significant.

I had intended to call a few pals and see if anyone was interested in a few sets of tennis or, in lieu of that, driving out to Wellington to watch polo practice while gargling something exotic like a Singapore Sling or a Moscow Mule. But instead I phoned Theodosia Johnson. If my choice was between tennis, polo, or her, it was strictly no contest.

I was hoping Hector wouldn't answer, and he didn't. But when Theo said, "Hello?" her voice had the tone of sackcloth and ashes.

"Archy," I said. "Good lord, you sound low. Anything wrong?"

"A slight disagreement with daddy," she said, "and I'm still seething. But I'll recover. I always do. Archy, I'm so happy you called. I was beginning to think you had forgotten all about me."

"Fat chance," I said. "Theo, how *are* you, other than suffering from the megrims."

"What are megrims?"

"Low spirits."

"I'm suffering," she admitted. "Cheer me up."

"How about this: I drop by around noonish and we drive down the coast. It's a super day and it would be a shame to waste it. We'll have lunch outside at the Ocean Grand and talk of many things."

"Of shoes—and ships—and sealing wax—" she said.

"Of cabbages—and kings—" I said.

"And why the sea is boiling hot—" she said.

"And whether pigs have wings," I finished, and she laughed delightedly.

"The only poetry I know," she said. "Thank you, Archy; I feel better already. Yes, I accept your kind invitation."

"Splendid. See you at twelve."

I went back upstairs to take off jeans and T-shirt, shower, and don something more suitable for luncheon at the Ocean Grand with a smashing young miss. I settled on a jacket of plummy silk with trousers of taupe gabardine, and a shirt of faded blue chambray. Casual elegance was the goal, of course, and I believe I achieved it.

Then I set out for my luncheon date with Madam X. A duplicitous plot was beginning to take form in that wok I call my brain, and if all went well I intended to start the stir-fry that scintillant afternoon.

I had imagined Theo would wear something bright and summery, but that woman had a talent for surprise. She wore a pantsuit of black linen. No blouse. Her hair was drawn back and tied with a bow of rosy velvet. Very fetching, and I told her so.

"No bra," she said.

"I happened to notice," I said.

She laughed. "Chauncey never would. And if he did, he'd be shocked."

"Surely he's not that much of a prig."

"You have no idea."

Her obvious scorn of her fiancé discomfitted me. She could think those things, but wasn't it rather crass to speak of them to others? As I soon learned, she was in a sharp, almost shrewish mood that day.

For instance, as we drove southward along the corniche I remarked, "I had the pleasure of meeting your father's business associate, Reuben Hagler, the other day."

"Rube?" she said offhandedly. "He's a boozer."

It wasn't her judgment that startled me so much as her use of the sobriquet "boozer." She might have said, "He drinks a little too much," but she chose the coarse epithet. It was not the first time I had noticed her fondness for vulgarisms. I hoped, for her sake, that her speech was more ladylike in the presence of Mrs. Gertrude Smythe-Hersforth. That very proper matron, I suspected, would be tempted to put trousers on the legs of a grand piano.

And not only did Theo seem in a perverse humor that afternoon but she made no effort to conceal her lack of restraint.

"You were right," she said. "It's a super day. Why don't we just keep driving."

"Where to?"

"Oh, I don't know. Miami. The Keys. Check into some fleabag hotel for the weekend."

"Theo, I don't think that would be wise. Do you?"

"I guess not," she said. "Just dreaming."

But I knew that if I kept driving and found a hotel that accepted guests without luggage she would have happily acquiesced. Her unruliness was daunting.

We arrived at the Ocean Grand and she was suitably impressed by the elegant marbled interior.

"This is what it's all about, isn't it?" she commented.

"You've lost me," I said. "All about what?"

"You know, Archy. Money. Comfort. People to serve you. No problems. The lush life."

There was such fierce desire in her voice that I didn't even attempt a reply. She had a vision and it would have been brutal to explain that what she sought was a chimera. She wouldn't have believed me anyway.

We dined on the terrace of the bistro, overlooking the swimming pool. And beyond was a larger pool: the Atlantic Ocean. I suppose that setting and that luncheon came close to matching Theo's ideal. The omelettes were succulent, the salad subtly tartish, the glasses of chilled chenin blanc just right. And while we lived "the lush life," I initiated my intrigue.

"Theo," I said earnestly, "I have a problem I hope you'll be able to help me with."

"Oh?" she said. "What is it?"

"First of all I want you to know that I have no desire whatsoever to intrude on your personal affairs. Whatever you do or whatever you plan is no business of mine, and I don't want you to think I'm a meddler. But willy-nilly I've been handed a decision to make that concerns you."

That caught her. She paused in the process of dredging a slice of smoked salmon from her omelette.

"Archy," she said, "what *is* it?"

"Well, Chauncey and I are really not close friends. Not buddy-buddy, you know, but more like casual acquaintances. However, on occasion he asks my advice on legal matters. I have tried to convince him that I am an ersatz lawyer— no license to practice—and he'd do better to consult my father, who not only has the education and experience but is the attorney of record for the Smythe-Hersforth family. But I think Chauncey is somewhat frightened of my father."

"Chauncey is frightened of many things," she said coldly.

"That may be, but I must admit Prescott McNally can be overwhelming at times. He is a stringent man of high principles. Unbending, one might say. Chauncey prefers to discuss his problems with me."

"And am I one of Chauncey's problems?"

I waved that away. "Of course not. Not you personally. Chauncey declares he is deeply in love with you and I believe him. He wants very much to marry you. What he is concerned about is the prenuptial agreement you have requested."

"Oh," she said. "That."

"Theo, I definitely approve of what you're doing to ensure your future, although I do think five million is a wee bit high."

"He can afford it," she said stonily.

"Perhaps not now," I said. "I don't think his present net worth could accommodate it. But he'd certainly be capable of a five-million settlement after he inherits."

"Yes," she said, "that's what I figured."

A cool one, our Madam X!

"But that's Chauncey's quandary, don't you see." I said. "I must tell you that Mrs. Smythe-Hersforth is not wildly enthusiastic about her son marrying. Not just to you but to any woman. You know what dominant mothers are like."

"Do I ever!"

"So if Chauncey tells her about the prenup, she may change her will and pull the plug on his inheritance."

"Can she do that, Archy? He's her only child, you know."

"True, and though I'm not too familiar with Florida inheritance law, I reckon Chauncey would be legally entitled to a certain percentage of her estate. I mean I doubt she could totally disinherit him. And if she tried, he could certainly contest the will. But what if she becomes so angered she decides to diminish her estate while she's still alive? Spend all her millions on a program for spaying cats, for instance. I'm jesting, of course, but it's her money and if she wants to give it all away, or most of it, to worthwhile charities while she's living, she's completely within her legal rights."

Theo took a gulp from her wine glass. "Jesus!" she said. "We hadn't thought of that."

Did you catch that "We"? I did.

She gave me what I believe she thought was a brave smile, but it looked rather tremulous to me.

"You don't think his mother will approve of a prenup agreement, Archy?"

"I don't. Do you?"

"I guess not," she said. "The old bitch doesn't even approve of *me*. I knew that from the start. What did you tell Chauncey to do?"

"I stalled him. Until I had a chance to talk to you about it and see how you felt."

She reached across the table to pat my cheek. "Good boy," she said.

We were silent while our emptied plates were removed. We both declined coffee, but I ordered bowls of fresh raspberries.

"You're a clever lad, Archy," Madam X said. "I'll just bet you've got an answer up your sleeve."

"There is one possibility," I admitted, giving her a straight-in-the-eye stare. "Have your own attorney draw up the prenuptial agreement for five million. My father doesn't have to know about it and Chauncey's mother doesn't have to know about it."

The simplicity of my solution stunned her and she took a moment to grasp it. "And you'll tell Chauncey to sign it?" she asked, almost breathlessly.

I switched into my enigmatic mode and didn't give her a direct reply. "Think about it," I urged her. "Talk it over with your father. Frankly, Theo, I think it's your only hope. But it's your decision. Now let's eat our raspberries. Don't they look delicious!"

"Archy," she said, "daddy is over at Louise Hawkin's place."

"Is he?" I said. "And when is he returning home?"

"Probably tomorrow morning," she said, and we smiled at each other.

I shall not attempt to apologize for my conduct during the remainder of that afternoon. I agree that "reprehensible" is as good an adjective as any to describe my behavior. But I do have an excuse: The devil made me do it.

We drove back to Theo's condo. Once again she led me to that appalling cretonne-covered couch, and once again I saw the blue butterfly flutter and take wing.

She was mystery incarnate. Ignoring her physical beauty—which I certainly did not—I sensed there was a fury in her convulsions. I do not believe I was the cause of her anger; it was her malignant destiny that enraged her, and she rebelled with puissance and a bravado that asserted her strength and independence.

I returned home exhausted and saddened, although if what I suspected was accurate, there was little reason for my sorrow. Still, I find it depressing when people with admirable attributes put their talents to wicked use.

I conducted myself with stately decorum during the evening routine of family cocktail hour and dinner. I do not believe either of my dear progenitors had any inkling of the deception I had practiced that afternoon.

After dinner I retired upstairs to work on my journal. I had hardly started scribbling when Sgt. Al Rogoff phoned.

"How many chukkers of polo did you play today?" he demanded.

"None," I replied.

"How many sets of tennis?"

"None."

"How many holes of golf?"

"None."

"Heavens to Betsy," he said, "what's happening to the primo playboy of Palm Beach? Then what have you been up to?"

"Investigating," I said. "I do work occasionally, you know."

"You could have fooled me," he said. "Hey, I told Lauderdale about Reuben Hagler and that Pinky Schatz. They can't locate him, but they've planted an undercover policewoman in the Leopard Club."

"Yikes!" I said. "Surely not as a nude dancer."

"Nope," Al said, laughing. "I guess she's not qualified. They put her in as a waitress. Her job is to buddy up to the Schatz woman and try to get her to spill."

"It might work," I said, "but I doubt it."

"Me, too," Rogoff admitted. "But one never knows, do one?"

"Al, will you stop stealing my line? You're infringing my copyright."

"Don't tell me you made it up."

"No," I confessed, "it's not original. I think Louis Armstrong said it first, or maybe it was Fats Waller. I don't remember."

"Talk about remembering," he said. "I just did. I owe you ten bucks."

"What?" I said, and then I recalled our bet and knew the real reason he had phoned. "You mean that sheet in the back of Marcia Hawkin's Jeep had acrylic paint stains?"

"Yep," he said, "but it wasn't a sheet. More like a drop cloth. Now tell me how you knew the stains were acrylic paint."

"Gut instinct," I said, and Al, who has as much contempt for that phrase as I do, roared with laughter.

"Bull*shit!*" he said. "You know something I don't know and you're holding out on me. This is a homicide investigation, you charlie, so let's have it."

"I really didn't *know,*" I said. "I was just guessing. Listen to this Al . . ."

I told him of my conversations with Luther Grabow, the art supply dealer, and how Silas Hawkin had purchased a palette of acrylics to paint a nude on a wood panel.

"Nice job, Sherlock," Rogoff said when I had finished. "You figure the nude on wood was the painting Hawkin labeled 'Untitled' in his ledger?"

"Yes, I think so."

"Oh, boy," he said. "Bubble, bubble, toil and trouble."

"It's 'Double, double toil and trouble,' " I told him.

"Whatever," he said. "Got any idea who the model was?"

"Nope."

"Could it have been his daughter? She ices him like she said in that letter and then swipes the painting because she's afraid it might incriminate her."

"Could be," I said. "You reckon she had it in the car when she went in the drink?"

"A possibility," Rogoff said. "I'll send divers down to look around and see if they can spot it. Maybe it floated out of the Cherokee."

"If it floated out," I said, "it would be on the surface, wouldn't it?"

"Yeah, you're right. That scenario doesn't wash. But I still think she had the 'Untitled' painting in her possession sometime during the evening she was killed."

"And now someone else has it?"

"Sure," he said. "Unless she burned it or hacked it to splinters. That's what I like about my job: Everything is cut and dried."

"I know what you mean. Al, did you hear anything from Michigan about Theodosia Johnson?"

"Not yet. Archy, tell me something: Do you think the Shirley Feebling kill in Fort Lauderdale has anything to do with Marcia Hawkin's murder?"

I hesitated. "Yes," I said finally.

"Uh-huh," he said, "that's what I figured. Are the Johnsons involved?"

"It's all supposition."

"Sure it is," he agreed. "Like meat loaf; you don't know what's in it. We're tracing Marcia's movements the night she was killed and we've got what we tell the newspapers are 'promising leads.' Maybe they are, maybe they're not, but I'll keep working my end, old buddy, and you keep working yours. Eventually we may take the gold though I'll settle for the bronze."

"Me, too," I said.

"See you," he said shortly, and hung up.

I sat there, stared at my open journal, and decided I didn't want to labor on a Saturday night. So I pulled on a nylon golf jacket (Day-Glo orange) and clattered downstairs to my wheels. I headed south on Ocean Boulevard to eyeball the Hawkin home, Villa Bile. I didn't have to stop to see that Hector Johnson's white Lincoln was parked outside.

Then I made an illegal U-turn and sped off to the Pelican Club. I was in dire need of a plasma injection, for what I envisioned had happened to Silas Hawkin, Shirley Feebling, and Marcia Hawkin seemed too awful to endure without Dutch courage.

It was still early so it was no surprise to find the club relatively quiescent. I tested Simon Pettibone by ordering an obscure cocktail from my antique Bartenders Guide.

"I would appreciate a Frankenjack," I stated.

He stared at me, rolled his eyes upward, concentrated a moment. Then he recited, "Gin, dry vermouth, apricot brandy, Triple Sec."

"You're incredible," I told him.

"Served with a cherry," he added. "You really want one, Mr. McNally?"

"No," I said. "A double vodka-rocks will do me fine, Mr. Pettibone. The good stuff."

"Sterling or Stoli?"

"Sterling, please."

He poured and placed the tumbler before me.

"First of the night?" he asked pleasantry.

"First and last," I said. "I shall not be a problem."

"You never are," he assured me. "Until you start reciting Shakespeare."

"Dear old Willy," I said. "What would I do without him? Tell me something, Mr. Pettibone: Do you believe that money makes the world go 'round?"

"Not entirely," he replied. "I do not believe it is money itself. After all, that is just metal and paper. No, it is the power money confers that makes the world go 'round."

"Power," I repeated reflectively. "Ah. As in comfort, people to serve you, no problems, the lush life?"

"You've got it, Mr. McNally."

"No," I said, "but I wish I did. However, I wouldn't kill for it. Would you?"

"Kill? Another person?"

"Yes."

"No," he said, "I would not do that. I enjoy my sleep too much."

"Well put," I said. "But I suspect there are those who would kill for money and sleep as soundly as you."

"Oh yes," he agreed, "there are those. But they will get their deserts on judgment day."

"And when will that be, Mr. Pettibone? Next Tuesday?"

He didn't laugh or even smile, so I ordered another belt. I finished that and departed. The Pelican was beginning to fill up with a riotous Saturday night throng and I was in no mood for revelry.

I returned home, undressed, and donned a silk nightshirt. But before I took to the sheets I consumed a dollop of marc and smoked one cigarette. To insure a deep, untroubled slumber, you understand. I finally went to bed absolutely convinced I would awake the next day with a clear head, a settled turn, a sweet breath—and possibly five pounds lighter.

Chapter 16

Of course my hopes were more than dashed on Sunday morning; they were obliterated. But I shall not weary you with a detailed account of my agonies. The only thing more boring than another person's dream is another person's hangover. Suffice to say that it was almost noon before the McNally carcass calmed to the extent that I ceased thinking of suicide as the only cure for my woes.

But my physical fragility was not the only reason I stayed at home that day; I was awaiting a phone call from Hector Johnson. I was certain his daughter had told him of our conversation during that luncheon at the Ocean Grand, and I was just as certain dear old Heck would gobble the bait.

A word of explanation is in order here. The reason for my scheming was that I had no proof. I had suspicions aplenty, but they might well have been skywriting, so ephemeral were they without a test of their validity and permanence. And the only way I could do that was by scamming the scammers. It may sound unnecessarily devious, but bear with me.

I was in my rooms and it was almost one-thirty before my phone rang. I grabbed it up.

"Archy?" he said. "This is Hector Johnson."

A surge of satisfaction dissolved the last remnants of my Katzenjammer. "Heck!" I said cheerily. "Good to hear from you."

"Likewise," he said. "Listen, Arch, I think you and I should get together for a little man-to-man."

"Oh? Concerning what?"

"I can't discuss it on the phone," he said brusquely. "It's about what you mentioned to Theo yesterday."

"Ah," I said, "that. Yes, I agree you and I should have a chat. Where and when?"

"I'm leaving in a few minutes for Fort Lauderdale. I've got some business down there and I'll be gone all day. But I should be home tonight. Is, say, ten o'clock too late for you?"

"Not at all."

"Suppose I come over to your place. I know the address. We can sit in my car and talk."

"Surely you'll come in and have a drink."

"No, thanks," he said shortly. "My car would be best. Private, know what I mean?"

"Whatever you prefer," I told him. "I'll be waiting for you."

"Just you and me," he said. "Right?"

"Of course."

"Good," he said. "See you at ten."

He hung up and I did everything but dance a soft-shoe, thinking my plot was developing nicely.

Is it elitist to recognize there are cheap people? There are, you know. I don't mean "cheap" in the sense of stingy, but cheap as meaning shoddy, of inferior quality. I thought Hector Johnson was a cheap person, and so was his old buddy, Reuben Hagler.

But sleazy people can sometimes be remarkably clever and remarkably dangerous. I do not take their tawdriness lightly. And so I spent some time devising and rehearsing my dialogue with Hector that evening. I knew the role I had to play. I believed I knew his and could only hope I was correct.

I recognized there was a certain degree of risk involved. Good ol' Heck did not impress me as a man who would accept defeat resignedly. But if he became physical, I was breezily confident I could cope. A perfect example of my damnable self-deception.

But before we met there was something I needed to do. Not because it might aid my investigation but because it was simply something I felt necessary. I dressed conservatively and went downstairs to my mother's greenhouse. She and father were still at church, I could not ask her permission, so I stole one of her potted begonias. It was the Fiesta type with red flowers. I was certain mother would forgive the theft when she learned the purpose.

I drove south to the Hawkin home, slowed to make certain Hector Johnson's Lincoln was not present, then turned into the driveway and parked. I carried the begonia up to the front door and knocked briskly. Nothing. I tried again and there was no response. My third attempt brought results; the door was opened slowly and Mrs. Louise Hawkin stared at me dully.

Oh lordy, but she was a mess. I did not believe she was drunk but she seemed in a stupor, and I wondered if she was drugged. I wasn't sure she recognized me.

"Archy McNally, ma'am," I said. "I want to offer the condolences of my parents and myself on your stepdaughter's tragic death."

But she wasn't listening. She was staring at the plant I was carrying and I thought she brightened.

"Glads," she said.

"No, Mrs. Hawkin. It's a Fiesta begonia."

"The red flowers," she said. "My mother always had fresh glads in the house. She went to the market every three days. All colors but mostly she liked red. So cheerful. I should have bought fresh glads every three days."

"May I come in?" I asked.

She allowed me to enter and watched while I carefully placed the plant on a glass-topped end table. Then she came forward to touch the rosettes tenderly. It was a caress.

"So lovely," she murmured. "So lovely."

I feared she had been sleeping and I had awakened her. She was wearing a wrinkled robe of stained foulard silk. Her hair was unbrushed and looked as if it needed a good wash. Her makeup was smeary, the polish on her fingernails chipped and peeling.

"Mrs. Hawkin," I said, "is there anything I can do for you?"

"Do?" she asked, seemingly bewildered.

I looked around the littered room. Overflowing ashtrays. A spilled drink. A tilted lamp shade. Newspapers scattered on the floor. An odor of grease and mildew. Total disarray.

"Perhaps a cleaning woman," I suggested. "I can find someone for you."

Unexpectedly she flared. "Everyone is always picking on me," she howled.

"Picking?" I said, and then realized she meant hassling. "I didn't wish to upset you, ma'am, and I apologize. Would you like me to leave?"

She calmed as abruptly as she had exploded. "No, no," she said, then added coquettishly, "Sit thee down, lad, and I'll get us a nice drinkie-poo."

I should have declined, of course, but at the moment a drinkie-poo was exactly what I needed. Unfortunately, Mrs. Hawkin returned from the kitchen with two tumblers filled with a clear liquid. After a cautious sip I discovered it was warm gin.

"Have the reporters been bothering you?" I asked.

"Everyone," she said. "Everyone's been bothering me. Reporters, policemen, photographers, friends, strangers who park outside to stare at the house."

"Awful," I said.

"I can't stand it!" she shrieked. She threw her filled tumbler away from her. The contents spilled, the glass bounced on the shag rug without breaking. Then she fell to wailing, face buried in her hands.

Shaken, I did what I could to clean up the mess. Then I went into the kitchen, a pigsty. I poured about a quarter of my gin into a reasonably clean glass and added ice and water. I made another like it for Louise and brought it to her.

She had stopped keening. "Thanks," she said huskily and gulped down half. "I don't know what's happening to me."

"You've been through a horror," I told her. "First your husband, then your stepdaughter. It would shatter anyone. It's amazing that you're coping as well as you are."

She stared at me blankly. "Coping? Is that what I'm doing?"

I nodded.

"I'm not," she said. "I'm dead. I can't feel anything anymore."

I didn't believe that for a minute. I saw that strong, determined face sagging and the heavy body gone limp. Sorrow was taking its toll; she seemed to be shrinking. But there was something else in her expression besides grief. Something I could not immediately identify that I had recently seen and could not recall.

"Mrs. Hawkin," I said, "don't you think it might be wise to ask Jane Folsby to come back to take care of you and the house?"

"No," she said at once. "Not her. She knows too much and might talk."

Then I knew Mrs. Folsby had been telling the truth but I feigned ignorance. "Knows too much?" I repeated. "About what?"

"Things," Louise Hawkin said darkly. She finished her drink and held the empty glass out to me. Obediently I returned to that smelly kitchen, realizing I was no better than Hector Johnson. But if I didn't fetch her lethe she'd get it herself. Still . . .

I sat across from her, leaning forward, intent on keeping up with her fleeting moods.

"Mrs. Hawkin, I don't know if you're aware of it, but I met with Marcia the afternoon before she died."

I saw her stiffen. "Did you?" she said. "What did you talk about?"

"It was a rather disjointed conversation. I didn't clearly understand it. She was obviously disturbed."

"Marcia was insane!" she said forcibly. "I wanted her to get help but she wouldn't. What did she say?"

"Something about a business deal she was planning. Very vague."

"Oh that!" she said, and her laugh was tinny. "Marcia had mad dreams. She thought Hector Johnson would lend her enough money so she could get her own apartment."

"Oh, that's what it was all about," I said. I relaxed, sat back, crossed my legs. "So I guess it was Hector she was going to visit after she left me."

Then that expression I had previously been unable to identify returned more strongly and I recognized it. It was fear, and the last time I had seen it was during my talk with Pinky Schatz in Lauderdale.

"It might have been," Mrs. Hawkin said, shrugging. "It's not important."

"Of course not," I agreed. "That's police business, not mine."

She responded hotly. "Police business? What do you mean by that?"

"Why naturally they'll be trying to trace Marcia's movements the night she was killed. I suppose they'll be talking to all her friends."

She looked at me. "Marcia didn't have any friends," she said flatly.

That might have been true but it struck me as a cruel thing to say. I remembered that poor waif telling me that I was her best friend.

I finished my drink and rose. "I think I better run along," I said. "Thank you for your hospitality and I hope—"

"No," she said. "Stay."

"I'd like to," I said. "I really would. But I promised my parents to accompany them to a croquet match."

"Too bad," she said. "I hate to be alone, and Heck's gone somewhere for the day."

"Why don't you call Theodosia to come over and keep you company."

"That bitch?" Louise Hawkin said tonelessly. "I'd rather be alone."

I could not reply to that so I made my adieu and departed.

"Thanks for the glads," she called after me.

I drove home slowly, trying to nuzzle things out. My visit to Louise Hawkin had been planned as an ostensible sympathy call, but as I had hoped, it had turned out to be more than that. Nothing conclusive had been learned, you understand, but I was beginning to see things more distinctly—as I'm sure you are also, for I have faith in your perspicacity.

It was during a long, lazy ocean swim that I realized my scam's risks, initially treated with sangfroid, could very well prove to be heavier than I had first calculated. They might, in fact, endanger the physical well-being of your humble correspondent. In spite of what I had heard from Mrs. Hawkin I had no intention of abandoning my cunning scheme, but now I recognized its dangers. I am not, I trust, a craven coward, but neither do I claim to be Dudley Doright.

The perils of what I planned disturbed me. If I should, by evil chance, suddenly be rendered defunct, what I knew and what I suspected would be sponged forevermore. I decided to insure against that unhappy possibility.

During the family cocktail hour I confessed to the mater I had purloined one of her beloved begonias and had given it to the bereaved Louise Hawkin.

Mother beamed, kissed me, and said, "That was sweet of you, Archy."

It was indicative of my mood that a bit of wisdom—"A good deed never goes unpunished."—popped into my mind.

"Father," I said, "could you spare me a few minutes after dinner?"

"How many minutes?" he demanded. He can be something of a martinet at times.

"Fifteen," I said, knowing it would be thirty and possibly more.

"Very well," he said. "In my study."

Dinner that night was another of Ursi Olson's specialties: medallions of veal, breast of chicken, and mild Italian sausage sautéed with mushrooms and onions and served with a wine sauce over a bed of fettuccine. Father contributed a decent merlot from his locked wine cabinet, and he and I shared that bottle while mother sipped her usual sauterne.

After a lime sorbet and coffee I followed father into his study and closed the door. He seated himself behind his magisterial desk, and I selected a straight-back chair facing him. I did not want to become too comfortable.

Ordinarily my liege does not request, nor do I provide, progress reports during the course of my investigations. He tells me he is only interested in results. That may be true but I suspect it is also self-protective. He is well aware that my detective methods, while not actually illegal, might be considered unethical or immoral. And he doesn't wish to hear the gruesome details. In other words, he wants no guilty knowledge. I don't blame him a bit; he has more to lose than I.

But my current inquiry, involving the Smythe-Hersforths, the Johnsons, Reuben Hagler, the Hawkins, Shirley Feebling, and Pinky Schatz, was a special case. I needed someone to share my information and my suspicions so that if I met my quietus (sob!) the investigation could continue and my labors would not be wasted.

I told him everything: what had happened, what I had learned, what I surmised, and what I planned to do. I spoke for almost twenty minutes and saw his face tighten. But he controlled himself; not once did he interrupt.

But when I finished, his wrath was evident. His courtroom stare was cold enough to chill all that merlot I had imbibed at dinner.

"If I thought it would do any good," he said in a stony voice, "I would absolutely forbid you to do what you contemplate. The potential hazards are too great. But I don't imagine you would obey my command."

"No, sir," I said. "I would not. There is no real evidence that what I suspect did, in fact, occur. The only way I can prove my hypothesis is to offer myself as a greedy dupe. If there was a less dangerous way of unraveling this tangle, I would happily adopt it."

"Archy," he said, genuinely perplexed, "what is your obviously intense personal interest in all this? It doesn't directly concern McNally and Son. It's a police matter."

"Not totally," I said. "There are connections to our clients. And two young, innocent women have been brutally murdered during an investigation we instigated."

He looked at me a long time. "Lochinvar," he accused.

"No, father," I said. "Nemesis."

His anger was slowly transformed to a concern that affected me. "Is Sergeant Rogoff aware of all this?" he asked.

"Some of it, but not all. I intend to tell him more tomorrow after my meeting this evening with Hector Johnson. I'm going to ask Al to provide some measure of backup protection."

"Yes," he said, "that would be wise. Do you think you should be armed?"

"No, sir. If a concealed weapon is found or suspected, it might prove an irritant. A fatal irritant."

His smile was wan. "Perhaps you're right. You're playing a very risky game. I know you're aware of it and I won't attempt to dissuade you. All I ask is that if things become too hairy, you shut down your operation at once and extricate yourself. You understand? If there is no hope of success, give it up and withdraw immediately. Agreed?"

"Yes, father," I said. "Agreed."

I think we both knew that if I failed, a safe withdrawal would be most unlikely.

I went upstairs and spent the remaining hour rehearsing my role once again. I tried to imagine what objections might be made and what my responses should be. I reviewed the entire scenario and could see no holes that needed plugging. I felt I had devised as tight a scheme as possible. The only thing I could not be sure of was luck, and it was discouraging to recall Hector's remark that when you really need it, it disappears.

But then I comforted myself with the thought that his dictum applied to him as well as to me, and perhaps his disappearing luck would be my good fortune. It was a zero-sum game.

A few minutes before ten o'clock I went downstairs and stood outside the back doorway. The portico light was on and I placed myself directly below it so he'd be sure to see I was alone. I lighted a cig and waited. He was almost fifteen minutes late but that didn't bother me. I was certain his tardiness was deliberate; it's a common ploy to unsettle one's adversary. I've used it myself on several occasions.

Finally the white Lincoln Town Car came purring into our driveway, tires crunching on the gravel. It stopped, the headlights went off, flicked on, went off again, and I stepped down to join Hector Johnson.

The first thing I noted after I had slipped into the front passenger seat and closed the door was the mélange of odors: 86-proof Scotch, cigar smoke and, overpowering, his cologne, a musky scent I could not identify.

"Hiya, Arch," he said with heavy good humor. "Been waiting long?"

"Just came down," I lied cheerfully. "How are you, Heck?"

"If I felt any better I'd be unconscious," he said and laughed at his own wit. "Hey, the reason I'm late is that I stopped at Louise Hawkin's place to check on how she's doing. She tells me you dropped by today and brought her a plant. That was real nice."

"From the McNally family," I said. "To express our condolences on the tragic death of her stepdaughter."

"Yeah," he said, "that was a helluva thing, wasn't it. First her husband, then Marcia. The poor woman is really taking a hit. Listen, would you object if I lighted up a stogie? If it would bother you, just tell me."

"Not at all," I assured him. "Go right ahead."

We were silent while he extracted a cigar from a handsome pigskin case. He bit off the tip and spat it onto the floor at his feet. He used an old, battered Zippo lighter, which made me wonder how much he knew about cigars. No connoisseur of good tobacco would use anything but a wooden match.

"I guess you and Louise had a long talk," he said, puffing away and blowing the smoke out his partly opened window.

"We did," I admitted. "She seemed in the need of a sympathetic listener."

"Uh-huh," he said. "That's what I've been trying to be. She tells me you talked to Marcia the afternoon before she was killed."

"That's correct."

"And that lunatic kid said she was going to ask me for money so she could get her own apartment."

"Heck," I said, "if Mrs. Hawkin told you that, she's confused. I said only that Marcia spoke of a business deal she was planning. It was Mrs. Hawkin who suggested she was going to ask you for money."

"That figures," he said, showing me a warped grin. "Louise is a little nutsy these days. But that's neither here nor there. What I really want to talk about is Theo's prenuptial agreement. Let's see if I've got this clear. Chauncey comes to you and tells you about it. But he's afraid to tell his mother because then she might put the kibosh on the marriage. Have I got that right?"

"You've got it."

"And what did you tell him to do, Arch?"

"Not to sign anything until I had a chance to think about it."

"That was smart," Johnson said. "So you thought about it and figured Chauncey could sign the agreement without telling mommy. That's what you told Theo—correct?"

"Correct." "

"Now I get the picture," he said. "He'll sign if you tell him to?"

"I think he will."

"Sure he will. We get a shyster to draw up the papers. Chauncey signs, and his mother and your father know nothing about it. It's our secret."

"That's right, Heck."

He turned slowly to look at me. "So why do we need you?" he demanded. "You've already told us how to handle it."

"Two reasons," I said. "First of all, I could tell Chauncey not to sign."

"Wouldn't work," he said, shaking his head. "If he wants my daughter— and I know he's got the hots for her—he'll sign regardless of what you tell him. You're just not built right, Arch; you can't compete with Theo."

"That's probably true. But the second reason is that you're asking five million. A lot of money. I'd like a small piece of the action."

At least he had the decency not to express sorrow that his image of me as a "straight arrow" had suddenly been demolished. He just bit down hard on his cigar and stared grimly through the windshield at the night sky.

"For what?" he said. "So you won't tell Chauncey's mommy?"

"Let's call it a finder's fee," I said. "Just like you wanted for telling me about Mrs. Hawkin's intention to sell her property."

His laugh was short and not mirthful. "You got a great memory, boy. Okay, let's say you tell Chauncey to sign the prenup and you agree not to squeal about it to Mrs. Smythe-whatshername. How much do you figure that's worth?"

"A hundred thousand," I said brazenly. "Two percent. Very modest."

"Sure it is," he said. "Cash, I suppose."

"You suppose accurately."

He tossed his half-smoked cigar out the window. "Doesn't taste so great," he said. "Tastes like shit."

"Too bad."

He turned his head to stare at me. "I guess I underestimated you."

"Many people do." I smiled at him.

"A hundred grand," he said. "Is that your asking price?"

"No," I said. "I don't enjoy haggling. That's the set price."

"Like the song goes: 'All or Nothing at All.' "

"Exactly," I agreed.

"That's a lot of loot to raise in cash," he said.

"You can't swing it?"

"I didn't say that. When it comes to my little girl's happiness I'd go to hell and back."

"Of course you would," I said approvingly. "She's worth it."

"Listen, Arch, let me think about this and make a few phone calls. Maybe we can work it out. I'll be in touch."

"When?" I asked.

"I should know by tomorrow. I'll give you a buzz."

"Can you make it early, Heck? I'm going to be running around all afternoon and wouldn't want to miss your call."

"I'll make it early," he promised.

I nodded and got out of the car. I stood at the opened door. "Sleep well," I said.

This time his laugh was genuine. "You're a nervy bastard," he said. "I'll say that for you."

I watched him drive away and then tramped up to my digs. I was generally satisfied with the way our face-to-face had gone. I believed he had taken the bait. Now all I had to do was set the hook.

My most worrisome problem had been to determine how large a bribe to demand. If I had asked for a million, for instance, or even a half-million, I knew he would have rebuffed me instantly. But a hundred thousand sounded reasonable: not too outlandish, not too covetous.

Of course I was gambling that there was no way on God's green earth that Hector Johnson could raise a hundred thousand dollars in cold cash. I had an approximate idea of his bank balance, I didn't think Reuben Hagler was rolling in gelt, and Mrs. Hawkin would be on short rations until her late husband's estate was settled. I calculated Hector would make a counterproposal, and I could launch the second part of my scam.

I thought my plan was brill. But if, by any chance, Johnson handed over the hundred thousand bucks I'd be a puddle of chagrin.

Chapter 17

There was a tropical depression moving slowly northward over the Atlantic about two hundred miles off the coast. It was no threat to South Florida, according to the weather wonks, but it turned Monday morning into a kind of soup. Well, consommé, at least. The air was choky, hard to breathe, and the sun gleamed waterily behind a scrim of clouds the color of elephant hide.

I awoke early enough to breakfast with my parents. It was an unusually quiet meal because a woolly day like that blankets the spirits and, if you're wise, you remain silent so you don't start snapping at other people or maybe tilting back your head and howling.

However, before father departed for the office he asked how my meeting with Hector Johnson had gone. I held up crossed fingers and he nodded morosely. That was the extent of our communication.

I returned to my journal, donned reading glasses, and began scribbling. I must confess that I mention my daily labors so frequently because the record I keep becomes the source of these published accounts of my investigations and brief romances. I just don't want you to think I'm making it all up.

I plodded along steadily, hoping for a morning phone call from Johnson. It didn't arrive until almost eleven o'clock, by which time I had begun to fear my crafty plan had gone awry.

"Listen, Arch," Hector said with mucho earnestness, "I know you're not an unreasonable man."

"No, I'm not unreasonable," I readily agreed.

"Well, to make a long story short, I can't come up with the total number you suggested. You capisce?"

"Yes, I understand."

"But I think I can swing half of it," he went on. "It should be available by tonight, and I was hoping we could work out a deal satisfactory to both of us. I'm ready, willing, and able to sign a personal note for the remainder to be paid over a period of time at regular intervals."

"You mean like an IOU?" I asked.

There was a brief silence. Then: "Well, yeah," he said finally, his voice tense, "something like that. How about us getting together and discussing this arrangement like gentlemen?"

"Suits me," I said.

"Hey, that's great!" he said, heartily now. "Let's do just what we did last night: I'll drive over to your place at ten o'clock and we'll sit in my car and crunch the numbers. Just you and me. And we'll both end up winners— right?"

"Right, Heck," I said.

I hung up and stared into space. I believed it extremely unlikely that he had raised fifty thousand in cash in such a short time. And I thought his offer of an IOU was a clumsy ploy. I reckoned he had another motive for wanting to meet with me and I suspected what it was. Definitely not comforting. So I phoned Sgt. Al Rogoff at police headquarters.

"What a coincidence," he said. "I was just about to give you a tinkle."

"Give me a *what?*" I said.

"A tinkle. A phone call. Ain't you got no couth?"

"I'm awash in couth," I told him, "but tinkles I can do without. Why were you going to call?"

"Good news for a change. The Lauderdale cops grabbed Reuben Hagler."

"That *is* good news, Al," I said. "You have no idea how happy it makes me. They're holding him?"

"Yep. He's in the slam."

"Very efficient detective work," I said.

Rogoff laughed. "I wish I could say the same but actually it was just dumb luck. He was beating up on that Pinky Schatz in her condo, and she was yelling and screaming so loud that neighbors called 911. That's how they nabbed Hagler. And the icing on the cake is that the Schatz woman is sick and tired of getting bounced around so she's talking."

"Wonderful," I said. "Did she identify Hagler as the killer of Shirley Feebling?"

"She can't do that, Archy," the sergeant said. "She wasn't an eyewitness and Hagler never told her that he had done it. But she's supplied enough to hold him on suspicion."

"Al," I said anxiously, "don't tell me he's going to walk."

"He probably will," Rogoff admitted, "unless Lauderdale gets more evidence. Like finding the murder weapon hidden in his closet wrapped in his jockstrap. Right now they haven't got enough to convict. Why did you call me?"

"Listen to this," I said, "and try not to interrupt."

I started repeating everything I had told my father: what I knew, what I surmised, what I planned to do. I was halfway through my recital when Rogoff interrupted.

"Why are you telling me all this horseshit?" he demanded. "I'm not interested in prenuptial agreements. What has it got to do with the PBPD?"

"Please," I begged, "let me finish. I need your help."

I described in detail the scam I had already set in motion and what I hoped to gain from it.

"That certainly affects your homicide investigations," I pointed out. "If my con works, you'll clear both the Marcia and Silas Hawkin cases."

He was silent a long time and I could almost see him, eyes slitted, calculating the odds.

"What you guess happened makes a crazy kind of sense," he said finally. "I can buy it. But what you're planning is strictly from nutsville. If you're right, you're liable to get blown away."

"And if I am," I said, "it'll prove I was right, won't it? Then you can take it from there."

"I always knew you were a flit," he said, "but I never suspected you were a total cuckoo. But if you want to take the risk I can't stop you. What do you want from me?"

"The showdown is tonight at ten o'clock. We'll be in Johnson's white Lincoln Town Car parked on the turnaround behind my house. He keeps insisting that just the two of us be present. I was worried he'd bring Reuben Hagler along, and then I'd really be in the minestrone. That's why I was so happy when you told me Hagler is behind bars in Fort Lauderdale. Now what I'd like you to do is park your squad or pickup someplace where Johnson can't spot it. Then be in our garage at ten o'clock—concealed, of course—in case I need assistance."

"Yeah," he said, "that's a possibility."

I ignored his irony. "If I need your help," I went on, "I'll give you a shout."

"Oh sure," he said. "But how are you going to do that if he's got his mitts clamped around your gullet?"

"He won't," I said with more aplomb than I felt. "I'm not exactly Charles Atlas, but I assure you I'm not a ninety-seven-pound weakling either. I mean brutes don't kick sand in my face on the beach without inviting serious retaliation."

"Cuckcoo," Al chanted in a falsetto voice. "Cuckoo, cuckoo, cuckoo."

"Your confidence in me is underwhelming. Just tell me this: Will you be hidden in our garage at ten o'clock tonight?"

"I'll be there," he promised.

I hung up, satisfied that I had done all I could to prepare to play Wellington to Hector Johnson's Napoleon.

I saw little reason to venture out into that scruffy climate so I decided to stay home, bring my journal up to date, futz around and wait for the great dénouement that evening. That plan evaporated, for my next phone call was from Theodosia Johnson. Southern Bell was having a profitable morning.

"Archy," she wailed, "I'm going cuckoo."

I laughed. "Two of a kind." I said. "What's the problem?"

"This miserable weather is suffocating me. And father has been a bear. He was bad enough last night but this morning he got a phone call—I don't know what it was about—and I thought he was going to blow a fuse. Ranting, raving, cursing. And he started drinking directly from the bottle. Have you ever done that Archy?"

"Thirty-six years ago. But it had a rubber nipple on it."

It was her turn to laugh. "You always make me feel better," she said. "Listen, I'm going to drive daddy over to Louise Hawkin's place. He says he'll be there all afternoon. The two of them will probably get smashed—but who cares? Anyway. I'll have the car and I'd love to meet you for lunch at that funky place you took me to."

"The Pelican Club?"

"That's it. Tonight I'm having dinner at the Smythe-Hersforth mortuary so I've got to build up my morale, and you're the best morale builder-upper I know. So how about lunch?"

"Sure," I said bravely. "Meet you at the Pelican in an hour. Can you find it?"

"I can find anyplace," she said, and I believed it.

I didn't bother getting duded up, just pulled on a navy blazer over the white Izod and tan jeans I was wearing. The snazziest part of my ensemble was the footgear: lavender New Balance running shoes.

Madam X was already seated at the bar of the Pelican Club when I arrived. She and Simon Pettibone were engrossed in a heavy conversation. They seemed startled when I interrupted.

"Glad to see you've met our distinguished majordomo," I said to Theo.

"Met him?" she said. "I've already asked him to marry me, but he says he's taken."

"I think I've just been taken again," Mr. Pettibone said solemnly. "Mr. McNally, this young lady could charm the spots off a tiger."

"Stripes," I said. "And she could do it. What are you swilling, Theo?"

"Vodka martini on the stones."

"Oh my," I said, "we are in a mood, aren't we? I'll have the same, Mr. Pettibone, if you please, and hold the fruit."

I took the bar stool next to Theo and examined her. She was dressed as casually as I. Her jeans were blue denim and she was wearing a black T-shirt under a khaki bush jacket. Her makeup was minimal and her hair swung free. Her appearance was enough to make my heart lurch.

"Mr. Pettibone," I said when he brought my drink, "do you recall the other day when you and I were talking about money?"

"I remember," he said.

"You stated that money in itself isn't important, it's the power that money confers. Is that also true of beauty?"

"Oh yes, Mr. McNally," he said, looking at Theo. "Beauty is power. And even in our so-called enlightened age, it remains one of the few sources of power women have."

"You got that right, kiddo," she said to him. "If a woman's not a nuclear physicist she better have elegant tits. Archy, I've got to pick up daddy in a couple of hours. Can we get this show on the road?"

"Sure," I said, and glanced around at the almost empty bar area. "Slow day, Mr. Pettibone."

"It's the weather," he explained. "The boys and girls don't want to get out of bed."

"Lucky boys and girls," Theo said.

I carried our drinks and we sauntered into the dining room. We were the only customers, and when no one appeared to serve us I went into the kitchen. I found Leroy Pettibone, our chef, seated on a low stool in his whites. He was reading a copy of *Scientific American*.

"Hey, Leroy," I said, "where's Priscilla?"

"Malling," he said. "She'll be in later. You wanting?"

"Whatever's available. For two."

He thought a moment. "How about a cold steak salad? Chunks of rare sirloin and lots of other neat stuff."

"Sounds good to me," I said. "Heavy on the garlic, please."

"You've got it," he said.

I returned to the dining room and told Theo what we were having for lunch. I suggested a glass of dry red zin might go well with the steak salad.

"Not for me, thanks," she said. "You go ahead but I'll have another marty."

I went out to the bar and relayed our order to Mr. Pettibone. He nodded and prepared the drinks.

"Dangerous lady," he commented. It was just an observation; there was no censure in his voice.

"Yes," I agreed, "she is."

I toted the fresh drinks back to our lonely table. It was not the one at which Connie Garcia and I usually dined. I had deliberately avoided seating Madam X there. Don't ask me why. Probably dementia.

We raised glasses, sipped, said, "Ah!" in unison, stared at each other.

"Archy," she said, "I'm caught."

"Caught?"

"In a pattern," she said. "My life. And I can't get out. Don't you find your life is a pattern?"

"More like a maze," I said. "But I must like it because I have no desire to change."

"You're fortunate," she said wistfully.

I wanted to learn more about her being caught but then Leroy brought our salads and a basket of garlic toast.

"Looks delish," Theo said, giving him one of her radiant smiles. I could see he was as smitten as I.

"Plenty more," he said. "If you folks want seconds, just yell."

It was as good as it looked: Boston lettuce, cherry tomatoes, hunks of cold steak, radishes, shavings of feta, cucumber, thin slices of red onions, black olives—the whole schmear.

"Garlicky dressing," Theo said.

"My fault," I confessed. "I asked for it."

"I'm not complaining," she said. "I love it."

I snuck glances at her as she ate. Mr. Pettibone was right; beauty *is* power. I mean she was so lovely that one was rendered senseless. I could understand why the Chinless Wonder would sign *anything* to win her, to have and to hold, till divorce doth them part.

"Do you think I'm wanton, Archy?" she asked suddenly.

That puzzled me because I thought she had said *wonton* and I couldn't see how she could possibly resemble Chinese kreplach. Then I guessed she had said *wantin'* as Leroy had just asked, "You wanting?" Finally I decided she had really meant *wanton*: lustful, bawdy. I think my confusion is understandable. *Wanton* is a written word. Have you ever heard it spoken?

"No, Theo," I said, "I don't think you're wanton. Just a free spirit."

"*Free?*" she said with a crooked grin. "Don't you believe it. It costs."

Did she mean it cost her or cost others? I didn't know and couldn't guess. This woman never ceased to surprise and amaze. I was no closer to kenning her essential nature than I was the first time we shook hands at the Pristine Gallery.

"Theo," I said, "something is obviously troubling you. Would you like to tell me about it? Perhaps I can help."

"No," she said immediately. "But thanks. I can handle it. I always have."

"You're very independent," I told her.

"Yes," she agreed, "and I think that's my problem. It just kills me to have to rely on other people. I know I have to do it, but I don't like it."

"You're referring to Chauncey?"

"Chauncey. His mother. My father. You."

"Me?" I said, astonished. "What on earth do you rely on me for?"

"A four-letter word beginning with F."

I pondered. "Fool? Fuss? Fill?"

She laughed. "You know what I mean. I wish we had time this afternoon. But there will be other afternoons. Right, Archy?"

She was more riddles than I could count but the largest made me groggy when I tried to solve it. Was she aware of my role in her affairs and enlisting my support by letting her blue butterfly soar? Or was she genuinely attracted to me and needed my enthusiastic cooperation as an antidote to the numbing company of forbidding mama?

The enigma I faced was hardly original or unique. It faces every man when a woman acquiesces. Is it from profit or desire? The Shadow knows.

We sat quietly in that deserted room for another half-hour. I had a second glass of wine, but Theo declined a third martini. I don't recall what we spoke of. I have a dazed memory of murmurs, small laughs, a few sad smiles. I had a feeling, totally irrational, that this afternoon in a waning light was a farewell. I can't explain it but I had the sense of a departure, a leave-taking.

I believe Theo had the same impression, for just before we rose to leave she reached across the table to pat my hand.

"Thank you, Archy," she said softly, "for all you've done for me."

I was grateful for her sentiment, of course, but it did nothing to unravel the mystery of Theodosia Johnson.

I signed the tab at the bar and we went out to our cars. I think there was much we both wanted to say and neither had the courage. But perhaps I was fantasizing. There's a lot of that going around these days. I wondered if we would kiss on parting but we didn't; we shook hands.

I drove back to the beach in a dullish mood. It seemed to me that our luncheon conversation had been inconclusive to the point of incoherence. I had to admit I simply didn't know Madam X. And so, when I arrived home, I reacted as I customarily do when confronted with a world-class brainteaser: I took a nap.

It was an uneventful evening at the McNally manse. Casual talk during the cocktail hour and dinner was mainly concerned with Lady Cynthia Horowitz's buffet on Tuesday night. Her engraved invitation had specified informal attire, and I declared that permitted Bermuda shorts and no socks. Naturally my father objected strenuously to such an interpretation. His idea of "informal attire" is appearing in public without a vest.

I returned to my cell after dinner to prepare for my ten o'clock brannigan with Hector Johnson. I was tempted to phone Sgt. Rogoff and remind him of his assignment as a confederate concealed in the McNally garage. But on further reflection I decided not to call. Al hates to be nudged. He said he'd be there and I knew he would.

I spent the remaining time rehearsing my lines, attempting to imagine Hector's responses, and devising my rebuttals. It all seemed so simple, so logical and neat, I saw no way he could escape the trap I was setting for him. I might as well have pledged allegiance to the Easter Bunny.

When my phone rang about nine-thirty I plucked it up, hoping it was Rogoff calling to confirm our arrangement. It was Hector Johnson.

"Arch?" he said. "Listen, I think we better change our schedule."

"But you—"

"I just don't feel comfortable driving around at night with this much cash in the car."

"We could—"

"Too many outlaws on the road these days," he charged ahead, ignoring my attempted interruptions. "The best thing is for you to come over to my place. Theo is having dinner at her guy's home so we'll be able to have a one-on-one and maybe a few belts to grease the wheels of commerce, if you know what I mean. So you just drop by at ten o'clock."

"Heck, I don't—"

"I'll be waiting for you," he said and hung up.

I sat stunned, my battle plan reduced to shredded wheat. I now had no doubt whatsoever that Hector had never intended to replay our first meeting. His last-minute change of setting was made to insure that he would not be caught in a snare, which was exactly what I had planned for him. No dummy, our Mr. Johnson.

It appeared to me that I had few options. I could phone him back immediately and postpone our get-together. But to what avail? We could set a different time, a different place, but Hector would surely make yet another revision at the last moment. I might curse his strategy but I had to admire it. Skilled one-upmanship.

Naturally I phoned Sgt. Rogoff. I tried his home first and received a curt reply from his answering machine. I left a message. Then I called police headquarters. He wasn't in his office and the duty officer informed me his present whereabouts were unknown. But if he called in, I was assured, he would be told to contact yrs. truly at once.

Snookered.

Deep, deep thoughts. Pros. Cons. The odds. The risks. Did I dare? Reuben Hagler was in the Fort Lauderdale clink so Johnson would be my sole antagonist. Could I take him? Could he take me?

I suspect you may think me an epicene lad with an overweening interest in wine, women, and song. (Not too heavy on the song, and I could live without wine.) It is true I am something of a coxcomb but I am not completely incapable of self-defense or violent physical action should it become necessary. I have played lacrosse at New Haven and rugby in South Florida. What I'm trying to convey is that my muscles are not spaghettini even though my brain may be Silly Putty.

And so I sallied forth to dance a pas de deux with Hector Johnson, papa of the unknowable Madam X.

The first thing I did after exiting was to search our three-car garage, hoping to find Al Rogoff lurking in the shadows. He was not. And during the early moments of my drive I tried to spot Al's parked squad car or pickup. No luck. I was on my own.

The Johnsons' condo was brightly lighted and Hector opened the door before I knocked. He was grinning, and he grabbed my arm and pulled me inside with a great show of boisterous good-fellowship.

"Glad you could make it, Arch!" he shouted. "Sorry about the change of plans, but I figure it's better this way. Am I right?"

"Sure, Heck," I said.

He practically pushed me onto that cretonne couch of recent fond memory.

"Hey," he said, looming over me, "I'm having a Chivas. How about you?"

"No, thanks," I said. "I've been drinking wine and it's instant blotto to mix the grape and the grain. But you go ahead."

"I was just pouring a refill when you pulled up," he said. "Be right back."

He went into the kitchen. I didn't think he was sozzled, but he wasn't stone sober either. I wanted him to keep drinking, figuring it might impair his coordination if things turned nasty. He returned with a full glass and no ice cubes that I could see.

"Your daughter is having dinner with her fiancé?" I asked.

"Yeah," he said, plopping down in an armchair facing me. "She drove the Lincoln. That guy of hers is a real stiff, isn't he? What Theo sees in him I'll never know."

"Maybe she sees five million dollars," I suggested.

His expression didn't change, but he took a deep gulp of his Scotch. "I'm glad you brought that up, Arch," he said. "Listen, I got bad news. I know I told you I had fifty grand and I did, but now I don't. I was depending on a pal to help me out, but he's in a bind and can't come up with the gelt. Arch, I'm really, truly sorry about this, and you have every right to be pissed. I mean I think you're in the right to ask for a finder's fee and if I had it I'd be happy to hand it over with a smile. But like they say, you can't get blood from a turnip. I only wish there was some other way we could work this out."

The opening I had hoped for . . .

I was silent a moment, looking at him thoughtfully. "There may be, Heck. And it won't cost you any cash."

He took another swig. "No money?" he said. "Then what do you want?"

"That painting you bought from Marcia Hawkin."

"What painting?" he cried. "What the hell are you talking about?"

"Heck," I said, "let's stop playing games. I know Marcia sold you a painting."

"Are you calling me a liar?" he said menacingly.

"Of course not. I just think you're making a very chivalrous attempt to protect the reputation of that poor, unfortunate girl."

He suddenly switched gears. "Yeah, you're right," he said. "That's exactly what I want to do. Louise has enough problems without that. How did you know?"

Then I went into my rehearsed spiel, speaking slowly in a grave voice. Don't let anyone tell you that you can't con a con man. His ego is so bloated that it never occurs to him that anyone would even try to swindle him. Bankers have that same fault.

"Heck, when I spoke to Marcia the afternoon before she was killed she made a confession. I didn't ask questions; she just wanted to talk. You know what a flake she was.

"She told me she arrived home while the housekeeper, Mrs. Folsby, was on the phone reporting to the police she had just discovered the body of Silas Hawkin. Marcia went directly to the studio and saw that her father was dead. Murdered. She said he had been working on a nude portrait of her, acrylic on a wood panel, and she was so proud and happy that he wanted her to pose because it was the first painting he had ever done of her.

"So, she admitted, she stole it. Just wrapped it in a drop cloth, carted it away, and slid it under her bed in the main house before the cops arrived. What she did was unlawful, of course: removing evidence from the scene of a crime.

"But Marcia said she didn't care. She felt the painting belonged to her. Not only had she posed for it but it would be her only remembrance from her father. You can understand how she felt, can't you, Heck?"

"Yeah," he said, finishing his triple Chivas. "Sure I can."

"But then the hostility between Marcia and her stepmother became more venomous. After the death of her father Marcia had no money of her own; her only asset was the last painting by Silas Hawkin. So she decided to sell it. To you. Because she thought you were wealthy and would be willing to help her out. I tried to convince her that what she planned was illegal. She really didn't own the painting; after her father's death it became part of his estate and Louise was his beneficiary. But Marcia insisted on going ahead with it. How much did you pay, Heck?"

The direct question shook him. He gripped his empty glass with both hands and leaned forward tensely. "She told you the painting was a nude of her?"

"That's what she said."

Then he relaxed, sat back, nodded. "I paid her twenty thousand," he said. "A bargain."

"It certainly was," I agreed. "And now I'm going to offer you another bargain. I'll take that painting as a finder's fee instead of the hundred thousand dollars I asked. A nice profit for you, Heck."

He rolled his empty tumbler between his palms while he stared at me closely. "You're so generous," he said, not without irony. "Why?"

"Because I like Silas Hawkin's work. I already own some of his watercolors. And I want to own his last painting, especially since it's on wood, something he hadn't done since he was a student in Paris."

Johnson kept staring and I still wasn't certain he had bought my fairy tale. I added more.

"If you're afraid of getting involved in the police investigation of Marcia's murder, forget it. I figure you paid her and she went out to celebrate with some of those crazy dopers and bikers she knew. They partied, things got rough, and she ended up dead."

"Uh-huh," he said. "That's the way I figure it, too."

"Another consideration is this . . . What we're talking about is stolen property. Marcia started by stealing the painting from her father's studio. You committed an illegal act by purchasing stolen property. But you get out from under by turning it over to me. Then I have the hot potato. Do you think I'm going to hawk it, lend it to an exhibition, or even show it to anyone else? No way! That nude goes into my private collection and stays private for the rest of my life."

He was silent and I knew it was his moment of decision. Snowing him as I had was the only way to uncover the truth. And if what I suspected was correct, he would be forced to react.

He pondered a long time, not speaking, and I didn't know which way it would go. Finally he said, "Clue me in on this, Arch. What's my downside risk?"

That was Wall Street jargon and I remembered he had been a stockbroker cashiered for securities fraud.

"Your downside risk," I told him bluntly, "is that the cops question me and I repeat what Marcia told me of planning to sell you a painting. The stained drop cloth was found in her Cherokee when they hauled it out of the lake. That implicates you. Also I'd feel it my duty to inform Chauncey's mother that her darling son intends to sign a five-million-dollar prenuptial contract with your daughter, contrary to my advice. There goes Chauncey's inheritance.

"Your upside potential is that the cops never learn from me what Marcia said, and I advise Chauncey to sign the prenup immediately. And everyone lives happily ever after. *If* I get the painting."

He twisted his features into more grimace than smile. "I don't have much choice, do I?" he said.

"Not much," I agreed.

"I need a refill," he proclaimed hoarsely, hauling himself to his feet. "Be right back."

He went into the kitchen. I waited patiently, satisfied that I had given it my best shot. If it didn't work I'd be forced to consider enrolling in a Tibetan monastery.

It worked. Hector came slowly out of the kitchen, not with a drink but with a revolver. It looked like a .38 but I couldn't be sure. I don't know a great deal about firearms. Badminton rackets are more my speed.

I rose to my feet. "Judgment day," I said. "And it's only Monday. I suggested to Mr. Pettibone it might be tomorrow."

"What?" Johnson said, completely bewildered.

You may not believe this but the sight of him carrying a handgun was a source of exultant gratification more than fright. For I knew I had been right, and what is more pleasurable than saying, "I told you so," even if they're your last words.

He was holding the weapon down alongside his leg, not brandishing it, you know, but gripping it tightly. I took one small step toward the outside door.

"Is that the gun that killed Shirley Feebling?" I asked him.

Oh, but he was shaken! His face fell apart. Emotions flickered: disbelief, consternation, fear, anger, hatred.

"You're a real buttinsky, aren't you?" he said, his voice an ugly snarl.

"A professional buttinsky," I reminded him. "I get paid for it."

I took another small step toward the door. He followed as I hoped he would. He was my sole assailant but little did he know that I had two allies: Desperation and Adrenaline.

I took another step. He came much closer, raising the gun and pointing it at me. When I saw the muzzle I realized it wasn't a .38; it was the entrance to the Lincoln Tunnel.

"Don't try to make a break for it," he warned harshly. "I'd just as soon drop you right here."

"And stain your beautiful shag rug?" I said.

I took a deep breath and made my play, a fast, feint toward the door. It was a singularly adroit move if I say so myself, and I do. His gun swung to cover my anticipated departure. I whirled back and rushed, knocking the revolver aside and embracing him. We hugged, straining, tighter than lovers. He was heavy and he was powerful. It was like pressing a grizzly to one's bosom.

I feared this monster was capable of collapsing my ribs or snapping my spine, and so I craned and fastened my teeth, uppers and lowers, onto his nose. Of course I had no intention of amputating his beezer. That would have left me with a mouthful of nostrils, an unappetizing prospect. No, I merely hoped to cause him intense pain. And I succeeded admirably. His roars of anguish were sweeter to my ears than Debussy's *Clair de Lune*.

I increased the pressure, hearing the creaking of cartilage in his beak. His groans became gasping whimpers. I opened my mandibles, disengaged myself from his clutch, and stood back. He fell to his knees and I stooped and plucked the revolver from his nerveless grasp. He put both hands to his bleeding proboscis and continued to moan.

I looked down at him and was tempted to utter a dramatic proclamation, such as *"Sic semper tyrannis."* Instead, I just said, "Tough shit," and rapped him on the occiput with the butt of his gun. It seemed to have little effect so I slugged him again and this time he slid face down onto the carpet. Kaput.

I began my search, starting in the bedroom at the rear of the condo. Only one bedroom: that perplexed me but I continued to toss the entire apartment. Every few minutes I returned to see if the comatose Hector was stirring. If so, I'd give him another sharp tap on the noggin and he would lapse into deep slumber again.

I was beginning to ransack the living room when I heard a heavy pounding on the front door. I rushed to the window and saw a police car parked outside, roof lights flashing. I yanked open the door to find Sgt. Al Rogoff with a young officer behind him. Both men had hands on their holsters.

"You okay?" Al asked anxiously.

"Dandy," I assured him. "How did you find me?"

"I was a few minutes late getting to your garage. I stayed in there for almost half an hour. When neither you nor Johnson showed up I knew something had gone wrong. His condo was the obvious place to start looking for you. Did everything go like you figured?"

"Pretty much," I said. "Come on in."

They followed me into the living room and looked down at the prone Hector Johnson. Rogoff knelt and rolled him over.

"What happened to his nose?" he asked. "Did you bop him?"

"No," I said, "I bit him."

Al looked at me sorrowfully. "And I thought you were a gourmet," he said.

The two cops hauled Johnson to his feet. He regained a groggy consciousness, but they had to hold him upright. The sergeant cuffed him and they hustled him outside and thrust him into the back of the squad car. Rogoff returned, leaving the front door of the condo open. I handed him Johnson's revolver.

"This might be the gat used to kill Shirley Feebling," I told him.

"*Gat?*" he said. "I haven't heard that word since Cagney died." He examined the gun. "It could be," he admitted. "It's the right caliber. I'll send it down to Lauderdale for tests. What about the painting?"

"Haven't found it yet," I said. "I was just starting on this room when you showed up."

We searched and came up with zilch. Rogoff went into the kitchen and came back with two tumblers of Chivas and water on the rocks. He handed me one.

"Drink it," he advised. "You look a little puffy around the gills, and Johnson will never miss it."

He sat on the couch and I fell into the armchair recently occupied by mine host.

"Maybe he burned the painting," the sergeant said. "Getting rid of incriminating evidence."

I shook my head. "I don't think so, Al. That nude is valuable, and I can't see Johnson destroying anything that might prove profitable."

"Then what the hell did he do with it? Put it in storage?"

"Maybe he left it at Louise Hawkin's place," I suggested.

"That's a possibility. Or maybe—hey, why are you grinning like that?"

"I know where it is," I said. "Not exactly 'The Purloined Letter' but close to it."

"Cut the crap," Rogoff said roughly. "Where is it?"

"You're sitting on it."

"*What?*"

"The one place we didn't look. Under that ghastly couch."

I flopped down on my knees and dragged it out. I propped it up in the armchair and we stared at it. It seemed in good condition, a bit smeared but easily restored. The composition was classic, the colors vibrant, the pose almost lascivious. Perhaps wanton would be a better word: The model was more naked than nude. I looked for the tattoo of the blue butterfly and there it was.

"Sensational," Al breathed. "Better than that portrait of her at the Pristine Gallery. She was making it with Silas?"

"Whenever it pleased her," I said. "She's a free spirit. But she admits it costs. Naturally Silas was eager."

"That's why his daughter did him in?"

"Motive enough, wouldn't you say, Al? Marcia was a woman scorned. Daddy had brief affairs before, but Madam X was an obsession. I can understand that."

"Who?" he said, puzzled. "Madam X?"

"That's what I call her. So Marcia killed him, just as her letter said, and swiped the painting that infuriated her. But then she needed money and realized she had the perfect blackmail bait. If she showed the nude to Chauncey and Mrs. Smythe-Hersforth, the marriage would be canceled. Hector didn't have the cash she demanded so he had to put her down and grab the painting. I imagine Reuben Hagler helped him. It would be a two-man job to strangle Marcia and push her Jeep off the pier into the lake."

Rogoff took a deep breath. "All because of a beautiful broad," he said.

I was about to quote. "Beauty is power," when, as if on cue, we heard a car pull up outside. We moved to the open door to see Theodosia Johnson slide out of the white Lincoln. She paused a moment when she saw my Miata and the police car. She went over to peer in at the manacled Hector. Then she came marching into the house and confronted us. How I admired her! She was erect, shoulders back, eyes angry.

"What's going on here?" she demanded fiercely.

The sergeant showed his ID. "I'm afraid I'll have to take you in, miss," he said.

"Do you have a warrant?" she said stiffly.

"No, ma'am," Al said, "but I have probable cause coming out my ears. Do you wish to resist?"

She considered for the briefest of moments. "No," she said. "I'll come along."

Rogoff took her arm lightly, but she turned to me.

"Archy," she said, "I'm very fond of you."

"Thank you," I said faintly.

"And if you feel sorry for me I'll never forgive you."

I felt like weeping but a cliché saved me. "You're a survivor," I told her.

"Yes," she said, lifting her chin, "I am that."

She gave me a flippant wave and Sgt. Rogoff led her outside to join Hector. Eventually he returned. By that time I had finished my drink and his as well.

"What are you going to charge her with?" I asked him.

He shrugged. "Enough to convince her to make a deal. You had eyes for her, didn't you?"

"I did," I said, "and I do. I can't see where she did anything so awful. I think her father was the main offender."

Al didn't look at me. "Archy, Hector isn't her father. I heard from Michigan this afternoon. Her real name isn't Johnson; it's Burkhart or Martin or Combs or whatever she wants it to be. She was a cocktail waitress in Detroit. Model. Party girl. Arrested twice for prostitution. No convictions. She's been Hectors live-in girlfriend for the past three years."

"Oh," I said.

Chapter 18

I arrived home shortly after midnight. Lights were still glowing in my father's study. That was uncommon; usually m'lord is abed by eleven o'clock. He met me at the back door.

"You're all right, Archy?" he asked.

"Yes, sir, I'm fine."

"Good. Did things go as you hoped?"

"Mostly."

He nodded. "Let's have a nightcap."

We went into his study. I was hoping for a cognac, but he poured us glasses of wine. That was okay; any port in a storm. We got settled and he looked at me inquiringly.

I started with a brief description of the murder of Silas Hawkin.

"Marcia actually killed her father?" the patriarch said, aghast.

"Yes, sir. But she had been sexually abused from childhood. Now I think she was more than disturbed: she was psychotic. Understandable. Her father's affair with Theodosia Johnson was, in Marcia's raddled mind, his final act of cruelty and betrayal."

"What about the Johnsons? What was their role?"

"I think the three of them—Theodosia, Hector and Reuben Hagler— came down to Palm Beach from Michigan about a year ago with a definite plan. Their financial resources were limited but their main asset was Theo, her beauty and charm. The idea was to marry her off to a wealthy bachelor and take him for whatever they could grab."

"An intrigue as old as civilization."

"Yes, father, it is. The only difference was that these creatures were willing to murder to achieve their goal. I believe they thought of Shirley Feebling and Marcia Hawkin merely as impediments to their success. Shirley threatened to make Chauncey's love letters public unless he married her, and so she had to be eliminated. I suspect it was Reuben Hagler who shot her. And Marcia Hawkin threatened to show her father's nude portrait of Theo to Mrs.

Smythe-Hersforth. That would have resulted in the marriage being called off or Chauncey being disinherited. And so Marcia also had to be eliminated. I have the feeling that Hector Johnson was guilty of that homicide."

"Despicable!" father said and rose to refill our glasses. When he was seated again I told him of the personal history of Theodosia Johnson.

The pater looked at me keenly. "You were attracted to this woman, Archy?"

"I was," I admitted. "Still am."

He sighed. "It never ceases to amaze me when talented people, intelligent people, imaginative people turn their energies to crime. One wonders what they might have achieved if they had devoted their talent, intelligence, and imagination to legal pursuits. The waste! When virtues are put in the service of vice it becomes not only a societal tragedy but a personal disaster."

I nodded gloomily. I was really in no mood for his philosophizing. We sat in silence for several minutes, sipping our port, and I could see he had gone into his mulling status. I wondered what was stirring in the dim recesses of his mazy mind. Finally he spoke.

"I think you have done an excellent job, Archy, and you are to be commended."

"Thank you."

"Not only have you cleared up a disagreeable mess but I believe it quite likely you have prevented one and possibly two homicides."

I stared at him in astonishment. "Prevented? Homicides? How so?"

"Hasn't it occurred to you that if Chauncey had signed the prenuptial agreement and married the young woman he might have suffered an early demise, perhaps in an accident craftily planned by this gang of miscreants. Or, in lieu of that, they might have plotted to arrange the death of Mrs. Gertrude Smythe-Hersforth first. Chauncey would inherit, and *then* he would be exterminated."

I sucked in my breath. "Leaving Theodosia Johnson with the Smythe-Hersforth millions."

"Exactly."

"Do you really believe they planned that scenario, father?"

"I do," he said decisively. "From what you have told me, I am convinced these people are sociopaths. They are totally devoid of any moral sense. Nothing is good—except money—and nothing is bad. Things just *are*. And if you believe that, you can commit any heinous act carelessly without a twinge of guilt or remorse."

I finished my wine and rose. "I think I better go up," I said. "It's been a long, tiring night."

"Of course," he said, looking at me sympathetically. "Get a good sleep."

But it was not a good sleep; it was fitful and troubled, thronged with visions I could not identify except that I knew they were dark and menacing. My bed became a battleground on which I fought demons and constantly looked about for hidden assassins.

It was no wonder that when I finally slept I did not awake until almost

noon on Tuesday morning. I staggered to the window and saw the sky had
cleared, the sun shone and, I presumed, somewhere birds were chirping.

I took a hot shower, shaved, and dressed with special care. Not because
I had important social engagements that afternoon but I needed the lift that
nifty duds always give me. I went downstairs to a deserted kitchen, inspected
the larder, and settled on a brunch of a garlic salami and cheddar sandwich
(on pump) and a frosty bottle of Heineken. The old double helix began twisting in the wind.

I went first to my father's study, sat at his desk, used his phone, and called
Sgt. Rogoff.

"What's happening?" I asked him.

He laughed. "It's finger-pointing time," he said. "Hagler, Johnson, and
the bimbo are—"

"She's not a bimbo," I protested.

"Whatever," he said. "Anyway, the three of them are all trying to cut
deals. Johnson says Hagler shot Shirley Feebling. Hagler says Johnson strangled Marcia Hawkin. These are real stand-up guys. Not!"

"What do you think they'll draw?"

"You want my guess? I don't think they'll get the chair. The evidence isn't
all that conclusive. But they'll plea-bargain down to hard time."

"And Theodosia?"

"She'll walk," he admitted. "She's being very cooperative. And she agrees
that she'll get out of Florida and never come back. Good riddance."

"Yes," I said.

I wanted to tell him that I thought Madam X was a self-willed, undisci-
plined woman who just didn't give a damn. But she was smart, sensitive, and
fully aware of her excesses and how they doomed her. I didn't say it, of
course; Rogoff would have hooted with laughter.

"Al," I said, "thank you for your help and keep me up to speed on this
megillah. Okay?"

"Sure," he said.

I hung up and sat a few moments in the guv's chair, reflecting. I shall not
claim I was wading barefoot through the slough of despond. It wasn't true
and you wouldn't believe me anyway. Instead, I found myself in a remarkably
serene mood. Which made me wonder if I had truly been in love with an associate of killers, a woman soon to be banished from the sovereign State of
Florida.

I had been enthralled by her and still was. If she had used me, where was
the harm? I had enjoyed it. I knew I did have and still had a strong affection
for her. Was that romantic love? I didn't know.

I went outside into a brilliant noonday. I decided to drive down the coast
and let the sun shrivel and the wind blow away all complexities. I wanted my
life to be simple, clear, easy to understand. I really enjoy a broiled lobster
more than paella. And that jaunt did rejuvenate me. Except that I found myself touring past the Ocean Grand and through Mizner Park, places where
Theo and I had memorable luncheons. But I didn't stop.

I drove directly back to Palm Beach and arrived in time to visit the Pristine Gallery before it closed for the day. Silas Hawkin's portrait of Madam X was no longer displayed in the front window nor was it displayed within. The proprietor was wandering about disconsolately.

"Mr. Duvalnik," I said, "what happened to that beautiful painting by Hawkin?"

"Haven't you heard?" he said. "Theodosia Johnson has been arrested, the marriage is off, and now Chauncey Smythe-Hersforth refuses to pay. He commissioned it and I suppose I could sue, but I don't want the hassle."

"So it becomes the property of Mrs. Louise Hawkin?"

"I suppose so," he said glumly. "I talked to the widow and she really doesn't want it. Told me to sell it for whatever I could get. One of the tabloids offered a thousand dollars but that's ridiculous. I end up with three hundred? No thanks. I spent more than that on Hawkin's exhibition."

"I'd be willing to pay ten thousand for the portrait," I told him, "if you'd sell it to me on time, perhaps ten or twelve monthly payments."

"You're serious?"

"I am."

He brightened. "I'll speak to Mrs. Hawkin. I'll tell her of your offer and urge her to accept."

"Thank you, Mr. Duvalnik," I said. "I admire the painting and would be proud to own it."

"And why not?" he cried. "It's a masterpiece!"

"It is indeed," I agreed.

I tooled homeward, convinced that eventually I would become the legal owner of Silas Hawkin's painting of Madam X. Not the nude. I knew that wood panel would remain in police custody as evidence during a criminal investigation. I had no interest in its final disposition. I didn't want it. Too many bad vibes.

But I wanted the formal pose: Theo seated regally in an armchair framed by crimson drapes, her lips caught in an expression so mystifying that it made Mona Lisa's smile look like a smirk.

I would not hang the portrait on the wall of my bedroom, of course. That would be a bit much. I would hide it in a closet, and occasionally I would take it out, prop it up, and look at it fondly while remembering and perhaps listening to a tape of Leon Redbone singing "Extra Blues."

I had time for a curtailed ocean swim, then returned home to shower and dress in a slapdash fashion for Lady Cynthia Horowitz's informal seafood buffet. We skipped the family cocktail hour that evening, and at seven o'clock the McNallys set out. My parents led the way in father's black Lexus. I followed in my flaming Miata, feeling more chipper than I had any right to be.

The Horowitz estate was all aglitter with ropes of Chinese lanterns, and a goodly crowd had already assembled by the time we arrived. Tables had been set up around the pool and the buffet was being arranged by caterers, pyramiding seafood onto wooden trenchers lined with cracked ice. A small outdoor bar was already busy, and in the background a tuxedoed trio played Irving Berlin.

I sought out our hostess. Lady Cynthia was an old friendly enemy and she gave me a warm welcoming kiss on the lips.

"My favorite rogue," she said, tapping my cheek. "Have you been behaving yourself, lad?"

"No," I said, "have you?"

"Of course not," she said. "At my age naughtiness is a necessity—like Fiberall."

"At my age, too," I said, and we both laughed as she drifted away to greet newly arriving guests.

I looked about for Consuela Garcia but couldn't immediately spot her. So I ordered a kir royale at the bar and joined the gossiping throng of friends and acquaintances. You must understand that you are required to pass a Gossip Aptitude Test before you are allowed to live in the Town of Palm Beach.

That evening the only topic being bandied about was the Chauncey–Theodosia affair. There were many reports, rumors, hints, insinuations, and much ribald laughter. I listened but contributed nothing.

Finally I espied Connie. Zounds but she looked a winner! She was wearing a mannish suit of white linen, fashionably wrinkled, and a choker of black pearls I had given her. With her bronzy tan and long ebony hair she made the other women at that soirée look like Barbies. I hastened to her side.

"Hello, stranger," she said with a bright smile.

"Connie," I said, "you look marv. May I have the first dance?"

"I'll be too busy getting the place closed up after dinner."

"Then may I see you home, later?"

"I have my own car," she said and looked at me speculatively.

I interpreted that look to be half-challenge, half-invitation. "Suppose I tailgate you to make certain you arrive home safely," I suggested.

"If you like," she said. "Now go eat before all the prawns are gone."

I dined at a table for four with my parents and Mr. Griswold Forsythe II, a superannuated bore who had depleted his repertoire of anecdotes fifty years ago, which didn't prevent him from repeating them ad infinitum. The only things that saved me were that piscine buffet and the bottle of chilled sancerre on each table, replaced as needed.

After that yummy feast was demolished, dancing commenced on the pool verge and the cropped lawn. I watched affectionately as my parents waltzed to a fox-trot, and then I lured mother into joining me for a sedate lindy. We did beautifully, and it was a moment to treasure.

The night spun down, Mr. and Mrs. McNally departed, other guests shouted their farewells and were gone. The caterer cleared up, spurred on by Connie Garcia, and the trio packed up their instruments and left. The bar closed, lanterns were extinguished, and quiet took over. The hostess was nowhere to be seen and, knowing Lady Cynthia, I suspected she had retired to her chambers with the pick of the litter. And I assure you he would not be the runt.

Finally, only Connie and I remained. We met at our cars in the driveway and, giggling, she displayed her loot: two bottles of that sharp sancerre.

"Bless you, my child," I said gratefully.

She drove back to her condo and I followed closely. We arrived without incident and within fifteen minutes were lounging on her miniature balcony, gazing down at a shimmering Lake Worth and sipping sancerre. What more, I wondered, could life hold for a growing boy.

"Tell me, Archy," Connie said lazily, "what have you been up to?"

"Busy, busy, busy," I said. "Dinners, parties, dances, and licentiousness. And you?"

"More of the same," she said, and we both burst out laughing.

"Actually," I said, "it's been sluggish."

"A drag," she said.

"Nothing," I said.

"Zip," she said.

We were contentedly together.

"Must you go?" she asked in a wispy voice.

"No," I said, "I must not."

"Promise not to snore?"

"I never snore," I said indignantly.

"Perhaps not but you do burble occasionally."

"I'll promise not to burble if you promise not to kick."

"I never kick," she said firmly.

"Do so."

"Do not."

"Then you sometimes jerk in your sleep. You convulse."

"Convulse?" she said. "Is that fun?"

"It can be," I said. "Under the right circumstances."

She refilled our glasses. "I've missed you, Arch," she said casually.

"And I've missed you, Connie," I said, just as casually.

"It's been silly-time," she added.

"Too true," I concurred.

"Right now?" she asked.

"Barkis is willin'," I told her.

"Who's Barkis?"

"A close friend of mine."

"I think I've had enough of your close friends," she said.

I skinned down and had popped between the sheets before Connie finished locking up and dousing the lights. She left a single bulb burning in the bathroom and when she came out starkly naked I almost swooned with longing. What a delight she was! And no tattoos.

She climbed into bed and we moved close.

"Let's go for it," she said.

I still refuse to believe romantic love is a myth. But an intimate friendship between a man and a woman is better.

I think.